MELVILLE GOODWIN, USA

BY
JOHN P. MARQUAND

HAVEN'S END

THE LATE GEORGE APLEY

WICKFORD POINT

H. M. PULHAM, ESQUIRE

SO LITTLE TIME

REPENT IN HASTE

B. F.'S DAUGHTER

POINT OF NO RETURN

MELVILLE GOODWIN, USA

MELVILLE GOODWIN, USA

BY JOHN P. MARQUAND

LITTLE, BROWN AND COMPANY · BOSTON

1951

The lines from "If" are from *Rewards and Fairies* by Rudyard Kipling. Copyright 1910 by Rudyard Kipling, reprinted by permission of Mrs. George Bambridge and Doubleday & Company, Inc.

The lines from "The Highwayman" are from *Collected Poems in One Volume* by Alfred Noyes. Copyright 1906, 1934, 1947, by Alfred Noyes. Reprinted by permission of the publishers, J. B. Lippincott Company.

PRINTED IN THE UNITED STATES OF AMERICA BY
KINGSPORT PRESS, INC., KINGSPORT, TENNESSEE

To Cousin Lucy, with love

Author's Note

Anyone who has ever written a novel hopes that his work will convey an illusion of reality to anyone who may read it, and I am no exception. In attempting to achieve this purpose, I have, naturally, drawn on my memories of two world wars, but all characters appearing in these pages are imaginary creations. With whatever degree of success they may live in print, not one of them represents any person I have ever known or heard of, either living or dead.

Contents

MELVILLE GOODWIN, USA

I

You Will Love Its Full, Exciting Flavor . . . and Now, Mr. Sidney Skelton

I KNEW nothing about what General Melville A. Goodwin had done in Berlin until I read of his feat in my own script shortly before going on the air one evening in October 1949.

Because of a luncheon engagement in New York that day, I broadcasted from the New York studio instead of from my library in Connecticut. I entered the building at approximately six and while waiting for the elevator, I noticed that a personally conducted group of tourists had gathered behind me. They had all bought tickets for a quick trip through the works, and they were being guided by one of the studio ushers, a nice fresh-faced boy dressed in a tailless coat of Confederate gray and gold.

"Just about to enter the car ahead of us," I heard the boy say, "is Mr. Sidney Skelton, the commentator. He goes on the air at seven o'clock."

There was a low excited murmur, and I still had perspective enough to be confused and embarrassed by this sort of thing.

At the thirty-seventh floor there was another boy in gray and gold who also knew me.

"Good evening, Mr. Skelton," he said.

"Good evening, son," I answered.

Then I remembered a statement by the gamekeeper in *Lady Chatterley's Lover* — that males would be more emancipated and prouder, too, if a universal law could be passed obliging them all to wear coats that did not conceal their buttocks. I have forgotten why D. H. Lawrence's character felt so strongly on this subject, but the boy certainly looked very happy and very proud in his gray monkey jacket. He

3

must have been given a good briefing on his responsibilities and his bright future when he got his studio job, and he still believed so obviously all they had told him that he made me wish that I, too, were his age, dressed up like a Roxy usher, instead of the synthetic personality I had become.

Miss Maynard, my studio secretary, was waiting for me in my office.

"Good evening, Mr. Skelton," she said. "It's going to be in Studio A. Mr. Frary hopes you don't mind."

Miss Maynard meant that I was to read the script in the studio into which the public could stare through soundproof glass. I might have told her, though I didn't, that it made no difference where I read the thing. I had read it from the top of Pikes Peak and from the ballroom of the Imperial Hotel in Tokyo and from the press box of the Rose Bowl in Pasadena — a change of scene was all a part of the show. The success of the program lay in my voice and not my brains, and in an accepted tradition I was being turned into a world traveler who appeared in odd places gathering material. I was not even encouraged to give much thought to the preparation of the script myself, because it was my voice and personality that they wanted, and Art Hertz, who usually put the piece together for me, knew radio technique. I could trust him for the timing and I could trust his balance of language, too, but still I did like to read the whole thing over first instead of taking it on cold. After all, the latest sponsor was paying close to a million dollars for the program.

"You sound a little hoarse tonight, Mr. Skelton," Miss Maynard said.

"Oh no," I said, "I'm not, really, but I would like a little soda with a piece of ice in it."

Miss Maynard opened the door of a cellaret while I hung up my hat and coat. I glanced up at the electric clock with its relentlessly moving second hand, sharply conscious of precision and passing time, though all the rest of the office seemed designed to make one forget such things. The place had been redecorated after the new contract had been signed, and it now sported a hunter green carpet and green and chartreuse leather upholstered furniture. There

4

was also a collection of blown-up photographs on the wall showing Sidney Skelton, the commentator, looking at the Pyramids, gazing raptly at the Taj and at the Forbidden City in Peking, boarding the battleship *Missouri* and shaking hands with General Eisenhower. I had personally been against this final touch and I had said so — but it was a million-dollar program. There had to be a proper office, a hideaway where Mr. Skelton prepared his broadcasts. It was twenty-three minutes after six.

"If Mr. Hertz is anywhere around, I'd better see him," I said.

Of course Art was around because this was his business. If we were going on in Studio A, I would have to read without glasses, so I should go over the script carefully. I unbuttoned my vest and took a sip of the soda.

"Hello, Sid," Art said.

"Hello, you big bastard," I answered. "Let's see what you have, and pour yourself a drink if you want one."

This was only a conventional greeting. Art weighed two hundred pounds and he was not a bastard. He was a very able script-writer. He was so good, in fact, that it had occurred to me recently that it might be wise, all things considered, if I spent a day in the newsroom myself.

"I think it's all right," Art said, "and there's a cute little snap at the end about a boy scout in Cedar Rapids in an iron lung."

"Don't spoil it," I said, "let it just come over me," and I picked up the script. It began with the usual salutation, "Good evening, friends," but the next words startled me.

"What's this?" I asked. "I didn't know we were close to war today."

"Didn't you?" Art said. "Haven't you read the evening papers?"

Time was moving on. There was no time to be ironical about being out of touch. It was six thirty-three.

"Good evening, friends," I read. "We were close to war this afternoon. The long-dreaded flare-up occurred today on the border of the Russian sector in Berlin. We know tonight that war was averted, or at least the incident that might have precipitated war, by the clear thinking of one American soldier. What is this soldier's name? You

5

will hear it everywhere tonight. The name is Melville A. Goodwin, the man of the hour and the minute. Major General Melville Goodwin, whom you might call a GI's general . . ."

"Oh no!" I said. "Not Mel Goodwin."

"Do you know him?" Art asked.

"Yes," I said, "I know him. He was in the breakout at Saint-Lô, and I saw him later in Paris."

"I am sorry I didn't know that," Art said. "It would have warmed the whole thing up, but maybe we can wangle ten more seconds. You'd better get started — we haven't got much time."

I should have been there earlier. As it was, there was only time for one excision in the script and a single insert: "This all fits my old friend, Mel Goodwin, to a T, the Mel Goodwin I met when he was commanding his armored division before the breakout at Saint-Lô — none of the stiffness, none of the protocol which one associates with big brass. It's like him to want his friends to call him Mel."

Little warm bits like this, the statistical department had discovered, were apt to boost the Crosley rating.

If you have seen one bombed city in the phony peace that has followed World War II, there is small need to see the others. All those cities — London, Tokyo, Berlin, and even Manila, which is as bad as the worst — have struggled to erect a façade of decency which is pathetic and not yet convincing. Tokyo, for instance, would like it to appear that its burnt-out area was always vacant land. London unconsciously tries to convince the visitor that nothing much ever went wrong there. The extent of ruin in all these places comes over you gradually, even the spectacular devastation of Berlin. Throughout Berlin, however, there has remained the indescribable scent of rubble, the dank, dusty smell of stone and brick and plaster and rotting wood and rust, and a stale antiseptic chemical explosive odor has mingled with all the rest of it.

The Berlin street that marked the boundary between this particular part of the American and Russian sectors must still have had that smell when Mel Goodwin walked down it. I have forgotten its name or what it looks like, although I surely saw it when I was in the city

6

last. Berlin architecture from Bismarck's time through Hitler's has always impressed me as grotesquely unimaginative, and anyway if you have traveled enough by air, all streets in cities have a disconcerting way of mingling in your memory.

The trouble had started when a Russian patrol picked up a drunken American private who had wandered across the line and an American patrol had appeared a second later and grabbed a Russian sergeant. The Russians began readying their tommy guns. They were always fond of waving these weapons, and the American lieutenant got rattled. There had been a good chance that somebody would shoot, when Mel Goodwin walked around the corner with a correspondent from the Associated Press. Mel Goodwin had been ordered to Berlin from Frankfurt with an officers' group, for information and instruction, but no one in Berlin seemed to have heard about the group, much less its purpose, when it reached there, and the incident would never have made the news if it had not been for the presence of the AP correspondent.

When Mel Goodwin saw the trouble, as he told me later, he walked into the middle of the street and halted in front of the Russian officer, who pointed a tommy gun at his stomach. The Russian was a rawboned gangling boy who looked very nervous. In fact, everyone was very nervous. The thing to remember, Mel Goodwin said, was that troops are always troops in any army and that all troops act alike. The thing to remember was that no one wanted to start the shooting. He never knew whether or not the Russians recognized his rank, because quite often British troops did not know what stars on the shoulder meant. It may have been his age, he said, that influenced the outcome, or it may have only been his knowing that troops were troops; but anyway he stood in front of the Russian officer for a second or two, he said, looking at the tommy gun, and then he lighted a cigarette. He did not offer one to the officer because he was sick and tired of giving cigarettes to foreigners.

"Then I pushed that gun away from my stomach," he said, "and gave the boy a friendly slap on the tail."

That was all there was to the incident, Mel said. No one had wanted to start shooting, and the slap on the tail broke the tension.

7

He laughed and the Russian laughed and then they shook hands and the Russian sergeant was swapped off for the American drunk. No one should have given it another thought, and the story should have been stopped at headquarters. There had been too many civilian-minded people mixed up with the army during the war and afterward, and too much public relations. Personally he was sick of public relations. He had gone to headquarters immediately and had reported the incident, first verbally, then in writing. He was particularly careful to say that a news correspondent was present and to suggest that any dispatch should be suppressed. He did not prevent any war, he said. He did not know anything about the publicity until orders came over the teletype for him to return immediately to Washington. Nobody outside the army until then had ever heard much of Major General Melville Goodwin.

I have often wondered why any thoughts of mine should have lingered on Mel Goodwin that evening after the broadcast was over. I had only met him briefly in Normandy, and then there had been one turbid and rather ridiculous interlude in Paris when he had made an off-the-record ass of himself with my old friend Dottie Peale. It was even difficult to separate his face or words or actions from those of other American generals who were under instructions to be affable with the press and who customarily referred to war as though it were a football game. From my observation professional generals looked alike, thought alike and reacted in an identical manner. It made no difference whether they were in the Pacific or in India or in the European theater. No matter how genial they might try to be — and personally I was inclined to respect the disagreeable more than the jovial ones — you could not evaluate them as you evaluated other people. You could not feel the same warmth or pity or liking for generals, because they had all dropped some factor in the human equation as soon as they had rated a car with one of those flags on it and a chauffeur and an aide to get them cigarettes. After the first flush of excitement which came from knowing them, the best thing to do, I always thought, was to keep as far away from them as possible and to drink and play cards with bird colonels or lower members of the staff. *Attention! Here comes the general. We were just playing a little bridge, sir. Would the general care to take a hand?*

On the whole it was advisable not to play around with generals or to expect anything rewarding from generals' jokes, unless by chance the generals were doctors. Nevertheless, something between the lines of Mel Goodwin's story stayed with me, something I had half forgotten of that shifting, unnatural and regulated world in Africa and the ETO. I was thinking of this when Art Hertz and I went into Gilbert Frary's office after the broadcast. Gilbert was in official charge of the program and he acted as liaison between the studio and the sponsor.

"How do you think it went, Gilbert?" Art asked.

It occurred to me that Art had been pushing himself around recently more than was necessary. It was up to me, not Art, to ask that question. Gilbert inserted a cigarette in an ivory holder and lighted the cigarette with a gold lighter. We both sat watching him respectfully. After all, Gilbert was responsible for the program.

"Frankly," Gilbert said, "at first I was a little disappointed. That whole Berlin business seemed artificially exaggerated, though of course we were following the evening papers. I don't see why that news took hold the way it did, but then you warmed it up very nicely, Sidney. You got enthusiasm into it, especially about his being a GI's general and liking to be called Mel. That's interesting that you knew him. What is he really like?"

"He's like all the rest of them," I said. "Nobody ought to try to warm them up."

The telephone on Gilbert's Italian refectory table rang and Gilbert reached for it eagerly. "Yes," he said, "yes, George. I'm glad you liked it, George. I thought it was well balanced, and I thought Sidney put a lot in it." He hung up the telephone. "Well," he said, "George Burtheimer likes it, and George isn't like other sponsors. He doesn't often call up. Shall we go somewhere and eat?"

"I'm just having a sandwich in the office, Gilbert," I said. "I ought to start back home."

"You'll be doing it from home tomorrow, will you?" Gilbert asked.

"Yes," I said, "if that's all right with you, Gilbert."

"It's all right," Gilbert said, "if you don't do it too often, Sidney. There's value in the illusion of your moving around. I wish you'd think about going out to the West Coast again with me next month. People like to see you, and the customers always enjoy hearing something from Hollywood."

It had only come over me recently how ironic the relationship was that existed between Gilbert Frary and Art Hertz and me, though as far as Art went he was only on the edge of it. You could always get another writer. The town was full of writers—but between Gilbert and me the bond was closer. We were becoming more and more like two boys running a three-legged race at a Sunday school picnic, tied together, our arms about each other's shoulders. No matter what we thought of each other—and I had been growing somewhat suspicious of Gilbert lately—we had to love each other, we had to stick together.

Gilbert was looking at me affectionately now, yet in a speculative way that I could appreciate. Gilbert had made me what I was today. He had picked me out of nowhere for his own purposes. He was a very bright entrepreneur, one of those peculiar, highly astute products of the American entertainment world. Gilbert, I often thought, could have succeeded in any field which demanded negotiating skill and intelligence. He could have been as successful in the film industry as in radio. He could have run a racing stable or a fighter stable. He had theories which he could relate to reality, and best of all, he did not have enough perspective to engender doubt of self. He was the son of a Kansas City grocer, one of a family of eight. Occasionally, in an intimate mood and with the successful man's wonder at what had befallen him, he did not mind speaking of his background —but you would have had no idea where he had come from as he sat there in his tuxedo. He had what he called "changes" in his office dressing room, and he always appeared in a tuxedo at six o'clock.

Gilbert was always saying that he loved people. He needed them around him. He was always saying that he loved me, and I imagine he honestly believed this, though of course his handling of my career reflected favorably on himself. Love never did mean quite the same thing in the entertainment business as in less volatile circles.

Gilbert had picked my voice out of the air one night. He always liked to tell the story. He was just sitting casually in his suite at the St. Regis before going to the theater, and for no good reason he had turned his radio dial to a program from London put on by Army Public Relations shortly after V–E Day. My job with SHAEF at the time had consisted of personally conducting Very Important People to very important points of interest, and I had been ordered to introduce some of these personages on the air. There was no end to the strange things they made you do in those days. I had to compose an introduction for Valerie James, the actress, I remember, and God knows why any branch of the army had ever given Valerie James a free trip abroad, and I had also been ordered to prepare a few words about Mr. Hubert Hudson, who owned a string of Middle Western newspapers and who, I am sorry to say, had fallen in love with Valerie James at Claridge's. I had not minded writing the script, because I had been a newspaperman myself before I had gone down to Washington to do what I could for my country, but when a man named Major Marcus, who knew all about radio and who was going to read the script, could not be found at the crucial moment because he had disappeared somewhere with the little Wac who did the typing, I had objected violently to taking his place. There you have it, the whole little drama that Gilbert Frary always loved to re-enact. Sitting in his suite at the St. Regis, no doubt in his tuxedo, Gilbert had been impressed by my voice. It had new quality, he said, freshness, unself-consciousness and integrity.

"Sidney," he used to say when he told the story, and he had been telling it more and more often recently, "would you mind saying a few words, just anything, so that everyone can understand what I mean. . . . You see what I mean now, don't you? Sidney's a natural. You get the impact, don't you? You would believe Sidney if he told you he had stopped beating his wife. You see what I mean? His words stand out and at the same time hang together, and you see what I mean by his timing? It all makes up into what, for want of a better word, I call integrity. Sidney's voice is what Spencer Tracy and Gary Cooper are in the movies photogenically. Like Spencer

II

and Gary, Sidney has effortless sincerity, which is the same thing as integrity in the final analysis, isn't it?"

When Gilbert continued along those lines, it was best to listen to him as little as possible, but at any rate he had made me what I was. Another man, even an agent, would have left the St. Regis, gone to the theater and forgotten all about it, but Gilbert called up Washington, and now there we were, four years later.

"Well, good-by, Sidney," Gilbert said. "By the way, Marie and I are giving one of our Sunday night suppers at the St. Regis for George Burtheimer. He'll be in from Chicago. Just a few interesting people. I think Spencer may be with us. He's coming on from the Coast."

"That sounds wonderful," I said, "but I'll have to ask Helen. I don't know what Helen's planned for Sunday."

A year ago I would have simply said it sounded wonderful. I would not have said I would ask Helen what she had planned, and Gilbert knew it. The trouble was he had done too well with me. He had made me into a Frankenstein creation which might move out of his control. He now had to guard against my becoming a monster. My voice had too much integrity.

"Well, come if you possibly can," Gilbert said, "and if you and Helen are entertaining any friends over the week end, Marie and I would love to have them also, and you can come, can't you, Art?"

"Why, yes, Gilbert," Art said, "it sounds wonderful."

"That new chauffeur of yours is working out all right, isn't he, Sidney?" Gilbert asked.

"Yes, Gilbert," I said, "he's wonderful."

"I am glad the new chauffeur and the Cadillac are working out, Sidney," Gilbert said. "Well, so long. We must have a good long talk some day soon, the way we used to. I am very glad that George Burtheimer was happy about the general."

For a long while I had been struggling with an increasing sense of being far removed from everything which I had hitherto considered real. Quite suddenly I had been relieved of most of my old ambitions as well as of nearly every species of material want. If this unfamiliar condition was creating new ambitions and new desires, these did not appear to have the urgency of the old ones. It was all disorientating — the corridors with the ushers, the air-conditioned purity which banished even a puff of cigarette smoke, my own gay office, my secretary, who was very beautiful like all the front-row company secretaries, and certainly Gilbert Frary. If I had been killed in Normandy — hardly a possible contingency, but then something did occasionally happen to Public Relations officers — I would never have had to cope with present problems. My career might have formed the plot of the sort of slick story that women read in beauty parlors, when they are waiting under the dryer in another world of unreality.

"Sidney," Gilbert had said to me once, "this all — I mean what has happened to you, if you understand me — must seem to you very much like a fairy story, coming as suddenly as it has."

"If you mean that there are a lot of them around, you are right, Gilbert," I said.

"No, no," Gilbert answered, "I mean it entirely in a nice way, but if you were to write down what has happened to you, it would be unbelievable. It would not have true fictional value."

"You mean, Gilbert," I asked, "that truth is stranger than fiction?"

"You know I'm not as obvious as that, Sidney," Gilbert said. "I mean that few episodes in real life fit snugly into a fictional frame. They are too incongruous. Willie Maugham told me that once."

"I thought his name was just W. Somerset Maugham," I said.

"His friends call him Willie," Gilbert said. "Didn't you know? I call him Willie. Marie is devoted to him. You would like each other because you have one great trait in common."

"All right," I said, "what trait?"

"Integrity," Gilbert said. "Both you and Willie have great integrity, and what is more, you have something else that is even more valuable. You have loyalty, Sidney, great loyalty."

"If you mean I recognize all you've done for me and that I won't let you down . . ." I began.

"I know you won't let me down," Gilbert said, "and that's why I'll always love you, Sidney."

Perhaps he would always love me, but I knew he would let me down at any moment if it would do him any good.

Miss Maynard was waiting for me when I stopped in to get my sandwich.

"A call has just come in for you, Mr. Skelton," she said. "I sent one of the boys to page you. Didn't he find you?"

"I thought all calls were going to be stopped down at the board," I told her.

"I know," Miss Maynard said, "but this was personal. She said you would want to speak to her. It's Mrs. Peale."

"Oh, all right," I said, and I picked up the telephone. "Hello, Dottie."

"Hello," Dottie said, "how's your goddam voice?"

"It's fine," I said. "It's got me a chauffeur and a Cadillac."

"How's your integrity?" Dottie asked.

"It's fine," I said, "how's yours?"

There was a second's silence, as though she were thinking of something, but she would not have called me up if she had not thought already.

"Darling, how about your dropping everything and taking me out to dinner?"

"I can't," I said. "Helen's expecting me, but I'd like to some other time, Dottie."

"How is Helen?" she asked. "Why does everyone who gets anywhere move to Connecticut?"

"You never have," I said.

"You know me," she said. "I'm a city girl, but I'll motor out sometime if you'll ask me. How's Camilla? Did she get the copy of *Little Women* I sent her? I just saw it in a window and thought of Camilla. I was brought up on *Little Women*."

Her thoughts, I knew, were returning as they often did to her small-town girlhood, and as time had gone on, Dottie could tell about it very prettily.

"Camilla loved it," I said, "and now she's reading *Little Men*."

"I'm glad," she said. "Jo should have married Laurie, shouldn't she?"

"Everything pointed that way once," I said. "How have you been otherwise, Dottie?" There was another hesitation, not exactly a

14

silence. I knew she did not want me to take her to dinner and that she wanted something else.

"Darling," she said, "I just heard you on the air. Isn't it wonderful about Mel?"

"Oh — Mel," I repeated, and she laughed.

"Don't be so vague, darling," she said.

"Why, yes," I said, "it's swell."

"Don't sound cross about it, darling," she said, "just because he made you run errands for him at the Ritz and I made you run errands, too."

I shifted my weight from one foot to the other. I had never liked chatting over the telephone, and Dottie was never out of reach of one, but at least I knew what she wanted as soon as she mentioned Mel Goodwin.

"If you want his address," I said, "I don't know it, or his number."

"Oh, Sid," she said, "don't you know anything about him?"

Mel Goodwin belonged to the war world I had left.

"Oh, Sid," she said, "don't you even know if he is coming home? . . . Well, please let me know if you do hear anything."

"Why don't you leave that poor old guy alone?" I said. "He'll look different over here."

"Don't be so censorious," she said. "When can I see you?"

"I don't know," I said.

"Darling," she said, "how about lunch on Monday?"

II

So Jolly Boys Now . . . Here's God Speed the Plough
. . . Long Life and Success to the Farmer

GILBERT FRARY had always handled my contracts, documents
which, even when I tried to read them, left me intellectually unfulfilled. I cannot believe that Gilbert understood the verbiage either,
but he could put his finger on the basic points. A contract, he said,
was an instrument out of which you either made or lost money.
I needn't bother about any of this, he said. It was best to leave it
all to him, and I always had left it to Gilbert until recently, when
I had been having the whole business checked by an independent
law firm. Gilbert and I had always enjoyed some sort of a mutual
trust, and he had been deeply hurt when he found that I had been
doing this, because, he said, his own lawyers were protecting us.
At any rate, in the latest contract there was a large appropriation for
travel and business entertainment outside of salary, and somehow
even the house in Connecticut had entered into the transaction.
Also, a Cadillac car, "or any other motor in this general price range,"
and "a responsible and adequate chauffeur" were set aside in the contract for my business use.

This business transportation was waiting outside the building
now, directly in front of the main entrance between two No Parking
signs. The police understood the arrangement, and perhaps this, too,
was included in the contract, although I had never asked. Williams,
the chauffeur, was out on the sidewalk the moment he saw me, and
as always he impressed me as unlike the ordinary chauffeur who
drove cars for people who were used to cars. He was overemphasized
in every way — a sort of stage effect. He was too eager, too sober,
too reliable. He was both a friend and an old retainer, and he always

16

made me wonder how many other people he had retained for and who they could have been, because he did it all so perfectly. His uniform was too new, but there was no false detail. He was a nicely planned part of the program, and he was so far beyond criticism that I could only criticize my own uneasiness.

As he opened the door, the interior of the Cadillac was flooded with mellow light. When I stepped inside, he wrapped a robe around my knees as skillfully as a trained nurse. I never wanted Williams to do this because there was an excellent heating system in the Cadillac and there was no need for a robe, but Helen liked the robe. Somehow Helen could adjust herself perfectly to unreality.

There was a fragile white box in the car, tied with green cellophane ribbons.

"Where did that come from?" I asked.

"It's some gardenias, sir, for Mrs. Skelton," Williams answered.

"She didn't say anything about gardenias," I said.

"Mr. Frary had them sent down," Williams said. "Shall we start home now, sir?"

I had disliked the smell of gardenias ever since the time a large wreath of them had been placed around my neck by the Chamber of Commerce at Honolulu, but it was just like Gilbert to do such a thing. The gesture was what Gilbert called a grace note in human relationship. It always paid, he said, to do nice little things for people, and lately he had begun doing nice little things for people in my name without my knowing it. It was growing confusing to be thanked by comparative strangers for boxes of cigars, champagne and orchids, and now even Helen had begun making these little gestures. I leaned back in the car and closed my eyes, but I was not tired. I was not at all tired.

On the contrary I was too much awake, too keenly aware of everything, and that telephone call of Dottie's had remained in my mind. We drove up Fifth Avenue and crossed the Park at Seventy-ninth Street on the way to the West Side Highway, and I began thinking again of Mel Goodwin and this episode in Berlin. He had done something which had a universal appeal, but I could not identify myself with Mel Goodwin. The instincts of a participant in such

17

an action could only be explained in terms of conditioning and training.

I thought of a bird dog named Mac that my uncle had owned once, a very steady Gordon setter. I could see myself as a young boy on Saturday afternoons in just such clear October weather as we were having now. Uncle Will suffered from arthritis but he still liked to go out for woodcock if he did not have to walk too far. He would ask me to go upstairs and get his twelve-gauge Parker shotgun. The gun was in the paneled closet by the big chimney, resting against the bricks beside Uncle Will's rubber boots and his canvas shooting coat. We would go out into the yard and back the Model T Ford out of the carriage shed. As soon as old Mac saw the gun he would run around the car in circles. For once he was going to participate in something useful, in something for which his whole species had been created, and when you came to think of it, very few individuals nowadays, dogs or humans, ever had much chance of doing the things for which they had been made. Pekingese, for instance, and men on production lines, and possibly even Williams driving the Cadillac, had probably forgotten their primary purpose years before. Everything was so complicated and possibilities were so limited that perhaps you never did have a chance of knowing what you were made for, but old Mac knew. He would jump into the back seat of the Ford and sit there waiting for us to start, never wriggling his head when I tied a bell to his collar. There was a good covert at Johnson's Brook. To get there you had to cross a pasture and climb a stone wall and then walk through the brambles. Mac did not have to be told to come to heel any more than I had to be told to walk behind Uncle Will. I could never forget the clear afternoon sunlight on the junipers and the subdued tinkle of Mac's bell and the gentle complaint of my uncle's voice, saying that the woodcock flight was not what it used to be. Things were never what they used to be, as I was old enough now to know.

Uncle Will always took his stand on a little rise just above the alders, because he was not good any longer at walking through brush. I would stand beside him and I remember the strange, pungent odor of the frostbitten asters that grew there and the way he would tell Mac to go on in. Mac would disappear in the thicket, running carefully, not missing anything, but we knew where he was by the tinkling of his bell. When the bell stopped, Uncle Will would send me after Mac. The bird when flushed would be fairly certain to appear above the alders, giving an opportunity for a quick shot, and this was all my uncle needed. I would always find the dog in the alders, frozen motionless, obeying an instinct of his breed, which had nothing whatsoever to do with animal survival. It was a behavior pattern which must have evolved only after a few millennia of hunting with man. Mac always held his point patiently, tail straight and left foreleg raised, but at a word he would bound forward, and there would come that whirr of wings, always unexpected, even though we were ready for it. Then the shot would follow. Mac always seemed to know the exact point in the thicket where the bird would fall. It seldom took more than a minute for him to retrieve the woodcock, which he would bring back to my uncle proudly and gingerly, like a dog in an English hunting print, and again an instinct contrary to the primitive had taught him not to mar the bird or even to clamp his jaws too tightly upon it. He was a good dog, perfectly conditioned.

So, I was thinking, was General Melville Goodwin. I had worn a uniform for a while but I possessed few of the soldier's instincts. If I had been present in that Berlin street scene, my first and perhaps my only reaction would have been one of curiosity. I should immediately have selected some point from which I could see everything. I should not have done this because of physical fear but rather because I was trained for observation, and it would never have occurred to me that any action of mine could have altered such a scene in any way. If the Russian officer had pointed his tommy gun at my middle, I would not have felt in my pocket for a cigarette, and certainly I would not have pushed his tommy gun away, either gently or briskly. My presence would have had no calming effect upon the officer. He would have shot me through the guts because I would have been expecting it. I could even feel the bullet ripping through me now. I could not have done these things because, unlike Mel Goodwin, I was a civilian, not a soldier, and I had the civilian's fallacious point of view that a peaceful environment continued to exist, even in a war.

Until the year 1939, except for a rented room on Myrtle Street in Boston and considerably later a two-room walk-up on West Tenth Street in New York, I had never lived in a home of my own. If there had been anything that approached a home environment in my youth, it was the run-down farm which my Uncle Will had bought outside of Nashua, New Hampshire, when he had retired as manager of one of the smaller textile mills in that city. When I was in my teens I was there often, and the farm was always more of a home to me than the rented stucco house on Wilton Street in West Newton where I lived as a child. We had looked on this anyway as nothing more than a temporary dwelling from which we would move to something better as soon as my father got further along in the insurance business; so when my mother died and I had been boarded for a while with family friends, it was like home when I went to stay with my Uncle Will. When my father married again, he moved to Natick, and though my stepmother wished me to live there, too, there never seemed to be room for me in a new household in a new life with new children, and that element of security which child psychologists now consider of such importance was denied me.

Nevertheless when I finished college and went to work on a Boston paper, I seemed to be no more insecure than anyone else in the city room, where security rested mainly on individual ability. Looking back, I seldom missed the solidity of home, and I never cared much about possessions. If I wanted pictures, I could see them in a museum. If I wanted books, there was always the public library. All I needed in those days were some suitcases, two suits of clothes and some ties, and a typewriter and some copy paper — and you could always get all the copy paper you wanted in the city room if you cared to write in your spare time. However, there was always a deadline somewhere, which permitted little opportunity for considered contemplation or for a leisurely co-ordination of ideas. I never cared about food or gracious living in those days, because what I was doing was an adequate substitute, and even now, when I hear a linotype machine or smell that sweet pervasive odor of printer's ink up in some composing room, my old contentment returns.

I never cared what was in jewelers' windows or who rode in limousines, except in a purely academic way. I never thought seriously of marriage or of the future but only of seeing all I could while I was alive. When I was on the Paris Bureau, it was easier to sit still than it had been in America, but I never wanted to buy anything even there, except possibly a few books from the stalls along the Seine.

I returned to New York in 1939 after writing three magazine articles on the Middle East and I still did not care where I ate or slept until I married Helen. She was an assistant editor then on a home furnishings magazine, and her work had made her deeply conscious of *décor*. We rented four rooms on the third floor of a pretentious old dwelling in the West Fifties between Fifth and Sixth avenues. It was noisy but near to everything. Helen furnished the apartment with odds and ends from auction rooms and she was always rearranging them. She was always saying that I would get used to them in time and that I was the most undomestic man she had ever known, but actually there had hardly been time for us even to get used to each other. Helen could never manage to get my clothes in order, and even when Camilla was born in the winter of 1940 and was moved into the back bedroom with her bottles and her bathtub, we were still not used to the apartment. We left it in 1941, when I joined the army and Helen and Camilla went to live with Helen's parents in Delaware, and we never did have a home in the accepted sense until suddenly in the spring of 1949 we bought the place in Connecticut called Savin Hill.

Helen had said we had to start living somewhere, instead of just subletting one Park Avenue apartment after another, and now that we could afford it we ought to think about Camilla and move to the country. Besides, Gilbert Frary felt we should consider the personality value of such a change. Helen and Camilla and I needed a gracious, welcoming home that would look like something — something solid, perhaps with horses.

"Why horses?" I asked.

Gilbert said that he had merely suggested horses because they had a social significance that built up personality.

"Not that you haven't a lovely personality as it is, Sidney," he said, "but Helen knows what I mean."

He meant that we must have roots somewhere that had a build-up value, and it ought to be Connecticut, not Long Island, because Long Island was rootless. He knew exactly the man who could find us such a place, he said, and larger country places were going begging now, and most of the upkeep could come out of the expense account.

I first saw the house that we now occupied one morning early in the previous spring. Helen woke me up at eight o'clock, which has always seemed to me an ungodly hour for starting a day — five or six if necessary, or else eleven-thirty, but never eight o'clock.

"What's the matter, Helen?" I asked her. "Is it something about Camilla?"

"Oh, Sid," Helen said, "please wake up. I want to get there so you can see it in the morning sunlight. There are crocuses all over the lawn along the drive — orange, white and purple crocuses. Do you remember the boy with the crocus on that frieze in the Palace of Knossos?"

"What?" I asked her.

"The boy with the crocus," Helen said. "You used to talk to me about him before we were married. It made me think you knew something about art. You were going to take me to Crete."

"That's right," I said, "Crete."

I had seen the mountains of Crete from the deck of an American Export liner on my way to Alexandria before the war, and I had always wanted to explore the Minoan ruins but I did not see how we could very well go there now with Camilla.

"Please get up, Sid," Helen said, "and put on your tweed coat and your gray slacks. I do want you to see it when everything is fresh in the morning."

"All right," I said, and I got out of bed. "Now just what is it we are going to see, Helen?"

"I wish I ever knew whether you were being vague on purpose or because you can't help it," Helen said. "The place in Connecticut — I was telling you all about it last night. Remember?"

The place in Connecticut had slipped my mind, because I had given it no careful thought. I had not been able seriously to envisage Helen or me in the country any more than I could envisage the new vistas that only recently had begun to stretch before us.

We drove out, I remember, in the new Packard convertible with the top down. I still enjoyed the Packard because I had never owned anything larger than a Chevrolet until that year. The Packard handled beautifully on the Merritt Parkway, and Helen began talking about this place again. I mustn't be depressed by its general size, she said. She knew that it was hard to make new plans now that it was possible so suddenly to do so much.

"Oh, Sid," Helen said, "I do wish sometimes you would let yourself go and try to be happy about everything."

"I'm happy about most things," I told her, "but I can't seem to relax like you."

Of course there were a number of other people like us in New York, but Hollywood was where we should have been or some similar place where money was not exactly money.

Savin Hill, from the first moment I saw it, was a sort of sword of Damocles for me. Day and night the spirit of Savin Hill hung over me by a thread, a perpetual reminder of the existence of material instability. The house had been built by a Mr. Edgar Winlock, who had died very suddenly from a coronary accident, and it was up for sale, furnished, to settle the estate. At least it was not a remodeled farmhouse. Instead, it was built along the lines of a Virginia plantation. A shaded avenue led up to it with fields resembling paddocks or pastures on either side, enclosed by deceptively simple white board fences. The place was trying to look like a farm, but the driveway had a rolled tar surface.

"You see, the Winlocks kept horses," Helen said. "There's a stable and a three-car garage."

"My God, Helen," I began, but she stopped me.

"We can afford it, Sid," she said. "Gilbert says we can" — she was pathetically eager to have me like it — "and a couple and an upstairs maid can look after the house." She had learned all about such arrangements, of course, from playing around with the editors of fashion and home decoration magazines and from writing pieces about gracious living. Having me dressed in a tweed jacket and slacks was her idea of part of the *décor,* and it was just as well for both of us that Helen had some training.

"All right," I said, "I'm Mr. Edgar Winlock. Do the horses come with it, Mrs. Winlock?"

"I wish you wouldn't give up without a struggle," Helen said. "It isn't like you, Sid."

The truth was that I could think of no fixed line of argument. If she really liked it, I told her, and if she thought she could run a place with a sunken garden and crocuses and a swimming pool, we would try it.

"Aren't you going to argue about it at all?" Helen asked. "Do you like the furniture? Of course, the living room ought to be in Chippendale, but still the Winlocks did have good taste."

I wondered whether it was the Winlocks' taste or that of an interior decorator. The living room was Louis Quinze, with a brilliant Aubusson carpet and a crystal chandelier — but Helen would change all that — and the dining room opened on a terrace that overlooked the swimming pool. I could face it all objectively, but not subjectively. I almost felt that I was a reporter again, visiting the estate for some professional purpose.

"And here's the library," Helen said. "You can have the library."

"Why, thanks a lot," I said.

"And you can do it over any way you like."

The trouble was I had never had an opportunity to develop any individual taste, and the last thing I wanted to do was to do something over.

"Sidney," Helen said, "don't you like the books?"

I wondered whether Mr. Winlock had liked them. They looked to me like a wholesale acquisition from the library of an English county family — tooled leather sets of the British poets and the British novelists.

"Isn't there a bar somewhere?" I asked.

"No," Helen said, "this isn't Hollywood, but we could use the flower room and have it paneled."

"Oh, no," I said, "I don't particularly want a bar."

"Sidney," Helen said, "haven't you any suggestions at all?"

"Why, no," I said. "I can't think of anything — except that there ought to be some place where I could do some writing."

"You can do some writing in the library," Helen said.

"Oh, yes," I said, "I had forgotten about the library."

"Darling," Helen said, "don't you think it's about time you were housebroken? Isn't it time we stopped camping out and had a home of our own?"

Of course you had to start sometime, somewhere, having a home of your own, but I always felt as though I were camping out at Savin Hill. I could never entirely get rid of the idea that the Winlocks might come back.

"I wonder if there is any shooting around here," I said.

"Shooting?" Helen asked me. "Do you mean a war?"

"No," I said, "game bird shooting with a shotgun."

"What in heaven's name made you think of that?" Helen asked.

"Oh," I said, "I used to go out with my Uncle Will when he shot woodcock in New Hampshire. He had a dog named Mac."

"I didn't know you liked dogs," Helen said.

"I don't know whether I do or not," I told her. "I never had time to own one."

"Well, darling," Helen said, "you have time to own one now, and Camilla ought to get used to dogs. We could get a poodle."

"Why a poodle?" I asked.

Before I had married Helen, and in fact until Camilla was born, I had always believed that I understood quite a lot about women. It had never occurred to me that women, including young mothers, would need more than a moderate amount of sympathetic personal attention. I had never considered those demands of security which I now know directly follow the excitements of childbirth. I did not understand that urge for building up something and for making a

25

firm place for a child, but I was glad to give Helen Savin Hill if she wanted it.

As the Cadillac turned into the black-topped driveway that October evening, I had much the same feeling about the place that I had experienced in early spring when the Winlock executors had passed the papers. I was thinking, as Williams blew the horn and as the lights of the house became clear in front of us, of an advertisement for an expensive automobile which I must have seen before the war. It was entitled, "The Day That Took Years in the Making," and above the headline was a pretty picture of a nice middle-aged couple standing on a stair landing looking out of an arched window. The man, gray at the temples, appeared somewhat buffeted by life, but his wife beside him looked very, very happy and very, very proud. Outside on the drive stood a brand-new automobile with, if I am not mistaken, a Christmas wreath upon it — the apotheosis of the day that took years in the making. This couple, we were told, had moved shoulder to shoulder through the years, because he had faith in her and she had faith in him. First they had lived in a small bungalow with a wretched automobile, then in a somewhat larger house with a passable car, because he had faith in her and she had faith in him, and today we could see the fruition of that faith. The Car was at the door. I remembered this advertisement because it was an almost flawless piece of materialism, and now here I was in a Cadillac, approaching the gracious landscaped entrance of Savin Hill. Yet the couple in the advertisement had some advantages over Helen and me. They had struggled upwards through economic gradations, whereas Helen and I had come cold on Savin Hill.

When Williams blew the horn, the door opened as though the sound of the horn had released some electronic mechanism, and there was Oscar, the houseman, in the tan alpaca coat that Helen had selected for him. Oscar was smiling in his mannerly Swedish way. Williams handed him the box of gardenias and hastily but delicately pulled the robe from my knees as I began to struggle with it.

"There has just been a telephone call for you, sir," Oscar said, "from Washington — they had your unlisted number — from the office of the Secretary of the Army."

26

It seemed to me that Oscar might at least have waited until I had stepped indoors, but Oscar was always overhelpful.

"Who was calling?" I asked.

"It was a colonel, sir, a Colonel Flax," Oscar said, "from Public Relations. He asked for you to call him back the moment you came in. He said it was very urgent."

Everything, I remembered, was always urgent around there, but I was not in the army any longer and I had never heard of Colonel Flax.

"If he wants me badly enough, he can try me again," I said, and I dismissed the whole thing from my mind. Public Relations was always after something, but I was not in the army any longer.

"Are there any orders yet for tomorrow, sir?" Williams asked. It was nearly nine o'clock, and I wanted to think of the present, but Williams repeated his question very gently.

"Well, I won't know about tomorrow," I said, "until I wake up tomorrow morning, but I'll tell you what you can do. Take it up with Mrs. Skelton, Williams. She'll probably have some sort of schedule."

"Yes, sir," Williams said, "Mrs. Skelton was talking about Miss Camilla's going to a birthday party tomorrow afternoon if you weren't going to need me to take you anywhere."

"Oh," I said, "can't Miss Otts drive her over in the station wagon?"

"Miss Otts was going to New York for the day tomorrow," Oscar said. "That is why Madam thought that Williams could drive Miss Camilla, but if you need Williams, sir, why I could drive Miss Camilla in the station wagon. It is my afternoon off, but I would be pleased to help."

It was cool outside the car, and the air was very clear. Even though we owned three cars and a pickup truck, these problems of transportation still persisted.

"Whose birthday party is it?" I asked.

"It's at the Jacksons', sir," Oscar said, "at half past four o'clock."

I could not remember who the Jacksons were.

"Well, well," I said, "you'd better take up the whole problem with Mrs. Skelton. Mrs. Skelton will fix it so Miss Camilla will get to that birthday party, and I'll tell you what I'd like, Oscar. How about getting me a Scotch and soda?"

I was thinking that if Oscar wanted to be helpful, this might divert his mind into more useful channels.

Helen had done the hallway over, and now it was green. The wrought-iron railing of the winding staircase was bronze green. The noiseless stair carpet was a deeper green, and on the wallpaper was a design of large plantain leaves. I had told Helen when she was finished with it that all we needed were a few bird calls and it would be a jungle. It had the same quiet quality as the rain forest around Belém, but then it was not raining, and Helen had never seen Belém. She was standing in the hall waiting for me and she looked very happy and very pretty.

"Hi," I said. "How's everything going, Mrs. Winlock?"

This was a joke which had worn pretty thin by now, as I saw by Helen's changed expression.

"I am sorry," I said. "It just happened unintentionally," and I kissed her.

"Darling," Helen said, "what did you have for supper?"

"I don't remember," I said. "A glass of milk and a sandwich, I guess, just before I left."

"Hilda can get you something hot in just a minute."

"Oh, no," I said, "that's all right."

"You sounded wonderful," Helen said. "Did you write it or did Art write it?"

"Art wrote it," I said, "except the piece about my knowing that general. He didn't know I knew Mel Goodwin."

"I didn't know you knew him either," Helen said, "but it sounded wonderful. Your voice was much better than last night."

"That's good," I said. "George Burtheimer called up from Chicago. I thought it was corny about Mel Goodwin, but George liked it."

"Why, darling," Helen said, "that's wonderful." Of course she knew what it meant, hearing from the sponsor. "Now you had better go up and see Camilla so she can get to sleep. She's in bed with a book waiting for you, and don't stay too long with her. She really ought to be asleep by nine."

28

"All right," I said, "just as soon as Oscar brings me a drink."

"Sid," Helen said, "do you always have to have a drink in your hand when you go upstairs to say good night to Camilla?"

"Not always," I said. "I'm just feeling tired after a long day in the city."

"Did you see anyone you knew?" Helen asked.

"Yes," I said, "quite a lot of people. I had lunch with Bill Schultz. He's just back from London."

"Oh," Helen said, "he's the one you worked with when you were on the Paris Bureau, isn't he?"

There was no reason why Helen should have remembered him at all because he was a figure from the past that had nothing to do with Helen's and my life together. It always touched me that Helen was interested in my early struggles.

"That's the one," I said. "You made quite an impression on him when we were living on Fifty-second Street."

"I wish you wouldn't always conceal all your old friends," Helen said. "You have a place now where you can entertain them. Why don't you ask a lot of them out some Sunday?"

"It might be a good idea," I said, "some Sunday."

"And even if they break something," Helen said, "I won't mind — as long as they don't leave burning cigarettes on tables."

"Well, it might be a good idea," I said, "some Sunday." And then I saw Oscar carrying a highball glass on an Early American silver tray.

"Is that the Paul Revere tray?" I asked.

"Yes it is," Helen said. "Now hurry, and don't let Camilla keep you too long. You know how she strings things out before she goes to sleep."

I was just starting up the stairs when the telephone rang. I handed my glass back to Oscar and picked up the extension beneath the stairs in the hall.

"Is this Mr. Sidney Skelton?" an operator was saying. "Just a minute please, Mr. Skelton."

There was a buzzing on the line and nothing else. It seemed to me that if an operator finally caught you, you were always left hanging

29

in space for just a minute. Helen was not even curious about the call, and I did not blame her. Oscar was standing patiently, holding my glass on its silver tray. We were all waiting for just a minute.

"Is this Mr. Sidney Skelton?" It was a man's voice speaking this time, fresh, vibrant and young.

"Yes," I answered, "this is still Mr. Sidney Skelton."

"This is Captain Orde from the Secretary's office," the voice said. "I was asked to check to see if you'd returned home yet. Colonel Flax is most anxious to speak to you."

"All right," I said, "put him on."

"Unfortunately he has just stepped out for a few moments," the invisible captain said, "but he wanted me to check up to be sure you had returned home."

"That's very thoughtful of him," I said.

It was like the old days, listening to Captain Orde.

"He wanted me to ask you please to wait until he returns," Captain Orde said. "He is most anxious to speak to you on an urgent matter."

"All right," I answered, "when will he return?"

"He was just called from his office a few moments ago on urgent business," Captain Orde said, "but he should return at any moment."

"What does he want to talk to me about?" I asked.

"I believe the subject deals with General Goodwin, sir," Captain Orde said, "Major General Melville A. Goodwin, but it would be better for you to hear of it from Colonel Flax personally. He will return at any time now."

"Well, tell Colonel Flax to take his time," I said. "I won't run away from him. Good-by, Captain Orde."

"What was that about?" Helen asked.

"I really don't know," I told her, and I took my drink from Oscar. "You never can tell what's coming out of Washington."

Colonel Flax was certainly most anxious to get me, even though he had stepped out temporarily. Someone higher up was obviously pushing Colonel Flax, but I did not see what I could tell him about General Melville Goodwin. It was time to go upstairs and say good night to Camilla.

30

Miss Otts was in Camilla's sitting room reading a volume of Maria Edgeworth. She looked tweedy and natural beside Camilla's dollhouse.

"You should try Miss Edgeworth sometime, Mr. Skelton," Miss Otts said.

"I read *The Parent's Assistant* once," I said. "My stepmother had it in Natick. There was a story about a little boy, wasn't there, with a piece of string?"

"Oh, yes," Miss Otts said. " 'Waste not, want not.' "

"Maybe it's not quite in tune with the present," I told her.

Miss Otts laughed, comfortably far away in a world that was all her own.

"That is why I like Miss Edgeworth," she said.

Camilla was sitting straight up in bed reading Louisa M. Alcott's *Little Women* for the third time, and her black hair fell over her shoulders in two neat braids. I stood there for a moment adjusting myself to her. I could remember her in her crib, but I had been away so much that I was still surprised that Camilla could talk fluently or that she could have ideas.

"Oh, Daddy," Camilla said, "you've got a drink."

"You and your mother certainly notice it when I have one, Camilla," I said. I sat down on the edge of her bed and took an uneasy sip of the Scotch and soda and wondered what Camilla really thought of me.

"I wish you'd shut the door," Camilla said. "You see, I don't want Miss Otts to overhear everything."

"What's the matter with Miss Otts?" I asked.

"Oh, she's all right," Camilla said, "but she talks in a funny way."

"That's because she's English," I said. "She talks in a very nice way, Camilla."

"You don't talk like her and neither does Mummy."

"I know," I said, "but we ought to. What did you do at school today?"

"The same old things," Camilla said.

"Well," I said, "maybe it's time for you to go to sleep."

"No," Camilla said, and her voice was louder, "we haven't talked about anything."

"All right," I said, "what do you want to talk about?"

"I don't know," Camilla said, "about anything, just talk."

"Well, I don't know either," I said. "That's a nice school you go to, Camilla, and Miss Lancaster seemed very nice the time I saw her."

"Let's talk about something else," Camilla said. "Talk about when you were a little boy."

"Well, well," I said, "when I was a little boy . . ."

Camilla's round gray-green eyes, just the color of her mother's, were fixed on me unblinkingly with that utterly uninhibited stare of childhood. I tried to see myself as she must have seen me, an almost complete stranger who could share not one of her interests. I was also trying to walk backwards into a land that was closed to me forever, and I was not a Eugene Field, who could bring to life a little toy soldier red with rust, or a Robert Louis Stevenson, who could climb up in a cherry tree to look abroad on foreign lands, but then perhaps those two great authorities could only recall childhood in an academic manner. On the other hand, Freud and Jung and all their disciples seemed familiar with the pitfalls and terrors of that land but with none of its beauties, and surely it had certain charms. I sat there in my daughter's bedroom studying its chintz curtains and the infantile wallpaper designed by some other professional who had forgotten about childhood, and I was very certain that Camilla was enduring my presence politely simply because my being there postponed the hour of her sleeping.

"Well," I said, and my voice to my own ears sounded painfully sugary, "when I was a little boy I lived in West Newton."

"Did you have a dog?" Camilla asked.

"No," I said, "I didn't, but I did have a pair of roller skates."

Somewhere in the distance, on the very edge of my imagination, the horns of elfland mingled with the loud metallic sound of those roller skates.

"I wish I had some roller skates," Camilla said.

Childhood was a time of perpetually unfulfilled desire, and if by

32

chance you finally attained something, immediately you wanted something else.

"They aren't any good without a sidewalk," I told her.

"I wish we had a sidewalk," Camilla said.

"Well, we haven't," I told her. "It would look funny around here."

We were both silent. I moved uneasily. It seemed to me that I had said everything that I could possibly say.

"What else did you have?" Camilla asked.

I tried to think what else I had. I had once possessed a sense of time which was completely gone. Once an hour had been like a day and minutes had been interminable, and now I had an impression again of dragging minutes.

"Now let me think," I said. "What else did I have? I had a pocketknife. It had a chain on it and one end of the chain I could fasten on a button inside my trousers."

"What sort of a button?" Camilla asked.

She had completely broken my train of thought. "I don't remember, Camilla, but there was a button somewhere."

"What did your mother do about you when you went to bed?" Camilla asked.

What did my mother do about me when I went to bed? I could see my mother's face quite clearly. It had always looked drawn and pale in the evening, though I must have been completely oblivious to her worries. I had seen her once just as Camilla now saw me.

"Well," I said, "she always made me wash."

"Didn't your nurse wash you?"

"No," I said, "there wasn't any nurse."

"Didn't your mother hear you say your prayers?"

"Yes," I said, "when she wasn't too tired. She wasn't very well."

"What did you say?" Camilla asked, " 'Now I lay me,' or 'Our Father'?"

"I guess it was 'Our Father,' " I said.

"All right," Camilla said, "then I'll say that one."

"Wait a minute," I said. "Hasn't your mother heard your prayers?"

"Yes," Camilla said, "but I didn't say that one."

33

"Now wait a minute," I said, but Camilla did not wait. She was out of bed and kneeling beside me. Her pigtails made two straight lines on her flannelette pajamas. I wanted to tell her again to wait a minute, but she had started already.

"Our Father who art in heaven . . ." she began, hastily, as though she might forget it all if she spoke too slowly.

I should not have been sitting holding a highball glass while Camilla recited the Lord's Prayer, but when she was in bed again I felt somewhat relieved and rather pleased. I knew that Camilla was finished with me now, and somehow I was sure when I kissed her good night that I had behaved in a satisfactory manner, and the knowledge made me contented.

"Daddy," she said, "I think I'm going to lose a tooth."

"Well," I said, "that's fine, Camilla," and I thought of the last tooth I lost in West Newton two weeks before my mother's death, and no one had done anything about that tooth.

34

III

And Mr. Gilbert Frary Has Another Good Suggestion

HELEN often said that I was the most unsure man she had ever known, and I often told her that with things going the way they were I didn't see why it was worth while attempting to be sure of anything except of eventual dissolution. Obviously this was not a constructive attitude, and I did not blame Helen for being annoyed by it, because I have often thought that women in general admire and need order more than men. They are pathetically sure of generalities and pathetically certain that every game has an unchanging set of rules and that somewhere there is an answer to every problem.

My own uncertainties usually amused rather than annoyed Helen. In fact she told me once that she had married me because I was so funny about so many things. It had occurred to me, however, during the war, that she might grow tired of me and write me a nice letter saying, as so many other wives had said, that it was all a mistake, and I was still very grateful that she had not, because I had reached a point where I could not possibly get on without her. There had been plenty of other men she could have married when she had been working on that high-bracket magazine. In fact she had been as good as engaged to a lawyer when I had first met her.

It was at a cocktail party in one of those old brick houses down on Eighth Street, and I had thought when we stood together in a corner that it would all be over in a moment, that someone who was more her type would find her and take her away. She was an exceptionally pretty girl with dark hair and fine features, and pretty girls in my experience had always expected too much of other people. I would have left her on general principles two minutes after we had been introduced if she had not asked me very quickly, and in what seemed to me a gauche way considering her pleasing appearance, whether I was doing anything for dinner. I told her that I appreciated her being kind to me but that she would only be bored because I had never been able to get on well with pretty girls who worked on class magazines.

"I wish you wouldn't hold my looks against me," she said.

I told her that I was not holding anything against her and that it was not her fault that her looks unsettled me, but that I was not a novelty or a suitable vehicle for escape.

"It's nice to see someone who is so uncertain," she said. "It makes me feel absolutely safe."

I was glad that she felt safe with me, I told her, as long as she wanted to feel that way, but I did not want her to think for an instant that my character needed changing or guidance. I, too, felt perfectly safe with her, because she would lose interest in a little while. There were so many men who had wanted to marry her that I always thought it would be temporary, even after we were married. I could not understand why she wanted to have children. I explained to her that I was not a parental type and that it would be hard on children when she grew tired of the whole arrangement.

"Why don't you face facts?" she said. "Don't you know that if a girl loves someone, she wants to have a child by him? The first time I saw you, I wanted you to be the father of my children."

I have never been able to understand the eccentricities of natural selection. When I thought of that cocktail party on Eighth Street, it seemed to me indecent that any such thought should have crossed the mind of such a pretty girl, and instead of flattering me, it alarmed me, since it showed how sure Helen was about everything. She had been sure that I was the man for her after looking me over for sixty seconds. She was sure that I would amount to something. She had estimated all my latent capabilities, or at least she said she had, and she was right. Helen was always right, theoretically.

The house, the winding staircase, and Camilla in her pigtails, all proved her correctness, theoretically. So far she had been right as rain about everything. Yet as I crossed the hall that evening and entered the living room, many of my old uneasy thoughts returned.

"Helen," I said. The living room was large enough so that I had to raise my voice. She seemed a long distance away, curled up on the corner of the davenport, looking at the fire. "Did you get those gardenias that Gilbert Frary sent you?"

"Yes," she said, "Oscar brought them."

"I thought that was very kind and thoughtful of Gilbert. Didn't you?" I said.

Helen began to laugh. Her feet were on the floor, and she stood up. She looked like a Pre-Raphaelite painting in a velvet gown that was neither a housecoat nor a negligee nor a dinner dress. I did not know the name for it, but surely Helen did.

"Sid," she said, and she held out her arms to me, "you're awfully funny" — and all at once it was all funny, Helen and the house and everything. Holding Helen in my arms and kissing her had many obvious values, but I wondered whether she understood whatever it was in this encounter of our minds and bodies that made me want to laugh. There were still times, like the present, when I could not avoid the illusion that Helen and I had never recited marriage vows. She was so exactly what I had wanted that it seemed like a gay sort of interlude, an unexpected piece of good fortune that should be taken at the flood and remembered in drab days that were bound to follow.

I was funny and Helen and the whole room were funny. She had done the living room over largely, I imagine, because she had grown tired of hearing me refer to us as Mr. and Mrs. Winlock. She had understood what I meant, she said. She had disposed of the Louis Quinze furniture and the Aubusson carpet, because the house should be in our own taste. I was a little vague about our own taste because we had never been surrounded by any old possessions which might have reminded us of any other incarnations. Helen and I had never had anything but a few books and the silver-backed comb and brush upstairs in our dressing room, which her mother had given her when we were married. Now there were English drum tables and piecrust tables, and heavy curtains called *toile de Jouy* drawn across the tall windows, and the strange thing about it was that the room actually looked as though we lived in it instead of looking, as I thought it would, like one of those period rooms in the Metropolitan Museum. I never could understand how Helen had achieved this effect.

As far as I could see, her background did not fit her for her present efforts any better than my own. When I had known Helen first, she had shared a two-room apartment in New York with a heavy, red-faced girl whom she had known at Bryn Mawr, and they had cooked casserole dishes on a hot plate in the bathroom. There was nothing in her home environment either that could account for her decorative skill unless it was revolt.

The house occupied by her parents in Wilmington, Delaware, was a smallish brick structure in one of those blocks to the west of the Du Pont Hotel. It had been constructed near the turn of the century, before everyone connected with the Du Pont Company had found it advisable to move farther into the country. Helen's father had not been connected with the Du Pont Company, and neither had her brother, and now they were not connected with anything at all except with Helen and me. I remembered my first glimpse of their house on the occasion when Helen introduced me to her family in Wilmington. I remembered the gas fixtures wired for electricity and the narrow dark front hall in which there stood a combination hat rack and umbrella stand of golden oak with a mirror at its back and a commodelike seat that you lifted up for rubbers. I remembered the golden oak balustrade and the crimson stair carpet with Paris green leaves upon it and the golden oak of the sitting room and dining room and the two Tiffany lamps, also wired like the chandeliers for electricity. There was even, believe it or not, a china cuspidor decorated with glazed roses in the parlor by a rubber tree. Nothing about that house in Delaware afforded an explanation for Helen's ability to cope successfully with her present surroundings. She would have been a very good adventuress. In fact, perhaps she was an adventuress.

"What did you and Camilla talk about?" she asked.

"About when I was a little boy," I said, "and then she said her prayers."

"But she had said them already. I always hear her prayers."

"Well, she repeated them," I said. "Lots of people do, now that I think of it."

"Darling," Helen said, "I wish you would look more natural. Why don't you ring for Oscar and get your slippers and your smoking jacket?"

Helen had been trying in various ways for a long while to get me into that smoking jacket. It was a wine-colored velvet garment with quilted cuffs and lapels which she had bought for me shortly after she had done over the room.

"Well," I said, because I did not want to hurt her feelings, "all right, Helen, I'll settle for the smoking jacket but not the slippers. Why do you think it makes me look natural?"

"It doesn't," Helen said, "but it ought to," and she looked at me as though she were doing me over. "It might if you kept wearing it."

I did not ring for Oscar to bring me the smoking jacket and I don't believe that Helen expected that I would. One of the best things about her was that she was never nagging or insistent. I was never conscious of any sense of struggle or any battle between the sexes when Helen and I were alone together. Instead of ringing for Oscar, I picked up a copy of the *New York Times,* unbuttoned my double-breasted coat and loosened my tie and sat down at one end of the davenport. Helen picked up the piece of petit point embroidery on which she had been working. There was no sound in the room but the occasional snapping of the oak logs in the fireplace at which we would both look up simultaneously to be sure that no spark fell on the beautiful round hooked rug which Helen had bought from some deceased collector's collection. Then we would look back again, I to the last paragraph of the lead editorial of the *New York Times* on the British monetary situation, and Helen to her embroidery, but neither of us would speak. Helen had always understood the value of silence.

Somewhere down the hall I heard the gentle opening and closing of a door.

"What's that?" I asked.

"Oh," Helen said, "it's Oscar sending in Farouche to say good night."

Farouche was the gray poodle that Helen had bought because, as she said, I had spoken about a dog, and she had always wanted a poodle. Farouche was trimmed in the modern Airedale manner, and the fur on top of his cranium was tied together by a fresh red bow. Nevertheless Farouche did not look silly. He entered the room in a dignified manner without bouncing or slobbering, carrying a rubber ring in his mouth. He glanced at us both, pleasantly and expectantly, and assumed an alert sitting position in front of us.

"Hello, Farouche, darling," Helen said.

Farouche edged nearer, still holding his rubber ring.

"Aren't you going to play with him?" Helen asked.

Farouche had a one-track mind, and the ring was his obsession. When I got up from the davenport and approached him, he dropped it carelessly, but he always snatched it again before I could pick it up, and he was delighted by my clumsiness. In the end, Farouche was very generous with me. He deliberately allowed me to get the ring so that I could toss it across the room. I was very glad to do so because it gave Farouche great pleasure, but I could not go on with this indefinitely, and Farouche understood when I was tired.

"He's very gracious tonight," I said, "and I like his new bow."

"He isn't gracious," Helen said. "He loves us. Don't you love us, Farouche?"

I never understood why people take a dog's love for granted. Farouche's mind was on his rubber ring. He knew that I had given up, but there was always hope that I would try to snatch his ring again.

"My God," I said, "we seem to be a long way from anywhere tonight."

Helen looked up at me quickly, but she did not give the appearance of adjusting herself patiently to one of my moods.

"Where's anywhere?" she asked.

"Anywhere is where we used to be," I said.

Helen raised her eyebrows and smiled.

"You always used to say you didn't care where you were," she said. "Remember?"

"That's true," I said, "but that's when I was anywhere, not somewhere."

"Darling, what got your mind on this?" Helen said. "You were just playing with Farouche."

"That's exactly it," I said. "I never thought I'd own a poodle with a bowknot on his head."

"He doesn't have to wear a ribbon."

"Even without a ribbon," I said, "even with a crew cut."

"I wish you wouldn't try to make him into a symbol," Helen said. "Don't you like him?"

Of course, I said, I liked him. I had not intended to discuss any phases of our life together, but there we were. Helen was sitting up straighter and she was speaking more carefully.

"Well, darling," she said, "you got us here. I didn't. We ought to put that on the record, and we have to be somewhere like this."

"All right," I said. "I know. It just happened, but I can't help feeling queer."

"Now, Sid," Helen said, "of course we're strangers here and we're new, but all the neighbors have come to call on us. They're all very nice, and we're being taken into the Country Club."

"They're all different," I said.

Farouche picked up his rubber ring and edged closer to me.

"Darling," Helen said, and there was a catch in her voice, "don't you like *anything* you're doing?"

It was impossible to answer yes or no to her question. There were aspects to the radio program that I did not like at all, but there were also compensating factors. I liked to use my editorial judgment on Art's script and to work myself over the dispatches from the newsroom, but at the same time I hated the show business side of it. I did not like having been discovered and turned suddenly into an overnight wonder like a Hollywood star. I could laugh with my old friends about my situation and they could laugh back, but it was not the old give-and-take of other days. There was always bound to be that element of envy which one cannot help feeling toward

41

some contemporary who has suddenly hit the jackpot. It was uncomfortable being accidentally successful for no sound or adequate reason.

"I like it all right," I said, "as long as I know what I'm doing, but let's not try to fool ourselves."

"It makes me awfully angry when you take that point of view," Helen began, "and start running yourself down."

"It's all right," I said, "as long as you just admit there's money in it, and you don't try to make me think I'm an artist. We're just two people trying to get along."

"Well, it only takes you a few minutes every evening," she said, "and you were wonderful tonight."

"That's the way to look at it," I said. "Just a few mad minutes."

"Darling," Helen said, "whatever you do, you're wonderful, and I like being a long way from anywhere as long as you're around."

"All right," I said, "only let me know when you're tired — that's all." And I kissed her.

There was a cough in the hall. It was Oscar, who was always discreet. I always felt like a guest when he coughed.

"Hello," I said. "What's the problem, Oscar?"

"I came to take Farouche to bed, sir," Oscar said, "and there's the same gentleman on the telephone again from Washington, a Colonel Flax, Colonel Edward Flax."

It took me a moment to remember the urgent call from Washington.

"He's from the office of Army Public Relations," Oscar said.

A number of telephone extensions in the house left me a wide choice as to where I could best talk to Colonel Flax, whether in the hall, the library, or the office where Art and the studio staff worked whenever we prepared the script in the country.

"Don't you want me to take the message for you?" Helen asked. She was always convinced that I would bungle any conversation on the telephone.

"Oh, no, I'll speak to him," I said. "I'll take it in the library."

"Well, don't let him make you do something you don't want to do," Helen said. "You never can say no over the telephone."

42

Oscar and Farouche accompanied me to that room of my own, the library. The telephone stood on the tooled-leather surface of the Old English desk on which I was to do some writing some day and on which the microphones were set up when I went on the air at home. I walked across to it as gingerly as though I were apologetically taking a call in someone else's house. I was still sure that I did not know anyone named Flax and I could not imagine why anyone should want to talk to me about Melville Goodwin at ten o'clock at night. Consequently I used my best voice, full of the integrity that Gilbert Frary so greatly admired.

"Hello," I said. "This is Mr. Skelton speaking."

I was answered by a worried voice which I could place as belonging to someone accustomed to giving orders and who, instead, was obliged to be ingratiating.

"Good evening, Mr. Skelton. This is Colonel Flax. I am sorry to trouble you so late at night. I'm in Public Relations at the Pentagon — General Todd's office — your former chief."

"Oh, yes," I said.

People invariably felt that it built them up to say that they were speaking from the Pentagon, and I had to admit I had done the same thing often enough myself when I was in there during the war.

"The General would have called you himself," Colonel Flax said, " — he was anxious to speak to you personally — but unfortunately he is delivering an address before the American Legion tonight. He did want me, though, to send you his warmest regards. He speaks of you very often and about the old days in Paris."

"Well, now, that's very kind of him," I said. "If you happen to think of it, tell the General I think of him often, too. I hope he doesn't still suffer from indigestion."

I looked at the leather-bound rows of British novelists and poets in front of me. I did think of the General sometimes, largely because he had not been good at Public Relations. He had come from the Point at a time when no one had ever heard of Public Relations.

"He brought up your name himself this evening," Colonel Flax said. "When we were in conference with the Secretary, a certain matter came up, and it was the General's idea, in which the Secretary concurred, that it ought to be handled informally. I imagine you can guess what it is, Mr. Skelton. We don't want to pull too many strings from here, and the General was wondering, and the Secretary concurred, whether, because of your former connection and your fine record in the service and your continued interest in the army and also because of your closeness to General Melville Goodwin — cr — whether you couldn't help out personally on a little job of work, nothing difficult, you understand, but informal. I wish I could talk to you personally and not over the telephone. If it's agreeable to you, I can come up to New York the first thing in the morning."

The colonel was speaking with an anxiety which communicated itself to me. In spite of my distance from the Pentagon, I could tell that there would be trouble for the colonel if he did not get what he wanted.

"Well," I said, speaking with integrity, "all these things you say make me feel very happy. You're right — I have a warm spot in my heart for the army. I shall always feel I owe a great deal to my war experience. But exactly what is it that the General wants me to do for you?"

"Well, frankly," Colonel Flax said, "it's about Major General Goodwin. You've been in here with us so that you can understand, in view of recent news, that he presents a public relations problem that must be handled in just the right way. We're right in here carrying the ball, and we don't want to muff it, and since the war — quite frankly, the personnel here isn't what it was during the war."

"You mean there isn't the same old versatility?" I said.

The colonel laughed as though we were old cronies sharing a sly, delightful joke. "That's exactly what I mean," he said. "We haven't the same old first team any more. They're all with the Air Force and the Marines, and this time the Ground Forces are carrying the ball, and we need a touchdown."

The colonel's voice ended on a ringing note, and without seeing Colonel Flax I already knew everything about him.

"All right," I said, "but I still don't know why General Goodwin's a problem."

"This incident in Berlin," the colonel said, "and the way the whole

44

picture is placed before the public. General Goodwin's flying back to the States tonight for press interviews and possibly for reassignment. He'll be in Washington tomorrow morning to report at the Pentagon, but we are planning to send him up to New York directly. He should be at Mitchel Field at two tomorrow afternoon."

It was a break for the army, with the Congress in session and with appropriations coming up, and it was natural that they should want to use the Goodwin episode for all it was worth, Colonel Flax was saying. There was a fine play already, and the news magazines wanted a definitive story. The General was a new personality, if I saw what he meant.

"We don't want him to say the wrong thing," Colonel Flax was saying. "We want someone to handle him, and we know how well you've handled a lot of the VIPs over in the ETO. If you could just manage to be with him to give him a little good advice, especially after those fine things you said about him in your broadcast tonight. His wife is riding up with him from Washington and all the sound reels will be there. We don't want him saying the wrong thing to those news magazines. In the conference it was suggested that you might be willing to meet him at Mitchel."

It all went to show what might happen if you spoke rashly on the air. Suddenly, because of a bright thought of mine that evening, I was the old friend of Melville Goodwin, the GI's general, right in there with him pitching.

"Before going to you direct," the colonel was saying, "we got in touch with the broadcasting company and we've been talking to Mr. Gilbert Frary, who concurs in the idea of your meeting General Goodwin at the field."

"Now, just a minute," I began. "I haven't heard from Mr. Frary."

"He said he would call you personally," Colonel Flax went on, "and he has another good suggestion if you will concur in it. He suggests that you ask General and Mrs. Goodwin to be your guests for a day or two at your home in Connecticut. He seemed sure that you would be glad to have them, because of your friendship."

I looked up from the telephone to find that Helen had entered the library, and from her expression I was sure that she had been listening over some extension.

"Now just a minute," I said. "I haven't heard a word from Mr. Frary, and I'm too busy tomorrow to go to Mitchel Field."

There was a deflated silence, and I wished that Gilbert Frary would mind his own business — but perhaps it was his own business, since it was as necessary for me as it was for General Goodwin to be a seven days' wonder.

"I'll send my car for him," I said, "and if they're going to do a definitive piece about him, they can come out and work on it here, but I'm not going to meet him at Mitchel Field."

"Tell him you don't want them here either," Helen whispered.

"You're sure you can't change your mind?" Colonel Flax was saying.

"Yes," I said, "I'm sure. But I'm sure that Mr. Frary will be there."

I should have said that I would have nothing to do with it. It was weak-minded of me, but I had begun to feel sorry for General Melville Goodwin, not that I knew him at all well, or that I had ever felt sorry for him previously.

"There you are," Helen said. "You let yourself in for something invariably every time you go to the telephone."

"So do you, almost invariably," I said.

"Now, Sid," she answered, "there was no earthly reason for you to ask him up here. At least you could have asked him without his wife."

"Now, Helen, you were just saying that I never ask any of my old friends up here," I told her. "Nothing's too good for old Mel, and I know you'll love him, and besides, I know Gilbert will like it."

"I'm getting pretty sick of doing things because Gilbert will like it," Helen said.

Before I could answer, Oscar had opened the library door.

"Don't tell me. I can guess," I said. "It's Mr. Frary on the telephone," and I smiled at Helen. "You'd better go back and listen in the hall."

There was no one more adequate in telephone conversations than

46

Gilbert. It always gave him inordinate pleasure to be chatting with the Coast or arranging calls with the overseas operator, and he was never bothered by the expense.

"How is everything in Connecticut, Sid?" he asked. "Settling down comfortably for a quiet night, I hope?"

"It's delightfully comfortable out here, Gilbert," I said. "You can hear a pin drop at any odd minute."

"Ha, ha," Gilbert said. "If you drop one, tell Helen to pick it up and all that day you'll have good luck, as the old adage goes."

"Maybe you don't have good luck at night," I said. "It doesn't say anything about night."

"Any home with the graciousness of yours and Helen's will have good luck day or night, I'm sure," Gilbert said.

"That's sweet of you to say so, Gilbert," I answered. "And Helen loved the gardenias. They came as a complete surprise."

"They were but nothing," Gilbert said, "but it did seem to me that fresh flowers in the country . . . Oh, by the way, Sid, to be serious for a moment, did an army officer from Public Relations at the Pentagon get in touch with you about that general, General Goodman?"

"That's right," I said, "he's just been on the wire."

"Well, I thought he had some rather good suggestions, didn't you? Not that you don't know more about these things than I do, having served with the army yourself overseas. I told him you had great loyalty to old associations."

"That's right," I said, "loyalty."

"I knew we'd see eye to eye," Gilbert said. "Then you'll be down at the airport and I'll have flowers from you for Mrs. Goodman, and perhaps you can think of some slightly comical favor for General Goodman, something that will look amusing in a picture."

"What's that?" I asked, and I was fascinated. "You want me to give him something?"

"Just something for a gag, Sid, that will look well in front of the cameras and the newsreel. I was depending on your own imagination, but how would a floral hammer and sickle be, or maybe perhaps you present him with a tommy gun, muzzle foremost, something with a laugh to lighten up the newsreels, Sid, and to give you the spot."

Gilbert's mind was never at rest, and I enjoyed so much hearing him run on that I hated to topple over his house of cards.

"Now, Gilbert," I said, "let's quiet down. I'm not going to Mitchel Field."

"Now, Sidney," Gilbert said, "I appreciate your reaction perfectly, but before deciding definitely, please give it a second thought. It may be better to have the ceremony somewhat more dignified and impressive, such as a simple frank handclasp and a word or two. I will withdraw the gag gift idea — but I do feel, without the slightest ambiguity, that this is all a real build-up for the program, and I know that George will approve of it. He always attends the newsreels, and if Helen can't make it, I know there will be another lovely lady there."

"Who?" I asked. "The General's wife?"

"No, no, Sid," Gilbert said, "but you know who — someone in your past and General Goodman's past. You know who."

"Goodwin!" I said. "Not Goodman — Goodwin."

"I wish I had your sharp-etched memory, Sidney," Gilbert said. "I've been talking about General Goodwin with someone who is intensely interested in him. You know who."

"Don't make me guess," I said. "Who is it?"

"Now, Sid," Gilbert said, "don't be so ambiguous. It's Dottie Peale, Sidney. She called me after you left the studio. She guessed they would be sending for the General. There's no one with Dottie's public relations sense. She's the one who thought about the gag present. She'll be at the airport, too, and Dottie's still photogenic, the minx."

Gilbert's thoughts were off again, and it seemed a pity to stop them.

"Listen, Gilbert," I said, "I'm not going to be there, but I wouldn't have Dottie either if Mrs. Goodwin is coming."

"Oh-oh," Gilbert said. "Oh-oh — does that convey an implication, Sidney?"

"You put it very nicely, Gilbert," I said.

48

"I cannot see how I was so inopportune," Gilbert said. "You mean he's seriously that way about Dottie?"

"He was the last time I saw him," I said, "but he was under strain, Gilbert; we were all under strain."

"Oh-oh," Gilbert said. "I love the way you put things, Sidney — so completely devoid of ambiguity."

"All right," I said, "how about our going to sleep now, Gilbert? I'm not going to the field, but I'm sending for him. I'm asking him to stay here."

"I wish I had your restrained taste, Sidney," Gilbert said, "yours and Helen's. I can see that will be better. The gesture has so much more integrity, and you can broadcast from your library tomorrow night with the General beside you, and some photographs."

"You'll come, too, won't you, Gilbert?" I said.

Gilbert's mind was working again in a new channel. It was going to be quite a party, a warm, intimate party — two old friends meeting after the wars.

"And whoever is doing the definitive news story, it would be gracious to ask him to do it in your home, don't you think?" Gilbert said. "We mustn't have any slip-up. I'll arrange the whole thing, Sidney, and I'll call Helen in the morning. It will all be studio expense. Tell Helen not to worry."

I looked up to discover that Helen was still in the library.

"Helen won't worry," I said. "Helen loves parties. Call us in the morning. Good night, Gilbert."

Helen stood scowling at me, and I laughed.

"Let's go back and toss rings to Farouche," I said.

"I don't see what you think is so funny," she said. "What are you laughing at?"

"About the General," I said, "my old close friend, Mel Goodwin."

"Sid," Helen said, "you never told me about the General and Dottie Peale. Was it that time you took all those writers and people over in a plane?"

"Yes," I said, "it was that time, but it doesn't amount to anything, Helen. You know Dottie Peale."

"Well, as long as it was the General and not you," Helen said.

49

At least she was no longer worried about the party, and the evening was over and it was time to put out the lights downstairs, and once again you could almost hear a pin drop.

"Helen," I told her, "don't forget that Dottie gave Camilla *Little Women*."

IV

If Necessary, She Would Have Done Very Well
in Iceland

Now that I had become so suddenly the old friend and host of General Melville Goodwin, I began to be acutely conscious of the commercial side of the transaction. I had started by being amused — and it was best always to be amused by such things — but now a sensitivity, of which I could never get rid, gave me a faint distaste for all that shoddy contriving. I felt ashamed that I should have to defer to anyone like Gilbert, and I wished that I were not so facile or so dependent on tawdry artificiality. I thought of sitting on Camilla's bed with my Scotch and soda. I thought of my integrity. It was getting shopworn and so were my old friends and so were my ambitions. All at once I felt as weary as King Solomon when he wrote Ecclesiastes and besought his readers to remember their Creator in the days of their youth before the years came in which they took no pleasure.

"Sid," Helen asked me, "what's the matter?"

"Nothing's the matter. I was just thinking, Helen."

"What were you thinking about?"

"Oh, this and that," I said. "I was just thinking that life makes almost everyone into something that he never exactly wanted to be, and then the time comes when he can't very well be anything else."

"But you never knew what you wanted to be."

"That's right," I said. "I never gave it much attention — but look at General Goodwin. Everything's closing in on him, except he probably hasn't the introspection to realize it."

"You're just talking in circles again," Helen said, but as she went upstairs she must have been thinking about General Goodwin, too.

"Don't start worrying about the lights. Oscar always puts them out. Don't you remember? Now come upstairs and tell me about Dottie Peale and the General, and don't be delicate about it, and don't think I'm worried about Dottie. You're always so funny when you think I'm worried about Dottie. I'm only jealous of her for just one thing. I wish I had known you as long as she has."

"If you had," I told her, "you wouldn't like me any more than she does."

"But you liked each other once," Helen said.

I had first met Dottie when she was make-up girl for the special-feature pages, and we had seen a lot of each other when we both worked down on Park Row. Right from the start Dottie had been an ambitious girl, who knew exactly what she wanted, and it did not take her long to find that I did not answer her requirements. She wanted an older man, in those days, with money and sophistication. She also wanted power, and the combination of these desires afforded the best explanation for her marriage to Henry Peale, the publisher, a few weeks after I left to join the Paris Bureau. Henry was very sweet, she said when I had dinner at their enormous house in the East Seventies the first time I came back from Paris. Henry was very sweet, but he needed his night's rest in order to face his problems in the morning. Henry would not mind at all our going out somewhere and dancing, and Henry could find something better for me to do than rattling around in the Paris Bureau. It was time I settled down and did something serious, and she would have a talk with Henry about me in the morning, and after we had got back to Seventy-second Street at two o'clock in the morning, she knew that Henry would not mind my kissing her good night because Henry knew that we knew each other so well — almost like brother and sister — well, not quite like brother and sister, but almost.

"Sid," Helen said again when we were upstairs, "what was it about Dottie Peale and the General?"

"I think Dottie was a little bored," I said, "and Dottie learned how to get on terribly well with generals."

It was a long story, one of those rather mechanized sagas that arise out of too much living, but Helen wanted to hear it all, and I was still telling her about it long after the lights were out in the largest master bedroom at Savin Hill.

In February 1945 I had been obliged to cross the Atlantic with Dottie and a peculiarly ill-assorted group of literary and publishing geniuses in an Army C–54. The idea was undoubtedly part of the program to make the Ground Forces popular, but I never knew who thought up this particular stunt or why I should have been sent back to Washington from the European Theater of Operations to take those people over; but obviously someone must have suggested to some high and publicity-conscious source that a group of writers who represented the arts, not the papers, ought to see at first hand what the war was about in order to appreciate the effort that the Ground Forces, not the Air Force or the Navy, were making to win the war. The idea had obviously received very high endorsement, either from somewhere in the Chief of Staff's office or that of the Secretary, because the whole trip had been given every possible clearance. Besides, the Air Force had pulled off such a trip already, and there was no reason why the Air Force should grab everything in Public Relations. The Ground Forces needed Public Relations, too. Hemingway had been a combat correspondent, but it was about time that other novelists, poets and playwrights should understand that the Infantry was the key to ultimate victory.

There was at this period a belief, quite conceivably correct, that there were so many short stories and articles about flyers, Marines, and the Navy that the Infantry was being forgotten to the detriment of its morale. Near the front there was always a pathetic realization that no one at home faced the truth in spite of military artists, newsreels, documentary films, war histories, and combat reporters. In addition, there must have been the discovery that nobody who could write was allowed to approach the combat areas because of age and decrepitude. There was no reason at all, with the Air Transport Command what it was, why a really distinguished group of individuals, including men and women, should not be comfortably transported to the theater of operations and there meet face to face the leaders who could brief them on what was going on and who could arrange illuminating side trips to the front and the devastated areas.

The net result of such a trip would be in the nature of a long-term investment and one of great potential value, since out of it might emerge another *Red Badge of Courage* or another play comparable to *What Price Glory*.

The whole project had been completely set up by the time I was ordered to Washington from the ETO, and the lieutenant colonel in charge had already arranged the itinerary and suitable accommodations for all the Very Important People, and a timetable down to the last minute, with dinners, cocktail parties and receptions. The commands where we stopped would be responsible for the smooth running of all arrangements, so that I had to act as nothing more than liaison, and if successful, this would be the model for other similar expeditions. It was not the colonel's business to consider that a lot of temperamental literary and artistic figures might waste the time of a lot of people who might be better occupied with finishing up the war, and it was not my business to tell him.

"We want someone who understands this type of individual," the colonel told me, "and that's why you're here, Major. You'll leave with the party tomorrow morning, and your orders are to keep everybody happy and reassured. Explain things to them. Smooth over the rough places. Use tact and personality and always see to it that everyone gets what he or she wants. I can't possibly give you any definite orders except that you'll see that everyone has a wonderful time, Major — and if anything goes wrong, improvise. There will be a case of Scotch aboard — you had better look after the Scotch — and there's a fine crew on the plane."

"You mean I'm going over as a sort of cruise director?" I asked. He was a civilian colonel, and one did not have to be as careful with high-ranking civilian officers.

I did not like any of it because I could foresee all sorts of areas of trouble, and I was particularly unimpressed by the Very Important People who had been rounded up for the tour. These consisted of two male novelists of whom I had never heard, three female novelists, a short-story writer, two motion-picture scenario writers who called themselves dramatists and some publishers and subeditors of magazines. I was introduced to them all by the colonel at a cocktail

54

party given at a Washington hotel by Army Public Relations, and they all looked self-conscious and strained now that they were on the threshold of the Great Adventure. I was so busy trying to remember each name and face and trying also to appear kindly and official, and above all as though I were used to this sort of thing, that I was not in the least prepared to meet Dottie Peale. I had written her when Henry Peale died, but I had not seen her since the beginning of the war. She was wearing a very smart twill traveling suit, and she had the cryptically bored look that she always assumed when she was out of her element. She was drinking a double Martini cocktail, which I was quite sure was her second one, not that Dottie could not handle liquor.

"Why, darling!" Dottie said. "What the hell are you doing here?"

I explained my assignment and I thought she was going to kiss me, but she must have decided it was not the time or place.

"Thank God you're going with us," she said. "You look wonderful, darling. Oh God, you look wonderful. Who are all these dreadful people?"

"You ought to know," I said. "You've been playing around with them longer than I have, Dot."

"Darling, I'm so mortified," she said. "I understood when I accepted the invitation that at least there would be Names and not just a list. There isn't anybody in the crowd I want to be killed with except you. Please get me another drink."

"You're not going to be killed, Dot," I told her.

"I have an intuition," she said. "That is — it's a premonition, isn't it? It's been growing on me, Sid, all afternoon. Not that I'm afraid. I'm perfectly glad to die."

"Well, that's swell," I said. "If it happens, it will all be over very quickly."

"Sid," she asked, "on the plane — will you sit beside me?"

"Some of the time," I said, "but I'm a cruise director."

"Darling," she said, "you do look wonderful in a uniform. How's Helen?"

"She's fine," I said. "She and Camilla are in Wilmington."

"Are you happy with her?"

"Why, yes, up to the present," I said, and she smiled at me as though she were sure I could not be happy with Helen. She smiled wistfully and very understandingly now that we were facing eventual dissolution together on our way to the Great Adventure.

"Sid," she said, "I wonder if you're thinking what I'm thinking."

"I wouldn't know," I said, "unless I knew what you're thinking."

"Oh, Sid," she said, "of course you know. Doesn't it seem queer to meet this way? It's as though it meant something."

"Possibly," I said.

"Oh, God damn it," she said. "Go and get me that other drink."

We always knew each other too well to be fooled by each other. Nevertheless I was very glad to see her, and I needed to see a friendly face in that planeload of talent as much as she did.

Some experiences and memories have seemed to me to be a good substitute for material possessions. They may tarnish like old silver and require occasional polishing, but they never take up room, and they are seldom around when you don't want them. You have to pay for them, of course, by giving a part of your life away to the people or places from which they were acquired. Though this is not always a good bargain, your acquisition is sometimes worth the price, and certainly better than nothing, and above all, beyond the realm of conscious choice. If some such exchange as this took place with me on that Atlantic flight in the last winter of the war, it must have taken place with Dottie, too. Without intending it, perhaps we both gave something of ourselves to each other, and consequently that day and night will probably for a long while retain a permanence for both of us.

I do not mean by this that any ultraromantic element entered into our experience, although we both may have been aware that such a thing might happen and possibly would not have minded if it had. It had been a long while since I had been in love with Dottie Peale, if ever, and the same was true with her. We both of us must have realized previously that falling in love with each other would have been a harrowing and unsuccessful procedure which would have spoiled a more useful sort of competitive relationship. At any rate, that was our relationship on the plane. We were critical and at the same time fond of each other, and it did not matter whether or not we called a spade a spade.

"By God," Dottie said, "it's nice to talk to an obvious bastard like you, darling, and nice that we can see everything in the same way without anything's ever getting anywhere. I'm awfully sick of relationships that inevitably end up in bed."

"That's a lovely way of putting it," I said. "You make me see exactly what you mean."

"Well, we might end up that way," she said. "I wouldn't mind particularly."

"That's very sweet of you," I said, "but don't let it worry you, Dot."

"Don't be so God-damned complacent, darling," Dottie said. "I could make you fall in love with me any time I wanted. Any woman can do that to any man if she has any sexual awareness, and you know it, especially racketing around on a junket like this. God, what a lot of freaks there are on this plane!"

This was the sort of conversation in which Dottie excelled. She always loved to spread her influence over people like a blanket.

There was not much time to talk to Dottie, what with all the attention I had to pay to the other freaks. They were all stirred up by the Great Adventure and they wanted to know all about future details, and I could see that this annoyed Dottie, because wherever she was, she always wanted some man for her especial property. This all took care of itself, however, because when we reached Gander at about dusk, there was a big fuss made over the Important People, with cocktails and a very special supper before the take-off, and I was able to withdraw a while with the pilot and the rest of the crew, who had the bad luck to be assigned to us all the way. We had coffee together before I had to round up the passengers, who were being taken to the PX after supper to buy toothpaste and cigarettes just in case there weren't any in Europe, and we had a chance to discuss the implications of the trip. There was a chance to say that it was a hell of a way to win the war — taking a lot of freaks around in a crate. There was a chance also to be drawn together by a mutual sense of frustration.

When the passengers climbed up the steps in the frigid dark and the door was slammed shut and they were told to make themselves as comfortable as they could, and that there would be a blackout after the take-off, I was delighted to see that they all understood at last the stress and strain of war, not that they were not all brave about it and very debonair. I found Dottie a seat over the wing, and after the flight engineer and I had arranged blankets and safety belts before the take-off, I took the seat beside her. While the lights were still on, she applied lipstick, efficiently and savagely, like someone preparing to die in the grand manner. She looked at me furiously when I told her that it was not on straight, and I felt rather sorry for her, because no matter how inured one may be to air travel, a take-off over a large body of water like the Atlantic is always a solemn moment. When the plane made its run, her fingernails bit into my hand, and I knew she was thinking what a fool she had been to come, but when we were air-borne, her grip relaxed. The motors made a reassuring drone in the dark.

"Does everything sound all right?" she asked.

"Hell, yes," I said. "Everything sounds fine, and now you'd better go to sleep."

"Sid," she said, "do you mind if I tell you something? I keep thinking we're going to die."

"All right," I said, "if you want it that way, but you could be wrong."

"Don't be so God-damned superior. I can think what I want, can't I? I'm not afraid to die."

"Well, plan your last words," I said, "and go to sleep. A special effort is being made to keep you alive."

"Oh, shut up," she said. "God damn it, it's made me sick all day, watching you showing off."

We did not speak for a while, and at last I thought she was asleep.

"Sid," she said, "I wonder what everything's been about."

"What's the matter?" I asked. "Are you still dying?"

"Suppose I am," she said. "I've always wanted to amount to something, and that's more than you ever have."

"Well," I said, "I've tried to get along."

"But you've never cared. Why don't you ever care?"

"About what?"

"About amounting to something. If you'd ever had any ambition, we might have been married. I could have done a lot for you. I really could have. Oh, God, I wish I'd ever been able to find a man!"

"Well, you've done a certain amount of investigating," I told her, "and you did find Henry Peale."

"There you go," she said, "and I know what you think. You think I married Henry for his money."

"Yes," I said, "that's exactly what I think."

"Well, maybe you're right," she said, "but Henry was awfully sweet. He understood me. You never understood me."

"You're damned well right I did!" I said. "I understood that I didn't have anything you wanted."

"Darling," she said, "you had plenty of things I wanted. I have often thought about them, but you didn't have ambition. You were possible in so many other ways, but I didn't want to have all the ambition."

Instead of answering, I listened to the motors. Though it was a time one could say anything one wanted, I did not want to say too much.

"I told you not to go over to Paris," she said. "I told you the Paris Bureau was the kiss of death. You didn't really think I'd wait around for you, did you, after you went to Paris?"

"No," I said, "not for a single minute."

"Well, at least we've always been honest with each other."

"You're damned well right," I said.

"Well, darling, we did have a lot of good times together."

"Yes," I said, "we had quite a lot of fun."

"Well, don't say it in such a disagreeable way. It wouldn't have worked."

"What's the use in going over it, Dot?" I asked. "We've always known it."

Everyone was asleep except the crew up forward, and the knowledge that only she and I were awake somehow made the darkness heavy and palpable. There was nothing to Dottie in the dark except the intensity of her slightly husky voice and the pretentious scent of

59

the Chanel Five she used and had used even when she was working for forty dollars a week, and except also an aura of physical cleanliness and resilience. Without seeing her at all, you could feel her strength and her unbroken confidence.

"All right," she said, "all right. Maybe I have done some investigating. Who hasn't? You can't help learning a lot about men when they are always making swan dives at you, darling, but it's all a little discouraging. I'll tell you what I've learned about men."

"Don't," I said, "or I'll tell you what I've learned about women."

I found myself sitting up straighter and listening. One of the port motors had missed, but then it picked up again. It had been nothing, and she had not noticed it.

"You never learned anything about women from me that didn't make you disagreeable and conceited," she said, "but I'll tell you about men. Most men are stupid and incompetent. You aren't stupid, darling. You've always been a smarty pants, but you're incompetent."

"Well, it's nice I have a high IQ," I said.

"You know you're incompetent," Dottie said, and her voice blending with the motors sounded like my own conscience speaking. "You were never able to write as good a news story as I could, and you can't handle people. God, I wish I could ever have found a man!"

I found myself growing annoyed, but I had to admit she was partially right. She had one of those restless retentive minds that could read and assimilate everything. She had an instinct for order and organization and an insatiable desire to influence everyone around her. She should have been a man and not a woman.

"You've never wanted a real man," I said. "You've always wanted someone you could push, and then you get tired of him as soon as you find he's pushable."

"Darling," she said, "you're so damned exasperating when you oversimplify. Of course I like to compete with men and of course I've had to in the publishing business, but I've always wanted a man who can do better than I can. That's all any woman ever wants — someone she can always respect, and someone whom she can do things for and who will listen to her."

60

"Well," I said, "that's quite an order, considering what you are, Dot."

"All right," she said, "what do you think I am? Please tell me, darling."

"I think you're a type," I said, "common in any matriarchal civilization."

"Oh, darling," she said, "do you think I am all of that? I told you you were awfully bright."

"You're an ambivalent type," I said.

"All right," she said, "maybe I am, but at least I know exactly what I want."

"You want everything," I said, "and you won't give anything up. That's why you're out in this crate tonight, because you want everything. First you wanted money and you got it, and then you wanted authority and you got it, and now you want to be General Eisenhower or something, and now you'd better forget about yourself and go to sleep."

"Darling," she said, "you're the only man who ever tells me what he really thinks about me. You're wrong, of course, but it's heavenly. Do you think we'll see Eisenhower in England or France or somewhere?"

"Not unless he's a damn fool, but I wouldn't know," I said.

"Oh well," she said. "Now I lay me down to sleep. . . . Good night, darling."

I was half asleep when she spoke again and I stayed half asleep while she went on speaking.

"I wish I weren't always competing for something. It makes me so tired. I was such a simple little girl, Sid. Did I ever show you my school photograph? I was such a simple little girl in such a nice little Midwest town, but Father and Mother always made me compete . . . and those little bitches at Miss Shippin's school who always had newer dresses . . . Did I ever tell you about Miss Shippin's school?"

"Yes, you know you have," I said. "Now let's go to sleep."

She did not want to go to sleep. That drive and ambition of hers must have come from her parents, who evidently had not wanted her to share their mediocrity and who had made prodigious sacrifices in her behalf. It was a worthy little story, but I knew without listening that Dottie would never get what she wanted. There would always be her discontent and her constant sense of unfulfillment, and yet she would never lose her high courage and desire. She would always be the center of some drama as long as she was alive.

Dawn was filtering through the windows of the plane when I awoke, and Dottie was fast asleep in the reclining seat beside me. Her eyes were closed, and her face, though tranquil, was somehow still alert. She awoke almost as soon as I stirred and unlike most people, she knew exactly where she was. She smiled at me as she rubbed her eyes.

"Is everything all right?" she asked.

"Everything's fine," I said. "If you like, I can get you some coffee."

"Thanks, dear," she said. "Didn't we have a good time?"

"When?" I asked, and she laughed.

"Why, last night," she said, "last night, talking."

"Why, yes, we had a pretty good time," I said. Dottie always was good company.

The trip must have received a blessing from the highest echelons, because the women were not required to wear any sort of uniform. Dottie was straightening her tailored jacket and arranging the eighteenth-century-looking frills around her throat and patting the plain but heavy gold pin that held them, not that any of this was necessary, because asleep or awake she was impeccably, aggressively trim, and she always despised sloppiness in dress or posture.

"It's like spending the night on a park bench," she said. "It's disgusting," but she would have looked as neat and fresh and competent even if she had been riding on bucket seats.

"Anyway, you can both take it and dish it out, Dot," I told her.

Her nose tilted upward when she smiled, as it did when she was particularly happy.

"Darling, isn't it nice being with each other again?" she asked.

"Again?" I repeated.

"I mean being on each other's minds, the way we used to be once," she said. "I haven't got anyone else on my mind but you. It's the way it was when you were a nice boy and I was quite a nice girl, but I

62

wasn't really nice, was I? Now button your coat and straighten your tie, and you should have shaved when you had the chance. You didn't shave at Gander, did you?"

I was not flattered by her attention because it only meant that I was the only man available at the moment for her to put her mind on.

Just then the door to the crew's compartment opened, and the mechanic caught my eye and beckoned. He wanted me to help awaken the passengers because we were beginning to let down from nine thousand feet. We were not going direct to Prestwick because of a weather front. Instead we were landing in Iceland and we would start off to Scotland again in about two hours. I was too busy after that to converse any further with Dottie. It was cold and blustery on the sub-Arctic air strip, not a tree in sight, only rock ledges and a few sparse clumps of heather and overhead a leaden, threatening sky. As we climbed out of the plane and started to a group of Nissen huts for breakfast, I had a glimpse of Dottie on the level surface of the runway, hanging back from the rest of the passengers with her mink coat draped carelessly over her shoulders, alone, as all of us would be in the last analysis. She was standing straight with the breeze whipping at her hairdo but never pushing it out of place, staring aloofly at the stormy land. Yet she looked as much at home as though she were on Park Avenue waiting for a taxicab, and I was sure she would have done very well in Iceland, had she been obliged to remain there permanently.

V

The Army Couldn't Have Been Sweeter

SOME MONTHS before this junket with the VIPs I had been assigned the task of conducting three or four newspaper correspondents to the front in Normandy. This was in the summer of 1944 during the build-up before the breakout near Saint-Lô, and it was here that I first met Major General Melville A. Goodwin. General Goodwin was commanding a division known as the Silver Leaf Armored, and the word was that he was somewhat of an authority on mechanized warfare, though he was not a personality with news interest. Besides, he was too busy to be bothered by correspondents except to meet them briefly, thus obeying the directive not to be disagreeable to the press. He only favored me with his personal attention because he wanted to make it very clear that I was to get those people the hell out of his sector as soon as possible. Then it had occurred to him that as long as we were going back I might not mind carrying back with me several personal letters he had written, and he took me with him to his dugout to get them. On our way a mortar shell landed near us, causing us to dive side by side into a ditch, not a friendship-cementing experience but something that did make us remember each other. He seemed to take the incident quite personally, I remember, acting as though it were a reflection on his own management that I should have rolled in mud, but finally he had said it was something that I could tell my grandchildren, and it would serve as a lesson to me not to come monkeying around in places where I did not belong.

I was shaken enough by the exploding shell to answer him somewhat disrespectfully. I told him, I remember, that it was not my idea of fun, being up there, and that as far as I was concerned I hoped I did not have to play around with him any more. Sometimes if you spoke frankly to those people, they enjoyed it, and he warmed up sufficiently to ask me what in hell I was doing in this war anyway. I told him I was sure I did not know, but whatever I was supposed to be doing wasn't useful. For some reason, this struck him as amusing, and he repeated it to his aide, who had come to brush him off. Then he said that I might as well have something to eat as long as I was there, and enough give-and-take had resulted so that he remembered me when I saw him again in Paris.

During the Battle of the Bulge in December, his division, the Silver Leaf Armored, had inflicted severe punishment on the crack German units that had endeavored to overrun it, but it had taken a bad pounding in the process, and in February it was being overhauled, and the General was in Paris on short leave. It was at just this time that I was there with that personally conducted tour, and General Goodwin himself was called in to help with the Very Important People.

By the time our literary caravan had reached Paris, various military echelons had succeeded in making the Very Important People who comprised our group feel that they amounted to more than they ever imagined previously — a phenomenon that was becoming quite common whenever the taxpayers' money was freely laid out for public relations. Indeed a selective feeling of sensitivity had developed in our party by the time we reached Paris. The Very Important People were growing quick to recognize unintentional slights, casual receptions at airports, grade B means of locomotion, and hotel accommodations not wholly in line with their expanding conception of their position. They were even beginning to criticize the quality of wines and liquors supplied by hospitable rear-echelon headquarters, but only mildly, as I knew, since I was the recipient of these complaints. Actually, they were having a wonderful time. They were becoming old campaigners, face to face with war's hardships, and entrusted with strategic secrets. They had been given the treatment reserved usually for visiting congressmen and perhaps a little more. They had been given wistful, brave and eloquent talks by the high-ranking officers best equipped to do this sort of thing. They had stood personally in the operations offices of bomber commands. They had watched paratroopers, had visited base hospitals and the interiors of tanks. Generals, who asked them to call them by their first names, had entertained them at delightful dinners, and they had been allowed on the whole to chat freely with the enlisted boys.

They were realizing increasingly that they had a mission to perform and that they, too, were part of the Team. Their mission was to tell smug, self-satisfied and ignorant civilians at home what war was really like, civilians engrossed in their petty selfishnesses who had never seen a dead body upon a battlefield or had never heard a gun go off. True, our group had not seen a dead body yet, but they had seen the Omaha beachhead. Now that they were in Paris and soon to go forward to study the ruins of Aachen, they might encounter a dead body at any moment. They might even be in an air raid and be dead bodies themselves, killed in a noble cause. Since most of the group had been engaged at least in the fringes of creative literature, they possessed the vivid imagination that enabled them both to appreciate and exaggerate. Some of them, in fact, were discovering latent powers of leadership and, in the few leisure moments allowed them, were beginning to indulge in military critiques. Being guests of the army, they were allowed to buy uniforms without insignia if they wished, and it was even suggested that the girls should wear trousers when they got to Aachen. They were very, very tired. They were making their own small sacrifices. They were having a wonderful time.

As Dottie Peale expressed it, the army couldn't have been sweeter, and sometimes the army was so sweet that it almost made her want to cry. I must say I was sometimes surprised that the army was so sweet to them, not that this made me lachrymose, since it was my business to be sweet to them myself. Looking back, I believe that the army was really impressed and bewildered by our party, because no army had ever seen anything just like it, even from a distance. No one knew, except in the vaguest way, who any of our people were, but officers, old and young, always seemed convinced that this ignorance was their loss and that it betrayed a regrettable lack of personal cultivation. They were always saying — even the generals, when they asked me in subdued voices just who these people were

66

and what they had written — that they did not have much time to read — and somehow those pocketbooks issued by the army seldom included the works of these particular Very Important People. Finally the brass even began to respect me, the mere cicerone of a traveling circus, because I could tell them what it was my charges did back there in the States. Thus I myself began to live in reflected glory by the time we got to Paris. I, too, was almost a man of letters.

I do not recall who in our party wanted to hear all about the Battle of the Bulge. This affair was still a sensitive subject in some quarters, since it was feared that the American public had gained the impression, especially after some acid comments by old General Peyton March, the World War I Chief of Staff, that this German offensive may have come to our leaders as a nasty surprise. It obviously must have seemed very important to somebody that these Very Important People, who had so much influence in civilian life, should be handed the real truth. At any rate, I was very much surprised on our second evening in Paris to be summoned by a very high-ranking officer and told that arrangements were being made to give my whole group a definitive lecture on the Battle of the Bulge. This was to be a confidential talk, and intelligence officers were already collecting the material, and efforts were being made to locate some competent general officer to deliver the address. I was to have my whole party at the place named at three o'clock. The day's schedule would be changed accordingly, and transportation would be supplied to take the party from the Ritz. I knew that this idea would not be well received by my charges, since they were pretty tired and had been promised a trip the next afternoon to Versailles, but it was not for me to argue.

The group found itself in a cold and bare room at one of the headquarters buildings precisely at the hour named. The lecture being confidential, there was a guard at the door to check credentials, which gave an atmosphere of humorless melodrama. Collapsible chairs were arranged as in a university classroom. There was a lecturer's platform, and there were specially prepared maps, covered by a drawstring curtain, with two officers to shift them. A worried-looking lieutenant colonel from Intelligence directed all the doors closed after asking me in a low voice whether everyone had been checked in, and I could see from the faces of our group that they understood that they had finally reached an inner sanctum. This was one of those strictly military occasions when everyone concerned had a word to say, and I had been ordered to make the first remarks. It was amazing how much trips like these had taught me about extemporaneous addresses, and thus I was able to step onto the platform grimly and confidently and to speak in that voice which Gilbert Frary had yet to discover.

"Ladies and gentlemen," I said, "we are now in what is known as 'a guarded room.' It is here that the day-to-day situation at the Front is explained to suitably cleared personnel. I am asked to emphasize to you particularly that all you may see and hear during this hour is of a Confidential nature, which means that it is only just below the category of Secret. For this reason you are asked to take no notes. I believe that is all I was ordered to explain, isn't it, Colonel?"

"Yes, Major Skelton," the colonel said. "Thank you, Major Skelton."

I stepped off the platform, taking a place beside Dottie Peale on one of the uncomfortable folding metal chairs with which these rooms were always furnished, and the lieutenant colonel followed me on the platform.

"Ladies and gentlemen," he said, "in arranging this er — little show, which everyone hopes you will enjoy, we are fortunate in having with us a divisional commander who took an active part in this battle and who has been kind enough to agree to outline it to you personally." He paused and cleared his throat and nodded to a sergeant in battle dress, who stood by a door next the platform. "All right, Sergeant," the colonel said, "if the General is ready for us."

The sergeant opened the door with a snappy one-two movement and then stood at attention. As someone involved in such arrangements had said, if you are going to do a thing, you might as well do it right. The army couldn't have been sweeter, and it was quite a — er — little show, with everything ticking according to plan. As the door opened, a two-star general, who must have been waiting in the corridor, strode in, deliberately, calmly, and stepped solidly onto the platform.

It was General Goodwin, whom I recognized immediately. He was a man of about fifty, of medium height, and his uniform was smartly pressed, even though its elbows and his ribbons looked well worn. His step was firm but at the same time light and co-ordinated. His sandy-gray hair was freshly barbered in a crew cut. His eyebrows were heavy, and the lines around his mouth were as correct as the creases in his trousers. His class ring immediately suggested West Point, not that a ring was necessary. He had an aloof but agreeable look which you might have called boyish, in that it made you think he had been a nice boy once, but he was no longer a boy. He was a two-star general, and not a staff general either. You could be sure of this without being able to explain why. He looked very much as I had seen him at the front at Saint-Lô, reliable and competent.

"Ladies and gentlemen," the lieutenant colonel said, "this is Major General Melville Goodwin, commanding the armored division known as the Silver Leaf Division, which saw action in the Battle of the Bulge."

There was a faint ripple of attention but no applause. After all, it was a confidential meeting. The General looked thoughtfully at the map curtain flanked by the two lieutenants.

"Have you got a pointer here?" He spoke gently and agreeably like a mechanic asking for a monkey wrench. The lieutenants and the lieutenant colonel scurried about the platform, searching with a galvanized sort of consternation, but somehow the pointer that always accompanied maps had disappeared.

The General raised his voice only slightly.

"There ought to be one around," he said, "one of those things you point places out with, Colonel. I always feel more at home when I have a stick in my hand." He smiled in a very friendly way at the Very Important People, and they tittered, realizing at once that the General was an affable man.

"Well, go ahead and find one." His voice was a shade louder. "Run out and get one, Sergeant, a ruler or a cane or something. And now

69

while we're waiting, I might begin to tell you the whole secret of how to win a fight, now that we're going to talk about a fight in a minute. This little ruckus" — General Goodwin strode toward the front of the platform and looked as though he were enjoying himself — "that we found ourselves in around Christmas time has all the principles of any other engagement, and the secret of winning a fight has been, I think, very well described by an old fellow who was a Confederate general in the Civil War. Mind you, I don't call it the War Between the States, because my grandpappy fought in the Union Army."

The General paused and smiled again in a friendly way, and I knew what was coming. It would inevitably be the good old chestnut that invariably flashed before the military mind.

"The party's name was General Forrest, but maybe you know of him, because they tell me that you are all high-ranking writers here, though I didn't know we had so many lovely lady writers." I saw the General smile and I saw that he was looking approvingly at Dottie Peale. "Now this General Forrest was an uneducated old fellow. He didn't go to the Point like General Lee, but he knew about war, and this is what he said in his simple way, and the principles of war are pretty simple, as you know if you've read Napoleon or Clausewitz, not that I'm giving a literary talk to literary people. This General Forrest said, the principle of winning a fight is, and I quote, *to git thar fustest with the mostest men.* Well, in this Christmas time ruckus we didn't git thar fustest because the Jerries were attacking, but we did end up with the mostest and we rubbed their noses."

The General rubbed his hands together. The aphorism of General Forrest was successfully off his chest. The sergeant was back with a pointer.

"Well, sons," he said to the lieutenants, "what are you waiting for? Pull back those curtains if they work and let's take a look at the map. You people must excuse me if I run right on informally. I'm not a public speaker."

The lieutenants drew aside the curtain. Major General Melville Goodwin was squaring up to his task. The preliminaries were over.

"Sid," Dottie Peale whispered, "he couldn't be sweeter."

As far as I knew, Public Relations in the European Theater of Operations had never been called upon to "humanize" Major General Melville Goodwin — a term used quite without irony in certain quarters when it became advisable to seek out homely and endearing qualities in the character of a general officer for the purpose of making him better understood and more beloved by the American public. Thus in spite of our previous brief acquaintance, I had never endowed the General in my own mind with any particular individuality. Until that afternoon he had been for me more of a species than a person, and when one was in uniform oneself, sharing the symbolism of rank, it was generally advisable to consider higher ranking officers in this manner. Then when they started pushing you about, instead of disliking them as people, you could blame their actions on a great system far beyond the control of any individual.

Up there on the platform General Goodwin was true to his species. His use of the old chestnut, the "git thar fustest" gambit, was reassuringly characteristic, and more suitable for a major general than a brigadier. His whole talk had what you might term a two-star competency, good and solid, without trespassing on the realms of three-star brilliance. His explanations of mobility and logistics were concise and unclouded, because there could be no embarrassed stumblings in a major general's talk. Those people had been trained since they were shavetails to marshal facts and present them to increasingly critical groups. Everyone was always giving a talk about something in the army.

Personally I had developed a healthy imperviousness to tear-jerking orators and would-be humorists and melodramatists. The easiest to take were the plain talkers, and the General was good and plain. As I sat there wishing to goodness that I were in some cafe near the Luxembourg Gardens, I began, in spite of myself, to think of him as an individual. The neat threadbare quality of his uniform indicated a sort of self-respect not acquired by looking in a mirror. He did not try, like so many of his kind, to project his personality or to exhibit the dynamics of leadership. He had learned somehow that this sort of thing was unnecessary, and this was not always so with major generals, a lot of whom had never held a rank above

71

lieutenant colonel before the beginning of the war. He did not appear to have himself on his mind, although he was addressing Very Important People, an experience which often made the army make an ass of itself. He spoke sensibly, not once drawing on personal reminiscence or saying that the American soldier is the greatest soldier in the world. Without being especially impressed, I began to wonder what there might be behind this façade, where he had come from, and what he might be like if one simply met him without the chain of command interfering — but then this was inconceivable.

In the middle of a sentence General Goodwin's talk came to a full stop, which startled me because I had not believed that a faint bustling sound in the rear of the room would have disturbed him, but when I turned to look, I saw that he should have paused. A three-star general had joined us, the one who had in fact initiated the whole show. He was an elderly-looking man with horn-rimmed glasses, and he stood watching like a proud headmaster approving of one of his teachers' efforts.

"I was just explaining the position of the Hundred and First Airborne, sir," General Goodwin said.

The visitor gestured to a sergeant to bring him a chair.

"Go right ahead, Mel," he said, "don't mind me. I am sorry I wasn't here at the beginning — but now that I've interrupted I might make one slight contribution to this discussion. War is always war, ladies and gentlemen. The concept is always the same in spite of modern weapons, and that concept was ably expressed by a Confederate officer in the Civil War named Forrest. He said it was all a question of 'gittin' thar fustest with the mostest men.'"

It was an inspiration, almost, to observe General Goodwin's face, for he seemed to have heard these remarks for the first time, and he gave them a subordinate's prompt approval.

"Yes, sir," he said.

"Well, go ahead, Mel, and don't mind me," the Lieutenant General said, and he sat down.

"Yes, sir," General Goodwin answered. "Well, up here is the position of the Hundred and First Airborne. . . ."

Years of discipline and the instinctive respect for rank and for the flag gave that little interchange a quality all its own, and aspects that might amuse a civilian were utterly lost on those two officers. Perhaps at some secluded meeting, in a poker game perhaps, Mel Goodwin would have called his visitor Dick or Charlie, since sometime in the course of their careers they must have been thrown closely together. Perhaps they had played polo once or had swum together on some Hawaiian beach. They were obviously friends, because of the word "Mel," but here rank kept General Goodwin in his place. He had picked up his chain of thought again, exactly where he had dropped it, and the Battle of the Bulge went on, down to its triumphant conclusion.

"Now that's about all I have to say on the subject," General Goodwin finally said. "But in closing, I don't want anyone here to think that there is anything definitive about these statements. All the reports aren't in yet. It will take years to evaluate them. A confusion called the fog of battle always settles over any of these ruckuses and somehow just never lifts. There's still a fog over the Battle of Gettysburg." He coughed apologetically. "Don't you agree with me, sir?"

It was very nicely done. He had tossed the ball over to his superior, exactly as he should have, and now his superior could carry it or toss it back, and the Lieutenant General tossed it.

"That's quite correct," he said. "You people would be surprised at the study any battle involves, but General Goodwin is carrying the ball for us. Go ahead, Mel."

It was all very nicely done. The Very Important People were basking in the relaxed confidences of the two military men.

"Well, sir," General Goodwin said, "maybe I'd better put the ball down now." He smiled, and his youth came back to him when he smiled. "I don't want to stick my neck out with one of my bosses listening." There were appreciative chuckles from the Very Important People. "It's been a great pleasure talking to you like this, off the record, and I hope I haven't put you all to sleep. Now maybe we'd better start thinking how we're going to cross the Rhine. Of course we're going to cross it. Thank you, ladies and gentlemen."

There was a gentle scraping of chairs. Then someone clapped timidly, since it might not be right to applaud a confidential talk,

73

but finally everybody clapped until the Lieutenant General's voice rose above the applause.

"Thanks, Mel," he said, "for the fine exposition that I knew you would give. I know all you ladies and gentlemen, our distinguished guests, must feel as grateful as I do to General Goodwin for giving us his time. Personally, I must add my apologies. He's down here in Paris for a few days of well-earned relaxation, and I was mean enough to cut into his play hours and put the bee on him for this assignment — but now perhaps we'd better all relax and get a little of this — er — fog of battle out of our throats. If you care to follow me downstairs, I think there are a few refreshments waiting, designed to accomplish this, and if any of you have any questions you want to ask General Goodwin or me or anybody else, why we'll be there to answer them. Thanks again, Mel."

I watched the group file out of the room, and before following, General Goodwin did the right thing. Smiling, he thanked the young officers for handling the maps and shook hands with the lieutenant colonel of Intelligence.

"I'm sorry about the pointer, sir," I heard the lieutenant colonel say.

"To hell with the pointer," General Goodwin said. "What is it, Sergeant?"

"Would the General mind signing my short snorter, sir?" the sergeant asked, and he unrolled the collection of paper money which soldiers gathered in those days, in the various countries they visited, and attached together with scotch tape.

"Why, certainly," the General said. "Pull it out, son. I started one of those myself once, but I don't know where it's gone."

Cocktails were served in the offices downstairs. By this time the VIPs had grown to understand that refreshments followed nearly every event. They were to be entertained that night at a Military Government dinner, which would be preceded by another cocktail hour, but they were not allergic to refreshments at any time. I had been told that morning, greatly to my relief, that Military Government would take full charge of the party from five-thirty on, which meant that I need not attend the function and could spend an evening in Paris by myself, but this time was still far off. Weary as I was of cocktails and appetizers and hearing officers going through the same routine, I had to follow them downstairs, the last of the procession like the tail of a kite.

It had not been my intention to speak to General Goodwin, because he would be bothered enough with other contacts. In fact, I never thought that he would remember me, and it surprised me that he did, until I recollected that officers of field rank were obliged to file away quick dossiers of individuals and their aptitudes. Scotch was hard to find in Paris unless you were around with the big brass, and even the VIPs were beginning to run short and had begun hiding bottles in their suitcases. I was taking the precaution of ordering a double Scotch before the supply ran out, when the General spoke to me. He was right beside me with a double Scotch himself.

"Well, hello," he said. "Who let you in here?" and he held out his hand.

I shook hands with him and told him I was there looking after the VIPs because someone had to. He asked if I didn't wish we were eating K rations at Saint-Lô, and I said I certainly did. Then he asked me if I'd ever been in Paris before, and I told him I had worked there for several years before the war.

"I've only been here during wars," he said. "Always passing through. Last time was World War I, just passing through, but you were in short pants in those days."

Naturally I did not want to take up any more of his time, and I thought he would turn away and give his attention to someone else, but instead he went right on talking, in an easy, friendly manner. Perhaps he was not at home with writers, and my status bridged a gap and made it possible for him to be informal.

"Well," he said, "maybe you'd better introduce me to the company," but he did not look happy at the prospect and he seemed to have something else on his mind. "Look, Major," he went on, "I'm at loose ends here. How about having dinner with me tonight — that is, if you haven't got anything else to do? God damn it, you don't have to. Never mind the rank."

"I don't," I said, "unless you want to pull it on me." Sometimes

75

generals welcomed such a feeble joke. "Thanks for asking me, sir. I should enjoy having dinner."

"Well, that's fine," he said. "You're sure you don't mind?"

"It'll be a great pleasure, sir," I said. He had obviously asked me on the spur of the moment, and now he may have realized that the whole thing was irregular.

"Don't sound off about its being a pleasure," he said. "I owe you a dinner. Those letters I gave you got home all right. Remember that mortar shell?" He laughed happily. "I always jump myself when those damn things go off. You never hear them coming— they're just right there. Let's have another drink and then I'd better meet the crowd."

"Yes, sir," I said, "I'd better introduce you. That's my function, I guess, and I enjoyed your talk very much, sir."

"God damn it," he said, "let's forget about the talk."

"Especially," I said, "about gittin' thar fustest with the mostest men."

He looked at me in a shocked way, almost as though I had uttered a blasphemy.

"Take me over and introduce me to that pretty girl," he said, and he nodded toward Dottie Peale, who was standing arrogantly aloof in her tailored suit, drinking a double dry Martini cocktail.

As the General and I moved toward her, I remember thinking very favorably of Dottie Peale's qualities of neatness and durability. The rest of the VIPs, though still avid enough not to miss a single minute of their unique experience, were beginning to suffer from museum fatigue, whereas Dottie looked as she had when she had awakened in the plane that morning over the ocean, fresh and in perfect order. The French, I was thinking, almost had a word for her — *soignée* — except that Dottie's general appearance had never given me the impression of care or effort or made me feel that she did all the things to herself one reads about in *Harper's Bazaar*. I found myself calculating her age by subtracting three or four years from my own, a computation which showed that she must have been about thirty-four that afternoon in Paris. She had never been aggressively or meltingly beautiful, but she still looked like a Rosalind in a page boy's dress, if you wanted to bring in Shakespeare, and she might have been a better Rosalind than any I had ever seen. She was not as pretty as Helen, I was thinking, but she was the most attractive woman in the room, and General Goodwin obviously shared my opinion.

"There's nothing like a nice American girl," he said, "is there, Sid?"

It may have been that first warming glimpse of her that made the General call me Sid. It struck me at the time as one of those crude and forthright efforts at friendship that the big brass made occasionally, and all that surprised me was that he knew my first name. He must have heard the newspapermen call me Sid back there in Normandy.

Of course Dottie had been watching us edge toward her, although she smiled at us in quick, innocent surprise.

"Well," she said to me after I had introduced the General, "I thought you'd got lost, Sid," and she smiled again, not at me but at him, "behind those maps or somewhere."

"Sid doesn't get lost," the General said. "Sid knows his way around," and he gave my shoulder a quick, affectionate shake.

"Oh, I didn't know you knew Sid," Dottie said. ". . . Oh, thank you, sir."

She had turned to a colonel who had arrived with another double Martini and who relieved her of her empty glass. The tone she used when she called him "sir" was charming, and ingenuous, but the colonel knew his protocol. If he had forgotten even for a moment that he was outranked, he would have remembered when the General glanced at him, and he left us.

"That Martini looks pretty warm," the General said. "Here, let me call him back and tell him to get you a colder one."

"Oh, no thanks," Dottie said. "It's very nice."

"These Cocktail Joes ought to know enough to dish up cold cocktails," the General said.

When Dottie spoke again, her voice had a serious, respectful note.

"I thought your talk was intensely interesting, sir," she said. "I'm not much at military details, not that I oughtn't to be learning, with

77

everyone so sweet about explaining things, but I loved seeing someone as sure of himself as you were."

I still sometimes found myself believing Dottie when she was humbly serious. You might forget the words but never her sudden yielding manner of speech. Even though time and experience had given me immunity, I felt a slight pang of jealousy as I observed its effect on General Goodwin.

"Well, thanks," he said, "but I guess you haven't seen many soldiers, have you?"

"No," Dottie said, "not many."

"Well, out here, if we don't want to get sent home," he said, "we've got to be sure of ourselves and also of the whole works."

"If you don't mind, sir," I said, "maybe I had better bring some of the other people up to meet you."

He was on duty. It was no time to talk to Dottie, and he knew it.

"That's right," the General said. "Go and get them, but just stay here, will you, Mrs. Peale, and help me? I don't know about these writing people."

As a matter of fact, I did not need to get them. All the Very Important People were already gathering around the General, so closely that Dottie was pushed to the edge of the circle.

"Oh, Sid," she said, "why didn't you tell me? I didn't know you knew him."

"I didn't know I did either," I said. "It just came over us suddenly."

"Darling," Dottie said, "do you remember what I said about looking for a man?"

"He wears pants, all right," I said.

"Oh, shut up," Dottie said. "Darling, you've got to do something about him for me. I don't want to lose him in this crowd."

Of course she must have known very well she was not going to lose him.

That dialogue between Dottie and General Goodwin has remained fresh in my memory because of its very dullness, but then even dull conversation had a meaning of its own in a womanless war theater. I was struggling under a weight of satiety, wishing that General

Goodwin had not asked me to have dinner with him, and wondering why I had not immediately thought of some polite excuse.

"Look at him," Dottie said. "He must be bored to death, but he couldn't be sweeter."

"If you don't mind, Dottie," I said, "please stop saying that these people couldn't be sweeter."

"You never did like people, dear," Dottie said. "Why can't you be kind when someone is suffering? Just look at him."

"I'm suffering myself," I said.

"But not in a sweet way," Dottie said. "You're always nasty when you suffer. Sid, please look at him."

"I'm going to see too much of him," I told her. "He's asked me out to dinner."

"Good God!" Dottie said. "Why didn't you tell me? I think you're the most selfish person sometimes, Sid."

If General Goodwin was suffering, he did not show it. On the contrary, he seemed to enjoy the group around him, none of whom would have given him a moment's attention in days of peace. He would have been at some army post somewhere this minute if it had not been for the war, sitting on some veranda in officers' row or in some office doing paper work. Perhaps this party was a welcome change for him. The word must have been passed that General Goodwin was a genuine combat general, and that he had seen a lot of action beginning with the North African invasion. A combat general was still a novelty to our party. He stood there answering their questions courteously, nodding and frequently smiling, with what looked like honest pleasure.

"Sid," Dottie asked me, "what are all his ribbons?"

For some reason, although everyone in the party had been given an illustrated folder explaining service ribbons and decorations, none of them seemed able to keep them straight. They only knew that every officer was a walking totem pole and that they could not read the signs.

"They aren't bad," I said, "considering he's a line officer and not in the Air Force. He's been wounded twice. He's got the *Croix de guerre* with a palm, Distinguished Service Cross, Legion of Merit, and a lot of other things with stars and clusters. He hasn't done badly at all. They look like good, honest decorations, and they're not too ostentatious."

"Don't be so patronizing. You haven't any," Dottie said.

I told her she was perfectly right, that I was in no position to collect those things, but I explained to her that officers, especially in the Regular Army, passed those things around to each other and valued them greatly because they were a help professionally, and that ribbons were useful also in indicating places of service, exclusive of heroism.

"I wish you would stop being cynical sometimes," Dottie said, "and stop treating bravery as a joke."

There couldn't be enough bravery, I told her, to balance all the ribbons in the ETO, and a lot of brave men didn't get them, and I told her that the General would tell her the same thing — that he really did have a very nice collection, but not all for good behavior.

"He's looking at his watch now," Dottie said.

"That's true," I said. "I guess he's had enough. He's going to ask the boss if he can go now."

"Sid," she said, and she pulled at my sleeve, "Sid, he's coming this way."

"All right," I said, "all right."

"Sid, can't I go to dinner with you?"

"No," I said, "you can't. You're going on another party."

"Sid," she said, "I've got a dreadful headache."

"Then you can have something quietly in your room at the Ritz. You can't walk out on the program, Dottie."

"Oh, can't I?" Dottie said.

"No," I said, "and you're not going to throw a monkey wrench into the machinery just because you have a sudden whim."

"Oh," she said, "so that's what I have."

"I'm putting it in a nice way," I began, and then we both stopped because General Goodwin was back with us.

"Well," the General said, "it looks as though the little party is breaking up."

Dottie spoke quickly before I had a chance to answer.

"Won't you come along with us to the Ritz, sir?" Dottie said. "Sid says that he's dining with you. I'm not going anywhere tonight because I have a dreadful headache, but I have a sitting room."

"Yes, that's true," I said. "Mrs. Peale has a headache and a sitting room," but neither of them was listening to me.

"I'd love it," Dottie said, "if you two would keep me company while I take some aspirin. It's awfully lonely at the Ritz."

"Why, Mrs. Peale," the General began, "if you're not feeling well — "

Dottie laughed lightly and musically.

"It's only a diplomatic headache," she said. "I don't want to go out to that dinner party, and Sidney says if I don't go, I will have to stay at home or it won't be military, and it's awfully lonely at the Ritz, but I have got a sitting room."

She stopped and waited and I waited while the General considered the situation, and it only took him a second to put it all in order.

"Perhaps I might make a suggestion," he said. "As long as you have a sitting room, why don't we all three have a quiet dinner there, Mrs. Peale?"

Dottie laughed.

"I think it's a very good suggestion," she said, "as long as I didn't suggest it first," and then the General laughed as though Dottie had said something delightfully humorous.

"I've got a car outside that ought to get us there," he said.

"Sid, dear," Dottie said, "would you mind finding my coat for me?"

"I've got a coat and things around somewhere, too," the General said. "Would you mind telling somebody to look them up for me, Sid?"

As I left them, he and Dottie were talking as though I had never been there at all, and as though they were old friends who had met delightfully and unexpectedly and who had a great many things to say to one another.

Outside the General's car was waiting in a highly preferred position. When he saw the General, the driver removed the cover from the two-star plate and opened the door

"The Ritz, son," the General said to the driver, and when we were all seated and the door was closed, he laughed. "Now that we're all together, let's cut out this 'sir' business and this rank. We both know Sid, and my name's Mel. What's your name, Mrs. Peale?"

"It's Dorothy, sir," Dottie said, "but you can call me Dottie if you like."

"Dottie," General Goodwin said, "you can't know what it means to see a nice American girl again."

"You've certainly met one now, General," I said.

"God damn it," the General said, "didn't I tell you to call me Mel?"

"That's right. Excuse me, Mel," I said.

VI

Sid, Here, Knows What I Mean . . .

In Paris that February, the Bulge battle was such recent history that it was still a good subject for conversation. It was generally known that the armored division commanded by Major General Melville Goodwin was a part of the group engaged in what was called "blunting von Rundstedt's spearhead." The Silver Leaf Armored, so called because of the insignia placed on its rolling stock, had been rushed from the Vosges area to a small village named Maule, where the situation was so critical locally that the division was ordered to attack before any suitable liaison could be established with the forces on its flanks, and, through no fault of its own, the Silver Leaf had been cut off and in the subsequent free-for-all had sustained heavy losses. Indeed it had even looked for a time as though it might be wiped out as a fighting unit, and I had heard it said that it only got off as well as it did because of its high morale and its commander's great skill with mechanized matériel. Whatever the facts might be, General Goodwin came out of the Battle of the Bulge very well personally. In fact if it had not been for the spectacular stand of the Hundred and First Airborne, the Silver Leaf Armored Division might have figured prominently in the news in those grim days when both headquarters and the press were looking rather frantically for heroes. As it was, everybody said that it had performed its mission correctly, dishing out more than it took and effectively chewing up von Rundstedt's advance elements so that they could finally be contained.

For a few days correspondents in the rear areas had been curious as to who General Goodwin was, and about his previous service, and a few people who knew everything, or thought they did, began supplying information. Goodwin had been in North Africa. He had been a brigadier at Kasserine Pass and had done something or other in that unhappy affair that had been favorably mentioned. Someone recalled that General Patton had spoken highly of him and had referred to him as Mel and had even called him a two-fist slugger. He was in the Regular Army, a West Point graduate, but never on what was sometimes called the "first team." Yet first team men had liked to have him in their groups and everyone could not be a prima donna.

When we had dinner that evening in Dottie's sitting room at the Ritz, an extra trimming which Dottie insisted on paying for with her own traveler's checks, I knew these facts about Mel Goodwin. I felt the genuine respect for him that anyone in my position was bound to feel for someone who had been through what he had. I wanted just as much as Dottie to give him a good time and to take his mind off things that worried him. Dottie was always good at little dinners and she loved to show how much she knew about wines and food. As she told us, she might be stupid about some things, about French for instance, which she could read but had never learned to speak, but she did know how to make men comfortable, and we could be a lot more comfortable at the Ritz than we would be at the Tour d'Argent or any of those crowded restaurants. I could do the ordering because I could speak French, and I could be bartender, too.

"Sid and I are almost like brother and sister," she said, "we've known each other so long."

She took a key ring from her purse. I could go into the bedroom, she said, like a darling, and open the alligator-skin case, not the big one but the small one, that she kept the bottles in, and, like a darling, I could bring out the Scotch she had bought yesterday and the gin and vermouth. Then while we rang for ice and glasses, she would go in and put on something more comfortable than her old traveling suit, but we must be sure not to say anything interesting until she came out. I could hear her whistling a little tune as she closed the bedroom door. I never knew what the tune was, but it was one I had often heard her whistle when she was happy, and it reminded me of her little apartment in Greenwich Village in the days before I went to the Paris Bureau. I could almost see her studio couch and her armchair and her bookcase with the copy of T. S. Eliot's poems that I had given her, and the paper-bound volume of *Ulysses,* which I had never been able to read except in snatches, beside her Fowler's *Modern English Usage.*

Dottie had no need to worry. The General and I said nothing interesting while she was in the bedroom. The General sat down heavily in a French armchair with rather dingy silk upholstery.

"By God," he said, "this is a good soft chair."

It was the first time I had seen him relaxed, but he was not wholly relaxed. His feet were placed so that he could spring up quickly if he had to, and though he had leaned his head back and half closed his eyes, he seemed to be listening to the street noises outside, to the staccato sound of motor horns one always hears in Paris, and to the sound of a plane. The lines on his forehead and at the corners of his eyes and mouth had not softened. His face had the stamp of the other faces of people I had seen who had come recently out of action into a quiet area. They always reminded one of a half-erased page still bearing a few distinguishable words left there by mistake.

"Son," he said, "it's peaceful here. How about taking a touch of that whisky before we get the ice?"

I was thinking as he held out his glass that we neither of us were as out of place in that sitting room as we might have been, in spite of its marble-topped Empire tables, its Louis Quinze sofas and its gilded mirrors. Other soldiers had been there before us — French and English and American — when the Big Bertha had fired on Paris back in 1918. More French and British had been there twenty years later, and then Germans and again Americans. The Ritz was as inured to soldiers as Paris was to war and riot.

When the waiter came with the ice, I asked him to send up one of the maîtres d'hôtel. We wanted to order a very good and a very special dinner.

"He understands you, doesn't he?" the General said. "I learned some French at the Point but it never seems to work right for me over here."

85

I told him that he could speak French as well as I could if he were obliged to, that it was all a matter of necessity.

"I wouldn't know," he said. "Frankly, I have never gone in much for languages, because if you know a language your neck is out. Now when I was in Tientsin, a friend of mine went to language school in Peking. . . ." He stopped; he was not interested in what he was saying. "So you and Mrs. Peale are old friends."

He glanced at the closed door of the bedroom.

"Yes," I said, "we've known each other for quite a while."

At least Dottie was something for us to talk about, and I told about Park Row and about her marrying Henry Peale, and how she had taken over the publishing business.

"Why didn't you two kids get married?" he asked. "You sound as though you'd liked each other."

I had not meant to sound that way. I did not measure up to her specifications, I said, and then I laughed.

"She was looking for a man," I said. "What's that poem — about asking Abraham Lincoln to give us a man?"

He had not heard of it, though he liked some poetry, and he asked if I was married now, and the memory of Helen and Camilla came back forcibly, as it did sometimes. Then we started to go through that little ceremony of showing photographs of our wives and children, and I remember the General's saying, when he drew a wallet from his inside pocket, that he wished he had one of Muriel when she was younger. He had lost his snapshot of the two boys, but they were good boys, real army brats. One of them was a lieutenant in the Pacific and the other was getting ready for the Point.

"I wish I had a better photograph of Muriel," he said.

But I did not have a chance to see Muriel that evening, because, just as he was going to hand me the picture, Dottie came out of the bedroom wearing a black evening dress that looked as though it had never been in a suitcase.

"What are you doing with the wallets?" Dottie asked.

"Oh," I said, "just looking at our wives."

"Oh dear," Dottie said, "am I intruding?"

"As long as our wives aren't here," I said, "it's nice that some understanding woman is."

"Muriel has never seen Paris," the General said. "She's always wanted to. I wish you could both meet Muriel."

"I hope I can meet her sometime when the war is over," Dottie said. "I'm glad I'm not a soldier's wife, especially a handsome soldier's wife."

"Does that mean me?" the General asked.

Dottie's nose wrinkled as she smiled at him. "Sid, darling, you're not being a good barkeep," she said. "Mix me my Martini."

The shadow of that unknown Muriel dissipated itself quite rapidly as wives' shadows customarily did in the ETO. It was no one's fault that it was hard to keep memories of wives perpetually green in that extreme and changing environment, even with the aid of the photographs and love-gauges that one carried overseas. The European Theater of Operations was not a place where home ties fitted into a successful design for living. Memory interfered with work, and if you thought too much about past domesticity, you became a maladjusted burden. Instead it was advisable to think of home as a Never-Never Land, and of your present milieu as a region with drives and emotional values that no one at home could possibly comprehend. It was just as well to believe that the things you did and said in this milieu into which you were thrust in order to keep your land safe and your loved ones secure, would have no effect whatsoever on what went on at home. Some day we would all get safely back to that Never-Never Land. Some might never return, but this would not be true of us as individuals. We would get back, and this Great Adventure would be the tale of an idiot. If you did not have this philosophy, you would not be a useful soldier.

The shadow of Muriel was vanishing as the shadow should of any well-trained army wife, and if the shadows of Helen and Camilla remained a little longer in that apartment at the Ritz, they were distinctly my shadows, and I was simply an innocent bystander. The General was the central figure, and Mel Goodwin — I began calling him Mel occasionally because it fitted our escapist mood — was beginning to have a very good time. By the time our dinner arrived, he must have concluded that he was comparatively safe and that Dottie and I would not let him down, though of course he never broke security. He was equally good at handling military secrets and liquor. Our conversation, consequently, never touched on future operations, and we never said mean things about high commanders. Dottie always possessed a brand of tact and intuitive good sense that could guide her in any situation. If she had learned nothing else, she was often fond of saying, she had learned how to be a good hostess and how to make men comfortable, though perhaps not women — she never did have much of a faculty for getting on with protected women.

Dottie had a good tough mind that did not object to monosyllables or facing facts, but she could also be a nice-girl-among-grownups. She could twist and turn a man and adjust him by some sort of mental osteopathy so that he always felt he was unusually brilliant and remarkably gay. There was no reason why she should not have been caviar to the General because she had been to a lot of more complicated characters. The General was having a wonderful time, and so was I, for that matter. We were under the illusion that we were all old, reunited friends, and this was not wholly due to the Scotch and the champagne. It was mostly due to Dottie.

"I can't tell you what this means to me," the General said. "In fact I wouldn't want to tell you."

Maybe it was just as well that he did not try. He was a soldier there at the Ritz, the representative of a great tradition with all the attributes of professional soldiers, from the days of the Macedonian phalanx. Mel Goodwin was not handsome, and nothing he said had brilliance, but the close cut of his hair, the level assurance of his glance, and the molding of his face, so devoid of the softness and the flabbiness that creeps into middle-aged civilian features, made him a part of the ages. He was Ulysses having a little talk with Calypso, Lancelot chatting with Guinevere, or Bertrand Du Guesclin, fresh from the Marches, divested of his armor, drinking his mulled wine and cracking his filberts between his strong white teeth. Even when I told myself that he was just big brass, he still retained a faint mist of glory. Once or twice — not more I hope, and for only brief intervals — I even found myself wishing that I, too, might be something like Mel Goodwin — a warrior from the wars — though I realized that this was a very adolescent wish and I soon pulled myself together. Yet I had never felt so strongly about any other military figure. I had never felt this desire for emulation when I had met Eisenhower or Patton or Bradley, but then I had never dined with any of them quietly at the Ritz, with Dottie to sit listening to their discourse like Desdemona with Othello.

Dottie was always saying that she loved to entertain graciously, and by this she meant that she liked to do things with a sort of weight-throwing ostentation attributable to her simple beginnings. The maître d'hôtel played up to her as headwaiters and captains always did. She wanted to give us a good dinner, she said, a really memorable dinner, since we were staying with her instead of going out on the town. Expense was no consideration with Dottie. It never had been since she had married Henry Peale. She was a very expensive girl, she used to say, but she knew just what the costs were because she kept the checkbooks and added the bills herself. There was no fresh caviar, and what we did need was a pound tin of fresh caviar, and imagine Paris without it, but we would do with canned caviar. Then there must be very good soup, something clear and bracing, and then pressed duck, and they could bring the machinery right upstairs, and a good green salad — they could bring the oil and vinegar — she would mix it herself — and then *crêpes suzettes,* and that would be enough unless we could think of something else. Neither the General nor I could think of anything else except coffee, and the General wanted American coffee and not that stuff that the French call coffee. The duck, as Dottie knew, called for a fine, sound Burgundy, but if we did not mind, Burgundy always made her sleepy. What about champagne? She was still a provincial girl at heart who loved champagne. The buckets always meant that it was a real party. We might just as well have a magnum of Lanson, and the maître d'hôtel could decide himself on the vintage — Dottie smiled knowingly at the maître d'hôtel with the special smile she reserved for headwaiters and captains — and brandy with the coffee — she had almost forgotten the brandy. It must be the best in the house, and she knew the maître d'hôtel knew his *fine*. It must not be *caramélisé*. She shook her finger at the maître d'hôtel, and her simple diamond bracelet glittered, the only important piece of jewelry she brought on the trip. I could see that she was proud of the word *caramélisé*.

"Darling," she said to me, "do you remember when you bought me the first champagne I ever tasted?"

That was quite a while ago. I had bought her a bottle of Bollinger at a speakeasy on Murray Hill while she was still working on the newspaper, and her bringing it up made me feel like an old roué, now grown settled and harmless, raking for embers in the ashes — nothing to worry Mel Goodwin.

"Champagne but not the bracelet, Dot," I said.

"You're damned well right," Dottie answered, "not the bracelet, darling."

The mention of diamonds cast a small shadow over us, but it was soon wafted away like the shadow of Muriel.

It was really a wonderful dinner, and there was no further effort or worry about what to say to the General after the duck and the champagne, because the General had begun to talk about himself.

"Sid here knows what I mean," he kept saying.

Naturally I felt flattered each time he said it, and now and then I could almost believe that I had seen a lot of service, although I was always careful to tell him that the army had only picked me up because I knew how to run a typewriter.

"Just the same, Sid knows what I mean," the General said. "I wish I could take you up forward with me, Sid."

"I wouldn't be any good, Mel," I said.

"You were all right at Saint-Lô," he said. Even Dottie was pleased at this — in a maternal way.

He said that frankly he never felt at home when he was in a rear area. He was not a politician and he never had been, and that was why he could not thank Dottie enough for having him here. Otherwise he would have been at some mess with a lot of smooth manipulators and Cocktail Joes. It was better where the guns were going off. He knew his way around at the front, where things were simpler, and Sid knew what he meant. Up there people had to come across or they'd be sent back. He could always understand what motivated troops. You could look at men's faces and tell just how much further you could push them, and Sid knew what he meant. There was nothing like the feeling that you had the confidence of troops. Loyalty came from the bottom up and not from the top down, in his experience. Troops never went back on you if you knew troops, and Sid knew what he meant. The old Silver Leaf was a good division because it had good troops and battle-wise officers, not just paper pushers who were too good to die. That was what hurt, and Sid knew what he meant. You had to estimate casualties, but you never could get immune to them. Now for example, there outside of Maule, there was a situation with tanks. There was no time to mill around. You had to keep them moving. Sid knew what he meant. You had to treat troops like kids sometimes, if you were to keep them moving. You had to show them you could do it, too, even if it was childish. He drove his jeep out ahead of the tanks just to get them going. It was not good judgment and he had no business out there, but it worked. You had to keep them moving.

Dottie sat in an armchair with her feet curled under her, listening.

"You mean you were out ahead of everything?" she asked. She was listening but she could only follow part of it.

"I shouldn't have mentioned it," the General said. "It was a foolish sort of thing to do."

"I'm awfully glad you did," Dottie said. "It makes me sure that everything I think about you is true."

Her voice made me realize, now that dinner was over, that neither Dottie nor the General needed me any more. The thing that he hated worst, he was saying, was the period just before troops were committed to action, when you had to walk around among them and talk to them. He no longer said that Sid knew what he meant.

"You know," he said, "talking like this gets a lot of things clear in my own mind. That thing you said this afternoon about my being sure — that's an interesting thought. You've got to be sure of the whole works. You've got to know the whole thing behind you is going to move ahead. What is that poem about Ulysses?"

"What poem about Ulysses?" Dottie asked.

"That poem," the General said, and he snapped his fingers as though this would stimulate his memory, "that one by Tennyson."

"Oh, I know the one you mean," Dottie said. "It's about the rowers and Ulysses going to sea again."

"That's it," the General said, "because he couldn't sit still. . . . 'Push off, and sitting well in order smite the sounding furrows.'"

None of us spoke for a moment. I had not thought of General Goodwin as emotional until then. He sat staring in front of him, and then he looked at his watch.

"Don't," Dottie said, and she put her hand on his arm. "It isn't time to go."

"Well, maybe it isn't if you say so," the General said, "but I've got my car waiting. Someone had better send it away."

He was not suggesting that I should do it, but it was time for me to go. It was none of my business any longer how Mel Goodwin or Dottie spent the rest of the night. Things had moved to a conclusion, and a part of the conclusion was that it was time for me to go. Also, it was not a time to call him Mel.

"I'll tell your driver, sir," I said. "I've got to get some sleep. The group is going to do something or other tomorrow at half past nine."

"Sid, I simply can't go tomorrow morning," Dottie said. "I've got a dreadful headache, I mean a dreadful, diplomatic headache."

"Well, it was a good diplomatic dinner," I said.

"I'll see you tomorrow, Sid," the General said.

"I certainly hope so, sir," I said.

"Good night, dear," Dottie said, and she kissed me.

Neither Dottie nor the General spoke as I left the room, and their silence urged me to leave it quickly. It was a quarter to one in the morning I saw as I looked at my watch, and when I closed the door the echo of "the sounding furrows" lay there behind me.

The manner in which Mel Goodwin and Dottie Peale spent their spare time should certainly have been no concern of mine. I am convinced that I was not jealous, though Helen said I was when I told her the story that night at Savin Hill. I was not theoretically disapproving, for in wartime one developed a delightful tolerance concerning who was sleeping with whom and why. War, whatever it might do to improve broad-mindedness, fortitude and capacity for self-sacrifice, was not calculated to bolster the abstinences of the flesh. Besides, Paris was Paris, and even in peacetime that magnificent city, once one of the most gallant, and still one of the most tolerant in the world, acted as an aphrodisiac to foreign visitors.

The European Theater of Operations, even in its most antiseptic periods, was never conducive to the small refinements or the dalliances of romance. Emotions and desires were expressed there in very direct terms, and nobody cared much what you did as long as you didn't do it all over the place and as long as it did not interfere too much with the fixed routine of duty. Yet there were some limits in the ETO, particularly for generals. What annoyed me, I think, about those few days of pilfered bliss, aside from the blatant obviousness and the crudity of the whole affair, was the naïveté displayed by Melville A. Goodwin. It was unbecoming and absurd, at least so it seemed to me, that the General at his age should have acted like a first lieutenant. Granted he had fallen for Dottie like a ton of bricks, there was no reason why he should have fallen flat on his face in public. There was no reason, either, why he should have attached himself to the VIP group and have followed them to USO and Red Cross installations and even to the tomb of the unknown soldier. He need not have gravitated to Dottie's side on every possible occasion nor have displayed an air of lovesick comedy even in the way he helped her on and off with her mink coat.

There was no reason either for Dottie to look continually like the cat that had swallowed the canary. Granted he was a major general, there were plenty of others like him; but I did not mind about Dottie. After all, the General was a feather in her hat and something to talk about later, and you had to do something for the boys in those days, if only out of patriotism — but I felt sorry for the General, in his ostrichlike obtuseness. He should have realized that just as soon as I sent his driver home, everyone at the motor pool would know what had happened at the Ritz and he might have refrained from taking Dottie conspicuously around in his car afterwards — but I suppose she liked the two-star insignia.

At about noon the next day the General appeared at the bar of the Ritz and seeing me there made him slightly self-conscious, although he was very genial.

"Well, hello, Sid," he said. "We had a lot of fun last night, didn't we?"

"Yes, we certainly did," I said.

He looked at me uncertainly and then he smiled.

"Oh, hell," he said, "why not admit it?"

"Why not?" I said. "It's easier."

Then he looked at me in a hard way, because, after all, troops were troops.

"I admit it and I'm proud of it."

"Well, that's fine," I told him.

"I'm proud of it," he said, "but I don't want any of this to hurt anyone. You understand?"

He must have seen that I did not like the way he said it.

"I'm not referring to you, Sid," he said. "I don't see any reason why there should be any talk. Do you?"

"No," I said, "not particularly."

"What the hell do you mean," he asked, "by 'not particularly'?"

"Well, there's your driver," I said.

"Oh," he said, "don't worry. That boy's been around, but I wouldn't want anything in any way to reflect on . . ."

He did not finish what he had to say because Dottie appeared at that moment.

"Oh," she said to the General, "I'm sorry I've kept you waiting, sir. Oh, Sid, here you are, too."

"Yes," I said, "here I am."

She was in her tailored suit again with a gold pin at her throat, and as usual she looked as though she had slept for hours.

"Sid, darling," she said, "Mel wants to go with us to see Napoleon's tomb. He's never seen it. I think he ought to, don't you?"

"Yes," I said, "but don't you think it would be just as well if he saw it some other time?"

"Oh, Sid," she said, "don't be so stuffy, darling. This is Paris."

"You're damned well right it is," I said.

"Sit down, Dottie," the General said, "and let me take your coat. We ought to have a drink before we see the tomb. What do you want to drink, Dottie?"

"Oh, Mel," Dottie said, "imagine your not knowing — a double Martini, dear."

"That's right," the General said, "imagine my not knowing."

"Listen," I said. "Everybody else will be here in a minute. Why not put off visiting that tomb?"

"Oh, Sid," Dottie said, "don't be so sour just because you see I'm happy," and she scowled at me and then she watched the General, who had gone to the bar himself to order her double Martini.

"Well, stop looking as though you'd swallowed a canary," I said.

"Oh, Sid," she said, "he isn't really a canary," and then she held my hand for a minute under the table. "Darling," she whispered, "do you know, I really think I love him."

"Well, that's swell," I said, "but don't love him in the bar" — I spoke very quickly because the General was coming back, carrying her double Martini himself — "Just remember, Dot, he's a pretty simple guy."

"And I'm pretty sick of complicated guys," she said.

It was rather touching to see the proud, happy expression on the General's face as he carried the Martini. At any rate, it was none of my business, and we were going to Aachen on Wednesday. It would all be over on Wednesday.

My duties at that period were exclusively limited to interpreting the wants and desires of my company of trained seals and to seeing that everyone was reasonably comfortable and happy and understood and loved the army, and these duties were onerous and absorbing. What Dottie did and what Mel Goodwin did fell entirely beyond my sphere of responsibility, but when I told Helen that night at Savin Hill that I had been disappointed in the General, she said that I had not been disappointed but repeated that I was jealous — not actively perhaps, but at any rate subconsciously.

95

"You know," Helen said, "you used to be half in love with her. You were when I first saw you."

There was no reason whatsoever for Helen to make me into a character in that romance at the Ritz. I had evidently not given my reminiscences the proper values, something that often happened when I told things to Helen, though no one's wife, who had remained in the Never-Never Land with other loved ones, could be expected to grasp what one thought or felt in the ETO. She could not understand why I seemed to think of Mel Goodwin as being too good for what had happened to him at the Ritz, and then exasperatingly Helen went off on another tangent.

"Sid," she asked me, "were you faithful to me in the ETO?"

I did not even have to say that I was faithful to her, Cynara, in my own fashion, and if she did not believe me, there was nothing further I could add to reassure her, especially since Helen had been reading recently about the sex habits of the American male. She simply did not understand that there were not many women in the ETO. She seemed to have convinced herself that there had been Wacs and Waves and Red Cross girls and theatrical entertainers over there by the million. It was hard to make her realize that the competition had been terrific and that I had never cared much for competition.

"But, Sid," she said, "you know you're very attractive."

"You don't seem to realize," I said, "that a different sort of attraction was needed over there."

It did not reassure her when I told her that a surprisingly large percentage of men in the ETO had been faithful to their wives and sweethearts, if only through stress of circumstance or because they were not fast workers.

"You boys," Helen said, "always stick together."

It was just as well to leave it at that, and perhaps we boys always did stick together, and this may have been why I found myself defending Melville Goodwin. In fact, for a little while back there in Paris I was considered an authority on the love life of General Melville Goodwin by many high-ranking officers.

The morning I called to discuss the final arrangements for the

96

departure of the VIPs from Paris, I found that the officer in charge was one of Mel Goodwin's contemporaries, a harassed-looking man whose name was Struthers. At least he was harassed at the moment, as people usually were when they embarked on VIP planning. When we had finished with the details of our paper work, he asked me to close the door and offered me a cigar.

"Say, Skelton," Colonel Struthers said, "you must have quite a time running that three-ring circus."

I told him it was a very broadening experience. The colonel lighted a cigar carefully and looked at the ceiling.

"What's your reaction to all this about Mel Goodwin?" he asked.

"What about him, sir?" I asked.

He appeared relieved by my question, since it indicated that I had tact and discretion, even though I had not been educated at the Point.

"I have served with Mel," he said, "out in the Philippines. We used to have quite a time at Baguio — I wonder if those damn Japs have messed up Baguio."

"I wouldn't know, sir," I said, "but it must have been quite a place from what I've heard."

"Yes," the colonel said, "Baguio is quite a place — cool up there in the hills. You wouldn't believe there could be such a quick change in climate."

His thoughts had moved to Baguio, and I could not follow them.

"Mel's had a lot on his mind," he said. "This is off the record, you understand. I'm a friend of General Goodwin's, and she's not a bad-looking gal, not bad-looking at all."

"Yes, sir," I said.

"Someone was saying you used to know her," the colonel said, "back on a newspaper or somewhere. She looks pretty good-looking to have been on a newspaper."

"There are good-looking girls," I said, "on newspapers occasionally."

"It's all right for Mel to have a good time," the colonel said, "but I'm a friend of his."

"Yes, sir," I said.

"Not that Mel needs friends," the colonel said, "and he deserves to have a good time."

"Yes, sir," I said.

"But it isn't like him. I've never seen Mel step off like that. It's all contrary to his record."

"Yes, sir," I said.

"Men are damn peculiar about women, particularly when they haven't seen any for quite a while."

"Yes, sir."

"Well, maybe it's just as well she's moving out on Wednesday," the colonel said. "These things get around. It would be different if he'd been a ladies' man previously."

"Yes, sir."

"Well, I'm glad we've had a frank talk about this. There are always jealousies in the service, and there are some damn fools who don't like Mel. If there's anything you can do personally to keep things normal, it might be a help, Skelton. People like Mel and me have to stay in this army when the war's over."

"Yes, sir," I said.

"This is all confidential. I don't have to tell you that, do I?"

"No, sir."

"Well, come and see me," the colonel said, "any time you're in Paris. I've got a nice apartment with everything under control. I wish I'd told Mel about it. Well, good-by and good luck."

It was a relief to know that I was not being stuffy, but strictly professional, in worrying about Melville Goodwin's private life. Someone was always bound to notice when a general stuck his neck out. Someone was always looking for a flaw in a general's personal record.

VII

Always More Brass Where He Came From

TUESDAY was a very busy day what with checking orders and getting out mimeographed itineraries and briefing the VIPs on conditions in the forward areas. It was necessary to tell them that they would have comfortable, warm quarters, good food and occasional other forms of sustenance, but still, life would not be quite as soft as in Paris and they would have to excuse the army if the trip occasionally assumed a camping-out aspect. For example, each VIP would be issued an emergency ration just in case the system should break down. There was never any serious possibility of this happening, however, because of the interest taken in the trip by the high echelons. In order to make everything absolutely watertight, it was decided on Tuesday morning that Colonel Struthers himself, because of his familiarity with transport, should be put in general charge, but this did not take the personal details off my shoulders. I not only had to run errands for the colonel but I had to continue giving friendly advice about toothbrushes, cameras, shoes and foot powder. By four o'clock that afternoon, however, a short time was allowed me to do my own packing. I was up in my room right in the middle of it when the General knocked on my door.

"Go right ahead," he said. "Don't mind me." And he sat on the edge of the bed while I continued putting things into my kit bag.

"Dottie's packing up, too," he said. "She says I make her nervous watching. She told me to run out for half an hour. You don't mind my waiting here, do you?"

I told him to wait as long as he liked and that there was some rye in the bathroom but that I was short of Scotch.

"Dottie really knows how to pack, doesn't she?" he said.

Dottie was the only one in that crowd who could put things in her suitcases and know where everything was afterwards. She was one of those people who could move into a strange room for overnight and be all settled in ten minutes.

"Yes, she's certainly good at it," I said. "Has she got a headache?"

From the way the General hitched himself back on the bed you could see that he was used to making himself comfortable anywhere.

"Yes, another of those headaches," he said. "She won't be able to attend the dinner tonight. She's been quite a headachey girl lately, hasn't she?"

"Yes," I said. "They call it *migraine* in French."

The General laughed as though I had said something that only he and I could understand.

"That's right," he said. "Sid, did anyone ever tell you you're a damn nice guy?"

"Not very frequently," I answered.

"Well, I'm telling you."

"Well, thanks a lot," I told him.

"You know, once when I was finishing with Tank School at Benning," the General said, "I acquired a dog. He was just a mutt, but he kind of attached himself to me. I couldn't seem to get rid of him, and I remember how he looked when I was packing up to leave. He knew sure as fate we would never see each other again. He couldn't read but he knew I was ordered to Hawaii. He didn't know Mrs. Goodwin but he knew Muriel didn't like dogs. He knew he wouldn't make the boat, and I was packing. Well, that's the way I feel this afternoon."

"There's some rye in the bathroom, sir," I said.

"I don't need any God-damned rye," the General said. "I don't believe in drinking when I'm emotional. God damn it, I can't believe this is over."

The General stood up, paced across the room and back and sat down again.

"Maybe it's just as well," he said, "everything considered. You know how I feel, don't you?"

"Yes," I said, "I've got a working idea."

"You don't mind my talking to you frankly, do you?" the General said. "My God, I've got to talk to somebody."

"No, of course I don't mind," I said.

"Maybe I'm not used to this sort of thing," the General said. "It doesn't fall into any regular category with me. It's separate. It hasn't got anything to do with anything else, but I'm proud of the whole damn thing. You see what I mean?"

"Yes, I see what you mean," I said. "It's a pretty good way to feel."

The General stood up again.

"Sid," he said, "I've been thinking something over. Dottie and I were talking about it. My aide got killed last month. I consider aides expendable. If I asked for you, would you like the job?"

Dottie always liked to maneuver things, but it was also kind of the General to think of me.

"Yes, sir," I said, "I'd like it, but I don't think it would look well under the circumstances, do you?"

"No," he said, "I don't suppose it would, under the circumstances."

"Well, thanks just as much," I said.

Even though I was not sure whether it was Dottie's or his idea, it was the pleasantest invitation I had received in the course of the war.

"Sid," he said, "do you mind if I ask you a personal question? Why didn't you ever marry Dottie?"

"I told you before," I said, "that I haven't got what it takes."

"Well, I'd have done it if I'd been you," he said.

"Maybe she wouldn't have married you either," I said.

As I looked at him standing there in his worn, carefully pressed uniform, with its rows of ribbons and gold service stripes, I thought that he was safe as far as Dottie was concerned. After all, there were a good many major generals — but I had not expected him to follow my thoughts so closely.

"I know what you mean," he said. "I haven't got brass enough, have I? Why not let's go down to Dottie's room and have a farewell drink?"

"No thanks," I said, "I'm pretty busy, sir."

"Well, then I'll just say good-by," he said. "You're a nice guy. Good luck."

"Good-by and good luck, sir," I told him.

You were always meeting people and saying good-by and good luck in the ETO. I was reasonably sure that I would never see General Melville A. Goodwin again.

When his hand was on the doorknob, he turned back to me for a moment and he had changed subtly and completely. He looked again like any other general officer, composed, assured and removed from the ordinary strain of human relationships. He had withdrawn to the dignity of his rank, and whether you liked to admit it or not, rank did have a dignity and commanded respect, for it was almost the only reality on which one could depend in an environment of change and uncertainty. Although he smiled agreeably, his whole mood and pattern of behavior had altered in those few seconds. He was like an actor with whom one chatted in the dressing room, who suddenly became the playwright's character when told that he would go on in another minute.

"So long, young feller," he said. "I'll see you in church sometime."

He did not intend to put me in my place, but I do believe that he felt some need to put himself into his own and that he needed the reassurance of a sense of position. I felt in that last glimpse of him that many of the ordinary ties of human relationship and of friendship were denied him. He could have enemies and faithful subordinates and obsequious bootlickers, but he could have no friends in the conventional sense. He had attained the category of power that made friendship and sympathy a weakness. He was a piece on the chessboard again, remote, insulated and alone.

I saw Dottie for a moment the next morning outside the Ritz just before she took her place in one of the fine new automobiles supplied for the party. It was raining and nothing could be colder than French rain. She was dressed in a Wac uniform, because all the VIPs had been put into some sort of uniform for their forward journey. In addition she was wrapped in a trench coat that was too large for her and which I could guess the General had given her. If so, it was a useful going-away present. She had fixed things so that she could ride with Colonel Struthers at the head of the procession, and the colonel looked delighted. I don't know how she had arranged this without seeming to push or be arrogant, but Dottie was always expert at getting where she wanted, gently and sweetly, but firmly, and she always managed to look surprised when she got there. Her face was already wet from the driving rain and she must have known that this might happen. She must have deliberately discarded powder and lipstick, depending on the foul weather to give her color.

"Well," she said when she saw me, "that's that," and she wrinkled her nose and shook her head, and with that shake she seemed to have shaken off the Ritz and everything. She was off on a new adventure, riding up front with the colonel, and she had become very military. Dottie was always quick in picking up mannerisms from people around her, and I could see at once that she had learned a lot from General Goodwin. They used to say the way to learn a language was to have a sleeping dictionary, but I did not tell her that. She was looking at the row of automobiles with an expert and disapproving eye, and then she glanced at her wrist watch. It was a new waterproof timepiece which I had never before seen on Dottie, though I had noticed the General wearing one like it.

"Why can't we get rolling?" she asked. "Why don't we put the show on the road?"

These expressions, none of which Dottie had ever employed before, sounded crisp and convincing.

"Why don't you blow a whistle—" I told her—"two sharp blasts?"

"God damn it," Dottie said, "why don't *you* blow a whistle? That's what you're here for, isn't it?"

Her voice had a new ring of authority, and even the colonel, who stood beside her, appeared to feel its contagion.

"Major," he said, "get these people into the cars. Let's get cracking. We're due to take off at o-eight-hundred. Will you come with me please, Mrs. Peale?"

It was a rough, hard day, even in the new cars. The road had been churned up by truck convoys and the rain came down steadily, so that, in spite of getting cracking, the show stayed on the road two hours longer than scheduled. It was pitch dark and still raining when we arrived at a mediocre northern-France hotel in a provincial town on one of the main supply routes. As usual the red carpet was out for the VIPs.

We were met by officers of the Quartermaster Corps, who had everything taped up and rooms assigned, and there was even a Chemical Warfare general to greet us. The dining room was decorated with streamers — red, white and blue. There were cold-storage turkeys for dinner, and there was a Quartermaster colonel to give a talk with diagrams on the complications of moving supplies forward. I had no chance to talk to Dottie, and there would have been no opportunity later that evening what with the Chemical general and three doctors, if one of the lady novelists had not objected to her accommodations. She said that all of her windows leaked and she was not mollified until I offered to change rooms with her. I had not realized, though the colonel took it up playfully with me in the morning and several times later, that this room adjoined Dottie's and had a connecting door. As it was, the colonel only took it up playfully, saying I was pretty quick on my feet, what with one thing and another — but at any rate it was something which seemed unnecessary to explain to Helen at Savin Hill. I actually had no idea that Dottie was in the adjoining room until she knocked on the connecting door at eleven o'clock that night. I had hung up some clothes to dry near a radiator that did not work, and I was sitting in a sway-backed chair under a single electric light bulb suspended from the ceiling, reading the essays of Montaigne.

"Sid?" she said. "Sid?"

"Yes," I answered, "what is it?"

"After all that maneuvering of yours downstairs," Dottie said, "don't you think you might at least open this damn door?" The door was not hard to open. In my experience French hotel room doors seldom were, especially in northern provincial towns.

Dottie's room also was lighted by a single electric bulb. Her Wac uniform was carefully folded on another sway-backed armchair. Her trench coat was suspended on a hanger. She was heating some hot water in a canteen cup over a canned-alcohol burner, and there were two glasses and a bottle of whisky on the table beside it. Dottie was in a belted Jaeger dressing gown and slippers, and her hair was freshly brushed, and her gold-backed brush and tortoise-shell comb and traveling clock were on the bedside table. The alcohol flame gave a warm, pleasant glow, and the whole place smelled of Chanel Five.

"I wasn't maneuvering downstairs," I said. "I didn't know where they'd put you."

"Well, at least you might pretend you were," Dottie said. "My God, that colonel was maneuvering."

"Which colonel?" I asked.

"Any colonel," Dottie said. "Frankly, I'm getting a little tired of all these men without women. They have such one-track minds. Darling, I never seem to see you on this junket, and I'm awfully tired of coping with the unknown." She gave her head a quick shake and she sighed. "God, it's cold in here, and I feel awfully by myself tonight. I don't seem to know what I'm doing or why I've ever done anything or what I'm for. Do you ever feel that way?"

"Yes," I said, "a lot of people do, particularly around here."

"Well, you never seem to show it," Dottie said. "You never seem to struggle or try to get anywhere. You're so damn self-sufficient. What's that book in your hand?"

"Montaigne," I said.

"Jesus," Dottie said. "Montaigne in the rain. Well, anyway it's like you. You used to read that to me, remember?"

"Yes," I said, "I remember."

"Was that why you were reading it tonight?"

"Why, no," I said. "I've always liked Montaigne."

"Well, Sid," she began.

"Yes?" I said.

"I wish you'd put that damn book down, and would you mind kissing me, at least in a friendly way? I wouldn't feel so much alone."

I was very glad to kiss her in a friendly way, although it did not seem necessary to tell Helen about this either at Savin Hill.

105

"Darling," she said, "I wish we didn't know so much about each other."

"I thought you were tired of the unknown," I said.

"Darling," she said, "I don't know what I'm tired of. Let's have some whisky and hot water. God, it's cold."

Then she told me to sit down on the bed or on the chair, but to wait until she had taken the clothes off the chair and hung them up. She said that I was always so untidy she could not see how Helen stood me, but then maybe Helen was untidy herself in a wild, attractive way that absolutely suited her.

"At least we don't have to worry about what we're saying when we talk to each other," she said. "Sid, maybe you were right."

When I asked what I'd been right about, she took a swallow of her whisky and hot water and sighed again.

"You said he was pretty simple. Maybe you're right. It was all pretty damn simple," she said, and she sat on the bed and curled her feet under her. "Henry was simple in a way, but he wasn't in *that* way."

Of course I knew she would talk about Mel Goodwin, and curiously there was nothing indelicate about it, especially in that bare, ugly room with the sound of the trucks outside rolling steadily through the night.

"In what way?" I asked.

"Darling, he knows all the answers in his book of rules," she said. "He merely has to look in the index. He's so sure of himself — but maybe his book is wrong. Most of mine has been. It would be awful for him if his book let him down."

It was not a bad way of describing Mel Goodwin's certainty.

"He would still be right in there," I said, "smiting the furrows."

"Yes," she said, "and that's something. Right or wrong he would go right on smiting, wouldn't he? He was awfully sweet. He couldn't have been sweeter."

I winced at that old phrase of hers when she applied it to Mel Goodwin.

"I wonder why it is," I said, "that you always expect too much of everybody."

"I know, dear, I know," she answered, "but it isn't really expecting. I begin thinking how much I could do for a man if I had the chance. You know that, Sid. It isn't expecting. It's only wanting someone to be the way I want him."

She never had wanted anyone the way he was.

"Did you notice that he was all wound up?" she said. "Maybe you didn't because I didn't think so at first. God, darling, he simply couldn't unwind . . . and it was always out of the book. Do you know what he kept saying the answer to everything was?"

"*Git thar fustest with the mostest men,*" I said.

"No, no," she said, "but of course that came in, too. The answer to everything, he said, is to estimate a situation and then take action. Even if the something you do is wrong, it's better than doing nothing. Darling, he said it at least five times. I don't mean that it got on my nerves but I can't stop thinking of it, because it isn't so. I'm always doing something, but actually I'm doing nothing. What's the use in positive action?"

"It's pretty useful for him," I said. "Why can't you accept people for what they are?"

"Because I want them to be better," she said. "Darling, if I were to put my mind on it, I could do a lot for him. He kept saying he'd like to be a corps commander. Do you think he could ever command a Group?"

That restive energy of Dottie's was always disconcerting, or at least it had always disconcerted me. In any situation and in any place, however unfamiliar, Dottie was congenitally unable to leave things as they were. Weary though she may have been from coping with the unknown, she was still trying to find the pivots and the balances. She always liked to understand people, as she said. It made no difference that she did not know definitely what a Group meant in tables of organization. She had already acquired a smattering of knowledge from Melville Goodwin, and now she was devising some way to move him upward and onward. She had tried to move me upward once, and even the memory made me uncomfortable.

"Listen, Dot," I told her, "why don't you relax and stop trying to be a Joan of Arc?"

"God damn it," Dottie said, and her voice had a snap which sounded exactly like Mel Goodwin's, "what's Joan of Arc got to do with it?"

"Well," I said, "she tried to win a war."

"Darling," Dottie said, and she helped herself to more whisky and water, "I know perfectly well that war is a man's business. From my experience it's the most completely, utterly male pursuit I've ever seen, and I'm awfully tired of hearing about relaxing. I'm asking you a perfectly simple, intelligent question, and you do have brains if you want to use them. Or perhaps you don't think I'm intelligent enough for this sort of conversation?"

"Oh, yes," I said, "I think so."

"All right," Dottie said, "then answer me. Do you or don't you think Goodwin could command a Group?"

"If you're talking about an Army Corps, you might ask General Eisenhower," I told her. "He'd have some idea."

"That's a very thoughtful suggestion," Dottie said, "and I'll remember to ask him if I see him, but right now he isn't here."

"Then why don't you relax," I told her, "or else try General Marshall?"

"Darling," Dottie said, "I don't believe that Mel is a Marshall man."

It was always wiser not to underestimate Dottie's capacities, but I had never realized until then that Melville Goodwin might interest her more than temporarily.

"Now listen, Dot," I said, "Mel Goodwin has troubles of his own. Don't give him any more by asking questions about him. Things like that get around."

"Darling, I can't help being interested," Dottie said, "and you don't mind my talking, do you? I'm just pretending. You know I love moving things around. Now if I had been his wife . . ."

"But you're not his wife," I said. "You can't be everything."

"If I had been his wife," Dottie continued, "I would have seen that we saw a great deal of the Marshalls."

She sighed and stared ahead of her, lost in her own thoughts. She was Mrs. Melville Goodwin. She was undoubtedly arranging in her imagination a quiet little dinner with the Marshalls, prewar, preferably in Hawaii, and Colonel Marshall, or whatever rank he held in those days, was on her right, and she was telling him how brilliantly Mel had worked out his problem in the war games. She would not be pushing Mel too much. She would know exactly when to stop, but she would make George see Mel's future as she saw it. She looked as though she were thinking of a Christmas tree as she sat there silently. Mel could have been Bradley or Eisenhower just as well as not, if she had been married to Mel. She did not know much about army wives, but she could have learned, and now she was an army wife. Perhaps it was Washington she was thinking about or the United States Embassy in Berlin before the war, and Mel was the attaché, and they were giving another small dinner. She sighed and looked up at me.

"I wonder what his wife is like," she said.

"Now, Dot," I said, "leave the poor guy alone."

"Darling," she sighed, "he's so easy to get on with and he does have a certain kind of ambition. I think he has some very good ideas about fire power. He knows a lot about tanks and new weapons."

"For God's sake, Dot," I said, "leave that poor guy alone."

The urgency of my tone made her stop. She had laid the General aside for the moment, and now I was the problem.

"I don't know why it is you're completely lacking in ambition, darling," she said. "You've been complaining about all this public relations thing you're doing, and when I try to get you out of it, you refuse. Mel said he asked you to go up there with him. He said he could arrange it."

I pushed myself up out of the rickety armchair and took a step toward the bed where she was sitting with her feet curled under her.

"Now, Dot," I said, "I knew perfectly well why he asked me."

"Darling," Dottie said, "don't you like it when I try to do something for you?"

"No," I said, "it makes me very nervous, Dot."

"Oh dear," Dottie said, "I wish you were a little different, just a very little different — and we could have done so much together, Sid."

"Well, I'm not different," I said.

"Oh, Sid," Dottie said, "I don't know why you're so impossible. Sid, please don't look at me in that critical way. Pour yourself another drink. I'm just thinking out loud. You don't think I'm really serious about Mel Goodwin, do you? I know just as well as you do that he can handle a division, and that's probably as far as he can go. He can run around end with his damn division, and I'm pretty tired of hearing about running around end. Darling, it was officious of me, interfering, but that's because I've always been in love with you in a certain way. Sid, please don't be cross. I've completely eliminated Mel Goodwin."

"Well, that's something," I told her. "I was getting sorry for that poor guy."

"Darling," Dottie said, "I don't even see why you like him."

"Leave him alone," I told her. "Go to work on someone else. Forget about him, Dot."

"I'm awfully sorry I've been so dull, dear," Dottie said. "I didn't mean to be boring, just talking about myself. Let's talk about you and Helen and Camilla."

It was a ridiculous suggestion, and she must have known it was.

"Sid," she said, "you're not angry with me, are you? Or are you just disappointed?"

"Oh, no," I said, "I'm not disappointed."

"Oh, hell," Dottie said, and she stood up. "Here we are and we're not getting anywhere, and we never could. God, he was awfully dull once the brass wore off. They're all so damned dull and they have such fixed ideas. Well, you'd better kiss me good night now in a friendly way, and leave the door open. I feel so terribly alone."

"Well, good night, Dot," I said.

"Sid," she asked, "you aren't jealous about Mel Goodwin, are you?"

"No, not especially," I said.

"Oh, the hell with it and the hell with him and the hell with you," Dottie said, "but you might at least kiss me good night again."

I was very glad to kiss her good night again. It made the evening less boring than many I'd spent in the European Theater of Operations.

Every experience comprises both a loss and gain. This, you may say, is a hysterical discovery of the obvious, but this resounding fact was first brought home to me when I returned from an eight months' stay in China shortly before the incident at the Marco Polo Bridge which precipitated the Japanese-Chinese War. When I boarded one of the Empress ships bound for Vancouver, and when we began moving in the dark down the Hwang Pu River to the sea, I left many intangibles behind me on the Shanghai Bund, among them a glittering assortment of enthusiasms and illusions. I had gone to China for a news syndicate, imbued with the idea so prevalent among newspapermen that some day I would write fiction and that all I required was experience with exotic backgrounds. I was leaving this idea behind me and carrying away in its place the disturbing discovery that the more I saw of the Orient the less equipped I was to reach conclusions. You could not simply board somewhere. You had to have a permanent stake in a land before you really knew any part of that land's meaning. An observer could have no stake in anything.

I faced much the same series of reactions when I left the European Theater of Operations a few months after the German collapse, except that these were more acute because, when I left it, the ETO was already ceasing to be an entity. The pressures that had formed it had been removed, so that it was dissipating like bubbles in champagne. To those of us who had joined the army from civil life, its breaking up was not unlike the ending of a generation. We were all returning to the void of peace, and the regulations which had held us together, and even the friendships we had made, were losing most of their validity. Most of us would never meet again after leaving the ETO, and if we did, we would never remember what our relationships had been. We used to say, we uniformed civilians, that we could not wait for the time when we might encounter some of those Regular Army bastards who had arrogated superiority to themselves simply because they were part of the regular service and graduates of West Point. Yet oddly enough, when the occasion arrived, as it did now and then, for you to tell that so-and-so who had pushed you around exactly what you thought of him, you could scarcely remember what it was that had eaten at you so over there in Europe.

I remember, for instance, that there was a Public Relations colonel in SHAEF who impressed me back there as the most arrogant and disagreeable person I had ever known. Though I never cared much for picking quarrels, I frequently used to fall asleep toying with the idea of picking a fight with him as soon as the war was over. Then suddenly in the summer of 1946, I met him at the bar at "21" in New York, and he bought me a drink and called me Sid and asked me if I didn't wish we were back there again in SHAEF. We certainly did have good times in SHAEF, and I found myself calling him Earl — Earl G. Roberts was his name. He seemed to have forgotten that he had threatened to prefer charges against me the last time we had met in Frankfurt. The cork had been pulled, and the champagne was very flat there in "21." Instead of feeling resentful, I was sorry for poor old Earl. He had been restored to line duty in the infantry and was on his way to Fort Benning down one rank. He no longer had anyone like me to push around. The ninety-day wonders were gone. I felt sorry for poor old Earl.

The tumult and the shouting was dying, and the captains and the kings, all trained and postured at West Point, were departing to the dull routine that had made them — back to Bragg, back to Benning or the Presidio or Schofield or to any of those other places where they led their insulated lives, watching their rank, living on their base pay, or whatever it was they were always talking about, and being sure to dance with the CO's wife at the officers' club on Saturday night. They were gone, and a very good thing it was unless there was World War III, when assuredly they, or others like them, would come popping up again. They had performed a very necessary specialized function, but, thank heaven, the rest of us whom they had tried to mold in their schools and by their lectures did not have to play at being soldiers any more. We did not have to try to strike their attitudes any more, or give them smart salutes right up from the heel. We did not have to remember all those complacent axioms from Army Regulations any more. We did not have to read and digest their windy mimeographed orders or stand at attention on the carpet taking their artistic bawlings out. They could not chew our rear ends off us any longer. We had tried but we could never be like them. You had to be caught young, or you had to be a boy at heart, to acquire the military mind. Heaven knows, most of us had sat up nights trying to acquire it, and heaven knows, in Public Relations we had tried to interpret it. It was curious how fast we were forgetting these people already. The regulars had left their imprint on us, but the main outlines were growing dim.

When Helen said that night at Savin Hill that she could not tell what General Goodwin was like from anything I had told her, I suddenly realized that I no longer knew, myself. You had to see him in a war. He belonged with its sights and smells, with its obsequiousnesses and its brutalities.

"But you say you *liked* him," Helen said, "and he asked you to be his aide, didn't he?"

"You don't like anybody there," I told her, "in the way you like people here."

This was the truth. Liking in the ETO had an expendable sort of quality which you had to experience in order to comprehend.

Helen did not speak for a long while, and finally I thought she had gone to sleep as I lay awake in the dark. My own mind was moving too restlessly for sleep. I was thinking of the General's plane and of the General sleeping in his reclining seat. Those people were like Napoleon. They could sleep anywhere at any time and wake up in a second.

"Sid," Helen said, and I realized that I, too, was half asleep, "when he comes here, what are we going to do with him?"

I had no idea what you could do with anyone like Major General Melville Goodwin in a place like Savin Hill, and I really was asleep when Helen spoke again. For a second as I awakened it was a tossup whether I was in the ETO or at Savin Hill.

"Sid, I've been thinking," Helen told me.

"Don't think," I told her. "Go to sleep."

"You know, perhaps you could write something about General Goodwin."

It was not unusual for Helen to get such an idea. Ever since she had first met me, she frequently suggested subjects on which I might write, and she still retained rather touching illusions as to my latent abilities.

The thought of doing such a thing had never seriously crossed my mind. I never dreamed that night that the preparation of the condensed biography of Melville Goodwin by the employees of a weekly news magazine would cause me to attempt to write about him. It was only later that I saw him as a quasi-Grecian figure moving along lines of almost inevitable tragedy. There was something about his pattern that was classic. In spite of his lexicon of rules, his life was beyond his control like the lives of all the rest of us. He was a part of the tapestry that the Norns were always weaving. He was fallible and infallible, perfect in his own setting and imperfect in any other. As I think of him now, I still like best to remember him when he was there at Savin Hill, bewildered by a problem for which he was not trained. As he told me himself, he never knew what he had got himself in for when he had brushed that Russian tommy gun away from his stomach in Berlin.

VIII

It's Just the Old Man Taking Over

WHEN Phil Bentley reached me on the telephone the next morning and told me that he had been assigned the piece about the General, I thought he was a good one to do it and so did Art Hertz, who had come out to prepare my evening script. I had known Phil Bentley for a long while, in the half-close, half-casual way one does know people in newspaper work. I had met him first in Boston when he was a reporter on the *Post,* and later I saw something of him in Washington, where I had spent some time after I left the Paris Bureau. We had both helped out once at the same Senate hearing. I had seen him several times during the war, when he had gone out as a correspondent for the *Digest.* Like the rest of us, he had dropped by accident into his present position. He was an anomalous-looking person, thin, tall and dark, in his middle forties, wearing heavy tortoise-shell spectacles that indicated accurately his salary and editorial status. He had graduated from the catch-as-catch-can class and he deserved his promotion. He had a quick, concise narrative style and a flair for lighting on those personality trivia that weekly magazine editors love in profiles. He had been taken away from the *New Yorker* by his present employers, and he liked the change because he said the *New Yorker* style made him self-conscious. He was thorough and he was quick without the curse of too much facility. Without his ever having to get tight at press clubs, all the news crowd knew him and liked him, which was a good thing for an editor on a weekly magazine. Colonel Flax in Public Relations had told him to call me up.

"Well, I'm glad you know this Goodwin, Sid," he said, "because I never heard of him. Frary wants me to bring out photographers, but I don't see any point in it today. We've got two trailing him around in Washington. I'll follow him out from the plane. Are you sure you've got room for me?"

Then he wanted to know if there was room for the research girl who was coming out with him and who would take the notes. Her name was Miss Myra Fineholt.

"And I gather from Flax that you're going to be with Goodwin to hold his hand," he said.

I told him that none of this was my idea, that I had only been asked to help out, and that we all had to do those things. He said it was one of those things that would have to be done fast before people forgot about the General. He said if it wasn't one thing it was another but that it would be pleasant to be there in the country and that he would like to see me again, now that I was in the higher income brackets. We were playful with each other but polite. I told him that there was room for the research girl and everybody. When it came to photographers, the broadcasting company was sending some. I could see he did not like the idea of being tied up with radio, but then he was getting his board and lodging.

"Expect us at about four," Phil said. "It's going to be quite a cavalcade."

It was not as large a party as I had been afraid it would be. Gilbert Frary was coming but he was not bringing his wife. There would only be the General and Mrs. Goodwin, Phil Bentley and the research girl, Gilbert and Colonel Flax and Helen and myself. Art Hertz and all the rest of them would dine somewhere else on their way home after the broadcast. It would really be a quiet evening, and now that all the arrangements were made, Helen was looking forward to it. All she would have to do was to be nice to Mrs. Goodwin, and probably Mrs. Goodwin would want to take a nap before dinner, and that would leave only Gilbert Frary.

We had been sitting at breakfast in our dressing room when Phil Bentley telephoned. The morning was as clear as a bell and filled with the brooding calm of Indian summer, and I was still finding it incredible that Camilla was already nine and that Helen was still happy with me and liked having me around.

"Sid," she said, "look out of the window. Isn't it beautiful?" It was one of those days that made you say, without thinking that it had been said before, that October was the best month in the year. "I wish we could have it to ourselves, without extraneous things and people spoiling it. We always seem just to be starting having a life of our own and then something interrupts it. Perhaps we ought to have another baby."

Helen had been talking quite a bit recently about having another baby, saying that we would have had one or two others by now if it had not been for the war, and Camilla herself had entered into the controversy, having just read an antiseptic little book entitled *A Baby Is Born.*

"We haven't been here very long," I said. "You've just finished doing the house over."

"Yes, but it's pretty well done over," Helen said, "and now there's got to be some reason for it."

I did not object in principle. Helen was good at anything and she was a good mother. There was no reason why she should not have more children if she wanted them, but children were inescapable facts, as I knew from my experience with Camilla, and I could not see why Helen would want inescapable facts when they were connected with me. Her beauty still made everything seem impermanent. The illusion I had experienced the night before — that we were simply going through a passing infatuation — was with me again. I wished that I could fit into this environment as she did, but I was still unable to think of anything to do at Savin Hill. I had never had time to learn to play golf. The Winlocks had kept horses, and there were bridle paths everywhere, but neither Helen nor I could ride. It almost seemed as though there were nothing to do except to have a baby.

It was a long day at Savin Hill. I read the papers for an hour, and Helen read them, too. Then I went downstairs to the office and worked with Art Hertz on the script, and after lunch I met Helen in the loggia for a walk around the place.

"I wish you wouldn't wear that double-breasted suit when you go for a walk," Helen said. "Why don't you go upstairs and put on a pullover and some gray slacks and crepe-soled shoes?"

"I can't," I said, "the General's coming."

The General's impending visit had been on my mind all day, and I began talking to Helen about him again, as we walked through the garden by the empty swimming pool. I told her it was always queer meeting someone at home whom you had only known when you were in uniform, but at any rate the General would probably be in uniform. Farouche, I remember, was walking with us through the garden, carrying his rubber ring, and I had told Helen that Farouche was as good as in a double-breasted suit himself. Then Helen began to talk to Mr. Browning, the gardener, who was spreading salt hay over the flower beds. I could never talk sensibly to Mr. Browning and I very seldom tried, because I had never been able to tell one flower from another, but somehow Helen had learned all the names in Latin as well as English. Farouche and I stood there like strangers from the city, which was exactly what we were, while Helen and Mr. Browning began to discuss moving plants in an herbaceous border. The feeling of impermanence was beginning to rise again and with it my incredulity that I should ever have ended up at a place like this, and then I saw Camilla and Miss Otts. It was later than I had thought. Miss Otts had apparently given up her day off to take Camilla to that children's party.

Somehow Camilla's pleated party dress and her coat with its squirrel collar pulled everything together and proved that Helen had been right — Savin Hill was a nice place for Camilla.

"Daddy," Camilla said, "you look funny standing there."

"We'd better be starting now," Miss Otts said.

Helen put her arm through mine, and we all walked back to the house and to the drive in front, where the new station wagon was waiting. Just as we reached it, I saw the Cadillac and another car behind it coming up the avenue with the deceptively simple white fences. General Goodwin and all the satellites were arriving. We stood there waiting and all at once Savin Hill became quite a place. Helen was my wife and Camilla was my child, and I began to wish that everything were on an even larger scale. I had the rank for the moment. I felt gracious and benign. I would not have wanted anything to be changed.

"Just a little home in the country," I said to Helen, "just a little home."

When I saw Mel Goodwin's expression as he observed the house and Helen and estimated the situation, I was increasingly delighted that everything was just the way it was.

"It's been a long drive for you, I'm afraid," I said to Mrs. Goodwin. The photograph of Mrs. Goodwin had been put away that night at the Ritz, before I could see it, but she looked very much as I had often imagined her — a general's wife in a newsreel, with a conventional expression of pride, and a sense of its being her day at last. She had the durable, well-traveled appearance that a general's wife should have, combined with the assurance that came of knowing her rank exactly. She looked as though she had spent a lifetime packing and unpacking and arranging things on short notice. She wore gray gloves and a sensible black tailored coat on which a large corsage of orchids seemed elaborately out of place. She was about the General's age, a more difficult time of life for a woman than for a man. Her hair, freshly waved, was frankly gray, with a beauty parlor's light bluish tinge that matched her eyes very nicely. You could see that Mrs. Goodwin had been pretty once in a rather petite manner, and her expression was agreeable and, I imagined, more interesting than it had been earlier. She had gained in weight and character, and she had seen the world. Eventually the services left their mark on their women as they did on their men.

When I shook hands with her, I had the uncomfortable impression that she was mentally taking off my double-breasted coat and putting me back into uniform and that I was not receiving a high mark in the test.

"Mel's told me all about you, Major Skelton," she said. She might have still been at the airport, greeting me as a part of a committee, and I admired the brisk way she managed me.

"How do you do, my dear?" Mrs. Goodwin said to Helen. "And what a sweet little girl, all dressed up for the occasion just like me. I hope you haven't felt that you had to make an effort about the General and me, my dear. Please don't. We're used to taking things as they come." Her duty was to put anxious people at their ease, and she was doing it well and quickly, and next she turned her attention to Farouche.

"What is that dog holding in his mouth?" she asked.

"It's a rubber ring. He wants to play," I said.

"The General will play with him. I won't," she said. "Mel, here's another dog for you to play with."

It was obviously the sort of small talk that she had learned to use gracefully before she climbed to the stand with the General to watch army post reviews. Another entourage had gathered behind her — the General, and a stout, genial-looking officer who was undoubtedly Colonel Flax of Public Relations, and behind them at a respectful distance, Gilbert Frary, Phil Bentley and the research girl and a photographer.

"Well, well," General Goodwin said, "so he wants to play, does he? And what's your name, sister? I remember Daddy told me that he had a little girl."

"Mel adores children," Mrs. Goodwin said. "You must excuse him for speaking to her first, my dear. Mel forgets everything when he sees a child."

"Just a moment," Gilbert Frary said. "Burt, come over here. How about a picture of the General kissing Camilla?"

I was the only one who was disturbed by the suggestion. All the brass in the ETO had learned to expect photographs.

"No," I said, "let's go inside."

"Yes," Helen said, "let's go in, and perhaps you and the General would like to go up to your room before we have tea, Mrs. Goodwin." The ladies moved into the hall, but everyone else held back.

"Go ahead, all the rest of you," the General said. "I'm going to stay out here a minute and talk to Sid. So this is Camilla, is it?"

"And this is Miss Otts," I said. "They're going to a party. Williams can drive you now that he's here, Miss Otts."

The General stood beside me, examining the house and the beech trees.

"This is quite an installation you have here," he said. "Are those the stables?"

"Yes, sir," I told him, "but we haven't any horses yet. I'm afraid

Helen's going to do something about them in the spring. You must be tired. Wouldn't you like to come in and have a drink?"

Although he had been doing a lot of plane travel, he hardly showed it.

"It's nice to see you, son," he said. "God damn, all of a sudden having this thing blow up in my face. You should have seen what I've been through today, not to mention being given only about four hours to turn things over in Frankfurt. I don't even know whether I'm to go back. I don't know what the hell anything's about. I suppose maybe I would like a drink." He took me by the arm, and we walked into the hall. "This all confuses the hell out of me," he went on. "Nobody said anything when I was cracking the line at Saint-Lô. This is a hell of a thing for my record. Just because I was walking down a street in Berlin . . ." He paused and laughed shortly. ". . . And now I'm under orders to do what these reporters want. I don't know how to answer these questions. Maybe we'd better have a drink. Oh, there you are, Flax."

"Let me take your hat and coat, sir," Colonel Flax said.

The General would not have to think himself of such things as his overcoat and his garrison cap now that someone in uniform was around. He was secure in his knowledge that they were now the colonel's responsibility, and I seemed to be following him into a new headquarters with his chief of staff. The General raised his arm quickly to look at his wrist watch. So did the colonel and so did I, instinctively, to be sure that we checked with the General's time.

"Sixteen hours thirty-five," the General said. "What's the program now, Flax?"

The General had not asked me what the program was, because he had been running around with the colonel all day, but he picked himself up immediately and patted my shoulder. "Excuse me, Sid," he said. "It's just the old man trying to take over. Next time, slap my ears back, will you?"

In spite of his hours of travel and all the wear and tear of his day in Washington, he did not look his age. His short crew cut concealed the gray of his hair. His body was still tough and resilient, and he had a quick, hard smile.

121

"Anything Colonel Flax suggests will be fine," I said. "Put the General's hat and coat on a chair, Colonel. Oscar will hang them up."

I saw Oscar out of the corner of my eye, moving toward us with three highballs on the Paul Revere tray.

"Thanks, son," the General said to Oscar. "This certainly looks good." The General glanced at the curving staircase and at the hall's tropical wallpaper and smiled again. "It's nice to see one of my old boys doing so well outside," he went on. "I didn't tell you, did I, Colonel, that Skelton was with me at Saint-Lô?"

"Why, no, sir, I didn't know that Mr. Skelton was with you," the colonel said.

There was no mention of the shortness of the time I had been with him in Normandy. Perhaps he had forgotten this, and I, myself, was beginning to believe that I had been with him quite a while. I was almost positive of it when he patted my shoulder again.

"I don't need to tell you, do I, Sid," he said, "what it means to me, your taking Muriel and me into your home here? It gives a kick to everything. It's like old times, being back with one of my old boys."

Colonel Flax cleared his throat in a tentative way, as though he hesitated to break up a reunion of comrades in arms.

"Perhaps if the General would like a few minutes to himself," he said, "Mr. Skelton and I might run over the arrangements for this interview. I'm afraid we've had the General jumping through a good many hoops today."

"Now that you mention it, it occurs to me that I have been traveling," the General said. "I might go upstairs and take a shower and put on a clean shirt while you boys collect my wits for me, provided you can find them. When does that man in the horn-rimmed glasses want to start asking me questions?"

"There isn't any hurry, sir," I said. "I don't see how any of us can do much until after dinner. Don't worry. You'll get along all right with Phil Bentley."

"I'm not worried," the General said. "If I put my foot in my mouth, you boys are the ones who will have to pull it out."

* * *

122

When Colonel Flax and I were alone in the library, we were like doctors in consultation, fresh from the bedside of our patient.

"Now my idea of presenting him," the colonel said briskly, "has been roughly this — and I hope you will agree with me: to show General Goodwin as a salty character with a lot of guts. I let him have his head all day, and I think he's come across. He's got the human touch, and these general officers all have to have something of the actor in them, don't you think? I've never seen one yet who was bad in front of cameras. He makes a good impression, but I wish we could locate something individual in him with a memory value that we could play up. I wish he had more of the Patton quality — pearl-handled pistols, something that would raise him above the norm — but I wasn't able to find anything. Of course he's got guts, but then they all have."

"Yes, they all have," I said. "I know what you mean about individuality, but I don't believe that people expect too much. The main point about General Goodwin is that he answers everyone's preconceived idea of what he ought to be."

Colonel Flax nodded.

"That registers in the newsreels," he said, "and that thing you said last night about his being a GI's general isn't bad at all. I was able to find one or two enlisted men who had served with him, and we had them talking together. He was good with them, too. He ribbed one of the boys about cleaning up in a crap game at Algiers. I don't know how he remembered."

"General Goodwin has a fine memory," I said. "He understands troops."

Colonel Flax looked at me questioningly and nodded.

"Do you know him well?"

"Not very," I answered. "Does anybody know a major general well?"

"That's the problem, isn't it?" the colonel said. "You can't translate them into ordinary terms. Did you ever meet Mrs. Goodwin before?"

"Not until right now," I said.

The colonel looked at me again and nodded.

"She fitted right into the picture," he said. "The General was hard to handle at first. He was against all the fuss that was being made, and he wanted to make it clear that the whole incident in Berlin was blown up out of all proportion, but Mrs. Goodwin enjoyed the show. Wives always do, don't they? They like to christen battleships and put wreaths around race horses."

I laughed, and the colonel laughed.

"He was all right after he got to the Pentagon. We had him meet the press there, and he gave a good account of the Berlin street scene — straightforward, from the shoulder. He even got a few laughs, intentional ones, I mean. He said, 'You boys have made me what I am today, and I hope you're satisfied,' and it wasn't a bad line. He did all right, but I'm worried about this definitive cover story."

"Why are you worried?" I asked.

Colonel Flax leaned back in his chair and looked at me again very carefully.

"Well, frankly," he said, "he's so damned simple — not that simplicity isn't all right in its place."

At last we were getting down to cases, and it proved that great minds thought alike. As I nodded without replying, I remembered I had said almost the same thing to Dottie Peale back in Paris.

"Don't misunderstand me. I don't mean this in a derogatory sense," the colonel said. "I've never seen General Goodwin until this morning, although I have read his record, but you get to know someone pretty fast under these circumstances. Now in these cover stories, the news magazines always start digging and they want to get an angle, and the public's pretty tired of generals now. I don't want them to make a monkey out of Goodwin. Now I know Bentley, and he worries me. He's got to turn out a line of goods. It's the way he earns his living."

"Phil Bentley's pretty serious-minded," I said.

"He's not so serious that he didn't write for the *New Yorker*," the colonel answered. "I wish there were some way of protecting Goodwin. Do you think it would do any good to give Bentley a briefing on the General's background? I've got his service record here, but it hasn't much appeal."

Public Relations officers, even when they were as good as Colonel

124

Flax, constantly toyed with the idea that you could influence writers. They seldom seemed to realize that this was the worst possible tactic. When you were dealing with someone in Phil Bentley's class, it was never even wise to hover around too much or to be overhelpful. The only thing to do was to give him everything there was, on and off the record, because in any event, he would get it by himself. No doubt an investigative crew was out already, asking the General's friends and enemies what they thought of him.

"I know," Colonel Flax said. "You're perfectly right, of course. These boys are always looking for odd bits, mild pieces of dirt that look bad out of context." Colonel Flax lowered his voice. "Did you ever hear about General Goodwin going overboard over an American girl in Paris, a writer or a publisher or someone?"

The story would attach itself like a burr to someone of Mel Goodwin's reputation, and Colonel Flax was only repeating it. You could never get rid of such a thing once it got started.

"Yes," I said, "I know all about it. As a matter of fact, I was there at the time."

I was glad that the colonel did not ask me what I knew, and I had no intention of asking him what he knew. We sat silently for a moment, and then the colonel moved uneasily in his chair.

"I don't like monkeying with anyone's private life," he said, "but I've got General Goodwin on my hands. This sort of thing, if it's used in a certain way . . ."

He left the sentence unfinished, but both of us knew how maliciously the material could be used, seemingly without libelous intent.

"Phil's all right," I said. "I'll tell him the whole story off the record. Phil and I know each other pretty well."

"That takes quite a weight off my mind," Colonel Flax told me. "I'd be much obliged if you don't mind carrying the ball on that one."

That evening had its peculiar aspects. For one thing we were none of us entirely at home in our surroundings, not even Helen, which afforded me some amusement since she had created them. I do not mean by this that the persons seated around our beautiful double-pedestal dining table, on the austerely graceful Chippendale chairs that matched it, did not know which fork to use. I do not even mean to imply that anyone present was rendered uneasy by the atmosphere. None of us had been reared in this environment — that was all. Helen knew all about silver and glass and linen and place plates, and she loved those things, but she had not entertained with them herself until very recently. In the old days — and they were not so old after all — Helen and I had allowed our friends to eat off their laps or off anything that came handy in our old apartment in the West Fifties, but you couldn't eat that way in our new dining room. We had given only two parties that might have been called dinners at Savin Hill. One was a dinner of eight for some people by the name of Bishop, who owned some sort of factory in Waterbury, Connecticut, and who had been kind to us. The other had been for the Gormans, who lived about a mile away and who had a daughter Camilla's age. Neither of these occasions had taught us all it should have. As we were preparing for the evening, Helen did not seem exactly nervous, but she did have an air of facing something, as I could tell from the way she was going over her dresses.

"What's the matter? Do you feel shy?" I asked her.

"Of course I'm not shy, but I do like everything to be right, and nothing's quite broken in yet," she answered.

"Well, everybody else here will be in the same boat," I told her. "Nobody's broken in."

"I know," Helen said, "but I don't want them to know that we're in the same boat with them, and that Mr. Bentley is so observant. He was walking around downstairs just a little while ago, looking at everything and whistling pointedly."

"You can't blame him," I told her. "I whistle sometimes myself."

"But, Sid," she said, "you know it's fun entertaining in our own house. Sid, I think you'd better put on a dinner coat."

"Why?" I asked. "No one else will."

"Because Mrs. Goodwin will expect it," she said, "with the General and everything. Have you a piece of paper and a pencil in your pocket? I'd better draw a seating diagram. I'd like to put Gilbert Frary next to Mrs. Goodwin. He can talk to her about Hollywood."

If I had to wear a dinner coat I wished that mine might have had a well-worn appearance, giving the impression that I customarily dressed for dinner, instead of looking new and glossy. But Helen was right, I think. Mrs. Goodwin expected to see me in a black tie. Her manner was approving when we all met downstairs in the living room. I only hoped that Phil Bentley would manage not to whistle.

"I didn't know you'd be dressing, Sid," he said, "or I'd have done something about it."

It was hard to think of an easy answer, because Phil knew all about me.

"It's a simple reflex," I said, "my old respect for rank."

Phil took off his glasses, pulled a little packet of polishing papers from his waistcoat pocket, rubbed the lenses carefully and blinked at General Goodwin, who was standing in front of the living room fireplace talking to Helen.

"Now I see why Sid behaved himself in Paris," I heard the General saying. "Did Sid ever tell you about Saint-Lô, Mrs. Skelton?"

Phil Bentley looked like a connoisseur peering across a gallery at a canvas.

"How much did you see of him at Saint-Lô?" he asked.

"Oh, not very much," I answered.

"Why do you respect him," he asked, "enough to put on a black tie? I never think of you as respecting anybody."

It was one of those disagreeable questions which people like Phil learned how to ask when they began writing profiles.

"Maybe you and I ought to respect a few more abstractions," I said, "such as courage and honor and duty."

"Do you think he respects those things?" Phil asked.

"He has to," I said, "and maybe you and I ought to."

"That's right," Phil said. "Maybe we ought to. Maybe I will later in the evening. He doesn't look too bad, does he? But then, none of them do. You'll get us alone right after dinner, won't you? I haven't got much time to horse around."

"Right after dinner," I said.

"Is there anything special you want to say about him?"

"Not right now," I said. "He's all yours. I don't want to influence you, Phil."

There was a slight atmosphere of tenseness as we talked and a trace of professional jealousy between us, but Phil Bentley was to do the work, not me.

"That Public Relations colonel looks pretty nervous, doesn't he?" Phil asked. "Why should he be so jittery?"

"Wouldn't you?" I asked. "He wants you to do a good piece about him."

"I'll do a good piece about him. We have quite a lot of material on him already, haven't we, Myra?"

"Yes," Miss Fineholt said brightly. "The fun of this work is seeing what material comes in. You saw something of General Goodwin in Paris, didn't you, Mr. Skelton?"

"Yes, when I was in Paris I heard him give a lecture on the Battle of the Bulge," I said. "I wouldn't press the Paris angle if I were you, Phil."

"I want to talk to you about it sometime while we're here, just to fill in background," Phil Bentley said, "if you don't mind, Sid."

"No, I don't mind. Any time at all," I said.

Miss Fineholt smiled, the weary, studious smile of a raker in dust heaps.

"I wonder whether Mrs. Goodwin knows anything about the General in Paris?" she asked. "Nobody seems to know if she does."

"Maybe she does," I said. "She seems to be quite an authority on the General."

"This is a very lovely room," Miss Fineholt said. "Are all these antiques original?"

"They're all certified," I said. "They give you a pretty good idea of my income, don't they?"

"Oh, I didn't mean to be rude," Miss Fineholt said, "and of course we know your income anyway. You know the bad habits we get, snooping, in this business, and besides, Phil and I might have to do a piece on you sometime."

"I can't wait," I told her.

128

I was back in an old world that I understood. I knew all about the proclivities and loyalties of research girls, but I hoped that Miss Fineholt would never be on a team doing a piece about me.

Time was moving on. Just before my broadcast I could always feel an inevitable pressure.

"Oh, Sid." It was Gilbert Frary speaking, and I saw that one of the company technicians was with him. "Excuse me please, Miss Fineholt, for interrupting an interesting conversation. It is ten minutes to seven, Sid. Perhaps we had better go in and settle down."

"Oh, it's the broadcast. May I come, too?" Miss Fineholt asked.

I told her that of course she could, that I would feel hurt if she didn't. It never did any harm to be kind to research girls.

"Sidney is never embarrassed by anyone," Gilbert Frary said. "He is utterly uninhibited before the microphone. Without intending to promote anything, I hope that before long you and Mr. Bentley will be working on a warm and friendly little piece about Sidney."

"Come on, Gilbert," I said, "let's get going."

"I have suggested to General Goodman that he might sit at the desk beside you," Gilbert said, "for the photographs afterwards. He is enthusiastic about the idea, Sidney."

The minutes were beginning to press closely around me when the General and I walked into the library. Often as I had gone through the motions, there still was a ceremony to sitting down at the microphone. Often as I might tell myself it was superficial and ridiculous, still a great deal depended on the smoothness and perfection of this act. Without having to make any mental checkup in case something was forgotten, I still found myself doing so, not out of nervousness but out of habit. The microphones and all the paraphernalia were in place. Art Hertz was standing near them ready to take the pages from my hand so they would not rustle. A technician stood near him with his watch, ready to give the signal, and the adjustments had already been made for my voice. Approaching the microphone, I was like a prize fighter climbing through the ropes. The little show, I saw, impressed the General because he understood the value of formalities.

"Imagine me walking into anything like this," he said.

129

"It's the way I pay for supper," I told him, "but it's too bad they bother you with it."

It was the way I paid for everything. I was lucky, if you wanted to call it luck. I might have been doing the same kind of work as Phil Bentley, but not as well — not possessing his facility or insight. As I saw him watching the tableau before the microphone, I was positive that much the same thought was crossing his own mind, and then I observed the General sitting beside me. He and I were in somewhat similar positions, in that we had each reached a climax in our careers. The only difference between us was that the General's career had reached a logical climax.

"We will be on the air in just one minute," Gilbert Frary said. "Will everyone please settle down?"

There was a ridiculous, churchlike stillness in the library. The eyes of everyone were on me and General Goodwin. The show was on the air, and the voice of Stanley Rose came through from the studio speaking for the sponsor.

"In just a moment Mr. Sidney Skelton will be with you with his personal interpretation of the day's news, but before hearing Mr. Skelton I should like to ask you a single question: Do not your thoughts often turn to a fine full-bodied soup in this crisp autumn weather? . . ."

Soup or shaving cream or hair tonic — it would have made no difference. We were riding the waves of free enterprise again.

". . . and so tomorrow morning, drop in at your nearest dealer's and look for that simple, friendly name on the can. You can't miss it. And now . . . Mr. Sidney Skelton."

It was Gilbert Frary who insisted on the "Mr." — just one more little grace note to give the program quality and integrity.

"Good evening, friends," I said.

The machine was moving in high gear. I could hear my own voice dealing with the revelations of a congressional investigation, and I had to admit it sounded well. Without my understanding where my incisive enthusiasm had come from, it was there, and the sentences did reflect my personality. If I stammered or stopped, Savin Hill would go up in smoke, but I knew I would not stop. I had a measured assurance which never exhibited itself in everyday living. I was completely at home in this ridiculous show.

"And what about the situation in Berlin tonight?" I was saying. "Thanks to Major General Melville A. Goodwin, the big brass is saying tonight, the situation in that city is less tense, and General Melville Goodwin reported on this situation personally in Washington this morning. It has been quite a day for Mel, a name his old army friends, and lots of the GIs, too, know him by. Mel got off the plane this morning to be greeted by a kind of barrage with which he's never had to cope, a barrage of cameras and of popular acclaim, but he plowed right through it. As a matter of fact, Mel Goodwin is right beside me here, as I am speaking to you from my home in Connecticut, and — well, he's still the same old Mel I used to know when his division, the Silver Leaf Armored, was knifing its way through France and rolling across Germany. He wishes the newspaper boys, as he calls them, would let him alone, but they won't. They've even followed him right up here. They can't wait for this broadcast to finish before asking what makes him tick. Well, good luck, Mel. . . . And now, out in San Francisco this afternoon on the great Golden Gate Bridge . . ."

I was finished with Mel Goodwin — his spot was over. It had been of value. Somehow an unseen presence by the microphone always helped to create dramatic effect.

"And now," I was saying, "thanks for listening, and I'll try to tell you how things look to me tomorrow."

The program was off the air and I stood up.

"You see what I mean," I heard Gilbert Frary saying to Mrs. Goodwin. "The intimate touch is what does it. It's just as though Sidney were chatting to us informally. And now, Sid, if Burt could take a few candid shots of you and General Goodman, just telling some little anecdote to each other by the microphone."

"I'm sorry about this, sir," I said.

"Cut out this 'sir' business," Melville Goodwin said. "Why didn't you tell me in Paris you could put on a show like that?"

"Because I never knew I could, in Paris," I told him.

"That's beautiful," I heard Gilbert Frary saying. "Don't mind the lights. Just keep talking to him naturally, General Goodman."

If Mel Goodwin was annoyed by being called Goodman, he did not show it.

"The truth is, nobody knows what he can do until he squares up to it," he said. "I have noticed that quite often. Let's get the girls over, too. They'd like to be in the picture. Come on over, Muriel."

"Oh no, Mel," Mrs. Goodwin said, "you know how I look in photographs."

I had forgotten there would be photographs until it was too late. I would have looked much better in country clothes. Phil Bentley was watching us, critically, but at any rate the show was almost over, and dinner had been announced.

It was a strange little dinner, with all of us there for the ghoulish purpose of prying into the workings of General Melville Goodwin and all pretending that we were not. I can recall almost verbatim everything that Mrs. Goodwin said. She had changed into a long dress of sturdy lavender crepe, and she still wore the orchid corsage, because, as she said, she wanted to get all she could out of it. The last time she had worn orchids was six years before, when she happened to be visiting some service friends stationed in Philadelphia, and she had been asked, since the General was at Salerno and would get his second star soon, to christen a Liberty ship. There had been orchids then, but nothing like these orchids.

"This dining room reminds me of a dining room in Georgetown," she said, "belonging to a service friend of ours, Colonel Ainsley. You may have met him as an attaché somewhere abroad — of course he has a comfortable income beside his army pay. Such a nice dining room, and your wife looks so delightful in it, Mr. Skelton! I hope someday soon the General and I can have a permanent home where we can receive our friends. We keep picking up odds and ends for that home. I have some lovely lacquer that we bought once in Tientsin, but that must wait until the General retires. Until then home must always be where we're ordered."

"I have moved around a good deal myself," I said. "I know pretty well what it's like."

132

"But you're permanently fixed now," she said. "This all looks very permanent."

There was always a gap between people in and out of the service, and Mrs. Goodwin was as aware as I that she was here in line of duty.

"Everyone's been so nice to Mel today," she went on. "I only wish he weren't disturbed by public attention. You wouldn't think he was shy to look at him, would you?"

"Why, no," I said.

"He doesn't like taking credit for anything that he doesn't think he deserves. He keeps saying that this is all a fuss about nothing, and perhaps it is, but it's about time Mel received some recognition. He's done a great deal that nobody outside the service knows about. I hope you'll help that newspaperman to find it out, but you'll have to lead Mel on."

"I'm sure he'll find it out," I said.

She looked down the table at the General. She was a good army wife, so good that it was hard to tell what she was like herself.

"I think the General looks well, don't you?" she said. "You wouldn't know that he'd flown the Atlantic and been in Washington all morning, would you? I always tell Mel he's very durable. When he got up to that delightful guest room of yours this afternoon, he just sat down in a chair and closed his eyes and was asleep before I could finish talking to him, and when I woke him up he picked up the conversation again, just where we had left it, wanting to know the latest about Robert and about our son Charles — Charles is still at the Point, you know — and all our closer friends. It's amusing in the service how you make friends and lose them and find them again . . . that is, if they're not killed. We lost so many good friends in the war. . . . I wish I could sleep at any time like Mel."

I wished that I could myself, I told her. I did not need to put my mind on what she was saying.

"Mel is so durable," she said, "that he still looks very much like the pictures taken when he graduated from the Point. I should know. You see, Mel and I were married the day after he graduated."

"Were you really?" I said, "the day afterward?"

"We were in high school together," she said. "He doesn't look so very different, a little heavier perhaps. Of course, I always knew he'd be a general someday."

"Why were you so sure?" I asked.

It was a careless question, but she answered it literally.

"Because I always wanted it. If you want something enough, you get it. Don't you think that's true?"

"Maybe it's true," I said.

"I always wanted to marry Mel, and I married him. I wanted two boys, and the children were boys. If you think of something long enough and hard enough, it comes true. At least I've found it that way."

"You have to do a good deal about it besides thinking," I said.

"Doing is part of the wanting, I think," Mrs. Goodwin said, "or perhaps not doing too much is part of it. The General never likes it when I try to do too much."

"And what do you want now?" I asked.

It was impertinent to ask her but I could think of years of wanting in Hawaii and Manila and Tientsin.

"I want him back," she said, "but now that I've got him back for a few days and now that Robert's back from the Pacific, I don't know that I want anything except to have Robert and Charles here tonight. . . . Oh yes, and I want them to find something worth while for the General to do — something beside returning him to his command in Germany, though it's hard to leave a field command, when a war is over. I don't mean that we like war, but after all, that's what the service is made for."

She stopped and looked down the table again at the General.

"I don't suppose I should have said that," she said, "but I won't take it back."

Her expression as she watched her husband — a complete understanding that was both devoted and detached — made me see why they had married the day after Melville Goodwin had become a commissioned officer. In fact, if I had been Melville Goodwin, with all my career ahead of me and in a period of youth when anything must have been possible — I might very well have wanted to marry her myself. At any rate, I was able to move back through time for a second or two and to imagine what their early years must have been like in spite of her lavender crepe and her orchids.

"Why shouldn't you say that about war?" I asked her. "It seems to me like a very sensible remark."

Her glance moved away from the end of the table, as though she had just seen me.

"Because you're not in the Regular Army," she said. "Of course you have been in the service, but temporary service isn't the same thing. It only sounds ugly to you to think of people living and waiting for a war, but I don't mean it in that way" — she spoke as though she wanted to hurry quickly to some firmer ground — "I only mean that a service wife has to be prepared for her man to go when a war starts, in a different way from an outside wife. Now directly after Mel and I were married, he sailed to France with a school detachment in the First World War. I learned my lesson then. I learned that I must want him to see front-line service with troops because I had to want it. . . . He went in at Château-Thierry, which is more than most of his classmates did. He was lucky and what he did I am sure has always helped on his record. All we live for is a service record, even if it's always concealed in a file, and a wife has to be a part of it."

She stopped and I was no longer aware of the voices of the others at the table. I was thinking of young Melville Goodwin and the guns of Château-Thierry and of the first time he saw Paris — just passing through.

"We all have to live by some sort of record," I said.

"Yes, but not in black and white, the way we do," she answered. "Mel has what I like to think of as a straightforward record. I don't want anything to spoil it." She stopped again. "You like Mel, don't you? . . . I can always tell when anyone likes Mel," she went on before I could answer. "Now this incident in Berlin will go on his record. I suppose there will be some sort of decoration, but he won't want it because he will say it isn't a sincere decoration. He doesn't believe in collecting medals." She leaned toward me and lowered her voice. "I don't like to ask this, since I hardly know you, but I hope you'll help him with these newspaper people. He has to see them, and it's in line of duty, but Mel isn't the kind of officer who likes his name in print. Please don't let them twist things he says. Please don't let them hurt his record."

I wanted to tell her not to worry, but instead, I began to worry myself, for fear she might be implying more than she had said. Dinner was almost over, and there was an abrupt silence at the far end of the table. Then I heard Colonel Flax speaking in a way that instantly caught my attention.

"Of course by that," I heard the colonel saying, "the General doesn't mean he's sorry the war is over."

Then I knew that the General had been meeting the press all by himself at the far end of the table while Mrs. Goodwin and I had been talking. Phil Bentley and the others were staring at him in a bewildered manner, and the General's face was set in conventional lines.

"I'm not speaking in the broad, humanitarian sense," the General said. "William T. Sherman was right. War is hell, and war is a hell of a profession, but looking at it from a professional point of view, it's pretty tough on professionals when a war stops and we're not wanted any more. Now old Clausewitz would understand me and so would Julius Caesar. War's an art. We professionals start getting good and just when everything gets cracking right the war's over. Look at the old Silver Leaf. That was a sweet division, a co-ordinated, battle-wise division, and where is it now? Can you blame me if losing something like that hurts me artistically? You can call it fascist if you like. I haven't had much time to study ideology."

Philip Bentley's glasses glittered in the candlelight, and I saw him glance meaningly toward Miss Fineholt.

"I see what you mean," Phil Bentley said. "I never heard it put quite that way before."

"Well, you asked for it," General Goodwin answered. "You said I almost seemed sorry that the war was over. I say I have mixed emotions on the subject, and so would you if you were in my shoes."

"Perhaps I would," Phil Bentley said, and the candlelight was reflected again from his glasses.

"You're damned well right you would," the General said.

Helen pushed back her chair and stood up and I looked at Phil Bentley as anxiously as if I were Colonel Flax.

"To use an old military expression," I heard myself saying in my sincerest voice, "perhaps we'd better put the show on the road. I'm sure the General would like to get started. We can go into the library any time now if you want to, Phil."

I was relieved that Phil Bentley and the General both laughed.

"Yes, let's put the show on the road," Phil Bentley said. "Go ahead and get your notebook, Myra."

We waited for the ladies to go first, and as the General followed them, Phil Bentley shook his head.

"Don't be so God-damned jumpy, boys," he said to Colonel Flax and me. "He's starting out all right."

"We're not jumpy," Colonel Flax said. "You see what he is — sincere."

I wished that the colonel would not explain. It never did any good to interfere with anyone like Phil Bentley.

I told Phil Bentley to take the whole thing over himself, once we were in the library, and he did it very well. He asked the General to sit down near the fire and he asked us all to relax and be comfortable, and everyone did look comfortable except Miss Fineholt, who sat at the desk with her notebooks.

"Now that we're all here," the General said, "I've said I'd be co-operative, but I don't like this sort of thing."

I had to admit that Phil Bentley was adroit and reassuring.

"That's the way everyone feels when we start," he said. "It does look rather like being interrogated, doesn't it? But you won't mind it after we get going, General. Just think of us all being here talking, and anytime you say anything you don't want on the record, let me know."

"All right," the General said, "let's get going."

"All right," Phil Bentley said, "it doesn't much matter where we start. Let's begin with your walking along that street in Berlin."

"I wish to God I'd never walked along that street," the General said. "It was just another street in a bombed-out town."

He glanced about the library without much curiosity, but at the same time with approval. The books were in good order, their leather backs well oiled. Helen had been augmenting the library by frequent visits to auction rooms and in the last analysis it was her idea of what a man's library should be, based on the best conservative tradition and approved by a dealer in definitive editions. If Miss Fineholt had been interested in the appraisal, she would have found that the books and furnishings amounted to more than the General's yearly pay. The mahogany book ladders on squeaking casters, the terrestrial and celestial globes, the so-called cockfighting chairs, were all Helen's idea, not mine, and so were the other chairs, which, I am glad to say, proved that some thought had been given to physical comfort in the late eighteenth and early nineteenth centuries. My sole contributions to the room consisted of two refusals. I had asked Helen to remove a rug made out of the hide of some African animal from in front of the fireplace, and I had not allowed her to put above the mantel an ornate map of the world showing my travels.

Miss Fineholt, Phil Bentley, Colonel Flax and I sat there listening to the General, all of us as unaccustomed to the library as the library was to us. We were not scions of old county families. As far as the General was concerned, circumstances had made him oblivious long ago to material surroundings, but still he did give the room a moment's thought.

"One of the things I like least about bombings," the General said, "is the way home furnishings get scattered. I don't like seeing chewed-up pages of books in the rubble, but then, Berlin is pretty well picked up, and paper sells for something."

"Why did you happen to be walking down the street?" Phil Bentley asked.

"Because this AP correspondent said he'd take me to see the sights," the General said, and he went on from there easily if not brilliantly. He was completely at home giving an account of any concrete action, and I imagine Phil Bentley had understood this. As the novelty wore off, General Goodwin's words became less stilted and less considered. By degrees his personality began to dominate the room, so that in a little while it made no difference that all of us were entirely familiar with the Berlin incident. Melville Goodwin's reaction to it was all that was important. He was a book, if the pages could be turned properly and if we could interpret his self-revelations.

"You see it was all nothing to make a fuss about," he was saying. "It doesn't make any difference what language they talk, troops are troops."

I watched Miss Fineholt's hand moving smoothly across the pages of her notebook. The General was becoming more interested in his own words, more absorbed in himself and less conscious of effect. You had to pay attention to him. In the end he was like the Ancient Mariner. You could not choose but hear.

"Now that we've broken the ice," Phil Bentley said, "how about telling us where you were born and about your family. Just tell us anything you want, as though you were trying to remember it all for yourself."

"All right," the General said, "I don't mind, if you don't. I was born and raised in Hallowell, New Hampshire, about ten miles away from the town of Nashua, New Hampshire, in the Merrimack River Valley. The town of Hallowell is at the falls of a small stream called Blind River, which flows into the Merrimack. The Hallowell hat factory is there, still using water power. Maybe you have heard of Hallowell hats."

He waited expectantly, but no one had heard of them.

"It's a town of about three thousand population, a small mill town. There have always been Goodwins in Hallowell, I guess, but I haven't been around there much since I left for the Point. I sometimes think when I retire I might go back, but you have to keep living in a place like Hallowell in order to stay with it. It's a specialty in itself, living in a place like Hallowell."

Our paths must have come very near to crossing at some point in Nashua. I remembered the town of Hallowell very well, one of those half-forgotten towns off the main highway with a single small industry to give it an excuse for existing.

IX

It Must Have Been Those Decoration Day Parades

THERE were always Goodwins in Hallowell, General Goodwin was saying, above ground and in the cemetery. There had been Goodwins in Hallowell in the French and Indians wars, and the Indians had burned down a Goodwin farm on one of their raids down the Merrimack. You still can find their arrowheads and the wigwam sites along Blind River where they camped when the salmon and alewives were running. There was no history of Hallowell that he knew anything about except for word-of-mouth history and the records on the stones in the cemetery. His great-great-grandfather, Amos Goodwin, had been in the Revolutionary War, and there was always a flag by his slate headstone on Decoration Day. His grandfather on his mother's side had been in the Civil War, but he was buried in Nashua. That was about all there was to say about his family, except that his own father, Robert Goodwin, had owned the drugstore, and when Melville Goodwin attended the Hallowell grammar school, there must have been ten other Goodwins there, including his two elder brothers and his sister Celia. His elder brother George ran the drugstore now, and his brother Harry was settled in Michigan. Celia was married and in California, which went to show that Hallowell had been pretty much a place to move away from.

Without wishing in any way to criticize West Point, which was the greatest school of its kind in the world, nevertheless a kind of iron curtain did fall, when you entered there. Many a time in his plebe year at the Point he had longed to return to Hallowell in a violent, homesick way. Many a time he had put himself to sleep

140

recalling the fishing and the skating on Blind River, and even the chores that had been assigned him before and after school. He had been able, in those unhappy periods when discipline had been kicked into him, to close his eyes and walk down every street in Hallowell, in the same way an expert could play chess without looking at the board. Yet frankly, by now Hallowell and his days there had begun to lie in a region which people in the service sometimes referred to as "outside," a disagreeable term which he knew was also employed by Sing Sing convicts.

You might as well face the fact that you saw civilian life through different lenses after you had been to the Point. You were constantly being disturbed by its lavishness and laxness, though he did not want to imply for a moment that army people did not have human weaknesses. Take the Hallowell high school, for instance. The school committee, of which his uncle had been a member, had never thought of giving Hallowell boys close-order drill and good setting-up exercises. These would have been more of a help to them in later life than Caesar's Gallic wars and Virgil, and there might also have been a course in map reading. Yet he could see, because he certainly was not a martinet, that innovations like these would never have been accepted in Hallowell. The disciplines of Hallowell were of a milder sort.

"Robert," he could remember his mother saying, "don't call the boys in yet. Supper can wait for ten minutes. Remember, children are only children once."

That was why he loved his mother and her memory. She had never exhibited maternal worries about her children. She always seemed completely certain that the future would look out for itself as long as one received a good education and went to church on Sunday. It was amazing how you were let alone to work things out for yourself in Hallowell.

Hallowell was a long distance away, but Melville Goodwin could still give a ground plan of the place. An aptitude for analytical observation of contour, water courses and cover, degree of slope, and condition of roads and fences, was now part of his professional equipment, and full knowledge of terrain had often meant for him

the difference between life and death, but his mind's picture of
Hallowell could never be objective. He never, for instance, fought
an imaginary war in Hallowell. He never thought of the Rowell
Memorial Library as a communications center or of the hat factory
as a strong point or Carter's Woods as offering suitable concealment
from the air. Nevertheless, he still could do a sketch map of it if
you would give him a pencil and paper.

Most of the country was a sandy glacial moraine covered by a
scrubby growth of pine and oak. No main motor highway ran
through Hallowell even now. The railroad junction was two miles
out of town, and only a freight spur ran to the hat factory. Once
an hour in summer and once every two hours in winter a trolley
would leave the square in front of the hat factory for Nashua.
Shute's General Store and Richards's Meat Market and Gray's Dry
Goods and Notions Store and Goodwin's Drugstore were all grouped
around this open space. The houses along Prospect Street, where he
had lived and where Muriel Reece's family had lived, had mostly
been built in the sixties, when the hat factory had enjoyed unusual
prosperity because of the Civil War. They were comfortable houses
with porches painted gray or white, and the largest of them, of an
earlier period, was the one occupied by Mr. Oakes Hallowell, the
owner of the hat factory. It stood behind a white picket fence just off
the common, adjacent to the brownstone Romanesque building of
the Rowell Memorial Library. The grammar school, a small yellow
structure, stood at the end of Prospect Street just where it ran into
the country.

What he remembered best were the sounds and smells of Hallowell, the whistle of the hat factory at seven and noon and closing
time, the constant sound of water over the dam, a clamor that rose
to a roar in spring, the steamy smell of felt and dye by the river,
the smell of wood smoke from the kitchen chimneys when the fires
were being started in the morning, and the sound of sleigh bells
in the winter. When he came home later on leave and when cars
were parked along the common and along Prospect Street, he was
still listening for the rattle of wagon wheels or for the ringing of
sleigh bells. The whole place was on the "outside" but somehow,

even down to the granite Civil War soldier in front of the town hall, it was different from any other place on the outside.

That soldier, with his cape and little visor hat, gave Melville his first impression of his country's wars, but there were other immediate wars in Hallowell. When he was a little boy, there was always the prospect of physical collision, beginning with the morning right after breakfast when his mother had packed his lunch box and kissed him and sent him off to school. His brothers were of no great help to him. George was eight years older and in high school already. Harry was three years older and did not want to be seen with a kid Mel's age, and Celia was so much older that she often, in speaking of him to other girls, referred to him as her cute little brother. Perhaps he was a cute boy when he came to think of it. His round face and his wide, innocent eyes and the length of his yellow hair may have had more influence on his development than he ever imagined. He never dreamed of telling anyone that he dreaded the twenty-minute recess period when his contemporaries would gather around him and call him "baby face."

There must always be some scene when the curtain rises on anyone's career, and a September morning in about 1903, when the family were having breakfast, may be as good a medium as any other for introducing the life and times of Melville A. Goodwin. It was the period when the mail-order house of Montgomery Ward and Company offered a free trip down the Mississippi to the boys who could sell the most Montgomery Ward buggies in their communities. George Goodwin had seen the advertisement two weeks before, and he was endeavoring to start his Mississippi trip that morning by inducing his father to buy a buggy, but Mr. Goodwin was in a hurry.

"I've told you 'no,' George," Mr. Goodwin said, "and I don't want to have to tell you 'no' again. How do you know there's any trip down the Mississippi River? Advertisements are only made to make a boy like you discontented."

"But you have advertisements in the store," George said. "What about Old Home Elixir?"

"Young man," Mr. Goodwin said, "you're too young to know about Old Home, even if this is a no-license town."

"Oh, it's got booze in it, has it?" George asked.

"It has an alcoholic content," Mr. Goodwin said, "but it's a medicine. Never mind about Old Home."

"Celia, dear," Mrs. Goodwin said, "bring the coffeepot over to your father."

"Well, if you won't buy a buggy," George said, "can I have fifty cents?"

Mr. Goodwin put a little cream in his coffee and a spoonful of sugar before he answered.

"Thank you for the coffee, Mother," he said. He always called her Mother at breakfast. "What do you want fifty cents for, George?"

"I want to send for an Indian snake's-eye ring," George said. "It's a lucky charm."

"What do you need luck for?" Mr. Goodwin asked.

"Why, any fella needs luck," George said.

Mr. Goodwin sighed. "You ought to stop reading advertisements, George. . . . I'll have two eggs and one piece of bacon this morning, Mother, but I'm in sort of a hurry. I've got to make up a prescription for Dr. Byles. . . . Now when I was a boy I used to read good books. George, did you ever read *The Last of the Mohicans,* by James Fenimore Cooper?"

"Who is the prescription for, dear?" Mrs. Goodwin asked.

"For Mrs. Perkins," Mr. Goodwin said.

"Is it her stomach again?"

"Yes," Mr. Goodwin said, "it's the digestive prescription — Dr. Byles's bismuth one." You could learn what was wrong with every-one if you listened to Father at home.

The family were having breakfast in the kitchen, as they cus-tomarily did on school days. Celia and Harry had set the table, and in the chilly September morning the stove was warm and pleasant. Melville ate his oatmeal in steady silence. His mother had packed his lunch box already with a jam sandwich, a hard-boiled egg and an orange. Soon it would be time to go to school.

"Mom," he said, "I don't feel very good this morning."

"Why, Mel," his mother said, "where do you feel sick?"

He tried to think of a good place to feel sick, but he actually felt very well all over.

"Sort of everywhere," he said, but he never was good at acting.

"Come here, Mel," his father said, "and stick out your tongue — 'way out, and now say 'ah.' I thought so. It's the old school complaint. I used to have it myself." He smiled and rubbed his hands together. "And I know the cure for it. The cure is, go to school."

Melville returned to his chair at the kitchen table and ate his soft-boiled egg. The cure was to go to school, and ten minutes later Harry and he and Celia started. The sun was bright on Prospect Street. It had been a dry summer, and the leaves were already falling from the elms. When you scuffled your feet in the dead leaves, they had a pungent, dusty smell.

"Harry," he asked, "can I walk with you?" If he went with Harry past the Stickney house, he knew that he would reach school safely. The main danger always came from the Stickney house, a hundred yards down the street.

"What's the matter?" Harry asked. "Do you need a nurse?"

"No," Mel said.

"Then don't keep tagging after me," Harry said.

"Go ahead, Mel," Celia said when they reached the Jacques house. "I'm going to call for Emily. Please go on, Mel, and don't hang around listening to us."

Mel Goodwin continued on his way, walking alone down Prospect Street, not alone technically, because there were grown-up people in the yards and there were dogs, but alone practically, from the point of view of childhood. He walked steadily and carefully toward the Stickney house, and each step brought him nearer. He could already see the gray mansard roof and the umbrella tree in the Stickney front yard and the iron fence and the drive leading to the gray barn. Every detail was assuming a painful distinctness as though he were looking through the focused lens of a spyglass. He never could be sure what might happen, perhaps nothing or perhaps nothing much, depending on whether Joe Stickney was waiting for him or not, and depending on Joe's whim. For one bright second he thought that Joe Stickney had started off ahead of him, but just as he began feeling that everything was all right, Joe ran down the front steps, and Mel knew that Joe had been waiting. Mel could shut his eyes and still see the active nine-year-old Joe Stickney, the merry, volatile Joe Stickney in his corduroy trousers and his red jersey. He could see Joe Stickney's short black hair and his brown eyes and his expectant smile. Joe was carrying a light switch with which he had been whipping at the elm leaves on the lawn.

"Hi, Baby Face," Joe said.

"Hi, Joe," Mel answered, politely and placatingly, because he could never be sure of Joe Stickney's mood.

"You're a buffalo," Joe Stickney said, "and I'm Buffalo Bill. Run for your life."

The switch struck Mel Goodwin's calves, and he began to run obediently, trying to think it was a game and even pretending that he liked Joe and that they might be friends; and it could have been a game if Joe Stickney had stopped whipping him. He felt the humiliation of it, but then it was a part of life, being bullied by Joe Stickney, and curiously enough he felt no anger or resentment. It was not as bad as it might have been, being a buffalo, until they reached the school yard and the older boys. He remembered that he asked Joe to stop, please to stop hitting him, but he asked with no particular hope. He remembered that the older boys began to crowd around him as they often did before the school bell rang.

"Hi, fellas," Joe Stickney called. "He's a buffalo and I'm Buffalo Bill. Let's see you go for me, Buffalo."

Mel Goodwin had seen plenty of that sort of thing later — at the Point, for instance, on a more elaborate scale. It was a part of life, being able to take it, if you could not dish it out, although he was not aware of this at the time. He only remembered that he faced a hopeless situation as he stood alone in the center of the circle, wondering where Harry was because Harry occasionally broke up these episodes. He had discovered that if he did nothing, pretty soon they would grow tired, and he would have done nothing if Joe Stickney had not switched him across the face.

There was a time and place for everything under the sun. He was not conscious of the pain of the switch across his face, but everything inside him stopped. He heard someone call to Joe Stickney to let the kid alone, and probably Joe had never meant to strike him there, because he saw Joe drop the switch. He had never known until that second that he was born with an athlete's coordination of hand and eye. He only recalled that he felt cold and still, and he was no longer conscious of sound or faces around him. He only saw Joe Stickney, taller than he was and older. Mel Goodwin had never struck anyone before. He did not even know that he was going to strike, and he was even surprised when he did, but instantly he knew that he must hit again. The thing to do when you were in a fight was to get there fustest with the mostest. He did not have an Indian snake's-eye ring that morning but he had luck. He heard Joe Stickney give a roar of pain and saw that he had landed square on Joe's nose and that blood was streaming down Joe's freckled face.

You were either born with an instinct for fighting or else you weren't, and he must have been born with it because he knew that the boy was off balance and that time was wasting. He had no acquired skill but he was on top of Joe before Joe got his balance, and he did not kick and claw. He knew enough to concentrate on Joe's thin nose. He pounded on it with short, sharp blows as they rolled on the hard ground of the school yard.

They were shouting to him to give it to Joe again, but he was cool enough to leave off when Joe began to cry. He was cool enough to reach in a dreamlike way into his trousers pocket for the clean handkerchief his mother had put there. He was cool enough to go to the pump for cold water to wash his face and hands, and by the time the school bell rang he had even brushed the dust off his clothes.

When Harry said at supper that Mel had been in a fight at school, no one in the family took it seriously because Mel did not even have a bruise or scratch. No one was sure of what had happened until Dr. Byles knocked on the door that evening and asked if Mr. Goodwin would open up the drugstore. The Stickney boy had been hurt fighting. He had a broken nose.

147

"Whoever did it kept pounding him in the same place," Dr. Byles said. "They say Mel did it, but it couldn't have been Mel."

Mel was studying his spelling by the lamp on the kitchen table. "If I hadn't kept on hitting, he'd have got up," he said.

It was a childish little story, and he had dwelt too long upon it, and yet later whenever he studied decisive battles in which everything had moved correctly, as at Austerlitz, Mel Goodwin used to think that his battle with Joe Stickney was also a model of its kind.

He had studied boxing like everyone else at the Point. He had learned the quick one-two, the swing, the side step, the uppercut and how to ride a punch. In fact, in his last year he had been one of the best lightweights at the Academy. He had always preferred at the Point to be knocked down attacking rather than to cover up when he met a stronger opponent. He had developed this taste, of course, from that first fight at Hallowell, when he had faced with tactical correctness a heavier, stronger boy. He liked to think, however, that if things had gone the other way, if Joe Stickney had smashed his nose, he would have gone on fighting without crybabying. In fact he was sure of this because when he had been whipped several times later, usually by bigger boys, he had stayed on his feet as long as he had kept his senses, but these incidents had all occurred when he was bigger and stronger. At any rate, those few minutes in the school yard at Hallowell formed a sort of base line and a reference point which controlled him in the future in any kind of fight.

As time went on he learned a number of simple skills at Hallowell — how to handle a canoe, how to hitch the family horse, how to milk a cow and even how to plow. He also learned how to make a banana split and how to measure and to use the balance when he helped his father in back with the prescriptions. He could still wrap a package beautifully and seal it with hot sealing wax if necessary.

He wished he could see the people in Hallowell, including his father and mother, his sister and brothers, as an adult should, but unfortunately he was still an adolescent when he left. In memory his father would always be a mild, careworn man, whose problems were remote from his own. His mother would always be someone irrationally devoted to him. The last time he ever saw her, she had told him to be sure to button up his overcoat. In his few brief return visits with his parents his life and theirs had fallen into the old design and they talked about school and about the neighbors as though he had never left.

"It always beats me," his father had said on one visit, "what made you want to be a soldier. I always sort of hoped you'd be a doctor and take over old Byles's practice. I saved up money for you to go to medical school. It must have been those confounded Decoration Day parades. I guess you're doing all right, Mel, but I wish that you had stayed home."

His father had been right. He never had recovered from a certain Decoration Day when the family had gone to Nashua to visit his mother's parents.

The whole family had been asked to spend the day, and they were leaving at nine in the morning in order to reach Nashua in time for the parade. So many other families were leaving, too, for the day's outing, that the square was very crowded. Mel Goodwin could remember the starched dresses and the big bow ribbons of the little girls, and the billowy sleeves and long skirts of their mothers. He could remember particularly how hot and uncomfortable his own Sunday suit was, and that his father had not wanted to go, and thus leave his clerk, Elmer Thomas, alone in the store.

"It's hot, and there will be a big run on the soda fountain," Mr. Goodwin said, "and Elmer's always dropping glasses."

"Now don't be hard on Elmer," Mrs. Goodwin said. "He can run the store for once, and you can have a good time with the children and me for once. They'll be grown-up and gone before we know it, and besides it's educational for the children."

"What's educational?" Mr. Goodwin asked.

"Why, the parade."

"What?" asked Mr. Goodwin. "Seeing a lot of old men out of step?"

"The militia will be marching, too," Mrs. Goodwin said, "and besides, Father and Mother want to see the children."

The boys were playing tag around the open trolley cars in the square, climbing on the running boards, whistling and yelling and getting ordered off again.

"Robert," Mrs. Goodwin said, "don't you think it would be nice to give the children a soda at the store before they start? They'll all be thirsty before they get to Nashua."

As soon as she asked if it would be nice, Melville knew that his father would agree.

"Well, all right, Mother," he said, "but I don't want the children thinking they can go in any time and get free sodas. I caught Harry yesterday behind the fountain helping himself to Moxie. They'll have to have sarsaparilla today. We're overstocked on sarsaparilla."

Melville still enjoyed sarsaparilla when he could get it, not root beer but regular sarsaparilla, although it was never as good as it used to be in Hallowell.

The store was cool and shadowy that morning, full of the clean smells of perfume, soap and chemicals.

"Sarsaparilla for everybody, Elmer," Mr. Goodwin said, "and you can have one for yourself. Easy, Elmer, on that syrup. Here, I'll fix these up myself."

"Now, Robert," Mrs. Goodwin said, "Elmer is fixing the sodas very nicely."

"All right, Mother," Mr. Goodwin said, "but just remember we have to get a living off this store. Melville, take your drink right down, and don't blow bubbles through the straw."

"Now, Robert," Mrs. Goodwin said, "don't worry over everything. Melville's only trying to make it last."

"By jingo," Mr. Goodwin said, "it's lucky somebody worries in this family. What are you looking at over there, Harry?"

"At the candy," Harry said. "How about a licorice stick, Pa?"

"Oh well," Mr. Goodwin said, "seeing it's a holiday, give them each three pink gumdrops, Elmer, and hurry with your sarsaparilla, Melville. It's time the cars were starting."

Four veterans of the GAR were going to march in the parade,

and everyone hung back to let them get on first. They were old men but still able to get around without canes, and their black felt hats and blue uniforms gave them a dignity which they completely lacked at other times of the year. Then Sam Jacques, the motorman, began calling to everyone else to get aboard, and he said the little ones could ride with him up front.

"You, Melly," he said, "you can get up front."

Melville found himself sitting next to Muriel Reece but he did not consider it a privilege. Muriel was a dumpy, fat little girl, with hair the same color as his own.

"Melville Goodwin," Mrs. Reece called to him, "you take good care of Muriel."

"Yes, Melville," Mrs. Goodwin called, "you take good care of Muriel," and then she said to Mrs. Reece loud enough for Melville to hear, "Don't they make a cute little couple?"

"What are you chewing on in your mouth?" Muriel asked.

"It's a gumdrop," Melville said.

"Well, give me one," Muriel said.

It was not fair, having to give up his last gumdrop. As far as he could recall, he did not say another word to Muriel all the way to Nashua. When she said it was nice riding up front, he did not bother to answer, and when she told him to stop squirming, he did not bother to answer. If anyone had told him that Muriel Reece would be his best girl someday, he never would have believed it; but it was nice riding up front in the trolley car to Nashua with the singing and the shouting behind him, with the soft May wind on his face, with the buds of the oak trees reddish pink and with the apple blossoms out and with a dizzying sense of speed. Trolley cars moved very fast in those days.

He hardly recognized his Grandfather Allen in his GAR uniform. The old man had kept his figure and he looked tall and straight in it, and he had spent good money to have it tailored to fit him. Furthermore he wore riding gauntlets which were not regulation, but they were a part of his old cavalry equipment.

"Well, well," he said. "Melville, ask your grandmother to give you a quarter of a dollar, and take your hat off when the flag goes by. I must be getting down the street. Will you have a cigar, Robert?"

"No thanks," Mr. Goodwin said.

"Well, I will," Mr. Allen said, "and there's a little something in the parlor cupboard if you're thirsty, Robert." He walked away down the street with his riding gauntlets stuck in his belt, blowing rank puffs from his Pittsburgh stogie.

"Oh dear," Melville heard his mother whisper, "I'm afraid Father's started drinking."

If he had, Melville often thought, the old man knew how to hold his liquor and it had done him more good than harm that day in Nashua.

Perhaps it was not a good parade according to later standards, but Melville had no basis for comparison that morning. It was the first time he had ever heard a military band — if you could call the Nashua band military, when it played "Marching through Georgia." It was the first time he had ever seen the colors on parade. The beat of the band had put life into the wavering marching columns, even into the GAR. He had no way of knowing then that the volunteer militia company, sweating in their thick dress uniforms behind the veterans of the recent war with Spain, was an unimpressive outfit. He had never seen shouldered muskets. He had never heard an order given. The sight of that uneven marching company took Melville's breath away, and before he knew it he found himself on the street following the parade with other boys from Nashua. The band was like the flute of the Pied Piper playing its tune to childhood. He would have followed the band anywhere and perhaps that band was playing for him still.

He was still "Marching through Georgia" when he sat on the steps of his grandfather's front porch later listening to the old men talk. There was no doubt by then that old Mr. Allen and his contemporaries had been drinking. Their coats were unbuttoned, their hats were off and their tongues were very loose. One of the old men was talking about Malvern Hill and another was speaking of Fredericksburg, and his grandfather was saying that he had personally seen General Grant.

"Well now, Melville," his grandfather said, "maybe you'll go to a war sometime yourself — but maybe you'd better run inside now. . . . Wait a minute. Here's a twenty-five-cent piece for you."

"Melville," his grandmother said to him in the kitchen, "leave those old men alone. They're only telling stories." And then she said to his mother, "They ought to be down at the Hall where they'd be out of the way."

The next Saturday, when there was no school, he went alone to the Rowell Memorial Library, a small musty building in spite of its large Romanesque windows, and he asked Miss Fallon, the librarian, if he might take out a book.

"The children's shelf is over there," Miss Fallon said. "I suppose you'd like a nice boys' book."

He had never been in the library before. He walked timidly to the children's shelf, and in this manner he encountered *Under Otis in the Philippines* by Edward Stratemeyer and the rest of the *Old Glory* series and also *Bob Raeburn at West Point*.

"Can I sit here and read one now?" he asked.

"Why, yes indeed," Miss Fallon said.

She did not know that she was talking to General Melville A. Goodwin or that she was directing his first steps on the road to war.

X

Time to Call Him "Mel"

THE time was close to half past eleven. We had sat listening for the last three hours while Melville Goodwin searched through the memories of his childhood, and when he paused we all remained attentively and respectfully silent. Our respect, I think, stemmed more from the complete honesty of his effort than from its picturesqueness.

Melville Goodwin pushed himself out of his chair, squared his shoulders, glanced at his wrist watch, and the folds disappeared instantly from his blouse.

"Twenty-three twenty-eight," he said, but the spell he had cast over us was not entirely broken. His distinct and occasionally monotonous voice was still with us. A part of General Goodwin had not yet returned from Hallowell, New Hampshire.

"Of course," he said, "there was plenty of time to think back there in Hallowell. Do any of you like ballads?"

A sudden authority in his voice snapped us all to attention.

"Ballads?" Phil Bentley asked. "What ballads, General?"

Our minds were still snared by *Under Otis in the Philippines*, and it was an effort to follow the General's new train of thought.

"Macaulay," the General said, *"Lays of Ancient Rome."* He cleared his throat, and I glanced at Phil Bentley, who appeared bemused. He obviously could not believe that Mel Goodwin was about to give us a recitation, but this is exactly what was happening.

> *Then out spake brave Horatius,*
> *The Captain of the Gate:*
> *"To every man upon this earth*
> *Death cometh soon or late.*

> And how can man die better
> Than facing fearful odds
> For the ashes of his fathers,
> And the temples of his Gods?"

The General paused as though he expected that some one of us would make an intelligent comment, but no one spoke.

"You know," he said, "I was able to recite the whole thing once. Of course, whoever was handling the Rome defense perimeter shouldn't have depended on Janiculum, and it wasn't true that a thousand could well be stopped by three. Cavalry could have cleared the bridge, and Lars Porsena had cavalry. We had the same situation at Remagen — but there's real thought in that poem."

"I'm afraid I haven't read 'Horatius at the Bridge' for quite a while," Phil Bentley said.

Mel Goodwin smiled in a bright chilly way.

"It was just a stray thought," he said. "I've never had orders before to pour my ego all over the place, but you asked for it — I didn't."

Phil Bentley laughed nervously.

"It is getting late," he said, "and I don't want to get you tired, sir. We might close up now and start again tomorrow morning if you don't mind. All this material is really very useful."

"Oh, I don't mind," Mel Goodwin said. "This is like a prisoner interrogation, isn't it? And you're pretty good at it, too, Mr. Bentley."

"I ought to be," Phil Bentley answered. "You see, it's the way I earn my living."

"Come on, Flax," the General said. "They're going to let us off now."

He and Flax could find their way upstairs themselves, he said. If it was all right, we would have breakfast at eight sharp, and he would be glad to start again directly after breakfast.

"Well, good night, young lady," he said to Miss Fineholt. "Good night, Sid." He stopped at the library door as though he had forgotten something. "I wouldn't say I'm obliged to you for this," he said to Phil Bentley, "but just the same, it's quite an experience. I have been before a lot of examining boards and a couple of investigative bodies, but I have never been through anything quite like this. Good night. I suppose you want to sit around and have a Goodwin session, don't you?"

Of course it was exactly what we were going to do, but Melville Goodwin spoke again before any of us could answer.

"Well, go ahead. I don't blame you," he said. "I didn't know I'd remember so much. It's a funny thing — the past." His voice trailed off, and his gaze was not focused on anything. "Maybe there isn't really any past. Maybe it's all back there waiting for you to find it. . . . Well, good night."

The door closed on General Goodwin, and Phil Bentley looked as though his efforts as Master of Ceremonies had tired him. He took off his glasses and put them in his pocket. Without them his face looked blank and naked. He glanced at Miss Fineholt, who was arranging her notes, and then he found his handkerchief and rubbed it across his forehead.

"Sid," he said, "did you ever go through anything like that?"

"No," I said, "not exactly." And for a second we were bound together by some unspoken sort of understanding.

Phil Bentley and I had been trained in the same practical school and spoke the same trade language. I was familiar myself with the problems of an interview. I knew that he was trying to find some salient feature in Melville Goodwin's character which, when properly stressed, would make the General stand out as an individual, and I could almost see Phil's mind retracing those last three hours in search of a central theme.

"You know," he said, "I have a certain reputation for these pieces I do. I've worked on actors and artists and producers, judges, politicians, labor leaders, industrialists and pugilists, but I've never seen anyone like Goodwin."

"Well," I said, "everyone's different. At least everyone ought to be."

"Yes," Phil Bentley said, "but with everyone I've done up to now, there has been some sort of reference point. I wish I knew what bothers me about this. I can't seem to put my finger on it. I don't know whether he's bright or stupid. He's all there, but I don't know how to begin taking him apart."

"Listen, Phil," I said, "maybe you've never done a general. Generals can't afford to be individuals until they get three stars, and this one has two. He's only a major general."

Phil Bentley did not answer me directly.

"Maybe I've underrated him," he said. "Maybe he's got a sense of humor and his tongue in his cheek. Maybe Horatio Alger had a sense of humor."

"What's Alger got to do with it?" I asked.

Phil Bentley stood in the center of the room looking lost without his glasses.

"You see what I mean, punching that boy in the nose and the parade, and the 'Old Glory Boys' and 'Horatius at the Bridge.' It's all too good, Sidney. If Horatio Alger had wanted to write a boys' book about a military hero, that's exactly the sort of stuff he would have used. That's what I mean. It's too damned perfect to be true. Goodwin can't be the way he describes himself. No one can be a complete 'Old Glory Boy.'"

We stared at each other silently, each trying unsuccessfully to identify himself with Melville Goodwin.

"Look, Phil," I said, "maybe we were 'Old Glory Boys' once ourselves. The Alger books made a lot of sense to me once."

Phil Bentley shook his head impatiently and his hands moved in quick, nervous gestures.

"Yes, Sidney," he said, "yes — I'm not a damn fool; but everyone outgrows that sort of thing. No one could possibly stay that way and keep out of an institution. Nothing is as simple as that, Sid. Goodwin isn't as easy as that."

"I don't know," I said. "It's just possible he might be."

It was just possible, I was thinking, that Bentley and I had both become too complicated to appreciate any longer the simplicity of a single driving purpose.

"No, no," Phil Bentley said, "no one could be like that."

Yet I was still thinking that we should face the possibility, and

157

that memoirs I had read written by military men all fell into the same harsh pattern.

"Just remember, he isn't like you and me, Phil," I said. "He hasn't had to be worried by the same things. He's led a very protected life."

Phil Bentley shook his head. He was laying aside his problems for the night.

"Come on," he said, "let's close up shop for a while. Make a note to call up the office tomorrow morning and have them send someone down to take candid photographs of him, will you, Myra?"

After putting out the lights, and before I started upstairs, I saw Farouche in his large, comfortable basket beneath the table in the hall. As soon as he saw me, he leaped up and seized his rubber ring and walked toward me wagging his plumed tail.

"Go back to bed," I told him, but instead of going, he dropped the ring carelessly at my feet and only grabbed it when I stooped to pick it up. Farouche himself had a simple mind and in his own way was an "Old Glory Boy."

The lights were out in our room upstairs, but Helen, like Farouche, was still awake.

"Is that you, Sid?" she asked.

"Who did you think it might be?" I asked her. "The Joint Chiefs?"

"Naturally," she said. "I've been learning a lot about rank."

"Oh," I said, "you mean you've been talking to Mrs. Goodwin?"

"Who else would there be?" she said. "We sat up until half past ten. She was very sweet to me, but I didn't have the rank."

"What else did you talk about?" I asked.

"Mostly about the General when he was a younger officer at a place called Fort Bailey," she said. "It was before they were ordered to the Philippines. Robert was born at the base hospital. Sid, it all gave me a very funny feeling."

She had to think for a while when I asked her what sort of feeling.

"I seemed so detached from it," she said. "I couldn't place myself in it at all."

It is not wholly fair to say that Melville Goodwin intentionally made a command post out of Savin Hill. Actually he did his best to be a guest and not an occupying force. His only difficulty was that he had not been obliged for years to adjust himself to any environment, because circumstances had invariably compelled him to manufacture his own. He was most appreciative at breakfast the next morning. If I felt rebuked at finding him waiting with Colonel Flax when I arrived downstairs at four minutes after eight, this only arose from old habit on my part and not because of his attitude.

"I should have told you to sit right down, sir," I said, "and to ring for breakfast."

He smiled in a gracious way that indicated that no apology was necessary. His face shone from assiduous shaving, and he did not need to say that he had slept well.

"Think nothing of it, Sid," he said. "Bentley and the girl aren't down yet either. I guess I ran that writer ragged last night."

Nevertheless I had kept him waiting, and without meaning to do so, he was implying that Phil Bentley, too, was keeping him waiting—but there was no need for apology, he said. He was a grateful guest in a civilian house and he was not a martinet. He was only accustomed to having things run on schedule.

"You didn't run him ragged," I said, "but these newspaper people are always late in the morning. What would you like for breakfast, sir?"

"Bacon and eggs and coffee," the General said, "the eggs sunny side up. I'm just a country boy, and I like a country breakfast, but I can settle for anything, as long as there's coffee."

"It's just the same with me, Mr. Skelton," Colonel Flax said, "as long as there's coffee."

"Are you just a country boy, too, Colonel Flax?" I asked.

"Yes, sir," Colonel Flax said, "I was raised in Kansas."

"Is that so?" the General said. "Whereabouts in Kansas?"

"Forty miles outside of Topeka, General," the colonel said.

"Topeka?" Mel Goodwin said. "I saw Topeka last back in '40 on my way to Texas when I was with the Inspector General's office. There was a hotel there with pitchers shaped like birds."

"You mean the Jayhawk, sir?" the colonel said.

"That's right," the General said. "It was summer and it was hot as hell."

"It does get pretty hot there in the summer," Colonel Flax said.

"But I had a fine T-bone steak," the General said, "and it was reasonable. I was trying to save money out of travel pay."

"They still have good steaks in Topeka, sir," the colonel said.

The conversation moved in a well-worn groove. We were back in an officers' mess where one talked politely about nothing, while one thought of the day and the timetable.

"I wonder where that writer is," the General said, and he rose abruptly and placed his napkin on the table.

"Maybe I had better go and find out, sir," I said.

"Oh no," the General answered, "don't disturb him, Sid. Let's you and I go for a walk. I like a walk after breakfast. You wait for the writer, will you, Colonel? Tell him we'll be back in twenty minutes."

It was another fine bright morning with a cool faint haze over the fields around us.

"Come on," he said, "let's get moving. I want to see those stables."

"There's nothing in them," I said.

"That's all right," he answered, "let's see them anyway," and then he added, "I'd like to get this interviewing over. Muriel says I ought to be down in Washington, finding out what's cooking."

He was walking rapidly, and I fell into military step beside him.

"It looks as though you're all fixed here, son," he said. "I wish I knew what's going to happen to me."

Somehow I was disturbed when Mel Goodwin said I was all fixed.

"I don't know," I told him. "This is all new to me. We only bought this place this spring, and as you said last night, it's quite an installation."

He was striking out at a four-mile-an-hour marching clip, eyes front.

"You want to take it easy, son," he said. "That's what I keep telling myself, and that's what I've been telling Muriel. She ought to know there's a shake-up whenever a war is over."

160

"I don't like being tied down," I told him, "but Helen does."

"You can't blame her," the General said. "Women don't like uncertainty. I don't blame Muriel, but she ought to know that I can't tell her what the score is. I'm a combat leader, and there isn't any combat, and I'm too young to retire. I can't pick up the marbles yet."

We had reached the stable. The door stood open, and we walked inside and looked over the empty box stalls that still smelled of Mr. Winlock's vanished horses.

"I feel sorry for horses," Mel Goodwin said. "They were bred and trained for centuries as a means of locomotion and now they're ornamental pets. Maybe I'm like horses. Anyway, right now I feel empty like this stable. I've spent all my life learning how to fight in a war. Being in the field has spoiled my taste for desk work. Well, I've had my chance, and now the whole show's over."

"Maybe there'll be another one," I said.

Mel Goodwin turned on his heel, striking out again at the same cadence. "I was just getting to be good," he said. "Son, I can handle a division the way a chauffeur drives a car, and I could do the same with a corps, and now I've got to forget it. I don't want to sit around waiting for another war."

The way he spoke of himself aroused my sympathy but obviously it was impossible to maintain a continual state of war to give him happiness.

"A lot of other boys are growing up," I said. "You can still teach them, Mel."

I had used his first name again without thinking of it, but then we were on a different basis from any we had been on since his arrival.

"I suppose Muriel was talking about me at dinner last night," he said.

"Yes," I answered, "of course she was."

"Did she ask you questions?"

"No, she just told me about you," I answered.

"I wish she wouldn't always tell about me," he said.

"Why, she's proud of you, Mel," I answered.

"Sid," he said, "I wish I weren't so restless. By the way, there's something I've been meaning to ask you."

I knew immediately what it was that he had been meaning to ask me. He had been intending to ask it ever since he arrived at Savin Hill, and the question stood between us like a tangible shape, of which we were both painfully conscious.

"Has — er — Dottie Peale ever mentioned me when you've seen her?"

"Why, yes," I said, "occasionally."

"I suppose she's heard about this Berlin thing. I suppose she's in New York now," he said.

"Why, yes, Dottie's in New York," I answered.

We were both trying to speak casually, and suddenly I felt old and weary of the world. I wanted very much to tell him not to make a fool of himself and to forget Dottie Peale.

"Well," he said, "let's get back and get started. Maybe that writer's awake. I really ought to be in Washington."

As a matter of fact, Phil Bentley, who only took orange juice and coffee in the morning, was down and through with his breakfast by the time we reached the house.

"Are you ready for me, General?" he asked.

Melville A. Goodwin was himself again. He fixed Philip Bentley with a steely eye before replying.

"Yes," he answered, "I've been ready and waiting for some time, Mr. Bentley."

"Well," Phil Bentley said, "then let's get going, General. Is it all right to use the library, Sid?"

It was perfectly all right to use the library.

"Now let's see," Phil Bentley said, "where were we?"

Physically we were just exactly where we had been the night before. The General had seated himself in an armchair in the half-relaxed, half-alert way that I remembered in Paris. If it had not been for Phil Bentley and Miss Fineholt, we might have been in any army office talking over a military problem.

"General Goodwin was talking about the books he used to read," Miss Fineholt said, thumbing through her notes.

"Oh, yes," Phil Bentley said, "that's so," and he adjusted his horn-rimmed spectacles. "I wonder, General, if you read the personal memoirs of U. S. Grant back there in Hallowell."

It was clever of Phil Bentley.

"I read them when I was about fourteen," the General said. "The book was in the Memorial Library along with *Battles and Leaders of the Civil War.*"

Phil Bentley smiled faintly, and I knew that he liked the answer.

"I had never read it until last evening," he said. "Sid has it here, and I took it upstairs with me. It's a good book, isn't it?"

He was like a trial lawyer as he asked the question, moving gently into a telling phase of a cross-examination.

"It's a great book," the General said. "I've read it a good many times since. Personally, I think many military critics underrate U. S. Grant."

Phil Bentley nodded, but his voice was quietly impersonal.

"How do you think he compares with Robert E. Lee, General?"

There was a careful silence before Mel Goodwin answered.

"I don't like making broad pronouncements," he said carefully, "and maybe we still use the Civil War too much in military thinking. I don't want to stick my neck out in print and I know that Lee said that McClellan was the best Union general he fought against by all odds. Mars' Bob must have been losing his memory when he said that. For my money Grant was a better man than Lee any day in the week and twice on Sunday. If Grant had been Lee at Gettysburg, that Fancy Dan, J. E. B. Stuart, wouldn't have ever kited off to Carlisle, Pennsylvania, and Longstreet would have moved when he was told in the Peach Orchard, instead of tidying himself up. Otherwise he would have been busted home and Pickett or some quick boy would have replaced him — but don't quote me. Sam Grant doesn't need me to back him up in print."

"Would it be right to say he's a special hero of yours?" Phil Bentley asked.

Mel Goodwin passed his hand over his closely cropped hair.

"I haven't any heroes now," he said, "but every kid has heroes.

When things weren't going right for me at the Point, I used to think that I was Grant."

"So you used to try to be like him?" Phil Bentley asked.

Melville A. Goodwin stared at his questioner with a reserve that I had seen on the faces of other officers speaking to someone outside the service.

"That's too easy, and don't put that in your article, son," he said. "I'm not another Grant. He had small feet but his boots are too big for me, but — all right — every kid has to have a hero. All right, I used to think about him quite a lot when I was there in Hallowell."

XI

Clausewitz Would Have Concurred

HE liked Grant, Melville Goodwin said, because young Grant had been brought up like him, in a small provincial town, the child of plain parents. Grant's father kept a tannery, and his own father ran the local drugstore, and this gave them a bond in common. In many ways Sam Grant's small Ohio town resembled Hallowell. Everyone had about the same standard of living in Hallowell, and even today Melville Goodwin was frank to confess that he did not understand much about large sums of money, except in terms of military appropriation. His life there in Hallowell, he used to think, helped him with troops later, because he was always able to identify himself with the backgrounds of most enlisted men. No one in the service was provincial, except possibly in a service way, yet underneath the service polish lay the small-town mark, and he was proud of it. The youth in Hallowell were just boys together and later boys and girls together, when they began pairing off. He was never a leader, because he had never liked to stick his neck out in Hallowell or anywhere else. He was not even a conspicuous figure there, because he never wanted to be different from the crowd. He would never have lived it down if he had told anyone that he wished to go to West Point, because everyone would have called him "Soldier" Goodwin or something of the sort. He never did tell anyone except Muriel Reece, but as he had said earlier, the world of Hallowell lay behind him intact.

He was fourteen years old when he told Muriel that he wanted to be a soldier, and then he was in high school, but he was small for his age and he still wore knickerbockers. One cold afternoon in March, his father had asked him to help out in the drugstore because Elmer Thomas was ill at home with the grippe. The afternoon was so gray and dark that his father had turned on the new electric lights. Melville could still remember the green shades and the quivering carbon filaments of those early light bulbs, each of which had its own individual switch. No one he had ever known, Mel often thought, had his father's eye for detail. Mr. Goodwin would have made a fine sergeant. He could carry the whole store's complicated inventory in his head, he could find dirt and dust anywhere, and nothing ever quite suited him. Melville was polishing the glass of the showcases for the third time, and his father in his spotless white coat was standing watching him, when their congressman, Mr. Orrin Curtain, entered the store.

"That's better," Mr. Goodwin was saying, and he leaned sideways to view the glass from another angle, "but it isn't done yet, Melville. Don't pretend that you don't see the streaks. Oh, good afternoon, Orrin," and his father and Mr. Curtain shook hands. "When did you arrive, Orrin?"

"On the four o'clock trolley, Robert," Mr. Curtain said in a fine ringing voice. "I arrived in Nashua yesterday from Washington and I cannot go back again without seeing my good friends in Hallowell. . . . And how are Mrs. Goodwin and the young people?"

"They're fine, Orrin," Mr. Goodwin said. "Everyone is fine."

"And how is business?" Mr. Curtain asked.

"Well, it isn't all I'd like it to be," Mr. Goodwin said, "but I'm still keeping busy."

"I was mentioning your store only the other day to Senator Lodge in Washington," Mr. Curtain said. "I met him buying a headache powder on F Street. I told him you had the best-run store in my district, Robert."

"Well, that's kind of you," Mr. Goodwin said. "What sort of headache powders does he use?"

"It's interesting that you ask that," Mr. Curtain said. "I don't remember. What do you recommend for headache powders? I'd like to pass the information on to Senator Lodge."

Melville was working hard on the glass showcase, but he still

166

could listen and feel a glow of pride that Mr. Curtain in his tight-fitting overcoat and derby hat and gloves talked to his father in such a friendly way.

"I was just thinking, Robert," Mr. Curtain was saying, "that it will be time soon to do garden planting. The Department of Agriculture has a very fine assortment of vegetable seeds this year, and I might be helpful along these lines, if you could bring the subject up to any customers, Robert, and forward their names and addresses to me. I'm almost certain they'll get seeds promptly and a much better selection, too, than were available before I was elected."

"Why, certainly," Mr. Goodwin said. "I'm always glad to help in any little way I can."

"I know," Mr. Curtain said, "and when I say I don't forget my friends, I mean it. Look at those electric lights. You and I know how electric lights got to Hallowell, don't we, Robert? There's no use being in my position if I can't be helpful. And who's your young assistant, Robert? Wait, don't tell me. He's your own boy, isn't he? Why, this is young Melvin."

"You certainly do remember everything," Mr. Goodwin said. "That's pretty near to it, but his name is Melville, after his grandfather Allen."

"Melville," Mr. Curtain said, "of course it isn't Melvin. I apologize, young man. Well now, Melville, when I was a boy, I used to like to plant radishes. How about some radishes, Melville? You'll get them as soon as I get to Washington. I'll see about it personally."

"Thank you, sir," Melville said.

"It's fine to see a boy who isn't loafing," Mr. Curtain said, "but helping his daddy out around the store."

Melville was working on the showcase again but he could feel their eyes on him.

"How old is Melville now?" Mr. Curtain asked. "About fourteen? If everything goes right, I might help out with Melville. I'm not promising but there might be an appointment to West Point."

It sounded exactly like one of the books he had read at the Memorial Library. He kept working on the showcase, but his head felt light; all of him felt light.

"Well, that's kind of you to think of it, Orrin," he heard his father say, "but I'd sort of like Mel here to be a doctor. Dr. Byles and I talk about it sometimes."

Then the telephone rang, and its bell cut through everything like a knife.

"Hello," he heard his father saying, "yes, I can send Melville right up with it, Mrs. Reece."

"Nothing wrong at the Reeces', I hope," Mr. Curtain said.

"Sam Reece has grippe," Mr. Goodwin answered, and he deftly wrapped a small bottle and put an elastic around it. "This is the grippe season. Here, take this up to the Reeces', Melville, and then you'd better go home and do your studying."

"Good-by, Melville," Mr. Curtain said. "I wish I were a boy again, with everything ahead of me."

Melville took the neatly wrapped package and went out in back for his overcoat and his rubbers. When he left the square and the green and then turned to Prospect Street, the slushy ground beneath him was completely devoid of its old texture of reality. His wagon was hitched to a star in the shape of Mr. Orrin Curtain, that big-hearted, selfless man upon whose word you could rely implicitly because he was a member of the Congress of the United States. It was as though the Constitution of the United States had assured Melville that it would send him to West Point, and it made no difference whatsoever that his father had dismissed the promise. From the moment Mr. Curtain had spoken, he knew that he would go to West Point.

Dirty melting snowdrifts still covered much of the sodden ground. The eaves of the Congregational Church were dripping icicles, and the air was so thick with the damp humidity of the river that it seemed to stick in his throat. No climatic condition in any other country he had known compared to March in the northeastern United States, but Melville was not conscious of climate. It might as well have been June with peonies blooming in the flower beds. He passed his own house without noticing that it was there and he hardly knew he was at the Reeces' until he had passed the ornately turned pillars of the veranda.

"Hello, Melville," Mrs. Reece said, when she opened the front door. "My, you got here quickly."

When she asked him to step inside and get warm by the parlor stove, he must have thanked her, but he was still in his daydream. The Reeces' parlor off the front hall was comfortably warm. He could see the coals glowing through the isinglass in the door of a hot-air stove, ornately trimmed with nickel, and Muriel Reece was sitting at a table working at her algebra.

"Here's Melville, Muriel," Mrs. Reece said. "He's coming in to warm himself up for a minute. I'll just run upstairs now with the medicine."

"Take off your rubbers, Mel," Muriel said, "so you won't track mud on the carpet."

Seeing Muriel was no novelty. They both had desks in Miss Macy's room at the high school, and neither of them had ever taken the slightest interest in the other.

"I'm only going to stay a minute," he said.

"You'll track in dirt just the same," Muriel said.

The Reece parlor was a very nice, comfortable room, somewhat more elaborate than the Goodwin parlor, which was natural because Mr. Reece was sales manager and vice president at the hat factory. There was a handsome Brussels carpet on the floor and a comfortable sofa and a Morris chair, with a smoker's stand beside it, and a bookcase near it containing Ridpath's *Great Races of Mankind*. The lamp on a cherry table in the center of the room was already lighted, and Muriel, with her yellow hair in two long braids, leaned over her book, half in the shadow and half in the lamplight. She looked exactly like any other girl in high school freshman year. She was wearing a brown, useful-looking dress, with a pleated skirt reaching halfway between ankle and knee. She had not put up her hair and she was not yet wearing a shirtwaist. Girls usually did these things only in the second year at Hallowell High.

"I'm doing my algebra," Muriel said. "Have you done yours yet?"

If you were a boy at Hallowell High, it was fashionable to be sloppy with your homework, and Melville had done nothing on his algebra.

"Why don't you sit down and do it now?" Muriel asked.

"All right," Melville said. "I may as well, now that I'm here."

They were on simultaneous equations, and he remembered the example still.

"You haven't got it right," he said.

Muriel had always been pretty dumb at algebra. He pulled a straight-backed golden oak chair to the table beside her and picked up a pencil.

"Now look," he said, "you do it this way."

The great thing about figures was that they were either right or wrong. There was no middle ground. There might be two ways about *Ivanhoe,* which they were studying in English, but there were no two ways about algebra.

"You smell all over drugs," Muriel said.

"Well, I've been working down to the store," he told her.

"I don't mind," Muriel said. "It's a nice smell. What girl do you like best in school, Melville?"

"I don't know," Melville said. "I've never thought."

"It's just the same way with me about boys," Muriel said. "All the girls are beginning to talk about boys. I don't know what boy I like best either."

He had never conversed for such a long while with a girl, and it occurred to him that Muriel had changed without his having noticed. She was no longer fat and dumpy. Instead, she was almost thin, and her hair was the color of pulled molasses candy. She did not have as many freckles, and her mouth was no longer as big as it had been.

"You're awfully good at algebra," Muriel said.

"Oh," he said, "algebra is easy."

"I guess we'd better keep on with these old examples," Muriel said. "It's silly just to sit talking, isn't it?"

"Yes," Melville said, "I guess it's kind of silly."

"When you grow up," she said, "I suppose you'll work in the drugstore."

"No, I won't," he said. "I'm going to West Point."

He had told her without thinking, but he was glad that he had told her. She turned quickly in her chair to face him.

"Oh, go on," she said. "You're fooling."

"You wait and see," he said. "It's a secret. Don't tell anyone, but you wait and see."

He could remember the next moment as though it had just happened, not that anything in particular did happen. He was back again in the Reeces' parlor and Muriel was looking at him, and he could hear the ticking again of the clock on the mantel.

"Of course I won't tell anybody," Muriel said. "Oh, Mel, I think that's awfully nice. You look sort of like a soldier."

It wasn't a memorable speech, but somehow nothing that anyone had ever said to him had ever sounded quite that way.

General Goodwin colored slightly and cleared his throat.

"Bentley," he said, "you have certainly got me going. I don't know why I should run on this way about Muriel in front of strangers but you've got me thinking about those days. We were just kids like any other kids. Hell, you've got me thinking of it and I like to think of it. I'm proud of it, and kid stuff is pretty funny sometimes, but just you mind, Bentley, all of this is off the record — strictly off the record. I don't know why but I consider you cleared. Do you understand?"

"Yes, sir," Phil Bentley said.

Generals liked to talk off the record. If anyone was cleared, they often enjoyed being confidential, and the words "off the record" always had a magic of their own for the military mind.

The next morning, just by accident, Melville happened to be starting for school just as Muriel walked by his house, and he walked to school with her, and when school was over, they started home together at the same time — but he was always sure that walking to school with Muriel had started just by accident.

Sex was something that every normal individual had to encounter sometime, and it always seemed to Melville Goodwin, from hearing others talk of their adventures, that a good deal of an individual's future and his attitude toward women in general depended on this first encounter. Perhaps, looking backward, it was reasonable to assume that his innocuous conversation with Muriel Reece that afternoon was his first true encounter with the biological urge and that he and Muriel had really chosen each other as they sat there doing algebra. From that time on Muriel had always kept a cool eye on his behavior. When Eunice Rogers, who was the prettiest girl in the high school class, passed him a note in the hall that April which read, "Somebody loves you," Muriel asked him on the way home from school what the note had said, and he showed it to her. When Muriel made a disgusted face at the contents of the note, he could sympathize with her distaste, though it was not his fault that Eunice had given it to him. He had never paid any attention to Eunice Rogers, though her hair was up and she wore shirtwaists with little butterflies and things embroidered on them. Eunice might be goodlooking, Muriel said — certainly Eunice was thinking about her looks all the time. She even kept a pocket mirror, a comb and violet talcum powder in her desk. The truth was that Eunice and her friend, Helene Dumont, the French Canadian girl, could not talk about anything but boys and kissing. The truth was, and Melville might as well know it, Eunice Rogers was getting boy-crazy. She was always writing those "Somebody loves you" notes and giving them to boys. Muriel was sorry for Eunice Rogers and sorry for her father and mother; her own mother said that the Rogerses were very ordinary. Nothing was sillier than writing flirt notes, and Muriel hoped that Melville had not answered the note . . . but then if he wanted to be silly, too, it was entirely up to him . . . but she knew that Melville was not the silly kind.

If you were a girl, Muriel said, and if you liked a boy and thought that you might marry him someday, after you had finished with high school, you did not have to send him flirt notes — if he was the sort of boy you wanted to marry someday. You did not have to kiss him either until you were engaged to be married — but then perhaps boys were different from girls. If Melville ever felt as silly as that, if Melville ever felt that he had to hold somebody's hand, he did not have to make himself laughed at by sending flirt notes to Eunice Rogers. If Melville ever felt silly that way, and she hoped he never would . . . Muriel stopped talking and stared grimly and coldly in front of her, while they passed the Memorial Library.

"If you have to be silly," Muriel said, "you can hold hands with me, but if you try to kiss me, I'll slap you."

"I didn't say I wanted to kiss you," Melville said.

"All right," Muriel said, "then don't be silly."

Melville was embarrassed and confused. It was not his fault that Eunice had passed him that note. He wanted to escape into a simpler world, uncomplicated by Muriel or by any other girl. He had never wanted to hold Muriel's hand, and there was no reason for her to suggest that he did, and the last thing in the world he had ever thought of was kissing Muriel Reece. Yet in Hallowell, if you did not want to be peculiar, it was just as well to have a girl friend. If the boys began jesting with him in a clumsy way about Muriel Reece, he could come right back at them because they were not immune themselves. It was due to Muriel, after all, that other girls let him alone, because they began to understand that he was Muriel's property, and he learned a lot about women from Muriel, not as much as the man in Kipling's poem, who took his fun where he found it — but quite a lot about women.

A few changes in the links of circumstance might have altered his life. If he had not delivered Dr. Byles's standard grippe prescription at the Reeces', he might have answered that note of Eunice Rogers's, and if he had answered the note, he might have been the one who had married Eunice, instead of his brother Harry, who began to grow silly about Eunice toward the middle of the ensuing summer.

His brother Harry, as soon as school was over, went to work in Mason's garage at Nashua, and shortly afterwards Harry induced their father to purchase a secondhand Model T Ford, the first car the family ever owned. Melville would never forget his first sight of the brass radiator and the brass carbide lamps as Harry drove it into the yard, or how the whole thing shook and pulsed when you cranked the motor after you set the spark and gas. No one worried much about licenses in those days, so Melville had learned to drive it right away, and he was fascinated by the mechanism and by its power. When he was in that Ford with the windshield open, feeling the wind on his face, he could almost forget about West Point.

In time all his ambitions might have been changed by that Ford, if it had not happened that during the summer a regiment of New Hampshire militia had made a practice route march from Manchester and had camped on the old fairgrounds at Blair, five miles away from Hallowell. There were always first times for everything. He went to the fairgrounds at Blair, driving the Model T, and for the first time he saw troops. It was the first time he was fifteen years old and he would never be fifteen again. It was the first time he had worn long trousers, even if they were only work pants bought in Manchester. It was the first time, too, that he and Muriel Reece had been anywhere alone together, because he had asked Muriel to drive with him to Blair.

It was an August afternoon, so still and hot that the leaves on the elms hung motionless and exhausted. Now that the older boys were working, his father had thought that Melville also ought to find something to do during his vacation, but his mother had said that Melville had been growing pretty fast and that before long he would have to work all his life like everyone else. He had received good marks his first year at high school, and she thought he deserved a rest. His father said that boys got into trouble doing nothing, especially when they were around Melville's age. It would be all right if he did not want to work indoors in the drugstore, because maybe he ought to have fresh air and exercise but playing ball on the common and going fishing were not what he'd call exercise, and there was no reason why Melville should not earn a little pocket money — but his mother said Melville would only be a boy once. Finally he had worked on the Sawyer farm during the haying season, but when haying was over, his father had said it would be enough if he did the chores around the house.

Melville had finished mowing the lawn at three o'clock that afternoon, and Celia had watched him all the time from the hammock on the porch while she read a novel written by Mrs. Humphry Ward. Though he was not resentful, it had made him hot to see her sitting in the shade and looking up from her book every time the lawn mower stopped. When he had finished and had put the mower in the barn and had washed himself under the pump, he went upstairs and put on a clean blue shirt and his long pair of khaki work trousers. When he came down, his mother was out on the porch, too, with her darning.

"Where are you going, Melly?" his mother asked.

He told her he was going down to get an orange phosphate at the drugstore.

"He wants to show off his long trousers downtown," Celia said. "Doesn't he look funny in long trousers?"

When he thought of it now, Celia looked pretty funny herself that afternoon with rats in her hair and a large black bow. There were a number of replies he might have made to Celia, but his mother spoke before he could answer.

"He looks very well in them," she said. "He's growing so, it's time he wore long trousers. Come here, Melly, and let me tighten your belt."

It was one of Harry's old belts. It needed another hole to be tight enough, and his mother made one with her scissors. He could always remember the simple things she did for him.

The trolley from Nashua was just in, and Mr. Jacques, the motorman, was in the drugstore drinking a root beer. Mr. Goodwin was out back in the prescription room but he heard Melville ask for an orange phosphate.

"Is that you, Mel?" he called. "Remember to take his money, Elmer."

"Oh, go on, Robert," Mr. Jacques called, "you don't take money from children, do you?"

His father stepped out of the prescription room, cool and neat in his white coat.

"Melville isn't a child," he said, "he's got on long pants."

Mr. Jacques laughed and fanned himself with his visor cap.

"That's so," he said. "I'll tell you what I'll do. I'll blow him to that orange phosphate."

"No, no, Sam," Mr. Goodwin said. "It's just a family rule — but Mel's a pretty good boy. Give him the phosphate, Elmer."

175

Then he stepped around the counter and put his hand on Melville's shoulder.

"Melville's a pretty good boy," Mr. Goodwin said again. "I'm going to make him into a doctor someday."

"Is that so?" Mr. Jacques said. "It will take a lot of money educating him into a doctor, won't it, Robert?"

"Maybe I can do it," Mr. Goodwin said, "by taking Melville's nickels away from him at the fountain."

Mr. Jacques finished his root beer.

"Well," he said, "it's a hot day for the soldier boys to be marching."

"What soldier boys?" Mr. Goodwin asked.

"The militia," Mr. Jacques said. "They're coming up along the river road. They're going to camp at Blair tonight on the old fairgrounds." What news there was usually reached Hallowell by trolley.

Blair was only five miles away, and the Ford was in the barn, and no one had ever told Melville expressly not to use the Ford. He had never driven it far by himself, but it was an easy road to Blair. Besides, it would do the motor good to be used. At least this was what he told his mother when he returned to the house and he could hear the anxiety in his voice, because he was not at all sure what she would say.

"Why, I don't know why you shouldn't, dear," she said. "You've been working so hard on the lawn."

"Harry won't like it," Celia said. "Melville really doesn't know how to run an automobile."

He did not wait to hear what his mother answered. The Ford started without any difficulty. He backed it out of the barn, turned it correctly into the yard, and went in low out to the street. He had driven to Blair once before in a horse and buggy, but now he was dealing with mechanical force. The pulsing, shaking engine felt immensely powerful. He squared his shoulders, pulled the little gas lever, and let the clutch drop back into high. It was up to him and no one else to get the car to Blair and back.

It was not due to any plan that Muriel happened to be on the front porch of the Reeces' house, and he stopped the car to wave to her without any idea of consequences. He thought he only wanted her to see him in the Ford.

"Hey, Muriel," he called, "would you like to take a ride?"

He waited with the engine running while Muriel walked slowly toward the car.

"Oh, Melville," she said, "I'd like to, but I don't know whether I ought to, and I can't ask Mother because Mother's gone to Nashua. Are you going a long way?"

"Oh, no," he said, "only down to Blair" — but it seemed like a thousand miles to Blair.

"Why are you going to Blair?" she asked.

She listened carefully while he told her about the militia camping at the fairgrounds, but a long while later she told him that of course she had already made up her mind to go.

"Do you think it's safe?" she asked.

"Safe?" he answered. "Of course it's safe."

"Do you think I need a coat or anything?" she asked.

He looked at her braids and her cotton print dress.

"No, you don't need a coat," he said, "we're only going to Blair."

"Well," she said, "maybe you ought to see some soldiers," and then she smiled. "It's silly, but I'd like to go."

Any good leader had to develop a sense of premonition. Premonition, after all, was only a peculiar sort of sensitiveness, not unlike that mysterious prescience that stopped you sometimes from running into an object in the dark. When, as a young subaltern, he led patrols in France and when he was older and examined dispositions on a map, instinct often told him to concentrate in the center or to move by the left flank. When Muriel climbed up beside him to the worn upholstery of that Ford runabout, Melville Goodwin had his first encounter with premonition. There was nothing sharp or definite about it, but he had a reasonable certainty that if he and Muriel went to Blair they would go to other places, and an equal certainty that if he did not go to Blair his life would follow quite a different pattern.

"Why are we waiting?" Muriel asked. "Why don't you make the thing go?"

"All right," he said, and he pressed the little pedal by the steering post and the car began to move down Prospect Street.

"Melville," she asked, "are you sure you know what you're doing?"

"Yes," he said, "of course I'm sure."

No one was ever entirely sure — at best you could only be partly sure — and perhaps Muriel always understood this better than he ever did. Perhaps in all the years they were together she was never convinced of his infallibility.

"My goodness," she said, "we're out of Hallowell already."

They were only traveling at twenty miles an hour, but the Ford was eating up the distance. They were a mile out of Hallowell, beyond the unpainted buildings of the Sawyer farm already, and over the bridge that spanned the Sawyer Brook. The sun was at his back and was dropping low, and he and Muriel were approaching the wooded, rolling country that lay between Hallowell and Blair. His mind was concentrated both on the management of the Ford, which had raised him to another plane, and on the curves and contours of the road. With his instinctive memory for terrain, even at that unaccustomed speed, he was storing away the landmarks, roughly measuring distance, noting down a curve, a white pine, a glacial boulder, a woods road to his right, or a stone wall in the oak thicket to his left.

"Melville," Muriel asked — they both had to raise their voices so that they could be heard above the rattling of the car — "do you think I'm too old for braids?"

He had no fixed ideas on the subject, and he could both watch the road unfold and tell her so.

"I think I ought to put my hair up," Muriel said, "something like the way Celia has hers."

"It might look all right," he said, "if it wasn't in a hard knot."

"How do you mean, a hard knot?"

"I don't know," he said, "all squeezed up tight with pins in it."

"It's got to have pins in it if you put it up," she said. "If I had known you were going to ask me for a ride, I'd have put it up."

"You look all right," he said.

"Oh, you're just being polite, Melville," she said.

"No," he said, "you look all right."

A blue farm wagon drawn by two dapple grays was approaching him, and he kept well to the right.

"Melville," she asked, "do you like poetry?"

"Yes," he said, "some kinds, but not love poetry."

"I know a poem called 'The Highwayman,' by Alfred Noyes," Muriel said. "It has love in it but it's about fighting. Shall I say it?"

"Yes," Melville answered, "go ahead and say it."

"All right," Muriel said. "I wouldn't say it to just anyone because some people would say that it sounded silly . . ." and she started it correctly, beginning with the title in the way one had been taught to recite poetry at Hallowell:

The Highwayman
by Alfred Noyes

The wind was a torrent of darkness among the gusty trees,
The moon was a ghostly galleon tossed upon cloudy seas,
The road was a ribbon of moonlight over the purple
moor . . .

The purple moor seemed to wrap itself around them both until he became Mr. Noyes's highwayman and she was Bess, the landlord's black-eyed daughter, and he was after a prize that night, and the redcoats were after him, but she could look for him by moonlight and he would be around though hell should bar the way. They were moving toward Blair, not in the Ford but on the misty wings of moonlight, until he lay in his blood on the highway with a bunch of lace at his throat, but even then, his ghost would come and knock on the old inn door. When her voice stopped, Melville came to himself almost with a jolt.

"It's kind of a silly poem," she said, "but it sounds nice, doesn't it?"

"It's all right," he answered, "except that with all those soldiers after him, he would have waited until there wasn't any moonlight, if he'd had any sense, and if the road was white, he'd have kept off the road. There's no use standing around in the moonlight to let someone take a shot at you."

His thinking was absolutely sound, and he was pleased that he could criticize the poem.

"I don't see why you have to spoil it all," she said. "It would be braver to come by moonlight."

There was no time to argue with her. While she was speaking they had come around a bend, and he could see the buildings of the fairgrounds with the roofs of Blair beyond them and a cloud of dust on the river road.

"Gosh," he said, and he hardly recognized his own voice, "the place is full of soldiers."

He was like the boy in the novel by Stendhal, looking at the field of Waterloo. He had no experience to guide him in estimating the number of troops. He could only see that columns of infantry and khaki-covered wagons were moving through the main street of the village and filling up the fairgrounds, and that tents were already being pitched in rows.

"What are we going to do now?" he heard her ask.

"We're going to see them," he said. "That's what we came for, isn't it?"

He wished for the first time on that journey that he had not taken Muriel along. He wanted to see this sight by himself without having to answer her questions, but after a few minutes he hardly gave a thought to Muriel.

Blair was scarcely a town; it was only one of those crossroad clusters of small white buildings that you so often passed in New England, wondering how it had come to be there in the first place and how anyone living there could manage to support himself. The fairgrounds were on level space next to the church and general store, but the boards of the fence which had formed the façade for its main entrance had nearly all disappeared, and the grandstand for the trotting races had been demolished. However, a few of those barnlike structures so euphemistically known as "exhibition halls" were still intact, and, that afternoon, life had returned to the fair-grounds and to Blair itself. Its inhabitants were lining the single street and clustering on the porch of the general store and post office, watching the volunteer militia end its march and enter camp.

Melville stopped the Ford on the grass by the side of the road not far from the ruins of the fair gates. He could still remember the heat of the waning sun on his bare head, the rumble of the wagons, the sweating, weary faces and the shuffling medley of tired footsteps, but his military status obtruded itself on these memories, cynically, like an artist's reducing glass. He could see himself and Muriel, a gawking boy and girl in country clothes, staring in mute respect at a ludicrous spectacle. He remembered the sun on Muriel's molasses braids, and he remembered that her mouth, usually firm and confident with the assurance of a girl who does the right thing and studies her lessons carefully, had fallen slightly open. He knew now, and Muriel would, too, that the New Hampshire Volunteer Militia was really nothing to gape at, except with charitable pity. As an officer in the regular service, Melville Goodwin now had his own opinion of the National Guard. Troops could not be even passably trained by evening drill in some armory and then by a week or two of summer camping. It was all very well to play at being soldiers, but basically it was a waste of time and tax money, and nothing exemplified his beliefs better than that militia moving into camp at Blair.

It was a hot day and the troops were soft as butter, though heat was no excuse for sloppiness. They all were straggling; all the precepts in that little black field service book had been lost along the way, and the commissioned officers and the noncoms simply did not know their jobs. There had been a pathetic effort to call companies to attention. The regimental band, if you cared to call it a band, was endeavoring to play them into camp, struggling painfully with "The Stars and Stripes Forever." The colonel, red-faced and perspiring, mounted on a bony black horse that must have been hired from some livery stable, had taken his position with the colors to watch the troops file past. The collar of his blouse was unhooked. He was slouched in the saddle like a melting mold of jelly, and of all things, he was smoking a cigar with the band still on it, not bothering even to remove his cigar from his mouth when he took the salutes. Moreover, he seemed satisfied with the miserable showing the men were making. As they attempted to come to attention and shoulder their Springfield rifles in some sort of alignment, he shouted rustic words of encouragement, which Melville could hear occasionally above the discords of the band. Melville could squirm now with professional pain as he recalled them.

"Freeze, boys, you're rubbering," the colonel shouted. "Hooray for Company C! Dress them up, Charley! Keep time to the music, fellas — one, two, three, four."

If the colonel had seriously wished to make any sort of show with those sad troops, he should have halted them for fifteen minutes before they entered Blair and he should have given orders — if anybody obeyed orders — to have packs adjusted and the men cleaned and buttoned up. As it was, they were winding slowly forward like the lowing herd in Gray's "Elegy," groaning and cursing while presumably at attention, using expletives which grew louder when they heard their colonel's voice.

"God damn it," he heard one of the spryer privates shout, "he's riding, ain't he?"

Melville stood utterly bemused by the moving column, boyishly unaware, at that time, of this lack of discipline, fascinated by the Springfields, by the officers' service revolvers, by the felt hats and blue braids, by the packs and the blankets and by the heavy, rumbling wagons. His heart beat hard with the excitement of it, and rightly so perhaps, for there was always something stirring about any regiment equipped for the field. He lived for a minute or two in a haze of make-believe, no longer a boy in his first long trousers. Instead, he was a young officer just graduated from West Point, young U. S. Grant himself, who had dropped over from Hallowell to take a look at the New Hampshire militia. He was so lost in the beauty of all he saw that he had forgotten Muriel until she tugged at his sleeve.

"Oh, Mel," she said, "aren't they lovely?"

Melville glanced tolerantly at Muriel. He had read *A Plebe at*

West Point and its sequels and all the historical fiction he could find in the library and was working on *Battles and Leaders of the Civil War*. He was an authority, and it was necessary for him to be critical and restrain his own enthusiasm.

"They're all right," he said, "but they aren't regulars, and some of them are out of step."

"You couldn't march any better," Muriel said.

He looked at her pityingly from the ivory tower of his experience.

"They haven't even any pickets out," he said.

"What are pickets?" Muriel asked.

"What are pickets?" he repeated. "They are lookouts for the enemy."

He spoke wearily and condescendingly, and his tone put Muriel in her place.

"What are they going to do now?" she asked.

His irritation evaporated beneath her wide-eyed ignorance, and he felt kindly and protective.

"They're going to pitch their tents for the night," he said. "I guess it will be all right to watch them."

He was not wholly sure of this. Though he walked with her unhesitatingly to the fairgrounds, he was afraid they might be ordered off at any minute until he saw that the militia was too occupied to notice the presence of civilians. Occasional groups of those uniformed citizens were slumping down, pulling off their shoes and feeling of their feet. Tolstoy, drawing on his memories for *War and Peace*, could never have seen anything as disorganized as that militia. Yet slowly, painfully, with groans and oaths, the company streets were taking shape. The headquarters tents were up. The wagon train was rumbling to a suitable location, and fires were being lighted near the cook tents. There were always some able individuals in any organization, and this regiment had its quota. Arms were being stacked after a fashion, and a small army city was rising. If the execution was clumsy, Melville did not know it then. No one alive, he thought, could have helped being stirred by that smell of wood smoke and of cooking, by the scurrying of the water and kitchen details and the guard, and by the strings of draft horses being led to drink. Both he and Muriel must have forgotten about the time, until the bugles blew assembly and the ranks began forming for retreat — not that he understood the formality then. Muriel had stayed beside him quietly and uncomplaining as they wandered here and there, but now her voice was plaintive.

"It's getting awfully late," she said. "I don't know what Mother's going to say."

"Oh," he said, "in the Ford we can get back in no time."

Nevertheless he knew they had stayed too long. It was six o'clock, and he could feel a faint evening chill in the air already. They hurried through the old fair gates. They were almost running when they reached the Hallowell road, but when they reached it, he could see no sign of the car, although he remembered exactly where he had left it. His father's Ford was gone.

At one time or another, Melville Goodwin had been exposed to all the components of surprise and disaster. Now they were like old acquaintances; yet his personal reactions had not changed greatly since that moment at Blair when he stared at the track left by the Ford's wheels. There would always be the same grip at his throat, the same taut dryness in his mouth, the same hideous, hollow tension in his stomach that he felt that day. The main remedy was always quick, decisive action. His reactions were slower at Blair than they were later, but he did not behave badly. There was, of course, a nauseous second of indecision, combined with sickening thoughts of consequences, and then Muriel's presence beside him began to exert the same stimulus that the presence of troops did later.

"Melville," he heard her wail, "it's gone. Why didn't you leave it in a safe place? What are we going to do?"

With her words and his own thoughts buzzing savagely through his head, he examined the tracks of the vanished Ford, and already common sense was returning to him. While Muriel was still speaking, he began tracing the tire marks through the long grass to the dust of the road. He only had to follow them for a few yards to discover that the Ford had been driven into the fairgrounds.

"It's all right," he said to Muriel, "it's around here somewhere."

Then he grabbed her by the hand, not to console her but because he was in a hurry. Whoever had taken the car, he was thinking, had not seriously intended to steal it, and it would not be on the company streets or near the officers' tents, but rather in the neighborhood of the wagons. It was the first estimate he had ever made of a serious situation, and it had been correct. Not more than three minutes could have elapsed before he saw the Ford down by the wagon park. It stood beside a confused heap of packs and harness, with its engine running, and four militia men were examining it, making obvious and humorous remarks. He was out of breath as he drew near them. One private, he remembered, was drinking from a whisky bottle and another was trying to pull it away.

"That's my automobile," Melville said.

He was ashamed that his voice quavered in his first experience with troops.

"Say," one of the men said, "look at the two little sweethearts."

Melville found himself blushing. He had forgotten that he was holding Muriel's hand, and he dropped it like a hot potato. He could still remember the red hair of the man who had spoken and the exact tilt of his mouth. The two top buttons of his shirt were open and he had one gold tooth.

"That's my automobile," Melville said again.

"Why, you little snotty-nosed bastard," the redheaded private said. "You're too young to own a car."

"It's my father's automobile," he said.

The soldier moved closer to him.

"Fresh, aren't you?" the soldier said. "How do I know it's your daddy's automobile?"

"Because I told you so," Melville said, and he was glad that his voice was firmer.

"So you told me so, did you?" the redheaded soldier said. "And what are you going to do about it?"

It was a sensible question, and it looked as though there was nothing he could do about it, but he did not want Muriel to know it. He swallowed and he felt his heart beating in his throat.

"I'm going to drive it home," Melville said.

185

"Now listen, bub," the redheaded soldier said, "you drag your little ass out of here before I slap your ears back."

"Oh, leave him alone, Jake," someone said, "he's only a kid."

"You heard me," the redhead said, waving an open palm at him, "drag ass out of here."

Melville knew that he could not walk away. It would be better to have his teeth knocked out or be killed than walk away. Probably, on thinking it over, nothing would have happened. Someone not as drunk as the redhead would have moved between them, but at just that moment Muriel tugged his arm.

"Here, Mel," she whispered to him, "take this."

Muriel was holding out a bayonet to him. She must have found it in the heap of equipment near the Ford, and she must have drawn it from its scabbard herself because he saw its ugly blade in the dusk. He had never held a bayonet before, and subsequently it was never part of an officer's equipment, but at that moment it seemed completely natural to be holding it.

"Keep away from me," Melville said.

"Why, you murdering little son of a bitch!" the redhead shouted. "You ought to go to jail."

The others around the car were laughing, but it was not all a joke.

Melville backed away carefully and climbed behind the wheel of the Ford, put the bayonet on the seat beside him and accelerated the motor. He felt as though he were moving and talking in a dream after he had told Muriel to get in beside him. That was all there was to it. No one spoke. No one shouted after them as he drove the car toward the fairgrounds gates. The only sound that he could remember was Muriel's convulsive sobbing.

"Don't cry, Muriel," he said. "There's nothing to cry about," and he threw the bayonet out of the car when they reached the Hallowell road.

He was never embarrassed after that when anyone in Hallowell said that Muriel Reece was his best girl.

The truths in the old book of Field Service Regulations had once been as much a part of his fixed beliefs as paragraphs on guard duty and the school of the soldier. Action, correct or not, was preferable to immobility. Muriel had never read the Field Service Regulations, but what she had done was in keeping with their essence. She had estimated the situation and had taken action when she handed him that bayonet. Most of his life having been made up of fighting or considering the problems of fighting, it was his habit to review the actions in which he had participated, and the action at Blair fell into a classic pattern. It could readily be incorporated in a textbook. Essentially, it had been fought by Muriel Reece, who had brought the weight of reinforcement to bear at the critical point.

XII

"If You Can Dream and Not Make Dreams Your Master . . ."

MELVILLE GOODWIN's words came to a standstill — for no artistic reason. His attempts to describe his life and his family had been prolix, humorless and dull; yet when he stopped speaking, I could feel not only the stark outlines of Hallowell but something of its depths and lights and shades. At any rate, his personality, or perhaps his utter lack of narrative skill, made Hallowell and young Mel Goodwin much more real to me at the moment than anything at Savin Hill. He was standing on firmer ground than all the rest of us.

Perhaps the others were thinking as I was — that compared to Melville Goodwin we were febrile and superficial, driven easily by light motivations and ambitions. Phil Bentley wore the rapt expression of someone who loves music listening to the last notes of a symphony. Miss Fineholt sat motionless behind the desk gazing at the General in a way that made me wonder for a second whether she could be thinking of herself as another Muriel Reece. Colonel Flax's expression was slightly different. He had obviously prepared himself as a good officer should for an interminable military lecture that had turned out to be something else, and he was plainly puzzled by the result.

We were still right there with Melville Goodwin when he moved his arm and looked at his wrist watch.

"Only nine-fifty-five," he said. "I thought it was later than that." Somehow, like Dr. Einstein, he had proved that time was variable. "Well, I guess it was that summer that I went to a Sunday school picnic. I guess I remember it because it was the last one of those

188

functions I ever attended. All our crowd was getting a little old for Sunday school picnics. There was a grove and a lake halfway to Nashua. We went there in the trolley car — but maybe it isn't important. Maybe everybody would like to get up and stretch."

"Oh, no," Phil Bentley said, "let's hear about the picnic."

"Well," the General said, "there always was one of those things every summer."

A gentle knock on the library door cut the General's sentence short. It was Oscar in his fawn-colored alpaca coat. He did not belong in Hallowell or on the Hallowell trolley. His presence was a jarring note and created a guilty sort of silence.

"Pardon my interrupting," Oscar said, "but Mr. Frary wanted to know if he could speak to Mr. Skelton for a few minutes. He's upstairs in his room."

I had completely forgotten that Gilbert Frary was still with us.

"Go ahead, Sid," the General said, "it's all right, I can get along."

"Well, I hate not to hear this," I began, "but I imagine Mr. Frary's going to town."

"Come back when you're finished," Phil Bentley said. "Now what about the picnic, sir?"

"Well," the General said, "there was a lake and a pine grove on the trolley line about five miles outside of Nashua, called Rodney's Grove. It was owned by the trolley company, I guess. There were a few rowboats and some swings and tables and benches. . . ."

Then as I closed the library door behind me, I heard him say, "But none of this has any real bearing on anything."

When I saw Helen in the upstairs hall, she was carrying a pad of paper and a pencil, which indicated that she was on her way to the kitchen to plan meals and her intent look showed that she was dealing with some complicated problem.

"Where are you going?" she asked.

When I told her that Gilbert Frary had sent for me, she nodded toward the door of our dressing room.

"Come in here for a minute first," she said, "and tell me what we're going to do for the rest of the day."

I followed her, not with any great alacrity, because I never could seem to see domestic problems through Helen's eyes.

"I woke up this morning," she said when she closed the door, "to realize we're running a sort of hotel. At least, I know now how people must feel who take in paying guests at a dude ranch or somewhere. Everyone is so — so extraneous."

"I know what you mean," I said. "The only difference is, ours aren't paying."

"Well, don't be so aloof from it," Helen said. "You asked them here."

"You know I had to ask them here or at least I thought I did," I told her.

We were speaking fixed lines, going through a routine of dialogue that other husbands and other wives had spoken a million times before, and neither of us, if we had tried, could have avoided a single line.

"I wish you weren't always so indefinite, dear," Helen said. "You mean Gilbert Frary made you ask them? . . . Oh, Gilbert and his publicity!"

"Well, maybe he did partly," I said, "but I don't see how I could be more definite."

"You could have put your foot down," Helen said.

"I didn't want to put my foot down," I told her. "There was nothing to put it on — that is, nothing in particular."

"Well, I don't mind especially," Helen said, "and I know this is the first time you've ever had your friends here, except they're not strictly your friends."

"That isn't exactly so," I told her. "Mel Goodwin's a sort of a friend of mine."

"I know," Helen said. "General Goodwin's awfully sweet. He couldn't be sweeter."

"What's that?" I asked her.

"He couldn't be sweeter," Helen said again. "Gilbert is in his room using the telephone so I can't use it, and Mrs. Goodwin is in the living room crocheting a washcloth."

"Is she really crocheting a washcloth?" I asked.

"She's making a whole set of them," Helen said. "She finished one last night after dinner, and now she's on another. How long do you think this is going to last?"

"I don't exactly know," I said, "but it won't be so long."

"I can't seem to make any plans," Helen said. "Please try to say something definite, Sid. Will they be here for another day, or for two days and two nights? How far is the General in his life?"

"When I left him he was just fifteen," I said. "He was taking Muriel to a Sunday school picnic. They were high school sweethearts."

"Do you mean to say," Helen asked, "that after all this he's only fifteen?"

I could think of the General unrolling himself like a film against a fixed time limit.

"Don't worry," I said, "at the rate he's going, he'll be much older by evening. Who knows — he may be twenty-five or thirty."

"All right," Helen said, "how old is he now?"

"He's fifteen — I told you."

"No, no," Helen said. "I mean how old is he really?"

"Oh," I said, "somewhere around fifty."

"And you mean he'll only be twenty-five or thirty by evening?" Helen said. "Sidney, can't we get this straight?"

"No," I said, "I don't know how we can. It's going to take him time to get older."

"Well, if he only gets to be thirty by evening," Helen said, "perhaps he'll only be forty tomorrow. Darling, what *am* I going to do with Mrs. Goodwin until he gets to be fifty?"

"Listen, Helen," I said, and I really wanted to be helpful, "the best thing to do is to relax — and besides, just remember that everyone's busy."

"Mrs. Goodwin isn't busy," Helen said.

"Well, take her for a drive," I said, "take her to do the marketing. She'd be interested in that."

"Williams is driving Gilbert back to town in the Cadillac," Helen said.

Somehow most of our recent conversations ended with the problem of transportation.

"Well, take her in the station wagon," I answered.

"Miss Otts will need the station wagon later to bring Camilla home from school," Helen said.

"Well, all right," I said, "there's still the Packard runabout."

"That's true," Helen said, "I'd forgotten about the Packard."

We looked at each other for a moment and then we both began to laugh.

"Darling," Helen said, "we do have a good time, don't we?"

"Yes," I said, "always, Mrs. Winlock."

Somehow the whole situation was eased simply because Helen had forgotten about the Packard.

At intervals during the last few weeks Gilbert Frary had been suggesting that he and I should get away somewhere and have a good long talk, or, as he liked to call it, "an exchange of ideas." He had been vague, I remembered, when I had asked him what sort of ideas he wanted to exchange. He had said they were not ideas, essentially, but merely a few thoughts that he had been storing in the back of his mind, none of which had any immediacy. He did not mean that we were to hold a conference. All he wanted was to think aloud with me along a few lines, to get my frank reaction to a few thoughts that were still nebulous. He could not tell me what these thoughts were until he thought them aloud with me.

I wondered again where these thoughts might lead as I made my way to Gilbert's room. As he liked to say himself, he was a very clever negotiator, and at the end of a long talk, if you were not careful, you were apt to find that you had been moved through unexpected mazes, like a ball in one of those glass-covered puzzles, until you found yourself in some unanticipated position. It was necessary not only to follow the eloquent, even flow of Gilbert's words but to search for implications, without being confused by the clichés of the moment with which Gilbert always adorned his comments. With some people perhaps he was devious, but not with me, he always said. With me it was like talking to his own brother Cedric, except that my mind was more incisive than Cedric's and utterly devoid of ambiguity. He sometimes thought, just between us both, that his brother Cedric, whom he had set up personally in the producing business, was lacking in a species of integrity, and I always had integrity, and there was nothing that he valued more than integrity. He and I could talk without make-believe because we were devoted to each other and devoted to the same objective. There was nothing he enjoyed more than sitting with me and having a good exchange of ideas. I was relieved by Helen's news that Gilbert wished to return to town in the Cadillac during the morning, since this would mean that the thought exchange would not be as complicated as it might have been otherwise.

The jump from the mind of Melville Goodwin to the mind of Gilbert Frary was as long as a passage by plane across an ocean. It was like moving from a temperate to a tropic zone, and it was no help, as I was preparing for the meeting, to encounter Farouche bounding toward me on the green carpet of the upstairs hallway. His smoke-gray coat was unsnarled and magnificent, and a bright new bow gathered the fur together on the top of his cranium. His dark eyes were limpid and thoughtful, and when he saw I was not interested in his ring, he accepted my reaction in a gentlemanly way and stood quietly beside me as I knocked on Gilbert's door. Inside I could hear Gilbert shut off his portable radio.

"Come in, come in," he called, and when Farouche and I entered he smiled at us. "Oh, excuse me, Sidney," he said, and he rose hastily from an easy chair. "I didn't know it was you. I thought it was Oscar. That makes a very pretty entrance, you and the poodle. It makes me want to pinch myself to be sure that I'm awake."

"He often makes me want to pinch myself, too," I said. "Did you have a good night, Gilbert?"

"A very restful night as always, in your home, Sidney," he answered, "though frankly I am not a country person and I miss the street noises — but I took half a grain of Luminal, not that I believe in sedatives, and then I knew nothing, absolutely nothing, until I was awakened by the sunlight on these delightful chintzes. It's an adventure, waking up in a strange and lovely room. All of this seems such a part of you and Helen, Sidney, that I cannot help but love it."

Except for his coat, Gilbert was fully dressed, but he still wore his silk dressing gown. His pigskin fitted suitcase on its stand by the foot of his bed, though open, was already packed. He only had to remove the dressing gown and fold it, put on his pin-striped coat, leave a bill on the bedside table, and there would be no trace of him left in the guest room except for the odor of his shaving and hair lotions.

"Why do you have to go to town?" I asked.

"I wish I might stay longer," Gilbert said. "There is nothing I would like better than to sit here all day dreaming dreams as I have this morning. I've been lounging in this easy chair since eight o'clock, toying with my breakfast, mulling over the papers and turning the radio dial. Have we time to sit down for a moment? I don't have to leave for another half hour, and we haven't had a talk for a long while. No, you sit in the comfortable chair."

"No, you sit in it," I told him. "This house is full of comfortable chairs," and I pulled a chintz chair closer to his. "What have you been dreaming about, Gilbert?"

Gilbert sighed and sat down in his armchair again and placed the tips of his long fingers together.

"Frankly," he said, "I've been dreaming a little about you, Sidney, not actively, just letting my mind run vaguely."

"I hope they were sweet dreams, Gilbert," I said.

Gilbert smiled at me affectionately.

"That dry humor of yours always pulls me together, Sidney," he said. "Frankly, without the least ambiguity, it makes me very happy to think that you and I are both here and both in a position where we can love people without being relentless. Come here, you smart doggie." He snapped his fingers playfully at Farouche. "Does it want to play with its ring?"

Farouche moved toward him in a dignified, impersonal manner. I liked to think that Farouche was somewhat bored and that he preferred me to Gilbert, though I could not be sure of this — but I also liked to think that Farouche, along with Gilbert and me, knew where his bread was buttered.

"All right," I said, "what were you dreaming about, Gilbert?"

"Nothing definite," Gilbert said, "but frankly I was dreaming somewhat about the program and a stray remark that George Burtheimer passed the other day and about a slight reservation of George's, not adult, just a stray remark. George is whimsical sometimes."

Gilbert shook his head and smiled at his memory of the whimsey, but I felt a slight uneasiness. There was obviously something definite on Gilbert's mind which he knew I would not like and which he desired to present to me in a sugar-coated way.

"Go ahead, Gilbert," I said. "What is it about the program?"

I felt the gentle impact of something being dropped on the toe of my shoe. It was Farouche's rubber ring, and I gave the ring a kick and Farouche bounded after it, and Gilbert laughed.

"Oh, oh," Gilbert said, "you might think it was a rat or something. I wish I might have a dog, but they hardly fit at the St. Regis, although I do encounter them occasionally in the elevators."

"Go ahead," I said. "What's the matter with the program?"

"Now, Sidney," Gilbert said, "if I have disturbed you, please forgive me. It's only a whimsical idea of George's. You and I know there's nothing the matter with the program, and I told George, quite caustically, to look at the rating — but you know a sponsor's line of thought, and the little restivenesses they sometimes have when they sign the checks for a million-dollar appropriation."

I found myself dropping automatically into Gilbert's own vernacular.

"And if they have, so what?" I said.

"It's just a little matter," Gilbert said, "but I have been dreaming over it for several days, and this morning at nine I checked myself by turning on 'Alan Featherbee and the News,' because George has been mentioning him a little wistfully lately. There may be something in the voice that has escaped me up to now, not that it compares with yours for an instant, Sidney, but frankly I was impressed by Alan."

One of the reasons I have always hated show business is the jealousy that it engenders; and now, when Gilbert mentioned another commentator named Alan Featherbee, I actually felt a sharp, half-hysterical twinge of anxiety. Subtly, indirectly, this unknown Featherbee was rising as a threat to my existence, merely because he had been noticed by my sponsor and because he had attracted Gilbert's attention. It did no good to tell myself that morning commentators, especially nine-o'clock ones, were worth nobody's attention. I still knew that Gilbert would not have mentioned Featherbee without a definite purpose. I was sure of it when I noticed Gilbert's hard and studious look. He was mentally comparing me with this Mr. Featherbee, weighing us in his mind as competing pieces of property.

"Well . . ." I said, "what the hell about him?"

Gilbert laughed in a merry, controlled way, as though we had been telling each other droll stories.

"Oh, oh," he said, "Sidney, don't tell me you're acting like a prima donna."

"Well, what the hell about him?" I asked again.

"Absolutely nothing about him," Gilbert answered, "and please believe I'm being candid. He has no future, no build-up possibilities at all, and no color or stature, as I explained to George very definitely and unambiguously. Yet he does do one thing which is conceivably interesting, and that was all that George was speaking about."

"What does he do," I asked, "bird calls?"

"Sidney," Gilbert said, "please understand me and please forgive me, without showing pique or employing persiflage."

"God damn it," I said, "let's get on with the situation, Gilbert!"

Gilbert made an eloquent soothing gesture with both hands.

"There is but no situation," he said, "or only the merest touch of a situation. George is merely wondering about the high price of the program, the same old conventional complaint."

"Well, the customers listen to it, don't they?" I asked.

"Of course they listen to it," Gilbert said, and his voice had a wounded note, "but do they buy the product after listening? That's what seems to be worrying George, and he has simply advanced an idea, very tentatively, and humbly."

"My God," I said, "are you and he going to start monkeying with the program again?"

Gilbert moved his hands upward this time, in a comical manner, as though warding off an unexpected blow, and then he pulled his flowered dressing gown into place.

"Sidney," he said, "I know you know me well enough to be sure I'll never let you down, with loyalty the keystone of our relationship. I am with you in the final decision, Sidney, but I honestly think we should entertain a sponsor's suggestion. I was speaking of it to Art Hertz yesterday, and Art thinks we should entertain it."

He intended his remark to be deliberately disturbing: he should not have spoken to the script-writer about the program before discussing it with me. I was almost sure that his speech contained a hint that I was not wholly indispensable, and I found myself speaking more carefully.

"All right," I said, "what is it you want me to entertain?"

"Well," Gilbert said, and his words also were more measured, "it falls into the commercial category. It is no reflection on your work. Everyone is immensely happy with your work. George himself was speaking of your mail only yesterday, but there is frankly a little feeling in the sponsor's office that not quite enough emphasis is being placed upon the commercial side of the program."

"God damn it," I said, "we've been through all that before. If they had their way they'd put the whole fifteen minutes into advertising."

"Sidney," Gilbert said, "I love it when you speak your mind, but after all, we live by the program, Sidney. We live by it, and so does the doggie here. What is your name, Doggie?" and Gilbert snapped his fingers. "You know that I love everything about you, Sidney — you and Helen and Camilla and your intemperateness. They don't want more commercial time, Sidney. George has merely advanced a little thought, and I promised that you would consider it. It is suggested that you should speak the commercials yourself, weaving them in with the news, as Alan Featherbee does."

"My God," I began — "wait a minute, Gilbert!" — but Gilbert interrupted me, speaking very quickly.

"Now, Sidney," Gilbert said, "you and I possess exactly the same variety of integrity. It shocked my integrity just as it does yours when I first faced it. In fact, I was almost rude to George; but as you consider the suggestion, Sidney, in an unbiased way, it is not so bad, basically. Please give me just a moment. I've made a few notes . . . oh, here they are." Gilbert picked up a piece of paper from the breakfast tray. "You see, Alan Featherbee does this commercial thing and he does it very adroitly with a real ring of conviction. Will you please, Sidney, not assume a nauseated look until I have finished? These notes are merely a little dream, not in your words but merely in mine. But just suppose you were to open this way. . . ."

Gilbert cleared his throat, drew a pair of horn-rimmed spectacles from his waistcoat pocket even more ponderously heavy than those of Philip Bentley, and began to read:

"Good evening, everybody. The news is very important and very critical tonight, but first, before I give it to you, let me tell you a little personal adventure of mine that was news to me. Sitting in my Connecticut home this evening, I was faced with a plate of onion soup. Its very aroma reminded me of the restaurant near the Rue de la Paix where I love to dine when I am gathering news in Paris. Its taste conjured up the vision of old Pierre, the chef, whom I had congratulated on his onion soup when I was last in Paris at the time of the breakup of the cabinet. Its stock had that same full-bodied, that same invigorating authority. . . ."

Gilbert took off his glasses and put them back in his pocket and waved the sheet of paper in an expansive fanlike motion.

"That's my dream, Sidney," he said, "a commercial with news action in it. It needs hours of careful thought, but you understand it, don't you?"

I could understand it and I sat for a moment without speaking. At least I was considering it. I was considering roughly what I had lived for and what everything had meant and when it was time to start and when it was time to stop.

"How serious are you about that, Gilbert?" I asked.

"Why, not serious at all," Gilbert said. "I was merely advancing the idea."

"Well," I said, "why don't you get Alan Featherbee to do it?"

"Now, Sid," Gilbert said, "don't take it that way. It was merely a suggestion — but there is Clause 28 in the contract."

"What the hell is Clause 28?" I asked.

"George considers it an escape clause," Gilbert said, "though frankly I consider this legally debatable."

"Well," I said, "then why do you bring it up, Gilbert?"

Savin Hill and my present situation had never seemed so ephemeral. I could imagine the house and everything being carted away in box cars as I sat there contemplating Gilbert Frary. He was like a magician holding an object in his hand. It had been there for one instant and now it had completely vanished and you could not be sure whether it had ever really been there. I had felt that Gilbert Frary and I had been about to reach the cleavage point that we probably would reach someday, but now magically there was no cleavage point and no tension between us. It was all very confusing, but then, Gilbert always loved confusion.

"Sidney," he said, "I have brought up absolutely nothing."

There had been something and now there was nothing. Gilbert looked hurt and reproachful, and I even had a feeling of remorse. I realized again that he was fond of me in a certain way.

"Gilbert," I said, "I don't understand all this."

"Sidney," Gilbert said, "I have to say something very humbly. I have been very devious with my very best friend. Forgive me, please forgive me, Sidney."

It was still hard for me to tell exactly where we were, and I could never be as good as Gilbert at playing out a scene.

"I don't see that there's anything to forgive," I said.

There were tears in Gilbert's eyes and Gilbert cleared his throat, and I had a sickening dread that Gilbert was going to cry.

"Sidney," he said, "I should have known before I started what your reaction would be. I should have known that this was a suggestion that could have never stood before integrity. Forgive me and let's forget it, Sidney."

"All right," I said, "let's forget it, Gilbert."

"The cheapness of it . . ." Gilbert said. "I feel indignant about it myself. When I get to the office I shall call up George and tell him so personally. I'm completely with you, Sidney."

"Well, that's fine," I said.

199

"Sidney," Gilbert said, "I won't be devious again."

"That's all right," I said, "you can't help it, Gilbert."

"I always feel better when we've had a talk," Gilbert said, "and you do forgive my crudeness, Sidney?"

"Don't ever worry about being crude, Gilbert," I told him.

"When you and I are together," Gilbert said, "I have no sense of time. It's actually a quarter before eleven. I must be leaving, Sidney, and please let me steal downstairs — without fanfare — and give my love and thanks to Helen, and I'll be in touch with you later in the day."

Gilbert whipped off his silk dressing gown and snatched up his pin-striped coat.

"No, no," he said, "I'll fold the dressing gown. Isn't it a nice piece of silk? I'll have one like it made up for you if you think Helen would appreciate it. By the way, how is everything going with the General?"

"They're working on him downstairs. I suppose I'd better go back," I said.

"Well, don't waste too much time," Gilbert said, "although it is nice to keep in well with the magazines. I think we ought to go to the Coast next month, but we can chat about it later — and, Sidney — "

"Yes?" I said.

He held out his hand and we shook hands.

"Don't worry about Clause 28. There's absolutely nothing in it. George only mentioned it playfully."

"I'm not worried about it as long as you're not," I said.

"And you feel happy about everything?"

"Yes," I said, "absolutely happy."

Gilbert snapped his suitcase shut and picked it up before I could reach it.

"Oh," he said, "I nearly forgot. Here's a little something for Oscar," and he dropped a five-dollar bill upon the bedside table.

I felt weary when I stood outside the house watching the Cadillac leave with Gilbert for the city, though our talk had been no more disturbing than other talks with Gilbert. I was a valuable piece of property and in a sense a negotiable security, and a contretemps like this was all a part of the climate in which I lived.

When he was gone I remembered Melville A. Goodwin in the library, but returning to him seemed to involve a considerable effort, including the process of getting rid of Gilbert Frary mentally, now that he was gone physically, and to manage this I needed a few minutes to myself. It was this need that made me wander into the living room. I had forgotten that Mrs. Goodwin might be there, and I had already walked past her when I heard her voice behind me.

"Good morning, Mr. Skelton," she said.

She was sitting on the corner of the long sofa crocheting a washcloth, just as Helen had said. She was wearing her useful traveling suit minus the orchids. Her soft, plump hands moved deftly and noiselessly.

"Oh," I said, "good morning, Mrs. Goodwin. I'm sorry, I don't know why I didn't see you."

"Were you looking for something?" she asked.

"No," I said, "I was just walking around."

"Perhaps you are thinking of something to write about," she said.

"No," I said, "I was just seeing Mr. Frary off and then I was walking around. The General is in the library."

"How is everything going?" she asked. "I hope the General isn't saying things he shouldn't."

"Oh, no," I said, "everything's going very well," and then I sat beside her on the sofa. "He was telling us how you handed him a bayonet, when the militia took his father's Ford."

"Oh," she said, "that was a silly thing for him to tell."

She frowned, but her needles still moved steadily. Her hair was blue-gray now, no longer the color of pulled molasses candy.

"I don't see why Mel should have remembered that," she said. "Mel and I haven't spoken about it for years. He always had a stubborn streak, and I was afraid the man was going to strike him, and then I saw that thing lying on top of a pile of knapsacks. Our son Robert has that same stubborn streak. When he was fifteen he looked very much as Mel did."

"How did he look?" I asked.

201

"Oh, like any towheaded boy of fifteen," she said. "He's taller than Mel and he has his father's features, but he has my eyes. He's stubborn but I'm afraid he hasn't his father's character. The General has a strong character and he's difficult when he's restless. It's queer he should think of that afternoon at Blair. Of course we never told about the trouble when we got home. That was Mel's and my secret." She looked at me and smiled. "I was glad to have some sort of secret with him."

XIII

Don't Say You Didn't Mean It, Mel

It was undoubtedly a washcloth she was crocheting — white with a green border — and she was doing the border now with quick, even plunges of her needle. I could understand as I watched her why mythological fates always seemed to me to be spinning, tatting or embroidering. Mrs. Goodwin would inevitably finish that washcloth. She would not thrust any half-completed work into a bag and forget it as Helen often did. Yet while the washcloth grew and expanded, it was only a methodical accompaniment, because her whole mind did not have to be upon it. A slight relaxation about the corners of her firm, small mouth showed that she enjoyed what she was thinking. She was like someone opening a box of old letters — in order.

"The General was speaking of a Sunday school picnic," I said. "You all rode somewhere on the trolley."

Helen had said that she did not know what to talk about with Mrs. Goodwin, yet I was entertained, feeling, at the same time, a sort of military deference because she was a general's wife. She glanced up at me, but she did not forget the washcloth.

"Are you being polite or are you interested?" she asked.

"If you really want to know," I told her, "I started by being polite, but I like putting things together. It's a habit, I suppose."

"Are you trying to put me together?" she asked.

"Not seriously," I answered, "only out of habit."

"You're not much like Mel, are you?" she said.

"I suppose that's why I'm interested in him," I said.

She nodded and I straightened myself uncomfortably, and felt like a younger officer paying a formal call upon the commanding officer's wife.

203

"I suppose you think the General's a type," she said.

"Why, yes, of course I do," I answered.

"And I suppose you think I'm a type."

"Why, yes," I said, "the idea occurred to me."

She smiled, and I understood her much better when she smiled.

"I'm glad of that," she said, "because I've always tried to be. So few people outside the service ever try to understand the service. Of course Mel has to be a type, but I wish he enjoyed being one as much as I do."

"Doesn't he?" I asked.

"Not when he's restless," she said, "and of course he's restless now." She smoothed the washcloth on her knee and probed at a stitch with her needle. "The General calls you Sid. Do you mind if I do?"

"Why, no," I said, "I'd like to have you."

"If you call him Mel," she said, "I don't know why you shouldn't call me Muriel. How long were you with the General in Paris?"

I was almost sure that Dottie Peale was coming next, and I was thinking of loyalty from the top down and from the bottom up. Helen had said that men always stuck together, and Mrs. Melville Goodwin was crocheting me like her washcloth.

"I only saw him off and on for a day or two," I said.

I waited for her to twist me further into the design, but the design changed.

"But you saw him at Saint-Lô first, didn't you?" she said. "That was Mel's great chance, of course, the sort of chance that everyone in the service dreams about. I wish I'd been there to see him."

"He looked very well," I said.

"Mel always appears well when he's with troops," she said. "I know what you mean by liking to put things together. I was in Washington before Normandy, sharing a home with a dear friend of mine, Enid Joyce, the wife of Colonel Joyce. We had quarters next to each other at Schofield when Mel was there in '34. Poor Bud Joyce had a disk in his back and he never had his chance. He was in G-2 in the Pentagon, wearing a brace, and Enid and I would spend off moments in Alexandria working over a five-hundred-piece picture puzzle on the bridge table. After D day, sometimes I used to creep downstairs at two in the morning and turn on the light and look for pieces."

She paused and smiled at me, but I was on the outside and she was on the inside. We sat there silently. It was a peaceful sort of silence.

"So I see why you like to put things together," she said. "If Mel and I were a puzzle all cut up by a jigsaw, I suppose that Sunday school picnic out at Rodney's Grove would be a corner piece."

She stopped and I was afraid that the balance of things was gone and that she would not get back to Hallowell. I was relieved when she went on.

"It was a very hot day," she said. "I made enough sandwiches for Mel and myself, but I wasn't sure that Mel would eat them with me because Mel was always shy with girls, especially in a group . . . and the night before, I sat up late, reading *A Plebe at West Point,* with a candle and the shades down so that Mother couldn't see the light from my bedroom. Did you ever read *A Plebe at West Point?*"

A Plebe at West Point belonged in a phase through which most boys passed, and my father must have understood this because he had given the book to me for my birthday when we were living in West Newton.

"You see," she said, "Mel always liked to talk about the Point. It was another of our secrets. There was only one thing that used to bother Mel about going to the Point. It's queer to think of now. Can you imagine what it was?"

I could not imagine what it was that had bothered him.

"What worried us was that there might never be another war. It *is* queer to think of now, isn't it?"

I was afraid that she might lose the thread, so I asked her what chance there had been to talk to Melville Goodwin about the Military Academy at a Sunday school picnic.

"Of course there wasn't much chance," she said, "and the Senior Bible Class was pretty old for picnics. We played Bible quotation games with Mr. Atherton while all the others were wading in the pond or swinging or playing hide-and-seek, but the first time Mel ever kissed me was at that picnic. I was half afraid he would and half afraid he wouldn't, and I kept wondering what I would do if he did."

There was nothing I could say about that fragile memory, which had traveled all the way from Hallowell. It was not for me or for anyone else to touch. I only remember my surprise that she should ever have revealed it to me, because this was the sort of personal experience that a man would have always kept to himself; but then, women faced reality in a very different way from men and their confessions regarding love were inherently objective. I had never told a living soul of the first time I had kissed a girl and never would — but Mrs. Goodwin's needle was moving again and I could almost smell the sweet scent of pine needles in the August sun of the picnic grove.

"Mel was always slow with girls, compared with other boys at school," she said. "He was awfully slow at hay rides and Halloween. Did you ever play that game at a Halloween party with a long thread and a raisin in the middle of the thread? When Mel played that game he would always chew up to the raisin and get it while the girl was still feet away. I thought those games were silly myself, and sometimes I wished . . . but it doesn't make much difference — all the things I used to wish. It takes a long while to learn that you can't have everything."

"A lot of people never learn it," I said, "maybe no one does."

"That may be true with civilians," she said, "but I don't think it's true with service people. You learn pretty quickly in the service that you can never get anything unless you give up something else."

Anyone could see that she had given up everything, including all her might-have-beens, to follow General Goodwin.

Melville had once told her, she said, that he had to wear long trousers to the picnic because all the other boys in the Bible Class would be wearing them, but Melville was in a transient stage, and he only owned two pairs of long trousers. One was his pair of khaki work pants, and if he had worn them the other boys would have started singing "Reuben, Reuben, I've been thinking . . ." His only others went with a suit of blue serge handed down from his brother

Harry, which had been altered by Kunik's Tailor Shop in Nashua for one dollar and seventy-five cents out of Melville's own savings. The suit was too heavy for a hot August day, but if he removed the coat, everyone would see how his shirt, also inherited from Harry, kept billowing around the middle, and everyone would observe the tucks his mother had made to shorten the sleeves and the way the neckband was folded here and there to accommodate the celluloid collar that was too small for it. The coat, when buttoned, concealed these defects completely, particularly when Melville had snapped a ready-made bow tie under the collar. Melville's hair had been cut for the occasion at Bedard's Barber Shop on the square — bushy on top but shaved in a neat geometric arc at the neck. He did not wear a hat because he had no summer hat, but he looked very neat and nice, Muriel thought, as they climbed onto the open trolley up front with the rest of the Bible Class.

When Mr. Atherton suggested that the boys who were wearing coats might take them off, Melville said he did not feel hot at all, that you only got hot when you exercised, and riding in a trolley was not exercise. He made this last remark to Muriel and not to Mr. Atherton. He was very polite and he carried her picnic basket and helped her on and off the car. As a matter of fact, all the boys in the Bible Class were constrained to be polite, and there was very little hair pulling or whistling up front in the trolley where Mr. Atherton was seated. Muriel was glad of this because she was wearing her best embroidered shirtwaist with some real lace sewed down the front, and her hair was pinned insecurely into a loose knot, which Melville had said he liked. If there had been hair pulling, the whole thing might have come to pieces. It might have been more fun without Mr. Atherton, in some ways, but she was glad he was around because there were none of those songs using real names like "Melville and Muriel going for a ride, and Melville said to Muriel, 'Won't you be my bride?'"

Melville offered her a stick of Beeman's gum from a pack which he had purchased at his father's drugstore. She said she might like some later but not in the trolley car, and she hoped that the boys would not begin throwing wads of gum at the girls' heads. When some boy blew one of those round mouth whistles loudly in Melville's ear, Melville did not even bother to turn around, and when the boys started a game of One Old Cat in the grove, Melville did not play because he said that he had lamed his shoulder. Of course he had to leave her when all the other boys left the girls, but he came back when Mr. Atherton suggested that they all sing "Onward, Christian Soldiers." Although Melville said that he was not hot at all with his coat on, there were beads of perspiration on his forehead, and undoubtedly his collar would have wilted if it had not been celluloid. When she found that he had forgotten to bring a handkerchief, she offered to lend him hers, and told him to use it when no one was looking. It was nice to have Melville sit next to her — but there was no chance to have a private conversation.

It may have been that Mr. Atherton, from previous experience, was against private conversations among the older group. On earlier picnics when she was too young to be interested, search parties headed by Mr. Atherton had been obliged to run through the woods calling for lost couples, and once the trolley car had waited for half an hour overtime before the picnic was intact. At any rate Mr. Atherton thought of a long succession of games and songs in which everyone was obliged to join, and there was not a single lull until about a half an hour before the scheduled time for departure. Then Mr. Atherton had to stop in order to see that the younger children were present and accounted for, and at this point Melville suddenly suggested to her that they take a walk on the path around the pond. She told him that it would be very hot walking, but Melville said the path was in the shade and it was cool beside the water. She said there would not be time, because the trolley was leaving in half an hour and she was afraid Mr. Atherton might not like it. Melville said if that was the way she felt about just going down to the pond, she could stay right where she was and that he was going by himself. Then she said that she would go, too, as long as he wanted to go so much, but that it was awfully hot.

The walk hardly seemed worth while, once they had started, because neither of them had anything to say. She did tell him that she had read *A Plebe at West Point,* and he had answered that it was just a kid's book. After that they said nothing until they were a quarter of the way around the pond, when she said they really ought to be getting back or else people would begin calling for them. They stopped under a maple tree near the water's edge, and there was a little patch of lily pads and one white pond lily on the water a few feet offshore. She remembered the silvery look of the sunlight on the lily pads and she remembered saying that she wished he could get that water lily for her. Melville tried to reach it with a stick, and then she pulled him back because she saw he could not reach it without getting wet.

"I just said I wished you'd get it for me," she said. "I didn't say I wanted it. I can wish without wanting, can't I?"

"I don't see what's the use in wishing for something without wanting it," he said.

Perhaps that was the difference between girls and boys. Perhaps boys always wanted what they wished for more than girls.

"Muriel," he said.

"Yes," she said, "what is it, Melville?"

"Oh, nothing, I guess," he said.

Then before she knew that anything was going to happen, he bent down and kissed her cheek. She was startled because she had not thought of such a thing happening and the kiss made her jump just as though it were a sudden noise and not a kiss.

"Muriel," he began, "I didn't mean to . . ." and he looked very confused and hot. "I'm sorry, Muriel."

"We've really got to go back now," she said, "or else people will start calling . . . but don't say you didn't mean to."

They walked back down the path without either of them saying another word and without either looking at the other, but there was nothing awkward about the silence.

Mrs. Goodwin smoothed the washcloth on her knee, examining the stitches. It was as compact and complete as that small moment, but the sunlight on the lily pads was gone.

"Well, that's three of them finished," she said.

An illusion of having been present at a time and place in which

I did not belong was so strong that I gave a start when I heard a footstep and saw the General crossing the living room.

"Well, well," the General said, "have I interrupted something?"

His voice was heavily playful, and he smiled at us, but at the same time he gave me a sharp questioning look. He was no longer in a celluloid collar, and his hair was no longer yellow. He had traveled a long way since the Bible Class. His rough edges were worn smooth and his uniform was not a hand-me-down, but a part of the young Melville Goodwin was there still.

"We were talking about kissing, Mel," Mrs. Goodwin said.

The General laughed, and I found myself laughing dutifully with him.

"Well, well, it's about time I broke off and came in here," he said, "if you've got right down to kissing."

"I wouldn't say we were right down to it, sir," I said, and the General laughed again.

"How's everything going, dear?" Mrs. Goodwin asked.

"Well, frankly, you'd be surprised," the General said. "It's the first time I've been able to get in a word edgewise in about twenty years."

We all three laughed conventionally.

Husbands and wives always revealed more than they thought they did. You could usually perceive the grooves of habit and the old methods of give-and-take and you could catch them picking up all sorts of things, just where they had left them off.

"How far are you along with it, dear?" Mrs. Goodwin asked.

"Well, frankly," the General said, "that magazine fellow ought to be in the Inspector General's office. I've only got to where I'm taking exams for the Point."

"Oh dear," Mrs. Goodwin said, "can't you get on faster, Melville?"

"It's funny, they don't seem to want me to get on faster," the General said. "I can dish it out if they want to take it, Muriel."

"I hope they're not making a fool of you, Mel," Mrs. Goodwin said.

"You'd be surprised, Muriel," General Goodwin said, and he frowned.

"The General's doing very well," I said. "You don't have to be worried. If Phil Bentley likes someone, he's always this way. He wants the full strategic background."

Melville Goodwin nodded, and his mouth and eyes took on the official expression of an alert officer receiving and weighing intelligence.

"I don't understand writers," he said. "As I think of my career, it's like a doctor's or a lawyer's. It doesn't make good copy, or a news story, or whatever you fellows call it. There's nothing in me that fellow Bentley can jazz up. I'm not a character like George Patton."

"But just the same," I said, "you people don't get around very often where we can see you. You regulars always stick together."

"You're damned well right we do," the General said. "We don't like having people look at us as though we were witch doctors. Do you think I'm a witch doctor, Sid?"

"No," I said, "but you're all of you conditioned and you're all in a clique."

"That's a fancy, disagreeable word," the General said. "Everyone's conditioned in some way or other. I do have certain skills and certain developed capabilities, but so does that radio fellow who was here last night, the one who kept calling me General Goodman."

"Oh yes," I said, "Gilbert Frary. He has capabilities."

"If I were you, I'd watch that fellow, Sid," the General said. "He acts like someone in some big headquarters . . . but getting back to me, maybe I'm an easy mark when I get outside what you call my 'clique.' Just the same, I wish that Muriel here wouldn't always be afraid I'm going to make a fool of myself with strangers."

In the end it was only the old interplay between any wife and husband, and just then Melville Goodwin was any husband, but still, there were overtones of another way of life. The General was still a general, though off his guard.

"Now, Mel," Mrs. Goodwin said, "sometimes you don't understand people outside the service very well. Do you remember that couple we met when we were in Atlanta, the man you played golf with who wanted to interest you in the orange grove in Florida?"

"I always told you," the General said, "that I hadn't the remotest intention of buying that orange grove. What about that man's wife in San Francisco who got you buying stocks when I was in the War College" — the General smiled at her officially — "and second-hand cars? It doesn't do any good to tell you to get in touch with Harry if you want a car — that's my brother Harry, Sid. He has a Buick agency in Michigan."

"Yes, I know, Mel," Mrs. Goodwin said. "When it comes to civilians, we're both babes in the wood."

"All right," the General said, "as long as you're a babe, too, baby," and then he laughed because I was there — the outside audience.

"I never worry about you when you're with troops," Mrs. Goodwin said, "only when you're in Berlin or Paris or somewhere."

"Or waiting around here?" the General said very brightly.

"I hope you'll hurry things here as much as you can," Mrs. Goodwin said. "Don't you think perhaps tomorrow I'd better go back to Washington? I won't start pulling wires."

"All right," the General said, "maybe it would be a good idea if you looked over the lay of the land — but don't wrap up any package for me before I get there, Muriel."

The idea of her going to Washington seemed to have lifted a weight from the General's mind.

"Now go back and tell them how you got into West Point," Mrs. Goodwin said. "Do you remember when we went to Nashua to call on Mr. Francis J. Garrity and I stayed outside and talked to the girl who was doing the typing?"

"Now wait a minute," the General said. "I know you can do a lot, Muriel, but you didn't make that congressman put me into the Point."

I believe they had finally forgotten I was there until I spoke.

"I thought Mr. Orrin Curtain was the congressman who got you into the Point," I said.

Both of them looked as surprised as though I had walked into their room without knocking.

"What a memory you have, Sid," the General said. "Orrin Curtain was defeated when he ran again. Francis Garrity, a Democrat, beat him, and maybe I wouldn't have dared go see Garrity if Muriel hadn't made me."

"Melville," Mrs. Goodwin said, "your *Croix de guerre* ribbon is twisted, and I think the palm is coming loose. Come here and I'll fix it."

"That leaf is always coming loose," the General said, and he reached instinctively to the left side of his blouse.

"Don't," Mrs. Goodwin said. "I can fix it, Melville."

He walked to the sofa and bent over Mrs. Goodwin and then as her hands moved toward the ribbons he kissed her cheek.

"Why, Melville," Mrs. Goodwin said, "you startled me."

The theory so prevalent in American art forms, that it is the matriarchal little woman who runs the world by outwitting the preposterously dumb menfolk around her — who fall like sitting ducks before her patience, wisdom and manipulative cleverness — has always seemed to me suspect. Admitting that most women believed this legend, in my limited experience they were not completely successful in following it. Yet I was not quite sure about Mrs. Goodwin. It was just possible that she might always have managed Melville Goodwin instead of merely thinking that she managed him. There were depths to her character that were not perceptible on the surface, and shoals and rapids beneath her placidity.

The General, too, was deceptive. He was never as dumb as you thought he was going to be. When he wanted, he had a poker face.

He straightened up and bent down his chin so that he could examine the alignment of the ribbons on the left side of his coat. It would have been an awkward pose for a civilian, but not for him.

"Thanks, Muriel," he said, "it looks fine now."

I hoped they would say something more, but Helen came into the living room just then, and broke up the little scene. She looked fresh and beautiful, an emissary from the inscrutable civilian civilization of which the Goodwins had been speaking.

"Good morning," she said. "I thought the men were all doing that *thing* in the library."

"The men ought to be," the General said, "but men can't get on without women."

"It's nice to know that," Helen said. "I was just wondering whether Mrs. Goodwin wouldn't like to take a drive with me and see the country. It's such a lovely morning."

"Why, yes, dear," Mrs. Goodwin said, "I'd like to very much if it isn't any trouble."

Helen said that it would be no trouble at all. She was going downtown to do some shopping and they could drive along the ridge, and we were going to have luncheon at half past one if it would be all right for everybody. Yet on the other hand, if Mrs. Goodwin would rather not go for a drive there was no reason, absolutely no reason for her to go, but Mrs. Goodwin was glad to go for a drive, glad to get some fresh air. It was amazing how two women could construct a situation out of nothing. The General and I fidgeted slightly while Mrs. Goodwin tried to ascertain whether or not it really would be convenient for Helen to take her for a drive, and while Helen endeavored to discover whether Mrs. Goodwin really wanted to go for a drive, or whether she would be happier staying in the living room, because it made no difference which. Neither of them seemed able to estimate the situation.

"Make up your minds, girls," the General said.

"Why don't you two run along?" Mrs. Goodwin said. "I'll just go upstairs and put on a hat."

"You don't need a hat," Helen said, "unless you'd rather."

"Come on, Sid," the General said, "let's put the show on the road." He took my arm and we walked out of the living room.

"Muriel's never happy unless she's running something," the General said, "and usually it's me. I ought to be on wheels and then she wouldn't have to push so hard. What were you and Muriel talking about?"

"About you," I told him, "and about the service."

"Did she ask you anything about Paris?"

It was the old problem of loyalty again and perhaps men always did stick together.

"She was just asking if I had seen you in Paris," I said.

"Oh," the General said, "well. . . . Was that all she said about Paris?"

"That's all," I said. "We didn't talk about you all the time."

"Say, Sid," the General said, "when this project is over here, I think maybe I'll spend a day or two in New York before I go down to Washington. It's been a long while since I've seen New York."

"If I were you," I said, "everything considered, I would go right down to Washington."

"I don't know whether you would or not," the General said, "but then you're not me, are you?"

"No, I'm not," I answered.

"God damn it, Sid," the General said, "we've got to be ourselves. Let's go back and answer questions."

Miss Fineholt and Philip Bentley and Colonel Flax were waiting for us in the library and when we appeared they all stood up. It was natural for the colonel to do so, but I was surprised to see Miss Fineholt and Phil Bentley snap into it, too, exactly as though they were troops.

"Please don't get up," the General said. "I'm sorry if I kept you waiting."

He was not very sorry. He was only acknowledging a military courtesy, telling the troops to rest and carry on, and he immediately sat down in his chair by the fireplace.

"Well, let's go," he said. "Where were we?"

"You were just starting up to Nashua to see that congressman," Phil Bentley said.

"Oh, yes," the General said, "Congressman Francis J. Garrity. Let's see . . . I didn't want to tell my folks what I was going to do. Father was talking college, now that I was finishing high school. He had that doctor business on his mind. I told him I couldn't work in the store that day because I had promised to take Muriel to Nashua to the movies, which was technically true. It's funny what a big town Nashua seemed like."

The General picked up a cigarette from a box on the table beside him. Colonel Flax leaped up with his lighter, but Phil Bentley was ahead of him.

"Here, let me, sir," Phil Bentley said. He would never have thought of making such a gesture a day before.

XIV

Your Congressman Always Knows Best

IT occurred to Melville Goodwin that most of his reminiscences about Hallowell started at the plainest place in that plain town, the square. Overshadowed by the volunteer fire-engine house on one side, the square was protected on another by the brick façade of the hat factory, which was adorned with a white bell cupola and plumes of steam. Melville always seemed to be leaving that square on the trolley, and perhaps this was eminently as it should be. Already the boys around high school were saying that Hallowell was a dead little dump without even a motion-picture theater; if you wanted to get ahead, you had to go to Manchester or Nashua. Hallowell gave you an American boy's healthy restlessness. Even if he had not gone to the Point, he would never have stayed in Hallowell. He could not have been a Dr. Byles. He had not the limits to ambition nor had he developed the inner contentment that allowed someone of his own father's latent ability to live out his life in Hallowell.

One Thursday afternoon toward the end of the spring vacation of his high school senior year, Melville met Muriel at the square and they took the two-o'clock car to Nashua. It was another of those gray afternoons in late March, the beginning of a rather early spring, and the rain of the night before had washed away most of the snow. Melville was seventeen then. Although he had another inch to grow, and his hands were too big for his wrists and his feet too big for his ankles, he wasn't so badly set up for his age. He had worn a blue suit again, but it was his own and not a hand-me-down, and he had learned from his older brother George, who was now the prescription clerk at Olmstead's Drugstore in Nashua, that celluloid collars and ready-made ties were small-town. He wore high starched collars now, and his sister Celia had given him a blue tie for Christmas with large white dots, and his mother had given him a solid gold stickpin with a moonstone in it. His shoes were not small-town either. He had bought them at Solomon's Shoe Shop in Nashua, high russet shoes with pointed toes. He had brushed his hair carefully, using some soap to keep it down, particularly on top, and he remembered wishing that his hair were not such a corn-silk yellow, because it gave his face an innocent, unmilitary look — but then he could do nothing about his hair. If his overcoat was not new — it was a brown overcoat of Harry's with what they called raglan sleeves — at least his dark green felt hat was, and he did not wear rubbers. He was not going in to call on Congressman Garrity wearing rubbers.

When he saw Muriel crossing the square, he wished she had not wanted to go with him because it meant that he would have to pretend he was the hero of one of those West Point stories. At least he was familiar fictionally with the mechanics of getting into the Point.

"Oh, Melville," Muriel said, "you forgot your rubbers, and you'll get your feet sopping wet. But anyway, you look slick."

He was pleased that Muriel thought so because at that time Muriel had been examining illustrations of men in *Everybody's Magazine* and had begun comparing him with them. For that matter, Muriel looked pretty slick herself. She was at least the next prettiest girl in high school, and her yellow hair looked better than his yellow hair. She had borrowed her mother's coat with the squirrel collar and she was wearing one of the dresses she had learned to make from Butterick patterns.

The Nashua car still had the stuffy, overheated smell that it had all through the winter. They sat side by side on one of the red plush cross seats in the middle, and Mr. Jacques, the motorman, nodded to them from the front platform. Mr. Mason, the conductor, rang the starting bell.

"Now, Melly," Muriel said, "what are you going to tell him?"

They had been over this several times before.

"Don't call me Melly," Melville said — he was feeling nervous already — "I'm going to ask him about getting into the Point, and I don't see why you want to go with me."

He was pleased that already he could refer easily and casually to that great institution as "the Point."

"Don't you want me to go with you?" Muriel asked.

"I didn't say I didn't want you to," he answered. "I said I don't see why you want to."

"If I don't go with you to his office," Muriel said, "you might get shy."

He wished she wouldn't act so much as though he belonged to her right there in the trolley car, and it was not going to be any help having her watching him get shy.

"Just look him in the eye," Muriel said, "and tell him that you want an appointment for West Point, and don't scratch at yourself. Remember, he's there to do what people ask him."

Perhaps Muriel was partly right. If congressmen did not often do what their constituents wanted, they always enjoyed being asked. Mr. Garrity was the only congressman of whom Melville Goodwin had ever asked patronage or favor. Frankly, he did not have a high opinion of congressmen, senators and politicians. They always made him feel that he was one of those pampered people battening on public funds that could more usefully be appropriated for the improvement of local rivers and harbors; or else he was in the position of having done some grievous injustice to some deserving local boy from some congressman's constituency. As Clausewitz said, all parts of war are easy but at the same time very difficult, and politicians were one of the elements that helped to make difficulties. Frankly, in Melville Goodwin's opinion, though he did not wish to be quoted, politicians, particularly congressmen, were narrow-minded, suspicious men who were always trying to withhold necessary funds from the army and who even hated seeing officers drive about in motor cars. Perhaps he should have felt differently about Mr. Garrity. In fact, he had sometimes tried to feel so, but he was afraid that Mr. Garrity was like all the rest.

Once back in the thirties, on one of those rare occasions when he had spent a few days in Hallowell, he had taken the trouble to go to

Nashua, in uniform, wearing his *Croix de guerre,* his Distinguished Service Cross, his Overseas Service Ribbon and his Purple Heart, to call on Mr. Garrity at his home. Mr. Garrity was a very much older man than the one he remembered and he was wearing pince-nez glasses attached to his waistcoat by a broad black ribbon. Mr. Garrity had not remembered Melville at all — in fact Mr. Garrity at first had thought he was a member of the New Hampshire National Guard, and the recollection was still painful to Melville. He finally had to remind Mr. Garrity of the appointment to West Point, and then Mr. Garrity did remember. He was always proud of His Boys, he said. It was one of his greatest pleasures as well as his gravest responsibility to see that the right boys in his district should have the privilege of attending those fine institutions, West Point and Annapolis. He always knew that Melville Goodwin would turn into the fine man that he was, and he was going to attend a little party that evening, given in his honor by the Lions Club, and he would like Captain Goodwin to come along with him.

Melville had gone with Mr. Garrity to the Lions Club banquet out of a sense of loyalty, but it had been a cloying experience to stand up before that crowd with Mr. Garrity's hand upon his shoulder — especially since, by now, Mr. Garrity had refreshed his memory.

"And I have with me tonight," Mr. Garrity had said, "a dear young friend of mine, Captain Melville A. Goodwin, from Hallowell. Melly, stand beside me so that your friends and mine can see you. Look at him and at the well-earned ribbons on his chest, won in the crusade for democracy." At this point Mr. Garrity had referred to some notes in the palm of his hand. "He is wearing, as we all here know, the *Crux de gerry* awarded him by those Frenchmen we won the war for, and our own Distinguished Service Cross, and the Purple Heart for the wound he suffered — where was it they hit you, Melly? — up near the Moose River? Take a step forward so they can see you, Melly, and don't mind if your friends here give you some applause. They are as proud of you as I am, Melly.

"Now, friends, it was back in 1914 — but I remember as though it

219

were yesterday — when I first laid eyes on Melly here. He came walking into my office, the same plain little office whose doors are still open to one and all, with his high school sweetheart — don't blush, Melly! — (she's Mrs. Goodwin now!) and he asked me simply and honestly for an appointment to the United States Military Academy. My dear niece, Patricia Flynn, who is now my valued assistant down in Washington, was typing in the front office then. 'Uncle Francie,' she said, 'it's just as well he brought his sweetheart in with him or I would have fallen for him myself. . . .' But seriously, why should I have given Melly Goodwin here his opportunity to attend West Point? I knew he was the son of my dear old friend, Bob Goodwin, who, God bless him, still runs Goodwin's Drugstore in Hallowell, and who, fine citizen that he is, has one little failing. He voted and he still votes, God bless him, a straight Republican ticket. Why did I give Melly that appointment instead of giving it to the son of some more enlightened voter? I know as well as you that a small-minded minority say that Francie Garrity is always looking for where his bread is buttered, but I am ready now as then, to stand or fall by my record. There was nothing to be gained from doing a favor for young Melly Goodwin. I knew this when I looked into the eyes of this fine young man in March, 1914. Then why did I give him the appointment instead of just a few kind words? I'll tell you why, good friends. I believed then as I do now that the nation's good rises above all local patronage! I wanted my friends and enemies to be aware of this belief, and so, regardless of the advice of many fine, well-meaning friends, I selected Melly Goodwin here instead of some other fine young boy with Democratic connections, because he was the best boy applying. I took his hand in mine then as I take it now, and I said these simple words to him which I now repeat, 'Good luck and God bless you, Melly Goodwin, God bless the Stars and Stripes and our great country, which you and I in our own ways serve.' "

Melville Goodwin could not recall that Mr. Garrity had said any of those simple words to him in his simple Nashua office, but he did remember people in Hallowell saying that Garrity could not be as bad as he was painted if he sent a Republican boy to West Point.

It all went to prove that you could seldom put your finger on the motives of a congressman.

Mr. Garrity's office was on the second floor of a business block on the main street. It consisted of an outer waiting room with a typist's desk and a single golden oak bench, and there was a small private room in back. The only decoration in the outer room was a campaign poster displaying an extraordinarily youthful and vigorous photograph of a square-jawed, determined man, beneath which was the simple bold device, "Garrity for Congress." There was nothing about the office to make anyone feel out of place or ill at ease, yet Melville's hands were clammy when he and Muriel entered it. He was offering himself for the first time to a waiting world and he was already alone with his own misgivings.

As they stood in the corridor in front of the ground glass door marked "Francis J. Garrity, Attorney at Law," it had suddenly occurred to him that he had not thought of any way of explaining Muriel.

"Well," Muriel whispered, "aren't you going to knock?"

"Maybe you'd better wait outside," he said.

"What would people think," she asked, "if they saw me waiting there alone?"

He wanted to ask her what people would think if they went in together, but he could not very well argue there with Muriel. He turned the knob of the door without knocking and walked in ahead of her, forgetting that it would have been politer to let her go first. At the end of the outer room, beneath a green-shaded electric light, a redheaded, freckle-faced girl was pounding on a typewriter.

"Is Mr. Garrity home?" Melville asked. With a slight sensation of nausea he realized that he had meant to say "in" instead of "home."

"He's not home; he's inside," the redheaded girl said. "Did you want to see him?"

He nodded without speaking.

"Well then," the girl said, "why don't you take off your hat and coat and stay a while?"

"Oh," he said, "excuse me."

"I guess you don't live in Nashua, do you?" the girl said. "What do you want to see Mr. Garrity for?"

His mind was a perfect blank as he struggled for an answer.

"I want to ask him about getting into West Point," he said.

"Well, all right," the girl said. "Take off your coat and sit down. Is this your sister with you?"

Melville felt his face turn beet red and he wriggled out of his overcoat.

"I'm not his sister," Muriel said. "I just rode up with him on the trolley to keep him company — from Hallowell. He's going to take me to the moving-picture show when he gets through with this."

"Oh," the girl said, "they don't have pictures down there in Hallowell, do they?"

"No," Muriel answered, "they don't have anything in Hallowell," and she giggled. "His name is Melville Goodwin. He reads about history and battles and he's very good at algebra and geometry. His father owns the drugstore. My name is Muriel Reece. My father is vice-president of the hat factory. It isn't much. There are three vice-presidents."

Then Melville finally found his voice, although he hardly recognized it when he began speaking.

"Say," he said, "can I see Mr. Garrity?"

"Oh," the girl said, and she and Muriel both began to laugh, "another county heard from."

Melville drew a deep breath.

"I asked you," he said, "can I see him or can't I?"

"Well, don't get mad," the girl said. "Mr. Garrity will have to ask you questions. So your name's Melville Goodwin."

"Melville A. Goodwin," Melville answered.

"What does the A stand for?" the redheaded girl asked.

"If I told you what it stood for," Melville said, "what difference would it make?"

"Oh my," the girl said, "another county heard from."

"You said that before," Melville told her.

"Well, anyway," the redheaded girl said, "you'd look kind of cute

222

in a uniform, all over buttons. If I see you get one of those uniforms, will you give me a button?"

"I'll see he gives you one," Muriel said. "I guess I didn't get your name."

"It's Flynn," the redheaded girl said, "Patricia Flynn."

She rose and opened a door beside her.

"There's the cutest young couple outside, Uncle Francie," he could hear her saying. "They come from Hallowell, and the boy wants you to send him to West Point."

Thirty-five years had passed and a curtain had fallen between him and the indisciplines of his boyhood, but the interview with Patricia Flynn and with Mr. Francis J. Garrity remained in his consciousness uneroded by time.

Mr. Garrity wore a conservative dark gray suit and he was smoking a long thin Pittsburgh stogie. The rank cigar smoke in the small office almost made Melville choke, and Mr. Garrity's whole appearance was an anticlimax after the campaign poster. His hair was thinner. His jaw was not as firm and his mouth was more mobile. Instead of looking like a leader of men, he looked like one of the older clerks in Osgood's Haberdashery.

"Well, young man," he said, "so you come from Hallowell. It's a fine place, and I have many fine friends there. What did you say your name was?"

His name was still Melville A. Goodwin.

"And what does A stand for?" Mr. Garrity asked.

"For Allen, sir," Melville answered.

"Well, well," Mr. Garrity said, "don't tell me that your grandfather was my dear old friend, Mel Allen. You couldn't be the son of Robert Goodwin who owns Goodwin's Drugstore in Hallowell Square?"

"Yes, sir," Melville answered.

"Now let me see," Mr. Garrity said, "didn't your father have Orrin Curtain's poster in his window last election time?"

"Yes, sir," Melville said, "my father is a friend of Mr. Curtain's."

"Well, now," Mr. Garrity said, "have a seat, Melville. There's nothing I like better than seeing a fine boy who wants to enter the

United States Military Academy, but this is election year. What will people say if they hear that Francis J. Garrity has sent a Republican boy to West Point?"

Melville pushed back his chair and stood up.

"Wait a minute," Mr. Garrity said. "Do you love your country, Melville?"

"Yes, sir," Melville said.

"And so do I," Mr. Garrity said. " 'Breathes there the man, with soul so dead, Who never to himself hath said, This is my own, my native land!'. . . Stand up straight and let me look at you."

Melville braced himself, and Mr. Garrity walked around the desk and stood beside him.

"Melville," Mr. Garrity said, "you wouldn't mind being in a picture with me in the papers, would you?"

"No, sir," Melville said.

"I want to figure this," Mr. Garrity said, and he pulled a pencil from his pocket and drew a pad of paper toward him.

"Now let's see," he said, "the name is Melville Allen Goodwin and your grandfather served in the Civil War. Goodwin's a fine old Yankee name. It couldn't be that any of your family fought in the Revolutionary War?"

"Yes, sir," Melville said, "my great-great-grandfather. His name was Amos Goodwin."

Mr. Garrity wrote carefully on the pad.

"That is a help, Melville," he said gently. "What year are you in high school?"

"The last year, sir," Melville said.

"And you wouldn't mind if I asked the principal for your marks, would you?"

"No, sir," Melville said.

"Well, now, Melville," Mr. Garrity said, "you did the right thing coming here to see your representative. I'm not promising, but maybe you'll get a letter from me next week. I'm glad to have met you, Melville, very glad and very proud."

Mr. Garrity put his arm around Melville's shoulder and walked with him into the waiting room.

"Say, Patsy," he said, "don't you think Melville and I would go well together in a photograph?"

"Why, yes," Patricia Flynn said, "you'd look lovely, Uncle Francie."

It was never safe to discount luck because luck was an element that might intrude itself suddenly into any planning. You had to allow for it. You had to give it what you might call operational room. Luck was the unexpected that appeared almost invariably in some phase of battle. The best thing to do was to treat it like liquor, as something you could either take or leave alone.

He was pretty hot that spring, as troops would have said about a crap shooter, and possibly he had never been quite so hot again. There was only one thing that remained on his conscience. He should have told his family, or at least his father, all about Mr. Garrity and West Point. He simply had a feeling that his dream was so fantastic that speaking of it might shatter it into a thousand pieces.

"I guess I wanted to be sure it was so," he said, when his father finally asked about it, but he was always sorry that he had not told his father.

The letter arrived one afternoon while he was still at school, and it had been placed on the table in the front entry with his father's correspondence. No one in the house except Mr. Goodwin ever received much mail, because the time was past when Melville, like other boys, clipped coupons and wrote for catalogues. For some reason he had not asked if there was any letter for him on that particular day. Probably he had concluded that it was not good luck to ask.

It was six o'clock on an April evening, and they were having boiled corned beef for supper. Celia was dressed up because she was going to a euchre party at Emily Jacques's but Melville had been splitting wood and raking trash in the yard and he came to table in a sweater. His father had said that he was getting old enough to wear a coat, even if they were having supper in the kitchen.

"Now, Robert," he remembered his mother had said, "Melville has been working hard all afternoon."

"That's no reason," Mr. Goodwin said. "Melville, go up and put on a coat and brush your hair, and, Celia, get me the mail and the paper."

When Melville came downstairs his father, wearing the nickel-rimmed reading spectacles that Dr. Byles had made him order that year, was opening catalogue envelopes with his penknife and laying them in a neat pile without removing their contents.

"More stuff comes in the mail all the time," he said. "I wish I had the money it takes to print and send it out. Oh, here's a letter for you, Melville." He was holding a long government-franked envelope. "It's from Garrity. I guess he doesn't know that Mel's too young to vote."

Melville took the letter quickly and put it in his inside pocket.

"Aren't you going to read it, dear?" his mother asked.

"I guess it isn't anything much," he said.

"Why, Melville acts as though it were a love letter," Celia said.

"Well, it isn't a love letter," Melville told her.

"I guess it isn't," Mr. Goodwin said. "It's garden time. Be sure to tell him you want radish seeds, Melville."

Melville ate slowly. He said he was not going anywhere that evening because he had to study his geometry, and he remembered that his father had said that he did not see what good geometry could do for anyone who was going to be a doctor. Melville could feel the envelope crinkle in his inside pocket as he leaned over his plate of corned beef and cabbage, and even now when Melville smelled boiled cabbage he could feel the excitement all over again.

"Now here's a chance to order a window display on spring bitters," Mr. Goodwin said. ". . . That reminds me, it's time to start pushing tonic."

Melville helped his mother with the dishes, and when she asked him if he was going to do his geometry in the parlor, he said he would take a lamp upstairs to his bedroom because it was quieter up there. He could still remember the crackling sound of the envelope when he opened the letter. If he shut his eyes now, he could still see its two terse typewritten paragraphs.

Dear Mr. Goodwin:

It gives me great pleasure to inform you that I am nominating you for my principal appointment to the United States Military Academy. As the Hallowell High School is not on the accredited list, you must take examinations at Fort Banks in Boston in the early part of February of next year.

Would you please call on me at my office at ten o'clock next Saturday, when I wish you to meet the representative of our local newspaper.

Very truly yours,
FRANCIS J. GARRITY

Naturally he had experienced other triumphs later, because his career, though not spectacular, had not been a complete bust either. For example, there had been his decorations, and of course there was the time at Casablanca when he was told that he would be a part of the Salerno show and that his two stars were coming up. Admittedly there were plenty of other good brigade and divisional commanders, and he hoped he had acquired enough stability never to allow promotion to go to his head, though on such an occasion you could not help but feel lightness and elation and a sense of gratitude to whatever had kept you alive and in the groove. Yet none of those later triumphs compared with his feeling as he read the congressman's letter. It was a kid-stuff moment, but then he was no better or no worse than the juvenile character in *A Plebe at West Point,* and maybe his development was still arrested here and there. As Kipling wrote in his poem entitled "If" — "If you can meet with Triumph and Disaster and treat those two impostors just the same . . ." The beauty of it was that he did not know that triumph was an impostor then, or that you had to pay for triumph. His thoughts became luminous. He was in gray, parading with the Corps. He was young Lieutenant Goodwin with his company, charging into cannon smoke. He was General Melville A. Goodwin, mounted on a horse not unlike Robert E. Lee's Traveller, and Old Glory flew above him and the bands were playing. A kid was only a kid once, and he still felt a little that way sometimes, when troops passed by him in review.

He wanted to run downstairs and shout the news, but some

shadowy suspicion that there might be a catch to it must have stopped him. Instead, he finished all his solid geometry — you had to be good at math and history and geography to pass the exams for West Point — though all the time he was reasoning an original problem point by point, he knew that he must tell Muriel before he went to sleep.

He remembered walking softly down the creaking stairs to the narrow front entry, and he seemed to arrive on the Reeces' porch by some sort of levitation. It was lucky for him, in his condition, that Muriel opened the door herself.

"How about going for a walk?" he asked.

"Oh, I couldn't," she said, "at this hour of night."

It could not have been more than nine-thirty, but that was an hour of night for Hallowell.

"I've got to tell you something that's happened," he said, and he said he could not tell her unless she came outside.

She put on her mother's coat with the squirrel collar, and neither of them said a word as they walked down the path to Prospect Street.

"Mel," she said, "don't walk so fast. I can't keep up," and he told her he was sorry, he did not mean to walk so fast. It was dark because there were no street lights then on Prospect Street.

"Mel," she said, "what is it?"

"I've got the letter," he told her. "I'm going to West Point."

"Oh, Melly," she said, and then she linked her arm through his and pressed his arm against her.

"Muriel . . ." he began.

"Yes," she said, "what is it, Melly?"

"Muriel," he said, "will you marry me if I get through West Point?"

It had come over him all of a sudden when he heard that he was going to West Point — he had fallen in love with Muriel Reece.

"Why, Mel," she said, "I'd like to very much." She sounded exactly as though he had asked her to go for a ride in the Ford or to go to the pictures in Nashua. It was going to be a long, long ride, but after all, there was no way for kids to know about anything like that.

228

XV

A West Pointer Looks at Hallowell

ONCE when he was in Baguio during his second tour of duty in the Philippines, Mel Goodwin had come across a book by an author named Harry Leon Wilson. He had gone up to Baguio for a week end to join Muriel and the two children, who were spending the summer in the hills away from the heat, and he must have picked up the book at the club or somewhere. At any rate, this Wilson was quite a writer. The book was called *Merton of the Movies*. Most of it was comedy, but in one part young Merton knelt down and prayed that he would be a great Hollywood actor and Melville had done almost the same thing in Hallowell after he returned home that night.

"Oh, God," he had prayed, kneeling down on the round braided rug that had come from his grandmother's house in Nashua, "help me pass my examinations and make me a good officer in the United States Army, for Christ's sake, Amen."

It was not a bad prayer either. He had made the same supplication with only a few variations many times in Cadet Chapel at West Point, and God had been kind to him. He had finished in the first quarter of his class at the Point, and some people were of the opinion that he was not such a bad soldier.

Of course he should have told his plans to his father immediately, instead of deciding to put it off until after his high school graduation. He never thought about the article in the Nashua newspaper, or even that there would be much of an article, until his father showed it to him. When his mother told him one afternoon in May that his father wanted him down at the store, he thought he was only needed to open packing cases.

His father was out in front waiting on Mr. Hallowell, who wanted to buy a new safety razor and was trying to decide between a Gem and a Gillette. Two of Melville's friends from high school, who were eating strawberry sundaes at the counter, had abandoned their spoons, and Elmer had stopped polishing glasses behind the fountain while they all listened to the conversation between Mr. Goodwin and the great man who owned the hat factory.

"It takes such a long time to get the blade out from that thing and clean it," Mr. Hallowell said. "The blade keeps falling in the wash basin, and I never can seem to do well with it under my chin."

Mr. Goodwin picked up the little razor expertly. He looked thin and neat and much more adroit than Mr. Hallowell.

"Some people like Gillettes," he said, "and some like Gems, and then there's the Durham Duplex and the Autostrop, but I don't know much about them personally. I've always used an old straight razor. If you have to bring up three boys, there's nothing like a good strop in the bathroom."

Mr. Hallowell smiled and so did Elmer and the two customers at the fountain.

"If I had three boys, perhaps I'd use a straight razor. I never thought of razors as being so closely connected with parenthood," Mr. Hallowell said.

"Well," Mr. Goodwin said, "I wish I could advise you, Mr. Hallowell. Why don't you take both a Gillette and a Gem and try them on different days?"

"That's a very good idea," Mr. Hallowell said. "Will you wrap them both up for me please, Mr. Goodwin, and I'd better have a bottle of shaving lotion. I wish I didn't always keep cutting myself, even with a safety razor."

"How about taking a styptic pencil along, too?" Mr. Goodwin asked. "I find them very handy." He was beginning to wrap the package, but his hand stopped in wordless interrogation while he waited for Mr. Hallowell's answer, and everyone else in the store waited with him.

"That's a very good idea," Mr. Hallowell said.

A deep, respectful silence followed Mr. Hallowell as he left the store. Even when the door closed, no one made any remark about him. After all, none of them would have been there if it had not been for the Hallowell hat factory.

"Elmer," Mr. Goodwin said, "get out another Gem and Gillette and put them in the showcase. Melville, come with me to the office."

His father kept his account books and papers in a small room behind the prescription counter. His ledgers and his invoices were symmetrically arranged on his roll-top desk. One wall was decorated by a patent-medicine calendar, and the whole place had the clean smell of chemicals. This was the room in which his father talked privately to salesmen about discounts and payment dates, after he had finally decided to place an order. Mr. Goodwin closed the door and seated himself in his swivel chair by the desk and pointed to the salesmen's chair beside it.

"Sit down, Melville," Mr. Goodwin said, "I want to have a little talk with you. I guess I keep forgetting that you're growing up. You may find, if you have a boy of your own, you'll forget he's growing up, too. All of a sudden before you know it, there he is, grown-up, and this will make you sort of sad. You'll wish you hadn't been so busy keeping shop and trying to make both ends meet. You'll wish you had got to know your boy and what he is thinking of, and about the time you get to wishing, it will be too late. It was like that with George, and now he's away in Nashua. It was like that with Harry, and before I even knew he was a man, he was working in that garage. I ought to have seen my boys more and taken more time off to be with them instead of just seeing them around the table at mealtime. Maybe I've been here at the store too much, Saturdays and Sundays and everything, and now it's too late. Someday you'll know, too, that something's too late, Melville, and it's pretty hard to take."

His father sat there straight and handsome in his white coat, as though he were talking to a salesman, and he looked as though he had not slept well for a long while. It was the first time that Melville had thought of him as anything more than a figure in his background.

"When I used to correct you children," his father said, "your mother would tell me that you wouldn't be children for long. Time's something that's pretty hard to handle. I used to think when the store was making a little money — and now the store is doing pretty well — that there would be time for you and me to kind of get acquainted, before you grew up like the other boys, and that I could tell you about how things were, and what I used to do when I was a boy — but I guess I've worked too hard in the store. I couldn't do much for the other boys, but I wanted to save some money so that you could have a chance. Well . . . if you put your mind on one thing, you have to take it off another. Time's a mighty funny thing."

He almost looked as though he were saying words that he had learned by heart, and his lack of eloquence made the words more touching.

"I used to think," his father went on, "that you and I would tell each other what was on our minds someday. I've never even known what you wanted to do or be — but then I guess my dad never knew I wanted to be a druggist. Still I might have guessed why you ran off in the Ford to see the militia that time down in Blair. . . . You haven't seen today's paper, have you, Melville?"

His father took down the Nashua paper from the top of the desk. His chair squeaked, but he still sat up straight as he handed it to Melville. There it was, on the front page, a picture of Melville standing beside Congressman Francis J. Garrity.

"Garrity picks Hallowell lad for West Point," he read. " 'Not a political choice,' says congressman. . . . In a surprise move that has silenced many critics in this city, Francis J. Garrity announced this afternoon that he has ignored the expectations of many supporters by bestowing his principal appointment to the United States Military Academy upon the son of a Republican voter who worked for his opponent in the last election. The lucky lad is Melville A. Goodwin, son of Robert Goodwin, popular Hallowell druggist. Commenting on this selection, Mr. Garrity said today that it was made solely upon merit. Young Goodwin's grandfather, the late Melville Allen, well known in this city, saw service in the Civil War under General Philip Sheridan, and the young appointee's great-great-grandfather was a hero of the Revolution. 'I am fully aware that many friends may be disappointed by this action,' Congressman Garrity said, 'but there are times when I ignore political expediency. After all, there are Republicans in my district. . . .'"

Melville looked up from the paper and saw that his father was watching him.

"Garrity's pretty smart," his father said. "This will get him a lot of independent votes. It's funny . . . I never knew you wanted to go to West Point."

It would have been easier if his father had been angry. As it was, his coolness and reserve showed the deepness of his hurt.

"I was going to tell you, I really was," Melville said, "but I was afraid there might be a catch to it."

His father took the paper and folded it.

"It's my fault; it isn't yours," he said. "That's all I've been trying to tell you, Mel. Anyway, you did it all yourself. Let's not talk about it now, but I'll tell you what, suppose you and I take the Ford on Saturday and ride down along the Merrimack and maybe you'll tell me all about it then . . . and now, if you want, you can help me with some prescriptions. I'm pretty rushed today."

His father must have realized that the family would not see much of Melville Goodwin again, but no one at the age of eighteen could have possibly known, and eighteen was his age when he left Hallowell for West Point. It was in June 1915 and he had twenty dollars for traveling expenses and a post-office money order for one hundred and sixty dollars made out to the Treasurer of the United States Military Academy, to pay for his uniform and equipment. This money order was about all he needed to ask for from his father, so at least he was no burden on the family. He carried nothing but a small traveling bag — he would not need more than he was wearing — and his family drove him in the Ford from Hallowell to the Junction. As the train pulled out, he watched his father and mother and Celia standing against the background of oak and scrub-pine hills, waving to him from the bare wooden platform. Only later did he value the memory — after he came to realize how complete that parting was.

If you got through plebe year you had been malleable enough to be beaten to a mold. They really dished it out to you that first year

233

at the Point. He did not see Hallowell again until the day before Christmas, 1916, when he had a short Christmas leave and he returned in his cadet's uniform with its long gray overcoat and cape all buttoned and fitted to a T. He wore his uniform partly out of vanity but also because he had grown too tall and broad for his old civilian suit, and the uniform was a part of him by then, anyway. He had developed the posture to wear one correctly. He knew how to hold his gloves. He knew instinctively about the slant of his visored cap and all about buttons and buckles. A regard for personal appearance had already been beaten into him at the Point and he looked an integral part of the Corps.

December twilight had fallen over Hallowell. Walls of snow bordered the sidewalks. The hat factory was running on a night shift because of French and British war contracts. Gray's Dry Goods and Notions Store, Richards's Meat Market, Shute's General Store and his father's drugstore were all open for final Christmas buying, and candles were burning in the windows of the Congregational Church. It was a picture that he had created in his mind all the way from West Point, except that when he saw it the size of the whole canvas had diminished. It was his home town but he would never fit there again and he would never have a home again, as he had formerly understood the word.

When he entered the drugstore everyone was glad to see him, but his father's look was like that of all the others, welcoming but incredulous. His father was smaller and older, and the boys he had known needed haircuts and appeared untidy and round-shouldered. The house, all fixed for Christmas with the tree, had not changed, but he had not realized how small the rooms were. All the family were there, George and Harry and Celia, down for Christmas — and they, also, regarded him with uneasy, questioning expressions. Celia looked very pretty, but it was hard for him to remember much about her. When his mother kissed him, he was deeply moved, but he had been away for such a long time, and he would only be there for such a little while, that he knew it would be hopeless to explain his life at the Point to her. They were all fingering his uniform and asking questions, but there was no sense to the questions. They were his family, and at the same time he was a stranger. It had to be that way, and you could blame it all on the Point. It had to be that way.

The only person in Hallowell who did not seem changed was Muriel, and even with her there was a moment of uncertainty. When they stood alone in the Reeces' parlor, he felt very shy. He had forgotten how beautiful she was.

"Well," she said, "well," and she stood staring at him.

"You're looking fine, Muriel," he said. "You've got a new dress, haven't you?"

"Yes," she said, "and so have you. You look just like the pictures."

"I ought to. You've got to look like that there," he said.

"Well, you look all right."

He realized that he was standing at attention, and he shifted to at ease.

"You've got to look all right," he answered.

"You've got a new haircut, haven't you?" she asked.

"They make you get them once a week when you're a plebe and once every two weeks thereafter," he told her, and then she began to laugh. "What's so funny?"

"Just you," she answered, "looking as though you weren't real. Is it against the rules for you to kiss a girl?"

XVI

The Color's Getting Lighter Every Year

THE reticences of women, as I have said, were very different from those of men. Women had another doctrine of security. They, and not the men, were usually the ones who kissed and told. Melville Goodwin, for example, only said that Muriel was just the way she had been and he let it go at that. It was Muriel Goodwin who gave me the full details of this meeting, and it was she, too, who told most about that earlier walk in the dark, when the General had asked her to marry him — but perhaps those episodes had meant more to her than they ever had to him.

"Melville never was a great lover," I remember her saying, while she and I motored to New York the next morning, "but I must have always thought he was going to be. I wish you could have seen him when he came home that Christmas. He was so handsome, so distinguished. I didn't know then that he had just the usual polish that any boy gets at the Point. At first I thought I couldn't ever be what a boy like that would want — girls, when they're in love, are so much more romantic and imaginative than boys — but it made me want to cry when I found he was still Melville, at least he was with me. The Point makes leaders but it can't take men away from women."

Melville Goodwin only touched briefly on West Point's relationship to love, although this aspect of life seemed to have a place in the curriculum, judging from the popularity of hops and of Flirtation Walk at the Academy. He skipped over the subject hastily when he described his career to Miss Fineholt and Phil Bentley, just as most officers did in their memoirs — including General Grant.

"It was certainly great to see Muriel again," he said. "Nobody knows what love is who hasn't been through plebe year at the Point, and that remark isn't original with me."

His mind was back with us again in the library. He was no longer Cadet Goodwin. There appeared to be a physical change in him as he adjusted himself rapidly from one environment to another. His eyes narrowed slightly, and the lines around his mouth deepened and everything he was telling became remote.

"Well," he said, "I'm afraid I've sort of gone overboard about all this kid stuff. Maybe we'd better break off for a while."

A second or two moved by us before anyone answered.

"General," Phil Bentley said, "do you mind if I ask a question?"

General Goodwin turned toward him slowly.

"All right," he said. "That's what I'm here for."

"Do you think civilian love is different from military love?" Phil Bentley asked.

"That's a smart one, isn't it?" the General said. "But I'll tell you one thing, son. Those girls who marry shavetails the day after graduation don't know what they're getting into. Somebody ought to give them a briefing. I don't believe Mrs. Goodwin knew."

It was "Mrs. Goodwin" and not "Muriel" now. The General's mind was back in the library, and he was watching Phil Bentley with cool disapproval.

"You see, son," he said, "different individuals have different aptitudes. I could never write like you, but then as I look you over, without meaning to be too personal, I'd say you wouldn't last six months at the Point."

Phil Bentley flushed slightly and then he laughed.

"Frankly, I wouldn't want to last three minutes."

"All right," the General said, "then don't ask smarty-pants questions about military love, and keep your tongue out of your cheek. I'm pretty tired of some of the cracks that boys like you make about the Point. There may be things wrong with it, but Grant, Lee, Pershing, Eisenhower and Patton and Bradley — they were all turned out by the Point."

Colonel Flax glanced at me uneasily. It was close to lunchtime. It was clearly advisable to break up the meeting.

"How about me?" I said. "Do you think I could have got through the Point?"

The General examined me impersonally, appraisingly, as he had once or twice in Paris.

"It's queer you asked me that, Sid," he said, "because I was just thinking about it. Maybe they could have kicked some sense into you. Yes, you might have gone through the Point."

I felt ridiculously pleased to have him say so. I believe I was about to thank him, and not ironically either, when a knock on the door interrupted me. It was Oscar saying that lunch would be ready in fifteen minutes.

"And Mr. Skelton," Oscar said, "Mrs. Peale has been trying to get you on the telephone all morning. She asked especially that you call her before one o'clock."

I did not want to look at the General or anyone else in the room, certainly not Phil Bentley or Miss Fineholt — not after Phil Bentley's question about military and civilian love.

"Go ahead, Sid," the General said, "go on and make your telephone call. There's nothing we can do here until after lunch, and remember me to Mrs. Peale, will you?" General Goodwin cleared his throat. "Mrs. Peale was over in Paris with a writers' group in the winter of 1945. I had to give them a lecture on the Battle of the Bulge."

There was no reason for him to have said anything and of course he should have known better. Perhaps, I began to think, there was a difference between civilian and military love.

"Could you make them understand about the Battle of the Bulge?" I heard Phil Bentley ask. "It must have been a pretty complicated subject."

"General," Colonel Flax said, "there's only a quarter of an hour before lunch, sir."

I was not in the least surprised to hear from Dottie Peale. After she had called me at the studio, I knew that I would hear from her again, because persistence was one of Dottie's greatest assets, and if she wanted something, she could never exercise the virtue of pa-

238

tience. Obviously she wanted to find out what the General was doing and how he looked and what was happening and how much he still remembered about everything. It was impossible to prevent her from gathering this information. It was inevitable that she and the General would meet eventually, now that he was on her mind again. There was no way of explaining the forces that drew two people together, but I did wish she could have waited for what might have been a more decent interval, and I wished that I were not the catalytic agent.

I decided to call Dottie from the privacy of the upstairs dressing room, and when I got there and closed the door, I found myself thinking again of the completeness with which General Goodwin and his interests had taken over the house since he had entered it. It was not my house any longer but a temporary headquarters in a theater of operations. In fact I should not have been in the least surprised, on looking out of the window, to see a headquarters company parking jeeps and command cars on the lawn and a signal detachment taking over the stables and an antiaircraft outfit digging slit trenches and gun emplacements in the garden. The past and the present and the future of General Goodwin had completely engulfed the place, and Helen and I were like a bewildered French couple I had once seen in a commandeered château just behind the Seventh Army. All at once the General's problems outranked my own. Instinctively I was snapping into it again, becoming a cog in the machine, although I owed him nothing, and there were no longer any army regulations to govern my behavior. He had asked me to be his aide once, and now I was in exactly that position, diplomatically and adroitly protecting the interests of my chief. I was devoted to those interests, or to put it in another way, if you had once been in the army, perhaps you always were.

It was five minutes to one when I called Dottie Peale at her publishing company office. She must have delayed one of her inevitable luncheon engagements to wait for the call. Dottie liked to transact the more critical angles of her business at lunch, and she must have had to rearrange her whole day's schedule, since she customarily left for lunch at half past twelve. She had undoubtedly told them at the switchboard to put the call through to her directly because the operator said, "Oh yes, Mr. Skelton, just a moment please," and then I was connected with Dottie rather than with her secretary first.

"Darling," Dottie said, and her voice sounded a little edgy, "are you in any sort of trouble? . . . Then what have you been doing that you couldn't take a minute all morning to answer a telephone call?"

It was exactly like her to take such a thing personally. Women in business were always personal.

"I've been busy all morning, Dot," I said.

"I suppose so," Dottie said, and she laughed gently. "You're such a VIP now, darling, that you forget that other people may sometimes be busy, too. It just happens that we're giving an authors' luncheon today at the Waldorf, and I ought to be at the head table right this minute."

"Well, well," I answered.

"Don't say 'Well, well' in that disagreeable way," Dottie said. "What in hell have you been doing all morning, darling?"

"It's nice of you to ask," I said. "I've been locked up all morning in the library."

"Oh, in the library," Dottie said. "Don't tell me you're writing a book or something, and you haven't told me about it, darling."

"No, no," I said, "I was just in there."

"Hell," Dottie said, "you were in your library and you know I don't give a damn."

"Yes," I said, "I know."

"At least not much of a damn," Dottie said. "I wish I could ever remember that you're a VIP and that I ought to have my party manners with me. You know what I want, don't you?"

"Yes," I said, "I know what you want — in a general way."

"You're getting so cryptic and so very funny, dear," Dottie said. "All right. . . . Is the General still with you — in a general way?"

"You don't mean General Melville A. Goodwin, do you?" I asked.

"Oh, please shut up, Sid, and pull up your socks," Dottie said. "How is he, darling?"

"He's fine. He looks about the way he did in Paris," I said. "They don't change the way other people do. We've been in the library all morning, working on that profile."

"How's Phil Bentley doing?" she asked.

"I don't know," I said. "I'm a little afraid he's going to be funny with it."

"Darling, you know what friends I used to be with Phil. Do you think it would do any good for me to have a talk with him?"

"No, I think it would be a very bad idea," I said.

"Oh dear, do you think he . . . ?"

She did not finish the question, and she did not need to.

"Yes," I said, "I do. You know Phil."

"Oh dear," Dottie said, "I don't see how things get around the way they do. Has Mel asked about me, darling?"

"Yes, he's asked about you."

"Well, give him my love and tell him I can't wait to see him, will you?"

I did not answer. There was nothing I could do about it. It was not even worth while to tell her that it would not be a very good idea.

"Well, darling," she said, "you know I never want to interfere with anything, and I suppose you'll all be working on the profile all afternoon, but it's such a nice day. How do you think it would be if I motored out and we all had tea at five o'clock? I haven't seen you and Helen for such a long while, and I'd love to see Camilla, and I'm dying to see the new house."

If Dottie wanted something, she could never wait.

"You stay right in town," I said. "There isn't any reason for you to mix things up, Dot. Mrs. Goodwin's here."

"Oh dear," Dottie said, "oh dear. Sidney you don't think she . . . ?"

Again there was no reason for her to finish the question.

"I don't know," I said, "and I can't very well ask her."

"Oh dear," Dottie said. "Sidney, what is she like, darling?"

"Mrs. Goodwin's very nice," I said.

"Hell," Dottie said, "do you know what you sound like? You sound like one of those general's aides, trying to cover up."

Dottie was always very quick, but it was disconcerting that any-one else should have thought that I sounded that way.

"Listen, Dot," I said, "what do you care about Mel Goodwin? Why don't you run along to that luncheon? You know this isn't a good time to see him, don't you?"

"Darling," Dottie asked, "how do you know whether I care?"

"I've got a pretty good idea," I said.

"Well, darling," Dottie said, "I've got to see you. If I can't see Mel, I've got to see *you,* and there's something I want to see you about besides Mel."

It was impressive that Dottie could shift so rapidly from one thing to another, but I knew that she would find out everything by hook or crook, and it was better to tell her personally than over the telephone.

"Well, all right," I said.

"We never seem to see each other any more, do we, darling?" Dottie said. "How would it be — if you won't let me come out to tea and of course I wouldn't dream of doing that if Mrs. Good-win's there — how would it be if you met me at the office and we had lunch quietly tomorrow, just you and I? We haven't seen each other for a long while."

They would be working on the profile, but after all, Colonel Flax was there.

"All right," I said, "I'd like to have lunch, Dot."

"You don't think you could bring Mel, too, do you?"

She never could drop anything once she had started.

"No, Dot," I said, "no, no," and she laughed as though I had said something very funny.

"Darling, I do love you, you know," she said. "Come at half past twelve, and please come promptly. It will be heavenly to see you."

Then before I told her that it would be heavenly to see her, too, I thought of something else.

"What was this other thing you wanted to see me about?" I asked.

"Well, darling, I don't suppose it's any of my business. It's just a little something that worries me about you and Gilbert Frary."

My own voice had changed. I was no longer General Goodwin's aide.

"What about Frary and me?" I asked.

"It isn't anything. It's just something that worries me a little bit, darling. You're so obtuse about some things and so trusting, dear, but I can't tell you over the telephone."

I tried hard to believe that she probably had nothing to say about Gilbert Frary and that it was only her way of making sure that I would come for lunch — and yet I remembered certain aspects of my last conversation with Gilbert. Occasionally I was not as obtuse as Dottie thought I was.

Helen and I never took cocktails before luncheon except on non-working days. In spite of my having spent years in a rigorous newspaper environment, I had never learned to handle liquor in the daytime, and cocktails invariably made me sleepy in the afternoon. Nevertheless I was very glad that day to see standing in front of the living room fireplace one of Helen's latest and more dubious purchases — our new bar table, with wheels instead of legs. Apparently Miss Fineholt and Colonel Flax and Phil Bentley and the General had enjoyed the sight of it, too, because they had all gathered around it, and their voices had the merry note of children's after school. General Goodwin himself was mixing Martinis, and Phil Bentley was trying to help him.

"No, no, son," the General was saying, "put that jigger away. I like to play this sort of music by ear. That's the way a good barkeep does it. He listens for the glug in the bottle and he judges strength by color. Do you remember Corporal Jones at the officers' club at Leavenworth, Muriel, and the night Jonesy taught old Bish and me how to mix them at that dance we threw on Effie's birthday? Why, Bish and I ended by chucking the corporal out and running the bar ourselves, and I've never gone wrong on a Martini since. Move to one side, son, and give me room."

The General waved the bottles expertly but not like an ordinary barkeeper. Instead he mixed the Martinis in a military way, moving by the numbers.

"That's the way," he said, "glug, glug, one, two, three. Now front and center with the vermouth. There's nothing as formal as a good Martini."

"The General is very fussy about his cocktails," Mrs. Goodwin said to Miss Fineholt. "He always goes by the color, and the color's getting lighter every year."

Mrs. Goodwin shook her head as though she were watching a small boy's antics, and Miss Fineholt laughed.

"Phil," Miss Fineholt said, "did you hear what Mrs. Goodwin said? The Martinis are getting lighter every year. When the photographers come, we might have a candid shot of the General stirring. It would make a lovely caption — 'The color's getting lighter every year.' "

Colonel Flax laughed heartily, and the General joined in the mirth.

"Flax," he said, "there doesn't seem to be any lemon peel. Run out, will you, and see if you can get somebody to cut off the outside skin of a lemon."

Helen indicated with raised eyebrows that she wanted a word with me alone.

"He suggested the drinks," Helen said softly. "I wasn't planning for them — and we were having a soufflé for lunch!"

"Well, that's fine," I said heartily, "I'm glad he asked for them."

"Did you hear him send out for lemon peel?" Helen said. "It's just as though you and I didn't live here any more."

She smiled at me in a Mona Lisa way, and we stood there like maladjusted guests, somewhat apart from the group around the bar on wheels.

"It means that he feels at home, Helen," I said. "He's trained to take control. You want him to feel at home, don't you?"

"It's funny," Helen said, "I keep thinking we're in some sort of war. Do all generals act like General Goodwin?"

"Some do more than others," I said. "They can't help it."

"I wish you'd wait on me sometime," Helen said. "You run after him as though you were Oscar."

"You don't understand, Helen," I said. "It's a sort of reflex. You can't help running around when you see a general. Look at Flax."

"Well, how far is the General in his life now?"

"I wish you wouldn't keep asking, Helen," I said. "He's moving right along. He's somewhere in West Point."

"Hasn't he even got out of West Point?"

"Maybe he has never really got out of it," I told her. "Lots of those regulars never do, any more than All-Americans ever get off the football team."

"Darling," Helen said, "it's awfully nice when we see things the same way, and I'm glad you got out of the army while there was still time."

"He said I might have got through the Point," I told her.

"And then I'd have watched you, like Mrs. Goodwin," Helen said. "Look at the way she's watching him."

"She's proud of him," I said. "Maybe it's nice to have someone to be proud of."

"Well, I'm glad I don't have to be as officially proud of you in public," Helen said. "Sid, we really ought to have another baby."

"Not right now, Helen," I said, "not right at this very moment."

The General was about to tell a story. I was sure of this from the intent expression that Mrs. Goodwin and Colonel Flax both wore. If he were to tell a story, it had to be good and they had to help make it good.

"Speaking of liquor," the General said, "do you remember Svenson, Muriel?"

"Svenson, dear?" Mrs. Goodwin said. "Let me see, was he an officer or an enlisted man?"

"Svenson . . ." The General spoke more loudly, welding us all into an audience. "You remember Svenson at Schofield, the one who was my orderly, Muriel, who used to play catch with Bobby out in front of the house. Don't you remember the day we found that prisoner who should have been mowing the lawn knocking out flies to Svenson and Bobby?"

"Oh yes, Svenson," Mrs. Goodwin said, "the one you were always going to give a court to and never did. Melville is always indulging his orderlies."

245

"Say, Sid," the General called, "didn't I ever tell you about Svenson? I have a lot of Svenson stories. There's nothing like those old goldbrickers who have served five or six hitches. They're sagas in themselves."

"No, sir, I don't think you ever told me about him," I answered, and I found myself moving nearer the cocktail table, smartly and almost without my own volition.

"I thought maybe I told you some Svenson stories in Paris at the Ritz." The General checked himself and cleared his throat and laughed at his memory of Svenson while we all waited to hear the anecdote. We had to wait. General Goodwin was in control of the situation.

"Well, there was still Prohibition back at Schofield," the General said, "at least in the first year of my tour there, but just the same, they used to turn out a fine native beverage in Honolulu. If it was aged, it could be as good as bourbon. The native name for it was 'Okulehao.' You remember that Oke, don't you, Colonel?"

"Yes, sir," the colonel said, and both he and the General smiled.

"Flax has been there," the General said. "Five dollars for a one-gallon jug — but you didn't want to get fooled on your Oke. Do you remember when General Hanson asked where I got my Oke that time we had them to dinner, Muriel?"

"Oh yes," Mrs. Goodwin said. "Tom was so sweet when you got to know him, but of course we didn't have the rank to know him very well at Schofield."

"Do you remember what I told him about that Oke?" General Goodwin asked. "I said, 'Sir, if you want my brand, you'll have to take over Svenson,' and old Hanson said, 'If I have to do that, Mel, I'd rather choke on my old brand. You keep Svenson and your Oke.' "

The General grinned at that ancient quip of General Hanson's. Heaven only knew who General Hanson was, but we all laughed, knowingly, as though we, too, had done our duty tour at Schofield.

"The main thing in dealing with enlisted men is to know how far to let them go and just when to pin their ears back. That's all there is to it, isn't it, Colonel?" the General asked.

"That's about it, sir," the colonel said. "It isn't all regulations, it's the human touch. Now when I was a kid I used to have a striker named Judkins when I was serving with the Tenth Cavalry at Bliss . . ."

Colonel Flax stopped abruptly because it was clear that the General did not want to hear about Judkins at Fort Bliss. He wished to continue the subject of Svenson at Schofield Barracks.

"You know the way an old soldier is, Flax," the General said. "Keep on his right side and he'll do anything for you. Old soldiers can get you anything. When they like you they show it in little ways. Svenson didn't have to get me that Oke. He just said one day standing at attention — he always stood at attention when he was going to get off something good — 'Sir,' he said, 'we ought to have better Oke at your quarters. I don't think that stuff you have is good for Mrs. Goodwin.'"

"Oh, Mel," Mrs. Goodwin said, "you never told me that Svenson said that. I never did like Oke."

"Now don't stop me — let me finish, Muriel," the General said. "That's just what Svenson did say, and after that when we were going to have a Saturday night poker game I used to tell him that things were sort of dry, and I would pass him five dollars and he'd come back with the Oke. I suppose he got it around Nuuanu and the district. I never asked him, but he had a very special source. We got to calling it 'Svenson's Oke' on Saturday nights. We used to have pretty high-class poker games at Schofield, didn't we, Muriel?"

"I wish we could play some poker now," Mrs. Goodwin said, "only it would be like taking money from children, wouldn't it, Mel?"

But the General was still thinking about his orderly and the Oke.

"As time went on," the General said, "I began to get the idea that I was handing out those five-dollar bills to Svenson at shorter intervals and that Oke was becoming more and more expendable around my quarters. Finally, one day Svenson came in with a gallon and put it on the upper shelf of my clothes closet, and the very next morning when he brought my riding boots and opened the closet door I happened to look up and discover that one third of that gallon was gone. It was time to do something. It was time to put Svenson on the carpet.

" 'Just a minute, Svenson,' I said, 'I know that this is a hot tropical climate, but look at that gallon of Oke.'

"Svenson came right to attention and looked at it, just one squint and then eyes front.

" 'It certainly is a hot climate,' I said, 'to have one third of a gallon of Oke evaporate in twenty-four hours with the cork in it, don't you think so, Svenson?'

" 'Yes, sir,' Svenson said, 'but I can account for it, sir.'

" 'I thought you could,' I said. 'How do you account for it?'

" 'Well, sir,' Svenson said, 'it's a liquid, sir, and liquids flow downhill to find their own level, and I was standing under that shelf yesterday afternoon. It kind of started leveling off before I thought much about it, sir.' "

The General looked at us mirthlessly, and Colonel Flax and I both gave way to merriment. It was all part of an act that we had been through with other generals.

"What did you say to Svenson then, sir?" the colonel asked. "It certainly was a logical excuse."

"I just told him not to get below it again," the General said. "I just told him in the future if he wanted to look at the Oke to get a stepladder and stand above it. The Oke lasted longer after that. I wonder what ever happened to old Svenson."

Oscar had opened the door to the dining room. The General put down his cocktail glass and smiled at Helen.

"I guess you'd better lead the old man in to lunch, my dear," he said, "and see that he doesn't stagger." Helen took his arm, and he patted her hand. "Let's stay like this and let the others go in first," the General said. "It's been quite a while since a pretty girl took me in to lunch."

No one sat down in the living room when we returned there after lunch. I saw Phil Bentley look at his wrist watch and the General saw him, too.

"I'm ready to go back there if you are," the General said. "We may as well put the show back on the road."

"Sidney," Helen said, "do you have to be in there all afternoon?

Camilla was saying this morning that she hardly saw you yesterday. Can't you take a walk with her later on or something?"

There was no reason why I should sit in at all the conferences now that everything was moving reasonably well.

"All right," I said, "if the General will let me off."

It was the conditioning. There was no reason why I should ask his permission to see Camilla. Then before Helen could answer, Melville Goodwin joined us and slapped his hand on my shoulder.

"Let's step outside for two minutes, Sid," he said, "and get a breath of air before we start."

We were both embarrassed when Helen asked the same question again about Camilla. There was no reason at all for me to be there, he said. He realized that he was monopolizing me too much. He realized that he had just moved in here and Helen mustn't ask any such fool questions again or he would move right out. When all this was over, he and Muriel and Helen and I would have to get to know each other. We would have to have a long visit together as soon as things were arranged in Washington. He had said just the right thing and Helen said the right thing back, but I knew why he wanted to see me for two minutes.

"Say, Sid," he said, when we stood outside in the drive, "did you call up Dottie?"

He had passed the stage of bringing her name casually into a conversation, and perhaps it was better to be direct about it.

"She wanted to know how you were," I told him. "As a matter of fact I'm having lunch with her tomorrow."

"God damn," the General said. "She understands how I'm fixed here, doesn't she? Tell her I want to see her as soon as I get to New York."

"All right," I said, "I'll tell her."

"This is the damnedest thing I've ever been through," the General said, "having the Secretary ask me to sit around here and talk. Well, let's go in and keep on talking."

249

XVII

"Nor Certitude, nor Peace, nor Help for Pain"

IT HAD occurred to me several times while the General was retailing his reminiscences that the simplicity of his childhood and the uncomplicated quality of his background must have been of great value to him in all his subsequent adjustments. He could not have been unduly or neurotically enmeshed in the lives of his parents, whose lives as he described them had been unspectacular and happy. If there had been any clashes or frustrations, they had escaped his power of observation. In fact the Goodwins without ever knowing it must have been ideal parents for a soldier. Except for a few precepts and simple rules, they had never interfered with Melville's development. As far as I could see, they had never loved him too much or worried over him too much. The whole social pattern of Hallowell, too, made it a suitable cradle for a soldier and a hero. There had been no violent distractions, there had been an even distribution of everything, and leadership demanded an unconfused approach and a fixity of purpose. Melville Goodwin's had been a normal life with few intense joys and sorrows and few areas of fear or regret. If it could have been described in a graphic form, you would have seen only a gradually ascending curve.

If any boy wanted to go to the Point, the General said, it was a pretty good thing for him to start as a pretty simple kid with just a few essential loyalties. It was a good thing for this hypothetical young lad to have been used to eating plain food, to sleeping in a cold room, to manual labor, and above all, to telling the truth. It was also desirable for him not to have a swelled head or too many preconceived ideas that would only have to be knocked out of him. Rich boys had a harder time than poor boys at the Point. You threw away your past the minute you started walking up the hill from the railroad station, and everyone was like everybody else once the crowd was all checked in. It would not be such a bad idea to have an arch at the entrance to the Point on which would be written some statement to the effect that you brought nothing inside there with you except yourself. Pocket money, family and chauffeurs did not matter at the Point. You didn't give a damn what any other plebe had been, at least not for quite a while, when you met him at the Point.

He was Mr. Dumjohn or Mr. Ducrot just like you and he would have his past kicked out of him just as yours was going to be. You all went through the same necessary hell together, right by the numbers. It was dished out by experts and you took it. It was up to you how well you took it, but all of you had to be pretty much alike when you came out the other end, more alike, perhaps, than you ever believed. This was what the Point was for. You learned to love and respect it, but perhaps respect was greater than love, at least it was for him.

One's experience at West Point was something that its graduates seldom discussed at length later, because discussion was needless. Personally Mel Goodwin had never put his thoughts about West Point into any order until once, some years after graduation, when he had accompanied his commanding officer there, a Colonel Savery, who had written three articles on the First Battle of the Marne for the *Infantry Journal* and who had also collected a nice set of lantern slides on the subject. The colonel had been invited to give a lecture on the battle to the cadets, and he had brought Lieutenant Goodwin with him to handle the projector. They had arrived early one spring afternoon and to kill time before the lecture Lieutenant Goodwin had walked about by himself for nearly an hour. He had not seen the place since he had left it after his graduation, and he had never been so deeply impressed by the Gothic mass of the buildings or by the unforgettable vistas of the Hudson. He could have moved blindfold on the double from place to place, but never before had he seen it all of one piece. He had never before been so conscious of the institution's permanence or of the memories enshrined within it. He had never realized the enormousness of what the Point had done to him and for him, until he stood by the Battle Monument that afternoon, breathing the fresh scent of growing things and listening to the bells and calls. The Point was oblivious to his existence now. Yet he was still a unit of the long gray line that marched endlessly back to the dawn of its history, and by God it was something to be a part of the Corps.

The Point had made him earn all that it had given him, but while he stood there by the Battle Monument doing nothing, he made a rough list of what he *had* been given. For one thing there was the resilience and co-ordination of his body. Even as he stood at ease his posture was correct. He had learned to ride and fence and box and swim. He had become passably proficient in golf and tennis. He had learned personal order and cleanliness and how to look anyone in the eye. He had learned truthfulness and respect. He had learned the whole school of soldiering and a good deal more besides, not that schooling ever stopped in the army. He was well grounded in mathematics. He had a good working knowledge of general history and geography and of law and a reading knowledge of French and Spanish, although he had always been poor at languages. Also he could express himself satisfactorily in expository English. He could go further with the list, but all these accomplishments could be summarized in one way. He had learned that if he were obliged to do so, he could turn his mind and hand to almost anything.

You could not possibly, the General said, explain the place satisfactorily to an outsider, any more than you could explain what went on inside yourself. West Point's primary function was to turn out leaders who could win wars for their country. It was not intended to turn out philosophers or artists. West Point was neither a boys' school nor a university. It was a professional institution for professionals. Its product was a soldier who could fight, who could submerge his individuality in prompt implicit obedience and still be an individual. If you wanted him to be frank — off the record — West Point was a hell of an experience. If he saw a cadet now, he could feel both sorry and glad for him and also proud of him. If officers seldom talked with each other at great length about the Point, certainly he was not going to talk about the Point at length to amateurs. Of course if he wanted, he could tell a lot of stories, especially about plebe year. No one could forget "beast barracks" or "bracing" or the formal jokes that plebes must learn by heart. They were an integral and useful part of the whole system. No one could forget his first sight of a perfect upperclassman. There would never be such neatness and polish again. No one could forget, either, the exhaustion and discouragement of the first weeks. Well, he had come through it all, and you could look upon him as an average product.

Certain harassing memories beset him as he stood by the Battle Monument. One was his fear that he would be busted out. He could still hear the voice of the cadet adjutant in mess hall, reading off the names of classmates who would leave the Corps. Often he would dream that his name was on the list. That fear of separation was always his greatest drive and it impelled him toward elaborate care and conservatism. He had never been as relaxed as some of his other classmates, and there had not been much time for ordinary friendship on account of that fear. Yet if you were to ask any of his contemporaries, he believed that they would tell you that Mel Goodwin had not been such a bad Joe. He could afford to feel a little sorry now for Cadet Goodwin at the Point, worrying about his haircut, about his shoeshine and the crease of his trousers. Outwardly he had been adjusted, but he sometimes wondered whether anyone was completely inwardly adjusted to the Point.

Another factor of course was the imminence of war. At his time at the Point — he was in the class of '19 that graduated a year earlier — you always knew that war was coming and this gave everything a grimness and an urgency that was not there in peace years. There was certainly not the gaiety and lightheartedness, in his time, to which other graduates alluded, yet the ordinary routines remained. He could see Cadet Goodwin as Mr. Ducrot wiping off his smile and stepping on it and announcing in the mess hall the number of days till June graduation. He could see Cadet Goodwin braced on the edge of his chair, and running upstairs two steps at a time. He could see Cadet Goodwin in recitations and Goodwin on parade. He could still see Cadet Goodwin as a stag at one of the hops.

He had never been a "spoonoid" but like any cadet he had been obliged to learn his way around the dance floor at West Point. M. Viset, a French dancing instructor, was there especially to teach clumsy, gangling boys, and he had learned both to lead and follow, dancing with other cadets. Though his ear for music was always poor, he had been able to perform adequately in the waltz, two-step and fox trot — not sensationally but adequately — and the girls were always kind in those war days. Though he had never been around country clubs and had never been to the theater, still the veneer of the Point was on him and he had learned the rudiments of party manners by his last year there — but those girls at the hops meant very little to him because Muriel Reece was his one and only, his OAO, as cadets put it.

What with the study hour and taps, there was not much time for abstract thought or active discontent at the Point, and the pressure of time and the necessity for making the best use of it was something that was hard to lose. If he had done any reading in his spare moments, it had been in military memoirs and the history of battle. He had been exposed like everyone else there to the rudiments of poetry, including selections from the *Oxford Book of English Verse,* but the poetry he remembered best was the Scripture reading in Cadet Chapel. He only learned the value of poetry later when time was heavier on his hands.

In the South of France when he was recovering from the bayonet wound he had received in the Argonne, he had stayed in a Riviera hotel taken over by the army for convalescent officers and he had shared a bedroom there with a reserve officer, a Captain H. T. Wilbur, who was a graduate of Princeton University. This captain's mind, though it was a good one, had seemed amazingly undisciplined, and Melville had been almost shocked by the tales he heard of lax student life at Princeton — of late hours, of clubs and of elective courses. According to what that captain told him, Princeton or any other civilian university was a sort of intellectual Garden of Eden where you could wander at will, plucking fruits from any tree of knowledge and tossing them away after a few swift bites. As far as he could see, you did not have to bother about where you stood in your classes or whether you were drunk or sober. When Captain

Wilbur produced a bottle of cognac smuggled into convalescent quarters contrary to regulations, it took Melville some time to find the courage to tell the captain that he had never tasted liquor at West Point. He had never forgotten Captain Wilbur's surprised look. In fact they had each looked upon the other as a freak. He was fascinated by civilian gripes about the army and its discipline. H. T. Wilbur could not wait, he simply could not wait, to get through with the whole business and to get home. He would tell in detail what he would do at home. He would take the family car and take a girl out to dine and dance. He would see all the shows in New York and he would sit up all night in a restaurant called "Jack's." H. T. Wilbur was speaking of a world of which Melville knew almost nothing, and though it fascinated him, Melville could not help but be uneasy. He was in a different class with a different rating.

"Haven't you ever read this?" Captain Wilbur used to say. "Frankly, Mel, haven't you ever heard of that?"

Of course, H. T. Wilbur was an amateur, being one of those ninety-day wonders from Leavenworth, yet his capacity for learning was as good as Melville's own and his mind was attractively adorned. Wilbur really showed him what poetry was while they drank illicit cognac. He had never realized until he read Wilbur's copy of Housman that the music of words could have a power as great as cognac, and sometimes in his memory he could still see the Mediterranean in the twilight and catch the lilt of Wilbur's voice. It was just as well not to keep too much poetry in your quarters, because some commanding officers might get odd ideas about you, but Melville had always kept the Housman and the Rupert Brooke books which H. T. Wilbur had given him.

On that spring afternoon by the Battle Monument he discovered that a stray couplet of verse was moving through his mind for no good reason. It came from "Dover Beach" by Matthew Arnold — a sad poem, and he could think of no logical reason for being sad on his return to West Point.

Nor certitude, nor peace, nor help for pain;
And we are here as on a darkling plain . . .

255

He liked words that made sense and the meaning of these restless words was annoyingly vague to him, except that the Parade Ground was always called the Plain. Perhaps he had learned at the Point that there was no peace nor help for pain, but he had been surrounded by certitude, even certitude of the hereafter. If you were sad, it was best to get your mind on something else — but he was puzzled by that phrase, "a darkling plain."

Then suddenly as he had stood there thinking, he heard his name called and he turned to see an officer walking toward him. Melville's mind moved like clockwork. The officer was Major H. A. Holton, in the Infantry like himself, and they had met once at Coblenz in the Army of Occupation.

"How did you get up here, Goodwin?" the major asked, and Melville looked at him straight and respectfully, explaining why he was there, and the major in reply said that he was serving in the tactical department on the usual four-year tour.

"Is there anything special you'd like to see?" the major asked, "or did you see too much of it when you were here?"

"If it's all right, I'd like to see the barracks," Melville said.

They walked side by side in careful step, and the closer they approached the barracks the faster the clock turned backwards. There was the usual meticulous, spotless order in the corridors. When the major rapped on a door, the hasty scuffling inside conveyed to Melville exactly what was going on. Two cadets stood at attention in their quarters, each behind his chair, correct in his carefully buttoned coat, though ten seconds before, Melville knew, they had been studying at their table with their coats hung on the chair backs. Either of those two cadets might have been an old image of himself. He was a first lieutenant now, with his service ribbons and his decorations, but at the same time he was young Mel Goodwin, who had been writing a letter home before the "Tac" had knocked. He could look at those two cadets impersonally, as he had learned to look at soldiers, but at the same time they were as familiar as old shoes. He had not realized that cadets could be so uniformly beautiful, so clean and so precise. He had forgotten how perfect the curtain of impersonality had been that you learned to draw at any second.

He was almost back in his own old quarters, with its regulation furnishings, clean, bare-walled, uncarpeted, devoid of almost any individual possessions. As he saw the straight-backed chairs, he realized that during his whole stay at the Point he had scarcely ever sat in a comfortable seat — except in the First-Class Club Room and the quarters of the Dialectic Society — but then his posture had never made him feel the lack. He saw the iron beds with the mattresses folded back and every bit of property ready for sudden inspection. He saw the shoes, spotlessly clean, all in their proper order, uniforms all hanging in alignment, and other garments neatly folded on their shelves, nothing out of place by a fraction of an inch. He saw a framed picture of a girl on the upper shelf on which it was permissible to keep a photograph. He was surprised that it was not his old picture of Muriel.

When the major introduced him to the cadets, he saw their eyes move from his face to his ribbons, and he smiled at them mechanically. Those cadets had their own problems and he did not want to waste their time, but he asked them a few agreeable questions, suitable to the occasion, such as "Where do you come from, Mister?" and he saw that one of them had been writing a letter.

"A letter home?" he asked.

"No, sir," the cadet answered, "not exactly."

It was the first and only crack in the veneer. It might have been the same room from which he had written to Muriel twice a week, seldom more often. It might have been the same room from which his thoughts had escaped to Muriel for an allotted space. He might have been one of the cadets, and the other might have been his roommate, Spike Kennedy, who was now down in Texas with the Cavalry.

"Thank you very much, sir," he said to the major, because the major was the one to thank and not the cadets, but he smiled again at the boys and wished them both good luck. It was a great experience, being a cadet at the Point, though you could hardly write a "sweet college years" song about it.

"Would you like to go through it again?" the major asked.

"No, sir," Melville told him, "not exactly."

They both grinned because it was something that was behind them now like World War I, and when something was behind you, its outlines generally softened — but not the outlines of the barracks. He remembered studying after taps by an electric light bulb concealed in the leg of a pair of trousers. He remembered going with Spike to an illicit food party, known in cadet slang as a "boodle party." They had not been caught, but you could not get away with much.

During his particular years at the Point, you studied tactics and engineering and the handling of small bodies of troops, for good and sufficient reasons. You had a thirst for knowledge and you said your prayers in chapel, for good and sufficient reasons. You studied maps and orientation, knowing that you might have real use for them in the next few months. There was less time in the war days for social functions and consequently Muriel had not come to West Point often. She had only been there for one week-end hop, for Hundredth Night, and for a Summer Camp Show, until she came with her mother and the Goodwin family for the graduation and their wedding. He and Muriel were married, like a good many other girls and graduates, in the chapel, the day after his graduation. He was to report at Merritt in two weeks' time to proceed to France in a school detachment. In a way this was a compliment, and he was delighted to get overseas, but, even so, he was afraid that he would not see action before the war was over.

Everything was compressed like a jack-in-the-box in those last few days, what with parades and the graduation and the ball and the details of his new uniforms and equipment, and at the end of it, marriage. He could never forget the confusion of the time. He was a cadet and an army officer and a bridegroom all at once, and strangely enough he seemed to know very little about anything, almost nothing about routine troop duties, for instance. Nevertheless he could stand up straight and answer when he was spoken to, and he had learned how to take prompt action after estimating a situation. If he did not know how to win a war singlehanded, he knew as much as a lot of others in his class.

The graduation order list had already been printed, and he stood in the middle of the first quarter. Some people were surprised that he had chosen Infantry instead of Artillery or Engineers, but he supposed he was simply one of those individuals who was born for Infantry. He had always been an infantryman at heart, just as he had always been an admirer of U. S. Grant.

It had not seemed possible that Muriel could be at the Old Hotel when he signed out of barracks to meet her on the afternoon of the graduation hop. He would have two hours to be with her, and when he saw her with her mother on the porch of the hotel, it was like a moment in a dream — but he was trained to handle it.

"Why, Melville," Mrs. Reece said, "you look just as though you had stepped out of a bandbox."

"That's just a part of everything here," he said. "I hope that you and Muriel had a good trip down, Mrs. Reece, and I hope your room is comfortable. Would you and Muriel care to walk around the grounds?" Other cadets were around him saying the same things to other girls and mothers.

"I think I'd better take a little rest and unpack Muriel's wedding dress," Mrs. Reece said. "Why don't you take Muriel about the grounds of the Academy? She loves it so."

There was nothing pleasanter in a cadet's life than taking his One And Only around the grounds, and there he was with Muriel, with an hour and a half to spend.

"Melly," Muriel said, "don't stand here showing off in front of everybody. Do you want to go walking or what do you want to do?"

He was not showing off in front of anybody. He was simply trying to behave in a polite and natural manner. He was in the graduating class and he could not behave like a lower classman.

"Why, anything you want, Muriel," he said.

"Well," Muriel answered, "let's not stand here like two bumps on a log."

They walked past the equestrian statue of George Washington.

"Aren't you going to say anything?" she asked him. "Aren't you glad to see me?"

259

"Yes, of course I'm glad," he said.

"How glad?"

"Very glad," he said.

"Well, I'm glad to see you, Melly darling, and I'm awfully proud."

He was very proud of her, too, in her broad-brimmed picture hat, but it seemed strange to have anyone call him "Melly."

"Do you know yet where you're going to go — or anything?" she asked.

"No, not yet," he said. "We're still waiting to hear."

"Well, I hope you're going to get overseas." It was the right thing for her to say. From the very beginning Muriel understood the army.

An officer was walking toward them as they passed the statue, Captain Folsom, the Tactical Officer of Melville's company. It was a compliment that the captain stopped after returning his salute. Captain Folsom during the last year had asked him several times to his quarters. They were almost friends and now they were almost brother officers. If the captain had often run him ragged, this was all forgotten. It had all been for Melville's good.

"Well," the captain said, "aren't you going to introduce me?"

Melville blushed but he remembered the etiquette.

"Miss Reece, may I present Captain Folsom?" he said.

"How do you do, Miss Reece?" the captain said. "I recognized you from your photograph."

"Oh," Muriel said, "on Melville's shelf." She knew all about the Point from his letters.

"It's always been a pleasant moment in my inspection, seeing it," the captain said. "I'm the one who checks Mr. Goodwin's locker, and I know he'll never forget it . . . will you, Goodwin?"

"No, sir," Melville answered.

"It's a great pleasure to meet the photograph's original. You see, Mr. Goodwin and I have been through quite a lot together," the captain said. "May I make a suggestion, Mr. Goodwin?"

"Yes, sir," Melville said.

"If I were walking with Miss Reece," the captain said, "I know where I'd be going — or are you on your way to Flirtation Walk?"

The memory of the captain smiling at him just as though he were not a cadet was one of his happiest memories of the Point, and the incident taught him a lesson that he never forgot. It paid to be kind to subordinates. He would have done anything for Folsom, but he was only to meet him twice again in the service, once in the War College at Washington and once dead in Africa at Kasserine Pass.

"Yes, sir," Melville said. "I have had that in mind."

"And thank you very much for bringing it up, sir," Muriel told Captain Folsom. "I'm not so sure he was thinking of it."

Right from the beginning Muriel understood the army. She always knew what to say to superior officers, and she very seldom said too much.

"He's the one who's your Tac, isn't he?" Muriel said. It was wonderful that she even knew the slang.

"Melly," she said, "I'm glad we're going to be in the army. Now take me to Flirtation Walk."

It was worth going to the Point just to be able to take a girl on that semirestricted walk along the Hudson. It was worth all the beating that you took to do it. Muriel always understood the service and she understood, too, that there wasn't much time to learn about it back in June 1918.

You had to remember that 1918 was some thirty years in the past and he had never kept a diary, so the weeks before he went overseas had become scrambled in his memory like the eggs of an omelet. He could not remember exactly when he received his orders or much either about his wedding in the chapel. When you were caught up in the tides of war, you simply moved, a part of the machine. Their wedding in the chapel moved, too, by the numbers. The chaplain's usual advice was to wait a while and think it over and not get married the day after graduation. Theoretically, of course, no one had any business turning into a shavetail and a husband simultaneously, but as far as he could remember, no one listened seriously to the padre, and personally he was glad he hadn't. Nothing developed a capacity for enjoyment like a few years at the Point. What more could he have asked than what was given him that June? He was marrying the girl he had always wanted to marry. He was a soldier, and the biggest war the world had ever seen was getting bigger all the time, instead of petering out as he was afraid it might after the German breakthrough in March. He was like a football player who had been sitting on the sidelines, and now the coach was waving to him. That was the way he felt and it was the way any shavetail ought to feel. It was a great time to be alive — in June 1918.

Muriel had gone to a secretarial school after he had left for the Point, and she had been in the front office of the hat factory for two years, working for Mr. Reece and sometimes for Mr. Hallowell. It was a great relief that Muriel was able to take over the details of lodging and transportation. Muriel purchased the railroad tickets after the wedding and arranged for a reservation at the old Waldorf-Astoria Hotel on Thirty-fourth Street in New York. She had always wanted to go to the Waldorf. He had never realized what a capacity for leadership Muriel had developed until they took that wedding trip. Frankly, the old Waldorf was a big jump from the barracks and he was only a kid, still self-conscious in his officer's uniform. Everything around him was new, including his clothing roll and bedding roll and foot locker, but you'd have thought Muriel had been to the Waldorf a hundred times. Somehow she knew all the finer points about porters and taxicabs. Perhaps girls developed more quickly than boys in some ways.

"Just follow the bellboys and me," Muriel said, "and ask for our reservation when you get to the desk."

All he had to do was to follow Muriel, eyes front, along a corridor with marble columns and to tell himself that he was an officer in the United States Army, legally married to the girl ahead of him, and that he could prove it by papers if necessary. He had to make a deliberate effort not to stand at attention when he asked the room clerk if there was a reservation for Lieutenant and Mrs. Goodwin. He was not sure whether he should refer to himself as "Lieutenant" or plain "Mister," but "Lieutenant" sounded better, and, after all, the Waldorf was not a military installation. It was a shock to him when the clerk called him "sir," and he finally signed the register as "Melville A. Goodwin, 2nd Lt., Inf., USA, and wife."

He was still so dazed when they went up in the elevator that

Muriel had to whisper to him to take off his garrison cap. For a moment he felt she was wrong until he realized that he was wearing no side arms.

"Give each of the boys a quarter," Muriel whispered as they stood in the center of their room.

In all the years they had been married he never had asked Muriel how she had learned about tips and hats in elevators.

"Why did you sign your name 'Melville A. Goodwin, 2nd Lt., Inf., USA, and wife'?" Muriel asked. "You should have signed it '2nd Lt. and Mrs. Goodwin, USA.'"

He had never asked her either how she knew that one.

"It's all right, Mel," she said, "you don't have to go back to change it. What are you looking at now?"

"The room," he said. "I should have asked how much it costs."

The truth was you never thought much about money at the Point.

"It costs a lot," Muriel said. "It costs eight dollars a day."

"With food?" he asked.

"No," she said, "without food. It's all right, there's the wedding-present money."

It was true that Mr. Reece and Melville's father had each given them a hundred dollars, but it would not last long at that rate.

"Just give me the money, Mel," she said. "I'll look after the expenses. It doesn't have to last long. We'll go back to Hallowell before it's finished, and then you're going overseas."

"What's in that room there?" he asked.

"It's the bathroom," Muriel said.

"What," he said, "a private bath?"

He did not mind when Muriel began to laugh. He did not even mind feeling like a plebe again in front of Muriel.

"Look," he said, "it's got a tub."

"Of course it has," she said. "Don't they have tubs at the Point?"

"We take showers," he said. "There wouldn't be time to let the water run into a tub."

"Well, there's time now," Muriel said. "Why don't you take a bath?"

"What," he asked — "right now?"

"Oh, Mel," she said, "don't be so silly. Go in and turn on the water, and I'll unpack our things."

"Not my things," he said.

"Mel," she called, above the running of the water, "hand me out your breeches."

His hearing was as good as his eyesight, but he had felt that there must be some mistake.

"Your trousers or whatever you call them," Muriel said. "I want to count our money."

He walked into the bedroom in his shirttails and handed her his breeches.

"Don't," he said, "don't wrinkle them, Muriel. What's so funny?"

"Just being married," Muriel said, "and I guess it's particularly funny being married to somebody from West Point."

A long time later, when he was a captain, he and Muriel discovered that many incidents in their abbreviated New York honeymoon, including that bath at the Waldorf, made a story that would set a dinner party into roars of laughter. He never suspected until he began observing other youngsters reporting for duty that their experience was in many ways universal. Now that he thought of it, once when he had dined in London with the big boss himself, someone had suggested, how about his telling about him and Muriel at the Waldorf, and it went over very well. It made the big boss laugh, and it even amused an admiral and a field marshal. Muriel's teaching him how to smoke a cigarette made a good story in itself. He had never heard of breakfast in bed and he never knew that Muriel smoked, either, until she asked him to get her purse and pulled a pack of cigarettes out of it. Muriel had told him it would be a good thing to learn to smoke if he were going to France, and as usual she was right. That was Muriel's story, but he had one of his own, too, and it was pretty good, if he did say so.

The first night they were in New York, they had gone to a musical comedy. All you had to do was to pick up the telephone and order the seats at the Waldorf. Just as they were going to get in the taxi for the theater, he took his first salute. Two enlisted men went by and their hands snapped up when they saw him, and Muriel had to tell him that they were saluting him. The name of that musical comedy, he thought, was *Going Up,* all about aviation. Between the acts the street was full of officers, and an artillery major asked him for a match. Muriel was the one who supplied it out of her pocketbook, and she told him to light it for the major. Then the major saw his ring and thanked him very elaborately. The major's collar insignia was "USR" not "US." It was his first encounter with the wartime service and with its individuals from civil life. The officer had been drinking, and it hurt Melville to see that one of his pockets was unbuttoned. He almost thought of mentioning it but he refrained, because of age and rank. A regular had to take his orders, no matter what he thought.

After the show, he and Muriel walked down Sixth Avenue and passed an open-air shooting gallery. Some enlisted men behind them were singing a snatch of a popular song, "If you can fight like you can love, good night, Germany!"

"Melly," Muriel said, "let's see if you can shoot like you can love."

As a matter of fact, when he came to think of it he was a better shot than lover, or at least he had had more practice. It was a big elaborate gallery with strings of ducks, revolving pipes and balls bouncing on jets of water. He would not have shot if two Infantry privates had not called out to move back and give the lieutenant a chance. At least he knew what he was doing when the attendant handed him a twenty-two, even if the weapon was chained to the counter. It was a nicely balanced little rifle, warm from a lot of shooting, but very dirty.

"All right," he told Muriel, "I'll try the ducks," and he knocked all the ducks over, snap, snap. Now that he had the feel of the rifle, he went on to the revolving wheels of pipes and cleaned out three wheels of them, but by that time he had shot fifty cents' worth, which was enough money for that sort of thing.

"Jesus," the men were saying, "look at that lieutenant. Go ahead and clean it out, Lieutenant."

He was better at snap shooting later. There was a trick to it like anything else.

"Go on, Melville," Muriel said, but he told her they were wasting money.

"I'll tell you what I'll do, Bud," the proprietor of the gallery said. "If you knock off the balls from the fountains from left to right, you can have all the shooting for nothing."

A crowd had gathered behind him. The balls were erratic, but Muriel was there and he decided to shoot fast, even if he missed.

"One," the men began to chant, "two, three, four; Jesus, look at the lieutenant — five, six, seven, eight," and then there was a groan.

"Oh, Melly," Muriel said, "you missed the last one."

"That's all right," one of the infantrymen said, "don't you mind what she calls you, Melly."

Melville set his rifle down carefully on the counter. It was his first experience with troops except for the well-trained personnel at the Point. If Muriel had not been there, he would have let the matter drop, but now he had to do something, and this was the part of the story he liked best, because it had a moral. The man was a green soldier on leave, and even then Melville could see that he meant no harm.

"What's your first name?" he asked. He spoke quietly like his Tac, Captain Folsom, at the Point.

"Charlie," the soldier said.

"Charlie what?" Melville asked.

"Charlie Thompson."

"Yes," Melville said, "but Charlie Thompson what?"

"Charlie Thompson, sir."

"Atta boy," the soldiers called, "give it to him, Lieutenant."

A good officer, he knew, should never get mad at troops. He was glad to remember that he had been adroit enough to smile.

"That's right," he said. "You guessed the answer. I'll give you five dollars if you'll knock off that last ball, Charlie."

"Go ahead, Charlie," the men called, "take his five dollars, Charlie."

"I couldn't shoot that good, sir," the soldier said.

He had been smart enough to know that he was as young as any

266

of those boys and he had made his point, and he had done right, calling the soldier "Charlie."

"Well," he said, and he had the sense to smile again, "you're going where you ought to learn. Remember to squeeze and not to jerk, and hook up your collar and button up your pockets."

He smiled again at the troops and pulled out the bill that Muriel had left him to pay the gallery.

"If there's anything left over," he said, "let some of these soldiers use it. Come on, Muriel."

The moral of the story was, you had to learn to handle troops right if you were going to the front and didn't want a shot in the back. Never let them get away with anything, but remember the human equation. . . .

"Say, Lieutenant, sir," one of the men said, "what outfit are you with?"

The man, being a sergeant, should have known better. According to military courtesy, he should have phrased his question in the third person, but then he was not in Melville's outfit.

"I haven't been assigned to any yet, Sergeant," Melville said.

"Well, I hope to God you get into ours, sir," the sergeant said.

"Why, thanks, Sergeant," Melville said, "and here's wishing you a lot of luck. Come on, Muriel."

"Why, Melly," Muriel said, "you sounded just like an officer."

It was not an intelligent critique, seeing that Muriel could not really know yet how an officer should sound.

"I mean," she said, before he could tell her so, "you sounded just like your Tac at West Point, that nice Captain Folsom."

It was a good idea to have a model when you started in the army, and he had been trying to sound like the captain, though he felt slightly deflated because she had guessed.

"It might be just as well," he said, "if you didn't call me Melly."

"Yes, sir," Muriel said, "and I'm pleased you're assigned to my outfit, sir, and take off that hat when we get into that elevator."

It all made a pretty good story, if you told it among old friends, or even if you had to make yourself agreeable to some gauche young officer and his wife, and there was another moral to that story, and he always liked to end it with that moral. The moral was, don't let your wife control the situation all the time. Let her handle you but you handle troops, and don't push troops too hard when they're on leave, especially in the States.

XVIII

Who Pants for Glory Finds but Short Repose

THE mass of American manpower that poured into France that summer left much to be desired from the point of view of training. It was basically excellent material but very raw, and admittedly even some of the regular divisions were not yet the smoothly working units that they should have been. One of the most peculiar things in the whole picture was the difficulty experienced by a well-trained officer in ever reaching a position within the range of enemy small-arms fire. This was ironical, but when you came to think of it, natural enough, since there was a demand which simply could not be filled for personnel to instruct green troops. If you exhibited any unusual skills and abilities in those days, someone was apt to grab you. All you had to do was stick your neck out a quarter of an inch and you did not have to fight. Instead you would be teaching others the theory without ever having had the practice. It was marvelous in view of this that the percentage of West Point graduates killed was in the end higher than that of any other group. It spoke volumes for their keenness and anxiety to do what they were trained to do, namely to lead in battle. When Melville Goodwin came to think of it, he was lucky ever to have seen the fighting. A lot of his classmates never even got overseas.

Melville Goodwin was ordered to France in a school detachment of officers from a new division which was still being organized in the States. The officers of the school detachment were to receive various sorts of technical instruction in France, after which they would meet that nebulous division at some debarkation point and assist in its final polishing. This would have been an excellent idea if the demand for manpower had not become pressing after the German breakthrough in the vicinity of Château-Thierry in July. If the

Ludendorff concentrations had not been effective, Lieutenant Goodwin might have studied the theories of the machine gun and of trench-mortar fire all summer. He was always grateful that the German general staff had come close to solving the problem of the breakthrough and that something close to open warfare had precipitated a sudden crisis.

However, he had no way of knowing the plans of the German general staff when he received his orders to report at Camp Merritt. He only knew that he was going to France for training after a few days' leave at home. Most of his able-bodied contemporaries had left Hallowell months before as volunteers or draft troops and the sooner he went, too, the better. People on Prospect Street looked curiously and sometimes bitterly, he thought, at his gold bars, and there seemed to be a feeling that he had become an officer as a result of some sort of pull or juggling. The implication was that here was Melville Goodwin all polished up and an officer and married, too, with a nice soft place for himself when he should have been out in the mud with all the other boys. Muriel was furious when people did not understand that it was more dangerous to be an officer than a private soldier, particularly a West Point officer.

"Well, Melville," his father said, when Melville had explained to him about the advance school detachment, "I thought you had been working at West Point learning about those same things."

His mother, however, was glad that the army was taking care of him. She had been terribly worried for fear he might go into the fighting right away, but now she could look over all his equipment, his beautiful puttees, his sleeping bag and all the things in his green foot locker without feeling any more that they meant he was going to be killed. She was glad at last that he had gone to West Point and that the army knew he was valuable. He hoped that she would not say things like that around town, and he asked her not to, but of course she did when she worked at the Red Cross center. The truth was that civilians never could understand about the army.

Muriel wanted to go with him and to stay somewhere in New Jersey outside of Camp Merritt until the detachment finally sailed, but he told her that it was better to say good-by right there in Hallowell. She would be all right because she could go to work again in her father's office at the hat factory. Yet even Muriel could not wholly understand his point of view.

"I know it's awful for you, waiting here," she said, "but I wish you wouldn't act as though you were so glad to leave me."

The thing to do in wartime was to get away from home. Women, even Muriel, were only a complication when you were going overseas. It never helped to remember the look on a woman's face when you were leaving her, even if she were as brave as Muriel. It was demoralizing to see a woman trying to be brave.

"I'd hate to have you stay," Muriel said, ". . . but you'll think of me sometimes, won't you?"

Women, even the best of them, could not help but be jealous of war. They never did wholly believe it when you said you would always be thinking of them and you never believed it either. He even thought at times that he should not have married Muriel, that it was not fair to her, but thoughts like that were bad for the morale. There was no use describing the details of parting because the thing to do was to get going and get away from home and to try to forget as much of those last moments as you could. He hated to admit when he finally said good-by, that he was glad to go.

When he saw the wooden barracks and the mess halls of the embarkation center at Camp Merritt and turned in his orders, he was happier than he had been for days and days. It was like coming home, to arrive at Merritt. There was a beautiful, restful simplification. An American army post anywhere in the world would be more like home to him in the future than any other place.

"Orderly," the major on duty said, "take the lieutenant to Quarters C, Square 5."

All he had to say was Yes, sir, thank you, sir, and then salute and about face, one, two. The President of the United States had reposed special trust and confidence in his patriotism, valor, fidelity and ability, and he was going to the war.

Army life had its dull moments, but no new assignment was ever dull. An assignment to a new command even today was a personal

271

challenge, and a fresh, blank page on your ledger. An embarkation depot always reminded him of that quatrain in the *Rubáiyát* about the tent where took his one night's rest, the Sultan to the realms of death addressed. Other guests had come before you and others would follow, and you only waited there in a sort of limbo before you marched aboard the transport.

He had hardly entered the barracks at Merritt and had scarcely started to look over the officers of the school detachment, who were checking their equipment, or sleeping, or reading or playing cards, before he saw Spike Kennedy, his roommate at the Point. He had never been so glad to see anyone as he was to see Spike, and they stood there for a while laughing and pounding each other on the back. Spike had only been there six hours ahead of him, but he already had the swing of everything.

"Say, Mel," Spike kept saying, "we've got to stick together."

The thing to remember, Spike said, was that they were in a pretty funny crowd. Lieutenant Colonel Redfern, the detachment CO, came from the Point himself and had seen service in the Philippine insurrection and the Boxer Rebellion, but aside from him there were no other regulars in the detachment unless you included a former enlisted man, now a lieutenant. All the rest of these birds who were going over, Spike said, were either from the National Guard or from Plattsburg or somewhere. They had not been for more than six months in the service, but some of them seemed pretty bright. Some of them had been lawyers and things like that, and one of them, an Artillery captain named Tucker, had been a college professor. It was comical seeing all these poor birds trying to be soldiers. Those guys simply did not have a West Point education, and the only thing to do was to help them.

Lieutenant Colonel Redfern exhibited approximately the same attitude when Spike took Melville around to the colonel's quarters to report. The colonel had a small box of a room to himself at the end of the quarters with a cot, two chairs and a table. He was in his middle forties, lean and stringy, with pale blue eyes and a long, reddish face. It was only when the colonel got quietly drunk by himself on the transport that Melville began to feel that he had failings. He must have been very lonely with that school detachment, or else he would not have expressed himself as frankly as he had.

"Sit down, gentlemen," the colonel said. "This is a hell of a war. God damn it, I never thought I'd end up taking a zoo across the ocean. My God, there's even a college professor. Do you play bridge, Goodwin?"

"No, sir," Melville said.

"That's right," the colonel said, "I forgot the attitude toward cards at the Point."

The colonel stared at the table in front of him.

"We're getting out of here in forty-eight hours," he said. "Any questions?"

"No, sir," Melville answered.

"Well, if you have any," the colonel said, "don't bother me with a damn one of them. The main thing is don't bother me. Do you understand?"

"Yes, sir," Melville said.

"You get that, too, do you, Kennedy?"

"Yes, sir," Spike Kennedy answered.

"Then repeat it."

"The main thing is not to bother you, sir, about anything."

"That's right," the colonel said. "All the rest will, but you won't, because you're from the Point. I don't understand civilians. Do you understand civilians, Goodwin?"

"I don't know, sir," Melville said.

"Don't say you don't know," the colonel told him. "Never try to understand them. Have as little to do with them as is reasonably possible. You'll only get yourselves confused, fraternizing with those ninety-day wonders. That's my considered advice."

"Yes, sir," Melville said.

"Now one thing more," Colonel Redfern said. "Our association will be brief, but I might be able to teach you the rudiments of bridge. It calms the mind, it teaches patience and self-control."

"Yes, sir," Melville said.

"Well," the colonel said, "we've got to get this organized. That damn professor, Captain Tucker, plays bridge. We can sweat

273

Tucker. Kennedy, give him my compliments and tell him to report in here after supper for bridge with you two young gentlemen. You understand?"

"Yes, sir," they both said, and they stood up.

"Very well," the colonel said, "that's all for now."

Lieutenant Colonel Redfern was quite a card. Heaven only knew what became of him later. He had no future and he never told about his past, but all the way over on the old *Kroonland,* Colonel Redfern had them playing bridge whenever they were not on submarine lookout. Sometimes even now when Melville played a no-trump hand, he could think of himself in his life jacket aboard the *Kroonland* and he could see the whole convoy again, spread out like ducks on the gray Atlantic with an old battle cruiser leading them, and he could see the old four-stack destroyers that came to meet them when they reached the danger zone.

"If you had counted your cards," he could hear the colonel say, "you would have known that there would be an eight against you."

Yes, Lieutenant Colonel Redfern was quite a card. Melville could remember him more clearly than he could remember the docks at Saint-Nazaire. This was not peculiar, because one day after landing, he was on a train, and three days later he was at the headquarters of a division north of Château-Thierry, and an hour after that, with no food in his stomach, he was on a truck moving to the front as a replacement officer for an Infantry regiment which was to attack at dawn. The Germans were retreating then in the Château-Thierry salient, and there was no time for school detachments.

There had been a momentary view of Brittany, then a six-hour wait in a Paris station and then a trip through villages with all their roofs blown off and unburied corpses in the fields. Then there was a road in the dusk jammed with French cavalry. It was the first and last time he ever saw cavalry in any war. Next there was the sound of shells bursting in a patch of woods, and he was walking through the woods in the dark. Then he was behind the blankets of a dugout in a regimental Post of Command. It was like a bad dream, but it was the army.

"Take this officer up to C Company," the adjutant was saying.

Then he was outside again with a guide stumbling through the dark. His locker trunk and bedding roll were nowhere. He did not even have a pack or blanket but he did have a web belt and a forty-five automatic and one of those flat tin hats of World War I. He did not know where he was going and he had not even seen a map. The company command post was in a shell hole in the woods and he was told to stay there until morning, and join his platoon at dawn. Almost without his knowing how he got there, he was in the middle of an artillery duel. The seventy-fives were firing over him and machine guns were chattering out ahead. There was nothing he could fit together, but it was a great experience.

General Melville Goodwin paused and lighted a cigarette, and there was dead silence in the library.

"It was quite a mess at Château-Thierry," the General said. "Any advance with green troops like that is always that way. Everything in back keeps pushing you. God damn, you've got to go."

Melville Goodwin was out of his chair and on his feet as though everything were pushing him still, and perhaps his memories were. His face was bright and he seemed to enjoy every one of his memories. He reminded me of a football player describing a touchdown.

"That company wasn't a bad outfit, considering, but maybe I'm sentimental. You always love your first outfit. It always seems to be the way it was originally, even when it gets the hell shot out of it. God damn!" He began to laugh. "We really didn't know anything. Most of those troops were like kids playing cops and robbers against professionals."

He tossed his cigarette into the fireplace.

"Well, anyway, we're up at the front," he said. "I admit it's taken a long while to get there. Suppose we all take fifteen minutes out."

He looked at Phil Bentley and Miss Fineholt, but no one answered.

"Do you remember the song," he asked, " 'The colonel got the *Croix de guerre,* and the son of a bitch, he wasn't there'? Well, this son of a bitch was, but let's take fifteen minutes out. Come on, Flax."

Colonel Flax stood up instantly and followed the General out of the library.

"I was there myself, sir," I heard the colonel saying, "at a place near Le Charme, but it wasn't charming then."

Miss Fineholt and Phil Bentley and I still sat silently, considering the life and times and metamorphosis of Melville Goodwin. He had changed himself from a schoolboy at Hallowell into what he was today in the course of a very brief time, without mirrors or deception, but it was hard to follow the process in retrospect. He had not known enough to take off his hat in the elevator, and now there he was, in the shell hole in the woods, with nothing to hold the tale together but a feeble string of anecdotes.

"God," Phil Bentley said, "what a life!"

"Whose," I asked, "yours or his?"

"His," Phil Bentley said. "Anyway, I guess we have something to be thankful for. We never had to go to the Point." Phil sighed and took off his glasses. "And that Lieutenant Colonel Redfern — my God, he can't be real."

I might have explained that any of the rest of us would have seen Colonel Redfern in a different light.

"People like him keep cropping up over there," I said. "You must have seen a few yourself."

"I never knew how lucky I was before," Phil Bentley said. "Oh, God — there'll be another day of this and he'll be back in fifteen minutes."

Then I remembered that I had promised Helen to take a walk with Camilla. It was after four, and the machine guns were still chattering in the woods north of Château-Thierry. Everything was still really a mess around Château-Thierry, but some of Company C had been first-team material. . . .

Until I saw Camilla in jodhpurs and a light-brown pullover sweater, I had not faced the fact that Helen had started her on riding lessons. All Camilla's class at the Country Day School, Helen had said, were going to a place called the Winding River Riding Academy conducted by an Anglo-Irish gentleman from Galway named Mr. Delaney. Mr. Delaney was also master of an organization known as the Winding River Hunt, which Helen said was popular in the neighborhood, and Helen said that Mr. Delaney was popular, too, and that he was not an ordinary riding teacher. He came from an old Galway hunting family and he was asked everywhere and we should have him over sometime and talk to him about our stables. I had learned lately that a number of people, even in our age group, had taken up riding because of the social contacts the sport afforded. In fact Helen had taken me to a hunt tea recently, where everyone was in riding clothes like Camilla's, and I had not known what to talk about at the tea, never having ridden myself. It was curious to see my own child looking like a miniature of all those extrovert strangers. It made me realize what a specialized place a child's world had become since I had grown up — at least out here in Connecticut. It was necessary now for children to become proficient in all sorts of skills. They could not simply bat a ball around or paddle in the creek. They had to learn how to volley and smash in tennis and how to perform the eight-beat crawl in a swimming pool.

Camilla seemed to be growing away from me already and, as often happened these days, we both struggled to find a common subject for conversation.

"Daddy," Camilla said, "why don't you carry a cane when you go outdoors?"

"Why should I?" I asked.

"Because other children's fathers around here always carry walking sticks when they go walking in the country," Camilla said.

There was a time when you struggled to have your parents appear like other parents, and I was conscious of my own inadequacy, but there was nothing I could do about it.

"Well, I haven't got a walking stick," I said.

Camilla took my hand and it always made me happy when she did.

"It's all right. I only suggested it," she told me. "You don't really need it, Daddy."

She did not sound like a daughter of mine. She spoke with the

277

fine clipped accent of Miss Otts, but then Helen had employed Miss Otts for exactly that purpose. On the other hand, if I had adopted Miss Otts's manner of speech, I would have been taken off the air, and there would have been no Savin Hill or riding lessons. It occurred to me that I must go back in a little while and look over the script.

"Well," I said, "what did you do at riding school?"

"We rode around in a circle," Camilla said. "Mr. Delaney stood in the middle. My horse's name was Daisy."

It was exactly what a horse should have been named, and I told her it was a quiet name and I hoped that Daisy was a quiet horse, but I had never ridden around any Mr. Delaney in a ring.

"Daddy," Camilla said, "we never have time to have a talk. What are we going to talk about?"

I had planned to walk through the garden and then up the hill to a patch of woods and then through the woods and back down to the stables, but I had not thought of any subject of conversation.

"We've got to talk about something," Camilla said. "We can't just walk."

"Why can't we?" I asked. "Everybody talks too much, Camilla."

"It isn't any fun just walking," Camilla said.

As a matter of fact we did not have to work this out immediately because when we walked around the house to the garden, we encountered the General and Colonel Flax, standing together on the path, staring intently at some marks the General was making in the gravel.

"The emplacement was up there," the General said, "at the edge of the trees, and this area here was open. There was a dead space here where you could crawl on your belly if you wriggled like a snake, and they couldn't cover the whole sector all at once."

He looked up from the marks on the path. He had not seen us and I don't believe that he had heard us, but something must have told him that he and Colonel Flax were no longer alone fighting World War I.

"Well, well," he said, "and here's Camilla. Come here and shake hands with the old man. I've hardly laid eyes on Camilla.

We haven't had time to get acquainted but we'll have time someday."

"Camilla's pretty busy," I said. "She runs on a very tight schedule."

When I saw Camilla looking at the General's stars and ribbons and timidly holding out her hand, something in her wide-eyed expression reminded me of Rudyard Kipling's little Una on Pook's Hill. The outlines of the garden were soft in the late October sunlight, and she might have been meeting Kipling's Roman centurion or his kind old knight. I wondered whether she knew enough about English history to understand *Puck of Pook's Hill* if I should ever have time to read it to her.

"Well, well," the General said, "so you've been out riding, have you?"

"Yes," Camilla said.

"When you speak to General Goodwin," I told her, "remember to call him 'sir.'"

Both the General and Colonel Flax looked self-conscious.

"Don't you mind your pappy, darling," the General said. "How'd it be if you call me 'Uncle Mel'?"

There was no way of telling how it would be, because Camilla stared at him without answering.

"I used to have two little boys once myself," he said. "They were always full of dirt and devilment. I'll tell you about them someday, Camilla. They were always riding bareback. They started riding at Benning. Did you ever see the children's riding class at Benning, Flax?"

"No, sir," the colonel said.

"The instructor there was a nice old stable sergeant, an old-time cavalryman. They're as rare as whooping cranes now."

Colonel Flax looked at his wrist watch.

"I think they may be waiting for us in the library, sir," he said.

"Oh, all right," the General said, "all right. Are you coming, Sid?"

It was a question, not an order, but nevertheless I felt apologetic.

"I'll be back in a little while, sir," I said, "but you're right in the groove now and you don't need me for a while. I'm just going to walk up that hill with Camilla."

"What hill?" the General said.

"Just up to the woods there," I told him, and I pointed beyond the garden and General Goodwin examined the hill.

"Well, don't be too long, Sid," he said. "I don't like it in there without you, and you'd better send a patrol out first. There might be a machine gun in those woods."

Camilla took my hand and we walked across the garden.

"Daddy," she asked, "who is General Goodwin?"

Probably no one had explained him to her except possibly Miss Otts, whose knowledge of the American army would have been rudimentary. I wondered what the General looked like through Camilla's eyes and from the point of view of an age in which fact and folklore were always coming into collision. She must have seen him as a new recruit might, but with even greater awe, since all his brass had been designed through the centuries to impress trusting childish minds. This, in the last analysis, was the only reason for uniform and spit and polish. It was difficult to tell in a few words who General Goodwin was. I could not tell Camilla that he was a resultant of a disturbed political order or one of those people you had to maintain as an insurance against dangerous contingencies.

"He's a man who tells soldiers what to do," I said. "He has those stars on his shoulders so that anyone can tell that he's a general. Now Colonel Flax only has eagles because he isn't a general yet. The more important a general is, the more stars he has and the more of those ribbons over his pocket. Some poor generals only have one star. General Goodwin has two."

"How many stars can you get to have," Camilla asked, "if you get to know everything?"

I could see where her mind was moving. They must still have been giving out stars in school as rewards for scholastic attainment.

"They can get up as high as five stars," I said, "but hardly any of them do, Camilla, and when you get five stars, you can have them in a circle and not in a row."

"Will he get five stars?" Camilla asked.

"I don't think so," I said, "but don't tell him I said so, Camilla. That might hurt his feelings."

"Isn't he bright enough?" Camilla asked.

"I don't know," I said. "It's hard to tell."

I really did not know. I was already beginning to revise my early estimates of him. Automatic fire could not cover every inch of ground because of natural contours. The traverse of a machine gun only had a limited number of degrees, and General Goodwin's capacity also had its limits. There were blind spots in him, egregious gaps, but then I was becoming conscious of extraordinary areas of acumen.

"Is he anything like Samson?" Camilla asked.

"Who?" I asked.

"You know, like Samson in the Bible."

"Oh, Samson," I said. "Samson wasn't bright at all or he wouldn't have let Delilah cut his hair off. I don't think Samson would have been a two-star general."

Then I began to think that I might be wrong about Samson. High physical courage always had its blind spots, and even if you had five stars, perhaps there was always some Delilah in the background sharpening up the shears.

When I had returned to the library, I could tell from the General's voice that I had missed something.

"I was waiting until it was firing over there," the General said. "The damn thing couldn't be everywhere at once, and I had time to get up on my knees and . . . Oh, there you are, Sid. Did you have a nice walk with Camilla?"

"You made quite an impression on Camilla," I said.

"What's that song?" the General asked. " 'I love the ladies . . . and the ladies all love me'?"

I was a disturbing influence, and everyone looked impatient.

"How about it?" Phil said. "Did you throw in the grenade?"

"You're damned well right I did," the General said, "and it landed on the button, or I wouldn't be here now."

I had missed a good deal by taking time out. I had left Lieutenant Melville Goodwin in the shell hole in the woods at the PC of C Company, but I caught up with the story later when I read Miss Fineholt's notes.

XIX

His Neck Was Out a Mile

ARTILLERY fire, even under optimum conditions, had not developed the precision it attained in World War II and there were no conditions at all in the Château-Thierry salient, optimum or otherwise. It was no joke in those days to be out in front of American artillery. The artillery was firing short that night, though this was no one's fault particularly, since no one had located the front lines. Even though Melville Goodwin was in a so-called regular division, a lot of company officers had not yet learned how to determine their positions on a French one-to-twenty-thousand map, and there weren't enough maps anyway. In the pitch dark you could hear the shells crashing among the trees. The company command post was trying to get the regiment whose code name was "Banana One," but the line was dead. There were no bananas and he was told to stay where he was instead of trying to reach his platoon in the dark.

In the morning he first saw gray in the sky and then the treetops and then figures moving in the woods. The night seemed to rise up slowly like a curtain, on a scene of distorted confusions. No one could adequately describe the disorder of a battlefield with its litter of equipment and the senseless distribution of matériel. The captain of Company C had been killed on the previous afternoon and the commanding officer was a first lieutenant who spoke with a broad "A." There was not much chance to exchange any ideas with him because this officer ended up a few hours later by being dead himself. Melville Goodwin could only remember that he was not a regular, that his name was Johnson and that he was covered with mud, but even if he was not a regular, he might have been a good officer, because he was as much in touch with all his company as anyone could have been under the circumstances. The orders were to advance at dawn through the woods, and Melville Goodwin went forward to take the command of the Second Platoon from a sergeant. It was not the best way to begin with troops, walking in among them out of nowhere. In fact he did not reach his platoon until after the sergeant had blown his whistle and all he could do was to tell the sergeant to go ahead. Fortunately the sergeant was an old army man, thickset, in his late thirties, with a face like a side of beef. His name was Riley and Melville did not need to tell him anything.

"They've pulled out, sir," the sergeant said. "It's all clear just ahead."

There was nothing arduous in walking with the sergeant beneath the trees because there was not much underbrush to cope with in those French forests. The Frenchmen were always cutting brush for firewood, always saving everything. There was always a lot of griping about the French, and he had to admit they *were* a funny race — and unsanitary. For instance they all enjoyed collecting large heaps of manure right in their front yards, usually beside the well. It seemed the richer you were in France the bigger your manure heap, and he should know because he kept falling in manure heaps as the outfit fought its way up to the Vesle. Yet at the same time their farms were neater than any around Hallowell.

The country they advanced over that morning was not cut up by hedges like the land around St. Nazaire. It was hay and grain fields and pastures and orderly patches of woods on top of rolling hills. When the infantry pushed ahead, it was like a pleasant practice maneuver. Though a mist was rising from the valleys, the sun was breaking through the clouds and there were patches of blue sky — and his uniform was drying. The artillery fire was slackening, because the guns were moving forward. Everything was moving forward, and the Germans were pulling out of that salient so hastily that only light forces were engaged.

Of course no officer, least of all a lieutenant in the first wave, could get the whole picture of an operation. Yet some individuals were born with a tactical seventh sense. It was an indescribable gift — "the feel of battle" Melville Goodwin had called it in a paper he had once read before the War College. You had it or you did not have it. He could see nothing except the men of his platoon walking through the woods, but at the same time he could feel whole divisions moving — reserves, artillery and supply. Attack was in the air and attack was in his blood. The feel of battle was impersonal, inexorable.

His platoon was a machine and he was already beginning to examine it and to estimate its capabilities. The men were wet and their faces were drawn. They were tired but not too tired. They moved ahead cautiously but not nervously. They had left their heavy equipment but they carried gas masks, rifles, grenades and bayonets.

"Sergeant," he asked, "did the men have breakfast before they started?"

He thought that the sergeant gave him a peculiar look and he realized that "breakfast" sounded odd out there, though the word was quite correct.

"They had corned willy and hardtack, sir," the sergeant said.

They were better off than he was, but he no longer felt hungry.

"What about water?" he asked. "Are their canteens filled?"

The sergeant gave him another look. "We've about run out of drinking water," he said.

"Have they got chlorine tablets?"

"Yes, sir."

"Then have them fill their canteens the next place where there's a well or any running water, and see that each of them drops in about six tablets."

"Yes, sir," the sergeant said, peering into the woods ahead. He knew that the sergeant must have thought he was a little snot, but still it was a sensible order.

He saw that the trees were thinning and that they were reaching the edge of the woods. Everything was quiet, except for the rustling of branches and the snap of small twigs underfoot and the dripping from the trees and the distant artillery, until suddenly he heard machine guns on the right front and the crack of bullets passing close overhead. The sound, he always had thought, was like his mother's sewing machine — a mechanical staccato that frayed the nerves.

"Tell the men to lie down, Sergeant," he said.

Perhaps he should have given the order himself, but then the men had hardly seen him. They were approaching a line of resistance, but it was only a hasty improvisation by the enemy to afford a delay which would facilitate his retreat.

"Come with me, Sergeant," he said, and they crawled to the edge of the trees.

"Easy," he heard the sergeant whisper. "You gotta watch it, Lieutenant."

The sergeant did not need to tell him. He was crawling as he had been taught, wriggling and propelling himself with knees and elbows, taking advantage of the tall grass at the edge of the wood. A pretty pastoral scene lay before them, a broad open field of hay which had not yet been harvested but which was too short and trampled to afford cover. The ground ahead rose gradually to a low ridge crowned by another patch of woods. The whole scene was surprisingly peaceful, but still his breath was coming fast and his heart made a drumming sound in his ears, from excitement rather than fear. Frankly, he could never remember feeling fear in action. It was a thing that came before or afterwards rather than in the middle. Besides, his mind was concentrating on a simple problem. He was observing an almost classic defense position. It was a good two hundred yards across that field to the woods on the crest. When he looked to his right he saw why the gun there had revealed its position, because a handful of bodies lay sprawled in the open field. Then in his interest he raised his head too far — two inches higher and he would have been dead. Another machine gun had opened fire from the woods directly on his front. He lay flat with his face in the moist earth, but he had seen its flash near the trunk of a large oak tree and the fresh earth of the emplacement.

"It's right up there," he said.

"You ought to know, sir," the sergeant answered, and they crawled back to the platoon.

Just then a runner came with word that Lieutenant Johnson

wanted to see him. Even in this short interval everything had been moving up behind them until the woods were jammed with troops. Lieutenant Johnson was talking to a freckled, sandy-haired major who, Melville guessed, would be the battalion commander. Lieutenant Goodwin saluted smartly.

"Never mind that now," the major said. "Who's this officer, Lieutenant?"

"He just came up last night, sir," the lieutenant answered. "I can't remember his name."

"Well, a name helps," the major said, and he turned to Melville. "What is it?"

"It's Goodwin, sir."

"All right," the major said. "What have you stopped for, Mr. Goodwin, are you tired?"

Melville reported the situation quickly and concisely. He was even able to take a pencil and paper and sketch the position in the major's notebook.

"Very pretty," the major said. "Take me up there and show me the original. We can't wait here all day."

They were faced with the same old problem that cropped up in any battle, the balance of loss of life against the element of time. That light defense in front would be overrun eventually. The only question was how soon and at what cost. Obviously it was necessary to test the strength of the position before deciding whether or not to wait for heavy weapons. In a few minutes there must be an approach.

That defense could have been brushed aside in modern war with its profusion of supporting weapons always close at hand, but in World War I the machine gun was still an ace that was hard to beat. With a few well-placed automatic weapons, a handful of enemy specialists who were willing to die could delay a whole division and snarl up the timetable. When you came to think of it, you had to admire those German gunners, left alone to hold up the advance. It took guts and devotion to duty, and you might as well face it — Germans were born soldiers.

The plan was improvised right there in the woods. The attack was ordered along the regimental front and his platoon was in it. He had only time before the show started to find a haversack and fill it with four grenades, those stylized iron ones that looked like pineapples. He was to lead the platoon, of course, and he remembered that he was shaking — you often got involuntary shakes before a jump-off — but he was also conscious of a detached academic interest through the minutes of preparation. He had the sense to examine the contours of the slope ahead and to take note of a fold of ground about seventy-five yards in front that might afford some shelter. Beyond this he saw there was a depression, not a watercourse or even a gully, but still a depression that wound toward the tall oak on the hill. He could see the fresh earth of the gun emplacement on his front, and to the right he could see another. Haste had denied the Germans the refinements of concealment, and luckily neither of those guns supported the other perfectly — two facts which explained why he came through that attack alive.

He pointed out the fold of ground to the sergeant and also the depression beyond it. When he told the platoon to follow him, his voice had an unwelcome quaver. He had often dreamed, both asleep and awake, of leading a real attack, but now that he was in motion, the ground was not solid and he seemed to move with exasperating slowness. Then he found himself flat on his belly behind that bulge of ground with half the platoon there with him. German machine guns had rather narrow traverses and they could not fire everywhere at once, and the gunners had no time to pick up the whole weapon in order to fire at a wider angle. This explained why half the platoon reached the shelter.

As he lay there catching his breath, he saw that the whole advance had been checked halfway across the field. He could see the dead and wounded on the open ground and small pockets of the living pinned down by the fire. His platoon was out ahead and a glance at the woods behind him showed that the attack was not being pressed. His men lay in temporary safety, although bullets were gouging the crest in front of them. It might have been better judgment to have stayed pinned down instead of attempting to reach the depression winding up the hill. He was not thinking in the least of himself, but only of the minor tactical problem. If they could wriggle up that hollow toward the oak tree, they might knock out the gun with grenades. It would have been more correct if he had balanced the chances, and he might as well admit it now that they were fifty to one against him, but his whole mind was focused on a single desire to get up the hill. There were twenty yards of open space between the rise that sheltered them and the winding hollow.

"Follow me," he called. The Jerries did not quite catch him before he reached the hollow. Only the sergeant and a private went with him. He never could blame the others for staying where they were.

He would not try to describe that crawl up the hill. He could only admit that he was shot with luck and besides the nearer you got to an emplacement the harder it was to get you. When he reached the crest, he remembered rising to his knees with a grenade in his hand and pulling out the pin and seeing the newly dug earth and a German helmet. Then he threw the grenade and fell flat. He got up again directly after the explosion. He had hit the nest right on the button.

"Come on," he heard himself calling, "come on." He had another grenade ready in his hand as he ran through the trees to the emplacement on the right. Perhaps he was two minutes in reaching it. He had no way of checking the time, but he came on it suddenly from the rear. The gun was firing, and its noise must have prevented any of the crew from hearing him. As he crouched behind a tree before tossing the grenade, he had a glimpse of the gray backs of the gunners. The air was full of dirt and stones and the gun had stopped before he could throw another. The Germans who weren't dead were in a daze. There was one thing in particular he did not like to remember — a German officer smeared with blood, staggering toward him with his hands above his head and then the sight of Sergeant Riley running him through with a bayonet. He could still remember his amateurish wonder at the sergeant's struggles to pull the bayonet out. Then it seemed as though everyone had followed him, not just the sergeant and the private. The attack had carried through.

He grew accustomed to the sight of corpses later — since sudden death and mutilation were sequels to any action, and after all, war in itself was a grotesque abnormality — but this was his first day in a practical school. The mangled bodies of those Germans around their gun brought home to him, all in a rush, the enormity of what he had been through, and a spasm of nausea swept over him. He staggered weak-kneed to a tree, leaned against it and retched. Fortunately there was nothing much to come up as his stomach had been empty for many hours. Though later he had seen other good men succumb to this and to more humiliating forms of bodily weakness, he could never quite forgive himself. It was all well enough to explain that exertion and emotion had put an undue strain on him. It was a mortifying anticlimax to find himself puking in front of troops. He had a frantic wish to crawl away somewhere with his seizure but there was never any privacy at a time like that. All he could do was to lean against the tree, shaking with the spasm. At any rate that was how the regimental commander found him, and later he had to admit that it made a good story at his own expense.

H. J. Jeffers was commanding the regiment then. If you were interested in military bibliography, he was the same Jeffers who had written a useful book, *A Foot Soldier's Notes,* which had been used in army schools before the war. Later, after the armistice, when the colonel once alluded to their meeting, at brigade headquarters mess, Melville was glad that he was able to laugh about it.

He had been leaning against the tree only half conscious of what was being said or done around him when he heard a voice ask if this was the officer. Someone slapped him hard on the shoulder and told him to go on with what he was doing, that there was no hurry, and when he turned around, he saw that Colonel Jeffers, in a muddy trench coat, had been addressing him. Beside the colonel was a French officer in horizon blue, looking extraordinarily neat under the circumstances, and the major was also with them, and a few paces behind were some other officers. It was his good luck, of course, that the colonel and the Frenchman should have arrived at that particular time.

When he saluted, his diaphragm and intestines were still chasing each other inside him.

"I'm sorry, sir," he said.

"That's all right," the colonel said, "quite all right, Lieutenant. What did you say his name was, Major?"

"He told me but I've forgotten, sir," the major said. "He just came up last night . . . but it ought to be Frank Merriwell."

As soon as the colonel laughed, everyone else joined him hastily and the joke settled Melville's stomach. There was nothing like a joke at a time like that. Later it always reminded him of a line in *What Price Glory.*

"Who is it," the Frenchman asked slowly, "this Frank Merriwell?"

"He's an American folk hero," the major said.

"Oh la-la," the Frenchman said, and everybody laughed again. Nothing ever sounded right in French.

"Sergeant," the major called. "Where's the sergeant? Come here, Sergeant."

Melville found himself standing with the sergeant as though they were two schoolboys led out before the class, and of course the major was vicariously pleased.

"This is Sergeant Riley, sir," the major said, "Second Platoon, C Company. Tell the colonel what you told me, Sergeant."

The sergeant was an old-timer but he was also overwrought.

"No crapping, sir," the sergeant said, "the lieutenant got the both of them."

Then Melville found his voice.

"There was a private with us, too, sir," he said.

"Jackson, sir," the sergeant said. "He's dead."

The colonel pulled a notebook from his pocket. Melville remembered that he had to hold it almost at arm's length because of the farsightedness that comes with middle age.

"What's your name, Lieutenant?" the colonel asked.

"Goodwin, sir," he answered, "Melville A. Goodwin."

"What's your class at the Point?" He had noticed Melville's ring.

"Nineteen-nineteen, sir," Melville said, "but we graduated this year."

"Do you feel all right now?"

"Yes, sir," Melville said.

"Then walk along with us, Mr. Goodwin. We'd better catch up

with things. This is Captain Bouchet, and we don't want Captain Bouchet to tell his general that we're loafing around here."

There was a gentle undercurrent of appreciative merriment.

"It is a pleasure to meet the lieutenant," the Frenchman said.

There was no use trying to imitate his accent, but those French liaison officers were all smooth and hand-picked for the job of establishing cordial relations. It was only good luck that the captain was there, itching to pass out *Croix de guerres*. Melville never knew until later that he was getting the Distinguished Service Cross out of it, too. He was pretty hot that day; it was all good luck.

On the other hand, there weren't any colonels or Frenchmen around to see him when he led a patrol across the Vesle River and returned with sixteen German prisoners. No medal except a Purple Heart was passed out when he got his bayonet wound in the Bois des Rappes. Actually both those occasions had demanded more in the departments of skill and guts and leadership than that episode in the Château-Thierry salient. Further, he had seen a lot of others, both officers and enlisted men, who had done more than he ever had beyond the call of duty, without even getting a word of commendation. He was luckier than a great many others, and that was about all there was to say. From his experience many soldiers who did most said the least, and he had described that episode only to give a tactical picture.

His service in France had taught him that he was adequate according to certain standards, and from the very beginning he had loved the life. He had been right when he had followed that parade in Nashua. He loved marching columns and pup tents and foxholes, and he loved to serve with troops. He never forgot the lessons he had learned in World War I about team play and the soldier. He had learned how to speak the enlisted man's language, and he could speak it still. He learned to get the best out of troops simply by letting them know that he placed their physical comfort and safety above his own and making them learn that he would never order them to do anything he would not do himself. In many ways enlisted men were a lot of kids. He was never bored with fussing over their food and equipment. Any little thing you could do for them, such as talking over their home problems or their gripes, paid dividends. Right now he could still make a good estimate of soldiers because of his experience in France. They were in the end the raw material with which you had to work.

Everyone, of course, had his own theories about bravery, an abstract quality which he had heard discussed interminably during his years in the service. Bravery, he was sure, was not a constant attribute but one which changed from day to day under varying climates of leadership. In the final analysis, willingness to face death and to toss one's life into the scales in order to achieve a result depended on pride and conviction. There were two kinds of pride, one that emanated from position and responsibility, which training could develop, and the other, greater pride that had its roots in loyalty to the outfit. If your unit was a good team whose members believed in themselves and their leader, death became preferable to letting down the crowd. You could take your outfit anywhere, and you would even be reluctant to stay behind as long as you could put one foot in front of the other. In the end personal courage depended almost exclusively upon mass emotion. You could do anything if you had a good team, though in the beginning you had to sometimes show the boys the way.

There had been a lot of time to think while he lay in the hospital, and he had gathered enough ideas so that he was neither restless nor lonely. He had been indoctrinated with the theories of offense and defense, but he began to think seriously about weight of fire power. He never forgot the columns of cavalry he saw on the road from Château-Thierry, pathetically waiting for a chance for action that never came. He knew, without anyone's telling him, that cavalry was on the way out, in the face of automatic weapons; and he would never forget the thrill he experienced when he first saw a line of tanks clanking through a French village toward the front. They were ponderous vehicles and they did not have the power next day to get them where they should, but unlike a lot of young fellows around him, he never discounted the potential of the tank in a future war. The Germans knew it, by God, better than the British, who invented tanks. As General Forrest had so aptly said, the secret of war lay in gittin' thar fustest with the mostest. He was already thinking of combinations of fire power when he lay in the base hospital before he went to convalesce on the Riviera. Of course other men were also thinking, and abler men than he, in English and French and German — but the armistice was signed while he was on the Riviera, and an era was ended.

Lieutenant Goodwin was with the Army of Occupation for a while at Coblenz but he was detached and sent home as a casual officer from Brest in June 1919, and it was only later that it struck him that his experience in France had suffered certain limitations. Often in the years between the wars, when he heard officers discussing their leaves in Paris and the wine and the women and the sights of France, he was surprised at how little he could contribute to this sort of conversation. He had hardly looked at a cathedral or a French château except through field glasses. While others had enjoyed themselves, he had either been at the front or in base hospitals. He had never learned the difference between Burgundy and Vouvray. All his pay went home. Even when he was convalescing at that swell hotel in Cannes, he did not have the money to go on parties with the Red Cross girls and the nurses — and besides, there was always Muriel.

He still remembered clearly one illustrative incident. Late one afternoon in November, after the armistice, he had gone on a walk by himself through Cannes to exercise his leg, which was still stiff, though he no longer needed a cane. He was trying not to limp and though he looked somewhat shabby compared to the aviators, a French girl spoke to him, a pale, hungry-looking girl. She spoke loudly and slowly as the French sometimes did to a foreigner.

"*Vous êtes tres chic, mon lieutenant,*" she said.

He had to turn the words over painfully in his mind, and his answer was like a tough recitation at the Point.

"*Non,*" he said, "*je ne suis pas chic.*"

"*Le lieutenant est blessé,*" she said.

"*Oui,*" he said, "*je suis blessé.*"

"*Mais pas malade,*" she said.

"*Non,*" he said, "*bonne santé.*"

It was like walking in a labyrinth, trying to pick up the words, and he was pleased that he remembered the phrase for "good health."

"*Voulez-vous venir avec moi?*" she asked.

The implication of the question escaped him entirely because of his mental efforts at translation, so she patted his arm playfully.

"*Vous et moi,*" she said, and raised two fingers in front of him, "*ma chambre, cognac, pas loin d'ici.*"

He still did not know what it was all about until she spoke again more loudly.

"*L'amour,*" she said, "*couchez avec moi.*"

He never forgot his feeling of embarrassed confusion. In many ways it was worse than being under shellfire, and to make it still worse, there was the problem of answering in French.

"*Mais je ne veux pas, mademoiselle,*" he said.

It was funny as he looked back on it but it was not humorous at the time because he had sense enough to know that he was not handling the situation correctly.

"*La-la,*" she said, "*monsieur est serieux.*"

He liked to remember that she had been neither angry nor contemptuous. On the contrary, she was very nice about it and he never forgot what she said before she left him.

"It is a pity always to be serious when one is young."

Perhaps she had been right. Perhaps she had known more about life than he. Sometimes he wished that he had relaxed a little more in a civilian way when he was young. Perhaps he should have thought more of picture galleries and architecture. Perhaps he should have listened to music, but the only music he liked then was band music and the notes of the bugle at retreat.

He was glad that he was a part of the real army. The others who had swelled the ranks were like water in a sponge, which was being squeezed as hard and as fast as the management could arrange it. He returned to the States on an antiquated passenger ship filled exclusively with other unattached officers from every branch of the service, most of whom hoped to leave the service as soon as they got across, particularly the junior officers. The war was over and to hell with the army.

In many ways Melville Goodwin learned more about personnel from those ten days at sea than he had in the front lines. The ship was so crowded that only officers of field rank were in first-class quarters, and the juniors were in the steerage. He would stand on the forward deck in good weather and watch those higher officers on the promenade, while below in the steerage he was in a mass of totally undisciplined young college graduates from every state in the union, all of whom were fed to the teeth. He was the only West Pointer in that crowd, and he was shocked at the things those others said about the army.

There was a second lieutenant near him in the steerage, he remembered, whose name was John J. Weather — a graduate of Yale, who lived in Westbury, Long Island. This Weather had come aboard with a dozen bottles of cognac in his bedding roll. He had a gold cigarette case and gold-backed hair brushes, and he and his crowd were always playing poker. One night Melville remembered seeing seven hundred dollars in the pot — on a blanket in the steerage — and when he spoke to Weather about the size of that pot later, Weather was frankly amused.

"Listen, baby," Weather said, "where have you been all your life?"

It was an interesting question, because although they had talked for hours, neither of them could make his life exactly clear to the other. They had the same rank and that was all. Weather had not been in combat, but still he had called him "baby," and once Weather said that he ought to show him around.

"You ought to learn about things, baby," Weather said, but of course as soon as they reached New York he forgot about showing him around. Weather and all his crowd disappeared in a golden haze. Melville never saw any of them again, but he remembered some of their strange codes. When he refused to get drunk and disorderly with Weather and his crowd, they all understood when he explained that he had to stay in the army, but they could not understand why he wanted to stay.

"All you have to do," Weather said, "is to get out, and my old man will get you a job, baby."

He did not know who the old man was and he never knew. He

was only glad that he could not resign from the service, for he had a feeling that he was not equipped for that wild world outside. He remembered a single taste he had of it early on the morning that the ship steamed into New York Harbor.

That morning a major general, the senior officer on board, ordered the lieutenants to assemble on the bow and addressed them from the promenade deck. He had a fine resonant voice and he needed it.

"I have a word to say to you young officers," he shouted. "We are now coming into New York Harbor, and I know that you will all be anxious to see the Statue of Liberty."

As the General paused a faint chorus of catcalls arose from the crowded deck. The officers had not enjoyed the steerage, but even so, Melville could not believe his ears, and perhaps the General could not either because he went right on.

"You will all want to see the Statue of Liberty. This will mean that you will run simultaneously to the port side, and this may endanger the ship."

The young men around Melville Goodwin broke into a cheer, but the General's voice rose above it.

"So all of you will stay below," the General shouted, "until we're docked."

It was not a sound or well-considered order. Still it was an order, and the reaction was amazing. It was as though a lid had been lifted from all suppression. Hundreds of voices were shouting back to the promenade deck telling a two-star general of the army to go to hell and what he could do with the Statue of Liberty. It was an interesting example of a complete breakdown of command.

"That will do," the General shouted, "you are all under arrest."

The General must have known that he could not court-martial several hundred officers now that the war was over. If you could not back up an order it was better not to give it. You had to be careful not to stick your neck out in the army, and the General's neck was out a mile.

Major General Goodwin paused. Personally I was delighted by the anecdote and so was Philip Bentley. Both of us had identified ourselves completely with that crowd on board, and so had Miss Fine-holt, but Colonel Flax looked grave, and the General was not smiling.

"That must have been quite a scene," Phil Bentley said.

Melville Goodwin nodded slowly.

"Yes," the General said, "I suppose it's funny to civilians."

"Yes," I said, "it's pretty funny."

"I suppose it is," the General said. "I have never looked at it in quite that way. I have often tried to figure what I'd have done if I had been the senior officer on that ship."

"What would you have done?" Phil Bentley asked.

The General still looked very grave.

"Insubordination is not a joke," he said. "If I had been that officer I'd have got to know those kids personally in the first place. I'd have been down there in the steerage with them twice a day. Maybe I'd have played a little poker with them, I don't know, but there wouldn't have been that type of trouble." Suddenly the General smiled. "In a citizen army you've got to learn to compromise with civilians. We always try to do the best we can for you when you get into the army — but I wish there weren't so damn many of you!"

We all smiled dutifully.

Come to think of it, he said, there were a hell of a lot of civilians in New York. You wouldn't think there had been a war, in New York, and getting back was like landing on the moon.

"What did you do when you landed?" Philip Bentley asked.

"Why," the General said, "as soon as I could get to a telephone I called up Muriel, of course, and she said she'd come down to New York. I needed someone to lead me around who knew the ropes. I am still sort of confused alone in New York."

"What did you do after you telephoned?" Phil Bentley asked.

"After I telephoned," General Goodwin repeated, "I took a taxicab and went to the Waldorf and got a room and took a bath, and do you know what I did that night?"

"No," Phil Bentley said.

"Well, son," the General said, "I didn't do any of the things you might think I would. I strolled down to that shooting gallery on

Sixth Avenue and knocked off all the God-damned pipes. It made me think of Muriel."

The General rose from his armchair. It was late in the afternoon.

"Let's break this up," he said. "Come on, Flax, let's go for a walk."

Phil Bentley looked at me and took off his glasses and polished them. School had let out when the officers had left the library.

"Do you feel the way I do?" Phil Bentley asked.

"I wouldn't know," I told him. "How do you feel?"

"Exactly as though I were in the God-damned army," Phil Bentley said. "I wish he didn't confuse me. Sometimes he sounds like the Rover Boys in Camp. He can't be as simple as he sounds."

"I wouldn't say he was exactly a Rover Boy," I said. "He's a specialist."

"I know," Phil Bentley said, "and he's damn near perfect."

"How do you mean 'perfect'?" I asked.

"I suppose I mean the military mind," Phil Bentley said. "I wish I didn't anticipate every one of his reactions." Phil Bentley was still groping for something human or individual, and the General's life was not conducive to individuality. "I wish I could get it straight in my mind why in hell I should begin to like him."

Miss Fineholt closed her notebook.

"He's sort of cute," she said. "He's so clean-cut. It makes him sort of cute. I wish I had been there when he was shooting those pipes in New York."

XX

Just a Little Dutch Girl — with Her Finger in the Dike

HELEN was reading upstairs in our dressing room and when I came in she asked me how everything was going.

"Well," I said, "he's through World War I and he's back in New York."

"Oh dear," Helen said, "maybe they'll still be here when we're fighting World War III."

Helen's problem as a hostess seemed to me utterly unimportant. I was still thinking of the Horatio Alger success story I had been following — young Mel Goodwin, the hundred-per-cent American boy. The fresh-faced shavetail who had prematurely left West Point, young Goodwin at the front, knocking out those machine guns, the serious Goodwin at Cannes, recovering from his wound — all combined to make a juvenile hero; but there was something more. There was character behind those exploits, but then again was it character or simply a lack of imagination, or had he done these things simply because he was not familiar with other choices? No outsider could ever understand the drives of the armed services, any more than he could comprehend those of a dedicated monastic priest.

"Sid," Helen said, "just how long are they going to stay?"

Her question, of course, pulled me from my reverie.

"It can't be much longer," I said. "Phil Bentley will cut this short. The trouble is, he's interested. You can't help being interested."

"Oh dear," Helen said, "I hoped we could be alone over the week end."

"You won't have to bother about anything," I told her. "Mrs. Goodwin's leaving for Washington tomorrow. I'll take her into town myself, and you can leave the rest of them alone."

"You didn't tell me," Helen said. "Why do you have to go to town?"

I had forgotten. I had been so involved with Melville Goodwin that I had not told her of my telephone conversation with Dottie Peale.

"If I don't have lunch with her," I told Helen, "she'll drop out here at any minute. You know Dottie. We can't let Bentley see her with the General."

I did not mention my own concern about Gilbert Frary, because there was no immediate need to worry her.

"What do you suppose she really wants to do about him?" Helen asked.

This was something I could not possibly have answered.

"Well, anyway," she said, ". . . as long as she doesn't do anything about you."

Women were always competitive. There was no reason at all why Dottie Peale and Helen should have liked each other, but Helen had always been very nice about her. All through that time she was nice about Dottie Peale, and the General, and me, and everything, and it must have demanded a lot of self-control.

I was thinking next morning when Williams was putting Mrs. Goodwin's suitcase into the Cadillac, just before we left for New York, that the Goodwins had learned all the techniques of farewell. They had been saying good-by to each other through two wars and in the interim between, and they had learned how to do this officially before an audience — half playfully, half seriously.

"Good-by, Melly," Mrs. Goodwin said. "Now don't tell that Mr. Bentley anything you shouldn't, and call me up tonight."

Melville Goodwin smiled at Helen and then at Mrs. Goodwin.

"Don't you worry any," he said. "I'm only going to tell him how the CO caught us skin-swimming at Moultrie. I never told you about that one, did I, Sid?"

"Oh, Melly," Mrs. Goodwin said, "don't be so silly. Anyway it was almost dark."

300

"Well, good-by, Muriel," the General said, "and don't seduce any of the Joint Chiefs before I get down. Remember, they've got a lot of private rooms in the Pentagon."

"What about you?" Mrs. Goodwin said. "I don't know whether we ought to leave him alone here with Helen. Do you think we ought to, Sid?"

It was all good clean fun and it showed that the Goodwins felt at home. When Mrs. Goodwin kissed Helen, she said she had never thought we could all get to be such friends so soon, and she said we must come to visit them just as soon as they found out where they were going to be.

"You know, I can't wait," Mrs. Goodwin said when we started off together for the city, "for Mel and me to have a little place of our own somewhere after Mel retires. I can't wait to be settled somewhere instead of always moving from one post to another. Army houses are all alike, you know, even the furniture."

I told her that somehow I could not think of the General settled in a little house on retired pay and puttering about in a garden.

"But everybody does, you know," she said. "Almost as soon as you get started in the service you begin to make retirement plans. That's why I bought my Chinese things in Tientsin, as part of a sort of hope chest, and Melville bought a beautiful writing table once in Charleston, not that he ever writes much. Then there are all his books. It's about time they stayed in one place, even though books don't count against the freight allowance when you move — and I wish you could see the lace napkins we bought in the Philippines and the Meissen china Melville found in Germany."

Mrs. Goodwin was familiar with motor transport as well as with the art of making conversation. She took another washcloth from her handbag and began working on it. You never could tell, she said, what sort of car might be assigned to a general, and you would laugh, she said, about the way service wives went on about service cars. They were as watchful of quality in rolling stock as they were of their husbands' rank, but personally she made it a point never to bicker over transportation. There was enough bickering without this on an army post. The only time she ever complained was when by some mistake Melville was given an old Chevrolet and a major on the post was assigned a Buick. Melville had been a major himself then, but Melville had the seniority. Mrs. Goodwin's hook moved smoothly.

"It's so nice to be driving to New York," she said, "instead of taking a train, and you've been so generous, looking after Melville, Sid. I hope you don't mind my calling you Sid. I can't help thinking of you as one of the General's officers. I wish I could have been with you when the General was being interviewed. He seemed a little tired last night."

"I should think he would have been," I said.

"No one would notice it except me. I can always tell when he's tense, and he seemed worried about something last night."

"Worried?" I repeated.

Mrs. Goodwin glanced up. Though I looked carefully ahead at Williams's back, I could feel that she was watching me.

"Melville says you are going to have lunch today with a mutual friend, a Mrs. Peale. He wrote to me about her from France. She's a writer or a publisher or something, isn't she? She sounds very interesting."

"Yes, she's pretty interesting," I said. "We used to work on the same newspaper together once. That was before Dottie became a figure."

I could detect no change in her voice, no sharpness, no undue curiosity, but I could still feel that she was watching me and not her washcloth.

"It's queer how seldom Melville gets on, really gets on, with people outside the service," she said.

"I suppose it's because he leads a specialized sort of life," I answered. "Now personally I often find it hard to get on with people in the service."

For some reason she seemed astonished and her voice grew warmer, and at least we were off the subject of Dottie Peale.

"Why, you don't act that way at all," she said. "I always keep thinking you are in the service, and you get on so beautifully with Mel, but then of course you were an officer."

302

"Only by courtesy," I said, "but I did have to play around with the brass."

At least, I thought again, we were off the subject of Dottie Peale.

"I hate that expression 'brass,' " she said. "Sidney, don't you see we're really like everybody else?"

Of course I could not tell her that they were not like everybody else—they could not be or else they would not have been big brass.

"Back in World War I," I said—how small and antiquated that war had become, no longer the Great War, but simply World War I—"we were asking the General what he did when he landed in New York. He said he called you up in Hallowell."

She remembered all of it very clearly. We were going down the Merritt Parkway, but Mrs. Melville Goodwin was leaving Hallowell for New York to become an army wife, and, watching her expression, I could imagine how she must have looked. She must have looked both very competent and very pretty.

"I wish you could have seen Mel," she said. "Of course I had his photograph. I could shut my eyes any time and see the picture of him, but it wasn't the same as Mel. No matter how much you love someone, you begin to forget about him after he's been away for a long time. Finally he half turns into a stranger and you wonder what he'll really be like and how much he may have changed. Then there was all that fighting and the wound and all that talk you heard everywhere about Paris and girls in France . . . it would make anyone afraid and unsure.

"He looked taller to me, and of course all his class at the Point had been promoted to first lieutenants. He was in his overseas cap and his Sam Brown belt, and he had those ribbons and he had his hair cut short, just the way he wears it now. He looked a whole lot more like a soldier than anyone else in the Grand Central Station, but of course he had to, coming from the Point. As soon as I saw him I knew Mel was just the same. He always has been the same. We could always pick up things where we left them. He just said, 'Hi, Muriel,' and I said, 'Hi, Mel.' Then he told me we were going to have a month's leave and that then we were going to Fort Bailey. That was because of the medal. Everybody doesn't get to Bailey."

"Where's Bailey?" I asked.

"What?" she said. "Seriously, haven't you ever heard of Bailey? Why, whatever were you doing in the army, Sid?"

"Not much," I said.

"Well, that shows you weren't a line officer," she said. "Any line officer knows Bailey. It's where they used to have the small-arms school, out in Kansas."

That was where the Goodwins started housekeeping, down toward the end of officers' row, because they did not rank much else. Officers' row looked over the parade ground, and there was a flower bed of begonias in front of the colonel's quarters, then came the officers' club with a star of elephant ears and salvia, and then the barracks. It was scorching hot in summer and miles away from anywhere. You could hear the machine guns going every afternoon out on the range. Their quarters were in a double house with the Murphys next door — the "Slugger" Murphys. Slugger was in the class below Melville at the Point. He was the same Slugger Murphy I must have heard of in the Airborne. Lieutenant Colonel Crosby's wife had the rank because the post commandant was old Colonel Jones — "Jupiter" Jones, and he was a bachelor. Jupiter was his army nickname and I must have heard of him. Sometimes they called him "Arapaho" Jones because he had served in one of those last Indian wars when he was fresh out of the Point.

I had never heard of Fort Bailey or of Slugger Murphy or of Colonel Jupiter Jones, but I was at Bailey with Muriel Goodwin on the way to New York and the Pennsylvania Station. Robert, their elder son, had been born there at Bailey, and then somehow we were back in Hallowell and she might have been telling me about that Sunday school picnic and everything else.

I left her with a porter on the Pennsylvania side.

"Good-by, Sid, dear," she said, and though I was startled when she called me "dear," I felt that I had known her for a long, long time.

"Where to now, sir?" Williams asked me.

It was ten minutes before twelve but Dottie Peale had asked me to meet her at the office early. It was always a part of Dottie's stage

304

effect to show off that office of hers at Peale House. Anyone going there was bound to realize that Dottie should be taken seriously.

The Peale Publishing Company was what the book trade called "a fine old house" and sometimes "an old-line house." It published a sound backlog of textbooks and also a book called *Mrs. Gosling's Cookery,* which with occasional revisions had been a popular seller for fifty years — but the Peale money was only partially derived from this enterprise. It was a fine old house, but Henry Peale's grandfather had also been fortunate enough to invest his savings in Mr. Alexander Graham Bell's telephone and in Calumet and Hecla copper. Thus even by the time Henry Peale was seven years old there was no economic reason for the Peales to bother about printing books. Henry's father had been content to let the business limp along under the management of an unimaginative but conscientious executive named Mr. Royal, whom Dottie had never seen but whose name and career she had encountered when she had edited a brochure entitled *One Hundred Years of Peale House.* She was the one who had thought of calling it "Peale House," she told me once, shortly after she and Henry Peale were married.

Henry's father had never cared for books and authors. Instead he had collected pictures of the French school, and a part of the Peale collection was now in the Metropolitan, together with his portrait by Sargent. He had also been interested in yachting, and his forty-footer, the *Alexandra,* named after Henry's mother, had done very well in ocean racing. The house on Seventy-second Street, as well as the house in the country, which Dottie had sold, had once been filled with the *Alexandra's* silver trophies — mugs, cups and punch bowls, and, most spectacular of all, a two-foot figure of Neptune seated on a wave and blowing a conch horn — until Dottie had finally put them all away.

Henry Peale, on the other hand, must always have been what was called "literary." It had never been possible for me to reconstruct all the details of his early life, which had been led along the elaborate lines common to wealthy boys who lived out their early manhood around the turn of the century, and I am reasonably sure that Dottie

305

never understood much about Henry's background either. He had been a shy, retiring, serious-minded boy, educated by private tutors until he went to Yale. His career at Yale must have been quiet, too, and he was always quiet when I knew him. As Dottie often said, it was very hard for Henry ever to get out of himself, and you had to know him a long while before you appreciated him. Personally I had not known him as long as that, having only seen him occasionally after he and Dottie were married.

Though Henry Peale was in his fifties when he married Dottie, he looked much younger, and his face was unlined and youthful like the faces of other people who have led sheltered lives. In some ways, Dottie once told me, Henry had never grown up, but I had never asked her what those ways were. I only remembered him as being tall and rather frail, with a precise and gentle voice. I remember his laughing at Dottie's jokes, though I had the impression that he was not easily amused. He was very kind to me the few times I saw him, not on my account, I imagine, but because Dottie and I were old friends and because he was completely devoted to Dottie. He called her "Dot" I remember and once he told me that Dot had made him unimaginably happy and that he had never known there could be a girl like Dot. I did not understand how true this was until I learned more about his carefully insulated life. He never could have known that there was any girl like Dot except by the merest accident.

He offered me a job once because Dottie must have asked him to. When we talked it over in his library on Seventy-second Street, I gained the impression that I would not like to work for him, not because he was disagreeable or arrogant but because he had no fixed ideas. When I was with him I was always puzzled and uneasy, and always wondering why on earth he had ever married Dottie or rather how Dottie had ever arranged it, but I could see why he liked the family publishing business. It was a sort of ivory tower for him — a plaything with which he could do what he wanted without worrying over the financial angle — and books with the Peale imprint always had artistic distinction. His authors on the whole were devoted to him. He could afford to give them generous cash advances without a thought to manufacturing costs, and they must have loved dining with him at Seventy-second Street or spending week ends with him in the country. He had a reputation in the trade for sound editorial taste, though I imagine his assistant, Martin Dever, was the one who really picked the manuscripts — until Dottie finally took things over.

When he met Dottie Peale, I was in Paris, and the whole thing was an accomplished fact when I came back to New York on leave from the Bureau. Consequently I never knew exactly how it happened, and I was never sure that Dottie wished to be completely accurate when she explained.

"Darling," she said, "I want you to be glad. I want you to understand that Henry needs me and I love him, and I want you to realize that money and everything like that had nothing whatsoever to do with it. I was just as surprised as you are right this minute when I encountered Henry's background, and I want you to get this straight. He proposed to me before I ever saw Seventy-second Street. He proposed to me one afternoon at the office after lunch during Book Afternoon Week, and money had nothing whatsoever to do with it. I want you to know that I'm in love with Henry. Darling, I understand what love is now. It's having things done for you and doing things in return for someone you love. Henry needs me, darling, and besides you never did seriously think I'd sit around waiting, did you? We were all clear on that, weren't we, before you went to Paris?"

I told her that of course we were all clear on it and that everything was wonderful and that I was just as glad as she was.

"Besides," she said, "I told you that the Paris Bureau was the kiss of death, and now Henry and I can get you out of it."

I told her again never to mind about the Paris Bureau and that I thought everything was wonderful.

"And, darling," she said, "you mustn't have an inferiority complex about anything. It hurts Henry, and it hurts me, too, when people think that money means a different way of life. God damn it, darling, I'm just the same as I always was. I'm just a working girl in Henry's office, darling."

I told her again that I thought it was wonderful and then I asked her to tell me just how it happened, how she first met Henry Peale and a few things along that line, but she was always vague whenever I asked her.

"You needn't act so damned surprised," she said. "It happened because it was meant to happen. We were always congenial. You'll see why when you get to know Henry better. He's a little like you, darling, except he's more malleable and has more common sense."

I never did get to know Henry well enough to see in what way he resembled me, and I never knew what made them congenial except that Dottie wanted it to be that way, but I could see that she was happy and having a wonderful time. She was loyal, too, but then Dottie was always loyal.

Martin Dever, after certain disagreements had caused him to leave Peale House, was the one who told me most about Dottie and Henry Peale, though in a prejudiced way, since he never had been partial to Dottie. Actually he was the one who introduced them, he said, and he was damned if he knew much after that. It had happened after I had gone abroad, when Dottie was on the book page of the paper, working for old Waldo Edgill. She was immensely valuable to Edgill because she did have a marvelous dexterity and she was superb at make-up. She could read enough of any new book in an hour or two to get the sense of it, and besides she liked writers. She was the one who helped Edgill spruce up the whole Sunday book section, and when it was suggested that the paper sponsor a series of book-and-author afternoons, Dottie was all prepared. This had not been old Edgill's idea, but a brainstorm from the business office to increase publishers' advertising. Edgill had hated it, so it was lucky for him that Dottie was on the page, because Dottie was the one who finally organized those teas. It was the beginning of the era of book fairs and book-and-author luncheons, and never having been to any of these gatherings I cannot imagine what the teas were like, but Dottie did everything, right down to helping the publishers drag authors to them. That was how she met Martin Dever. Then one morning when she was in Martin's office, Henry Peale came in.

"That was all there was to it," Martin said. "He wanted to ask me about the design for a jacket, and Dottie said it ought to be plainer, and then he asked her into his office to look at alternate designs.

They stayed alone in there for about half an hour and then they went out to lunch, and the next morning he asked me for Dottie's telephone number, and next he asked her to the theater, and so they got married."

Martin did not know how it happened any more than I did. He could only say that directly after the honeymoon Dottie moved right in, taking over the office next to Henry's, and by God in a year she had taken over the whole damned editorial and production department. He did not want to criticize Dottie, because she was a friend of mine, but perhaps I knew what Dottie was like when she got started. He wouldn't say she was a bitch, because she was a friend of mine, and certainly she did not act like ordinary bitches. He could work for Peale — in fact he had run the whole editorial department for him and a good deal of everything else — but six months after Dottie showed up, there wasn't anything left for him to run. She had her finger in every pie. She was terribly sorry when he finally resigned. She begged him to stay and she felt his leaving was all her fault.

"Martin, darling," she had said, "you can't leave me all alone here with Henry. I'm just a little Dutch girl with my finger in the dike."

He had to admit she was nice about it, and she was the one who got him the job in Philadelphia, and she had not done too badly when she was left alone with Henry. In fact she was able to do more with Henry than he ever could. In fact she was a very smart cookie and some day she would take over the entire business. That was all that Martin could tell me. No one would ever know exactly how Dottie happened to marry Henry Peale, but I always did think that Dottie could do anything she wanted when she put her mind on it.

After Henry Peale's death, Dottie had moved the Peale House offices to a more modern building on Murray Hill, but she had not moved much of the accumulated *décor* with them. Dottie maintained that an office was a place in which you transacted business and not a place where you lounged and looked at antique furniture. After some of the offices I had seen lately, it was very agreeable to enter Peale House. The rooms were large, noiseproof and air-conditioned. The walls were painted in restful, unobtrusive tones. The equipment right down to the desk calendars was strictly functional and aggressively new. There were no comfortable libraries or directors' rooms, no couches or overstuffed chairs and, curiously enough, very few books. The volumes on the current season's list stood on three shelves in the reception office, but other publications by the Peale House press — Dottie had bought a printing and binding plant after Henry's death — were efficiently locked in a storeroom. Dottie's own office in a corner of the building was just as austere as that of the other executives, with a gray steel desk, a gray carpet, a bare oval table and six gray upholstered chairs. There was nothing on her desk except a clock, a calendar and a blotter. I could not help comparing the place very favorably with the offices of the home decoration magazine on which Helen had once worked.

There was no funny business about Dottie's secretary either. She was a plain girl with low heels and without any of the receptionist's manner, and she obviously had been told to show me right in, because she appeared about thirty seconds after I had given my name at the front desk. As I looked around, she might have been ushering me into a tooth extractor's instead of into the inner sanctum of Peale House. Dottie was dressed in a severe gray tailored suit, softened only by a ruffle at the neck, like a man's neckcloth in an eighteenth-century portrait. She wore no rings or bracelets — no diverting ornaments. She smiled at me brightly but she did not shake hands.

"It's awfully kind of you to pick me up here, Sid," she said. "You won't mind waiting a minute, will you, until I finish one piece of business? Sit down by the conference table. Miss Strode, will you please bring Mr. Skelton some cigarettes and an ash tray?" She gave me a winning smile. "We don't smoke at Peale House as a rule, but you can be an exception."

"Why, thanks a lot," I said.

"I won't keep you waiting more than a minute," Dottie said. "Miss Strode, will you tell Mr. Taylor I'm ready to see him now with that paper sample."

I knew that Dottie would not keep me more than a minute, if she said so, and I also knew that she had asked me there to impress me, out of habit and not because it was necessary.

"What are you laughing at?" she asked when Miss Strode closed the door.

"Nothing," I told her, "just hysteria."

"Darling," Dottie said, "don't be so damned funny. You can be funny at luncheon but not at Peale House."

It was really quite a show. Miss Strode returned with an ash tray, matches and a package of cigarettes, and behind her came a youngish man in a double-breasted suit carrying a sample of paper.

"Oh, Mr. Taylor," Dottie said, "you see what I mean, don't you, when you hold it to the light?"

"Yes, Mrs. Peale," Mr. Taylor said, "you were perfectly right about it, and Mr. Jennings has checked."

"Good," Dottie said. "Be sure to get Mr. Harris himself on the telephone. . . . Oh, have you ever met Mr. Sidney Skelton, Mr. Taylor?"

"Why, no," Mr. Taylor said, "but I've often enjoyed hearing him. How do you do, Mr. Skelton."

"You might call me up at home and tell me what Harris says," Dottie told him. "There isn't anything else, is there, Miss Strode?"

"No, Mrs. Peale," Miss Strode said. "I'll call you if anything comes up."

When Miss Strode closed the door behind her again, Dottie giggled suddenly, as though we were children.

"Darling," she said, "you must admit I make them snap into it. . . . We might as well be leaving now. Bernard and the car are waiting. Shall we have my Bernard take us uptown? Or shall we have your Williams? . . . What are you laughing at now?"

"You know damned well what I'm laughing at," I said.

She walked around the desk and put her arm through mine.

"No man can be a hero to his valet, Dot," I said.

"Darling," she told me, "I am really not preposterous. I don't know why I always like it when you think I am."

"Because I always have," I said. "It goes with the Chanel Five."

"Oh, Sid," she said, "I wonder why we never got married."

I looked at her and looked around the room.

"You know damned well why," I said.

"Yes," she said, "oh yes, I know, but we do get on so well together, don't we? We don't have to pretend anything. All the cards are on the table."

It was true that there never had been any make-believe, at least not for a long, long time. She walked toward the door and glanced at me over her shoulder.

"God," she said, "it's nice to see you, darling."

And I was glad to see Dottie, too. I had forgotten what good friends we were, and that there were no friends like old friends — with occasional reservations.

XXI

No Mothers to Guide Them

I HAD seen very little of Dottie since her marriage to Henry Peale and, except for that war trip overseas, very little of her after Henry Peale's death. When you stepped very suddenly from one category to another, you did not always have the capacity for bringing old friends with you. You no longer had the former common interests, or even the same kind of money. However, having found myself in ascending circumstances during the last two years, I could sympathize with Dottie's problems more than I had a year or so before. They were still more complex than mine, but now I, too, had been thrust unexpectedly into a style of life to which I was not accustomed.

It was preposterous to think of descending from my Cadillac, even if it was a company car, and walking with Dottie into the Peale residence and hearing Dottie say "Hello, Albert" to her butler. When the door closed behind us, I was thinking that we were in a larger, more complicated version of Savin Hill. We were both interlopers, not legally but spiritually. We were both intelligent enough not to make fools of ourselves, but still we did not belong. In the end we could only do the best we could, as other boys and girls do when they try to get ahead. Other poor girls had married wealthy husbands and other poor boys still came into the chips rapidly in some way or another. This, as they still said over the air, was America.

The house had been built in the early nineteen-hundreds along those pseudo-English, pseudo-baronial lines that were popular in the days when Robert W. Chambers wrote *The Danger Mark* and *The Fighting Chance,* and when the gay young blades quaffed champagne from the slippers of the girls of their choice and white doves were occasionally released at banquets at Delmonico's. The house had a frontage of at least thirty feet. The entrance hall was paved with marble. A dark oak double staircase swept upward. In one gloomy corner, near the door through which Albert the butler had retired with my hat and topcoat, was a suit of armor on a pedestal. I had never seen one of those things outside of a museum, except once, in an English country house during the war, but in the Peale house it looked moderately appropriate.

I had never made any comment on the house to Dottie because there had always been Henry Peale or company when I had been there before, but now I felt impelled to whistle softly in a slightly vulgar way.

"All right," Dottie said, "all right. What about that little shack of yours in Connecticut?"

"It isn't quite the same," I said.

"No," Dottie said, "it isn't but it's the same in principle. Darling, I can't help it. There's an income from a special trust fund running it."

"Don't apologize," I said, "don't exhibit social guilt."

"Oh shut up," Dottie said. "We might as well take the elevator up to my study. I don't believe you've ever seen it, have you? I did over the top floor after Henry died. I spend most of my time there when I'm not entertaining."

Of course there was an elevator, one of those automatic lifts with a row of electric buttons. When the door closed, she looked up at me.

"Sid," she said, "do you remember?"

"Yes," I answered, and I remembered that I had kissed her in that elevator when I had first dined there during the time I had been recalled for a month from the Paris Bureau.

"Sid," she said, "I really think just to be polite . . ." and she turned her cheek toward me. "Darling, I'm awfully glad to see you."

I had not seen Dottie's study. Nothing else in the house had ever looked like her, but the study did. Everything was in its place and there was a place for everything. The rear windows opened on a little terrace with a row of potted fir trees along its railing. The curtains were yellow brocade, and there were Chinese carpets and a sofa in front of the fireplace and a desk with her typewriter and sharpened pencils and all her favorite books along the walls — and two very good Renoirs. She had always liked Renoir because, as she said, Renoir's people were always having such a happy time.

"Sid," she asked me, "does it remind you of anything? I mean the fireplace and the sofa and the books and the typewriter."

"You mean your place in the Village?" I asked her.

"Don't you think it's like it?" she said. "Do you remember how you used to wait for me when I changed before we went out somewhere?"

I could see what she meant. Her general taste had not changed, and it was a little like her two-room apartment in the Village only vastly larger.

"Well," she said, "pour yourself a drink — everything's over there on the table — and sit down. My room's in front and I'm going to put on another dress, but I'll leave the door open."

It was a little like her old apartment in the Village and I also thought of the suite at the Ritz in Paris when I heard Dottie whistling in her bedroom.

"Darling," Dottie called, "are you all right?"

"Yes," I said, "I'm fine" and then she went on whistling.

"Maybe you'd better take sherry," she called, "we're going to have champagne at lunch," and then I heard her swear.

"What is it?" I called back.

It was only a run in her God-damned stocking but she would be finished in a minute. It was almost like old times, almost but not quite.

I never thought until I heard her whistling, what a difficult time she must have had at first being Mrs. Henry Peale. I had only thought before how well she had succeeded. She had told me once that Henry's family and friends had been very kind to her on the whole — as people were when obliged to make the best of an accomplished fact. They had never thought that Henry would marry, at least not so suddenly, but now that they saw her they said they could understand why he had, and they were so glad that Henry was happy, and now that Dottie was making Henry so happy, perhaps she could be on some of the family's charitable committees. Well, as she told me once, she was still on some of those committees. Nevertheless she had to face the fact that she had always felt gauche with Henry's family and friends and that basically she was shy. She simply did not fit. Yet on the whole she had succeeded with them. She had accomplished this through the book business, which was a world in itself, what with publishers and authors, and then there were her theater friends. The Peale family finally had liked to be asked to her Sunday supper parties, now that she knew everyone or almost everyone. Dottie had always been quite a girl.

I sat there waiting, under the illusion that I was younger and still working on the paper, and that there were no broadcasts and no Helen or Camilla, which I am sure was the effect that Dottie desired. It was as if everything we had gone through were still in the future when she came back into the room. She was wearing a purple dress and a gold bracelet and a topaz pin. She did not look at all as though she were nearly forty. The blatantly unobtrusive cut of the dress indicated that it had been made for her and that it had probably cost about three hundred dollars. She sat down on the sofa beside me with that prim sort of schoolgirl posture that I remembered from the days on the paper. For a moment, though of course it did not last, we were a boy and girl together, at the end of a working day, and I thought of the song "What street compares with Mott Street in July?" even though it was late October.

"Darling," she said, "it's just like old times, isn't it? Snap out of it and get me some sherry."

Of course I knew Dottie well enough to know that she was consciously setting this scene of old friendship and of enduring congeniality because she wanted something from me. It would not be anything tangible, I knew, since she had everything in that line she desired. It would be something more in the nature of affirmation, of sympathy and support. Though I could begin to make guesses already, it was entertaining and instructive to watch her create the setting. She did it so well, in fact, that occasionally I honestly believed that she simply wanted to see me, and this may have been partially true.

She had always understood men better than women. When she

316

wanted, she was like a dancer who could follow any lead, conforming without the least apparent effort to any taste or intellect. I had forgotten how utterly entrancing she could be if she wanted or how much she knew about things that interested me. She knew the broadcasting world a good deal better than I did, and she had some very good anecdotes about Soviet diplomats and domestic politics. I was reasonably sure that she did not listen to my broadcast every evening, but she gave the impression of having followed it consistently. She knew Art Hertz, and she felt just as I did about Art — that it was wise to talk things over with him carefully before he started on the script — and she knew Gilbert Frary, and she could imitate him perfectly. She even knew that new phrase of his, "without the slightest ambiguity," and then she used one of her own which I had not heard before.

"I wish you wouldn't keep saying it's only your voice," she said. "I always knew you could get somewhere if you ever wanted to. You're better than all the rest of them, because you have more developed mental capacity."

That was quite a phrase, developed mental capacity, something you could take or leave. She laughed when I told her it didn't mean anything at all.

"Darling," she said, "you still don't know much about women, do you? You don't know how happy a woman is to be wrong, really wrong, if someone she's fond of proves she's wrong. I'm so happy that I was wrong about you, Sid. It makes me respect you so much, and there are so few people I can respect. It used to make me furious when I thought you were wasting your time, but everything you did was subconsciously right, and here you are. That's what I mean by developed mental capacity."

She sat on the sofa with her feet curled under her and shook her head and smiled at me wistfully.

"I know I missed the boat," she said, "but still it makes me feel proud. I'm a little envious, too, when I see you and Helen together, but not in a mean way, darling. I keep wanting to help you still. You know how I used to try, and God, you were exasperating. Sid, I wish you'd admit something."

317

"I'll admit that you've always wanted to help some man," I said, "but then most women do."

"Darling," she said, "that's perfectly true, and the awful thing about it all is that I've never been able to help anybody except perhaps poor Henry. I wish you'd just admit that I could have done a lot for you. Please admit it, Sid."

She looked at me in her most appealing schoolgirl way. She had her chronology somewhat mixed but not entirely. She seemed to have forgotten how long she had been married to Henry Peale, and I might have reminded her that after Henry's death she had not tried in the least to help me. Instead, she dropped me like a hot potato. I was a failure without a future in those days.

"Why, yes," I said, "of course you could have helped me, Dot."

"Thank God you admit something sometime," she said. "Sid, it's queer, isn't it, that nothing changes when we see each other?"

Being with her had always been like a game, but now I could watch her playing it, unemotionally, as though I were an observer at a conference. I knew that she had manipulated our conversation exactly as she had wanted. She had talked about me, and herself and me, and now we were going to talk about her.

"Now just a minute, Dot," I said, "before I forget to ask you. Didn't you say over the telephone that you were worried about Gilbert Frary and me, or something along those lines?"

Dottie assumed an expression that was partly cryptic and partly amused.

"Oh dear," she said, "I wouldn't have dreamed of saying that if I had thought you were going to mull over it. Did it really bother you, darling?"

"Not much," I said, "but you probably wanted it to, didn't you?"

Dottie's cryptic expression changed and she looked delighted.

"Of course I wanted you to be worried," she said, "because I wanted to be sure you'd come to see me. There really wasn't anything else, but it is interesting if you feel a little uncertain about Gilbert."

"Are you sure that's all?" I asked.

"Well, darling," she said, "you know how I'm able to sense things

318

and how interested I always will be in you. When I think of you and Gilbert, I sometimes get intuitively worried, but I haven't really heard anything at all in any whispering gallery, and now that I've talked to you about the program, I know everything's in order, and I'm so glad. Let's forget it."

I was relieved that I had been right—that she had nothing to tell me that I didn't know.

"All right, he does disturb me sometimes," I said—"but let's forget it."

"Still if anything ever should come up—anything like a break with Gilbert—you'll promise to come right to me, won't you, darling?" Dottie said. "You know how dreadfully happy I'd be to help in any little way. Darling, I wish I didn't feel so unfulfilled. It's a most terrible feeling. I suppose I'm spoiled. I suppose I've always got everything I've wanted."

There was a discreet knock on the study door.

"Oh, hell," she said, "there's Albert with our lunch."

"That's tough," I said, "just when you were getting somewhere after all this build-up."

"Oh, what's the use," Dottie said, "in trying to be fascinating with you? I wish to God you didn't know so much about me. Anyway, it's going to be a damned good lunch, and we're going to have champagne."

"Then we'll pick it up where you left off," I said. "We'll just remember, you're feeling unfulfilled."

Dottie glanced at me and shrugged her shoulders.

"All right," she said. "Just remember you couldn't have ever fulfilled me. If you want to wash, you can use my bathroom in there. Come in, Albert."

Obviously Dottie preferred having her meals in her study, and I did not blame her after what I remembered of the dining room downstairs. Albert the butler and a maid came in, pushing tables on wheels like room service in a hotel, and they knew exactly how to turn one end of the room into a little dining alcove. Albert opened the champagne and took the tops off the lacquer soup bowls, and then Dottie told stories about the State Department until Albert asked if there were anything more and went away. It was a simple luncheon but it was very good — clear soup and squab and mixed green salad and Camembert cheese and coffee.

"I hope it's what you wanted," Dottie said. "I know you don't like much in the middle of the day. If you're finished, let's take the champagne over to the sofa. Do you remember the first time we ever drank champagne?"

"Yes," I said.

"I remember how it tickled my nose," Dottie said. "It made me awfully silly," and she giggled.

"No it didn't," I said. "Nothing ever made you silly." Suddenly I felt impatient. "Come on, Dot," I said, "let's get down to what you want to talk about. Why don't you tell me why you wanted to see me?"

Dottie put down her champagne glass on the coffee table and sat up straighter.

"Now, Sid," she said, "that isn't fair. You know I always love to see you, and we see so little of each other, but . . . well, all right. . . . Tell me about Mel Goodwin, Sid. Has he asked about me?"

"I told you he had," I said. "Why shouldn't he?"

"Oh, all right," Dottie said, "tell me some more about him. Tell me how he looks."

"He looks about the way he did in Paris," I said, "but you've seen his pictures in the papers, haven't you?"

"I mean does he look well?" Dottie said. "Does he look happy?"

"Didn't he look happy in the pictures?" I asked her.

Dottie shook her head impatiently.

"Darling," she said, "I know exactly what you're thinking and I know you don't approve, but it's none of your business, is it, really? I wish you wouldn't act like a buffer state and pretend you're so damn conventional. You know you can't stop my doing anything I want and at the same time you're the only one I can talk to about this. Darling, I really have to talk to someone. Why is it you don't approve of my seeing Mel Goodwin?"

We were getting down to plain facts at last, and I always liked Dottie when she was facing facts.

320

"Because I think it might upset him unnecessarily," I said. "I know it's none of my business, Dot, except I rather like him."

Dottie pushed a strand of hair back from her forehead.

"Pour me some champagne, will you, Sid?" she said. "That's right. Thank you, darling. . . . That's what I wanted to know. I wasn't sure. . . . I'm awfully glad he still feels that way about me."

"Oh, my God," I said.

Dottie smiled and took a swallow of her champagne.

"Why don't you pull up your socks, darling?" she said. "Your attitude really makes me a little annoyed. I wish you'd think about me just a little, Sid. Look at me. Can't you — a little?"

We both looked at each other for a moment without speaking.

"Listen, Dot," I said, "what else have I been doing?"

"Really, Sid," Dottie said, "you haven't really thought about me for years. If you had you'd know how little I really have in my life. I don't mean materially. To hell with material things! I'm pretty sick of materialism."

"Since when did you begin getting sick?" I asked.

"All right," Dottie said, "be nasty if you want to, but at least you might try to think of me. I know you're fond of me — don't say you aren't. Damn it, I was thinking of you the other night and I ended up by taking a Nembutal."

"Now wait a minute," I said, "don't get me mixed up with Mel Goodwin."

"Don't be so pleased with your own humor," Dottie said. "I wasn't thinking of you in that way. I was only thinking you have everything I've always wanted. You're married, you have a home and children."

"A child," I said, "not children."

"All right," she said, "a child, and you don't deserve to have one. You don't know what it means."

"Well," I said, "if I don't, you don't either. Since when did you start liking children, Dot?"

Suddenly Dottie began to cry. It was something I had not expected, and I was quite sure that she had not expected it either.

321

"Oh, Sid," she said, "can't you see I haven't anything? Damn it, I haven't even got you."

I would have laughed if she had not been crying. It was exactly like her not to have wanted something when she could have had it and then to end by regretting that she had not wanted it. It was like the ending of a rather badly written story to be there with Dottie Peale and to have her sobbing on my shoulder.

"Oh, God," she said, "oh, God," and for once I knew she was not using the name of the Lord in vain. I could not think of anything consoling to say and I patted her softly on the back.

"Oh, God," she said again, "I'm so sick of always thinking about myself."

"Dot," I told her, "everybody has to most of the time."

It was curious. She was tired of thinking about herself, and yet this was exactly what she continued doing as she lay against my shoulder weeping.

I found myself recalling a poem of Hilaire Belloc's in his *Cautionary Tales* — the one about the mischievous little girl who kept calling the firemen for fun, and finally, when she was actually being consumed by flames and shouted "fire," they only answered "little liar." On the other hand, her saying that she had nothing left, not even me, though personally annoying, had a ring of complete veracity, and I was glad that my reaction was close to complacency. I wished Helen could see how well I was behaving under the circumstances.

Dottie was not wholly responsible for what had happened to her. She was the finished product of a new age of competitive women and of a feministic epoch. There were no precedents and no rules in this new competitive arena, where bright girls were taught to invade all sorts of fields of endeavor that were once reserved for men. There had been Becky Sharpes at the time of William Makepeace Thackeray, but they had been creatures of convention, and there were no conventions now. The town was full of Dottie Peales, and female institutions of learning were turning out more of them annually, and the feminine periodicals were telling them what to wear in the way of girdles and nylons, even down to what scents they should select to bring them victory. The town was full of Dottie Peales, and there was no reason for them not to have been confused in their values because they had to get along as best they could and they had no mothers to guide them — or at least the guidance of their mothers was very seldom useful. I hoped she did not know that I was sorry for her in such a detached way, but of course she did know.

"Stop pounding my back," she said. "I'm not asking you to be sorry for me. I'm only asking you to be kind."

"Now, Dottie," I said, "how can I be kind unless I'm sorry?"

"Oh, nuts!" Dottie said, and she blew her nose. "Stop sitting here humiliating me."

"I don't see how I'm humiliating you, Dot," I said.

"You'd never say that," she answered, "if you had ever understood me at all. If you'd ever understood me in the least, you wouldn't put me in this position."

"I haven't put you in any position, Dot," I said.

"Oh, yes you have," she answered, "you've put me in the position of making me deliberately humiliate myself, and I can't stand it, Sid."

It was difficult to follow her logic, but when I was with Dottie, I was accustomed to having things end up by being my fault.

"All right," I said, and I could not help laughing.

"Stop it," Dottie said. "God damn it, stop it," and then she looked at me and blew her nose again. "Well, what's so funny about it?"

"I just remembered something," I told her.

"What?" she asked me.

"Well, it was quite a while ago," I said, "but I remember that you told me once it was all my fault you married Henry Peale."

"Well, it was," she said.

I could not help laughing again.

"Darling," she said, "I wouldn't take this from anybody else. Can't you think of me at all, Sid? Can't you see that I'm unhappy?"

"Yes," I said, "but then you've never been the contented type."

Her mood had changed and she smiled at me just as though she had not been crying.

"Darling," she said, "it isn't asking very much, is it, to talk to me

323

for a few minutes about Mel Goodwin without acting as though I were contagious or something? There isn't any reason for you to assume this protective attitude about him."

There was no reason at all, and yet I did have this attitude.

"Listen, Dot," I said, "why not face it? You're not going to help that poor guy at all by being interested in him."

"That's pretty condescending of you, calling him a poor guy," Dottie said.

"Well, he is when he gets in the ring with you," I told her. "He just isn't in your class, Dot."

"Why, darling," Dottie said, "that's the nicest thing you've said to me all day, not that I understand just what you mean by it" — but of course she understood, and we both sat there for a while thinking in our different ways about General Melville Goodwin.

"Why don't you admit," I asked her, "that you had forgotten all about him until he became a figure in the news? Why not be frank about it?"

Dottie sighed, and shrugged her shoulders again.

"Well, I remember him now," she said, "and maybe I'm just as much of an authority on him as you are. Come to think of it, I ought to be. Oh, Sidney, let's not be so silly with each other. After all, we're adult."

This was a timeworn word in certain circles. By being adult she meant that one could be freed from the trammels of convention and face facts fearlessly and now she was facing them in her own way.

"Darling," she went on, "I want to try to make someone else in this world happy. That's one of the rules of life, isn't it? . . . And I could do a lot for Mel Goodwin."

"His wife wants to make him happy, too," I said. "At least she has a few ideas. Why don't you try to put your mind on someone else. There are a lot of other men."

Dottie lighted a cigarette and blew a cloud of smoke toward the ceiling.

"He isn't happy with her," she said, "in the way he ought to be happy with someone, Sid. She's always managing him. He told me so in Paris, darling."

324

I could imagine without undue effort what Melville Goodwin must have told her in Paris, and I did not answer.

"Aren't you going to say anything?" she asked.

"Yes," I said, "and you know exactly what I'm going to say. For two days now I've been listening to him telling the story of his life. He's in a different category from you and me, Dottie. He doesn't know what is going to happen to him professionally. He's restless just like you, and that's about all that you and he would have in common. He's never had the chance to see people like you, Dottie, and he's a very nice guy basically. You can't help him. All you can do is upset him. The only way you can help him is to leave him alone."

I did not know that I was going to be so eloquent, or that I would feel so strongly, but what I had said couldn't have been more maladroit, because I had only aroused her interest.

"Can't you think of anything to call him but a 'poor guy' and a 'nice guy'?" Dottie asked. "But as long as you can't expand your vocabulary, don't you think that I'm a nice guy, too?"

"You know what I think of you," I told her. "No. You've never been a nice guy."

"Well," Dottie said, "for my money you've always been a bastard yourself, and you're getting to be more of one all the time."

"Maybe that's why we've always been reasonably congenial," I said. "We've lived in a tough world, Dot. We've never been to the Point. We've never won the *Croix de guerre*. We've never needed to develop a superiority complex, and we haven't been in any chain of command. Dottie . . . aren't you going to leave Goodwin alone?"

Dottie threw her cigarette into the fireplace.

"No," she said. "Aren't you going to talk to me about him?"

"No," I said, and I stood up. "I'd better be going now. I've got to get back to the country."

"Oh, darling," Dottie said, "when you're angry, you're like a hero in a juvenile, and I ought to know, because we're printing a lot of them."

"I wouldn't know," I said, and I thought of Melville Goodwin reading the *Old Glory* series in the Hallowell library.

"Darling," Dottie said, "I never said I didn't like boys in books.

Please don't go away. Can't you and Helen bring Mel Goodwin around to dinner?"

"No," I said. "When he's through with us, he has to go to Washington."

"Well, he can drop in here on his way, can't he?" Dottie said. "I'm going to call him up right now. What's your number in the country, darling?"

"I don't remember," I said.

"God, you're a chump," Dottie said. "You act as though I were going to give him a disease, and I know your number anyway." She walked over to her desk and picked up the telephone and smiled at me while she waited for the operator. "I want to make a person-to-person call," she began, "to Major General Melville A. Goodwin. . . ."

There was nothing I could do about it, nothing I could say.

"At least don't mention your name," I said. "Good-by, Dot."

"At least he's a man," Dottie said. "Darling, Helen has improved you a lot. Come here and kiss me good-by."

"No," I said, "not with the operator listening."

"Darling," Dottie said, "you can't go yet. You don't know how to run that elevator."

It was true that I was not mechanically minded, but I could try.

"Just keep your mind on Mel and forget about me," I said; and while I pressed the elevator button, I could hear her speaking in her gayest, sweetest tone.

"Mel," I heard her saying, "Sid's here and we've been talking about you all through lunch. Aren't you getting pretty tired of it out there with Sid? When are you coming here to see me and tell me how you won the war. . . ?"

I had not known what button to push, but at least the car started downward. Actually I had pressed the wrong one, and when the doors opened automatically, I found myself on the floor above the hall with the massive dark oak staircase almost in front of me. I had a glimpse of the Peale parlor with its carved Italian tables, and its gigantic pieces of tapestry-covered furniture, and also of the gold motif of the music room, and the dark splendor of the dining room with its wall of heavily framed Fragonard school pictures. My footsteps made no sound on the Oriental runners. I might have been in the enchanted castle of an old Gothic romance or even Ulysses in Circe's palace. I wanted to get out of there and Dottie must have rung some sort of bell, because the butler was standing at the foot of the staircase with my hat and coat.

"I got off on the wrong floor," I said.

"That's all right, sir," Albert answered. "I can turn on the lights if you would care to glance at the pictures."

"Thanks," I said, "some other time. I'm in a hurry now."

I wanted to get out of there. I was glad to be back in the clear sunlight of the October afternoon, and even Williams and the studio Cadillac seemed like very old friends.

"We'll go home now, Williams," I said.

I told him not to mind the robe, but still he wrapped it around my knees because, as he said, the air was sharper in the afternoon. He was not my chauffeur, strictly speaking, but at least he was not Dottie Peale's chauffeur. Williams was an excellent driver, and I felt entirely secure speeding along the West Side highway well ahead of the rush hour. Nevertheless I was thinking of a Grant Wood picture I had seen once when Helen had taken me to an uptown gallery — a picture of a car and a truck moving swiftly toward inevitable collision on a winding road, and I thought of the impending doom of Melville Goodwin. All the years of training and conditioning that had formed Melville Goodwin had taught him how to throw the Silver Leaf Armored into combat but not how to cope with Dottie Peale. Her problems had become grotesque, and I was safe from them and there was no longer the old reality to her tears or piety or wit, but I was deeply worried about what she could do to anyone like a Regular Army general who understood troops. I had never thought until then of Mel Goodwin as a classically tragic figure whom the fates were conspiring to destroy. I thought of him in the garden just before Camilla had asked me suddenly about Samson and Delilah. He was one of those Samsons ready and waiting for some Delilah to give him a haircut, and Dottie Peale was just the one to do it. Melville A. Goodwin was going to get his hair cut, and

.327

medals and stars and clusters would not help him. He had killed his lion and had carried away his own gates of Gaza, but he was going to get his hair cut. There would be no light or heavy weapons to help him now that Dottie wanted to do something for him. The Philistines would be upon him and he would not even know that the Philistines were there.

When I reached Savin Hill, they were still at it in the library. The General was still talking to Phil Bentley, and Miss Fineholt was at the desk with her notebooks, and Colonel Flax was listening.

"Hello, Sid," the General said. "It's a funny thing, isn't it, that Sid can bring himself to go away and see pretty widows in New York when they've been taking pictures of me all afternoon."

"I thought it was about time to call in the photographers, Sid," Phil Bentley said. "We're getting this thing pretty well cleaned up. We ought to be through by tomorrow."

Melville Goodwin shook his head impatiently.

"I don't know why we should have taken up all last evening and this morning with this stuff between two wars."

"It's very interesting to me," Phil Bentley answered. "Nobody ever knows anything about army officers in peacetime. They all go underground."

"Listen, son," General Goodwin said, "we have our work and our wives and kids and problems, just like everybody else. How about it, Flax?"

"That's right, sir," Colonel Flax answered. "The General is absolutely right. I hope you'll remember to make that point in the profile, Mr. Bentley. Damn it, service people are just like other people."

XXII

Brave Days on Officers' Row

GENERAL officers were not what you would call public characters in the sense that Hollywood stars, ball players, pugilists, district attorneys, channel swimmers or nominees for the Presidency were — unless there was a war. Then they appeared unheralded out of nowhere, and suddenly parents, sisters, sweethearts and even the GIs themselves wanted to be reassured about them. They wanted to be told that generals had been fun-loving, mischievous boys, who had led a good honest American life, and to know that they loved jokes, children, dogs and football and had a few good healthy hobbies. Granted that they were military geniuses, it was important to know that they had the common touch. In Public Relations you could get their records from the files but these were not enough. You could see your man through the Point and perhaps you could find someone who could tell a funny story about him when he was a plebe. You could trace his career in some subordinate capacity in World War I, but after World War I his trail vanished into such a maze of technical notations that it finally disappeared from view. There were no large-scale maneuvers or big parades under peacetime appropriations to keep the army in the public eye. The army was simply scattered all over its real estate in almost identical barracks.

Melville Goodwin could not list offhand the places he had seen or the sequence of his duties. He had served in Hawaii, the Philippines, China and Panama. He could remember the temples and the blue robes of the Chinese in Tsingtao, but none of this mattered greatly in retrospect. It might be true that if you joined the army you saw something of the world, and you learned, naturally, about sanitation and the care of troops in the tropics and about insect pests and dysentery, but most of the time you were concerned with a way of life. Most of the time you simply saw the army. The army was a closed corporation, and you had to learn its amenities and how to get on with difficult superiors and how not to stick your neck out. The officers corps, Melville Goodwin said, was largely personality, and as time went on you either got the hang of it or you didn't. He had heard it said by outsiders that army men gossiped like old women when they got together, always telling stories about Mike So-and-so or remembering something about Hank Somebody-else, but this was not all done to pass the time away. At any time there might be new orders and you might be thrown in with Hank and Mike; and then you might be very glad to know what they and their wives were like and whether or not they enjoyed playing Ping-pong and what they thought of a little Saturday's drinking. Muriel, as time went on, kept notes about army people, and these were very useful, though personally he had never kept a note, finding that he could rely on his memory. You could name almost anyone right now who had served as an officer in the peacetime army, and Melville Goodwin could give you a word sketch of him. No matter how dull the duty was, there was usually someone you could discuss Clausewitz with, or some new idea, confidentially, without sticking your neck out.

Then, too, there was nothing more solid than an army family. The boys had been a heavy expense at times, even with free doctoring, but he would not have missed having them for anything, and neither would Muriel. He could remember Robert in his play pen at Bailey waiting on the square of lawn in front of the veranda. Charley had come along later when they were out in Oregon just before they went to the Canal. He could remember Charley in his pen, too, on another square of lawn in front of another veranda. It was always great to get back to the quarters and see Muriel and the kids, especially after someone had been chewing on you. Also there were horses to ride and the tennis courts and the golf links and the Saturday nights at the club. It was not a bad life, the peacetime army, if you did not stick your neck out. A lot of it ran together now in his memory, but there was one thing you never forgot, and that was your first post. It was the beginning of your life more than any war, and he and Muriel started together at Bailey.

They were just kids and they had hardly been anywhere together and it was Muriel's idea that they should save on their travel allowance by going West on day coaches. The way you handled the various allowances that came to you over and above your base pay made a lot of difference in your living, and Muriel right from the start had a knack for squeezing out the last penny. In fact he often told Muriel that she knew more about finance than anyone in the Finance Department.

It was late afternoon when they got off the train at Bedeville. They hitched a ride on an army truck to Bailey, Muriel in front with the driver while he sat out in the dust with a quartermaster sergeant who answered his questions about the post. They jolted along the road for about half an hour across miles of uninhabited prairie before they saw the reservation. He had to hand it to Muriel that she was not discouraged by being so many miles from anywhere, but nothing, when he came to think of it, ever discouraged Muriel. At headquarters there was a mixup because they had not heard that he was a married officer, and the news made all the difference. When the colonel saw Muriel, he immediately asked them to supper. By the time they were moved into half a house at the junior end of officers' row, they were almost part of the family, and Mrs. "Silver" Crosby, the lieutenant colonel's wife, showed them around herself and called Muriel "my dear" and said they must have a long talk about everything in the morning. Colonel Jones — Jupiter Jones — the post commander, who attended to the housekeeping but who did not conduct the school, was a bachelor just reaching the retirement age and he looked every year of it. Yet when he saw Muriel, he told her that he would have been married long ago if he had ever seen a girl like her.

"Oh, Melville," Muriel said when they were alone that night, "it's like a story, isn't it? And I just love Colonel Jones. He was so happy after dinner."

Melville, too, had observed that Colonel Jones was happier after dinner than before. He had been suffering from a cough before dinner and had excused himself several times to gargle his throat, and each time he returned, his cough had subsided and he was happier.

331

The truth was that Colonel Jones was something of a problem, and the word was that everyone should cover up for the Old Man. You couldn't help but love him when he began to talk about Indians and the old army. Kansas was a dry state, and the nation was going dry along with it, but there were still the patent medicines. You should have seen the Old Man's cases of Old Home Elixir and other bracing medicines.

"Young man," he told Melville once, "the Civil War would have ended a year earlier if General Grant had known about Old Home."

He was always fond of Muriel. In fact when Muriel was having Robert, he would sometimes call on her himself with a bottle of Old Home.

Characters like old Jupiter Jones amounted to little in one's professional career, but you always came upon Joneses here and there, and it was useful to know how to handle them. There was one time, he remembered, when Colonel Jones began firing his automatic from his second-floor window because he believed that Arapaho Indians were skulking about the house. Melville was the one who got there first.

"Sir," he said, "please give that gun to me quick, there's an Indian attacking Muriel."

"Take it, boy," the colonel said. "I'll handle the rest of them barehanded."

Stories like that would last for years. People in the service would hear some story about you even before they knew you, and Melville could tell a lot of good Jupiter Jones stories.

Some of his oldest and dearest friends were among the younger officers who were on the post at Bailey with him. It was his good fortune, too, that he had been able to meet and converse with some of the ablest Infantry officers in the army who came there to the school. He could name them all now if he had to, but then what did names mean? He might, however, mention A. C. Grimshaw, and even civilians ought to remember Grimshaw's name in World War II. He came to the school for two weeks once to deliver a series of lectures. They called him "Foghorn" Grimshaw because he spoke in a low, deferential voice.

332

"Of course there may be a possibility that I'm wrong," he used to say, but by God, Grimshaw was never wrong.

Melville met him first over a chess game at the club, and he took one game off Grimshaw, too, which may have been why Foghorn took a liking to him. It was possibly due to knowing Grimshaw at Bailey as much as to his record in the War College that Melville got a staff job under "Tweaker" Beardsley in the middle thirties. It may have been a word from Grimshaw, too, as much as his record, that finally got Mel Goodwin into tanks and to North Africa.

There had been quite a ripple of excitement when Foghorn Grimshaw had appeared at the school. The word had gone around that both "Black Jack" Pershing and Peyton March had said publicly that Grimshaw had one of the finest tactical and organizational brains in the service. He had been one of the youngest regimental commanders in the AEF, serving with the Ivy Division and then with Corps and finally at GHQ. There was nothing he had not read and nothing he could not do. He could even paint pictures. Put him anywhere, even in a soap factory, and he would have been running it in the end. When Mel Goodwin took a game off him at chess and played another to a draw, he did not realize at all what this might mean to him until he happened to be standing outside his quarters one day after retreat. Melville had just bathed and changed into fresh khaki and had gone out to look over the square of lawn that was drying up, when Major Grimshaw rode by on horseback with an orderly. The school horse he was riding was a scrubby animal named Soby, with a cast-iron mouth and a bad habit of dancing sideways, but even Soby looked stylish with Grimshaw on him.

"Why, hello, Goodwin," he said. "Is this where you're living?"

"Yes, sir," Melville said.

"Have you a chessboard handy?"

Melville was very lucky. He had bought a pegged-in chess set when he was in Cannes and he had it in the house.

"It looks cool on that veranda," the major said. "How about a game if you've the time?"

It would have been conspicuous and out of line to have invited anyone like Grimshaw to his quarters, but it was different now that the major was inviting himself.

"Take my horse back to the stables please, Murphy," the major said, "and thank you for a very pleasant ride."

He never forgot an enlisted man's name, and when he spoke to enlisted personnel, you were never conscious of rank. Muriel was out on the veranda as soon as they were up the steps, and Melville was proud that she did not look surprised or flustered.

"I've just made some lemonade," she said, and then a while later, after they had finished a game, Muriel asked if Major Grimshaw would not like to stay to supper. They weren't going to have anything but cold chicken and salad and iced tea, but then perhaps it was too hot to eat much.

Right from the beginning Muriel was pretty good at things like that. He would not have dreamed of asking the major himself, and he nearly dropped through the floor when Muriel spoke of chicken, but Muriel had run out in back and had borrowed it from the Cromleys, and Muriel had also borrowed cigars. She had heard Mrs. Silver Crosby say that Major Grimshaw liked them, and she had run all the way up the row to borrow some from Mrs. Silver Crosby. She had also borrowed after-dinner coffee cups from the Buddingtons and had asked Colonel Jones if she could pick a few of his begonias.

During supper they began talking about the war, and Major Grimshaw apologized once, saying he was afraid the talk might be boring to Muriel, but Muriel said she had to learn about those things, being an officer's wife, and Melville simply would never tell her about them.

"Melville knocked out two German machine gun nests," Muriel said. "He threw pineapples into them — isn't that what you call them, dear?"

"Now, Muriel," Melville said.

"That's just like Melville, Major Grimshaw," Muriel went on. "He never wants to talk about himself. Melly, dear, aren't you going to smoke your cigar?"

He had only smoked one once, near Hill 302 in the Argonne. Still, he could not very well pretend he did not like cigars when Muriel put him in that position.

"It was north of Château-Thierry, sir," he said, "near a little town named Cerey, and Muriel shouldn't have brought it up."

"I've been through Cerey," the major said.

"Now, Melly," Muriel said, "don't change the subject."

He had to go on and tell about it after that, and as he did, he grew interested in the tactical problem and then the major began talking about tanks.

"I wish we had a sandbox here," the major said.

"Melly," Muriel said, "get a baking pan and get some sand from the Crosby baby's sand pile."

It turned out to be quite an evening when they mixed a little water in the sand. There were some things that were chores, such as paper work and language and administration, but he always did have an instinctive enthusiasm for terrain. He began to forget who Grimshaw was as they moved from one subject to another, and he began criticizing things more freely than he should have. For instance, he did not believe that horses could go anywhere that motor vehicles couldn't — if you had the right kind of vehicle. When Major Grimshaw left, it was almost midnight, and Melville did not realize how much he had been sounding off until the major looked at his wrist watch. Then he imagined Foghorn Grimshaw's telling how he had spent an evening listening to a cocky kid lecturing on logistics and fire power. Muriel was the one who had started him off and after the major had left he told her it was pretty flat-footed. It did no good to have her say that the major enjoyed the evening or he would not have stayed so long.

"You made me sound like a divisional commander," he said, "right in front of Grimshaw."

They were standing alone in that tiny living room filled with all the furniture that no one else on the post wanted — because of course they were kids and almost anyone could rank them out of anything.

"But, Melly dear," Muriel said, there at Bailey at midnight, "you're going to be a general *someday*."

The funny thing about it was that Muriel had hardly seen a general then, except at his graduation from the Point. It was a year later before she met one personally. Old "Blinders" Blake stopped in to inspect the school and there had been a review, of course, and the customary show on the range, and afterwards one of those receptions at the club. Come to think of it, Muriel had been pretty pregnant then. Wives on a post were always nervous about generals, just as though they might exercise seignoral rights, but Blinders Blake had not looked up to this sort of thing. He looked pretty sprung at the knees at that reception. Melville had worn his ribbons because Muriel had sent him home to get them. She was delighted when Blinders Blake had noticed his DSC.

"Where did you get that, son?" he had asked.

"Just outside of Cerey, sir," he had answered.

"And is this your wife, son?" the General asked. "It's nice to know we're going to have another soldier soon."

Things like that always got around. When "Tinhorn" Harry, who was the doctor then at the post hospital, gave Mel the news, he said that General Blake had called the number right. It was a boy. Muriel had told all the girls about the ribbons and about his trying to skip off to the reception without them. She had been right, Blinders Blake had noticed them, because generals were always checking up on medals, and it made a good story.

In fact General Newhouse, when Mel served down at the Canal Zone, had actually heard the story.

"Where did you get that, son?" he said to Melville. "I'm quoting General Blake."

It only went to show how word could get around.

It may have been dull in peacetime, but there were a lot of good minds and good men in the service. They were the framework around which the armies of World War II were built. They invented the system of instruction that finally turned out divisions like cars on a production line. All those army schools paid off in the end when everybody, even privates in the rear rank, had to become teachers handling raw material. Yet it took guts to stay with the army in the twenties, when there was no sign of another war. Out in Honolulu perhaps there was a certain reality to the war games, because there

336

was a possibility that the Japs might land there someday. The only trouble was that the navy would handle the Japs. The navy was always throwing its weight around, ready and willing to handle anything, particularly out in Honolulu — but then he was not going to criticize the navy, although he did know some pretty good stories about it.

Sometimes he wished that army wives were not always watching and worrying about their men, but then there was nothing else much for them to worry about. Their futures were inseparable from their men's futures, and they only had one horse to put their money on. When things went sour, you could not blame a lot of them for wishing they had married someone else. Maybe Muriel wished she had sometimes, but she very seldom showed it. Of course he could feel that she was watching him, but Muriel very seldom pushed him and needled him. She never showed the bitterness or competitive spirit of many other army wives. On the contrary, she was a good sport and she was popular. She was always helpful and sympathetic, and as time went on she was always kind to younger wives. There was never anyone like Muriel for speaking the army language and saying the right thing.

When he got promotions she never looked complacent like some of the other wives and when he got passed over for something good, she did not complain. She backed him up the one time that he disobeyed an order and came close to a court-martial. It happened at the Fort Jellison Demolition School when there had been a problem of blowing up a bridge. A Captain Burdock was the instructor, and Melville had commanded the detail that had placed the explosives. When the thing had not gone off, Burdock had ordered him to remove the charge immediately, and he had refused, because of post regulations, to risk the men. He had ended up under arrest in quarters. He still remembered Muriel's face when he told her why he had come home early, and he could only tell her that he was right according to the book. The charge should have been left for two hours before it was touched.

"Where's the book with it in it?" Muriel asked. "I guess I'd better go out and see somebody."

337

It was one of the few times they had seriously quarreled. He had told her that this was his problem and not hers — but he never forgot that she was right behind him.

"Well, anyway, you've still got me, Mel," she said.

Actually the charge blew up half an hour later and half an hour after that he was called to the post headquarters office.

"Now wait," Muriel said. "Before you go, take a shower and put on a clean uniform."

The captain was in the CO's office and the door was not even closed, so that everyone heard Captain Burdock get his orders to apologize and everyone heard Burdock do it. Muriel was the one who fixed it up later by asking the Burdocks to come in to supper. It was not his fault or Muriel's that everyone at Jellison called the captain "Delayed-action" Burdock after that. He was always called "Delayed-action" Burdock, and Muriel still sent a card to them every Christmas.

Melville Goodwin could go on endlessly with his stories once he was in the mood. He seemed to tell them for much the same purpose that a chain smoker smokes cigarettes, for their soothing effect on the nerves rather than for any individual point or moral, and most of them seemed to me to illustrate nothing except a certain mediocrity and a snail-like advance upward on the service list — a list which was governed entirely by seniority until 1935. The General kept saying that he hated nothing more than blowhard officers who pulled wires and who sucked up to their superior officers at headquarters, but you could have a glimpse of Muriel Goodwin through the General's verbiage, dusting him and brushing him and showing off his right points to the right people by skillful indirection. Yet obviously his own abilities and virtues were the factors in getting him where he was. No woman could push a chump up to two stars.

I remembered what she had once said — that she never worried about Melville when he was with troops, and I could think of her as breathing a sigh of relief and putting her mind on the children and the house when Melville was out somewhere on field maneuvers. Also, I had heard some of his contemporaries vaguely and guardedly

338

imply that the farther he was removed from basic realities, the less effective he became, but he possessed great reserves of clearheadedness, resilience and mental durability. Furthermore, he was fearless, not only intellectually but physically, in an unimaginative, unhysterical and dedicated way. This arose from what I had always thought about him — that he was essentially annoyingly simple.

Melville Goodwin was never happier in his life, he said, than when he was assigned to command a company in the Philippines in Colonel Curly Whittell's regiment — Curly was subsequently relieved after a visit from the Inspector General's office and ended his career at a G–2 desk in Washington. Before he was assigned to the Philippines, Melville had been attending a lot of schools. It was good, after all this theorizing, to get down to basic fact, and no matter what anyone said, Infantry was fact. All the special branches and the bright boys in them, the Artillery, the Signal Corps, the Tanks and Aviation, had no other basic purpose than to push ahead the Infantry, and you had better not forget it. He always resented the snooty attitude specialists took about Infantry.

One night at the club at Baguio, when he was up there in the hills for a week's leave to see Muriel and the boys, he got into quite an argument with his classmate, Phil Mitch — who was commanding a field artillery battery — and some flying officer who had something to do with a pursuit group on Nichols Field. This might not have happened if Muriel had been there, but Muriel had a low fever and had told him to go ahead to the Saturday night dance. Someone in a corner had been singing that one about caissons rolling along, and Phil had asked Melville why he hadn't chosen a *real* branch of the service instead of the Infantry. Their voices must have risen because quite a crowd began gathering around them, including some higher officers. Melville said plenty about Infantry and he quoted Henderson's *Stonewall Jackson* to prove it, just the way dogmatic ministers quote the Bible. Phil had said he sounded as backward as the late William Jennings Bryan and the monkey trial, and he had told Phil to keep the conversation away from monkeys, that they were talking about Infantry. He must have said more than he intended and perhaps he stuck his neck out because Lieutenant Colonel Dowel—that would be old "Gypsy" Dowel, who was infantry himself, but on a four-year tour as Inspector General—kept handing him drinks and saying he was a fundamentalist himself and thank God there were a few fundamentalists left in the army, and Melville had said thank God there were, sir, that sometimes he thought the army was drifting away from fundamentals; and some of the officers below field rank had said go ahead and give it to him, "Fundamental" Goodwin.

At any rate, he must have stuck his neck out all right because Muriel, who felt well enough by Monday to go out to a ladies' bridge luncheon, came back and said she had heard that he had been very noisy at the club and that maybe it would be just as well if he did not have such a chip on his shoulder about Infantry. Nevertheless he had been absolutely right, and he told Muriel then that she might as well face it, she had married someone who was going to be in the front lines if there was going to be another war, and never to mind the rank. He overheard her saying the next night that Mel was an eccentric, but as a matter of fact she was as proud as he was of that company. It was like owning something at last to have a company.

An Infantry company, when you came to think of it, was the sharp edge of all war weapons and the individual enlisted man was the the primary unit. You could not be a successful company commander or a successful anything in the field if you could not put yourself in the shoes of the average American soldier. No enlisted man in his right senses ever expected an officer to be his pal, but if you could get the confidence of your people, you could do anything with them. Even the worst of them wanted to be the snappiest soldiers in the best outfit in the service, and they would rupture themselves trying to be if they felt they had a chance.

Company A, when he took it over, was not bad, but its personnel were slowed up and were trying to cut corners. The food and the drill were mediocre and so were the uniforms. The first thing he did when he took command, even before he talked to the officers, was to interview the top sergeant, because the morale of the company and everything else was in the hands of the top kick. The top sergeant of A Company was a sullen-looking man named Politz, who had already served three hitches and who knew all about gold-bricking.

"Now, sergeant," he said, "I want to be frank with you. I'm ambitious and I want to get ahead, because I have a wife and two kids, and I'm going to make this the best God-damned company in the army. I want you to help me do it."

He could tell from Politz's expression that he had seen officers come and go, so he decided he had to make it stick, especially as he was still a first lieutenant, though a company CO.

"You think I'm handing you the old line of goods, don't you, Politz?" he said. "All right, I'll have to show you. I'll back you up if you'll back me, and if you don't, I'll bust you. First off, I want you to be the best-looking top sergeant in the regiment and so you've got to do something about your breeches and your blouse. Report here at two this afternoon, and I'll take you to the post tailor myself."

He could see that Politz did not like it and neither did the mess sergeant when he got after the cooks, but he really turned that company inside out and in the end it could do close order and extended order like a drill team. They were all a team from top to bottom, including the junior officers, one of whom, "Long John" Gooch, he asked for, later, as his chief of staff in the Silver Leaf.

Day and night he was out there. He would go over every man from head to toe, as though they were kids getting dressed up for a birthday party, and by God you should have seen his men at guard mount. Maybe Politz and some of them thought he would quiet down, but he didn't. There was always wife trouble and girl trouble and drinking trouble in the company, and he was always ready after retreat to listen to troubles personally. No matter what engagements Muriel had made for him, she had to break them on the nights of the regimental boxing matches, and it was the same with the company ball team. When the men began to spend their own money at the post tailor's so that they could have their breeches and blouses like Goodwin's, he knew that everything was in hand, and Muriel got the spirit of it and began doing things about the noncoms' wives.

341

When the word got around that Goodwin would go right down the line for anyone in A Company, he knew that he was getting where he wanted. He could always figure logistics in terms of live troops. They were never abstract figures but men with a certain limit of endurance. He could reach decisions by looking at the faces of troops. He had learned this from Company A.

He often explained such problems to Muriel when they were together in the evening, and it was amusing to hear Muriel quote him, as she did sometimes at routine official dinners. You certainly learned about social life in the army, starting right as a shavetail, because of all those calls and courtesies and functions. You learned how to enter a room without tipping things over and how to pull out chairs and handle teacups and how to carry on a meaningless, harmless conversation with the lady on your right or left. It might be dull, but by God you learned. If incidentally you learned too much about somebody's wife flirting with somebody else, you also knew when not to speak about it. Most officers might have started as small-town boys who had never seen a formal dinner table, but you knew your way around by the time you got to field rank, and no one could laugh at the army.

There was nothing that made him more pleased and proud than hearing from other people what a really top-drawer girl Muriel was. Formidable women in the higher echelons who had marched with their husbands from the Point up to the big house on the post and who ought to know, and frightened clumsy little lieutenants' wives who didn't know anything, all kept drawing him aside at dances and functions to tell him how much they liked Muriel. She knew all the stories and the jokes and the special type of flattery that made the big brass feel good, and yet she could also turn right around and make all the young kids just entering the service feel right at home. It made him very proud that Muriel had so much faith in him, though when they began to get a little rank and he overheard small snatches of what Muriel was saying about him to the big brass, he would sometimes be impelled to laugh and say that Muriel overestimated the situation; but at the same time, Muriel never went out of her way to tell anyone that he was an unappreciated wonder, as a lot of other wives did while building up their husbands. In fact she would always start by running him down a little. She would say, for instance, that she was afraid sometimes that Melville was turning into a martinet . . . sometimes she really wished that the boss would put him on the carpet and tell him to relax. She sometimes thought that man of hers, as she occasionally called him, was such a perfectionist that people under him would resent it. Yet back there in the Philippines the men in that company of his had really adored him, though she was sure she did not know why, and when he got orders to return to the States, Sergeant Politz and a little enlisted men's committee came calling at the house, bringing a silver cigarette box . . . it almost made her cry. . . . The box was presented to *her,* of course, to get around army regulations. . . . Melville was just as hard on his own two sons as he was on troops. She was sure she didn't know why his sons were always following him around and always calling for Daddy when they went to bed — except that he could tell them nice stories.

For instance there was the story of Corporal Hoskins and his dog. Melville was surprised when he heard Muriel telling this one to Colonel Frye at a formal dinner, because Muriel always disliked dogs and would not have one of them around the house. Somehow enlisted men always would go for dogs and monkeys and things like that. Every once in a while you'd have to have an open season on pets, or you'd find you'd be running a zoo. That mutt of Corporal Hoskins's was one of those queer mutts you saw running around the rice paddy villages in the Philippines with sores all over him, but Hoskins had cleaned him up. The mutt's name was Bolo, and Melville put up with Bolo because Hoskins was a good noncom, until one day at a battalion parade, when the company was passing in review and he had just given the command "Eyes right," he happened to see Bolo right behind the adjutant keeping time to the music. The battalion commander put him on the carpet afterwards, in a nice way — but on the carpet.

"I love you, Goodwin," Major Grundy said, "but I don't love your dog, and the colonel was right there, and the colonel doesn't love him either."

"Neither do I, sir," Melville said. "He isn't mine. I didn't know he was there, sir."

"Well," the major said, "maybe he thinks the adjutant's a hydrant."

"He didn't commit a nuisance on his post, did he, sir?" Melville asked.

It was all good fun and there was always apt to be kid and dog trouble around a parade when the band began to play, but still, he had taken a bawling out and when he got back to the company office, he put Hoskins and Bolo on the carpet.

"Hoskins," he said, "by tomorrow morning I want to see that pooch out of here."

"Sir," Hoskins said, "if the lieutenant would watch what he can do, the lieutenant might go easy on him."

"What can he do?" Melville asked.

"He can do it on his hind legs, sir," Hoskins said.

"Do what on his hind legs?" Melville asked.

"The drill, sir," Hoskins said.

It was the damnedest thing. That mutt could stand on his hind legs and do a rightabout, left face and right face and walk around the room, forward, to the rear march, and eyes right, all by the numbers. Something had to be done about genius, and eventually he took Bolo and Hoskins up to the major, who took them all to the colonel's. The colonel was giving a little dinner that night, and after dinner Bolo did his drill. After that Bolo entertained at a lot of parties, but he never did appear again at a formation.

If Muriel's ideas about him did not always coincide with what Melville knew about himself, they certainly were always favorable, and they always made him happy, and she certainly seemed to know better than he did how to get on the right side of individual superiors. To give just one example, when Lieutenant Colonel Witherell from the general staff came to Hawaii for the winter maneuvers, Muriel found out somehow that Witherell had a special weakness for the Civil War battle of Chancellorsville and that Witherell was particularly fond of everything that had happened on the Orange Plank Road. She had told Melville this several days before Witherell

344

dined with them at Kahala and she had urged him to study up in his Henderson for two evenings on Chancellorsville. Then Muriel had simply said in a most casual way that she did wish that Melville could think of something besides the Civil War. Any time those navy people next door wanted a bridge game — and it was fun to see Melville make money off the navy — why he would always excuse himself and sit under the lamp with one of those Civil War books. That was all that Muriel needed to say. Witherell came around a lot after that. She also told Witherell one of those Philippine Company A stories, the one about his playing parcheesi with Robert after his supper.

"Mummy," Robert had said, "Daddy doesn't try when he's playing parcheesi. He keeps counting out one, two, three, four, five, halt. He's thinking about A Company."

He could not remember Robert's ever having said anything like that, but it made a pretty good story.

Muriel kept after his bridge game, and then she went to work on his golf. That paid off pretty well when they were stationed around Washington, but by then Muriel had found out somehow that fishing and generals seemed to go together. When he finally got his majority, he could play good poker and bridge, not to mention chess. If he was not a good dancer, he was adequate. He could play fair golf and he could cast a fly and he always had been excellent at skeet.

"You really have the makings of a good field officer now," Muriel told him, "and don't say I haven't worked on it."

Of course this was partially a joke but not altogether. There was a lot to the army in peacetime besides routine duty and professional qualifications, and Muriel had recognized this much more clearly than he ever had. Some officers were good dancers and some were fine piano players and singers, but accomplishments like these, Muriel used to say, weren't sound, and Muriel may have been right. There was Sewell Beebe, for instance, five years after Melville's time at the Point. When Melville Goodwin was serving at Schofield on Tweaker Beardsley's staff, everybody wanted "Soo" around because he could play the ukulele and he had a fine baritone. Yet seriously,

345

Beebe was also a fine officer with brains and ambition. It surprised Melville, when a staff job was open, to find Tweaker Beardsley turning Beebe down. Though Melville hated politics, he had been serving under General Beardsley for about a year when Soo's name came up, and he felt that he was enough of a member of the family to stick his neck out for a friend.

"Soo's a good officer, sir," he said. "He wouldn't fit so badly in Operations."

Tweaker Beardsley took a cigar out of his left-hand desk drawer and chewed the end of it for a while.

"Give me a light, will you, Mel?" he said.

Melville was ready, because Muriel had seen to it that he always carried a pocket lighter when he went to work for the Old Man.

"He looks all right on his record," the Old Man said, "and maybe he is, except that he sings."

If Melville had wanted to stick his neck out a few inches further, he might have reminded the Old Man that he always sent his aide for Beebe and his uke when there were dinner guests at the big house.

"I don't mind music personally," the Old Man said. "Mrs. Beardsley always carries around a lot of red seal records and she chews on me if I break one, but to get back to Beebe, he's too good a singer. We'll scratch Beebe and take on 'Plugger' Hume. He played right guard, didn't he, his last two years at the Point?"

"Yes, sir," Melville answered.

"That's more like it," the Old Man said, "and, Mel, just as an older man to a younger one, don't go sticking your neck out for singing officers. You might be misunderstood."

"Yes, sir," Melville said.

The Old Man's cigar was out, and he asked Melville for another light.

"When you're choosing personnel," the Old Man said, "select a good sound poker player or a golfer or someone who likes fishing, and you know where you are, because those types have stability. Put the prima donnas in Intelligence but keep them out of Operations."

Of course, parenthetically, this prejudice about singing was some-

346

what personal with old Tweaker Beardsley. For over ten years the Infantry School had a glee club which put on two musical comedies yearly and two concerts also. He once bet Muriel that he could pick at least fifty generals who had sung in glee clubs between the wars, and what about the glee club in the Command and General Staff School? There was even a male quartet in London with a Catholic priest, a Protestant chaplain and a brigadier general in it. Nevertheless, Muriel always stuck to her guns. It might be all right, she had said, that evening when he told her about Soo, if officers sang in groups and choirs. She still did not think it helped if an officer was too funny alone with a ukulele or a piano, and she was very glad that Melville never sang with a uke. She would have been worried.

"But, Melly, dear," she said, "it might be a nice thing to ask Plugger Hume and Betsy over for Sunday lunch and we'll ask the Beebes, too, and Soo can bring his uke."

It was great to hear Soo singing that Sunday under the coconut palms with the trade wind blowing, but Plugger Hume walked right across the *lanai* and all the way around the living room and back on his hands. He was sound and he made a good assistant in Operations.

Those years had been like the moving belt on a production line, and Melville Goodwin and his contemporaries had taken their places on the belt by the numbers. Some had left to go into business in the twenties. Others had met with death, accident and illness, and one or two had been pulled off by the high command. The rest of the crowd had stayed on the belt until the very end, to be so shined, tightened and tested that they stepped off as logical candidates for a star, and even some of these end products broke down when a more than theoretical strain was placed on them. No matter how effective the simulation, combat was the final test.

Melville Goodwin, as he once said himself, was basically a competent military mechanic. He might not have the global approach of a planner in the Pentagon but he could look at the road and guess what lay around the curves. There was a lot that was wrong with the army. It had its deadwood and its paper-passers, but still it was a pretty good army to have turned out Bradleys and Pattons and MacArthurs just when they were needed. He did not mean to place himself in any of these echelons, because at some point or other every officer's professional clock struck twelve. Everybody could not be a Napoleon, and an armored division was just about his dish. That was a show he had really learned how to handle — but, without boasting, he could handle a corps or something larger. At any rate he had graduated from the Command and General Staff School at Leavenworth with a recommendation to command a corps in wartime.

Besides the Command and General Staff School, he had attended the Army War College, and he had done his share of staff work in Washington. He had sweated it out for years in the old Munitions Building, and he had not been bad at a desk. He couldn't be, with his rank, but somehow active service in the field had spoiled his taste for desks and for sitting around conference tables or reclining in map rooms, talking to a lot of Fancy Dans. Of course he had been at a desk in Frankfurt, but frankly, he did not want to be chairborne again if he could help it. He could take the Pentagon, if he had to, but frankly that building gave him a mild sort of claustrophobia. Sometimes he wished that Muriel would stop thinking about three and four stars. There just weren't many stars being passed around on platters now, not even in the Air Force. A lot of his colleagues were also shaking around loose like him, looking for stars — who had a lot more jokers up their sleeves and a lot more horseshoes in their pants than he had. Competition was pretty stiff around the Pentagon, but maybe someone would take a look at him in Washington and give him a job of work to do.

Actually he had been over the whole subject with Muriel last night, and he had pointed out one pretty good fact to her. The country had made use of him. He had been the doctor who had been allowed to practice, and just exactly where would they have been if there had not been a war? He was still a major back in 1940 and only a lieutenant colonel at the time of the maneuvers in '41. That was something for Muriel to think about. She had raised her boys to be soldiers, he had told her, and maybe in a year or two her oldest boy ought to put his sword and gun away so that she could give a little more thought to Robert, and to Charley at the Point.

It was interesting to remember how things started to chirk up in the service when there began to be a little distant gunfire in the world. Henry L. Stimson seemed to want us to do something about Manchuria, though nothing happened. Then, after Hitler's march to the Rhineland, and the blowoff at the Marco Polo Bridge, and Munich, you began to feel that maybe you hadn't missed the boat being in the army. Still, after Dunkirk it looked as though the whole show were folding up. It made him very restless and he found himself short of sleep. They were at Benning—he was on the Infantry School staff as Tank Instructor at the time—and there were new ideas every minute, and there was also the tactical aircraft angle.

"Melly," Muriel asked him, there at Benning, "have you heard from Foghorn Grimshaw lately?"

Of course, as everyone knew, General Grimshaw was in the office of the Chief of Staff in Washington.

"I suppose he's still living in Georgetown, isn't he?" Muriel said. "I haven't written Ellen Grimshaw a letter for a long while, and they sent us a Christmas card. I don't believe they even know that Robert has entered the Point."

When he got orders to go to Washington to attend a conference of observers back from Europe, he was sure that Muriel's letter had nothing to do with it. He was certain that Foghorn Grimshaw would have thought of him anyway, and the General was very glad to see him and asked him to come to Georgetown for the night. The truth was that things were chirking up. The General said he might be wrong, but confidentially he did not see how we could keep out of that show in Europe indefinitely. There were going to be a lot of chances for bright young men. The General was not as young as he had been back in Bailey, and neither was Melville, though he hadn't a gray hair in his head, but he was still a bright young man to Foghorn Grimshaw, and everybody began to see that this was the sort of war that demanded younger men in the higher ranks, instead of Papa Joffres.

349

XXIII

Right Under "H" in the Dictionary

SOMEHOW I found myself examining Melville Goodwin not as a friend but as a useful piece of material — as Foghorn Grimshaw must have, not to mention other members of the hierarchy in Washington. It was after eleven o'clock when he had reached those prewar months in Washington. He stopped after mentioning Papa Joffre and looked slowly around the room as though he were trying to gauge the effect of everything he had said. Then he smiled at Phil Bentley. It was not his sour smile, but that appealing smile that always made him look so young.

"Say, Bentley," he said, "right out of the horse's mouth — have I made a God-damned fool of myself up to date or haven't I?"

I could see that Phil Bentley liked it. The General had learned how to handle Phil.

"No, sir," Phil said. "On the contrary, you've made a lot of sense."

Obviously Mel Goodwin was pleased, but his glance did not leave Phil Bentley's face.

"In the army," he said, "you've always got to take loyalty for granted from the top down and from the bottom up. There's no reason why you should be loyal to me, but I'm trusting you, son, and I've got my neck way out. You can raise hell with me if you want to, and maybe there are some people around who would enjoy it if you did."

"You're going to see everything I write," Phil Bentley said, "and if you think any of it raises hell, I'll change it."

Coming from Phil Bentley, this meant a great deal, and I wondered if the General realized it. His eyes were still on Phil.

350

"You see, I'm just a simple guy," he said. His using that expression surprised me, because I had applied it to him so often myself. "You've got to be a pretty damn simple guy if you lead troops in combat, because combat's God-damned elemental."

"You're not as simple as all that, sir," Phil Bentley said. "You're complicated sometimes."

"Listen," the General said, "I know where I stand. I'm a pretty simple guy, Phil."

It was the first time in all those interviews that Mel Goodwin had called him "Phil." As I have said before, calling you by your first name was one of the beguiling habits of big brass. I remembered that he had called me "Sid" much sooner. He had shown perspicacity in waiting so long with Phil.

"Just the same," Phil said, "I'd hate to meet you in a poker game."

Phil Bentley knew something about the brass himself. Nothing ever pleased them more than being told they were good at poker, and Mel Goodwin laughed as though Phil had said something very funny.

"Phil," he said, "we'll really have to try it some day."

He had called him Phil once more to show it was no mistake. I was looking at Mel Goodwin again, as Foghorn Grimshaw must have looked at him in Washington. He had no excess weight. He was trained down like all the good ones, with just the right facial lines and a cheerful, extrovert look that you often saw on a good competitive athlete. He was a very finished product. He would rate as a piece on any chessboard and not an advanced pawn. He might not be a rook or a queen, but he was surely a knight or a bishop. He was the sort of person whose name would be bound to come up for some big spot.

The General flicked up his wrist to look at his watch.

"Well," he said, "just a few yarns about North Africa tomorrow morning and then you'll have the old man pretty well squeezed out, Phil."

Colonel Flax laughed at the General's little joke, and General Goodwin stood up.

"Let's plan to end this by lunch tomorrow if that's all right with you, Phil," he said. "Good night, bright-eyes." He smiled at Miss Fineholt, and then he turned to me and punched me softly on the chest.

"Sid," he said, "stay down here for a minute and explain me to them, will you, and you'd better come along with me, Flax. They might say something that will hurt our feelings, and, Sid . . ."

"Yes, sir," I said.

"Stop in and see me before you turn in, will you?"

"Yes, sir," I said.

General Goodwin had taken over.

"There isn't a thing to talk about, sir," Phil Bentley said. "You've laid it all pretty well on the line. To use an old army expression that I seem to have heard somewhere, it's only up to me to start carrying the ball."

The General had done very well or Phil Bentley would never have been so informal.

"God damn it," the General said, "cut out that 'sir' stuff, will you, son? You're not in the army, and my name's Mel. Come on, Flax, and let's get the hell out of here."

After they left, Phil Bentley took off his glasses and polished them carefully.

"Sid," he said, "he really seems to like me, doesn't he? Maybe I'm learning about the army."

Perhaps we were all understanding the army better than we had previously. Phil had seen something of it before, as an overseas war correspondent, but he had been exposed to the products of that great organization more than to its way of life.

"Those anecdotes," Phil Bentley said. "He pulls them out of a hat like rabbits. God, they are still running around the floor."

I am sure that none of us were thinking of Melville Goodwin's little stories individually as much as of the background that created them.

"There's one thing that interests me," Phil Bentley said. "Generals' stories are almost interchangeable among generals. Have you ever noticed that?"

"Yes," I said, "that's right. They're uniform."

352

Phil Bentley swung his spectacles like a pendulum between his thumb and forefinger.

"Then why do you suppose they keep on telling them?" he asked. He was obviously working out the structure of the profile.

"Sometimes I've thought it rests them," I said. "They convey some private meaning that we don't see. They're a sort of narrative shorthand."

"Maybe they haven't got anything else to talk about," Phil Bentley said. "Take someone like Goodwin. Take his humdrum stultifying little life, all that spit-and-polish and all that competition and all that existence by the numbers. Then suddenly he gets more power than anyone ought to have and an automobile and a plane and a permit to kill off people. I don't see anything in the life he's lived that makes him capable of using that power intelligently. There's a gap somewhere. I wish I could find the gap."

I could see it if he didn't. I had gained some sort of glimpse of it behind Melville Goodwin, but it embarrassed me to point it out to realists like Phil Bentley and Myra Fineholt.

"Don't you see, Phil?" I said. "You can't put him into any ordinary category. Don't you see he's a hero? It's the power and the glory. Now you and I wanted to be heroes once, and Myra wanted to be Joan of Arc, and we've all got over it, but Goodwin still has the virus. It's catching around there at West Point. I don't say that I approve of heroes. I don't say that they look so well in peacetime, but he's a hero and he can't help it."

I saw Miss Fineholt gazing at me tolerantly, but Phil Bentley looked startled.

"Listen, Sid," he said. "Don't you think you're going off the deep end?"

"No," I said, "the trouble is we don't like to admit there are heroes any more, outside of an epic."

"Any more than there are fairies in the bottom of my garden," Miss Fineholt said.

"Just the same, Myra," I told her, "you've been listening to a hero tonight, perhaps not grade A but grade B. They have to eat and get along and they have compulsions like you and me. If you take Goodwin that way, everything fits together. He wouldn't have put up with what he went through if he hadn't had the power-and-the-glory vision."

Phil Bentley put on his glasses.

"Now wait a minute," he said, "are you trying to make me believe that every officer in the Regular Army is a hero? Let's get down to facts."

"All right," I said, "the fact is that a lot of them have never got over that early fantasy. A lot of them think they may be heroes some-day, and that's why they like the life. Why not face it instead of gagging over a word?"

There was something behind all that Melville Goodwin had said that was dedicated and magnificent and undemanding of justifica-tion. Perhaps a psychiatrist would call it immaturity, but whatever the attribute was, it had its own splendor.

"Let's get it straight," Phil Bentley said, "instead of kicking it around. Just what is a hero?"

I walked to the bookshelf and looked for the *Shorter Oxford Dic-tionary,* which Helen had given me the first Christmas after we were married, and I handed down the first volume to Phil Bentley.

"Look it up. In case you don't know it, it's under 'H,' " I said.

Phil turned the pages over slowly. I heard the tall clock in the hall — the clock that Helen had bought when she began to like Chippendale — strike the half-hour, but the sound was aloof in the silence of the house. I had the ridiculous illusion that General Good-win was back there with us again, in his chair, actually leaning for-ward and waiting for what might be read.

"Well," Phil Bentley said, "well, well. Take this down, will you, Myra, on a separate sheet, and put it ahead of the notes? Here's an Oxford definition of a hero. Quote: 'A man who exhibits extraor-dinary bravery comma, firmness comma or greatness of soul comma, in connection with any pursuit comma, work comma, or enter-prise. . . .' Close quotes."

"You can't use that about Goodwin, can you?" Myra Fineholt asked.

Phil Bentley closed the dictionary and took off his glasses.

354

"Why not?" he said. "Anyway I'd like to think it over. I think I might use it in the lead."

"You know better than to do that, sweetheart," Miss Fineholt said.

Phil Bentley sighed and looked at the empty armchair where Melville Goodwin had been sitting.

"Well," he said, "maybe all this has put me a little off the beam. I don't go with it all the way, but still the definition almost fits him, doesn't it?"

Of course I had seen some heroes in the last conflict and although I respected what they had done, I had not always admired them or wished to be like them myself. The press was always looking for new ones, and there was a lot of hero competition between the Air Force and the Navy, and there was frequently considerable pressure on Public Relations from higher echelons to do something about Ground Force heroes. In fact I had once been assigned as a sort of valet to one of these — a Congressional Medal of Honor hero. He was twenty-two years old, from Ohio, and his name was Corporal Jacob Snodgrass — no relation to the former ball player.

It had been my duty to take him about the country for two weeks, arranging appearances before various civic groups so that they could see a hero. It was a pretty tough assignment for me but not for Corporal Snodgrass. He did not like being exhibited but he enjoyed the trip. When he was not drinking bourbon, usually supplied by me, he was taking money out of me at gin rummy or becoming emotionally involved with uninteresting women. When he was not doing any of these things, he was reading comics very slowly. It generally took him two days of cerebration to finish a book of comics, and he always needed to get drunk before he started on another. I have an idea that he modeled himself on Flash Gordon, Dick Tracy and Superman, and he may even have won his Congressional Medal because he could not let the comics down. He had killed almost a platoon of Japanese in a jungle, and he had walked back to the lines with a live Japanese major under one arm and his wounded patrol leader under the other, but he cost me nearly three hundred dollars for liquor, girls and gin rummy, for which I was never reimbursed by the government. I admired what he had done in the jungle, but to him it was only a slightly hilarious episode, and sometimes after he had polished off a pint of bourbon he would say, Hell, that I could have done it myself. I could not have done it myself. I did not possess his physical build, or his physical courage, or his lack of imagination. Perhaps it was not fair to use the corporal as a unit of measure, because the corporal did not answer the dictionary hero definition very well, but he did have one thing in common with other heroes I have known. He did not thrive in an ordinary environment. Take heroes away from their proper time and place and they became awkward and maladjusted.

Now Melville A. Goodwin was far from being a Corporal Snodgrass, but you could not see his virtues clearly when he did not have to employ them. You had to see him grinning and rubbing the mud off his uniform, as he had in Normandy when that mortar shell had exploded near us, or you had to see him in a jeep driving across a mine field in Normandy. It was not his fault that opportunity did not permit him to exhibit intestinal fortitude all the time. He would have been very glad to do so, as I endeavored to point out to Myra Fineholt and Phil Bentley before I said good night.

As I walked upstairs after putting out the downstairs lights, I was still thinking so intensely about heroes that I almost forgot that Melville Goodwin had wanted a word with me before I went to bed. I experienced a short sense of anticlimax when I saw him in the main guest room in his undershirt and trousers with his shoes off, but he still looked as though he could slip back into everything if a whistle blew. His shoes were in perfect alignment at the foot of his bed. His coat was on its hanger in the clothes closet. His military brushes were in the exact center of the tall bureau and through the half-opened door of the bathroom I could see his shaving brush, shaving stick, toothbrush, toothpaste and safety razor all in a meticulous row on the glass shelf below the medicine chest. There was only one detail that I found disconcerting. He was wearing steel-rimmed glasses, and it had never occurred to me that he might need glasses for reading. He wore them, I saw, because he was examining a pile of photographs.

"Sit down and look them over, Sid," he said. "This bunch has just been rushed up from Washington. I think the boys did a real job on me. What do you think?"

He watched me anxiously when I sat down and examined the pictures.

"News services do better than the Army Pictorial Service," he said. "Don't you think so? I had a lot taken of me in Normandy and a lot up with the Silver Leaf, but these are better."

There were candid shots of Melville Goodwin from every angle, Melville Goodwin gazing straight ahead, a stern Goodwin, a smiling and a laughing Goodwin, a sad Goodwin, a Goodwin looking slyly from the corners of his eyes and even a bored and yawning Goodwin.

"They were crawling around and snapping me all afternoon here, too," he said. "I never had time to brace myself because I never knew when they were going to push the button."

They had to be good photographs. Most of this series would be used, I supposed, as aids for the artist who did the magazine cover picture.

"They are certainly giving you the works," I said.

The photographers had obviously struggled for informality, but the strange thing was that not one of them showed him in a grotesque or ungainly pose or off balance. Smiling, frowning or smoking a cigarette, talking or tight-lipped, he was easily as photogenic as a Hollywood star. The uniform may have helped and the instinctive correctness with which he wore it, but still there must have been some sort of subconscious watchfulness inside him that not even a candid photographer could penetrate.

"You certainly look sharp," I said.

He accepted it as a fact.

"You learn to," he said, "with troops looking at you all the time. I'm used to having the privacy of a goldfish. I'm trying to pick out the best one to pass around."

I knew what he meant by passing one around. They always made a specialty of signed photographs in the service. I thought of the rows of them I had seen on walls or bookshelves in officers' quarters.

"Muriel collects them like postage stamps," he said. "She always carries a gallery with her. Maybe it's not artistic but it's good to look around and see your friends. . . . I think I'll use this one."

"That one looks fine," I said.

"You don't think it looks too much as though I were going to chew off somebody's rear, do you? It doesn't look too much like old Vinegar Joe?"

"You don't look like Vinegar Joe," I said.

"Muriel said to be sure to get one of you, Sid," he said, "preferably a picture of you and Helen together. We want you in the gallery."

"That's where we want to be," I said, "permanently in the gallery."

He took off his glasses and put them in their small black case, and I was curiously relieved to see him without them.

"Sid," he said, "I can't tell you what your seeing me through this has meant to Muriel and me. Muriel said she liked you as soon as she saw you. She knows a lot of people, but she doesn't like so many."

"Well, I liked Mrs. Goodwin, too," I said.

"God damn it," he said, "she's Muriel. Get used to calling her Muriel."

It was obviously the time to make a formal and graceful speech in acknowledgment of the General's tribute.

"Helen and I have enjoyed having you here tremendously," I said. "Helen loves company, and this has been quite a build-up for me. They always like it at the studio when I associate with Very Important People." I laughed to show that this was partly a joke, though basically serious. "I feel I've come to know you as I never would have otherwise — what with all this personal history and reminiscence. I've always thought a lot of you, just seeing you around, the way you do see people, and it's nice to know I had sound judgment."

It sounded a little laid on, but then, high-ranking officers usually were like artists, actors or writers, who depended, whether they admitted it or not, on a certain amount of adulation, and the flattery did not have to be so gentle either. They had all built up a tolerance for it, and undoubtedly a lot of people had dished out this sort of

358

thing to Melville A. Goodwin, because I could see him reviewing my little statement like a connoisseur, winnowing the chaff from the grain. I was glad when he accepted it at its face value, because I had felt it genuinely.

"I'm glad if I've made a hit with you, Sid," the General said. "I guess everybody likes to be regarded favorably in the right quarters, and I admire you personally. You've got a lot on the ball."

"Not as much as you," I said. "I'm superficial and you're not. You see, you don't need to be superficial."

The General was not thinking of me or my problems at the moment, and I was just as glad he was not.

"Brother," he said, "you certainly can lay it on with a trowel, but go ahead, I like it. Say, without pulling punches, how do I rate with Phil Bentley and that research girl?"

"You ought to know," I said. "They admire you, Mel."

"Well," he said, "that's fine. I thought it might pay off to hand it to them out of the horse's mouth. . . . Say, Sid, get me my fountain pen, will you? It's in my blouse pocket in the closet."

It was an order but it was not out of place, because his asking me showed that he considered me a member of his group.

"Here you are, sir," I said.

I had just called him "Mel" but now it was correct to call him "sir" and we both knew it. He picked up a photograph from the floor beside him, his favorite photograph, and wrote across it diagonally in a firm bold hand.

"Here," he said, "from me to you."

Across the photograph he had written, *To Sid with admiration and affection, Mel.*

"Thanks, sir," I said. "I'll value this always."

Again, it was correct to call him "sir" because the moment had been formal, involving a presentation, an award of merit, like the pinning of a medal, and all our talk had led up to it, but now the ceremony was over and we were out of formation.

"Oh, hell," he said, "forget it, Sid, but I mean every God-damned word of it." He coughed and cleared his throat. "So you had lunch with Dot in New York, did you?"

The elaborately weary way he leaned back in his chair and his careful unconcern were faintly amusing because subtlety was not one of his strong points. For some reason I did not look forward to what was coming, now that he was, with admiration and affection, my old friend Mel.

"She called you up, didn't she?" I said.

Without meaning to, I was adopting his own unconcern — talking casually about a girl we both knew slightly named Dottie Peale.

"That's right," he said, and he coughed again. "You didn't suggest she call me, did you, just to cheer the old man up or anything like that?"

"No," I said, "no, it was entirely her own idea."

It was disturbing to see him lean forward and to see his whole face light up.

"You mean she thought of it all herself?" he asked.

"Yes, all herself," I answered.

He was smiling his youngest smile. I was alarmed to see him look so happy.

"I'm having dinner with her tomorrow night," he said. "It really will be nice to see Dot again. I sort of thought she'd forgotten all about me. She never answered my last two letters."

There was no use warning anyone about things like that. Instead it was always advisable to get out from under, and the General was old enough to take care of himself, and I was probably overemphasizing the whole thing — but I felt that I had to say something.

"Oh, that's the way she is," I said. "It's off with the old and on with the new. You don't want to take Dot too seriously, Mel." It was about all that I had any right to say.

"Thanks for the briefing, son," he said. "I guess I wouldn't have had that invitation if I hadn't spanked that Russki in Berlin. I'm not taking Dot seriously, but all the same, it will be nice seeing her again."

"Dot's pretty good company," I said, "and she has a whole suit of armor in the front hall."

Melville Goodwin still looked very young.

360

"I certainly want to see it," he said. "Maybe I need a little relaxation — off the record, Sid."

"Well, don't forget you have a record," I said.

"Oh," he said, "everything doesn't get into a 201 file."

"Perhaps not," I said. "I was just thinking of Ulysses coming home from Troy."

"What the hell has Ulysses got to do with it?" the General asked.

"You recited a poem about him once at the Ritz in Paris," I said. "Remember?"

He looked at me hard, as though he wanted to pull his rank, but then he must have realized that he was out of the military zone.

"I'm still waiting to hear what Ulysses has to do with it," he said.

"Well," I said, "when he was sailing home to Ithaca to rejoin his wife Penelope, he put wax in his ears so he couldn't hear the sirens sing."

There was a moment's tension, and Melville A. Goodwin's face grew red, but suddenly he laughed. He was never as dumb as you thought he would be.

"God damn," he said, "it hurts me to see an educated boy like you fall down on mythology. He put wax in his crew's ears, son. He didn't use any wax on himself. He had his men tie him to the mast." Melville A. Goodwin had an almost flawless memory. "And anyway, there aren't any Circes or Calypsos or sirens around, either, son. There's only Dottie Peale, and I don't take her seriously."

Even in his undershirt surrounded by his photographs, Mel Goodwin possessed a quality in which I needed to believe. That must have been why I let myself go further.

"All right, you're not exclusively Ulysses," I said. "You're Major General Melville A. Goodwin, USA, graduate of West Point, the Infantry School, the Tank School, Command and General Staff School and the War College, but what's more, you're a combat general. I've even heard the boys call you 'Muddy Mel.'"

"Son," he said, "you ought to write citations. Go right ahead and lay it on. Don't let me stop you."

"And what's more," I said, "you're Horatius at the bridge."

361

"God damn," Melville Goodwin said, "I thought you were just telling me I was Ulysses."

"Well, you're Horatius, too," I said. "'And how can man die better . . . Than facing fearful odds . . . For the ashes of his fathers . . . And the temples of his Gods?'"

He had been smiling, lapping it up, as he listened to me, but suddenly he stopped and raised his eyebrows.

"No kidding, Sid?" he asked.

"No," I answered, "not in the strictest sense."

His face was graver and sterner and sadder than it had been in any of those candid photographs. He looked entirely off his balance, not ready for any camera.

"That's right," he said, "it isn't entirely kidding. Maybe I've got a little of that stuff. You need it in the show, and now the whole show's over. There's one trouble with acting in those shows. You get keyed up to them, and I'm not dead. That's the trouble with it — I'm still alive. You've handed me a pretty fast line, son, and maybe old Horatius Ulysses Goodwin had better turn in now and get some sleep. Good night, Sid."

"Good night, Mel," I said.

"Here," he called, "come back here. God damn it, you forgot your photograph."

What was it that I had felt that night about Melville Goodwin? I still cannot exactly set it down. I had reacted toward him as he himself had reacted long ago to that Decoration Day parade in Nashua. If he was not great, he had great memories, and he knew how to throw the dice, win or lose, both for himself and for a lot of other people. He had his 201 file and his record and I may have recognized its value, having so slim a record of my own. For me there was no sense of achievement. There were no 201 files or service dossiers in civil life.

I thought of him at the Ritz in Paris, reciting Tennyson's lines on pushing off and sitting well in order and smiting the sounding furrows. He was pushing off again, but he should have been in battle dress pushing off with the tanks. He had to keep on pushing because he had forgotten how to stay still. He had been in too many big parades to sit at home in Ithaca or Washington. A doctor might have said that he had developed an adrenal quality. He had drunk too long from the golden cup that held the wine of power and glory.

XXIV

A Short Quote from Kipling

I THOUGHT that Helen would have been asleep long ago, but she
called me as soon as I was in our dressing room. She was sitting in
bed wide awake reading Proust, a taste I had always found it impossible to share.

"I haven't seen you all day," she said, "except to look at you across
the table at the officers' mess."

"Don't be bitter," I said, "we've got to World War II, and the
circus ought to break up after lunch tomorrow."

"I'm not bitter," she answered, "but I didn't know you could be so
military. I'm beginning to feel like Mrs. Goodwin."

"You couldn't," I said, "not really."

"She wants him to settle down," she said, "and I'd just as soon have
you settle down, too. You look worried. Are you worried about Gilbert Frary?"

I had not been worried about Gilbert, and it was too late at night
to start worrying about him now. I told her I could not keep my
mind on both Gilbert Frary and the life and times of Melville
Goodwin.

"Well, tell me I've been wonderful through it all," she said. "I
need a little encouragement."

I told her of course that she had been wonderful through it all.

"All right," she said. "Now open the window. Things don't feel
right this evening. The house doesn't feel right."

Our bedroom still seemed too large for us, and there was that
country silence to which I was not accustomed, but the house felt to
me just as it always had. It was too new to have atmosphere or ghosts
except those of Mr. and Mrs. Winlock.

"You always start having premonitions whenever you read Proust," I said.

"There's nothing of Proust around at all," she said. "Everything's more like Shakespeare. I feel as though we were all in *Julius Caesar* with a lot of omens."

I hesitated to tell her that I had begun to feel that way myself.

"You can't have everything, Helen," I said, "and there aren't any omens in Connecticut."

"What were you doing up so late?" she asked. "I heard everyone come upstairs."

"Oh," I told her, "just saying good night to 'Julius Caesar' Goodwin"—but certainly Melville Goodwin had never been offered a golden crown in any forum.

"Maybe Mark Antony comes nearer," Helen said.

It was not so quiet outside as it had been. I could hear the wind in the bare branches of the ornamental beech trees. "Sid," she went on, "what's going to happen about him and Dottie Peale?"

Sometimes she was like Camilla and did not want to go to sleep.

"Now, Helen," I said, "what makes you think anything is going to happen?" In such circumstances men always stuck together.

She looked at me for a moment and then she shrugged her bare shoulders. She had beautiful shoulders, and the whole scene was getting more and more like Shakespeare.

"Sometimes you're awfully obtuse," she said. "Don't you know that Mrs. Goodwin knows all about it?"

"Now, Helen," I said, "there isn't any 'it' for her to know anything about. There was only Paris, and I told you about Paris."

"Oh, Sid," Helen said, "oh, Sid."

"I don't believe she heard anything about Paris anyway," I said. "What did she say to you that makes you think so?"

"Oh, Sid," Helen said, "of course it isn't about Paris. It's about now, and of course she didn't say anything. How could she?"

"You ought to put something over you with the window open or you'll catch cold," I said. "If she didn't say anything, how do you know she knows anything?"

"Oh, Sid," Helen said, "really."

At least Mrs. Goodwin had not been there when Dottie Peale had telephoned.

"I wish you wouldn't keep saying 'Oh, Sid,'" I told her.

"Oh, Sid," she said, "anyone can see she knows. You only have to look at Goodwin, Sid. I'd know if it were you."

"Well, it isn't me," I said.

"I know it," Helen said, "but it would be nicer if you said, 'It isn't I,' and besides, it used to be you."

There was no reason whatsoever for her to bring up the subject, and I had told her everything about Dottie Peale and me.

"That was before I ever saw you, Helen," I said. "How many times have I told you that it was all over as soon as I went to the Paris Bureau?"

"Oh, Sid," Helen said, "of course I know. Dottie's never worried me."

"Then why did you bring her up?" I asked.

"I didn't," she said, "but now we're on the subject, she made a pass at you this afternoon at lunch, didn't she? Not much of one but a sort of one, didn't she?"

We looked at each other for a moment. She was smiling. She had never been worried about Dottie.

"What makes you think so?" I asked.

"Oh, Sid," she said, "it's so easy to tell about those things — the way you looked before dinner when you said you had lunch in her study. Why else would she have you in her study?"

"Suppose we get back to Goodwin," I said.

Helen laughed, although I could not see what she thought was funny.

"Oh, Sid," she said, "you only had to see the way he looked after she called him up this afternoon. Sometimes I don't think you know anything about sex or about the subconscious mind or anything. It was like something in the Song of Solomon. Now kiss me good night and say you love me, darling, and then open the window wider. You never like fresh air."

It was always colder in the country than in the city when the window was open.

366

After the light was out, Helen spoke again. "Darling," she said, "he's such a nice old thing. He's just like Colonel Newcome."

"Goodwin's not in a wheel chair yet," I told her, "and he isn't a bit like Colonel Newcome."

"Well, I wish there were something we could do about it," she said. "Do you know what I think? I think she wants to marry him."

"Now, Helen," I said, "what should make you think anything like that?"

"Oh, Sid," she said, "anyone can see she's looking for a man."

"All right, she's looking for a man," I said.

When she spoke again, I was half asleep.

"Sid," she said, "another thing."

"What other thing?" I asked.

"Gilbert Frary sent me a big box of orchids this afternoon — not purple ones, yellow ones."

"Well, he was here the other night," I said, "and Gilbert always likes to send things."

"But he's never sent so many," Helen said. "There are twice as many as he's ever sent before. You can look at them tomorrow. They're in the icebox. Good night, darling."

"Good night," I said.

Gilbert Frary and the orchids and Julius Caesar Goodwin and Cleopatra Delilah Peale tangled restively in my thoughts, while I was falling asleep.

Women were usually more realistic than men in their analyses of other women, especially certain women. I had not taken a number of aspects of my luncheon with Dottie Peale seriously until after those remarks of Helen's. They had opened a new and curious vista of odd little possibilities. Of course Dottie Peale was one of those people who were always being talked about in the chromium New York Latin Quarter that had its center near the night clubs and the restaurants of the Fifties. I had never cared much for this area, but I did know something of it professionally, since professionally I had become one of those figures whom headwaiters and captains recognized, and Gilbert Frary frequently said that it was a part of my day's work to appear with Helen sometimes and to allow myself to be seen by what he called my "public." I did not like these expensive hot spots, but I was well acquainted with them because, one might as well face it, we were all of us hustlers in our different ways, and at least I was a piece of property who always got a table up front.

Everyone in this area had been wondering for a long while when and whether Dottie Peale would get married again. She was the sort of person, everyone said, who certainly ought to get married, and there were plenty of prospects with whom her name had been connected. There was Alfred Binghill, who had that big place at Manhasset and that winter place at Palm Beach, and if Alfred Binghill was too extrovert there was also a foreign composer who frankly was very anxious to marry a beautiful rich American girl. If he was too exotic, there was Mortimer Felcher, the British novelist, published in America by Peale House, a writer whom Dottie had always called another Galsworthy. I had not thought about Dottie's private life for a long while, and Helen's theory that Dottie had selected Mel Goodwin as a prospective husband did not seem wholly convincing. Still, I could not help remembering Dottie's wistful remarks about missing the boat and now not having anyone — not even me. If Dottie had been thinking along these lines about Melville Goodwin, at least I had come first, and somehow the idea made me quite cheerful.

These reflections returned to me as soon as I awoke the next morning. The army had taught me to set my mind like an alarm clock, and the General would be down for breakfast at eight sharp, prepared for his final session in the library. I immediately awakened Helen. She could not believe it when I told her it was half past seven.

"And what if it is?" she asked. "I've just got to sleep."

"It's his last breakfast," I said, "and we both ought to be down."

"How do you mean?" Helen asked. "He isn't going to be executed or anything, is he?"

"The last officers' mess," I said, "and I think you're all wrong, Helen. I don't think Dottie has any idea of marrying him. Why should she?"

"Oh, you're thinking about that, are you?" Helen said.

"It just crossed my mind," I said. "Of course she doesn't want to marry anyone."

368

"Well, why are you looking so cheerful?" Helen asked. "You're usually cross at this time of the morning."

"I was just thinking about you and your shape of things to come," I said.

"Darling," Helen said, "don't you see the General's new? He's different from all you other boys. Can't you put yourself in Dottie's place?"

"No, I can't," I told her.

"Well, I can," Helen said.

The General and Colonel Flax were already in the living room waiting for breakfast, and Melville Goodwin also looked cheerful. He must have been telling Colonel Flax some anecdote because I heard them both laughing before Helen and I arrived.

"Good morning, my dear," he said. "Did Sid make you come down here on account of me?"

"Oh, no," Helen said, "I love to get up early."

"So does Muriel," the General said. "It's nice we're getting Helen in the groove, Sid . . . and, Sid, we've really got to get activated this morning. I want to leave for New York this afternoon. Where are Bentley and Fineholt? Can't they ever wake up?"

"I'll send Oscar upstairs after them," I said.

"That's all right," the General said. "Flax has been up after them already. They answered you, didn't they, Flax?"

"They're rising and shining, sir," the colonel said. "They ought to be right down."

"Oh, Mel," Helen said, and she was right in the groove that morning, "Sid showed me your photograph and what you wrote on it. I love it." I had meant to remind her to speak of the photograph, but she had done it all herself.

"I meant every word of it, my dear," the General said. "I'm proud to think I'll be somewhere in this house."

"I'm proud, too," Helen said. "It's all been lovely, and sometime soon you and Muriel must come again without all this interviewing. It hasn't really been a visit, has it, Sid?"

Helen looked at me and smiled in a meaning way.

"No," I said, "of course it hasn't."

Helen smiled at me for another second before she turned again to Mel Goodwin.

"Muriel and I had such a nice time comparing notes," she said. "I love Muriel."

"That goes both ways," the General said. "You ought to hear what Muriel said about you, dear. She said she wished you had married someone in the service. You know what she means, Sid. Muriel couldn't say anything more than that."

"That reminds me," Helen said, and she glanced at me again. "I have a little present for you to take to Muriel — some orchids. They are in the icebox now but they'll keep until you get to Washington tonight."

At last I could see the way things were going. Helen was right in the groove that morning.

"Why, that's very kind of you, my dear," the General said. "Imagine your thinking of anything like that, but frankly I don't know how I can handle orchids."

"They won't be any trouble," Helen said, "as long as you don't bounce them around. They're all packed in a box."

The General had estimated the situation, and now he was taking action.

"I can't think of anything Muriel would like more," he said. "There's only one little hitch." He frowned and clasped his hands behind his back.

"What little hitch?" Helen asked.

"Well, it may just be," the General said, "that I won't be able to get to Washington tonight, and I wouldn't want to have those orchids spoil on me. I know what Muriel would say."

"Oh dear," Helen said, "they're yellow orchids. As soon as I saw them I thought of Muriel."

"The difficulty is, dear," the General said, "I have a few duty calls to make in New York. I ought to drop in at First Army Headquarters as a matter of courtesy and see Bud Hodgkins there. We were at the Point together, and Bud may ask me to spend the night. That's why I can't be sure about the orchids."

"Oh dear," Helen said, "but perhaps you could put them in the refrigerator. Colonel Hodgkins will have a refrigerator."

"*General* Hodgkins," Colonel Flax said.

"Oh," Helen said, "I'm sorry — General Hodgkins."

The ranks were forming already, and loyalty was starting in a military manner.

"I'll be going down to Washington tonight, sir," Colonel Flax said. "It will be a pleasure to leave the flowers for Mrs. Goodwin."

The General smiled. "Good," he said, "thanks, Flax. That's the best way out of everything."

I knew that Helen was looking at me, but I did not want to look at her.

"Let's go in and get breakfast," I said. "There's no use waiting."

"No use at all," the General said. "We've got to get moving. Say, Flax, you were in the landings at North Africa, weren't you?"

"Yes, sir," Colonel Flax said, "I went in with 'Bolster Two.'"

"'Bolster Two,'" the General said. "'Pinky' Perkwell was with 'Bolster Two.'"

"Yes, he was, sir," Colonel Flax said.

"Pink and I served at Benning once," the General said, "but we missed connections in North Africa. I was with 'Heinzy' near Tunis in 'Bullpup' and I never did see anything of 'Bolster Two.' . . ."

Once I heard someone say in France that any general above the one-star rank carried his headquarters around with him mentally, even if he was not attached to anything. General Goodwin had developed an instinct, of course, for imposing order wherever he went, for "tidying things up a bit," as General Montgomery had put it in the Battle of the Bulge, and Phil Bentley and all the rest of us had instinctively fallen into our proper echelons. Breakfast at the stroke of eight was part of the system, and following breakfast came the brisk ten-minute walk in the open air. The General had started by suggesting the walk, but by the third day it had become routine. He simply said, Come on, Flax, or Come on, Sid, according to his desire. When he finished breakfast, Phil Bentley and Miss Fineholt now knew that they would have just ten minutes to organize things in the library or the General would be displeased. This last morning, after technical dialogue with Colonel Flax about the mission of "Bolster Two" around Oran and various personalities in "Bolster Two," Melville Goodwin pushed back his chair and thanked Helen, dear, for a delightful breakfast. Then he did not even say, Come on, Sid. He simply said, Sid. Everything was running like clockwork at headquarters, and in thirty seconds we were outdoors in the fresh October morning. He had set a course for himself down the drive to the main road, then diagonally across the field to the deserted stables, which still seemed to attract his attention because of their lack of horses. We started down the drive in close-order cadence.

"There was a wind last night," he said, "but no rain. This is damn good maneuvering weather."

"Yes, sir," I said. "The ground's solid underfoot."

When he looked at me I felt like a young officer who had made a flip remark.

"Don't kid me, son," he said. "I'm not in a kidding mood. Those God-damned orchids! What made Helen ever think of sending me down to Washington with a bunch of orchids?"

"Well, you see," I said, "Gilbert Frary — he's the one who runs the program, you know — sent them to Helen. They're a very rare variety. It's what Gilbert would call a gracious gesture, and I suppose Helen wanted to make a gracious gesture."

"Well, God damn!" the General said. "If anyone sent Muriel a lot of orchids, I'd put an interpretation on it."

"Maybe I should," I said, "but Gilbert's always making gracious gestures."

"Now there was a colonel when Muriel was at Baguio . . ." the General said, " 'Slink' Somerby, ought-seven at the Point. . . . Some people always have woman trouble. It's like liquor. You can always pick the Fancy Dans." I waited expectantly for Melville Goodwin to go on about Slink Somerby, but he was silent, and we walked for a while in cadence. "Muriel was really a sharp-looking gal in Baguio," the General said, "but she never did have man trouble. There's only one thing wrong with Muriel."

The General was thinking out loud, but I wished he would not think out loud quite so confidentially.

"I wouldn't say this to many people, boy," he said, "but there comes a time when a man has to talk to a friend who has a broad-gauge, tolerant view. I don't know how to lay it on the line exactly, but you're about the only one I know as an intimate friend who is both on the inside and the outside."

"On the inside and the outside of what?" I asked.

"The service," the General said. "You have a service-type instinct and a service-type loyalty. I observed it the first time I saw you. You're like me; you're loyal from the top down and from the bottom up, and believe me, there aren't many who have the right team loyalty. There are a lot of pink-pants boys who have their knives out for guys like me. Now don't interrupt me. Let me make my point."

I had not the slightest intention of interrupting him, but I did wish he would do his thinking aloud along more conventional lines.

"Now let me make my point," he said again. "There's only one thing wrong with Muriel. She's always taking over. You know, sometimes Muriel reminds me of the British. Did you ever collaborate with the British?"

"No," I said.

"When you get around a table with them," the General said, "you shake hands with Sir Gordon Fewks, KCB. Then you shake hands with Field Marshal Sir Guy Douglas Jones-Smyth-Jones, KCB, CBS. Then before you know it, there they are, right in control, telling you what to do exactly. You must do this and you cawn't do that, really, old thing. You may have a few simple ideas of your own, but they always get lost somewhere, and you mustn't hurt the feelings of the British. Now up there near Antwerp there was a Limey division on my left flank, and oh my God, you wouldn't have known we had won the Revolution. I might have been a Canadian or an Aussie. Oh my God!"

We reached the main road and turned right oblique across the field to the stables, dropping into route step because the ground was rougher, and I wanted to ask him some more about the British, but I remembered he had not made his point.

"Now Muriel's like those Limeys," the General said. "She instinctively assumes control, if you know what I mean, and she always does it for the best. It may be — I don't know — that I'm not quite as adjusted to Muriel as I was, because I've been overseas for quite a while and sort of on my own. You know — compelled by circumstances to work out a few ideas by myself. I know Muriel can't help it. She assumed control just as soon as I stepped off that C–54. She's got it in her mind to get me a desk somewhere at the Joint Chiefs. God damn! I don't seem to be adjusted any more. You see what I mean?"

"Yes," I said, "I see what you mean. Now take Helen . . ." but I stopped. There was no need for bringing Helen into it, and besides, Helen's problems and mine formed no suitable basis for comparison. After all, a lot of other men had found they were not adjusted to their wives when they came back from overseas.

"That's exactly what I mean," the General said, "everybody has personality problems. I've had to go over plenty of them with a lot of the kids in France, and it's usually the same damn problem essentially — but I haven't really any problem."

I felt as removed as a doctor or a priest. His face brightened now that he had talked himself out of his problem.

"But there's one thing I'd like to get straight," he said. "I may be wrong, but it seemed to me that you had a sort of stricken look when I said I was going to have dinner with your friend and my friend, Dottie Peale, tonight. Now what the hell is the matter with it? You didn't have any stricken look in Paris. Why did you give me all that talk about my record just because I'm having dinner with Dottie Peale?"

I thought for a while before I answered. I might as well have tried to stop a fire horse from running to a fire. His men had not tied him to the mast, and he was hearing the sirens.

"Never mind it," I said, "but just take it easy, Mel."

He looked at me and I looked back at him. It was another of those rare moments when he did not have the rank.

"Say, Sid," he said, "has anything happened between you and Dottie since Paris? I get the idea that you don't seem to like her any more. You don't seem to understand her charm, her sympathetic quality or anything."

"Oh, let's skip it, Mel," I said. "I like her in a different way from you, that's all"—but of course he did not want to skip talking about Dottie Peale.

"There's one damn funny thing about me, Sid," he said, "that I don't understand. Any time I dance with a pretty girl twice on Saturday night, there's always a general air of disapproval up and down the scale, a raising of eyebrows and a lot of God-damned kind advice. I don't know why it is that other people seem to be able to raise hell and get away with it. There are a lot of high-ranking nonmonogamists—you'd be surprised—but when it comes to me taking a day off—God almighty! Eisenhower or Clark or Bradley or somebody gets me on the carpet. The whole damned army wants me to be true to Muriel. What are you smiling about? Do you think that's funny?"

"Yes," I said, "a little funny."

We had reached the stable, and now we turned right oblique to the house.

"You ought to get some horses, Sid," he said, "but let's get this straight. I know where I am and what I'm doing. Do you understand?"

"Of course I understand," I said.

"I just want a few moments off," the General said, "just a few God-given moments out of a hectic life to talk to someone who listens to my ideas. Dottie always listens. She even likes some of my ideas."

"That's right," I said, "Dottie always listens," and I wondered if he knew that he had opened himself like a book and had guilelessly turned page after page.

"Maybe I'm smoking too much," he said. "I always seem to have catarrh in the morning." The General drew a deep breath and cleared his throat. We had almost reached the house. "Well, that's all there is to it. I just wanted to give you a little briefing, Sid, so you'd see there's nothing serious about this at all," and then he smiled that very young smile and nudged me with his elbow. "And besides, everything's secured. Flax is taking those orchids to Washington."

There was something incredibly naïve about the boyish gesture of suddenly selecting a best friend to whom you could tell everything. General Goodwin had tossed the secrets of his life out casually and carelessly, just as though he were pulling objects from a hastily packed bag and strewing them helter-skelter around the floor. I was not in his age group and hardly a brother-in-arms, except by his own directive. I could only explain his action from what I knew of the way military figures dealt with material classified "Top Secret." Once they knew you had the proper clearance, they would shoot the works with pleasure, just to get it off their chests. By some eccentricity Mel Goodwin had decided that I was cleared. I did not want to be his intimate friend handling his top-secret files, but there I was, a voice of experience.

There were checks and balances, I supposed, in any marital relationship, which were always undergoing subtle change. Once the General had not minded Muriel's taking over the controls, and now he did. I wished I knew what had happened at their first meeting when he had descended from the plane at Washington, fresh from Berlin; something between them must have been unfamiliar. I thought of Muriel Goodwin in the living room working on the washcloth, one of the set they would use when they eventually started housekeeping again. She had always been crocheting for Mel Goodwin, but I had never dreamed that I, too, would be crocheted into Mrs. Goodwin's washcloth, somewhere on the margin, and that Dottie Peale would be a part of it as well. That episode in Paris had meant more than it should have to Mel Goodwin. I was more convinced than ever that he had not recovered from it in a normal way.

"Say, Sid," the General said, when we were walking down the hall to the library, "I was thinking of a poem last night."

"What?" I asked. "Push off and sitting well in order smite?"

I was certainly mixed up with the crocheting and there was no rank any longer, because the situation had grown fluid.

"No, no," the General said, "I'm referring to Kipling's 'If.'" He stopped and I knew I was going to hear a piece of it. "The part that goes this way. . . ." He was almost but not quite standing at attention.

> *If you can dream — and not make dreams your master;*
> *If you can think — and not make thoughts your aim;*
> *If you can meet with Triumph and Disaster*
> *And treat those two impostors just the same. . . .*

He was looking beyond me, not at me. I was thinking how heavily obvious that poem had always seemed to me, but it still fitted Melville Goodwin.

"Well, what's that got to do with anything?" I asked him. "Where's there any disaster?"

The lines around his mouth had hardened. Compared with his expression out of doors, he looked as though he were ten years older.

"Listen, son," he said. "You never want to underestimate a situation. Never discount disaster."

I could not tell whether he was thinking of World War II or of Dottie Peale, and I did not want to ask him.

"Come on," he said, "I want to get this over. One thing at a time, son, one thing at a time."

XXV

War Is Hell — in Alexandria or Anywhere Else

I FOLLOWED the General into the library and closed the door. He had a well-compartmented mind that could move effortlessly from one thing to another.

"Let's get this thing cleaned up, Phil," he said. "I have to be in New York by five o'clock. That means leaving here by three forty-five. Make a note of it, will you, Flax, and take it up with Mrs. Skelton. Where did we break off last night?"

"You were back in Washington," Phil Bentley told him, "in the summer of 1941."

Melville Goodwin laughed and sat down by the fireplace.

"It was really hot that summer," he said. "Everyone, as I remember, was sort of crazy with the heat. . . ."

In the final draft of his profile, Phil Bentley came up with only a paragraph on Melville Goodwin's pre-Pearl Harbor experiences.

With his deceptively boyish smile that softened but did not obscure the tough corners of his mouth, Melville Goodwin described those months of shoestring improvisations and basic organizational blueprinting as follows: "The whole crowd were like jugglers in a three-ring circus, keeping pie plates in the air. No sooner did you catch one than you had to get rid of it in time to get the next one that the Old Man was scaling at you — and you couldn't break them either. It was lucky for me I was a fast mover."

He meant by this that he was a sort of liaison trouble shooter down in Washington, shuttling back and forth among high echelons, because A. C. Grimshaw, who had already attained a temporary two-star rank, began using him more and more as a second pair of legs and eyes. Grimshaw would send him as his representative to policy conferences on training and plans, and he did a lot of doubling and tripling in brass that summer. He never mentioned Muriel's place in this picture to Phil Bentley, but he did take up the subject of Muriel with me privately.

Muriel, he said, came right up from Benning to Washington to win the war, and they had a few differences of opinion as to where he should fit in the scheme of things. Washington was quite a place, Mel Goodwin said, for an army girl that summer. Anyone who had what it took was bound to get more rank, and if you had some time for a little daydreaming, which he hadn't, you could dream yourself right up to four stars. Of course the whole town was overcrowded, not alone with service personnel, but with dizzy New Deal civilians who were beginning to spin like dancing mice when Congress began upping the appropriations. Though he was assigned to duty under Grimshaw at the Department, he could not rustle up any living quarters for Muriel and young Charley and it was lucky Robert was at the Point. He had wanted Muriel and Charley to stay where it was cool until he could at least find out what the score was. He even suggested that Muriel might take Charley to Hallowell to visit her mother, who was living all alone in the house there since Mr. Reece's death. He could not very well afford to keep them in some Washington hotel on his pay, and though Muriel and her mother never did get on well sharing a house together — because each of them was always taking over without consulting the other — he did hope Muriel would keep out of Washington for a while — not that he would not miss her.

He pointed out to her in several long letters, which he should not have spared the time to write, what with all the reports and directives he was always drafting for the boss, that he had no time for family life anyway. When he was not being sent somewhere around the country, he was at the Department during all his waking hours. Whenever he got back to the room he had occupied in "Shorty" Telfer's apartment, he was in his sack in five minutes. Shorty was on the training program then, and Shorty was so tired at night that his wife Beatrice couldn't get a word out of him, and even if there had been time for family evenings, you couldn't tell your wife what was going on, because everything was classified.

Of course he must have known subconsciously that Muriel would never keep out of Washington. However, he did think that she might have warned him that she was coming instead of just appearing at Shorty's apartment with Charley as though she had been airborne. It meant that for five days Muriel and Beatrice had to share the main bedroom while Shorty took over the guest room and Melville had the studio couch and Charley used a bedding roll on the living room floor. They all used one bathroom, and he was always forgetting about Charley and tripping over the bedding roll when he got home at night.

Finally, of course, they did get settled, because Muriel called up Enid, Bud Joyce's wife, whom she had not seen since Schofield. Bud had rented a little house in Alexandria, and Enid told them to move right in with them and share expenses, even before she took it up with Bud. He never forgot old Bud's expression when he came home to find the whole Goodwin family spread out, but then he had done Bud a good turn when Bud had begun feuding with "Bing" Bishop at Schofield. Besides, Bud was always a good sport, and he and Enid had always wanted a boy, and there was Charley. Bud's only remark was that war was hell in Alexandria or anywhere else. As a matter of fact, Bud and Enid kept Muriel and Charley right there through the whole war, and they were all still good friends at the end of it, though he never understood how they had managed it.

There was another complication when Muriel came to Washington. As Bud said, the gals made up a general staff of their own and began doing long-term planning. Bud, with his desk at G-2, and limited duty because of disability, was not much for Enid and Muriel to work on, but Melville was really good material for two bright girls. He had done all right at the Tank School and Leavenworth and the War College, and Muriel's thinking was always around the top of the heap. Still, if there was going to be a war, he did not want to be on any staff. As he pointed out to Muriel, somebody had to fight the war, but Muriel wanted him to be nearer the top and more on the administrative side, where the big brass might notice him, instead of being lost in some training area. When they wanted someone, she said, it was only human nature to look around and pick someone in sight rather than someone buried down in Texas. He did not have time to discuss these matters with Muriel except occasionally when they went for a walk on Sunday, but Muriel had lots of time to consider them.

One night in August when he had a few minutes alone with the chief in his office, he brought up the subject of the southern maneuvers and expressed a sort of wish, as definitely as you could express such a thing, that he might get down there with a regiment or something, but Grimshaw only said that he was needed right where he was and the situation was still fluid.

"And besides," he said, "I may be wrong, but I think Muriel has some pretty sound ideas about you. Why don't you leave things to Muriel and me?"

They had recently spent two Sundays at the Grimshaws'. When the General had the time, he liked to get a small crowd around and cook hamburgers in his back yard at Georgetown, and Muriel was very proficient with outdoor grills. He certainly did not want the General to think that he differed with Muriel, and it was quite a problem to think up an answer.

"Muriel really can cook hamburgers, sir," he said. "Muriel can stir up anything."

He was relieved that the Chief seemed to see what he meant.

"Don't you worry about Muriel," the General said. "Muriel intuitively knows what's cooking."

Grimshaw always did have a quiet sense of humor.

"Yes, sir, she certainly does," Melville said, "but I don't want her to overdo me on both sides."

This was about as far as he could go, even with anyone like Grimshaw.

"Mel," the Old Man said, "Muriel never overdoes anything, but maybe you and I both had better go down and look over those maneuvers. I may be wrong, but we might both get a few ideas."

It was the best news he had heard in a long while. You never knew how the Chief was going to jump. Actually, when they were down there he was able to fix things so that he did something with simulated tanks before he was yanked back to Washington. You could never tell what was in the Chief's mind, and he never knew why he was being kept on ice. When he asked for a job in the Philippines just before Pearl Harbor, the Chief turned him down flat, and twice that winter when he asked for something in the Pacific, the Chief turned him down again. Grimshaw was never a Pacific man. By the spring of '42 he was still sweating it out there in Washington, when suddenly the Chief sent him out to Arizona to observe desert maneuvers, but not to take command of anything. He only got the connection when work began on "Torch" and he was promoted to temporary colonel. Muriel was beginning to find him pretty hard to hold when they were in the middle of the North African planning, but it was not until September that the Chief said the word, and then he dropped it casually.

"Mel," he said, "some of you younger fellows will have to be going over. Maybe you'd better start thinking about packing."

Two weeks later his orders were cut for Paisley, where they were training the armor, and the best thing about it was that Muriel had known nothing whatsoever about it. She had cried half the night when she heard he was going to Paisley because she was certain he would be lost down there. There were lots of rumors, but "Torch" was all top secret. The truth was Muriel did not want him to be killed, and it did no good to point out to her that it was about time someone did a little fighting.

Her feelings were hurt when he gave her the word that she had better stay with Bud and Enid and not go to all the trouble of following him down to Paisley.

"But you'll be there for a year," she said, "before you go overseas."

Muriel could not be right about everything. She only got the point when he flew up to Washington to say good-by, and of course she could not ask him where he was going. Secret orders never did help home life, and curiously enough, Charley was the one who came closest to guessing it, because Charley was a smart kid. He had just turned fourteen and he really followed the war news.

"Say, Dad," he said, "I'll bet you're going after Rommel."

He always remembered this. Charley thought a lot of him and knew he could lick anyone.

"No," he answered, "I'm going up to the North Pole to help out Santa Claus."

"Shucks," Charley said, "you wouldn't be packing khaki pants along with your woolens if you were going to see Santa Claus."

Charley was smart and he had narrowed down the operation. The only thing to tell him was to believe in Santa Claus and to take care of his mother. Actually he had only an hour or two to talk over plans and this was just as well. Sitting there in the living room in Alexandria looking at Muriel and Charley, he realized how big the break was going to be, even though it was something for which they had all been waiting. He and Muriel had been together ever since he had come back from the AEF. They had been everywhere as a family unit, even as far as Tientsin, and now it was all over. There would be no Muriel where he was going, to guide him or to talk to the boss. It was quite a thing to consider, quite a thing.

"Muriel," he said, "don't you think it would be best for you and Charley to go up to Hallowell?"

"No," Charley said, "Ma gets into arguments with Grandma."

"We don't get into arguments, Charley," Muriel said, "but your grandmother is an old lady and she has rather fixed ideas. The schools are better in Washington, and maybe I can be of some help here in Washington. At least I'll be able to get some news."

Still North Africa was quite a way from Washington.

"All right," he said, "and say good-by to Robert for me, won't you? Tell Robert to keep his nose clean, will you?"

"You always pick up coarse expressions," Muriel said, "when you get away with troops."

"Well," he said, "he'll know what I mean."

"And what's your final advice to me?" Muriel asked. "What about my own nose?"

"Muriel," he said, "you always did have a pretty nose."

"I wish you wouldn't behave as though you were going to a surprise party," Muriel said.

"Damn it, Muriel," he said, "you don't want me to cry, do you?"

"I just don't want you to act as though you were going on a vacation," Muriel said.

He could feel the tension and he was glad Charley was there because it eased things somewhat, and it was unsettling to see that Muriel was on the verge of tears.

"Come now, Muriel," he said, "you wouldn't want me to be out of this show."

"For heaven's sakes, don't make a little speech," Muriel said. "I just wish you didn't make me think . . ." she stopped a moment . . . "that you're glad I won't be around."

"Now, Muriel," was all he could think of saying, "now Muriel."

"Melly," she said, "you're all I have."

"Now, Muriel," he said, "you've got the boys."

The mention of the boys pulled everything together, and besides, Muriel was a service wife who knew a wife must not upset things when the army was off to war.

"Forget what I said, will you, Melly," she told him. "Of course you're not glad you're going — except at the same time you can't help but be."

"Now, Muriel," he said, "now, Muriel."

"And now we're on the subject," she said, "just see you keep your own nose clean."

He saw plenty of other farewells. You could not avoid them when they took place, openly, all around you in every railroad station. They always created a personnel problem whenever troops were alerted for overseas, and every one of those scenes was characteristic of all the others. There was a staff sergeant, for instance, at Paisley named Cathgart, a well-set-up kid who had a lot of the army in him in spite of his having been an insurance agent on the outside. When the train was moving east from Paisley to the embarkation point, Mel Goodwin stepped off to get some air at some Middle Western whistle stop and there he saw Cathgart kissing a girl who was down at the station passing coffee for the USO and who acted like a wife, and he hoped she was, because she had a little two-year-old golden-haired kid with her. He never asked how Cathgart had arranged to have her meet the train. The man had broken security to do it, but sometimes it was advisable not to take cognizance of everything. At any rate there were Cathgart and the girl and the child in a three-way clinch on the platform, and when the word was given to get aboard again, Cathgart was sobbing like a baby, and he sent word to Cathgart to report to him in his compartment up in front. It was funny how you began traveling in style once there was a war. He had rated a private car and a driver at Paisley and plane priorities when he took trips from Washington. He rated a drawing room now because he had to do routine administrative business on the train.

"Listen, son," he said to Cathgart, "I happened to see you outside there."

"Yes, sir," Cathgart said. "Christ, sir, I had no idea she would be there."

"Oh, hell," Melville Goodwin told him, "that's all right, Cathgart, but everybody in this outfit has to say good-by to somebody. I had to say good-by to my own wife in Washington. I know how it takes it out of you, but we all go through it. Just remember that, and if you feel bad, son, and if you want to talk about it, just take your weight off your feet and light up a cigarette and tell me."

"Thanks a lot, sir," Cathgart said. "It just got me, seeing Milly."

"So her name's Milly, is it?" Melville Goodwin said.

"Yes, sir," Cathgart said, and then he went on for a while about Milly. It seemed that he had married Milly three years before, at a time when he was selling farm machinery.

"Well, here's something else to remember, son," Melville Goodwin told him. "We're all teammates, no matter what the rank, and nobody lets a teammate down." It never hurt to let men know you were a human being.

God had kept him safe so that he could hear the guns again, and now he had his chance to pay his debt to God and to his country. There was no wonder that he looked as though he were going to a party, as Muriel had said. He had been working for quite a while to get dressed up for that party. He was not a shavetail any longer. He had been to the War College with its extremely limited and selected enrollment of officers who were almost certain to become top brass. He had the equipment to make a stab at any job that was handed to him. There had been a lot of white-haired boys in tough competition at Paisley, and he had been able to keep his place. What was more, he learned when he got to Africa that he was able to say to hell with all this accumulated knowledge when necessary. He meant that he was not weighed down by all his intellectual equipment, like these pedants or theorists who bored the hell out of sensible people. By the time North Africa was secure, even though he got a shell fragment in his shoulder before the show was over (which fortunately did not keep him off the beach where those damned Greek temples stood near Salerno), he was pretty handy.

Frequently you had to learn fast in North Africa if you wanted to be around next day to absorb more knowledge. Uncle Sam needed every horseshoe he had in his pockets for that operation—with the best units still green and none of them battle-wise. Sometimes he felt like old Rip van Winkle himself when he saw the self-propelled guns and the tanks and the jeeps and the trucks and the tactical air cover and compared them with the stuff around Château-Thierry in the other war. Nevertheless the basic elements were all the same, and all the old logistics headaches.

After the landing he was up ahead on the way to Tunis with a tank unit known by the code word "Force Goodwin"—but there was no use being technical about groupings. If they didn't reach Tunis before the Jerries, you could blame it on the mud and roads, because they certainly tried like hell to make that play. He began to realize in a few days that you had to blow every instrument in the band. When it came to a pinch, you had to be an artilleryman or an engineer or a tank specialist, and you never knew how things would be balanced or grouped from one day to the next.

North Africa, in spite of its Frenchified cities, looked like something in a Sunday school picture book. He had read in ancient history that the country was semiarid, whereas, books to the contrary, it was always raining when you wanted air cover, and the gumbo on the roads was like glue—but somehow there was always good weather and good footing for the Jerries and the Italians. The Arabs fitted right into that mess. They could have the country any time as far as he was concerned, and anybody who wanted could have the Arabs. They were always around everywhere like flies.

Once when he was a whole lot farther away from everything than he should have been, trying to get a look himself at a German concentration — because nobody had sent any coherent word back — he and a walkie-talkie boy were suddenly pinned down by machine-gun fire. Just as he was trying to figure out some way to get some solid terrain between his party and the gun and was hoping the Krauts weren't going to open up with the mortars next, he felt a pull at his leg. You might have thought it was someone in the group with a bright idea about something, but instead of that it was one of those Arabs trying to sell him half a dozen eggs. That was the way it always was with Arabs. They came right out of the ground like prairie dogs, and when they weren't selling something, they were stealing, but he did not mean to deliver a travelogue. He never did see much of North Africa except for various portions into which his nose had been rubbed.

If he wanted, he could give a good lecture about Kasserine Pass, where we came so near to being pushed back on our behinds, but now he was not talking before the War College. His tanks and some other units that came under his command took a whipping there, but they pulled out all right, and maybe he had a little to do with this. Anyway, some people still thought that he had.

In order to refresh his memory about North Africa and subsequent operations, the General produced a packet of letters which he had written home and which Muriel had brought from Washington after hearing he was to be interviewed. He read excerpts from them to Philip Bentley and lent the whole lot to me later, and, though the letters did not shed much more light on North Africa, in certain ways they did help to round out the Goodwin picture.

DEAR MURIEL,

Babe, who just dropped in to say good-by, says he will give you this on his return to Washington, if he doesn't wet his feet. Don't ask Babe about his future plans because they won't be bright, if you know what

I mean. The poor guy just hasn't got what it takes out here, and he's on his way out. Poor Babe. I am replacing him, and naturally it hurts like hell. Funny, isn't it? Remember how you used to say you wished I got around the way Babe did? Well, well.

I don't need any socks or anything. Just now dry goods, including brassières, are running out our ears. However, if you can pick up a handful of new westerns and whodunnits, give them to Bud to give to Gerald if he's still in there with the Chief. Gerald can wangle them out here, but say to hold them with Smitty at Algiers. Maybe I'll get back to that dream town someday and hang out in the Aletti — maybe. They have sawed-off beer bottles for glassware there and wrapping paper for napkins, all except the Limey boys, who have silver and napery. Well, well. Whoever said Africa was hot? It's all mud. I'm even holed up in a mud hut with a mud wall around it. Goats jump over the wall and get in the yard. We ate goat yesterday and it still stays with me. Just now I picked a piece of him out of my back molar. Slim sends you his regards. He's a real comfort to me. If you're writing to Katie Burwell, tell her from me that Jim did fine. There wasn't enough of poor old Jim to pick up, and a piece of him landed on my helmet, but you needn't tell her that.

It's cold as Greenland here but last week it was hot in certain sectors. Don't worry about me and don't go around asking questions. I'm feeling fine, and everything's beginning to get in the groove. You know I've always liked this stuff, and everybody else here is beginning to like it. By God, they'd better. It's building up, and if they want to slap us down, they'd better do it quick. I have a hunch they're going to make a try for it, but don't ask questions. Old Heinzy called me in last night, five miles in the mud, and all the usual yakety-yak. I hope he doesn't drop it if he's given the ball.

It's nice to think of you in Washington. Give Charley my love and tell him we raised our little boy to be a soldier, and please tell Bob if he wants to try for the Pacific it won't hurt my feelings. It looks as though they need a little help there. There's something itching and I'd better read my shirt a while. We're out of lice powder.

Love, and don't worry,

MEL

DEAR MURIEL,

Shorty, who is going over to have a little talk about certain things that have happened, says he will get this to you, but don't go trying to get hold of him. He's got a lot on his mind. Oh yes, I'm in the base hospital with a piece of hardware in my shoulder, but I'm walking around already and playing gin rummy with the other hand, so don't worry. I was lucky not to get my block blown off, and I walked out of it under my own steam, without running to the nearest exit, and no one else did either. They were a fine selfless bunch of kids. All they need is a little straight talk and they'll do anything.

If you read the papers maybe you'll know what all this is about. I'd like to read the communiqué myself. It will have to be a masterpiece because we really got a bloody nose and a few right in the guts — and maybe the Limeys rather like seeing us over the barrel. The orders were to pull out and it was pretty late to pull. I took over the cover-up job, between you and me, without consulting Heinzy. It looked for a while like old Custer making a last stand with a lot of Sitting Bulls around us. In fact I thought maybe I was going to be Custer, but they dug in when I got some heavy stuff around their right end. I mean they thought it was heavy, and we walked off. Slim got himself killed, you may have heard. There never was a finer kid. Please write Edwina that I'm writing personally. Who do you think I saw when I walked off? Old Folsom, my Tac at the Point. Do you remember? The one who told us to stroll on Flirtation Walk. He was dead — air strafing — but I had time to gather up some of his letters and things personally. You see the hardware in the shoulder didn't slow me up, so don't worry and don't start pulling strings. I am not going Stateside because I shall be fit for duty in three weeks. I got the word this morning.

By the way, they came around this afternoon and pinned something on me and took some pictures. You can ask the Chief about it if you want. He or Gerald ought to have the details by now. Now don't worry, I'm feeling fine. I'm reading Agatha Christie when I'm not playing gin rummy. The word is the shoulder won't even be stiff. Give my love to Charley and Robert.

With love,
Mel

This letter was all he had ever set down regarding his part in the Kasserine Pass action, except for his report and recommendations now somewhere on file in the Pentagon, and a report would have been too technical to have made much sense — and he was not giving any military lecture anyway. The staff work was faulty, and a lot of people in back got the wind up. It was easy enough to give orders for a quick withdrawal, if you were sitting somewhere looking at maps — but this was off the record and he was not going to expert anything that happened. The order to withdraw came through at three in the morning — when anyone physically in touch with anything could see that there would have to be some sort of holding action along the high ground on the front known as Area 20, which overlooked a track along which the enemy would obviously move part of his armor. It was an elementary problem of buying time. When Melville Goodwin received the order, his chief, Arty Watson, who was commanding the area, saw as clearly as he did that a complete withdrawal would leave everything wide open. He had no criticism to make of Arty Watson, who immediately began sending back everything that was feasible, but half an hour later mortar and eighty-eight fire began dropping on them.

Mel Goodwin was still with his chief trying to straighten things out when one of those eighty-eights landed under a weapons carrier, and a minute later *he* was chief. He sent back everything that wasn't needed, and by the time it was daylight he was alone with his combat team all dug in, plus three one-fifty-fives and four tanks, one of them disabled. It was light enough by that time to secure some information. The Jerries were coming right down the track just where he expected them, tanks and trucks and everything, evidently thinking that it was clear ahead. Sometimes the Jerries weren't as bright as you thought they were going to be, considering their experience. It was something to remember, watching that column snaking toward their position over that Godforsaken country, with the sun just rising. The only problem was how to stop them for an appreciable period of time, and he waited until they were on the level ground in front before he let them have it with everything available. They were like sitting ducks, only there were just too many ducks. Nevertheless they certainly acted surprised, and their whole column was in an unholy mess. He always believed that if there had been more fire power available they might have turned back permanently. As it was, they overestimated his force, and they were confused when he got his tanks firing into them well on the left. It took personal persuasion to keep everything cracking, but just the same, it was a good fight. He only wished he could have had more time to observe it instead of being so continually busy.

At any rate by afternoon what was left of his group was still holding the high ground in Area 20. They had bought the time, and there was no use hanging around any longer. When the sun was setting, he sent back everything that could roll, and the rest of them began walking and they walked all night until they were picked up around daylight. He had brought off the wounded, but a lot of equipment and dead remained back in Area 20. He was not familiar with all of the night's events. His shoulder had been bandaged and it had stopped bleeding, but the wound may have made him lightheaded. Nevertheless he kept everything under control all the way personally, and he could still put one foot ahead of the other when he walked into headquarters and made the report. His memory was vague as to just what he said, but other people told him later, probably making it into a good story.

The story was that he saluted old Heinzy, which he probably did, since his right hand was all right, and then he said:

"There's been a little trouble up in Area 20, sir, but we'd all like to start going back as soon as we've had some coffee."

That was what they said he said, and it made a good story, but he never could have said anything like that to a major general who knew the score. Nevertheless he always did think that they should have moved forward instead of pulling back farther. There was nothing in any of this to be proud of because he was paid to work out problems like Area 20, but there was one thing he did remember that pleased him. When he walked out of the headquarters—and he was still walking—he heard a master sergeant say, "The God-damned fighting bastard."

That meant a lot to him, coming when it did, because his shoulder was full of red-hot needles and his left arm was numb. The man who had spoken was standing with three or four others beside a jeep, and Mel Goodwin walked right up to him.

"Son," he said, "if I go first, I'd like to have you write those words on my tombstone."

This was true, whether or not it made a good story, and he did not care who knew it.

He was in the hospital when Task Force Headquarters was reorganized. In May he did desk work in Algiers because the medics were still checking on his shoulder. He got his star in June '43 but did not see the Sicilian show or any more fighting until he was on the beach at Salerno as an assistant division commander. He was a specialist in armor by then and he knew it. When he was yanked out and sent to England to take command of the Silver Leaf Armored and whip it into shape in preparation for the cross-Channel invasion, he knew that he was equipped to take armor anywhere, anytime and anyhow, and that was all there was to it. He did not want to be technical, but he did know quite a little about contemporary warfare, and why not? He had spent most of his life studying war and he had been presented with fine opportunities to perfect himself in practice. He wrote some of his thoughts in a letter to his wife in April 1944, and perhaps the letter would cover most of what he had to say.

Dear Muriel,

I don't see what harm there is when you get this in asking the Chief or Gerald or somebody to tell you confidentially if they can what they've pinned on me over here. I don't mean any more chest spinach either, though sometimes they do seem to pass decorations here as easily as we used to pass the buck. I mean the job they handed to me. Old Skeet Shaw felt kind of upset when he got the word to turn it over to me, and I felt kind of mean about taking it from Skeet after he had shown me around, but you know Skeet, and he knows we have to take what's dished out to us on this picnic. Skeet said he would rather have it me than anybody else and he said kind words about me to the officers when he turned it over. The kids don't seem to mind the idea of having someone who's been there before help them get shaken down. They are nice kids, and Skeet has done a lot of pulling and hauling on them so they look about as much in the groove as they can be until they get their tryout. By the way, Bugsy Waters and Long John Gooch are both here with me. We're making up into quite a team. I even like the padres. They look like athletic babies who will hand out the good word right.

Do you remember when we bought Robert the electric train the Christmas we were stationed at Sykes and Bob didn't know he was going to get it, in spite of the carpenter setting up the table and Gooding working on the electrical gadgets? Do you remember how Bob looked, just as though the train and the tracks had dropped out of the sky, and how he kept walking around and around in a sort of daze as though he couldn't believe it and then how we couldn't pry him loose from that electric train for weeks? Well, that's how I feel about this Thing and all the lovely gadgets that go with it. I feel just like a kid at Christmas and maybe sometimes I act that way. I keep getting up in the middle of the night and hopping in a jeep just to see it's all pinned down and hasn't moved somewhere else. I keep wanting to go right over across the street and try it out on the other gang. Believe me, it's going to be good, and I think I'm going to know how to work it. I ought to after that Italian business, even if I finally bust a gut. Well, you go and ask the Chief, and you might tell Bob and Charley that they really handed the old man something. It won't hurt them to know that the old man has kind of made good on his own and that some people think well of him for all the scrabbling around he's done out here. I sort of wish you were here to see it.

Old Baldy is the number one in these parts, as maybe you can imagine if you've been talking to the Chief. The other night he asked a couple of us to his little shanty to dinner — it looked as though it belonged to a duke or something — to show us off to the Big Boy himself and some of the little big boys who were with him. I hadn't seen Big Boy since North Africa and he's grown some. Funny our paths never crossed, but you remember what Pershing said about him? He'd never known him either. Anyway, you'll be pleased to know he chewed the fat with me for several minutes and asked me to look him up if I was ever around the big city. I won't if I can help it. I'm an outdoor boy, and the high echelons always make me sweat, and when I sweat I stink. I can just hear you saying I always get coarse when I'm with troops. Everybody sends you their love, though, and a lot of them remember old times.

I laughed to read about you and Enid and the picture puzzles. Life is quite a picture puzzle in itself, isn't it? — one you never finish because something's always jiggling the table. Just take it easy now. I'm doing fine. All that worries me is that this island may sink with what we've got on it, even with the barrage balloons to hold it up, but that's an old one, isn't it? I'm glad Bob's moving out. I wish I might have seen him, but tell him from me I know he'll be good. How could he help it, considering who his mama is? The washcloths will come in handy the next time I have to hit the dirt. Give Charley a slap in the pants and tell him I'll write him tomorrow.

With love,
MEL

There were some other letters, too, but this one seemed pretty well to cover the situation. Anyone who had been in preinvasion England could add in all the color himself. Old P. T. Barnum should have been alive to have seen it because it really was the greatest show on earth. It was something to be a part of that show and to have been right in the first team with the Silver Leaf Armored and with the teammates. It was a page of history, and if he was just one of the punctuation marks, still he was on the page, and anyone could read it without his doing much further talking. However, in case anything more was needed, he did have a newspaper clipping which he could show for what it was worth. He never suspected at the time that he was talking for publication, since he was not one of those field runners who made the papers, and there were too many stars anyway on that all-star, all-American team. Yet maybe this was not accurate — the British were on the team, too. At any rate when a newspaper correspondent named Al Crouch came around, Mel Goodwin never thought seriously that this would mean any kind of feature article, and after all, it only appeared in the Sunday supplement of a newspaper in upstate New York, but it might as well be included in the record.

Actually it made me a little homesick for the great days when I read it. Its journalistic language was characteristic of those days, and I had participated in many similar efforts when I had been in Public Relations. I could remember no correspondent named Al Crouch, but then, accredited correspondents were as thick as flies before the invasion. It was utterly characteristic that he did not call himself Albert Crouch, but just plain Al. All those correspondents were always abbreviating their first names. They had to be tough even if they were 4–F and wore glasses. The dispatch was simply dated

"Somewhere in England, 1944," and it had appeared in print only after the invasion. The headline was "Al Crouch Looks Them Over. . . ."

Your correspondent took a busman's holiday today, spending his time visiting, instead of an Air Force outfit, an American armored division on a wind-swept English moor. He had the good fortune, on dropping into its headquarters, an uninvited guest, to ran smack into its commanding officer, Major General Melville A. Goodwin.

Some division!

If you have been around for a while on this tight little island you get hep to an outfit that's ready and rarin' to go, and, oh brother, this one was prancin'! And when you've rattled around enough among the big brass hats, you get to know when a man's a real guy.

Some guy, this cocky young fighting divisional CO, with his words that hit you like a punch in the midriff and his infectious, boyish smile!

Some guy, this Mel Goodwin, right from the top of his battle-buffeted helmet with the two stars riveted on it, down to the toes of his GI shoes. No funny business — all fight and a yard wide!

Maybe you folks around Syracuse have never heard of Mel. It's your loss if you haven't, but the Mel Goodwins that make this army strut its stuff aren't the kind you see at peacetime tea parties or handing out E award pins. In case you haven't heard of Mel Goodwin, here's the pitch, as Colonel "Long John" Gooch, his chief of staff, handed it to me hot off the griddle.

Melville A. Goodwin, born in the tiny town of Hallowell, New Hampshire (ever hear of it? I hadn't), where his father was for many years the local druggist and where young Mel once jerked a few sodas himself (but maybe this ought to be off the record!). Young Mel got out of West Point just in time to knock out two German machine guns personally in World War I, and win the DSC and *Croix de guerre* with palm. He may not mention it himself, but he got all these things again in World War II and a shoulder wound for refusing to be evacuated in a little mix-up with some of Rommel's bad boys, and then a couple of swift one-twos at Salerno.

"Hell," he says, with that smile of his, "forget about the ribbons, son! I think perhaps they shower down a little easier when you get pushed up to the top of the heap." Anyway, no GI in that armored outfit would agree with him. As Staff Sergeant Milton I. Hawker (Rochester, N. Y.) put it, when I brought up the subject, "That guy doesn't look in mirrors. He doesn't have to use mirrors."

At any rate, I ran smack into "that guy" just as I reached headquarters, and the word is you run into "that guy" everywhere. This division is definitely his baby, and every one of its GIs is one of Mel Goodwin's kids. Don't ask me how.

"Well, son," he said to me, "tag along if you want to look around."

We just hopped into a nearby jeep. The General did the driving himself, a lot of it on two wheels.

Funnily enough, everybody seemed glad to see "that guy" whenever he stopped the jeep. He just fitted in naturally with the GIs. For instance, there was Pfc. Martin J. Flynn (Albany, N. Y.) taking a BAR to pieces.

"Here, son," General Goodwin said, "let's see if I can still do that." A little group gathered around him just like kids watching teacher. "I haven't fussed around with one of those things since Africa," he said, tossing the BAR back to Pfc. Flynn. "It's nice to know I can still do it. It may be useful to me where we're going in case I see one lying around."

This one got a good laugh.

With all that automatic fire power — the General pointed out to that serious-faced little group — all you had to do was to spray it out in front of you and keep walking.

"And I'll be walking with you," he said, "whenever we aren't riding. We'll just stop now and then and stretch our legs this summer. Summer's a great season over in France — in case we should be going there."

This got another laugh. He could really tickle the boys.

"Of course it might be that one or two of us may sprain an ankle," he said, "but there'll be nurses to massage it and you can take it from me, a lot of very sharp-looking nurses are coming over."

And so it went for three hours all up and down the line. Hard-bitten, tanned, alert Mel Goodwin had the old army "pro" stamped over every inch of him. In spite of that quiet kidding manner, he always had the authority. He had so much that he could handle it carelessly, just as I have seen an old bar fly hold a glass. That was why he could rub shoulders with the toughest GI in the outfit, drop into a company mess hall as we did, scrounge a cup of hot java and sit exchanging salty wisecracks with the mess "sarge" and the KPs.

As Corporal Wally Sterner (Bath, N. Y.) laughingly confided: "You kinda don't mind the fact he's got stars and all the chicken gut over his left pocket."

A private with a paintbrush was stenciling initials on the side of a truck — RTA.

"What's that?" I asked.

Mel Goodwin regarded the truck quizzically.

"It's sort of alphabet soup," he quipped, "but it's the division motto — Right There Anyhow — RTA. Maybe it sounds simple to you, but combat is a pretty simple thing. In fact you can sum it up in just one word."

"What word?" I inquired curiously.

His eyes looked cold and icy blue. Maybe his mind was moving across the Channel to the Great Adventure.

"Guts," he said, "four letters, son. Don't laugh at it."

I did not laugh at it because it sounded all right coming from Major General Mel Goodwin on that wind-swept British moor.

"American troops when handled by competent command are in my opinion the best soldiers in the world," he said. "I think I know how to lead troops, with God's help. Sometimes in battle you get pretty close to God. What was it the Marine said? There ain't no atheists in foxholes. Yes, son, you wake up sometimes at night and think a lot of lonely thoughts when you wear stars and face the fact that you're in charge of all these men, with no excuses and only yourself to blame. I hope I know my business because I think I've got the best damned division in the world. I mean I *know*."

Then his mood changed. First he smiled and then he laughed.

"Hell," he said, "I wouldn't swap my job for Eisenhower's. You see, I like it here."

You had the feeling that everything in General Goodwin's division was squared away — oh, oh, I didn't mean to use navy talk.

Well, anyway, come D day, H hour and M minute, this scribe knows one rootin', tootin', shootin' outfit that's going to hit the beach and one general who isn't going to do his fighting in any dugout. When I left them the sun was going down, the bugles were sounding retreat, and Mel Goodwin was saluting his flag. There was a lump in my throat when I drove away from there, but my chin was a little higher. I was a little prouder that I was an American and I was good and mad, too, mad at that army doctor who found that I had a heart murmur and flat feet. You see, really and truly I wanted to go Right There Anyhow, too!

I wanted to throw in with that swell bunch! I wanted to hit the beach with Goodwin!

It was hard to see why this cracker-barrel sage had not driven Mel Goodwin nuts in May 1944. The General could not have been courting publicity. If he had been he would not have shot the works to an unsyndicated correspondent like Al Crouch. I could attribute part of his compliance to the respect and apprehension with which some high-ranking officers regarded the press, and also, perhaps Mel Goodwin had been lonely out there on his moor, not that I believed it was a moor. He may have leaned on this Al Crouch as he had on me in Paris, desirous of talking to someone who was out of the chain of command, someone to whom he could explain some of the things that everyone around him took for granted.

In spite of his clichés and ephemeral journalese, Al Crouch did have perceptive sensitivity of a sort. Despite the lapse of time, Al Crouch could make you see something of what he saw. Those direct quotes of his, one of modern journalism's greatest banes, he had doubtless drawn from his memory, but they sounded so real that I could hear Mel Goodwin's voice. In the end you began to distrust your own sophistication. If I had been there with Al Crouch, I, too, would have wished that I could throw in with that swell bunch and hit the beach with Mel Goodwin, even though I would have been of no great help had I hit it.

When Myra Fineholt read that piece aloud, I had the feeling that she, too, wanted to hit the beach and so did Phil Bentley. Naturally Phil concealed his emotions, and, as he had a good ear for prose, the piece must have hurt him even more than it did me.

"Well," Phil Bentley said, "Mr. Crouch certainly gave you all he had."

Mel Goodwin looked at Phil Bentley self-consciously.

"Well, frankly," he said, "I know you can do better than that, Phil. That Crouch, now I come to think of it, was a funny sort of Joe, but he liked the old Silver Leaf, and anybody who liked the Silver Leaf goes down all right with me. Maybe I'm a ham actor at heart. There's always that temptation in front of troops."

I could see Phil Bentley's face light up, and Myra was writing it down. It would make a good caption under one of the photographs — a ham actor at heart.

"Frankly," Mel Goodwin said, "I was surprised when I saw that clipping. He sent it to me and asked me for my photograph. I don't believe I said all those things, but just the same, it gives you a sort of working idea."

I saw Colonel Flax squirm uneasily.

"You're right," Phil Bentley said, "I'd have done it differently, but it does give you an idea."

"Well, there it is for what it's worth," Mel Goodwin said. "If he's shot the works, so have I. I've been shooting them all over the place for you, Phil, and you've got me pinned right down. I keep living things all over again."

Mel Goodwin paused, and we could see him thinking, half happily and half sadly, with much the same expression I must have worn when I told Camilla about my roller skates.

"You know," he said, "if I say so myself, I used to be a good pistol shot, not that I'm so bad right now. In fact I believe I could have made the army team once if Mrs. Goodwin hadn't discouraged it. She always had an idea it didn't get you anywhere going around to shooting matches. Well, I used to have the sweetest forty-five. It fitted into my hand so that every line of my palm seemed to fill some part of the grip. I really think I could have plugged the head out of a dime with it snap shooting. It got to be a part of me, that forty-five. I left it back in Washington when I went out on 'Torch' because I wanted Bob to have some personalized gift from me, even though he isn't any better than an average shot. Well, Bob mislaid it somewhere around Leyte. That's all right, but I still get thinking about that gun. Sometimes I wonder where it is now . . . all rusted somewhere in the bush, I guess."

The General held his hand in front of him as though he were gripping the memory of it.

"Now that gun," he said, "is sort of like the old Silver Leaf. Of course nothing can be precise that's made up of a number of thousand human beings all suffering wear and tear, but by and large the

Silver Leaf was an efficient unit according to any set of standards. At any rate my greatest moments were with it. I guess I was made to head a division like the Silver Leaf. Everybody's made for something, and maybe the better you get at doing one thing, the less good you are at coping with other things . . . maybe."

The General's face had a sad, half-empty look. It was the first time I had ever seen sadness in him, and the first time also that he seemed to be face to face with a situation that he could not quite estimate.

"Well,". he said, "where's the old Silver Leaf now? It's all in pieces like one of those alarm clocks I used to disassemble when I was a kid. It isn't anywhere. What's going to happen to people like me? Sometimes I think of all the casualties and dollars it cost to turn me into what I am. Maybe I was useful once, but what's the point of it now, when I'm not really wanted any more? Oh, yes, I'll get something. Maybe I'll even be a permanent colonel, pushing or hauling on something, but maybe — I don't mean to bellyache — but maybe I ought to be pushing daisies along the Rhine along with a lot of the old Silver Leaf crowd."

Melville Goodwin stopped. It seemed to me that his voice had ended on a note of surprise when he reached that logical conclusion, and the worst of it was I found myself thinking that he might have been right. The power and the glory were gone, evaporated into a thin haze of memory.

Colonel Flax looked uncomfortable. From the Public Relations angle such a conclusion indicated an emotional instability that was not for the good of the service.

"Now, General," he said, "you don't mean that."

Then the General must have realized himself that it was not for the good of the service.

"I guess I didn't phrase my thought quite correctly, Flax," he said. "The thought I was trying to convey is, I can never feel sorry for anyone who was killed clean in the line of duty, and that's how I should have put it. Frankly, I've never been greatly interested in death, one way or another. Old whiskers with the hourglass is always hiding around some corner, isn't he?" The General laughed, and looked relieved now that matters were back on a firmer basis. "Give me a cigarette, will you, Flax? My only thought, now that the old boy isn't chumming around with me as much as he used to, is that I've got to do some future planning, and I've kind of forgotten how to sit still."

"Now, General," Colonel Flax said, "you know that the bosses won't let anyone like you sit still."

Melville Goodwin smiled again. For years there had been someone around prepared to tell him the right thing.

"Well, anyway, Flax," he said, "I may be able to take a little time off to do some hunting and fishing. Did you ever try that wild boar shooting in Germany?"

"No, sir," Colonel Flax said.

"Let's see," he said, "where was I?"

There was a curious pause. For a second or two no one seemed to remember where the General had left off.

"I guess you were about ready to hit that beach in Normandy," Phil Bentley said.

"That's right," the General said, "it was Omaha."

We all waited for him to go on, but he did not continue, and then I knew that he was empty and finished. His clock had stopped at Omaha and he did not want to wind it up again.

"You know," he said, "I think you've got about all I have to give. Let's break it off at Omaha."

He glanced at his watch and stood up.

"What I want, Sid, is one or maybe two of those nice pale Martini cocktails and then a bite of lunch, and then I'd better kiss the girls good-by. Get yourself braced for it, Myra."

It was the first time that he had called Miss Fineholt "Myra" and that concession was like the dropping of a curtain. Phil Bentley must have known how things were. There must have always been a time in other interviews when it was useless to go further.

"All right, let's call it a day, sir," Phil Bentley said, but it was not quite a day.

Now that the show was over, we were reluctant to leave the show, and Melville Goodwin was like a gracious host.

"You get my point, don't you?" the General said. "There comes a time when you can't blow your own horn any more. The rest of it is what you might call straight military history, and Flax can give it to you if you want it, or you might get in touch with my old chief of staff, General Gooch."

"The Washington Bureau's covered that already," Phil Bentley said.

The General laughed.

"Well," he said, "let's hope I've lived right."

We all laughed, but the General was waiting expectantly, as though something were missing, and I knew what it was. There had been no formal speech of acknowledgment, but just as I was about to make it, Phil Bentley did it instead.

"General," he said, "I want to thank you for everything. You say you're a specialist, and I suppose I'm one, too. I must have done thirty or more of these interviews and some of them have been tough. Well, this one hasn't been tough at all."

"And Phil and I wonder if you'll sign us each a photograph," Myra Fineholt said.

It was exactly the right touch, the photograph, and as she pulled two out of her briefcase, I could see that Mel Goodwin approved.

"Well," he said, "I didn't know this was coming. Flax, lend me your pen, will you?" but Colonel Flax had his pen out and waiting before the General asked for it.

To Myra, he wrote on Miss Fineholt's photograph, *who took down all of Operation Windbag, With love, from Mel.*

To Phil, who made the old man stick his neck out, he wrote across Phil Bentley's picture, *and is too good a guy to chop it off, With admiration and affection, Mel.*

"Say, Flax," the General said, "how about going out and whistling for drinks." The operation was over but headquarters was still intact. In fact I was almost embarrassed when he remembered where he was.

"Forgive me, will you, Sid?" he said. "I'm just like Muriel. I'm always taking over."

402

XXVI

Once More the Sirens Sing

I HAD traveled extensively before, during and after the war. Many of my trips had been highly uncomfortable, combining physical fatigue, bad water, inadequate food, and insects; but when a trip was over, a mellow glow immediately began to dull its grimmer aspects. I would think of the sights I had seen, and the companions, whose eccentricities I had scarcely been able to tolerate, became warmly agreeable in retrospect. Small grudges and annoyances would be forgotten, and regrets would begin to arise that the party was breaking up and everyone would exchange addresses and promise everyone else to get together sometime soon.

We had all followed Melville Goodwin through a strange country, and the experience had drawn us together, but I personally was experiencing the sort of museum fatigue that comes when you have seen and heard too much. Somehow I had not been the casual observer that I had thought I would be — but it was almost over now. The portable bar was in the living room for the last time, and they would all be gone directly after lunch. One more of those peculiar meals, and Goodwin, Fineholt, Flax and Bentley would be drawn back to the orbits of their own lives. The old rule was already working. It had been quite a trip with Mel Goodwin and we were a swell lot of people, and we must get together sometime soon. I even remember suggesting to Fineholt that we have lunch so that I could show her the studio, and Helen herself was sorry now that the end was near, because I heard her telling Mel Goodwin, who was showing us for the last time how to mix Martinis, that nothing had been any trouble at all. He had not descended upon her. She had enjoyed every minute of it.

"I'm just beginning to understand the army," I heard her say, "and now you're going and I'll have to start understanding Sidney all over again."

"Say, Flax," the General said, "upstairs in my room there are two parcels on top of my kit bag — some things I've been saving for Sid and Helen. Would you mind asking Oscar to bring them down?"

Of course Colonel Flax did not mind, and Mel Goodwin took a swallow of his Martini.

"Just two little things I picked up after the surrender," he said. "They've been knocking around in my baggage. They don't amount to anything, but they do have an association value."

In spite of the casual way he put it, our journey together had meant something to him also. When Oscar brought the two parcels tied up in brown paper, I could not help remembering the postwar days when everybody began pinning medals on everybody else. The parcel he gave to me contained one of those ugly Luger automatics that had passed almost as currency in the early occupation.

"I suppose you own one of these things already," he said, "but this is a special Luger. It turned up when they were searching Goering's baggage — that time when they fed him chicken and green peas. It belonged to old Fatso personally, and here are the papers to prove it."

I held the thing as though it were a hot potato, and everybody laughed.

"Is it loaded?" I asked.

"That's funny," the General said, "I've had it all this time and I've never thought to look. Hand it over here, Sid."

It was impressive to watch him with the Luger. He handled it in an expert, half-contemptuous professional way, breaking out the magazine with a quick one-two motion.

"By God," he said, "it *is* loaded. I wonder what was the matter with our boys. Here, Flax, you keep the ammunition. Maybe Mrs. Flax might like it."

"She certainly would, sir," Colonel Flax said, "particularly if — er — Sidney would let me have a copy of those documents."

"Hand Helen her little bundle, will you, Flax," the General said. "It's a sloppy package. I didn't tie it up myself."

His words gave me a fleeting memory of young Mel Goodwin sealing packages in his father's drugstore.

"Why," Helen said, "what a lovely tea cloth."

"It was right on the table in the bunker in the room where Hitler shot himself," the General said, "but the stain on it is tea, and here's the paper to prove it, signed by the Russian Intelligence. I got it at one of those vodka parties when we were still hotsy-totsy with the Russians."

"Oh," Helen said, "it's lovely." I recognized the tone, though the General did not, as one she employed whenever I gave her something that she could not imagine how to use.

"Just from me to you, dear," he said, "and Muriel particularly wanted you to have it."

Then I wondered fleetingly what grisly relic he might be saving for Dottie Peale. It was bound to be good, although I could not think of anything that might outrank Fatso's gun and Eva Braun's tea cloth. It was the direct measure of his gratitude, and I could not help but be touched.

"Why, son," he said when we both thanked him, "they aren't anything. I wish they could be the Hesse jewels," and then he thought of Phil Bentley and Myra Fineholt. "I wish I weren't running clean out of souvenirs," he said. "Say, Flax, how about getting the powder taken out and then loosening up and handing Phil and Myra each one of Fatso's cartridges?"

It was the time for passing out the Legions of Merit.

"I'd love to have one for a lipstick holder," Myra said, "and Phil can put his on a key ring."

"It takes a woman to think up things," the General said. "Sister, you've got a lot of bright ideas."

We were all a swell crowd, and the trip was almost over, and now the General was in a reminiscent mood. He was about to tell another one of his stories, and it was sad to think that it would be the last of them.

"I don't know why I should have thought of this," he was saying. "There was a young officer at Maule. That was right in the middle of the Bulge show, and everything was pretty scrambled up. Goochy,

405

my chief of staff, sent him to report to me personally about some snarl up forward. I don't remember what, because it was all one big foul-up. He was just a kid, a nice first lieutenant, nice face, nice hands. He gave me his name and outfit, but I forgot his name because I was thinking of the tactical situation. He gave a good report, too, all the facts in order. Then I saw him swaying. I should have seen he was going out on his feet — just plain pooped — but I wasn't thinking about him until he fell down slam on the floor, out cold. Then I thought what a dead-game kid he was, and I wanted to make a note of his name personally so that I could pin something on him later. So I looked in the kid's pocket and pulled out a letter, and found myself reading it, forgetting I shouldn't. Well, do you know what the letter was? It was a 'Dear John' letter. The kid's wife was leaving him for a navy flier in Jacksonville. He reminded me of Robert, stretched out there on the floor, except he didn't have my kid's physique. Well, anyway I saw he got a bronze star out of it, even if he lost the gal. Maybe it helped a little, but it didn't fix anything permanently, because he was killed up on the Rhine. Well, I don't know how this crossed my mind. Who's ready for another drink?"

I wished that Oscar would appear with the news that lunch was ready, because the shadow of the young lieutenant lingered in the room, an uninvited guest, the ghost of an unknown soldier who should have stayed in the ETO where he belonged. I wondered myself how he had escaped out of the tight compartment in which Mel Goodwin kept the memory pictures of other officers and men, to run erratically across the General's mind. There was more in his mind than one ever thought. There were the scars of old decisions and old regrets, for instance, and the weight of responsibilities that still rested on him, which he could not shift from himself to any subordinate or superior. Those were the things he had to keep all buttoned up and packed away and which he could never allow to move up front. There must have been a lot of things that he had felt obliged to forget as rapidly as possible. It made me uneasy that the young lieutenant should have appeared, but Melville Goodwin was forgetting him again and remembering something funny.

"The blast lifted us right off the seat," I heard him saying, "and then we landed on it again hard, right by the numbers, and Goochy began to swear. Swearing was all right for Goochy, though it always hurt him when I used bad language.

" 'What's the matter, Gooch?' I said. 'Did you pick up one of the pieces?' You see, it was an HE shell and a lot of metal was flying around.

" 'No,' he said, and he looked as though he wanted to cry, 'but I sat down on that God-damned pint.'

"It was that pint of bourbon in his hip pocket. We hadn't seen bourbon for two weeks and I had told him not to carry it on his hip. Well, you should have seen Goochy doing his work that evening. He had to write his orders lying down flat while the medics were taking pieces of glass out of him. The glass was there but the bourbon was all gone. It was really a two-way operation."

Colonel Flax and I were standing a few steps away from the portable bar. We both joined in the merriment, relieved that things were back in the right groove.

"I think this has all been good," the colonel said to me. "Don't you think the General handled himself all right?"

He was appealing to me as a connecting link between the service and the eccentricities of civilians.

"I think Mel did a swell public relations job," I told him.

The colonel looked toward the portable bar and lowered his voice discreetly.

"I've been watching Bentley," he said, "and frankly I had my fingers crossed once or twice. The General is the type that's hard to put over public-relations-wise. You never know how the combat type is going to jump. They get too natural. He's getting pretty natural right now."

I did not answer. After all, the show was over.

"The hours I've sat with combat types, sweating it out in press conferences," the colonel said, "waiting for them to drop it all on the floor. The rough-and-tumble ones are never public-relations-conscious."

"They can't be everything," I said.

Colonel Flax sighed. "Someday," he said, "you and I have got to get together and tell each other stories. I don't know why they're always dropping bricks. They want to be liked and the public is all set to like them and indulge in a little hero worship, and then they drop a brick. Take Patton."

"Well, he was the greatest figure in the war," I said.

"I didn't say he wasn't," Colonel Flax answered, "but, oh brother — whenever he made a speech!" He cast a level appraising glance at General Goodwin. "He hasn't got the color but he's got a few of the Patton traits."

"Well," I said, "they've got to be the same piece of goods because they all have to do the same thing. Maybe the public understands them better than you think."

"Not the left wing," Flax said.

"Everybody isn't left wing," I told him.

"Sometimes it seems as though everybody is," Colonel Flax said, and he sighed again. "Somebody is always pulling the carpet out from under combat generals," and he glanced again at Melville Goodwin. "They have to put over their personality to a lot of twenty-year-old kids. They have to tell themselves they're good about a hundred times a day. They've got to hold that thought or else they'll crack. Look at Goodwin. He looks pretty good, doesn't he?"

Now that he had mentioned it, I had never seen Mel Goodwin looking better.

"He's got his mind on something else now," Colonel Flax said. "Boy, I'm feeling tired," but Mel Goodwin was not tired.

"Hey, Sid," he called, "come over here. I've been asking Helen the name of your tailor, and she can't remember."

"What do you want a tailor for?" I asked.

"That tweed jacket and slacks of yours," Mel Goodwin said. "I need something to wear on Sundays. The war's over."

I wondered whether it was a desire common to all army officers to get out of uniform or whether he was thinking of Dottie Peale. There was something preposterous in the idea of Melville Goodwin dressed in a tweed coat and slacks, minus stars and ribbons with only perhaps a small single enameled decoration in his buttonhole. I wondered what Dottie Peale would say if she saw him in gray slacks or a conservative double-breasted suit. Half of him would be gone and he did not know it.

"Well, what's so funny about it?" Mel Goodwin asked.

He could read my thoughts correctly at the most unexpected times.

"It would give you schizophrenia," I said. "You've been in uniform too long."

The General put his arm around my shoulders. "Sid always comes up with something good," he said. "Maybe Sid's got something." He finished his cocktail and set his glass down deliberately. "All you people on the outside seem to have queer notions about officers in civvies. Now I'll bet Sid here got out of his uniform as soon as he had the chance. Didn't you, Sid?"

"Yes, sir," I answered, "I certainly did."

"You're damned well right you did," Melville Goodwin said. "There's nothing more satisfying to an army man, after a hard day, than getting out of uniform into some everyday clothes. It's like taking off your corset and scratching — excuse me, Helen, my dear."

We all smiled at one another appreciatively.

"Just walking down the street like a plain citizen, without having to take a salute, means a lot. It's like getting out of school. . . . But do you know what Muriel told me as soon as I got off the plane?" He paused dramatically, but none of us knew. "She said that Charley — my kid Charley — had taken over all my civilian wardrobe — and it was a pretty sharp one — and had worn it ragged for the past two years. So here I am, without a fig leaf, except my uniform."

Something in his voice showed it was no time to be amused, even when he mentioned a fig leaf.

"But didn't you get some suits made during the occupation, sir?" Colonel Flax asked.

"I did have a couple of suits made over there," the General said. "There was a tailor in Wiesbaden — Bethge. Frankly, off the record — mind you, off the record, Bentley — that bird would make you up a suit for two cartons of cigarettes."

"What?" Miss Fineholt said. "For only two cartons of cigarettes?" Melville Goodwin shook his finger at her.

"Off the record, Myra," he said. "Well, those suits are with my baggage in Frankfurt. I was yanked over here pretty fast. They may be following me, but they haven't got here yet. . . . Anyway, I think they may look pretty Krauty over here. . . . I've really got to get some civvies."

He stopped, but his mind was already moving away from civilian clothes. They had reminded him of something else.

"Say, Flax," he said, "don't forget those orchids for Mrs. Goodwin, will you?"

"No, sir," said Colonel Flax, and then the General laughed.

"Look at old Flax," he said. "I've run him ragged, haven't I? Don't worry; it's almost over, son."

He must have been watching Flax and me very closely while we were talking. Then I saw Oscar standing in the doorway, and Mel Goodwin saw him, too.

"Come, dear," he said to Helen, "soup's on."

The house was very quiet after they all had left and Farouche began pushing his rubber ring at me more hopefully. The old routine was returning, but Mel Goodwin's personality was still in the house. There were echoes of it everywhere, and everything was at loose ends.

"Sid," Helen said, "what do you think he's going to do?"

"You know what he's going to do. He put on his 'A' uniform after lunch," I said.

"I don't mean that," Helen said. "What do you think he's going to do about everything?"

"I don't know," I said. "I don't care right now."

"Well, I care," Helen said. "I wish people wouldn't come here and throw their personalities around until I begin to worry about them."

It was about time that I looked over the script for the broadcast. It was about time I dropped the problems of Melville Goodwin, because I had problems of my own.

"Forget about him. He's all grown up," I said, and I wished that Farouche would stop dropping the rubber ring in front of me.

"Farouche needs another ribbon," Helen said.

"All right," I said.

I thought we were on another subject, but I was wrong.

"He's a lot younger than you are in a lot of ways. He's so innocent," she said, and I knew she was not speaking about Farouche.

"You shouldn't have done that about the orchids," I told her.

"I couldn't help it," she answered, and she smiled, and neither of us spoke for a while.

"I wonder why Gilbert Frary sent you so many orchids," I said.

"Maybe we'd better think about that, too," she answered, but the personality of Melville Goodwin was still with us.

Once when the dust of events had settled, Mel Goodwin told me quite a lot about that looked-forward-to evening he had spent with Dottie Peale.

Knowing them both, I was able to make for myself a fairly accurate reconstruction of their meeting, in much the same way that an archaeologist can make a model of some vanished Grecian shrine. Mel Goodwin told me about it in one of his embarrassingly confidential moods, and though much of his narrative made me acutely uncomfortable, I still think it fell into an artistic frame instead of being only another errant night away from the reservation. Perhaps because I have always been fond of the *Odyssey* I kept seeing in the Goodwin chronicle the return of a hero, weary of the wars. I always found myself thinking of Circe and Calypso, of palaces, fine wines, rare napery and of perfume in the air. Actually there was a wine list and Chanel Five and a new gown from Valentina and a silver-blue mink stole and diamond clips. Seen through Mel Goodwin's eyes, Seventy-second Street must have come as quite a shock. It certainly had been a shock to me when I had first seen it and I had not been to any war.

There had been a traffic jam on the West Side highway so that Williams and the Cadillac had been unable to bring the General to the Park Avenue entrance of the Waldorf before half past five o'clock, and this cut his timetable short, as he had arranged to meet Dottie at about six. He had decided to stay at the Waldorf out of loyalty to the name, though it was not the old Waldorf, and he could have taken an army discount at some other hotel. He had on his "A" uniform and frankly he looked pretty sharp. The clerks and the bell-hops made him feel like a VIP, yet at the same time he also felt like a kid. Someone who must have been a manager shook hands with him and took him up to his room himself and was sorry it was not a better one. It looked too good as it was, considering his budget, but he could only stay for a night because he would certainly have to check in next day in Washington. When he had left his canvas bag in his room, he went downstairs to the florist's shop with an idea of buying Dottie some of those yellow orchids, but he decided against this because it was too late to have the flowers delivered, and he did not want to walk up Park Avenue carrying them in a box. He had a fixed desire to walk up Park Avenue.

It was sunset when he started up the Avenue, and New York was still the magic city it had always been for him, rising into the clouds and pulsing with life and hope, never weary or disillusioned like Paris or London. Nobody had bombed New York, and by God, nobody would dare to touch it. The truth was it didn't give a damn for the past. It was forever reaching for something just around the corner, and this was his own mood exactly.

I had described Dottie's house to him vaguely, but he thought that I had been exaggerating until he saw it, and he found himself making a whole new evaluation of everything when he saw the suit of armor and asked the butler if Mrs. Peale was at home.

"Yes, General Goodwin," the man said, "Mrs. Peale is expecting you. May I take your hat, sir?"

"Thanks," he said, and he handed Dottie's butler his cap and gloves and followed him up that broad, noiseless staircase.

"General Goodwin, madam," the man said.

Dottie was waiting for him in that same monster salon with the travertine marble fireplace and Italian chairs and tapestries, where she had received me when I had returned from the Paris Bureau, and I remembered what she had said to me while I was still looking around at the sights.

"Very cinquecento, isn't it?" Dottie had said.

"Yes," I had answered, "unspoiled Borgia with a patina."

Some months after the armistice Mel Goodwin had been to Italy on a two weeks' leave, so he was able to take it without gulping, he told me. She held out both her hands to him and turned her cheek for him to kiss it. In a way it was half formal and half informal. He did not know exactly what the technique should be, since that butler was still there.

"Oh, Mel," she said, "it's been ages. Albert, would you tell Bernard to bring around the car?"

"What's the car for?" Mel Goodwin asked.

"You don't mind if I show you off a little, do you, darling?" she said. "Only cocktails at '21' and then a quick dinner at the Stork and then we'll come back home."

He was glad that he had thought to bring some cash with him.

"It sounds all right to me," he said.

She looked up at him. "I had completely forgotten you were so damned handsome," she said.

"Why in hell didn't you answer any of my letters, Dot?" he asked her.

"Because I never dreamed that anything could ever be the way it was," she said.

"Well, it is the way it was," he said.

"Darling," she said, "let's both be surprised for a minute, shall we?"

"All right," he said, "that isn't such a bad idea."

He had thought of her a great deal and there had been plenty of time for that sort of thinking. He had thought of her again and again as he had first seen her among those other civilians in Paris in that austerely tailored suit. He particularly remembered how she sometimes called him "sir" in what you might have termed both a kidding and respectful way, but he had forgotten what he called her resilience and her loveliness. Of course she was dressed for the occasion, but if she had been dressed in coveralls like an Army nurse, they would have been becoming. Her gown was made of plum-colored taffeta that was tight on top with a long billowing skirt that rustled, and every fold and flounce of it fell into formation. Everything about her was always a unit, even the diamond clip and bracelet. She always wore clothes the way a regular wore a uniform. You always thought of the individual first if the whole uniform fitted properly, and that was the way he thought of Dottie.

"Do you like it?" she asked him.

"Like what?" he answered.

"Why, my Valentina frock," she said. "I like the noise it makes when it swishes."

"That's right," he said, "it sounds like a wave running up a beach."

He was thinking of the waves on the windward side of the island of Oahu, where the crowd used to go sometimes for swimming picnics. Then Dottie began to laugh.

"As long as it's a beach and not a bitch," she said.

He had to laugh himself because they were right where they had been before, and you never worried about her language. If anyone else had said it, it would have sounded coarse, but not with Dot.

"Darling," she said, "I'd almost forgotten how nice it is to see a man again. I don't mean anyone in pants. I mean a man." She pointed to a record player that was finished like the Italian furniture. "Turn on that thing over there, will you? I was playing it this afternoon."

When he pressed the switch down the music was that old waltz from *The Chocolate Soldier.*

"Aren't you going to give me some of this dance," she asked, "my Hero?"

"Don't kid me, Dot," he said when he put his arm around her.

"My Hero" was still playing when Albert handed him his gloves and cap.

I had been exposed to similar evenings myself and I particularly remembered one occasion on which Dottie had taken me out to see the town. It was during my brief vacation from the Paris Bureau and on a night when Henry Peale was suffering from a head cold. I had never had the sort of money to go to the places where Dottie wanted to go that night and I was lucky enough to be in a

414

position to tell her so. I had suggested that we go somewhere in the Village.

"Now, Sid," she said, "of course I know you can't afford it. Take this, and if we run through it, I'll pass you some more under the table." And she handed me a packet of crisp new bills and told me to be sure to give ten dollars to the captain, at which point I told her that I was not a gigolo.

"Now, Sid," she said, "I know how confusing this is for you because it was for me once, but stop being silly and remember that some people play with different-colored chips. Consider it a social experiment, darling."

I finally let her give me the money to pay for the party on a social experimental basis and because she was anxious to show me how she was living. I had never before been so aware of the uneven distribution of wealth, and I learned a lot from the experience. As Dottie told me herself, people who played with different chips had different thought processes, but Dottie could still step down from her new environment, and she could see with malicious pleasure what the environment did to me.

"It will come easier the next time," she said, "when I pass over the cash. Naturally it's demoralizing, but why shouldn't I debauch you?"

That was exactly why there had never been a next time. I could see the corrosive influence of making free with someone else's money, but then I had known Dottie for so long that we were able to discuss the subject without the least embarrassment.

"You're always so damned difficult," Dottie said, "but I don't see why we can't still be friends."

I was not the one who was difficult. Friendship was usually complicated if you played with different chips and I had not been sea-green and incorruptible. I had taken the money — once.

In many ways this problem must have been even more confusing for Mel Goodwin than it had been for me. He had never seen much of New York high life on an army officer's pay, with a wife and two kids who needed food and clothing. He had been to "21" once on a big blowout two days before he had sailed with "Torch," but he had left the crowd before they reached the Stork. "21" was enlarged now and in front of it were all those iron jockeys that had once been hitching posts. He had never dreamed of going to the bar there with anyone like Dottie Peale and he had never dreamed that people would know who he was when she introduced him. Somehow Dottie made it all like something in those movies you kept seeing at the officers' clubs. They had double Martinis — he remembered that she always liked Martinis — and he looked curiously around the room at the checked tablecloths and the hurrying waiters.

"Mel," Dottie said, "why didn't you come back sooner?"

"Well," he said, "there are still pieces of an army over there, and I kept thinking the Russkis might act up. I like it with an army. It's simpler."

"Do you think I'm complicated?" she asked him.

"Yes," he answered, "but I don't mind some complications."

"What are you going to do now you're back?" she asked him.

"Dot," he said, "I wish I knew. I don't know what they can do with Joes like me, now we're back."

"Oh, Mel," she said, "you don't sound happy."

When he helped her into the limousine her skirts made that swishing sound and she laughed. "Listen to the wave," she said, "running up the bitch."

Dottie was the only woman he had ever known who could be completely feminine and still talk like a man. He seemed to have known her always by the time they were half through dinner. She was interested in everything he said, not that he could remember clearly what they talked about, except that most of the conversation was about the relationship between men and women and what made such relationships successful.

"You know," he remembered that she said, "every woman wants to make a man happy. That's all she ever wants."

Somehow she brought back to his mind all sorts of things he had forgotten — things about the Point and about when he was a kid — and then they began remembering things that had happened in Paris.

"It was all just something off the map, Dot," he said, "like the fourth dimension or the Einstein theory or something."

"Mel, dear," she said, "do you think we're off the map right now?"

"Yes," he said, "because it can't last, Dot."

"Why can't it?" she asked.

"Why, look at you," he said, "and look at me."

"It might," she said. "I'm looking."

When the waiter brought the check, he brought a pencil with him, and naturally he placed them before Mel Goodwin. What with the champagne and the caviar and everything, it was lucky he had brought that loose cash.

"Hand it over and let me sign it. It's my party," Dottie said. "There used to be a song about it, didn't there? — 'When the waiter came she simply signed her name; that's the kind of a baby for me.'"

The future must have hung in the balance, and the difference between Mel Goodwin and me was that he lived by regulation.

"Not my kind of baby, Dot," he said.

The strange part of it was that she seemed surprised, which rather offended him until suddenly she looked wistful.

"God damn," Dottie said — she was always picking up someone else's trick of speech — "it's awfully nice to feel helpless again." And then she said one final thing and Melville Goodwin told it to me.

"Why can't things be like this always?"

Calypso must have said it, and Circe, and Cleopatra undoubtedly said it to Antony, if not to Julius Caesar.

XXVII

There Could Always Be a Palace Revolution

THE details of this encounter were pieced together from what the General told me later, like so many other episodes in his career. I knew nothing of them at the time. In fact after Melville Goodwin had left for New York I believed that he had gone more or less for good. If he had made a strong impression on me, so had other people who had also vanished, and in the last analysis one can only give so much of one's energy to the affairs of other people. I had no way of knowing that Mel Goodwin's life and mine were each moving to an almost simultaneous crisis. I could only see long afterwards that coming events had cast their shadows during those days at Savin Hill. The General's interest in Dottie was of course a recognizable shadow, and I should have known that Gilbert Frary's oblique talk with me at Savin Hill, and the orchids for Helen were dangerous portents; but then, such shadows are usually difficult to perceive until too late. Whenever I thought of Mel Goodwin at all in the next few days, I simply thought of him as being in Washington caught up again in his own routine, disappearing like other friends and acquaintances from the ETO, now that the war was over.

Actually I had not been paying enough attention to my own affairs. As I told Helen, I had professional pride, such as it was. I had never expected to be a radio commentator, but now that I was one, I wanted to be a good one. I was tired of being only a front and a piece of property. I was delighted to have the assistance of an expert script-writer like Art Hertz, but I was beginning to wish to have a final say myself on the writing. I had noticed that Art Hertz sometimes exhibited pain when I made suggestions or asked for a few minor changes, but I had always accepted this reaction as natural, and I would not have respected him if he had not begun to look upon the script as his own property. Nevertheless I did think he should have admitted it was mine in the final analysis, if only because a great many people thought of me as a commentator who wrote his own opinions on world events.

I had never been as conscious of a sort of opposition on the part of Art Hertz as I was just after the Goodwins' visit. I should have seen earlier that Art and everyone else on the program knew something that I did not. I should have gathered, I suppose, from Art's manner that I was not as essential to him as I had been, but at the time I was exhilarated by a sense that I was beginning to pull more of my own weight in the boat and that things in the studio were going pretty well. I was also beginning to enjoy writing the script myself with Art and the rest of them to check up on it and I was finally getting the feeling of writing for the air. A welcome aspect of the situation was the fact that Gilbert Frary had left suddenly for the West Coast without asking me again to accompany him, and with Gilbert away I was not quite the Charlie McCarthy I had been around the studio.

One day in the latter part of October at four in the afternoon I was sitting in the elaborate office which the company had supplied for me, going over Art's revised notes, and I had asked Miss Maynard, the secretary whom the company had supplied for me, to get me some foreign dispatches from the newsroom so that I could check some of Art Hertz's statements. I had just decided that a lead on the situation in the Orient sounded better than Art's beginning, which dealt with a Washington investigation, when suddenly the door from Miss Maynard's office opened, and a tall, youngish man, whom I did not know, peered in. This would not have happened if Miss Maynard had been at her desk but she had just come in to me with the teletype copy.

Strangers were not supposed to pop in at the studio unless there was a visitors' tour, and I could not say that I was pleased. I had never seen this youngish man around, but something in the careful cut of his double-breasted suit and in the neat fold of the handkerchief protruding from his breast pocket gave me an idea that he knew his way about studios.

419

"Oh," he said, and he had a fine sincere voice that reminded me of my own when I heard a broadcast played back to me, "excuse me. I didn't know anyone was here," and then he was gone.

"Who was that?" I asked Miss Maynard, and I thought Miss Maynard colored slightly.

"Why, don't you know him, Mr. Skelton?" Miss Maynard asked.

"No," I said, "but he's got a voice and a presence, hasn't he?"

I should have known right then that Miss Maynard knew something that I did not, but at the time such a thought never crossed my mind.

"Why," Miss Maynard said, "it's Mr. Alan Featherbee. You know, he has the nine-o'clock-in-the-morning spot at Acme, the one that's called 'Alan Featherbee and the News.'"

I felt a twinge of the unreasoning professional jealousy that is unavoidable in the show business, particularly when I remembered that in my latest conversation with Gilbert Frary he had mentioned that Featherbee was the one who spoke his own commercials.

"Well, what's he doing here?" I asked.

"I really don't know, Mr. Skelton," Miss Maynard said. She looked unusually beautiful against the background of the green carpet and the gay upholstered chairs, but it seemed to me that she was speaking especially carefully and sweetly. "Mr. Featherbee has been around here a good deal during the last few days. Just visiting, I suppose."

"Oh," I said, "are we going to take him away from Acme?"

"I really wouldn't know, I'm sure, Mr. Skelton," Miss Maynard said, "but he has been around frequently."

I wanted to ask Miss Maynard some further questions, but I had learned that with studio secretaries there was seldom that loyalty from the bottom up to which Mel Goodwin had so often alluded. At least I had the common sense then to suspect the possible shadow of a coming event.

"Oh," I said. I wanted very much to ask Miss Maynard to try to find me a record of one of the Featherbee broadcasts, but I thought better of it because of the loyalty angle. "Maybe you'd better go out front and keep out visitors, Miss Maynard. I'm pretty busy now," but before Miss Maynard could reach her office the door was opened again by one of those nice boys in the Civil-War-gray, military-academy uniforms with all the braid.

"Forgive me, Mr. Skelton," he said. It must have been a part of the briefing those boys received that made them always ask to be forgiven and not excused. "A gentleman at the floor reception desk would like to see you personally, and your secretary's telephone did not answer."

"Oh dear," Miss Maynard said, "I'm dreadfully sorry, Mr. Skelton."

I smiled as sweetly as I could at Miss Maynard.

"All right," I said, "who is it?"

"Captain Robert Goodwin, sir," the page boy said.

"I can see him and find out what he wants, Mr. Skelton," Miss Maynard said, "and I'll really see this doesn't happen again."

"Oh, never mind," I told her. "Tell him to come in as long as he's here."

First it had been Art Hertz's script, and now I would have to let it go as it stood, and then it had been Alan Featherbee and the News, and now I was back again in the life and times of Melville A. Goodwin. I had never imagined that I might see his older son nor could I understand why he wanted to call. When Miss Maynard showed him in and left us and closed the door, it occurred to me that I had never received a guest of my own in my new private office. I was not at ease with all those blown-up publicity photographs lining the wall, and it did not help to observe that Robert Goodwin began to eye them immediately after we shook hands.

"Don't blame any of that on me," I said. "It's all a part of the show. How did you find I was here?"

Robert Goodwin smiled, and it was the Melville Goodwin smile on a younger face.

"It was really tough tracking you down, Major Skelton," he said, "but I called up your home in Connecticut and was able to reach Mrs. Skelton. I hope you'll forgive the intrusion. I'm only in New York for a few hours."

He was in a civilian suit that was too reddish-brown and tweedy.

No West Pointer had ever looked right to me in a business suit. They always went hog-wild in men's clothing or haberdashery shops. They always come out, even from a reliable tailor, with some garment that was slightly out of line or that jarred the notes of convention. Robert Goodwin stood as if he were entering an office in the Pentagon. He was Regular Army from his manner and in spite of his garish costume he almost made me feel like a colonel.

"Take any color chair you like and sit down," I said. "I thought you were a lieutenant. I didn't know you were a captain."

"It just came through the other day, sir," he answered.

He looked young for the rank until I looked at his eyes. His eyes were older than the rest of his face.

"Help yourself to a cigarette," I told him. "There ought to be some in the box on the fake Chinese coffee table."

"Thanks," he said, "is there an ash tray handy, sir?"

I could think of Muriel Goodwin telling him to be careful about cigarettes. When he saw a mushroomlike ash receiver in a corner, he started up to bring it nearer.

"Sit down," I said, "and drop your ashes on the carpet. The management cleans it every day."

"This really is quite a place you have here, sir," he said.

"That's right," I said. "I wish your father could have seen it. It might have built me up with him."

If I had been young Robert Goodwin with a few hours of my own in New York, I would not have consumed one minute of it looking up one of my father's civilian friends, unless I had called for a purpose. When he smiled, his eyes narrowed exactly like Mel Goodwin's. I could see that he was trying to size me up, and that he had probably never seen anything like me or the broadcasting studio. I found myself anxious to make the right impression on him, and I was curious about him, too, because just seeing him put Mel Goodwin in a different light.

He was taller than his father, yet he looked very much as Mel Goodwin must have looked when he was fresh from the Point. He still had a few rough edges but I was thinking that perhaps he had used his father as a model, because his hair was done in the same

422

crew cut and he had the same way of sitting, relaxed and yet not relaxed. His youth still concealed many of the qualities which would later give him the authentic stamp of the professional soldier, though I could tell from previous experiences with other younger officers that he had been in action many times. Action always left an indefinable mark on any face. Though they were not deep as yet, lines were already apparent around the corners of his mouth.

"It was nice seeing your father," I said. "We had quite a time up at my place with those magazine people."

Robert Goodwin flicked his cigarette ash on the impeccable office carpet and looked longingly at the ash receiver.

"We're looking forward to seeing that piece about him," Robert Goodwin said. "Mother can hardly wait. We all hope the old man didn't put his foot in his mouth."

"Don't worry, he did fine," I told him. "I suppose he's right in the groove now and settling down in Washington."

Captain Goodwin looked straight at me, with the same cool, searching look his father could assume.

"I wouldn't say the boss was quite settled down yet, sir," he said. "He's got some leave and he and Mother are still sort of camping out with some old friends in Alexandria, Colonel and Mrs. Joyce. Maybe you heard the old man speak of them."

"Yes, I have," I said. "Your mother and Mrs. Joyce work on picture puzzles, don't they?"

"That's right," he said. ". . . I've just got orders to go to Benning — instructor in recoilless weapons."

The ice was breaking slightly, and he looked more at ease. He seemed to expect me to make some intelligent comment about recoilless weapons, but when I did not, he went right on, still formally but more confidently.

"We played with those things some in the Pacific," he said. "The word is they're better now, but I sort of wish I could stick around Washington. I'd sort of like to get to know the old man again. I haven't seen him for quite a while."

Obviously he was planning to talk about the old man, now that the ground was cleared.

"Maybe you've noticed, sir," he said, "or maybe it's only my own impression, that the old man is sort of restless."

When our eyes met, I saw that he was watching me carefully, and I thought he handled himself very well. He did not fidget, as a civilian his age might have, but then he was an officer with a record.

"Everyone's restless sometimes," I told him.

"Yes, I know," he said, "I'm that way myself — but then I'm under thirty, if you get my point."

In the army you took more things for granted than you ever could on the outside. Now and then you had to put all the cards on the table with someone after a few minutes' acquaintance, and you got to know and to trust people quickly. I must have fitted some of his own standards, and I could not help being pleased.

"Yes, I get your point," I said.

He glanced at the electric clock on the office wall with its moving second hand, and I wondered whether it gave him the same inevitable sense of pressure that it had always given me.

"Maybe I'd better lay it on the line," he said. "The old man was saying the other night that you were the only noncombat civilian officer he knew who ever made full sense to him in a service way. Of course the old man's pretty naïve at some points, but I saw a lot of civilians out in the Pacific myself." He smiled at me again. "Now if the old man said that about you, I guess that means you sort of like my old man. Jesus, I'm making a long speech!"

Robert Goodwin crossed the room and dropped his cigarette in the ash receptacle, although he had just lighted one, and then he immediately lighted another.

"Perhaps you'd like a little Scotch," I said. "I have some right here."

"Thanks, I really would, sir," Robert Goodwin said.

I fetched a bottle and some glasses out of the cellaret and then I called Miss Maynard and asked her if she would please get a little ice and some soda from the small refrigerator that was in Mr. Frary's changing room. We talked about the Pacific until Miss Maynard left the room.

424

"That's a really nicely stacked up secretary you have, sir," he said.

"They all are, in the front offices," I told him. I was not old enough to call him "son" and he was too young to call me "Sid," but it was remarkable how a little Scotch always eased a situation.

"You know, I've seen a lot of generals, sir," he said, looking up at the clock again, "because I was Priestley's aide for a while on Saipan, and do you know when I looked my father over the other day in Washington, I was surprised?" He stopped and looked at his drink. "I may be prejudiced, but I think he's got what it takes, all the way around. I have a hunch he can handle anything right through a four-star job."

As I waited for him to go on, I found myself beginning to think that he possibly might be right. In the beginning I had discounted Melville Goodwin's capabilities, which were always getting lost behind his simplicities, but somehow Goodwin was always better than you thought he was going to be. He had always gained something from experience. He had always moved a little further forward and he was still young as generals went.

"A lot of officers can only push beyond a certain level," the captain was saying, and he moved his hands in a quick gesture to indicate a level. "You can get the feel of this when you meet them — but it's different with him. I'm not referring to guts. The boss has a mental toughness that is more than guts, and he's really got a future if he doesn't stick his neck out."

He glanced at me, but I did not answer. It was curious to hear him implying what had been so often in my own thoughts.

"There's nothing in this world quite so naked as a general," Robert Goodwin said. "He's up there where everybody can see everything about him including his private life, from every angle, and he must be right; he can't be wrong. Well, the old man's up there just now, and they're looking him over. Every one of them has his own crowd behind him. . . . All right, I'm naturally in the Goodwin crowd" — Robert Goodwin glanced straight at me again — "and I don't want to see him fall flat on his face, Mr. Skelton."

The room, like all the studio offices, was carefully soundproofed, and the silence all around us was distinctly artificial.

425

"What makes you think he's going to fall on his face?" I asked.

Robert Goodwin's face framed itself in that mirthless service smile. It was, of course, a useless question, and of course we both knew it.

"Listen," he said, "what about this dame he keeps seeing in New York?"

We were surrounded again by an artificial, antiseptic silence and I was conscious of blank helplessness. It was news to me that the General had seen Dottie Peale more than that once in New York.

"Keeps seeing?" I repeated.

"That's right, sir," Robert Goodwin said. "He's commuting up here all the time from Washington."

"How do you happen to know about this?" I asked him.

His lips twisted again into that mirthless service smile.

"I wouldn't say the old man was exactly a subtle character, would you, sir?" he said. "He's talked to me about the dame. He's one of those people who always has to talk to somebody. He says you introduced her to him in Paris."

It seemed to me that he was implying that, because of an introduction, I was the one who should do something about it.

"That was quite a while ago," I said.

"All right," he said, "that isn't all."

"What isn't all?" I asked.

We were beginning to sound like characters in a soap opera, in that soundproof office.

"Everybody's beginning to talk," he said. "They've been seen around. It makes a pretty good story. Everyone likes a good story when it's on a general, sir."

"Now look," I asked, and I sounded as cautious as a confidential family lawyer, "don't you think you're exaggerating?"

"Maybe," he answered, "but then, so is everybody else. That's the way those things go, isn't it?"

I wished he would not act as though I were responsible, but I could feel his cool accusing glance.

"Now look," I began, "these things happen sometimes."

"Yes, sir, you're damned well right they do," he answered, "but they ought not to happen to the old man right now."

"These things happen," I said again, "and nobody can do much about them, I guess."

"Well, the point is somebody ought to try. Don't you agree, sir?" he said, and he looked at me. I wanted to tell him that I had tried in my own way, but there was that gap of age between us and I had my own loyalties.

"Have you tried speaking to your father?" I asked.

"Yes, sir," he said, "I brought it up last night and it only made the old man mad. Have you ever tried to argue with him?"

"Yes," I said, "I've tried."

We sat in silence for a while, both supporting a Leaning Tower of Pisa — the career of Major General Melville A. Goodwin.

"Well," he said, "somebody's got to do something. I hope it isn't as bad as we think."

"I didn't say it was so bad," I told him.

"I know you didn't say it, sir," he said. "Well, what about this Mrs. Peale?"

"Well," I answered, "what about her?"

He sat up straighter and gripped his knees with his heavy fingers.

"Maybe she really likes the old man," he said. "Maybe she doesn't realize how this sort of thing might hurt him, from the service point of view, I mean. Maybe she doesn't know that the old man's slated for something big just now. I think I ought to meet her and have a talk with her myself."

It was exactly what someone of his age would have concluded, clear and logical and completely useless, and the worst of it was I knew that Dottie would love to see young Robert Goodwin and that anything he might say would only give Mel Goodwin a new value.

"Listen," I told him, "I don't think these things are ever helped by sitting around a table."

"Well," he said, "I don't see how doing nothing will help either, sir."

"All right," I said, "then you'd better talk to her. She always likes verbiage."

"Sir, would you consider going with me?" he asked.

"I think she'd like it better," I answered, "if you went alone."

427

"Would you mind telephoning her and telling her I'm coming over?" he asked.

There were a number of things I might have said about Dottie Peale, but somehow they seemed to have all been spoken, wordlessly, already, and I asked Miss Maynard to get Mrs. Henry Peale for me at her private number. It was five o'clock, and she would probably be at home, and it turned out that she was.

"Why, Sid darling," she said. "Where are you?"

"I'm at the office," I said.

"Well, it's a good place for you to be, under the circumstances," she said.

"What circumstances?" I asked.

"Oh," she answered, "not over the telephone, darling, but there is something I'd like to tell you someday soon."

"Well," I said, "Robert Goodwin's here with me right now. You know, Melville Goodwin's son."

There was a slight pause before she answered, which I rather enjoyed.

"Damn it," she said, "don't always explain everything with diagrams."

"There's no need for a diagram," I said. "He's here and he'd like to see you."

There was another pause.

"Why, I'd love it," she said. "I think it's awfully sweet of him to want to see me. Tell him to come right over if he'd like to . . . and, Sid?"

"Yes?" I said.

"Does he look like Mel?"

"Yes," I said, "quite a lot."

"Then tell him to hurry over," Dottie said.

"It's all cleared," I said to Robert Goodwin, ". . . and you know if there's anything else I can do . . ." but of course there was nothing that anyone could do, and I had my own life to lead. Besides being concerned about Mel Goodwin, I found myself wondering why Dottie had said it was nice I was in the office and what it was that she could not tell me over the telephone.

428

If I was disturbed after Captain Robert Goodwin had left, it was an indefinite sort of disturbance, not a single element of which could be isolated. Uncertainty had begun to lurk in the background of everything I touched. You could start with all the world events which I was trying to put, with the aid of Art Hertz, into an agreeable, intelligent capsule to fit within the limits of fifteen spoken minutes. Nothing was secure in the world any longer, where balances and beliefs were shifting and settling like the foundations of a badly constructed building. I had only to look at that broadcast script to observe how those one-world theories, once so eloquently outlined by the late Wendell Willkie, had flown out of the window. They reminded me of a balloon given me as a child, the string of which had been whisked out of my fingers by an unexpected gust of wind. I could remember staring in pained unbelief after that balloon, watching it rise and rise until it was only an unattainable speck. Europe was in a state of imbalance, and a single push could topple over governments and traditions. Asia was weltering in revolution, and at home our own government was seething with its own involutions. You could gloss over the details, but the facts remained. Once there had been a logical blueprint for the defeat of despotism, and now there was not even a plausible plan. The world itself was like the Leaning Tower of Pisa, and so was my own future.

Once I had been able to view all these matters detachedly, but that was before I had stakes in the future and before I had become involved with studios and contracts and people like Gilbert Frary. Now my thoughts moved like a modern statesman's, in all directions, facing a half dozen unpleasant eventualities. I did not like the broadcast and I did not like Art Hertz or anything in the studio. The work had amused me once, but not any longer. If I had been alone, I should have known exactly what to do and I should have enjoyed doing it, but I was not alone. I remembered what Gilbert Frary said about pinching myself to be sure it was not a dream, and it was not a dream. There was no sense of euphoria any longer.

I was not even alone with my own problems — there was also Melville A. Goodwin. When I toyed with the idea of reaching Gilbert Frary on the Coast and asking him a few curt questions about this

Alan Featherbee, who had popped suddenly into the office, along came the shades of Melville Goodwin and Dottie Peale. Again, when I had almost decided to call in Art Hertz and have a frank, tough talk, I found myself wondering about Robert Goodwin and Dottie Peale. Then I began thinking of Melville Goodwin in Washington struggling with his own uncertainties. I was reminded that before long I would be going down to Washington myself to give the broadcast there, thus creating the customary illusion that I was in close touch with the nation's capital. The details had all been arranged six weeks before. I was enmeshed in personalities and details.

Before I was aware of the time, Art Hertz came in with the final script, walking very softly considering his weight. It seemed to me that Art was more sure of himself and more aggressive than he had been a day or two before. I believed that he was looking at me in a speculative way, as though, like Miss Maynard, he knew something. At any rate, it was six-fifteen, too late for any alterations in the script. While I was reading it and Art was sitting waiting, I still felt that he was watching me, though every time I looked up from the boldly typed and spaced pages he was looking carefully at his hands or playing with a pencil.

"That's fine, Art," I said.

"I'm glad if you like it," Art said.

"I always like what you do, Art," I told him, "but no two minds ever think exactly alike. You mustn't worry if I intersperse a few ideas sometimes."

"Oh, no," Art said, "that's all right. I always liked working for you, Sid."

At certain times you noticed small details if you knew what was good for you. Art had used the past tense when he said he liked working for me, and the disturbing thing was that he noticed it, too.

"And I still like it, Sid," he said.

He sat waiting as if he expected me to continue on the subject. "Has Frary called up today?" I asked.

Art Hertz put his pencil in his pocket and smiled to show that we both understood all about Gilbert.

"Oh, yes," Art said, "he was on the telephone about half an hour ago. He was in a *cabaña* at some swimming pool. He just wanted to hear the lead of the script. He said the sun was shining and he must leave for his massage in the solarium. You know how Gilbert likes the sun. I could do with some of it myself."

"Did you tell him I was here?" I asked.

"Oh, yes," Art answered, "but when Miss Maynard said you were in conference, he just said give you his love. I guess he was in a hurry to get to the solarium. You know how he is about the sun."

"Oh, Miss Maynard was in your office when he called, was she?" I asked.

"She just dropped in," Art said. "You know Maynard; she's always around everywhere."

"That's right," I said, "everywhere."

I felt like a sultan in a palace, carefully guarded and yet aware of a palace revolution, and the feeling was all around me.

"You know we're going down to Washington on the thirteenth," I said.

"Yes," Art answered, "everything is set. Someone from the State Department is going to use three minutes, but we don't know who he is yet. Well, if you haven't got anything else on your mind . . ."

Art stood up and took his pencil out of his pocket.

"No, my mind's a perfect blank," I said, and I smiled at him.

He knew it was time for him to leave because I wanted to go over the script again by myself.

"By the way, it's going to be in Studio C," he said. "I hope you don't mind, Sid."

You noticed small details if you knew what was good for you. It was the first time I had ever broadcast from Studio C.

"No," I said, "I don't mind. I'd just as soon not have a crowd watching me."

I should have gone over the script again, but instead I began thinking about my contract and I remembered how hurt Gilbert had been when I had shown it, before signing, to a law firm I had selected myself. The firm was Frankel and Jacobs, well known for literary and theatrical work, and as a matter of fact Dottie Peale had introduced me to them. The contract was a long document which

431

I had never read carefully, seeing that I had paid the Frankel firm to read it, but I did remember a clause over which there had been argument, called a mutual dissatisfaction clause, permitting a termination of the contract by either party. The part about either party had been inserted by Mr. Frankel instead of simply applying to the sponsor, as Gilbert Frary had suggested. The clause was number twenty-eight in the contract, and I wanted very much to read it just then. I even thought of asking Miss Maynard for a copy until I thought that this might arouse needless suspicions. Instead I asked her to get me Mrs. Henry Peale again on the telephone.

"Darling," Dottie said, "I thought you might be calling me. Is anything the matter?"

It went to show that she knew too much about my voice and behavior. I was going to ask her if I might drop over later, and now I hated to ask, simply because she had thought I would call up.

"I was just wondering whether young Goodwin had gone," I said.

"He just left a minute or two ago," Dottie said. "He was so sweet. Don't you think he's sweet?"

"That's right," I said, "sweet."

"And he does look like Mel, doesn't he?"

"That's right," I said, "he looks like Mel."

"Why don't you stop in for a minute on your way home?" she said. "I could give you a bite of supper, darling, up in the study. I haven't anything to do until nine o'clock."

I was very glad that she had asked me, and then before I could get to the script again, Helen called me.

"Sid," Helen said, "is anything the matter?"

I wished that the women in my life did not understand all the inflections of my voice. I told her that of course nothing was the matter.

"Camilla has a temperature," Helen said, "and Dr. Gordon's just been here. It's only a cold, but she's been asking for you."

It was not one of my better days. Yet I was surprised by my own voice when I sat in Studio C and said "Good evening, friends." It sounded as though I did not have a care in the world and as though the world were going on delightfully for everyone.

*   *   *

432

Everything at Dottie's always ran like clockwork, although this may have been an archaic way of putting it. Albert, that butler of hers, greeted me like an old family friend and asked whether he should take me up in the lift or whether I cared to go by myself. When I told him that I would try to run the thing alone, he showed me which button to press.

"The doors open and close automatically, as you may remember, sir," he said.

Automatic elevators always reminded me either of the *Arabian Nights* or of a journey to a hospital operating room. When I pressed the button and when the doors closed, they physically shut out the immediate present and I seemed to have committed myself to a transition from one phase of life to another. When the elevator doors opened, I could see Dottie, across the entry to her study, sitting there on the sofa. Her feet were curled under her in that manner she had never outgrown, and it was easy to forget all the years and events that had separated us.

She wriggled off the sofa when she saw me, just as she would have years before. There was always something youthful about the way Dottie got herself off a sofa. She was dressed in a greenish afternoon frock which she had undoubtedly hurried into directly after I had told her about Robert Goodwin. In fact Dottie and that whole study hinted at the ending of a little scene. There was still a trace of cigarette smoke in the air and almost the echo of voices.

"Hi, Dot," I said.

She held her hands out to me, but before I could take them she threw her arms around me and kissed me. It was utterly unexpected, but I could not say I minded it.

"Well, well," I said, "say I'm weary say I'm sad, but Jennie kissed me."

"Darling," she said, "your feathers are all ruffled. You look upset."

There was no use concealing my feelings, and as I stood with my arm around her, I had to admit that I felt happy, because I suddenly realized that she and I were friends in spite of all our quarrels and competitions. I have never been able to understand exactly what constitutes a friendship between a man and a woman. There were still some echoes of old emotion, but they were not disturbing then. I only knew that Dottie would not go back on me, and that it was safe to tell her anything that worried me.

"Well," I said, "perhaps I am."

"Do you want a drink?" she asked me.

"No," I said, "not right now, thanks."

"All right," she said, "if you want to be strong-minded. I had Albert bring up chicken sandwiches and milk. Do you still like chicken sandwiches?"

It was kind of her to remember that I liked chicken sandwiches, but then if she wanted she could remember everything.

"Darling," she said, "I'm ever so glad you called me up."

There was no need to make any conversation. I felt again as I had in the elevator, the same sense of motion without my own volition. I was conscious of her possessive instincts. I knew that she always liked to run things, but I did not mind this then. She was back on the sofa again with her feet curled under her.

"Oh, hell," she said, "why not face it? It's awfully nice to know you still belong to me a little."

"I don't mind it either right now," I said.

I knew this was one of her moods, but then perhaps it was valid.

"We needn't be so damned strait-laced about it," Dottie said. "If two people have ever been in love with each other, they always do belong to each other a little, whether they approve of it or not. It isn't anything to be ashamed of. It's only an obvious sort of fact. I don't even mean that we were very much in love, because we always knew too damn much about each other . . . and now you'd better pull up your socks and tell me what's the matter."

"It's nice to be on such a friendly basis, Dottie," I said.

"God, yes," she said, "it's nice we're grown-up, darling."

Now that she mentioned it, I was almost sorry we were grown-up, which was probably exactly what she wanted. I did not love her any longer and she did not love me, but at the same time I could tell her some things about myself which I could not have told Helen.

"Well," I began, "this afternoon at the office . . ."

And there I was, telling Dottie Peale about Alan Featherbee and

434

Gilbert Frary and Art Hertz, moving back and forth, mixing the end with the beginning.

"I know," Dottie said, "they're all sons of bitches, darling."

I had always known they were, but it was very comforting to hear Dottie say so and to feel that I was talking to an expert.

"I don't want Helen to be disturbed," I told her. "I suppose I ought to do something. What alarms me is that I don't seem to care."

"Don't you care at all?" she asked.

"Frankly, no," I said. I would not have dreamed of telling anyone except Dottie that I did not like broadcasting the news and that I welcomed any opportunity of walking out and leaving it.

"God damn it," Dottie said, "it's just like you, after you've made a success of something. It's just the way you left and went on that Paris Bureau. God damn it, I suppose I'll have to make you do something."

She was delighted, trying to run someone's life again. She got off the sofa and mixed two highballs and while I watched her I was very glad that we were not married.

"You're so clever in some ways and so dumb in others," she said. "Seriously, darling, haven't you known that Gilbert was out to knife you? I've known it for the last six weeks."

"How did you know?" I asked.

"Because I'm not a chump like you," Dottie said. "You've got to start pulling up your socks. You've got Helen and Camilla."

"I know," I said, "I've given that a little thought."

"You always were so damned irresponsible," she said. "If you can't think of Helen and Camilla, I suppose I'll have to. There's plenty you can do about Frary. You're as important as Frary. What are you thinking of doing?"

I took a sip of my highball. I was perfectly glad to drink it, because I was not upset any longer.

"Frankly, I'm thinking of collecting my year's salary and getting out for good," I said.

"And then what'll you do?" she asked.

It was a pleasure to have her ask me instead of asking myself.

"I don't know," I answered. "Maybe I might do some writing."

"Oh, my God," Dottie said, "what sort of writing? Dog stories?"

"I've a poodle named Farouche," I said. "I might do poodle stories."

"Oh, Jesus," Dottie said, and then she saw that I was laughing at her. "It's just the way it was on the paper. All right, I'll go around myself and see someone tomorrow. You can forget about it now and let me run this."

It did sound exactly like old times.

"Well, that's fine," I said. "You sound exactly like Mrs. Melville A. Goodwin."

I had never considered the consequences when I mentioned Mrs. Goodwin until I saw Dottie's face redden and there was a moment's silence.

"Now just why did you bring her up?" she asked, but now that she was brought up, we both must have realized that the Goodwins had been with us all the time.

"Now, Dottie," I said, "I didn't mean to, but how did you like the soldier boy?"

Dottie sighed impatiently and picked up a cigarette and lighter from the table and balanced the lighter on the palm of her hand, as though it were the scales of justice.

"One of your worst troubles," Dottie said, "is that you never face up to anything. First you come here and tell me all your difficulties and then when I'm considering them, you ask about something else. What's the matter? Don't you want to have me help you?"

"Now, Dottie," I said, "talking this over has been a help, but I don't want you to go and see someone."

"Sid," she said, "I don't know why you don't understand that a woman's never happy unless she's useful to some man. Now just the other night I was talking to Norman Jones. You know Norman Jones in White Wall Rubber, don't you? Well, he was just saying the other night that they want to sponsor a news hour."

I could look into the future and see her talking to Norman Jones.

"God damn it," Dottie said, "I'm going to see him whether you want me to or not. You never know what you want."

"Dottie," I asked her, "does anyone know what he wants?"

"That's a silly question," Dottie said. "I know, I've always known and I don't flounder around like you."

"Well," I said, "you've never got it, have you?"

There is always something embarrassing about naked truth. She scowled at me and then she gave her head an impatient shake.

"That's right," she said, "but I'm still in there pitching, darling, and I don't just slide around."

I have never known where the talk would have gone from there—whether it would have continued with the White Wall Rubber Company and my problems on the radio or whether it would have centered on the desires of Dottie Peale. I never knew because I saw her move her head sharply and I heard the automatic elevator.

"My God," Dottie whispered, "what time is it?" and then she looked at the clock on the mantelpiece. It was exactly half past eight. "Darling," she whispered, "don't go. Don't go just yet."

XXVIII

But Don't Quote the General Personally

WE had both turned to the door that opened onto the hallway, and there was Melville Goodwin. He stood like a picture in a frame, and there was one of those uncertain silences before any of us spoke. His uniform, the ribbons and the insignia gave everything a new complexion.

"Why, Mel," I heard Dottie say, "you're early."

"That's right," he said, "a half an hour early. I was hoping to surprise you and turn up here like a plain citizen, but the tailor hasn't finished with my tuxedo yet. I hope I'm not interrupting a conference. Hello, Sid."

I think he was surprised because he must have expected Dottie to be alone, but at the same time he was glad to see me.

"Hello, Mel," I said, "I just dropped in for a minute and I'm leaving now."

"What's the idea of your leaving?" Mel Goodwin asked. "Dottie and I were going to see the town. How about taking him along, Dot?"

There was still an element of surprise. There was no reason why General Goodwin should not have appeared, but I had not expected him to be so completely at home. I had not expected his slightly proprietary air, and Dottie was looking at us both proudly, almost maternally.

"Sid just came around for some advice, Mel," Dottie said. "Career trouble."

Mel Goodwin smiled and walked across the room and patted me on the shoulder.

"Career trouble?" he repeated. "By God, that sounds like Washington. Well, Sid can tell me all about it while you go in and put on what you call an evening frock."

There was no doubt that Mel Goodwin was perfectly at home. Somehow we were in the middle of a family scene and I was the old and understanding family friend.

"God damn," the General went on, "are they knifing you in the back, Sid? It looks as though they're ganging up on all your boy friends, Dot."

Dottie shook her head.

"Mel," she said, "would you mind very much if we all stayed here?"

Somehow this simple question gave the scene an even more domestic note. Mel Goodwin looked at her quickly and the crow's-feet deepened around his eyes.

"Why," he said, "what's the matter, Dot?"

"Oh," Dottie said, "nothing, Mel, except perhaps I've been thoughtless. Darling, I never dreamed that people would begin to talk."

Mel Goodwin clasped his hands behind him and glanced at me and back at Dottie, and the lines on his face looked deeper.

"Well, well," he said, "so that's why Sid's up here."

"No, no," Dottie said, "it isn't Sid, but I imagine Sid agrees with me. I've been awfully thoughtless, Mel."

I admired that façade of Melville Goodwin's. It was easy to see how accustomed he was to environments in which anything might happen.

"Let's get this straight," he said. "If Sid hasn't been talking to you, someone else has?"

"Oh, never mind, Mel," Dottie said. "It really doesn't matter who."

"Wait a minute now, let's get this straight," Mel Goodwin said. "You didn't feel this way when I called you up at noon. Someone's been working on you since then. Come on, who was it, Dot?"

"Oh, it doesn't matter, Mel," Dottie answered.

Mel Goodwin did not raise his voice. There was only the slightest change in it.

"Come on," he said, "who was it, Dot?"

It was interesting being an innocent bystander, now that Dottie had finally found a man. I was sure that she did not want to tell and I was just as sure that she was going to.

"It's about time for me to be going home," I said.

"No," Mel Goodwin said, "I want you to stick around, boy. Who's been so interested in me, Dot?"

"Mel," Dottie said, "promise me you won't be mad at him."

"That depends on who it is," Mel Goodwin said.

"Oh, hell," Dottie said, "all right, have it your own way. It was Robert."

"Well, I'll be God damned!" the General said. "So Bob was here."

"He's awfully fond of you, Mel," Dottie said.

"Well, I'll be God damned!" the General said. "So it was Bob, was it? Did you see him, Sid?"

I heard the question, but I could read nothing from his face.

"I saw him first at the office," I answered. "He's worried about you, Mel."

The guileless eyes of Mel Goodwin held me for a second.

"Do you think he's got a right to be?" he asked.

"Yes, sir," I answered, "he made me think so."

"What did you think of Bob?" he asked.

"I liked him," I said.

Mel Goodwin smiled and the watchfulness left his eyes.

"That boy is going to get along," he said, "if he just learns not to stick his neck out. God damn, it's nice, his being worried about the old man. You know, I kind of like it. What did he say?"

He was asking me, not Dottie.

"He thinks you have a future, sir," I said, "if you don't stick your neck out."

"You know, that's sort of pleasant," Mel Goodwin said, "to know that the kid thinks that. Did you and Bob get along all right, Dot?"

Dottie smiled her warmest smile.

"He loved talking about you, Mel," she said. "He was so sweet about you."

"Well, well," the General said, "maybe I should have taken this all up with Bob myself, but there never seemed to be any opportunity around the house in Alexandria. Maybe Bob's right about being

440

around publicly. Well, let's all stay here and have a happy evening. I'm really glad you saw him. I'm pretty proud of Bob. Did I ever tell you about the last time I had to lick him? It was when he swiped my horse at Schofield. He was too much horse and he ran away for about two miles, but Bob stayed with him. He told me later that I made his rear end sorer than the horse did. Say, I sort of wish I knew where to find Bob. I'd like to have him around right now." Melville Goodwin smiled and sat down on the sofa. "Fetch me a drink, will you, Sid? This is certainly a welcome change from Washington. God, that crowd in the Pentagon! It's full of people with battle records now, but a lot of the boys look confused."

As I watched Melville Goodwin, my own affairs assumed a tawdry, humdrum aspect, involving only small minds and little people. Melville Goodwin's personality had filled the room, embracing and absorbing Dottie Peale and me. Although his weaknesses and failings were very clear, he was living more intensely and more honestly than Dottie Peale or I ever would; he had seen more and he had given more freely of himself and he still had more to give, and anything that might happen to him would have a greater significance in human terms.

I forgot that it was time for me to be starting home. I was in an atmosphere of suspense, as I watched Mel Goodwin and Dottie Peale, and every bit of byplay was portentous. It was fascinating, for instance, to observe that when he sat down on the sofa he unbuttoned two buttons of his blouse. When you thought of the buttons of West Point and of his subconscious preoccupation with appearance, nothing could have been more revealing than that unconsidered action. It told as clearly as words where Dottie and Mel Goodwin stood.

"This is a fine idea," he said, "sitting around in a home this evening."

The unbuttoning of his blouse confirmed his words. Obviously he had given all his trust and all his confidence to Dottie Peale freely and rapidly, but then he had grown accustomed to swift decisions. It was only left for me to wonder uncomfortably how far he had gone in his planning.

"How's Muriel?" Dottie asked. I moved uneasily. Her inquiry was as candid as the unbuttoning of the blouse and so obvious that Dottie must have intended me to see how things stood. At any rate they both had made it clear that there was no need for camouflage.

"Oh," the General said, "Muriel's as busy as a bird dog. She's giving a round of cocktail parties and we had a steak fry last night."

"Oh dear," Dottie said, "every time I see you, you seem to have just left some steak fry or other."

You might have thought that she had said something very profound, judging by the General's emphatic agreement.

"Ever since I was a shavetail," Mel Goodwin said, "there have been steak fries, but they're increasing lately. Women like them and a lot of the big wheels seem to like chewing meat in somebody's back yard. I guess I've had too many alfresco meals to get the point, but Muriel likes me behind a grill with a fork in my hand. Every man in Washington is turning into a God-damned chef."

"Does General Bradley grill steaks, too?" Dottie asked.

"Oh, hell," Mel Goodwin said, "Brad's good at anything."

"Did you see the President yesterday?" Dottie asked. "You said you were going to."

"I certainly did," Mel Goodwin said. "Muriel and I went there to tea and he gave me fifteen minutes in the office. You really should have heard Muriel telling how I won the war."

"Well," I told him, "I think I ought to be going now."

"No, no," the General said, "sit down, Sid. You know what I mean about Muriel. No one can set things up like Muriel."

"Don't go yet, Sid," Dottie said. "It's always fun when Mel gets started on Washington."

I would not have termed it all fun, but I was back again in the orbit of General Goodwin.

This was the second time, Mel Goodwin was saying, that he had come home from a war. He had been very junior on the other occasion and that was easy to handle, but it was no joke coming home as a general, with a lot of missiles being thrown at you, including custard pies and bricks. If you put up your head a single inch out of a slit trench in Washington, you were apt to connect with something. It seemed, down in Washington, even in branches of the Department, that everyone was forgetting there had been a war and Washington was sick to death of officers and their records. There was all the Pacific island-hopping crowd trying to muscle in ahead of the Africa and ETO crowd. The truth was, combat officers were selling for about a dime a dozen, and you couldn't see the desks for the battle ribbons. There were a lot of people in Washington who were anxious to cut major generals down to size, now that we were winning the peace. All the branches of the service were still jockeying for position down in Washington. The Air Force boys, for instance, all knew they could win without Ground Forces now, and the navy seemed to have an idea that they could win without the Air Forces. It made you dizzy to hear the talk in Washington. He would wake up sometimes in the middle of the night wishing that he were a shavetail again out somewhere with troops.

The chain of command was something which anyone must respect because it was the backbone, sinews and nerve force of the service. He was willing to grant that you should obey it automatically, and he always had, and you learned also to put up with any personality above you. Frankly, he had served under many mediocre superiors, but there was something new in the peacetime setup that made him gripe. There was a cream-puff quality about a lot of thinking down in Washington. He once had the idea that the army was primarily designed to produce efficient combat units, but this was old hat now in some quarters. Instead, coming to it cold, you sometimes got the impression down there that the army was a sort of social service institution designed to provide financial security, healthy outdoor sports and desirable civic works. The army seemed to have its finger in everything — recreation centers, adult education, scientific research. A lot of people who should have known better were fiddling around down there in such a mental fog that they were getting fouled up over basic training and manpower. You might think — you really might — that the principal activities of the Department would be concentrated on the equipment and development of a few first-rate mobile divisions that could be used as an expansion nucleus in future

443

emergency. Granted the best minds were developing insomnia over how to accomplish this in the face of dwindling appropriations, yet bringing up such a subject was not well received in some groups. You would even get yourself lectured sometimes in a nice way about new tactics and new weapons by a lot of theoretical so-and-sos, although he admitted there were a lot of good boys around who had learned a few basic facts of life from coming in contact with the enemy.

On his first day in Washington he had dropped in on the spur of the moment to see "Snip" Lewis, just for a friendly chat and some informal orientation, on the off-chance that old Snip might not be too busy. Maybe he should have telephoned. Snip had been in a key position since the war and as far as Mel Goodwin was concerned, he deserved everything he had, including the Legion of Merit and the DSO and his complimentary French and British decorations. He had nothing at all against anyone like Snip, who had been three years behind him at the Point. Snip was an old Grimshaw man, and they had worked together in Washington before "Torch." It was not Snip's fault that he had stayed on in Washington — somebody had to stay — and Snip had been a fine exec for Grimshaw. Personally, Mel Goodwin was glad that Snip had worked his way to something. Nevertheless he was surprised when he dropped into that Pentagon office. Snip's office had a lot of mahogany in it and was about as big as the Chapel at the Point, with map racks and conference tables and his general's flag, but the thing that struck him right in the eye was Snip's exec in the outer office. It was old "Froggy" Jukes, sitting right out there pushing all the buttons. It was hard to tell what would come up next when you saw a man like Froggy Jukes in a key position.

He wanted to make it clear that he had nothing against Froggy. It wasn't any man's fault if he suffered from emotional instability and did not make the grade in a front area, because this might happen to the very best. Nevertheless when Froggy Jukes was in "Bullpup" in North Africa, he had been indecisive at a moment when you could not wait for second chances, and old Heinzy had not taken him over to Italy, after that little mix-up. Yet here he was, a brigadier, in the Pentagon with three secretaries and secret filing cabinets and four telephones. He had nothing whatsoever against Froggy and and he had not been mixed up with Froggy's problems, but they had both been in "Bullpup" and he knew the score.

"Well, well," Froggy said, "I've been wondering when you'd come here."

"Well, well," Mel Goodwin said, "it's nice to see you, Froggy. How have things been going?"

You could see that things had been going pretty well. Froggy had his North African ribbon, the Legion of Merit and the DSO and a Caribbean ribbon.

"I'm just the Chief's errand boy," Froggy said, "but I'm busy as a bird dog, what with all this unification. Let's see, you were in 'Bullpup,' weren't you, Mel?"

Froggy knew damned well that he was in "Bullpup," if he had not lost his wits.

"Heinzy never understood me out there," Froggy said.

All you could do was to be nice about it, and say that a lot of others hadn't hit it off with Heinzy either, but it was peculiar to hear someone like Froggy treating "Bullpup" as a joke and you could see that he still had it in for the "Bullpup" crowd on general principles.

"I suppose you want to hit the Chief for something," Froggy said.

Of course he was saying it in a kidding way, but it was not a nice way of putting it, considering who had the rank and record, and it was time to put Froggy in his place.

"If General Lewis has about three minutes," Mel Goodwin said, "I'd like to pay him my respects."

"The Chief is pretty busy now," Froggy said. "It's a crowded morning but I think he can give you five minutes."

"All right, ask him," Mel Goodwin said. "I'm pretty busy myself, Froggy."

Froggy opened the door to the inner office and slid through and closed it softly behind him. There was nothing about any of it that Melville Goodwin liked, particularly the implication that someone

445

like Jukes could do him a favor. People like Froggy Jukes always got on well on staffs and Froggy probably did have the knife out for any-one who had been in "Bullpup," but of course Snip Lewis had time to see him.

"Sit down, Mel," Snip said. "I wish I didn't have to get out of here in five minutes."

"It's damn nice to see you, Snip," Mel Goodwin said. "How's Ethel?"

"Ethel's fine," Snip said. "We'll have to get you and Muriel over on the first clear night, and we'll get the Old Man. The Old Man wants to see you."

"Well, that sounds good," Mel Goodwin said.

"We've got to find a groove for you, Mel," Snip said. "I wish there were room for you on the team here — but a lot of people are going to be asking for you. If there's anything you'd like particularly, count on me to put in a word."

This was all said in a kidding way, of course, and Mel Goodwin laughed because it was the right thing to do and not because he felt like laughing.

"Well," he said, "if you've got a division running around loose, bear me in mind, will you?"

This was said in a kidding way, too, but it was curious to see the blank look on Snip Lewis's face. You could see that he had always been away from divisions except on paper.

"What in hell do you want a division for?" Snip asked, and Mel Goodwin felt as embarrassed as if he had asked for something off-color.

"Well, I know about them," he said.

Snip Lewis wrote something on his memo pad.

"Listen, Mel," he said. "We can cook you up something higher than that. Now you're safe home we don't want to send you out to Bragg or Bailey. What would you do with a division, boy?"

It was the damnedest thing he had ever heard and a funny sort of attitude. He wanted to ask Snip Lewis what he thought the army was about, but it was no time to sound off too freely, and besides, Froggy had just re-entered the room.

"General Councillor is outside, sir," Froggy said, "and the car's at the Mall entrance."

"All right," Snip said, "two more minutes . . . and take my briefcase," and they both watched Froggy close the door.

"Froggy has been quite a find," Snip Lewis said.

"I'm glad to hear it," Mel Goodwin answered. "I'd be damned if I'd want him."

After all, he could call a spade a spade with Snip, and Snip laughed.

"I know," he said, "but right now we need more brains than brawn. Just get it through your head that you've got brains, too. Goochy's here and a lot of your old crowd. We'll all get together. Take off the pressure, Mel, it's going to be all right."

They walked out of the office together, and it was quite a walk from Snip's desk to the door, but he was not sure even then that everything was going to be all right. There were too many major generals wanting something. He was always running into them along the corridors, all calling on their own Snip Lewises. Maybe there should have been a displaced persons camp. There was nothing more displaced to his way of thinking than a combat general without troops in the Pentagon.

When you came to think of it, Bud Councillor had been holding down a desk in Grosvenor Square until the Third Army was outside Paris and then he had warmed another chair in Paris until he had got himself promoted to the higher echelons in Frankfurt. There had been a time when things had been a little different around the Pentagon. He could remember, for example, when he had flown back just after Salerno as a member of a group of five to give a firsthand picture of certain situations. Everyone was running around in those days to light your cigarette and when you sat around a table there was a universal belief that someone who had heard a gun go off might conceivably contribute something worth while to a discussion.

He had hardly been able to wait until the plane took off again. There had been a little dinner before the take-off in a certain house at Fort Myer and it had flattered the hell out of him to have been in such company. He had been the junior to all of them, but some of them had looked wistful, and sometimes you could forget about the rank. That farewell party and the faces stayed with him in the plane all the way up to Gander, but he would not have wanted any of their jobs. They were in touch with everything and at the same time out of touch. That was always the trouble with high echelons. You had to delegate so much and trust so much to other eyes and ears that you were always locked away in some map room dealing with high logistical problems, surrounded by people like Froggy Jukes. You were more of a professor than a soldier, and he wasn't any professor.

I had never seen Melville Goodwin quite so completely frank. His face was more mobile than I had ever seen it, and it exhibited traces of uncertainty and worry that I had never observed previously. He was clearly talking to himself as much as to Dottie Peale and me, though at the same time he was conscious of both of us. He wanted us to listen, although there was nothing that either of us could contribute because we were not familiar with the practices of army administration. We could only sympathize inexpertly with his disturbance. Then all at once he looked guilty.

"This is all off the record, you know," he said. "I'm afraid I've been giving you a false picture of the Pentagon. Set it down to biliousness, will you?"

He was back with his loyalties again. He had given a false picture of the Pentagon and now he wanted to make it clear that there was the finest crowd of people there that had ever been in any damned army — only there was so much fine material that it was a little crowded together, even in the Pentagon. He knew everybody there, or almost everybody. Why not, after thirty-five years in the service? There had never been such a collection of people with fine battle records or so many good leaders. It was a thrill to be on a first-name basis with nearly all the big wheels in that fine crowd. When he spoke of theoreticians and cream-puff thinking, he was only referring to a very few. They were doing the best they could there in the face of public apathy. They all felt basically as he did about building up a combat force and he had been unduly hard on Froggy Jukes too. Froggy really had a lot to recommend him.

He had been talking out of school about old Snip Lewis, too, who had done everything for him in Washington. Why, Snip had even wangled it somehow with Public Relations so that he could have a car and a driver when he needed it, and God only knew how Snip had managed it. Snip's office wasn't really as big as the Cadet Chapel either, and of course he had not been hitting Snip for a job seriously. Snip was not Career Management, but maybe you did just run on about things when you were new around the Pentagon.

"I don't want to give you any improper picture," he said, "but Sid here knows you can bellyache about the Pentagon a little, even when it's full of old classmates."

He passed his hand over his closely cropped hair and unbuttoned the last button of his blouse.

"Why don't you take your coat off?" Dottie asked him.

I had never thought that I would be so much Melville Goodwin's partisan. I hated to think of his being disturbed in Washington. I did not want him to be vulnerable like other people.

"Maybe that's a very good suggestion," he said, "but I wish you'd get in the habit of calling it a blouse instead of a coat."

"Oh, excuse me," Dottie said. "I don't know why I always keep forgetting."

He rose and took off his blouse and hung it neatly on the back of a chair, and that homely action dramatized all that he had been saying. He obviously recognized this himself, because when he sat down again in his olive-drab shirt, I saw him gazing at his blouse.

"Come to think of it," he said, "it looks like part of my skin, doesn't it? Now if Sid took off his coat, it wouldn't look so much like skin."

He smiled at us expectantly, but neither Dottie nor I spoke.

"Come to think of it, everything's on it, isn't it?" he said. "Maybe that's all that anybody ever sees in me — right over there."

Dottie smiled, and I was glad that she answered quickly.

"Oh, no," she said, "you've still got some stuffing in your shirt."

Mel Goodwin looked sharply at Dottie, but he saw the joke.

"Well, there it is," he said, "and it reads like a book. How would you like it if I left it off for good?"

"You look more comfortable without it," Dottie said.

"By God," Mel Goodwin said, "I do feel more comfortable, as long as you're around here, Dot."

He stood up and walked toward the chair where his blouse hung, and walked around it slowly.

"Now when I was a kid at the Point," he said, "I often dreamed of ribbons. Maybe there comes a time when you get too many. Maybe I've reached that period. Maybe it's a sort of change of life. I've got a queer kind of a feeling."

"What kind of a feeling?" Dottie asked.

"That maybe I might kick and holler if anybody should happen to pin another cluster on me," Mel Goodwin said. "God damn, maybe I've been a kid all my life and now I'm growing up. Maybe Sid sees what I mean."

He was looking at me in his coolest way, and I could almost believe that he knew what I thought about ribbons.

"Mel," I said, "you'd better remember just one thing."

"What one thing?" he asked.

"You'd better remember that you're too old to grow up."

For a moment he looked deadly serious and then he smiled his very youngest smile.

"Son," he said, "that crack of yours shows you know a lot about me and about the service. I don't believe you know how deep that cuts. I'm too old to grow up but I can still feel myself growing. Now maybe you can tell me where it's taking me."

"I wouldn't know," I said.

He walked across the room to the window and stood with his back to us, looking out into the back yards of Seventy-second Street.

"All right," he said, "I wouldn't either, but something's got to give somewhere. That's right, isn't it, Dot? Something's got to give."

"Now, Mel," Dottie said, "don't worry about it now."

She must have been referring to something between them that they had often discussed before, and I could only listen, like an eavesdropper.

"I'm not," Mel Goodwin said. "I'm used to shoving off whenever I know what's cooking."

450

Then his mood changed, and I was very glad it did. All the lines straightened on his face.

"Why haven't you stopped me sounding off about myself?" he asked. "You were saying that Sid had something on his mind. Well, all right, what's your problem, Sid?" It was remarkable how quickly things could rearrange themselves. Melville Goodwin was back again and in control of the situation. I was very glad to unload my own troubles and to get away from his.

When I began telling how Gilbert Frary had discovered me — hearing my voice from the ETO — my story seemed painfully superficial. It was mostly an egocentric striving, punctuated by a few pallid efforts at escape. Once, I suppose, I had wanted to be a great writer or columnist, but the desire had never assumed the proportions of an emotional drive. There was a gap between mediocrity and greatness which I had never crossed. Mine had been the life of anyone in a protected peaceful era within the limits of what might be called free enterprise, but all the time I talked I could feel what it lacked in splendor. I had never been a selfless part of a cause. I had never tossed my life in front of me and followed it. If I had risked it once or twice, this had only been through accident and not because of concerted purpose. The ship ahead of me in a convoy had been torpedoed once, the windows in my hotel in London had been shattered once by the explosion of a bomb, but I had never advanced with a group of men on an enemy position. I had never commanded a lost hope. I had never obeyed a call. I was not a Melville Goodwin. All I could say in my defense was that I could see myself more clearly than Goodwin had ever seen himself.

Dottie Peale had heard my story before. She sat gazing abstractedly at the pointed toe of her slipper, but Melville Goodwin looked straight at me, following every word, and occasionally he frowned.

"You see, it's what I've told you, Mel," Dottie said. "Sidney is always drifting. He simply never seems to care."

"I don't know," Mel Goodwin said. "Sitting in on this with a purely outside point of view, I can make a few suggestions, but it

451

seems to me Sid's done pretty well, Dot. He's getting the facts together and waiting to take action."

Gilbert Frary and the broadcasting studio had finally reached a military level, and Melville Goodwin's voice had a ring of complete authority. He had taken over my problem, and curiously enough I actually felt a weight being lifted from me because Melville Goodwin was taking over.

"I'd like your advice," I began, "but there's no reason why you should know much about this sort of thing."

Melville Goodwin nodded. "That's all right, Sid," he said. "You've given me the information. All anybody ever needs is good straight information."

"Be quiet," Dottie said, "don't interrupt him, Sid."

"I wasn't going to interrupt him," I told her.

"Well, I'm glad you weren't," Dottie said. "Now, Mel, make a note that I know a man who wants a news program."

"I'm not forgetting," Melville Goodwin said. "Get me a cigarette, will you, Dot?" and Dottie handed him the cigarette box and picked up the lighter as quickly as Colonel Flax.

"There was an officer at the St. George Hotel in African Headquarters in Algiers," the General said, "named Sturmer, holding a temporary rank of brigadier general like me. He was just like this Frary, flexible and without loyalty. Did I ever tell you about Ed Sturmer, Dot?"

"No, I don't think so," Dottie said.

"Dottie always gets me talking," Mel Goodwin said. "I begin to forget what anecdotes I haven't told her. Now this Ed Sturmer was just like this Frary. You always find people like him around any headquarters. He wanted to get my spot in 'Bullpup.' He was always telling me what a fine guy I was and how he admired me, and then he was always finding little facts about me and getting in to see the old man when I wasn't there, and giving the little facts an unfavorable slant. Well, I let Ed run along with it until I was all ready for him. Ed and I were just old buddies until I was ready."

Melville Goodwin rubbed his hands together.

"I just waited until the Old Man had Ed and me alone with him there in the St. George," he said, "going over a map. I remember Ed was holding a pointer and arguing about some little track behind the mountains. I interrupted him right in the middle and spoke to the Old Man.

" 'Sir,' I said, 'may I make a remark before General Sturmer finishes?'

" 'Yes, what is it, Mel?' the Old Man said.

" 'Heinzy,' I said, 'Ed is going to ask you, if he hasn't asked you already, whether he can't have my spot in "Bullpup." If you want him and not me, I'd suggest you make the decision, instead of letting us both horse around like kids at a cocktail party.' "

Melville Goodwin fixed his eyes upon me as though I were Ed Sturmer, and I could feel indirectly the impact of his words.

"There are times when you've got to stick your neck out," Mel Goodwin said. "I was taking one hell of a gamble. Sturmer jumped so, he damn near dropped the pointer, but old Heinzy didn't say anything for a quarter of a minute. I had thrown the ball right at him.

" 'You're damned impertinent, don't you think, Mel?' the Old Man said.

" 'Yes, sir, I think so,' I told him.

" 'Well,' he said, 'there's no need for such shocking manners, Mel. Go on and consider there has been no interruption, Ed.' "

Melville Goodwin paused as though he had reached the end of the story, and he grew impatient when he saw we were waiting for more.

"That was all there was to it," he said.

"But what *happened?*" Dottie asked.

"God damn it, Dot," Melville Goodwin said, "nothing further happened. I was in 'Bullpup' until I got a piece of hardware in my shoulder, wasn't I?"

It seemed to me that it was one of Melville Goodwin's better anecdotes, because it ended in suspense, even if Melville Goodwin thought it ended perfectly.

"Is Ed Sturmer around the Pentagon now?" I asked.

"Hell, yes," Melville Goodwin said. "Ed's right there in the Pentagon, but that isn't the point."

"Then what's the point?" I asked.

"Either you or I must be pretty dumb tonight, son," the General said. "The point is, you've got to stick your neck out sometimes. You get another job lined up and then go and see this Frary."

"Did you have another job lined up in Algiers?" I asked.

"Listen, son," the General said, "I'm talking about you, not me. Three other people were asking for me, and Heinzy knew it. Maybe I'm not as dumb as you think I am. Dottie will go around and see that man for you, and now you'd better get back to Connecticut or Helen will pin your ears back. You have nothing further to worry about. Dot and I personally will handle your situation."

"Suppose I don't want you to handle my situation?" I asked.

Melville Goodwin smiled.

"I used to think you knew something about women, son," he said. "Don't you know that Dottie will do it anyway?"

Dottie was smiling at him affectionately, and I knew that Melville Goodwin was right. It was time for me to be getting home to Connecticut. They wanted me to go, but I still delayed for a minute, because of an incongruous piece in the General's thinking that aroused my curiosity.

"There's just one element that I'd like you to consider, sir," I said, "a rather personal element."

It was a suitable moment to call him "sir," and that mystic monosyllable was a warning signal, showing that what would follow had a formal and serious note. His eyes narrowed in alert interrogation.

"Suppose I'm sick to death of this broadcasting and that I'd welcome any opportunity to get out of it."

Dottie shrugged her shoulders impatiently.

"Sid's always sick of anything he's doing," she said, "and he always has been."

"Well," I said, "the same is true with you, Dottie. I've never thought of you as a contented type."

"Oh, nuts," Dottie said, "I always stick to what I'm doing and at

454

least I know what I want." She always would believe she knew—simply by affirmation.

Melville Goodwin looked as though I had uttered a heresy and he stood up. I noticed that he did not have to use his hands to propel himself upward from the cushions of the sofa.

"Now, Sid," he said, "now, Sid." He spoke in the gentle and fatherly voice that he probably used on subordinates whom he really liked. "You're bothered and tired, son, or you'd never have said a damn-fool thing like that." Then his voice changed. There was a ring in it of absolute and beautiful certainty. "Just take it easy, son. Of course you're not sick of what you're doing, because basically you have guts. You've got a fine position and look at that lovely home of yours in Connecticut. When I think of you running around loose in the ETO, only a Public Relations major, and I see you now, it's a real inspiration. Now listen to me."

In spite of myself, his voice instilled in me a sense of guilt. I felt like a college football player being addressed by the coach in the locker room at the end of a ragged half.

"I'm going to tell you something, son," he went on. "Do you remember when that mortar shell rolled you and me into the ditch in Normandy? When we got up and exchanged a few words afterwards, I knew I was talking to a man, even if you were only a ninety-day wonder from the Special Services. I'd have known it if you'd been an entertainer in the USO, and do you know what I said to Goochy afterwards? I don't think I ever told you what I said to Goochy about Sid, did I, Dot?"

Dottie shook her head; the echo of Mel Goodwin's voice held her silent.

"I said, 'Goochy, make a note of that officer's name and find out about him when we get the time. A lad like that ought to be in the line. It's too damn bad to think of his crapping around somewhere in back.'"

Melville Goodwin waited, and I cleared my throat.

"It's kind of you to tell me that, sir," I said. "It means a lot, coming from you."

And somehow it did mean a lot.

455

"The war's over. Forget it, son," he said. "You've got guts and you've got your directive too. Never neglect a directive. You've a lovely wife and a beautiful little girl, and you're not going to let them down. Now go on home and leave this to Dot and me. Good night, son."

The speech was ended, and Melville Goodwin strode over to the table and the bottles.

"Good night, dear," Dottie said.

But I said one thing more to Mel Goodwin before I left.

"I thought you sounded rather discontented yourself tonight, sir."

I should have been taking a general stock of myself, recalling the amount of money I had saved, and striving to remember Clause 28 in my contract instead of feeling a deep concern for Melville Goodwin. A part of that concern was undoubtedly a hang-over from the war. You had to be loyal in the army, and whether I liked it or not, I was loyal to Melville Goodwin, though perhaps I was not as loyal to him as to the idea he represented. Roughly speaking, I suppose I owed a debt to all the Melville Goodwins. They had been useful a short while ago and they might be needed again in an uncertain world. He was both an individual and a symbol and he had to do what I expected of him. He must not be a failure. I was one of the Goodwin crowd and right behind Melville A. Goodwin. I was sure that Mel Goodwin and Dottie Peale could not have anything in common that would last for any length of time. As long as there was some sort of sensible discretion and as long as he did not continue to quote Tennyson's "Ulysses" and as long as he did not row into the sunset with Dottie Peale, he would get it out of his system. Yet there had been some other sort of understanding between them. I remembered Dottie's telling him not to speak about it now and his saying that something had to give somewhere. . . . "That's right, isn't it, Dot? . . . Something's got to give. . . ."

XXIX

Time to Meet the Gang

It was after eleven and the wind around Savin Hill was rising, blowing the brown leaves off the beech trees by the front door and sending them scuttling across the tarred drive with a sound not unlike the scampering of mice or squirrels across a deserted attic floor. I could tell that the weather was about to change, a phenomenon which I never noticed in New York. There were no stars and the house, like the weather, had an ominous and foreboding look, even though the bronze lanterns on either side of the front door were lighted, as they always were when I was late. They were old ship lanterns that Helen had bought at an auction, and I had not the least idea on what type of vessel they had belonged or what exact function they had performed at sea, but they never had looked as expatriated as they did that night.

I unlocked the door myself because Oscar usually went off duty, as he called it, at ten o'clock, and Helen always tried to be careful about Oscar's hours. A single light was burning in the hall on a stand beneath the dim gold Chippendale mirror which Helen had also bought that summer. She had always said that antiques were an investment and something you could always sell if necessary — and it might be necessary. I began to think unpleasantly of the possibilities of a sale in case we should need ready cash, and my imagination was so acute that I could almost hear the footsteps of auctioneers and appraisers. There was no light in the living room or anywhere else downstairs, except in the hall, which made me believe that Helen must have gone to bed. I do not know why this should have made me feel hurt or disappointed except that she customarily waited up for me. When I heard quick footsteps in the upstairs hall,

457

I was sure it must be Helen, but instead it was Miss Otts with Farouche.

As soon as Farouche saw me, he bounded quickly upstairs again without bothering to greet me, and I knew where he was going. He had a one-track mind.

"Oh, is it you, Mr. Skelton?" Miss Otts said.

Of course it was I, and it could not well have been anyone else, but I could not understand why Miss Otts was still dressed in her tweeds because she usually retired early.

"I thought it might be Mrs. Skelton," she said.

"What?" I said. "Where is Mrs. Skelton?"

"Oh, she went out for the evening," Miss Otts said, "but she said she would be back early. She left you a note, Mr. Skelton, on the hall table by the lamp."

"Oh," I said, "thank you, Miss Otts."

The whole day had given me a sense of insecurity. When I picked up the envelope from the table, I could not help thinking of the "Dear John" notes in the ETO. I could not imagine where Helen could have possibly gone. The note was hastily scrawled in pencil.

"Darling," I read, "the Brickleys asked us over for dinner and bridge. You know — the ones two miles down the road who always keep asking us and you never want to go. When I said you were out, they asked me anyway. I thought I ought to go to be polite, and Mr. Brickley is calling for me, so don't worry, and he will bring me back. Farouche has been aired, but if you are in before I am, please look in on Camilla. The doctor says it's only grippe, but she has some fever."

I remembered that these people, the Brickleys, had come to call one Sunday in the summer, and I recalled the difficulties I had encountered in making conversation with them and that later they had asked us to a picnic. This had been kind of the Brickleys, and they had said that we must be neighborly. We had all been very cordial, but I could not remember much more about them — except that Mrs. Brickley raised dogs and that they had an apartment in town for the winter, although they always came to the country for week ends and whenever else they could. Also, I had thought that Mr. Brickley must have worked in town, successfully, judging from appearances. Nevertheless it was no time for the Brickleys to be complicating the picture, and I was very sorry that Helen had not stayed at home.

"How is Camilla?" I asked.

It was a question that other parents in other eras must have asked Miss Otts about other offspring, and she was ready for it.

"She's doing very nicely," Miss Otts said, "but she called to me a half an hour ago. She was restless when she found that you and Mrs. Skelton were both out, and she's still awake. I was about to call Mrs. Skelton when you came in."

I did not blame Camilla for being restless, alone with Miss Otts, because Miss Otts always made me restless, too. When I opened the door of Camilla's room, the light on her bedside table was carefully shaded so that the room was dim, and the dollhouse I had given her and her childish books on the shelves and all her other small possessions were vague and shadowy. Camilla was in her blue flannel wrapper, lying with two pillows behind her and with a braid hanging over each shoulder. She looked like a miniature of Helen.

"We've been reading," Miss Otts told me, "and we've had aspirin fifteen minutes ago. I think we will go to sleep in a few minutes now that Daddy has come home, won't we, Camilla?"

"Yes," Camilla said.

"Hello, dear," I said, and her cheek felt very hot when I kissed her.

"And Daddy mustn't stay too long," Miss Otts said.

It was a general observation rather than a command or a request.

"No," I said, "Daddy won't stay too long."

Camilla stared at me unblinkingly and did not answer until Miss Otts was gone.

"You sounded funny when you said that," Camilla said.

I could never be sure how much anyone Camilla's age saw or knew, and I seated myself carefully on the edge of her bed.

"Well, I felt funny," I said. "Why don't you close your eyes and try to go to sleep?"

"All right," Camilla said, and I took away one of her pillows.

459

It was almost the first time I could remember that I had ever done anything physically helpful for Camilla.

It had been quite a day, what with Miss Maynard at the office and Art Hertz and Dottie and Captain Robert Goodwin and General Melville Goodwin. It was difficult as always to move back to Camilla.

"Daddy?" Camilla asked.

"What?" I answered.

"You haven't got a drink."

"No," I said, "that's right, I haven't."

"Well," she said, "that's just as well."

"You'd better go to sleep," I said.

"Daddy?" she asked. "Where is that man?"

"What man?" I asked.

"That man who was a soldier." I had not known that the General had made any impression on her. She had not seen much of him, but it must have been the uniform and the ribbons. Besides, perhaps the memory of Mel Goodwin was still around the house and might stay there, as memories of Washington and Lafayette and Lee had persisted in other places. After all, Mel Goodwin had slept here.

"Oh," I said, "he's being a soldier somewhere."

"He was funny, wasn't he?" Camilla said.

"Yes," I said, "in some ways."

"You always laughed when he was being funny," Camilla said.

"That's right," I said, "he told a lot of jokes."

"Daddy?" she said.

"What?" I answered.

"Let's talk about something."

"All right," I said, "let's talk."

"About when you were a little boy."

Camilla was the only person in the world who was interested in that era. I was glad to see that her eyes were half closed. I did not know whether it was the aspirin that was making her drowsy or security. Then I thought of my balloon again as I had thought of it during the afternoon.

"Well," I said, "once when I was your age and I was staying with

460

my uncle in Nashua, New Hampshire, he took me to a county fair."

"What's a county fair?" Camilla asked.

There were always gaps in experience when one dealt with child-hood, and I had to improvise a definition of a county fair.

"There were all sorts of things there," I told her, " — farm animals and flowers and prize jams and a lady with snakes. There was a man who could walk on a tightrope and another man who could hang by his toes and drink a bottle of ginger ale."

I thought that this would interest her, but she let the phenomenon pass.

"And all the children there," I told her, "had whips with whistles on the end of them or windmills on sticks or balloons. My uncle bought me a balloon."

"What color was it?" Camilla asked.

"Blue," I told her, and I could see the balloon again as clearly as though I were holding it. Its strange rubberoid smell was in my nostrils, and I could hear the complaining squeaking noise when my fingers gently stroked against it. "It was on a string, and then I forgot it for a moment and I let the string go. It was gone, up in the air, and I could only stand there watching it until it was out of sight or almost out of sight."

"Where is it now?" Camilla asked, and I saw she was very sleepy.

"I don't know," I said, "but it must be somewhere. Everything that happens, everything you do, must be somewhere."

I had not intended to be metaphysical, but it made no difference because Camilla was asleep, and I left her sleeping by the shaded lamp. Everything seemed in order now that Camilla was asleep.

Farouche was waiting outside Camilla's door holding his rubber ring but he was not resentful when I paid no attention to him. He followed me downstairs patiently and hopefully, and there was still no sign of Helen. I had been to plenty of places without her in the last few years without feeling as solitary as I felt that night. It was, of course, the house. It had been too large for us in the first place and we should never have purchased it, especially with financial help from the broadcasting company. It was not reassuring to recall that

Gilbert Frary had made all these arrangements and that I had paid no particular attention to them. I was not even sure who would own the place in the event of difficulties. Without Helen there, it was only a memorial to my own bad judgment. I did not turn on the lights in the living room because I did not wish to face its impact, but I did go into the library, which Helen had so carefully planned for me as a place in which to write.

It still resembled a nook in a stately home of England and there was no reason why it should not have, since most of the room had come from stately English homes. It was a gentleman's library, and the trouble must have been that I was not enough of a gentleman for it. The chair in which Melville Goodwin had sat for so long was exactly where it had been. Actually the library had become more his room than mine, and the inflections of his voice still seemed to be in it. He had brought Hallowell to us there, and the woods at Château-Thierry, and North Africa and Bailey and the Philippines and himself. I could almost see that dripping fringe of woods on a July morning long ago and hear the machine guns chattering on the crest of the slope.

It was a quarter before twelve and there was still no sign of Helen. I took a book from one of the shelves without caring what it might be. It was entitled *General Sir Cyril Bulwythe, K.C.B., A Memoir,* and it had been printed in 1830 by someone on the Strand. I had never heard of General Sir Cyril nor did I particularly wish to know about him, but I did turn to the last chapter, and judging from the crisp resistance of the pages, this was more than anyone else had previously done. The memoir was written in the portentous style of the period connecting the eighteenth century with the Victorian era.

"The inactivity of retirement," I read, "despite the acclaim that was his, and the doors which were gladly open to him upon his return from India, and the charm and social graces of Lady Bulwythe, ill befitted, alas, the talents of Sir Cyril, who could accept only with reluctance, and indeed frequently with acerbity, the routine of a retired army officer upon half pay. The last years of General Bulwythe, instead of being replete with peace, and adding lustre to the honours bestowed upon him, were, alas, tumultuous, and the bottle, which he had eschewed as a subaltern and had faced later with a moderation amazing in the India service, became, alas, increasingly his companion. . . ."

The front door opened, and I was very glad of it, although I did want at some future time to learn about the social graces of Lady Bulwythe. Helen had returned, and Mr. Brickley in a dinner coat was with her.

"Now please come in for just a minute," I heard Helen saying in the front hall. "There's Sidney's hat and coat, and he'll miss not seeing you. Sidney's a dreadful night owl. He's never in bed at this time."

"Well," I heard Mr. Brickley say, "I keep country hours in the country, but I'd love to stay for a minute or two."

"Oh, Sid," Helen called. "Where are you, Sid?"

She did not need to call me. I was already out of the library and craving human companionship in any form. Helen was wearing her Fortuny pleated dress, and if I had been Mr. Brickley I would have wanted to stay a few minutes myself, in spite of country hours.

"Darling," Helen said, "you remember Mr. Brickley, don't you?"

As I have said, I did not remember Mr. Brickley very well, and certainly not in a dinner coat with pearl studs. The last time I had seen him he had been wearing some sort of a ranching or lumberjack's costume at his picnic, and the change from the country to the urban Mr. Brickley was dramatic. He was now like someone at the speakers' table at one of those dinners I used to attend when I was a young reporter — and you always worked hard for such an assignment because of the free food. He was bald, pinkish and good-natured, past fifty, about the General's age. Melville Goodwin must still have been on my mind, because I was comparing Mr. Brickley's smooth face with the General's chiseled features. Mr. Brickley had been leading a different life and one even more an enigma to me than that of Melville Goodwin.

"Of course I remember Mr. Brickley," I said, "and thanks for having Helen over."

"I did have a wonderful time," Helen said. "I wish you could have been there, Sid."

463

"It was just the usual crowd," Mr. Brickley said, "but I will say we have a nice gang around here. You've got to take some time off and see the girls and boys."

Helen had already turned on the lights in the living room.

"I always thought the Winlocks' room was perfect," Mr. Brickley said, "but this is even better. Your wife has a real decorative sense."

"Yes indeed she has," I answered in my sincerest voice, "and she has given the house a lot of thought all summer."

"The room only needs living in now," Helen said, "and Sid always keeps going into the library. Don't you think it would be nice if we lit a fire, dear?"

Helen could fit in anywhere, and I wished that I could. I examined the logs in the fireplace suspiciously. I knew something about open fires from living on my uncle's farm outside of Nashua and I knew how to lay logs and kindlings better than Oscar. In spite of the exquisite fans of paper he placed beneath them, the logs were always too close together. I adjusted them as well as I could, considering the tall andirons, and then struck a match while Mr. Brickley looked on with professional interest.

"There's nothing like puttering around with an open fire, is there?" Mr. Brickley said.

"That's right," I answered. "It teaches you self-reliance."

"Now for years," Mr. Brickley said, "a crowd of us have always gone up to the Restigouche — that's up in New Brunswick — to a little salmon-fishing club. There's a guide up there, old Walt Grant, who can make a fire out of almost nothing, just some birch bark and a few shavings he cuts with his jackknife."

"Have you been waiting for me long, dear?" Helen asked.

"Oh, no," I said, "only long enough to begin reading one of those books you bought at the Parke-Bernet, *General Sir Cyril Bulwythe, K.C.B., A Memoir.*"

Mr. Brickley was politely interested. I must have been as strange to him as he was to me, but then this was the sort of thing I would be expected to be doing — reading a good, unusual book.

"I don't think I ever heard of it," he said.

"Neither had I," I answered. "I just picked it out. There were a

464

lot of vacant shelves, and Helen bought an assortment at the Parke-Bernet to fill them up — you know, thoughtlessly — like filling in a pie."

"Well, I've got a lot of books myself," Mr. Brickley said, "and I always mean to get at them on a winter's evening, but all I ever have time to read is balance sheets."

"Darling," Helen said, "did you see Camilla?"

"Yes," I answered, "I think she's asleep now. Miss Otts said Daddy ought not to stay too long, and Camilla noticed I didn't have a drink with me. She spoke of it particularly."

"Oh, Sid," Helen said, and I was sorry, especially when I saw Mr. Brickley's expression. I was not doing right by Helen.

"It always seems to happen that way," I said. "Helen and I usually have a cocktail before dinner, and then it always seems to be our daughter's bedtime." This apparently explained everything to Mr. Brickley, and we were again becoming the nice natural couple that Helen wanted us to be. Talking to Mr. Brickley was like learning to ride a bicycle and finding it was possible.

"I'd better run up and see how Camilla is," Helen said, "and speaking of drinks, perhaps Tom would like one. Everything's all on a tray in the pantry, dear, except the ice."

For a moment I did not know who Tom could be until I decided it must be Mr. Brickley.

"Well, I don't know," Mr. Brickley said. "How about you — er — Skelton?"

"I think it would be a fine idea," I said, "just a nightcap. Or there's beer or ginger ale."

This put it up to Mr. Brickley. I did not especially want a drink and I was sure that he did not either, but we were caught in the vise of the amenities, and there was the danger that I might think the less of him if he wanted ginger ale or beer. We were like two strange dogs circling each other suspiciously and at the same time wagging our tails.

"Oh, I'll take anything you take," Mr. Brickley said.

He said it genially and jovially as man to man and he had handed the ball right back to me, as Mel Goodwin would have said. I thought of my unfortunate remark about Camilla, and yet it would not have been hospitable to have said that I would settle for ginger ale, although I would have very much preferred it — and I passed the ball back to Mr. Brickley.

"How about a touch of Scotch?" I said, "or bourbon if you'd like it."

Mr. Brickley gave the matter a moment's serious consideration.

"Oh, not bourbon," he said, as though bourbon were going too far, "but I might settle for a drop of Scotch, just a drop."

"I like Scotch better myself," I said, and everything was settled and the debate was over. "I'll be back with it in just a minute."

"Let me come and help you," Mr. Brickley said. "I know my way around here. I was always in and out of Edgar's pantry."

"Edgar who?" I asked.

Mr. Brickley coughed. "Oh, I forgot you didn't know him," he said. "Edgar Winlock. We used to have great times at the Winlocks'."

"I never saw him," I said, "but I always have a feeling that I've known him, living in the house. Sometimes I call Helen 'Mrs. Winlock.' "

Mr. Brickley laughed nervously, and I saw I had gone too far again and had not made quite the right impression.

"Just a bad marital joke," I said. "There's nothing more tiresome than conjugal humor."

The word "conjugal" made it sound better, and Mr. Brickley laughed.

"I know what you mean," he began. "Well, well, who's this?"

It was Farouche with his rubber ring. He had become discouraged when I had paid no attention to him and had gone upstairs to bed, but he must have heard our voices.

"We call him Farouche," I said.

"Here, boy," Mr. Brickley said, "come and give it to me, boy. One thing about the country — you can keep dogs. Maida — er — Mrs. Brickley, has two Scotties called Gin and Fizz. They're all over the house. Come here, boy."

He was tossing the ring to Farouche when I went into the pantry.

466

As I extracted ice cubes, I felt as though I were off stage. I hoped that Helen would be down when I returned, but Mr. Brickley was still alone.

"I suppose they keep you pretty busy with that broadcasting and everything," Mr. Brickley said.

"It's a steady sort of grind," I told him.

"Well, if you ever have any time on your hands," Mr. Brickley said, "I hope you'll drop in to see us. Maida — er — Mrs. Brickley, and I are always around over week ends, and we'd like you to meet the crowd."

I spoke in my sincerest voice. It sounded almost too sincere.

"I'd certainly love to, Mr. Brickley," I said. "I'm terribly sorry I couldn't come to your house this evening."

Mr. Brickley cleared his throat. "We were going to call you up about two weeks ago," he said, "but then we heard you had a house full of guests, including even a general. Your Oscar knows our Pedro. That's the way things get around in the country."

We had naturally been under observation ever since we had bought the place, and I was under observation now, and what Mr. Brickley thought about me would undoubtedly get around.

"He dropped in all of a sudden," I said, "an old friend of mine, Major General Melville A. Goodwin. Did you ever hear of him?"

"Oh, yes," Mr. Brickley said. "Everybody around here has heard lots about him. Whenever Pedro could get off, he came over here to lend a hand."

"Tell him to come often," I said.

Mr. Brickley laughed uneasily. I had been uncouth again, but I could not very well undo it.

"There's one good thing about it around here," Mr. Brickley said. "This is a real live-and-let-live community. You can see people or not, just the way you want. Do you know Maxwell Blenheim, the novelist? He has a place here."

"No, I don't believe I do," I said.

"He doesn't get around much either," Mr. Brickley said, "except to go down to the post office. It's a real meeting place, the post office. You've been there, haven't you?"

"No, I don't think so," I said, "but I'm sure Helen has."

Mr. Brickley looked disappointed.

"And there's Arthur Phillips Stroburt, the composer," he said. "You know him, don't you?"

"I think I've heard of him but I'm not sure," I answered.

"Well, if you once get going around, you'll meet a lot of interesting people here," Mr. Brickley said, "and some salty country characters, too. You mustn't mind our interest. We were all deeply concerned over what might happen to the Winlock place. When Edgar passed out of the picture and when we heard that someone in radio had bought it — well, frankly we had our fingers crossed, but that was before we met — er — Helen. You won't mind my saying, will you, that there's nothing much wrong with Helen?"

"She's always made the grade with me," I said.

"You ought to have seen her tonight," Mr. Brickley said. "The gang were crazy about her, and we hope she liked us as well as we liked her. We've all got to be neighbors from now on, real neighbors."

Mr. Brickley raised his glass. It was an accolade, a signal of approval by an ambassador visiting a migrant tribe, and we had qualified.

"It's nice you feel that way," I said. "I know this is a rather closed community."

"Not if you're inside it," Mr. Brickley said, "and that's what I'm here for. We all want to see more of the Skeltons."

Then the dialogue was over and Helen was back.

"She was asleep," she said. "I was just arguing with Otts about the light beside the bed. Farouche, stop bothering Mr. Brickley."

"He doesn't bother me," Mr. Brickley said. "No dog ever bothers me. Helen, I was just telling — er — your husband, that he's got to meet the crowd. You've got to pull him out of hiding. What about Saturday night? He has Saturday off, hasn't he?"

"Call him 'Sid,' Tom," Helen said. "Of course we'd love to do something on Saturday. Anything you think would be fun. Maida can call me."

"You gals just work out something between yourselves," Mr.

Brickley said. "I'll tell Maida to get in touch with you. Do you play poker, Sid?"

"Yes, a little, Tom," I said.

"Well, I've got to be pushing off now," Mr. Brickley said. "Good night, Sid. We'll look for you on Saturday. Good night, Helen dear."

Newspaper work, I always believed, placed one in contact with people from every walk of life, but Mr. Brickley must have been a type that never made the news. I could see, after I had followed Mr. Brickley to his new convertible, that I had been trying, oddly enough, throughout that whole innocuous conversation to be like Mr. Brickley, and yet I could not understand in the least why I had tried. What was it that had made me? Helen kissed me and she looked as though there had been some sort of achievement somewhere.

"Darling," she said, "it's wonderful, the way you get on with people."

"Do you think I did all right?" I asked.

"Darling," she said, "you were wonderful, and I was so afraid you wouldn't like him. It's been worrying me all evening."

There was an atmosphere of triumph, a sense of the bridging of a gap, and she was so happy and excited that she seemed to have forgotten that something had been distressing me when she called me earlier at the office. She was like a girl who had been a great success as a stranger at a dance and could talk about nothing else.

"What made you think I wouldn't like him?" I asked.

"Oh, I don't know," she said. "You're so unpredictable sometimes. I was so afraid you would think he was dull or stuffy or something."

"I don't see why you should think I'd think that," I said.

"I kept wishing you were there all evening," she said. "Everybody was so awfully nice and — outgoing."

"Outgoing where?" I asked.

"Darling," Helen said, "please don't spoil it all by being critical. They really were awfully nice. Oh, I know if I were to describe it, it would sound simple and corny — I wish no one had ever invented that word. We just talked about the neighborhood and power lawn mowers and tree infusions and things like that."

469

"Tree infusions?" I repeated.

"There's a new sort of thing they do for trees," Helen said. "There's a sort of liquid full of nitrogen and things that they force down among the roots under pressure." Helen laughed; she was very happy. "It sounded like forcible feeding."

"Why do they have to be fed forcibly?" I asked.

"I don't know," Helen said, "but I have the address of a man who does it."

"How much does it cost?" I asked.

"I don't know," Helen said, "but you don't have to do it every year and not to every tree. Darling, they were really awfully nice, and it was such fun talking about ordinary things for a change . . . like children's jodhpurs, and the Country Day School. . . . It was all so homey. I know how you object to the word 'homey' but I don't know any other way to say it."

"There must be some other way," I said.

"Darling," Helen said, "please don't spoil it all."

I took her hand and held it tight.

"I won't spoil it," I told her. "I'm awfully glad you had such a good time."

"I'm awfully glad you're getting used to everything," she said. "You are, aren't you, dear?"

"Yes, of course I am," I told her.

"And you did like Tom, didn't you?"

"Tom?" I repeated.

"Tom," she said, "Tom Brickley."

"Yes, I thought he was swell," I said. "I always like people, Helen, when I get a chance to know them."

"If you like him you can't help liking all the rest of them."

"The gang?" I said.

"Sid, please don't say it in that way. All right then, the gang."

"Of course I'll like them if you do, Helen," I said.

"Darling, I've been so worried ever since we've been here," Helen said, ". . . oh, not exactly worried, but wondering whether you'd ever get to like it and whether we could fit in or whether we'd have to move somewhere else. Sid, I can't tell you how happy I feel. You've never belonged anywhere and I haven't either, not in Delaware or anywhere. I've always been someone just passing through, and now I really think we're going to belong here. I can't tell you how happy it makes me feel. It's like having loose ends tied up tight."

I began wanting to find an end that was not tied up, but then I had always been that way and perhaps it was time to stop — as long as I did not have to see the gang too continually.

"Of course we're going to belong here, Helen," I told her.

I was still holding her hand. Melville Goodwin had been absolutely right. I had what he called my directive. I would have to do something right away about Gilbert Frary and Art Hertz. I could not let Helen down if she wanted to belong. If she wanted it, I wanted to belong myself, and if she wanted to feed trees forcibly, I wanted to arrange that she could do it. I wanted her to have everything she wanted. It was about time I pulled up my socks and put my mind on it.

"Darling," Helen said, "this is such a wonderful place for children. . . . I really do think we ought to think about having another baby."

XXX

It Was a Lot of Fun with Goochy

IT HAD been Gilbert Frary's pet idea, as I have said before — and Gilbert always did have an instinct for showmanship — to move the broadcast about the country. This gave the broadcast, as Gilbert said, an on-the-spot reporting flavor and what he called, in vaguer terms, the illusion of motion. It may have had its value, this illusion that I was doing my own leg work and contacting the news at first hand, as Gilbert put it. If I started a broadcast by saying, "Good evening, friends. I am speaking to you from Washington tonight" — or London or Paris or wherever Gilbert wanted me — perhaps the listeners did think of me as Sid Skelton, the news hawk, ferreting out his own facts after confidential talks with heads of governments, instead of getting them off the teletype and having Art Hertz prepare them.

It was an expensive process, but the Crosley rating of the program proved its value, and besides, George Burtheimer, the sponsor out in Chicago, was the head of a corporation that could write the expenses off on the tax return instead of giving them, as Gilbert Frary put it, to Uncle Sam for buying up potatoes. As Gilbert said, it was all just nickels to George Burtheimer, and Gilbert always did like to make arrangements for a show. Though he was still out in Hollywood, he had perfected all the arrangements by remote control. For instance, I was to be in Washington ostensibly looking into the Chinese situation, and somehow Gilbert had contrived to get the State Department interested, and finally a man from the Department named Hubert Stillwater was to have a three-minute spot in which he would tell me all about China.

"I just happen to be sitting now," I was to say, "with my old friend, Hubert Stillwater, one of our State Department's 'think men.' We have been just discussing the implications of Chinese Communism, and perhaps Mr. Stillwater would not mind repeating to you what he has just been telling me. How about it, Hubert?"

This was not an original idea of Gilbert Frary's, since other commentators had been doing this sort of thing for years, but, as Gilbert Frary said, a good idea was a good idea, and if it was good for them, why shouldn't it be for me. If somebody else started by saying, "Good evening, everybody," there was nothing to stop my saying, "Good evening, friends," which was also Gilbert Frary's idea and what he termed a warmer and more human salutation. After all, as Gilbert said, you had to start by saying something, and I had as much right to talk as any other commentator.

I had spent long periods of time in Washington when I had been on the paper and I knew the city as a reporter knows it. In those days I rented a single room without a bath in a lodginghouse on B Street, NE, in order to be near the Capitol, to which I was generally assigned. B Street, NE, was not much of a district, but then I was seldom at home except to sleep, what with all the calls I had to make. My evenings, if I had free time, I usually spent at the Press Club, where you could hear some pretty funny stories and get into a card game if you wanted. It had been a hectic life, with every day rushing into every other in a way that is difficult to describe to anyone who has not led it. Helen could never understand my activities when I tried to explain them to her. She only said it must have been dreadful, and she did not sympathize when I told her that I always wished I were back on the bureau again whenever I returned to Washington.

Well, things were different now. I did not stop at B Street, NE, any more. Instead I was lodged in one of those peculiar diplomatic suites at the Hotel Mayflower, all done in Empire and damask, designed apparently for foreign potentates with an entourage of equerries. We did not need the entire suite, because Gilbert would not be there, but still, there was the entourage. There was Sammy Kohn, who always traveled with the show to handle transportation reservations and general broadcasting arrangements. Then there was Miss Maynard, who always seemed to come along largely for decorative purposes but who answered the telephone and helped out Sammy more than she ever helped me. Then there was Art Hertz and Miss

Olson, his secretary, and one of the boy ushers named Jimmy, who handled bags and typewriters and poured drinks for callers and who looked like a Yale undergraduate, now that he was out of uniform.

The suite and the entourage were all there ready and waiting for me, when I arrived from New York at eleven in the morning, but there was not the customary flair to the expedition with Gilbert Frary away in Hollywood. We all seemed like automatons, without Gilbert's showmanship to pull us together, and there was also a perfunctory quality in everyone's attitude toward me which was even more noticeable than it had been in New York. The atmosphere seemed to be charged with impending change, and I felt somewhat as Bonnie Prince Charlie must have felt after the Battle of Culloden — still the boss but a falling star. Sammy naturally gave me the largest room, but he did not buzz around as he had formerly. Art Hertz was in the adjoining room, and I noticed that Jimmy, who was unpacking his bags, did not leave them to take care of mine. There were two adjoining sitting rooms, one for Art and Sammy and me, and the other for the girls, who had already set up their typewriters. We were all one big happy family.

"Art," I called through the connecting door, "is your room all right?"

Art entered my room in his shirt sleeves.

"Everything's swell, Sid," he said. "I've begun on a first draft — without waiting for you."

There was nothing to criticize in the way he said it except that his manner was unduly positive.

"Go right ahead," I told him, "and see this man Stillwater, too. I won't bother you with any thoughts today."

"I didn't mean it that way, Sid," Art said.

"Oh, that's all right, Art," I told him, "and when Gilbert calls up from the Coast, talk to him yourself, I have a lot of personal things on my mind."

"Sid," Art said again, "I didn't mean it that way."

"Neither did I," I told him. "I only mean this whole show runs like clockwork when I'm not here."

I smiled my sincerest smile. I had never enjoyed snide little wars of

474

words, but my instinct for self-preservation told me that the time had come for some serious personal planning.

"I don't know what's troubling you today, Sid," Art began, "but if I've done anything you don't like, I wish you'd specify."

Of course there was nothing to specify, and nothing could have been gained by having it out with Art Hertz, who was only a straw in the wind.

"Don't you ever get depressed, Art?" I asked. "I'm only undergoing a mild fit of depression, that's all. Don't worry about me. I'll get over it."

It was like asking the dealer for one card at poker and then tossing in a blue chip.

"Well, don't be depressed," Art said. "Everything is going fine."

I smiled my sincerest smile at Art again and walked into the sitting room and called Miss Maynard. I had already made my business plans and contacts. Dottie Peale had taken over as she had said she would, and I had seen my lawyers and Dottie's friend in White Wall Rubber. It was time to put my cards into order according to suit and value.

"Miss Maynard," I said, "will you get me Mr. George Burtheimer in Chicago, please?"

I said it loudly enough so that Art could not miss hearing it, and Art did not miss.

"Say, Sid," he said, "you know how Gilbert feels about anyone else talking to Burtheimer."

"That's all right," I said. "I'm feeling lonely," and I observed that both Miss Maynard and Art looked flustered.

"But there isn't anything to bother him about," Art said.

"Now, Art," I said, "I won't bother him."

The telephone was a wonderful invention. I only had time to sit down and smoke half a cigarette before Mr. Burtheimer was on the line, and by then all the connecting doors of the suite were open and everyone was listening.

"Hello, George," I said. "I'm here in Washington and I'm feeling lonely."

Then I asked him what he was doing for breakfast the next morning. I said I was lonely and I wanted to have breakfast with him and I told him that I could take a night plane to Chicago. Then I asked Miss Maynard to see about a reservation. I had been thinking over this plan for several days, and I was gratified by the general reaction. "Say, Sid," Art said, "have you told Gilbert anything about this?"

"Why, no, Art," I said. "The impulse just came over me," but I was sure that Gilbert Frary would hear about it in a very little while.

"But what about tomorrow night?" Art said.

"Oh, I'll be back in New York in time," I told him. "You write it and I'll read it, Art."

When it came to office infighting with all its ridiculous nuances, offense was always preferable to defense, and clearly no one had expected a definite step like this. At least Bonnie Prince Charlie had put the whole crowd off balance, and now that the lines were drawn, it was only necessary to let matters take their course. There was no need to embarrass Art Hertz by staying in the suite for the next few hours. All I required was some good excuse to leave, and I thought of Melville Goodwin as a valid one. I had the Goodwins' number in Alexandria, and I did not want to confuse the entourage any more by calling anyone whom they might think had something to do with Chicago.

"Will you please get me General Goodwin," I told Miss Maynard, and of course Miss Maynard would tell everyone else that I was only going to see an army general.

I reviewed, as I waited for the call, everything I had heard about the house in Alexandria which was owned or rented by Colonel Bud Joyce of G-2, and which had sheltered Muriel Goodwin and young Charley through the war years. It would certainly be in a new development and I could imagine the living room with its collection of signed photographs. There would also be some sort of sun porch, and somewhere the card table with its picture puzzle. When I did not recognize the voice of the woman who answered, I knew that Enid Joyce must be speaking. The General — that is, Mel — was not in, but Mrs. Goodwin — that is, Muriel — was right there, and she knew that Muriel would be so delighted I had called up, and she would get Muriel in just a second.

"Muriel," I heard her calling, "Muriel," and I gathered that Muriel Goodwin was doing something in the kitchen, because I heard the opening of a door.

There was often a discouraging anticlimax in the sound of a disembodied voice, but Muriel Goodwin's had a clear, executive assurance, surprisingly like that in the voice of Dottie Peale. Both voices had the same contagious warmth and enthusiasm, artificial perhaps, but nevertheless peculiarly effective.

"Now let's see," she said. "We must make plans. Mel will be furious if he doesn't see you right away. He's at the Pentagon, and I'll have him call you, and what are you doing after the broadcast tonight?"

I could see what Mel Goodwin meant about her taking over. She had read all about the broadcast, and she kept on planning even after I told her I was taking a night plane to Chicago.

"We'll take you to the airport," she said. "We're having a steak fry in the back yard tonight. If it's too cold we can eat them in the house, but everything always tastes better outdoors. . . . It won't be any trouble at all, Sid. Mel or someone can take you to the airport. It's really only a step."

She had all of Dottie Peale's executive powers, and an even greater certainty. It was impossible to tell her that I did not want to be in a dimly lighted Alexandria yard on a cold November evening, meeting strange people from the armed services, or that food, for my money, always tasted better indoors than out. I could smell the steaks as she was speaking. I could see myself coping with one on a paper plate while I also tried to handle one of Melville Goodwin's Martinis.

"That sounds wonderful," I heard myself saying.

No people in the world were more hospitable than service people. There was an invariable disregard for ordinary limitations. All I had to do was to wait right where I was, and she would get hold of Mel, and Mel would call me. All I had to do was wait until I had heard from Mel.

I did not have to wait more than a few minutes either, before the telephone rang. Muriel Goodwin had set the wheels in motion, and the army was in control. A captain by the name of Rattisbone was on

477

the telephone. General Goodwin was at a meeting which he could not leave, but the General was looking forward to seeing me the moment he was free. In the meanwhile, if I would wait just where I was, Captain Rattisbone would get a car from Public Relations and call for me. The army had taken over and Captain Rattisbone would be at the Hotel Mayflower in a very few minutes.

It was not so long ago that my own job in the army had included meeting Very Important People, an assignment taxing one's capacity to please and demanding tact and adroitness, but now I was the VIP and I was in a position to admire Captain Rattisbone's technique. He reminded me of a registered human retriever who could go on a complicated liaison mission and who could bring back VIPs alive, unruffled, and contented, to any designated point. He would get me where I was going, though he might agree to stop momentarily en route so that I might purchase a pack of cigarettes, razor blades or a pint of bourbon. He would get me there and he would do it no matter what. His uniform was impeccable. His European and his Asiatic theater ribbons and Infantry Combat badge were just enough and not too much for his rank. His hair was a golden molasses color. His eyes were discreetly gray and his nose, mouth and chin were ingenuous and beautiful, but firm. I could not help wondering what Robert Goodwin would have thought of him. They both looked the same age and they had been classmates, perhaps, at the Point — undoubtedly the Point.

"It's a great pleasure to meet you, Mr. Skelton, sir," he said.

His gaze moved incuriously about the sitting room until it stopped with Miss Maynard, but Miss Maynard did not deflect him.

"It's very kind of you to come and get me, Captain," I said.

"It's a real pleasure for me, sir," the captain answered. "Are you ready to start now, Mr. Skelton?"

I was in the army again, and I picked up my hat and coat.

"What about your baggage, sir?" he asked.

"Baggage?" I repeated after him. "I'll come back here for my suitcase, Captain."

A shadow of concern crossed Captain Rattisbone's face.

"The General said you were bringing baggage, sir," he said. "The

478

General is planning to see you off on the night plane to Chicago."

"The General must have misunderstood," I said. "I'll have to be back here later, Captain."

He looked as though I were the one who had misunderstood and not the General.

"I'll explain to him about my bag," I said.

"Thanks very much, sir," the captain answered.

We did not speak in the elevator or while we crossed the lobby, but I knew he was trying to place me, and my silence may have indicated to him that this sort of experience was not entirely new to me. The Army Public Relations car stood at the curb.

"No baggage," the captain said to the driver, who held the door open, and then he seated himself beside me.

"Would you care for a cigarette, sir?" he asked.

"No thanks," I said, and of course he could not smoke alone. Neither of us spoke again until we turned left off Constitution Avenue.

"We've been enjoying a wonderful autumn in Washington this year," he said.

"Yes," I answered, "it looks like a pretty good autumn. Are you with General Goodwin now?"

"No, sir," he said, "with General Gooch, but General Goodwin is using General Gooch's office for the present."

"General Gooch was General Goodwin's chief of staff over in France, wasn't he?" I asked.

"Yes, sir," the captain answered. "Did you serve with General Goodwin in France, sir?"

Captain Rattisbone had stuck his neck out slightly, which proved that he was not absolutely perfect. I was absurdly pleased that he had guessed that I had been in the army.

"No," I said, "but I did meet him there. The General isn't hard to meet, is he?"

"No, sir," he answered. "The General's really been around a lot."

"Yes," I said, "and he knows a lot of good stories."

The captain brightened. We were on safe ground at last.

"He really does," the captain said. "Did he ever tell you the one

479

about that orderly of his at Schofield who was drinking his liquor?"

"The one about liquids seeking their own level?" I asked.

"That's the one, sir," the captain said. "He really does know a lot of stories."

"Has he been given any sort of assignment yet?" I asked.

"I wouldn't know, sir," the captain answered, "but I don't believe so — not yet."

I should not have asked the question and his words became more measured, but suddenly he relaxed.

"We've all got our fingers crossed," he said, and his tone had changed. "Everybody's right behind the General, but you know the way those things are."

"Yes," I answered, "I have a pretty good idea."

I was back in the army again. I almost wished that I were back in uniform — almost, but not quite. We were drawing up to the River entrance of the Pentagon, with the two flagpoles and the Stars and Stripes on the bank in front. I glanced at Captain Rattisbone. The captain was not the sort of officer to be easily impressed. I remembered what the General had said about staff officers — that he never had been able to get along with them, although he had often been one himself. It must be that he had developed if he could impress a smoothy like Rattisbone. Somehow in the last few years Mel Goodwin had learned how to handle any sort of troops.

The Pentagon, I was thinking, was the greatest military monument in the world, dwarfing the Invalides and Napoleon's tomb in Paris. The whole intricate structure — complex yet severely designed corridors and moving staircases and ramps — was a stony tribute to military planning and as much a logical projection of its predilections as were the filing systems and the top-secret documents and requisitions all done in quintuplet. It was endless and labyrinthian and, characteristically, had already grown too small for the clerical staffs and the documents that occupied it. It was the glorified temple of the services, and I could feel the invisible arms of discipline surround us as Captain Rattisbone and I walked up the steps.

It was a relief to see that the captain was moving forward confidently, because I often lost my sense of direction in the Pentagon. He looked as though he had been made to fit the building. Exactly, I was thinking, who was Captain Rattisbone? What had he been once and where had he come from? I should probably never know, and if I did, this sort of knowledge would never help me to understand him any more than I understood Melville Goodwin. You had to make your sacrifices to be in his group. You had to turn your back on early associations. In a way, you had to develop a passion for anonymity when you became a part of the machine. Yet there were compensations for sacrifice — quarters, allowances, low prices at the commissary, retirement pay, opportunity to travel and opportunity to die with your boots on. The Pentagon itself was as much a monument to dedication as a monastery.

"This way, sir," the captain said when we stepped off the moving staircase. "Did you ever hear the story about the Western Union messenger boy who got lost in the Pentagon?"

I winced slightly, though I endeavored not to show it.

"It seems to me I have," I said, "but maybe I've forgotten it."

"The one about his being lost for a year," the captain said, "and coming out an Air Force colonel?"

I laughed politely.

"Oh, yes," I said, "I remember that one now."

The captain glanced at me doubtfully, and I remembered that a sense of humor was seldom a career asset below field rank. Still, it was not a bad story to tell a VIP.

"I suppose it is what you might call an old chestnut, sir," he said.

"Well, not entirely," I told him. "Did you ever hear the one about the officer who moved his desk into the men's room?"

Captain Rattisbone's step lost its briskness and his face looked redder.

"I guess maybe I've been sticking my neck out, sir," he said.

"Only a very little way, Captain," I told him.

"You see, you've got to watch your neck around here, sir," he said.

I knew how right he was. The corridor was taking us toward heights where every junior measured his words, if he knew what was good for him. We were nearing the thrones of the hierarchy. Young

Rattisbone was near the end of his assignment and we were soon to part, and I would never learn anything more about him. He was opening a door on our right.

"This way, sir," he said.

We entered the outer room of a suite of offices, but the captain did not pause. Having led me past a row of empty leather upholstered chairs, his hand dropped tentatively on the knob of a closed door. He turned it noiselessly and pushed the door cautiously, ready to close it discreetly if we had arrived at an unpropitious moment. If it were not for his uniform so immaculately pressed, Captain Rattisbone might have been a street fighter leading a patrol, but everything must have been all right inside because he turned his head toward me, nodded and opened the door wide.

"Will the General see Mr. Skelton now?" he asked.

Then I heard Mel Goodwin's voice.

"Hell, yes," I heard him say. "Don't keep him waiting outside."

"You can go right in, sir," Captain Rattisbone said, and he walked behind me as though I might turn and escape.

The offices were very comfortable in that part of the Pentagon. I have never heard who was responsible for the interior decoration, but whoever it was understood the value of setting. I was in a fine room carpeted in crimson. A massive mahogany desk stood in front of three broad windows that looked out over the Potomac. There was the inevitable leather couch that one seldom sat upon and the heavy chairs that one seldom used and the lighter ones which could be arranged in hasty groups around the desk. An oil portrait of a very antiquated soldier in a chokingly high-necked uniform hung upon the wall. Melville Goodwin was standing near the desk with the cold light from the windows upon him. In fact I was sure that he had been sitting on the corner of the desk gazing at the river when the captain had first opened the door. He was in his "A" uniform and he looked very well.

"Well, well, Sid," he said. "So you got him, did you, Captain? Did he come without making trouble?"

Captain Rattisbone laughed appreciatively.

"There wasn't any fuss, sir," he said.

Melville Goodwin smiled.

"You know, Sid," he said, "you can send this Rattisbone for anything, and by God, he always gets it." He smiled at the captain graciously. "And he's been very kind to the old man. Just a minute now
before you duck out and leave us here, Captain. I've never asked —
are you married, son?"

"Yes, sir," Captain Rattisbone said.

"Well," the General said, "Saint Paul said it's a fine institution, but
I don't see where he found the time to learn about it. We're frying
steaks at home tonight. Why don't you and Mrs. Rattisbone come
over if you haven't anything else to do?"

"Thank you very much, sir," the captain said.

"And when you go out, see if you can find General Gooch and tell
him I'm hungry, will you? Tell him Mr. Skelton's here, and it's time
for lunch."

"Yes, sir," the captain said.

The General and I stood watching the door as it closed noiselessly
behind Captain Rattisbone.

"You know, that's a very nice lad," he said, "when you get to
know him."

"He looks as though he might be," I said.

"And he's got a sense of humor," the General said, "when you get
to know him."

"I wouldn't put it beyond him," I said. "He started to go through
the whole Pentagon joke book."

"Oh boy," Melville Goodwin said, and the corners of his mouth
twisted, "wait until I tell Goochy that Rattisbone was trying to
tell you Pentagon stories. God damn, it's nice to see you, Sid. I was
just telling Goochy this morning that he can have this whole place if
he wants it, even this portrait here." He nodded in a friendly way
toward the picture on the wall and took a step toward it. "Do you
know who that's a picture of?"

"No," I answered, "unless it's Zachary Taylor."

"No, no, no," Melville Goodwin said. "You ought to bone up on
your history, Sid. I've been reading some lately. It puts me to sleep if
I wake up in the middle of the night. That's one thing about being

here — I'm getting time to catch up on my reading. . . . No, no, of course it isn't Zachary Taylor. It's General Winfield Scott — old 'Fuss and Feathers.'"

"Oh," I said, "well, it's quite a picture."

"Goochy always goes for old portraits," the General said. "He snaked this one out of the Secretary's office. It was sent down originally from the Point. Goochy had the choice of that or the Peach Orchard at Gettysburg. He picked out Scott. He says it's more inspirational."

"It certainly is an interesting portrait," I said.

Melville Goodwin cleared his throat.

"I've been in two meetings this morning," he said, "or I'd have gone over to get you myself. They're going to decide what to do with me any day now. It's been sort of tense here this morning. I wonder what's happened to Goochy."

We both were unnatural in the formality of the office, with Winfield Scott staring at us. Melville Goodwin cleared his throat again. I could see that he was waiting to introduce me to General Gooch and that he was rather reluctant to start talking when we would be interrupted at any moment.

"Come to think of it," Melville Goodwin said, "Muriel was pretty tense this morning, too. I wonder whether she knows something I don't or whether it's just this steak fry. I'm glad we're throwing a party, now you're here, Sid."

General Goodwin was an old hand in dealing with tensions. He knew only too well how to handle hours and minutes of suspense, each of which had its own peculiar agony. He had built up an immunity to tension until he could handle it as a heavy drinker handled whisky, and he was not abnormally gay or calm. Still he was talking more than usual, for example about that portrait of General Winfield Scott, and his voice sounded as it had at Saint-Lô after all the final orders had been given and the watches had been synchronized. I even began to feel tense myself.

"To go back to pictures," he was saying, "I've never had much to do with them but I did buy one in Tientsin once. A curio dealer brought it around to the quarters wrapped in a piece of cloth, the

484

way people carry things in China — one of those pictures wound on a stick." He swayed from his toes to his heels with his hands clasped behind him. "It was a painting of an old man in a blue robe. He had a poker face, if you ever saw one, and long thin white mustaches — what they call an ancestor portrait — and I'll tell you why I bought it."

He was growing interested in his own train of thought. The infantry barracks of that crowded treaty port and the bare, sharply defined landscape of North China were all undoubtedly filed away in his memory for future reference.

"I bought it because no one, not even a Chinaman, could have looked so disciplined. I paid thirty dollars for it — that is, thirty dollars Mex. It was an idealized picture. I used to look at it and wish that I could develop that discipline. Now I don't believe in unreality as a rule, but I grew to believe in that old boy in blue. He had more guts than old Winfield Scott here because he wasn't real."

"Mel," I said. He turned his head toward me quickly and he must have suspected that I was going to say something that was out of line with convention. I was verging on a familiarity that I would never have ventured on a few weeks before.

"Mel," I said, "has anything happened to you?"

It was the bluntest and most personal question I had ever asked him, and when he listened he looked like the old man in blue.

"What makes you think so, son?" he asked.

I was too old for him to call me son, but there was still that ten-year gap in our ages. There was no implied rebuke in the way he called me "son." On the contrary, it was more like an acceptance of a closeness in our relationship and an invitation to me to continue.

"Because I think you're pretty wound up this morning," I told him.

I could see him thinking it over, but something inside him had relaxed.

"Right," he said, "you're right on that one, son."

He walked over to the windows behind the desk and stared out at the river. Then he walked back to where I was standing, slowly, softly on that soundproof red carpet.

"I've been going through a lot lately, emotionally, I mean. I can handle it, but at the same time . . . Do you ever get hunches, son?"

"Yes," I said, "occasionally."

"Well, it isn't a bad idea to respect them," he said. "I've noticed the further along a man gets, the more he's got to live with himself and with a few hunches that come to him out of the air. There gets to be less and less to lean on except yourself and whatever it is that makes you go, and the hell of it is you don't know what that something is, except that it's a combination of everything that's behind you, and you'd better not get too analytical or you'll lose your grip. Do you think I'm talking sense?"

I nodded, and his glance moved slowly over the office and the woodwork and the leather upholstery.

"I don't usually run on this way," he said, and he squared his shoulders in a movement that was almost imperceptible, because his shoulders were always squared. "But this is all pretty new to me — all the setting around here, I mean — not the facts. This is up pretty close to the throne, a lot too close for comfort, and the air is God-damned rarefied, but hunches are hunches anywhere and I still know a hunch when I meet one. It begins in the stomach and travels through the liver and then gets up into the head. It runs all through you finally. Right now I feel the way I felt at Maule, for instance, when no information was coming in. There's something inside me that keeps talking from my guts. Something is saying, 'Listen, Mel, you're going to get it one way or the other. Be ready to take it, Mel.' "

I was so completely captured by his stark eloquence that I was bracing myself for whatever it was that was coming.

"The dice are coming out of the box, son," he said. "I'm either going to get patted on the head or get kicked in the pants, and it's about time, too. Jesus, the air's thin here, and I don't want to talk to Muriel about it any more either. By God, I wish there was a war."

He rubbed his hand over the back of his closely cropped head. It was one of his few indecisive gestures.

"Have you seen Dottie lately?" he asked.

He asked it abruptly, as though he were changing the subject, but his mood was not changed.

486

"No," I answered, "not since that night."

"I haven't either," he said. "Perhaps it's just as well."

He stopped, seeming to hope that I would make some answer that would be reassuring.

"This damn business," he said slowly. "It's funny how many times I've had to lecture other officers on woman trouble and now I don't seem to have the build to handle it myself. New York's too close to Washington."

He had passed me a memorandum for my comment and initials, and he was waiting.

"I could say something pretty obvious," I said, "but I don't want to make you sore."

"Now, Sid," Mel Goodwin said, "you won't make me sore. I've stuck my neck out, haven't I? It's right out there a mile."

"All right," I said. "It might be a good idea if you were to pass up Dottie Peale."

I thought he would be the old man in blue again and put on a poker face, but instead he waited anxiously for me to go on. Of course I could have given him reasons in chapter and verse, but he knew all the reasons as well as I did. When it came to woman trouble, he had a perfectly good academic knowledge.

"Sid," he said, "you're a damn nice boy."

"I'm glad you still think so," I answered. "You know I'm only talking sense, don't you?"

"You never did approve of this thing, did you?" he said. "Not right from the beginning."

"I wouldn't take Dottie too seriously," I said, "if I were you."

I was being disloyal to Dottie, and I knew how he felt about loyalty, but then he was having trouble with his own loyalties.

"All right," he said, "all right. I know how it all looks. Don't tell me. But there's only one trouble with your suggestion. I'm just not able to take it, son."

I had to admire his frankness. He had spent most of his life dealing in problems of fact and he could apply the principles to himself.

"Doesn't it occur to you that this is only a phase?" I began. "Nearly everyone goes through something like this sometime."

Melville Goodwin nodded and he stared at the floor as though it were a map.

"Yes, I know," he said. "You've got it all on your side. I've said that to other people and I've said it to myself, but I can only deal with the foreseeable future. I don't know whether it's a phase or not. The trouble is, I love her."

If he had only said it with more emotion, it would have been easier to discount. Instead he made the statement sound inescapable.

"All right," I said, "but do you think she loves you?"

"I wouldn't know," he said. "She says so, and I hope she does."

For a second the picture was all there in black and white, without a bit of shading. Then an instant later it was gone, because the door opened just as Melville Goodwin finished speaking, and Dottie Peale and all his storm and stress were snapped away into the compartment reserved for his top secrets. His face cleared and the whole office became bare and impersonal.

"Hello, Goochy," Mel Goodwin said. "Where the hell have you been? Let's go in to lunch, and I want you to meet my friend, Sid Skelton, General Gooch."

As soon as I saw General Gooch, I realized that I had met him before in Normandy but I had not placed him as the General's chief of staff. That absurd army nickname, "Long John" Gooch, was the reason for my error. It was one of those heavily humorous army efforts. Instead of being tall, he would have been in the shortest squad at the Point, which was undoubtedly the reason they had called him "Long John," unless they had given him the name because his face was long and concave.

Small army men always looked sterner and tougher than their larger counterparts. Their faces were always more mobile and more deeply lined. They always had a staccato quality, perhaps to compensate for size, or perhaps all small officers who got anywhere possessed a high emotional quotient. At any rate General Gooch looked very tough. His dish face was leathery and hard and it contorted itself in an almost painful way when he smiled, and even his smile had a sour tinge that fitted the rasp in his voice.

"Glad to meet you, sir," he said.

488

He did not look as though he were glad to meet me. He made me feel as though I were both an interruption and an unfortunate weakness of General Goodwin's. He seemed to be trying to figure out why under the sun a first-rate officer like his old chief wanted to give anyone like me a minute of his time, but then there was the loyalty. If Goodwin wanted it that way, Gooch could take it, too, and his face contorted itself again in his effort to take it.

"You got here all right, did you?" he asked.

"Yes, thanks," I answered, "I got here."

In the seconds of awkward silence that followed, I saw Mel watching us both affectionately, but at the same time professionally.

"Let's get lunch, Goochy," he said.

"Where do you want to go, sir?" General Gooch asked.

Melville Goodwin smiled happily and spoke with a sort of artificial carelessness.

"We're going to have lunch in there in the Secretary's Mess," he said.

"Jesus," General Gooch said, "who's shoving us into there? Why not the General and Flag Officers' Mess, where boys can be boys?"

Melville Goodwin laughed merrily.

"Goochy always swallows the wrong way when he sees civilian Secretaries," he said. "It's all right, Goochy, I asked Snip to fix it. I told him that Sid here is a VIP and that he ought to see the works."

"How about going to the Army and Navy Club?" General Gooch asked.

"No, no," Mel Goodwin said, "we're not dead on our feet yet, and I want Sid to see the top brass, too. Come on, Goochy."

I had never been to the Secretary's Mess, although I had heard of it, and judging from General Gooch's hesitation, he seemed to doubt whether I was up to it.

"I don't know whether we can get a small table, sir," General Gooch said.

"Then we can sit anywhere," the General said. "Maybe 'Sunny' Minturn will be there."

General Gooch glanced at his wrist watch, and then his beady eyes met General Goodwin's wordlessly. I did not know who Minturn was but his name appeared to convey something significant.

"He might be," General Gooch answered. "It's about his usual time."

"I have a hunch Sunny may have some news for me," the General said, and he and General Gooch exchanged another wordless glance.

"Yes, he might, sir."

Melville Goodwin gave a pull at his blouse, although it did not need straightening. "Well, what are we waiting for?" he said. "Come on, Goochy."

"Yes, sir," General Gooch said. "Has Mr. Skelton washed?"

"Thanks," I said, "I feel pretty clean."

Melville Goodwin laughed heartily, and so did General Gooch in a quieter and rather painful way.

"Sid looks all right to me," the General said, "but you inspect him, Goochy."

General Gooch laughed again, clearly in the line of duty.

"I'll pass him if you do, sir," he said.

Melville Goodwin slapped my back affectionately and opened the office door.

"Goochy knows the ropes around here," he said. "He is really settled into it. We'll be all right if we stick with Goochy."

I followed Melville Goodwin through the outer office and out to the corridor with General Gooch walking close behind us. Everything we had said in the office was over and finished and filed for future reference. Melville Goodwin looked happy out in the corridor.

"You know, this eating place is really something, Sid," he said. "Sometimes when I see it I wonder who let me in."

It was amazing how completely he could throw himself into any present. His adroitness in repressing himself would have been abnormal in me, but of course it was not in him. The drives within him might lead him up or down, but the surface was serene.

"Oh, by the way, Sid," he was saying, "I didn't tell you, did I, that I have a civilian outfit now?"

Those civilian clothes he had bought had finally arrived, he was saying, and he looked pretty sharp in them too, if he did say so him-

490

self. He had a blue double-breasted suit and a tweed coat — Harris tweed with grids — and slacks like mine.

"You wait, son," he said, "I'm going to wear the tweed tonight. You wait till you see it, Goochy."

All the while he spoke the heels of his polished brown shoes were also speaking. We were all in step together and the cadence beat into my thoughts.

"The trouble is, I love her," I could hear his boot heels saying. "The trouble is, I love her."

He was all right in the Pentagon — he knew where he was going — but unfortunately he was going further than the Pentagon, alone into a strange country where his instinct for terrain would not assist him — only his instinct for self-preservation or destruction, whichever it might be.

I followed Melville Goodwin into the Secretary's dining room and for the first time in a long while I felt shy and callow. The mark which the army had left on me was stronger than I had realized. Although I might try to look about me cynically, I could not avoid my old reaction to rank. I could be amused by the elaborations, but ingrained respect told me that the place was appropriate for the individuals who sat at the tables. It had taken them a long while to get there. That decorous club-like dining room was a suitable setting for the climax of careers. I cannot remember its details clearly, but I can recall its dignity and measured merriment. It was a room in which to sit up straight and to take your soup carefully and to speak in a modulated tone. In fact I found it difficult to speak at all. As Melville Goodwin had said, the air was very rarefied. It seemed to me that everyone whose picture I had ever seen was there, excepting Mac-Arthur, who was still in Japan. I could see why General Gooch had hesitated about introducing me.

"Gooch," General Goodwin said, and I thought that even his voice was low and tentative, "there seems to be a small vacant table over there."

It was not a statement of fact but a question.

"Yes," General Gooch said, "but I'm not sure . . ." His words trailed off beneath the firm voices and the discreet sound of knives and forks around us. Melville Goodwin cleared his throat, and spoke to a Filipino petty officer who stood by the door. "May we occupy that small table over there, Chief?" he asked.

"Which table, sir?" the Filipino asked.

"Over there in the corner," Melville Goodwin said.

There was not the slightest edge to his voice, but I was pleased to see that the navy snapped into it.

"Certainly, sir," he said.

"Thank you, Chief," the General said. "Come along, Sid."

I was impressed by the poise of Melville Goodwin as I followed him. He did not walk too fast or too slowly. He smiled and nodded to officers who looked up at him, graciously or deferentially, according to their rank.

We seemed to have walked a long way before we reached the table.

"Sit over there, Sid," the General said, "where you can see the show."

The faces at the other tables had a definite conformity, in spite of differences in features. They all bore the imprint of similar experience. They were all assured. They might have been arrogant once, but now they were assured instead, and some were benign and almost kindly — now that they could afford to be.

"There's Sunny Minturn over there," the General said. "Who's he sitting with, Goochy?"

"He's with General Candee, sir."

"Candee?" the General said. "That isn't 'Butch' Candee, is it?"

"There's only one Candee that I know of, sir," General Gooch said.

"Then it's Butch," the General said. "Where's Butch been keeping himself? I've never seen him around here."

"He's in from Japan, I think, sir," General Gooch answered.

"Yes, it's Butch all right," Melville Goodwin said. "It's been ten years since I've seen old Butch. . . . It looks like a roast beef day. The beef's good here."

"Coffee with the meal, sir?" the mess attendant asked, but the General wanted coffee later.

"The first time I came in here, Goochy," the General said, "do you know what I thought of?"

492

Neither General Gooch nor I knew what he had thought of.

"I thought of the first time I went to the old Waldorf with Muriel and walked into the dining room behind her. I didn't feel I was Mel Goodwin at all, and this place always strikes me the same way. It's nice to be some place where you feel young. How about it, Goochy?"

"That's right, Mel," General Gooch answered.

"Gooch," the General said, "how about telling Sid about the time that you were with Jenks in that jeep?"

"Which time?" General Gooch asked.

"Up near Metz, the time you rolled over the bank."

"You tell it, Mel," General Gooch said. "You can tell it better," and he smiled at me painfully. "I don't know why the General likes that story."

"Because it's a damn good story," the General said. "You see, it was this way, Sid. Goochy was riding in this jeep. A captain was driving him, named Jenks. Do you know where Jenks is now, Goochy?"

"He's home," Gooch said, "practicing law in Atlanta."

"I wouldn't have thought Jenks was a lawyer on the outside," Melville Goodwin said. "Well, anyway, Goochy was out riding with Jenks around Metz. I don't know why. Maybe Goochy was out for a good time. You wouldn't know it from looking at him, but he likes to amuse himself now and then. They skidded off the road and they turned a somersault in the air and landed right side up in the middle of a brook, and do you know what Goochy said? He just said, 'That's what I call service, Jenks, but after this we'd better walk.'"

General Gooch smiled in a tortured way.

"I don't know why the General likes that story, Mr. Skelton," he said. "There really isn't any point to it."

General Goodwin laughed.

"You're the point, Goochy," he said, "but maybe we'd better not tell any more jokes in here." He nodded genially to a friend across the room. "If G–1 or any of the Joint Chiefs heard them, they might not be able to work all afternoon."

"Right, sir," General Gooch answered.

"You know, Sid," the General said, "I always have a lot of fun when I'm with Gooch."

I could see why General Gooch might have been a good, efficient chief of staff. Officers I had met who occupied such a post were usually meticulous executives who were forced to lash out in disagreeable ways in order to accomplish missions and give life to the machine. I could visualize Goochy giving me an artistic chewing, but I could not see why Melville Goodwin always had fun with him. I could only perceive that they were devoted to each other, and far removed as I was from their friendship, I was drawn closer to them by its warmth.

"Was that the time General Gooch landed on the bottle?" I asked. They both stared at me blankly.

"On a bottle?" Melville Goodwin repeated. "What bottle?"

"Yes," General Gooch said, "what bottle?"

I felt like an officious junior who had let himself go too far, and I found myself adopting my most placating military manner.

"Perhaps I haven't got it right, sir," I said to Mel Goodwin, "but don't I remember your telling me that General Gooch sat down hard on a pint of bourbon in a jeep? I was only wondering whether it happened in this jeep."

They both looked brighter. They both remembered, and General Gooch looked as though he had just sat again on the bottle.

"I hoped the boss had forgotten that one," General Gooch said. "That was when I was with General Goodwin in another jeep—up near Remagen, wasn't it, Mel?"

"You see," the General said, "Sid's got a photographic memory, Gooch. I forgot I'd told him about that one. That's another of Goochy's jeep stories. He fragmented the bottle. He should have put in for the Purple Heart. It was a wound in the line of duty."

I saw that General Gooch did have the Purple Heart. His beady eyes were brighter and his lips were closely held together.

"A broken one, not purple, sir," he said. "When that bottle broke, my heart damn near did, too."

Time had been moving on its course. We had finished the roast beef and we were each working on a hard piece of ice cream, a

494

variety that seemed especially invented for an American officers' mess. I was back in the army again sufficiently to realize that General Gooch's bon mot had values that could not be captured in civil life. It had its own military breadth and freedom. It was just the sort of joke that slayed you in the army, and it worked on Melville Goodwin. His face turned red and he began choking into his napkin.

"Say, Goochy," he said, "make a note to tell that one at the steak fry tonight, will you? But don't tell any more now or I may bust a button. That's an order, Goochy."

Throughout the Secretary's dining room luncheon was nearly over. Chairs were being pushed back, but the ripple of merriment from our table was not lost. I was aware of curious smiling glances, and so was General Goodwin. I saw General Minturn, with his three stars, looking at us across the room, and Butch Candee, with his one star. Melville Goodwin sat up straighter and waved his hand at them in informal greeting. A tall, pallid, bean pole of a major general with an Adam's apple walked toward us, and he halted at our table, smiling at Mel Goodwin. General Gooch sprang hastily out of his chair, but Melville Goodwin remained seated for an appreciable moment. Then he, too, stood up.

"Hello, Snip," he said. "Sit down and join us, won't you? We're about to have some coffee, and Goochy's telling some pretty good ones. This is my friend, Sidney Skelton, I was telling you about. He used to be in the PRO. Major Skelton — General Lewis."

I kept forgetting that my old rank could be carried into civil life, if I wanted it, as a graceful acknowledgment of past services. In fact I could have been called Colonel if I had elected to join the reserves. I saw at once why General Lewis had been nicknamed "Snip" — a vestige also of old humor from the Point, when Cadet Lewis had stood tallest in the tallest squad. If he had later become another Napoleon, his classmates would still have called him Snip.

"It's a real pleasure to have you here with us, Mr. Skelton," General Lewis said. "I'm sorry the Secretary isn't here today, because he would have enjoyed meeting you — but perhaps some other time."

"Sit down, won't you, Snip?" Melville Goodwin asked again.

General Lewis smiled graciously and shook his head regretfully, but even that brief gesture conveyed ease and charm of manner. I could place him right away as just the sort of person who would be selected to accompany a chief on an overseas mission that demanded tact and adroitness.

"I wish I could," he said, "and I hope Mr. Skelton will forgive me, but I'm due at a meeting in five minutes." He smiled at me confidentially. "Unification. Mr. Skelton probably knows we're unification-conscious around here now. Mel, has Sunny Minturn seen you yet?"

Melville Goodwin's glance traveled across the room and back to General Lewis. He looked questioningly innocent, but General Gooch did not have his skill. Every line of his concave face was intent and intelligently watchful.

"How do you mean, has he seen me yet?" There was just the slightest emphasis when Melville Goodwin spoke the word "yet." We were all watching General Lewis, who had the concerned expression of someone who had said too much.

"You would think, wouldn't you, that I'd know enough not to let cats out of bags by now," he said, and then the full charm of his smile was turned on Melville Goodwin. "Anyway, it makes me the first to congratulate you, Mel. Step over here for a second with me, will you? Will you excuse us, Mr. Skelton, if two bad boys do a little talking out of school?"

I had observed that playful manner before in other quarters, and I could think of women speaking of that charming General Lewis. He had his arm through Melville Goodwin's, and they moved slowly toward the entry, speaking softly to each other, with inclined heads.

"Son of a bitch!"

I started. It was General Gooch beside me who had spoken, and immediately I knew that the expletive had been purely involuntary, and that he had forgotten I was there.

"Er," he said, "pardon me, Mr. Skelton."

"That's all right," I answered. "Don't mind me."

Of course he minded me, because I had no place in that scene. I wished I were not there myself, though I was caught in the fascination of it. General Lewis and General Goodwin were shaking hands,

496

and I heard General Goodwin say, "Thanks, I'll see you later, Snip." The tension and the waiting were over. The ghost had walked. The decision for Mel Goodwin's professional future must have been made that morning. The palms of my hands were moist. I was right in there praying for Melville Goodwin exactly as hard as General Gooch was praying.

"Son of a bitch!" General Gooch said again. Then I understood that his speech was only a release of nervous tension and that he had not been referring to General Lewis. Melville Goodwin was walking back to us.

"Well, Goochy," he said, and his voice was hoarse and he cleared his throat. "Well, Goochy."

"Come on — what's the score?" General Gooch asked.

Mel Goodwin smoothed the furrows on his forehead and policed the lines of his mouth. He sat down slowly and took a sip of water, and we all sat down. He put his glass down carefully and folded his napkin neatly and slowly.

"Merriwell's asked for me."

I saw General Gooch's face light up.

"Boy," he said, "it's Plans!"

"You said it," Melville Goodwin said. "Plans."

"Say," General Gooch said, and I could feel the depth of his pleasure and relief, "see if you can get me over with you, will you?"

Melville Goodwin rolled his napkin into a neat cylinder and dropped it in front of him.

"Goochy," he said, "I don't know what's the matter with me. I know it's more than I deserve. I know I ought to jump at it — but hell . . ."

"Say, Mel," General Gooch said, "how about coming to my office. We can scare up a cup of coffee there instead of having it here."

Plans and planning had always been breathless words for me when I was a PRO. I had always experienced a twinge of envy for any officer in Plans. Plans was so remote, so clouded and restricted that I had no conception what happened there, except that Plans was the brains of the army. You knew everything there was to know if you

497

were in there. You had to be outstanding in some line and cleared for everything. I had always believed that you had to have intellect plus the pure integrity of a Galahad to get into Plans, and once you were in, you were apt to stay for quite a while. It was the secret circle of the elite. I had felt pleased for Melville Goodwin. It seemed to me like a distinguished climax to his career and an ultimate reward for brilliant service. I was thinking of all the subtle comforts and emoluments that were awaiting Melville Goodwin, the son of Hallowell's late popular druggist. I was thinking how far he had gone and of the dignity which had finally reached him. I could see him on his way to another star. I could see him in an office still larger and more spacious than that of General Gooch and I could hear the respectful voices and the muted footsteps of junior planners when they came to hand him papers. I could see him passing the sentries as he entered guarded rooms. I could see him with his private motor on call day or night. I could see him in imagination in one of those comfortable houses at Fort Myer or in his apartment at the Kennedy-Warren — Muriel would like the Kennedy-Warren. I could see him at staff meetings extracting top secret papers from his briefcase. I could hear his telephone ringing on the private wire that connected him with the Pentagon, and there were lots of other little things. Nothing was too good for Plans.

My imagination was building up the vision, but instead of looking elated, Melville Goodwin looked tired and discouraged.

"To hell with the God-damned coffee, Goochy," he said when we were back again in the office.

"Okay, Mel," General Gooch said. "Rattisbone," he called, and his voice crackled like bond paper. "Where's Captain Rattisbone?"

"Right here, sir," I heard the captain answer.

"Wait a minute," General Goodwin said, "wait a minute, Goochy. I don't want any coffee, but perhaps Sid does. Do you want coffee, Sid?"

"No thank you, sir," I answered.

"All right," Melville Goodwin said, "excuse me. Carry on."

"We don't need coffee, Captain," General Gooch said. "Say I've stepped out if anyone calls. We don't want to be disturbed unless there's a telephone for General Goodwin." He closed the door softly and decisively. It had a lock and when Goochy locked it, for some reason rank dropped away. In fact I could almost call him "Goochy" and I could finally see why Melville Goodwin liked him.

"Listen, Mel," he said, "let's cut out the horsefeathers. Why the hell aren't you buying us drinks and cigars? You've just been given the snappiest damned job that anyone could hand you. What are you dragging your ass for? I haven't seen you this way since they ordered us out of Maule. Sit down and get whatever's biting you off your chest. Nothing you say in here is going any further unless . . ." His beady black eyes bored into me, "unless it's Mr. Skelton."

"God damn it, Goochy!" Melville Goodwin said, and I had never heard him raise his voice before. He did not raise it much, but it sent a shiver down my spine. "Sid's all right. Besides, we didn't pull out of Maule."

"No, we didn't and we God-damned near got a court for it," General Gooch said.

General Goodwin rocked back and forth on his heels.

"They couldn't give me a court," he said, "because we saved the whole God-damned corps, and you know it, Goochy. That's why when I was in Paris old Four-eyes got me to lecture to those VIPs. Do you remember, Sid?" I remembered very clearly. I remembered the lieutenant colonel and the pointer and Dottie Peale.

"Well, get it off your chest," Goochy said. "Get it out of your system, boy, as long as Sid here understands it's confidential."

I could see that a part of Melville Goodwin was enjoying the interplay between Gooch and me, even when another part of him was suffering.

"That's right," he said, "you call him Sid, and, Sid, you call him Goochy."

It was a childish directive from a civilian point of view, but it was the army's hopeful American way of settling any difficulty. "Go on, Sid," Melville Goodwin said, "call him Goochy."

I might never see General Gooch again. We were only ships passing in the night, but if we ever did meet again, we would know the countersign. We would be on a first-name basis ever after.

"All right, Goochy," I said.

"All right, Sid," General Gooch answered, but his mind was not on me. "Now listen, Mel, don't you know you never had it so good? What's the matter with Plans?"

Melville Goodwin made no direct reply. He stood in almost the exact center of the red carpet with his legs farther apart than regulations recommended. He jabbed his hand viciously into the side pocket of his blouse and pulled out his cigarettes and his lighter. Then he jerked a cigarette from the pack and lighted it, with the same sort of one-two motion that an infantryman used on the bolt of his rifle at inspection, and the lighter made an appropriate decisive click. I could have practiced for a year without being able to imitate that gesture. When he had taken off his blouse at Dottie Peale's, he had still maintained some of his rank, but there was not a sign of it now.

"I don't know what's the matter with me, Goochy," he said, "that I don't jump at a good thing when it comes my way. Hell, I was in with the Chief half an hour yesterday. Hell, he didn't say a word about moving me into Plans. I want to know what God-damned soft-bottomed Fancy Dan fouled me up in this. I even wish they'd ordered me out to SCAP. At least it would take me out of here for a while."

"And just who the hell would be wanting you in SCAP?" Goochy asked. "Why don't you get the lead out of your pants?"

I did not understand the technical significance of the last question, and Mel Goodwin paid no attention to it. Instead he began pacing back and forth across the office rapidly, as though there were no weight in his pants at all.

"I wonder how the wires got crossed," he said. "By God . . . do you know what I think? . . . I think it's Muriel!"

General Gooch laughed rudely. "Horsefeathers, always horsefeathers," he said, but Melville Goodwin paid no attention.

"You know, this is just what Muriel wants," he said. "She'll be crazy about this. Jesus — me settled down in the Pentagon with Merriwell to ride me — Jesus!"

"Oh," Goochy said, "when did you start getting so particular?

Just what the hell's the matter with Lieutenant General Merriwell? He was a damned good corps commander, wasn't he? I didn't hear you gripe about Merriwell in Normandy."

Melville Goodwin stopped his pacing. "He's a piddling old s.o.b."

"They all are," Goochy answered, "but he's only got another year."

"I know," Mel Goodwin said, "and maybe I'll get another star out of it if I live right, but, Jesus — a year with 'Fuss' Merriwell!"

I knew that I was hearing more about the Pentagon than I would ever hear again, but the conversation was too technical and intimate to follow, since I knew nothing of the eccentricities of Fuss Merriwell.

"Don't you know when you have it cushy?" Goochy said. "You and I can't be buzzing around forever — and we've had a lot of fun."

I had not known that General Gooch could speak so gently. His words seemed to make Mel Goodwin feel his age. I would not have called it fun that he and General Gooch had been having, but they always called active service fun in the army, and perhaps it had been fun for Goodwin and Gooch. They had been lucky, I was thinking, when you recalled what had happened to many of their contemporaries. They both of them were shot with luck to be there in the Pentagon at all.

"God damn it, Goochy," Melville Goodwin said, "this place is getting you calcified. Pull in your belt. You and I aren't through just yet."

"I didn't say we were," Goochy answered. "You'll end up with a corps when you get out of Plans."

"Hell," Mel Goodwin said, "I know I don't make sense, but after paper-passing for two years in Frankfurt, I supposed I could be connected with troops in some way."

"God almighty," Goochy said, "can't you ever get troops off your mind?"

Melville Goodwin moved toward the desk very slowly and ground the end of his cigarette hard into a glass ash tray.

"Say," he said, "no matter what they shower on me, I know what I'm meant for and what I'm made for."

501

"Horsefeathers," Goochy said. "You'll go where they send you, Mel."

Melville Goodwin smiled his most mechanical smile, but for once it concealed nothing. For once I had seen the whole of Melville A. Goodwin, and I had to hand it to him. At least he did not want it soft.

"Will I?" he said. "Maybe. . . . But I could retire."

There was a dead, queer silence, and he seemed to hold and control all that silence.

"Say, Mel," General Gooch said very slowly, "has that little skirt in New York been getting to you again?"

It came so suddenly that I caught my breath.

"Never mind that now, Goochy," he said, and that peculiar silence was back with us.

"And at your age," General Gooch said. "God almighty!"

"I wish you'd stop referring to my age," Mel Goodwin said. "I'm not in a wheel chair yet."

Then the telephone rang with a discreet, muted sound, and the spell or whatever it was that had held us was broken. Before the ring was over, General Gooch was at the desk.

"General Gooch speaking," he was saying. Then he closed his wiry hand over the mouthpiece and nodded. "For you, Mel," he said. "The Chief's office calling."

Melville Goodwin snatched the telephone out of his hand.

"General Goodwin speaking," he was saying.

The rank was back. The world was moving again by the numbers. There was a sharp decisive click as General Gooch unlocked the office door.

"Yes, sir," General Goodwin was saying. "I'll be there directly, sir." The telephone gave a little thump as he set it down.

"That makes it official," he said. "I'd better say so long, Sid. I'll see you tonight, and bring your baggage; someone will get you on board that plane. Wait for me, will you, Goochy?"

"Thanks for the lunch and good luck, sir," I told him.

General Gooch smiled his sourest smile.

"Congratulations, Mel," he said, ". . . on everything!"

The sound of the wish was as acid as the smile that had gone before it, but Melville Goodwin was already out of hearing.

"That old bastard," General Gooch said, "off the beam for a floosie . . . and when he starts he always goes. By God, he always goes!"

XXXI

It Was Almost a Celebration

I was not without my own private sources of information in the broadcasting business, and these all indicated that Gilbert Frary was definitely planning to throw me over. He was only being true to his reputation, and if one lived in such uncertain surroundings, one had to be ready for anything. Knowing that I possessed a certain commercial value, I realized that I could continue without Gilbert if I handled matters in the right way, and I felt obliged to do something after my last talk with Helen. It was time to plan very carefully what I would say about the program to George Burtheimer in Chicago, and what I would say to Gilbert Frary either in New York or Chicago, for it was certain that Gilbert would fly east promptly. Yet somehow I could not do any of this after I had left the Pentagon.

Again, the intrigues in which I was engaged seemed petty and insignificant. The dilemma of Melville Goodwin was larger and more tragic. I could see myself worrying along in some way, but it would be different with Melville Goodwin. I did not possess his intensity, or his liking for personal risk, or the belief in myself that would allow me to throw over a comfortable future for something indefinable.

Instead of keeping my mind on myself, I thought all afternoon of his infatuation for Dottie Peale. His personality was like a cloud that obscured everything I did, and I did not want to see him end in nothing. I did not want to see small things ruin him. Perhaps I had read too much about the "Old Glory Boys" when I was young. Perhaps I had always loved the uniform and the brass without knowing it.

All that afternoon and evening, I went through the motions of my own living, but I did not recall a single detail of the broadcast ceremony or what there was in the script or how I read it. I only remember that I wanted to know what was happening in Alexandria.

People in the service seldom displayed much imagination about their home surroundings, perhaps because they could not afford imagination. When my taxi stopped in front of the house in Alexandria, I could not escape the idea that I had seen the whole picture many times before. It was about eight in the evening and rather cool for a steak fry, but in the small back yard a good many people were clustered around the outdoor grill, and there were more on the sun porch and in the living room, all eating slabs of steak — commissary steak — from plates spilling from their knees. Everyone was talking loudly and having a wonderful and half-off-the-record time. It was a military party, but like many others of its sort it had, to an outsider, the quality of fancy dress, if only because so many of the male guests were out of uniform. Released from duty, they were pretending to be civilians, just as civilians often pretended to be pirates or monks or Spanish grandees. They would have all been highly indignant had their attention been drawn to this parallel, but still, the parallel existed.

I had been to the Joyces' house in my imagination many times, and there it was, illuminated by the street lights, and with lights blazing in the windows. It was in a uniform real-estate development, one of those contractor-designed dwellings that had sprouted like mushrooms around Washington during the war and postwar years. The evergreen shrubbery around the brick front steps was all according to planned convention, as were the self-consciously broad clapboards, and the solid green shutters with their cut-out crescent moons and imitation wrought-iron fasteners. Equally conventional was the sign at the edge of the minute brick walk that read "Col. Joyce" in letters that glowed when headlights were cast upon them, and the lantern above the green front door, a grotesquely modernized version of one of those illuminating fixtures that had been hoisted in the tower of the Old North Church at the time of Paul Revere.

When no one answered the doorbell — because everybody was having too good a time to hear it — I opened the door myself and entered the living room, followed by the taxi driver carrying my suitcase. The living room completely confirmed my educated guess. The fireplace was correctly centered, with knotty pine paneling and a mantel with a Chinese god of happiness in its center. Two fanback chairs, and the sofa, which I was sure could turn itself into a bed if some friends dropped in from somewhere suddenly, were crowded close to the wall. The rather flashy Chinese rugs had been rolled back, presumably for dancing, but I could rearrange everything mentally. The card table with the picture puzzle was intact, I was glad to see, and three middle-aged men were around it, grimly fitting pieces. The piano, too, was in the orthodox corner with framed signed photographs upon it, and a wall-hanging behind it of dark blue silk embroidered with gold dragons. Someone would start playing on the piano in a minute — someone who would never get far in the service — and a group would gather around singing a few good songs. There was a glassed-in sun porch and there were glass doors to the small dining room, and beside the staircase leading to the upper floor was a carved teakwood chest aromatic from its camphor-wood lining. The house of Bud and Enid Joyce was an authentic army home and it would be the smaller counterpart of a future residence of General and Mrs. Goodwin.

"That's all right," I said to the driver, "just put down the suitcase," and he was gone in an instant.

No one noticed me immediately, because everyone was having a wonderful time. I was about to move out to the sun porch to look for my host and hostess, when fortunately my eye lighted on Captain Rattisbone, who was sitting in a corner beside a frightened brown-eyed pregnant girl, who must have been Mrs. Rattisbone. When he saw me, he sprang up instantly.

"General and Mrs. Goodwin asked me to keep an eye out for you, sir," he said. "I'll tell the General, if you'll wait here. May I present you to Mrs. Rattisbone?"

Mrs. Rattisbone's hand was cold and damp. She smiled at me in a hasty stricken way, as though she were frightened at being left alone with me without a suitable topic for conversation, and I did not blame her. She was conscious of her condition and besides, she was very, very junior.

"Roy said he was sent to get you this morning," Mrs. Rattisbone said.

"That's right," I said, "Roy got me."

"It's a treat for Roy and me to be here," she said. "Isn't it a lovely party?"

It was not necessary to go any further, because Captain Rattisbone always could find anyone, and he had returned with Melville Goodwin. It took a second for me to adjust myself to the General's appearance. He was out of uniform and he fitted into no preconceived pattern, because I had never seen him that way before and I had not prepared myself to face the unknown.

I was accustomed to thinking of him as endowed with an indestructible compactness. There had been a tenaciousness in the set of his head and shoulders and a repressed calmness in his whole posture that had indicated complete co-ordination. I had never known him to assume an awkward pose, and now mediocrity had suddenly overtaken him. He looked like a plump and middle-aged nonentity, whom you might meet at a golf club and immediately forget, and whose face you could not place.

Of course it was the cut of the clothes. A good tailor might have set off his figure stylishly, but even so, Mel Goodwin would not have known how to manage a civilian coat; and at any rate, a service budget demanded ready-made clothing, hastily and perfunctorily altered. The General wore the Harris tweed coat and gray slacks, because after all it was a steak fry, and I recalled how wistfully he had often eyed mine. I wished that I might have gone with him when he had bought his outfit, but then he would not have settled for quiet colors. After years of olive drab, he would have revolted against monotones. The coat he had selected was a viciously heavy and unkempt garment. I could think of him picking it off the rack because of its unusualness. Its main color was russet brown, approaching the hue of an autumn oak, but a grid of violent green had been woven into the brown texture. Its lapels rose in points like the clipped ears of a bull terrier. It was belted in the back and full of pleats, and it had round buttons of green leather that looked like misplaced olives. Even the pockets had olive buttons, but this was not all. His ready-made gray slacks were a hideous imitation of an English motif, with accordion pleats around the beltless waist — and then there were his shoes. These were of a heavy brogan type of darkish cordovan colored grained leather, with an infinite number of curlicues and decorations and with jumbo-sized soles of light yellow crepe. His soft shirt was a rich blue. His tie was red with green diagonal stripes.

Where was the Goodwin gone, I was thinking, who had stood there in the Pentagon prepared to resign if he could not serve with troops? Where was Goodwin of North Africa and Goodwin of Saint-Lô and Goodwin of the Bulge? I might have been seeing his brother now, a prosperous small-town merchant at a lodge outing, who had never shared the advantages of Major General Melville A. Goodwin. He may have read some of my thoughts, because he often had an unexpectedly sensitive insight.

"So you got here, did you, Sid?" he said. "How do you think I'm looking?"

"Like something off a Scottish moor," I told him.

"That's right," he said, and he appeared delighted. "It's Harris tweed, and you can smell it and it says so on the label. Once when I was around Prestwick I bought some tweed almost like this, but the plane took off a half hour early and I forgot it." He stroked the coat affectionately. "This really keeps you warm outdoors. I've got a quieter suit, a double-breasted pin-stripe blue that reminds me a little of yours, but I didn't want to wear it frying steaks. I might have got grease on it."

"You haven't any grease on this one," I said.

"Muriel took that angle over," he said. "She made me wear an apron — you know, army cook issue — but I've got a cook out there doing all the real work. Goochy found him. Wait till you get in the chow line and see him juggling steaks."

"I can hardly wait," I told him.

"Well, we'll take that suitcase of yours upstairs," he said, "before someone falls over it, and then you can meet the crowd. . . . Here, give it to me. I'm not in a wheel chair yet."

The Goodwins and the Joyces must have been completely congenial to have lived together in that small house, which was clearly designed for a single family. Upstairs there would be, I was sure, the so-called master bedroom — a resounding term indissolubly connected with the modern American home — the smaller double children's room, a communal bathroom, and finally a hall-bedroom, which at one time would have been called a sewing room.

"Here," Melville Goodwin said, pointing to the hall bedroom, "we can stick the suitcase in my dressing room."

I wondered how they had arranged who should have the dressing room — General Goodwin or Colonel Joyce — whether they had tossed coins for it or whether its assignment had been a question of rank. It must have been Charley's bedroom during the years before he had left for the Point, and a part of Charley was still left in it — a baseball bat and a fielder's glove in a corner, a photograph of a juvenile football team, and a Luger automatic hanging on a nail, proof that Melville Goodwin, when he was overseas, had remembered his younger son. He had referred to it as his dressing room, and it doubtless was, for the time being, but it was really a spill-over room, with a denim-covered studio couch available at any moment for any unexpected guest, and Melville Goodwin's possessions there could have been moved out in five minutes. His brief-case and a few papers and his garrison cap and three volumes of Clausewitz and a Bible lay on a battered little table. His clothes, perhaps including that double-breasted suit, were in the narrow wardrobe concealed by a blue denim curtain. Melville Goodwin was only stopping there on his way to somewhere else.

Until I saw the evidence, the transientness of his life was something that I had accepted without understanding its significance. That shared house in Alexandria was as permanent to him as any other home, because he had never lived anywhere for long since he had left Hallowell. Melville Goodwin's sense of home was as mobile as an army column. His home was where his orders took him, and he was perfectly content camping out with the Joyces.

"There certainly is a crowd downstairs," he said, and he set down the suitcase. "You never can tell who's coming when Muriel throws a party. Let's go."

"Just a minute first," I said.

He seemed to have forgotten everything we had been through.

"Oh," he said, "excuse me, Sid. I should have asked you. The bathroom's down the hall, the second door on the right."

"No, no," I said, "never mind about the bathroom." I could treat him almost brusquely now that he was in that tweed coat.

"Well, what the hell do you want then?" he asked.

"I know it isn't any of my business, Mel," I said, "but I can't help being curious about what happened to you this afternoon."

"Oh," he said, "oh, that."

"Yes," I answered. "Are you going to take that job or aren't you?"

He gave me his blankest, dullest stare.

"Listen, boy," he said, "in the army when the boss puts you in a good spot, you don't argue. I did tell him I was disappointed, for personal reasons, just a little disappointed."

The anticlimax fitted perfectly with Melville Goodwin's tweeds and slacks, but it also was a relief.

"So you're not retiring?" I said.

Melville Goodwin still looked at me blankly.

"Listen, son," he answered, "you don't do things that way. You don't show any immediate superior when you're browned off. You pull the lines together first and get organized and do a little quiet cerebration. I'm waiting and thinking for the moment, son, and, you know, I've got quite a lot to think about."

"Well, that's fine," I said. "I've been worrying about you."

He glanced down at his crepe-soled oxfords and clasped his hands behind him.

"There's one thing I always tell the boys," he said. "Worrying never makes decisions. You have to wait and then everything comes to you all at once."

"I don't suppose it's any of my business," I said again, "but maybe I'd better not get wires crossed. Have you explained your reactions to Muriel?"

He rubbed his hand over the back of his head.

"God damn it," he said, "I suppose you'll think this is funny. I started to, but she's so damned happy that I couldn't. This whole party's by way of turning into a celebration. Maybe I haven't any guts when it comes to Muriel. She's been through a lot and I don't like to spoil it for her — at the moment. I can't seem to do it this evening, Sid. God damn it, this is what always happens when you get mixed up with women. Let's go downstairs and get a drink."

He put his hand on my shoulder and pushed me toward the stairs, and his thoughts were off on another tangent. "I've got a case of the smoothest Scotch you ever tasted, and I bet you could never guess who gave it to me. Lieutenant General Merriwell."

"You mean the son of a bitch?" I said.

He first looked shocked and then amused.

"That's right," he said. "I never knew that guy could loosen up like that. He's downstairs drinking some of it now. Muriel asked him over."

It should have been the end of a perfect day, but no one could ever evaluate the reasons for another's discontent. He belonged with that crowd downstairs. He would have been a fish out of water anywhere else, and I had to tell him so — no matter what the repercussion. The time had come when it was impossible to evade things by polite deferment and intentional blindness, but I had never foreseen that I would tell Melville Goodwin off on the second floor of a jerry-built house in Alexandria.

"Wait a minute," I said, "wait a minute, Mel," and his hand dropped from my shoulder.

"What the hell's the matter now?" he asked.

"Mel," I said, "don't you know you belong right here, you God-damned fool? If you try to fit anywhere else, you'll have two strikes against you just as you have right now in those clothes."

"Now wait a minute," he said. "What's the matter with my clothes?"

"They're grotesque," I said.

"Now, Sid," he said, "let's get this straight. What's wrong with you tonight?"

He was reaching for the center of the situation, and perhaps there was more wrong with me than there was with him, because I did not have his capacity for adjustment.

"What do you think you'll look like," I asked, "if you leave this for Dottie Peale?"

"Sid," he said, "what makes you think I'm going to?"

"Because I've been watching you," I said. "You've been thinking about it, haven't you?"

"Yes," he said, "I've been thinking."

"Well, think some more," I said. "Think what you have and what you'll lose."

The moment that followed was one of those uncertain beats of time. Neither of us took his eyes from the other.

"You see a hell of a lot more than you ought to, boy," he said.

"You're pretty obvious sometimes," I answered.

Melville Goodwin drew a deep breath.

"Boy, it's funny," he said. "I ought to be mad as hell at you." Suddenly he clenched his fist, moved his hand upward slowly and tapped me gently on the chest. "There's just one thing I want straight from now on out. I don't need any more advice, son. You understand?"

"You won't get any more," I said, and we stood facing each other for another moment.

"Everyone has to run things for himself, boy, in the final analysis. You understand?"

"Yes," I said, "I understand."

"It's funny I don't get mad at you," he said. "I would, except you mean well."

"That's right," I said, "I mean well."

"Come on," he said, "let's go downstairs and get a drink."

At least we knew where we were, and there was no further need for double talk. General Gooch undoubtedly knew, too, that it was Dottie Peale who had tipped the scales. The word had gone around already about that little skirt in New York. Melville Goodwin must certainly have realized that the shadow of scandal was right behind him. I was pleased with myself that I had again had the intestinal fortitude to bring up the subject of Dottie Peale.

"Just one thing more," I said, and I paused at the head of the stairs.

"Sid," he said, "I'm pretty well browned off right now."

"Use your imagination," I said. "Try to think how you'd look with Dottie Peale in New York."

"I could find a good civilian job," he said.

"Yes," I told him, "Dottie can find you one all right."

"We could get a ranch somewhere," he said. "We could travel."

"Yes," I said, "and how would you look carrying the bags?"

Then I knew I had gone too far. I had trampled on the edges of his dream. I had desecrated something that he had to keep inviolate. His face had grown brick-red and his voice shook.

"Come on," he said, "get going before I kick you in the pants downstairs."

"Just see you don't kick yourself downstairs," I said.

Someone was beginning to play the piano, and he grasped my arm just above the elbow.

"Wait a minute," he said. He had controlled his face and voice, and he shook his head slowly. "I told you" — and his voice was very restrained — "I told you to stop riding me. Don't do it again, son. . . . Don't you see there are some things I can't help?"

"Yes," I said, "I see."

"Then shake hands," he said. "Damn it, you and I didn't make this world. . . . Come on."

As General Gooch had said that afternoon, when Goodwin started going, he always kept on going.

"Bud," he called as we were going downstairs, "come here, I want you to meet Sid Skelton, and call to Joe to fix him up a steak — rare." We were back at the party, back from our rough trip together, and it was quite a party — almost a celebration.

As you grew in experience, and grew to understand people and their motives, you also developed a sense of discrimination and a comprehension of your own tastes and limitations. A few years previously I might have been happy with all that group, because I would not have known any better. Now I had lived too long, and I had become too specialized. I was like a child at a strange party. They were all as polite to me as they would have been to a strange child, but I was not in the service and I possessed none of the drives and worries connected with it. I knew none of its gossip and only a few of its anecdotes and I could not draw on my days at the Point or any gallery of mutual acquaintance. A few years before after a few drinks my separateness would not have disturbed me, but that evening I was an insoluble element.

This did not mean for an instant that I did not like the crowd. I knew enough about them to understand that they were more valuable by far to the world than people like Art Hertz or Gilbert Frary or most of the newspaper crowd and the writers I played around with. I both admired and envied them. I envied their security, their own specialized sort of freedom, and the firm bonds of their companionship. I might have been one of them if I had shared their years of apprenticeship and indoctrination, but now it was too late. They were all polite to me and cordial because I was a friend of the Goodwins, but I floundered there like a fish out of water.

"Bud," Mel Goodwin was saying again, "I want you to meet Sid Skelton. Get him a Scotch, Bud, will you? Where's Mrs. Merriwell? I'd better skip around and see if she's taken care of. Take Sid to find Enid and Muriel, will you, Bud? Or else we'll both catch hell. Hasn't Goochy set up those bridge tables on the sun porch?"

Colonel Joyce shook hands with me warmly, and obviously he had heard all about Paris and Savin Hill. He, too, was in civilian clothes. He was one of those round, jolly officers who had put on weight because of desk work, and he had a quick smile that could be wiped off promptly. He was saying it was certainly a pleasure to meet me. Any friend of Mel Goodwin's was a friend of his, right by regulations. The Goodwins were his and Enid's oldest, closest friends, and no one was as good as the Goodwins, and wasn't it fine about Mel, because I'd heard the news of course. No one deserved the recognition as much as Mel, and it was about time, just between us both, that somebody recognized Mel and his record. There was only one aspect of the situation that made him sad. Now that Mel was all set in Washington, the Goodwins would have to move away into a bigger place. He really didn't know what he and Enid would do without them, and Enid and Muriel were just like sisters, and Charley was just like a kid of his own.

"Well," he said, "we'd better find the girls. They'll either be in the kitchen or outside at the grill."

We found Enid Joyce first, on our way across the sun porch. There were streaks of gray in her dark hair, but there was no age at all in her eyes. Once she must have been as pretty as Muriel had been, and she was still the life of the party.

"Why, Sid Skelton," she said. "Excuse me, I *have* to think of you as Sid, Mr. Skelton. Muriel still talks about how sweet you were to her and Mel in Connecticut. . . . Bud, dear, see if you can't get some ice, and see if you can't round up a detail to get dishes into the kitchen before people begin stepping on them. . . . There's too much rank here tonight. Muriel and I should have asked more young officers and their wives. The kids can always be so useful. . . . Mel says you were in the service, so I guess you don't mind service parties."

"No," I said, "I always like them very much."

"You see us all being very informal," she said, "and very natural. We're all old friends here, at least almost everybody. Muriel wanted to ask some of the navy, because of the Joint Chiefs, but I said let's leave the navy out of it for once and avoid the strain. Isn't it wonderful about Mel?"

"It sounds fine," I said.

"Dear Muriel," she said. "I was so afraid Muriel would have to go to Texas or somewhere, and now she can settle down and uncrate some of that lovely furniture of hers that's been in the warehouse, and make a home for Mel and the boys. Dear Muriel. Mel never tells about anything until after it's happened. Thank goodness Bud has never been that way, except about all the Intelligence things he does, of course. Bud called up as soon as he heard. Mel was too busy, I suppose, and I don't believe he *ever* knew how anxious Muriel was. It's everything she's ever wanted."

515

To Melville Goodwin, Plans meant the end of the good life, and to Muriel, it was the ultimate triumph. Perhaps always there was a cleavage between men and women. No woman could ever know the lure of a command. She could only know academically the beauty of well-executed maneuver.

The steps from the sun porch descended onto a small lawn bright under a floodlight that might have been borrowed from some nearby installation. It was not unpleasantly cool outside, and some of the women in evening cloaks, and some of the men without them stood around the dying embers of the charcoal grill.

"Do you remember the Rossiters' parties at Shafter?" someone was saying. Everybody except me seemed to remember, but this did not matter, because I saw Muriel Goodwin coming toward me, completely in command and with a look of fulfillment.

"Sid," she said, "this makes everything perfect."

There were so many people she wanted me to meet, she said, and she was so sorry that Helen was not with me, but there would be another time — and before I met anyone, she was going to be selfish and talk to me for just a minute. She drew me away to the edge of the light so that we stood apart from the guests on the lawn.

"Have you seen Mel?" she asked. "It's the first time in years that Mel's got anything he deserves. I've been afraid for weeks that they were just going to shove us away somewhere and forget us, and I can't tell you how many people were after this place in Plans. . . . Well, I'm the one who ought to know." She laughed very happily. "A wife can be useful sometimes, and Mel never will put himself forward. . . . I've hardly had a chance to say a word to him. It's queer the way he acts."

"How does he act?" I asked.

"He's been going around all evening like someone at a surprise party. I don't think he's really had time to think what this is going to mean to us. He doesn't seem to understand that at last we're really going to be able to settle down." She lowered her voice. "He's right on his way to almost anything there is and he doesn't know it."

I nodded but I did not answer. I could not say anything to spoil it for her.

"He's been so restless," she said, "and he's been so repressed lately. He's never let himself unwind since he got back from Germany. It's been so hard wondering how I could help him."

It was difficult to be loyal.

"He still seems pretty restless." That was all I was able to say and the only way I could put it.

"I know," she said. "They all are at loose ends when they come back from overseas. It takes a little while to get settled. . . . I'm going to start house-hunting, and then Mel will have time to work on his golf. All he needs is to get back into a routine."

She sounded very much like Helen on the subject of Connecticut. "It's pretty hard to settle down," I said.

"It will be all right — now things are fixed," she answered. "He never can believe that he has a future. I won't have to sit and wait any more and wonder where he is. You don't know what waiting and watching means, because you're a man."

He was the hunter home from the hill with all his field service behind him, absolutely safe.

"And now you'll have to meet everyone," she said. "Do you really have to leave tonight? You could sleep in Mel's dressing room just as well as not."

Hardly anyone in the house was below the rank of colonel. I saw a general doing card tricks, and two other generals, surrounded by officers' wives, exhibiting Roman wrestling.

"That's 'Skid' Gabriel playing the piano," Mrs. Goodwin said. "It's just as though we were back at Schofield."

Again I thought of Muriel's theory about music and the army. The officer was only a major.

Melville Goodwin had already gathered a group in the living room and they had been singing "Smiles" and "I Want a Girl Just Like the Girl" and other songs of World War I. Melville was standing beside the piano, and General Gooch in a pepper-and-salt suit stood on one side of him, and General Snip Lewis in a dinner coat was on the other side. Suddenly, I heard his voice, entirely off key, but booming with deep fervor, "Bless 'em all, great and small." One of the beauties of that song of the Pacific was a secret meaning

517

you could put into it, which acted as a balm to lacerated feelings.

"And now I want you to meet General Merriwell," Mrs. Goodwin said. "He's Mel's new chief, you know."

General Merriwell was the only three-star general present and he, also, wore a dinner coat. He stood alone, three paces behind the crowd at the piano, not singing but listening tolerantly, like someone who had no ear for music or too few drinks.

"Muriel, my dear," he said, "this is a delightful party. Do you remember the night years ago when Gertrude and I dined with you? Where was it?"

"Wasn't it at that little place of ours at Kahala?" Muriel Goodwin asked.

General Merriwell thought carefully. His face lacked the harsh lines of the singers around the piano. It was both shrewd and pedantic.

"No, no," he said, "of course I remember Kahala, but I was thinking of when I was in G–3 in Manila and Melville was a company commander."

"Oh yes," Muriel said, "Company A. Melville still goes on about Company A."

"And let's see," General Merriwell said, "there was a trick dog that walked on his hind legs. What was his name? Don't tell me. I mustn't forget names. His name was Bozo; that's it, Bozo."

"That's right," Muriel said. "I'd almost forgotten his name myself."

"I wonder where Gertrude is," the General said.

"I think she's playing bridge," Muriel answered.

"If Gertrude's playing bridge, I may as well sit down," General Merriwell said. "Gertrude says you play a very sensible game, my dear, and Gertrude ought to know. You've been playing enough together lately."

"There's no one who's more fun to play with than Gertrude," Mrs. Goodwin said. "She has instinctive card sense and she's improving all the time."

"Let's sit down," General Merriwell said. "Would you care for a cigar, Mr. Skelton?"

"No thank you, sir," I answered.

"When I took my last physical," the General said, "I was told to slow up on cigars. It's what might be termed a routine suggestion. Just one cigar. Well, here it is, just one cigar. That's easy, because I've never learned how to smoke two at once." General Merriwell smiled and waited, and we all laughed. "You don't mind cigar smoke, do you, my dear?"

"I love it," Muriel said. "I wish Melville would learn to smoke cigars and not those cigarettes."

"Well, I'm relieved to hear it," the General said. "We'll have to see what we can do with Mel's smoking. I hope Mr. Skelton will excuse me if I talk shop for just a moment. No, don't go, Mr. Skelton," and he patted my arm. "I just wanted to say, Muriel, how pleased I am to get my hands on Mel and to have him next door. The work has been crowding up lately. It's time we had more men in Plans with long and practical combat records, but I'm a little afraid, from something that transpired this afternoon, that Mel is reluctant."

"That's just the way Mel always is when he starts with desk work," Muriel said. "He always expresses doubts."

"Somehow or other," General Merriwell said, as though he had not heard her, "officers with combat records are often restless. Well, if Melville did not want this, he should not have rated so high at the War College. I went over all Mel's qualifications off the record with Foghorn. By the way, his arthritis has been pretty bad lately."

"Yes, I know," Muriel said. "Mel and I called on him yesterday afternoon."

"I made that pilgrimage, too, yesterday," General Merriwell said. "Whenever anything important comes up, I like to get the Grimshaw angle. There's always that jump between combat and no combat — a different thought pattern, as Foghorn put it. Foghorn told quite a funny story about the first time he saw you and Mel. Where was it?"

"Why, at Bailey," Mrs. Goodwin said.

"Bailey, that's right, at the old Small Arms School," General Merriwell answered, "and you fixed a sand box for him. Well, Grimshaw says not to worry about Mel. He says put Mel anywhere and he can do anything."

"That's awfully sweet of Foghorn," Muriel Goodwin said. "Melville, come over here."

Melville Goodwin stood attentively in front of us.

"Yes, what is it, dear?" he said. "Does the boss want some of his Scotch?"

"The boss has just told me what Foghorn has been saying about you," Muriel Goodwin said. "He says, put you anywhere and you can do anything. Now aren't you pleased?"

"Yes, dear," Melville Goodwin answered, "very pleased. Thank you for passing that on, sir. Sid, I think you and I ought to leave for the airport pretty soon."

I had never thought that General Goodwin would take me to the airport. I had thought that I could simply call a taxi, but he seemed anxious to go with me, and somehow I still rated a Public Relations car, which Goochy had ordered. People were leaving already, the General said, and his ducking out for a few minutes would not break up the party, because Muriel and Bud and Enid would still be there.

"Airport, son," he said to the driver, and then he added, "the commercial planes," and he turned up the glass window that separated us from the driver's seat. I was a little constrained, but he acted as though there had been no words between us, and I remembered that he must have lived through lots of torrid scenes. Someone in the army was always bawling out someone else and then forgetting it.

"Driving out here makes me feel as though I were pushing off somewhere myself," he said. "I wish to God I were — anywhere."

He must have been thinking of Hangar 6, at which army transport planes had previously been loaded, and from which I had left, myself, with Dottie Peale and that troupe of VIPs for Europe — and it would have been better for Mel Goodwin if that C–54 had never made the flight.

"I used to like these parties of Muriel's," he said. "I don't know

520

why I'm not in the mood for them now. Sid, do you ever feel as though you'd missed something? I mean something you've never known about?"

"Yes," I answered, "I suppose everybody feels that way sometimes."

"I keep thinking what in hell have I been doing with myself all these years," he said. "Do you know when that idea first came to me?"

"No," I said.

"Well, it came over me in Paris when I saw you and Dottie Peale. That's why I began reciting about old Ulysses. Old Ulysses must have felt just that way, and he had the brains to recognize it."

"That only goes to show that people like you should never mess around with civilians, Mel," I said. "You can't be me, and I can't be you. Nobody can have everything."

"All right," he said, "let me ask you this one question. You wouldn't want to be me, now would you?"

"No," I said, and then I was afraid that I had sounded rudely fervent. "I wouldn't have what it takes."

"All right," he said, "then you ought to see why I don't want to be myself. Dottie sees."

I seemed to be standing in front of a mental fluoroscope watching the simple motives of General Goodwin.

"Yes," I said, "Dottie would. Dottie doesn't want to be herself either."

"Poor kid," he said. "I know Dottie's never had a break."

"How's that again?" I asked.

"You don't understand Dottie," he said. "You don't try to. She's like a . . ."

He stopped. He was not good at similes.

"Like a what?" I asked.

"Like a bird fluttering in a cage," he said. "And Dottie knows what I'm going through. She's got a lot of insight, Sid . . . and I'll tell you something else about Dottie."

"What else?" I asked.

"Dottie's got guts," he said. "Dottie and I have that in common.

521

If we had to, we could both go down the line together. Dottie wouldn't be afraid."

Dottie had done what she wanted with him, and he was sewed up now. He was at peace with himself momentarily, because in his thoughts he and Dottie were walking away from the Pentagon together, away from General Merriwell and Plans, away from humdrum fact and into a roseate future where details did not matter — because Dottie had insight and infinite patience and they understood each other. It did not occur at all to Melville Goodwin that there could be a morning after.

"Mel," I began, "take hold of yourself, for God's sake," but he stopped me. He wanted nothing to spoil his dream, and I was glad to see that we were pulling up at the airport.

"Don't give me any more advice," he said. "I told you I'm handling this myself from now on out. Push off and sitting well in order smite."

"For God's sake, don't recite that thing again," I said, as the driver opened the door, and I made one last remark. "Don't bother to come inside with me, Mel. Go back home where you belong and try to stay there."

I wished again that Dottie and the VIPs and I had never left from Hangar 6. When all the Melville Goodwins were making their European crusade, they should have been left to do it alone, entirely alone.

"Well, good night, son," he said. "Just remember, we have to work out these problems by ourselves. Happy landings, son."

"Happy landings, Mel," I said.

Fortunately I was leaving as I was sickeningly certain of where he was going to land. I felt as though I were walking away from a wreck, but I was leaving.

XXXII

The Service Takes Care of Its Own

OF COURSE I should have known that you paid a price for becoming a confidant, just as you paid admission at the box office of a show. After an initial sense of compliment in being singled out as an adviser, you invariably ended up like Sindbad the Sailor with a helpless and beguiling Old Man of the Sea clamped upon your back. There was no escape from a friend's problems. They aroused you in the watches of the night. They assailed you unexpectedly in the leisure moments of the day, until finally you faced the timeworn truth, that good or bad advice was inflated currency. Friends only wanted reassurance — never advice. I had made an unintentional commitment by sitting there at Savin Hill watching General Goodwin unroll the scroll of his career.

The Chicago plane was excellently equipped. Two beautiful uniformed hostesses, smiling rich lipsticked smiles, put each passenger at his ease as he climbed aboard, if only by making the gentle, playful remarks that hostesses customarily learn at hostess seminaries. We were all to relax on that happy plane and we were all to partake of a delightful mutual experience, flying in a pressurized cabin northwestward through the stratosphere. Coffee and meals and chewing gum would be served aloft, and fasten your seat belts, please, and no smoking until the signal is given. Beside the door of the Monel metal kitchenette where the hostesses stored hot meals and coffee, there was a squawk box, and when the plane was off the ground and had started on its skyward climb, the system addressed the passengers so softly and sweetly that I felt that the pretty hostess was speaking just to me. Good evening, I was being told;

we were being welcomed one and all to a pleasant journey which would end at the Chicago airport near the late Al Capone's Cicero. We were planning to cruise tonight at sixteen thousand feet, but due to the clear weather conditions, we would have glimpses of the great cities on our flight. The captain's name was Arthur J. Ballinger. The copilot's name was Hugh Munroe, and the rest of the crew up forward had names also, and so had the two hostesses, lovely names. During the flight, arrangements would be made for passengers who might so desire, to go to the forward compartment to view the workings of the aircraft. We were off, and pleasant journey, everybody.

We were off, up three miles in the air in a land of Wynken, Blynken and Nod, flying before the approaching dawn. After a moment of tension, which I always felt whenever a heavy plane left the runway, everything became smooth. The night was very clear, and as I was dozing off to sleep, I began to think of Melville Goodwin as taking off on a trip of his own, exercising no more control than I did over that Chicago flight. Melville Goodwin could unfasten his seat belt now. The army would handle his personal difficulties. The army had its ways of taking care of its own, when it came to woman trouble. I could see them already, in some Pentagon office, dealing in the broad generalities of love and life and then coming down to particulars. I could almost hear old classmates at the Point and old associates in the field talking about Melville Goodwin.

From a military viewpoint, the subject of woman trouble fell into several categories, and you ought to take a broad-minded attitude about it. Officers weren't meant to be plaster saints. There were always a lot of pretty fast-moving gals and boys in any installation, and gals had to be gals and boys, boys, within limits; but it was necessary to face the fact that some officers could handle woman trouble better than others. Some could shed it as ducks shed water. Some were always getting in and out of it — and this was perfectly all right within limits — and overseas extramarital complications usually settled themselves automatically. Back in the States it depended on the officer and the general setup and on how you handled woman trouble. Some people could handle a lot of it just the way some others could handle whisky, and not a word against them.

524

Gals had to be gals and boys had to be boys. For instance, some excellent officers had been unfaithful to their wives for years, and others had been cuckolds for a generation, without any of this sort of thing interfering with their general efficiency or their record. Frankly, anyone might take an unpremeditated roll in the hay by accident — where you had war you had to have sex — and anyone who got anywhere in the army could face the fact. Even the chaplains could face it, and army chaplains weren't all jerks. You could get away with a lot in the army if you handled it in the right way and kept it within limits. For instance, everybody knew about Captain So-and-so and Colonel So-and-so's wife, and none of this ever hurt Captain So-and-so, and he was a general now — all because it had been handled in the right way.

But then, there were some officers who were different. Take Mel Goodwin, for instance, and I could hear them already taking Mel Goodwin in the Pentagon. It was all very well back in the ETO, but you would never think anything like this of Mel Goodwin. He had never been off the deep end before. He had never shacked up anywhere. At his age it was somehow not right to start a shack-up job in New York, although the old motto: "Don't play around within a mile of the flagpole" still held good. There were plenty of other arrangements he could have made that would have had a regulation quality. He should have known his way around, considering his age. You had to face it. What he was doing quite frankly denoted emotional instability, and emotionally unstable officers did not look well in Plans — not that there were not maritally unfaithful officers in Plans, but somehow these officers knew how to handle these problems. It was different when someone like Mel Goodwin suddenly took a stray. It was hard to explain the difference, but it shook one's faith in institutions of regularity.

Such a conclusion was not fair, perhaps, but conventions very seldom were, and somehow I was sure that he had broken a convention. I could not define its limits, but he had done something unexpected when he should have been predictable. He had become an unknown quantity, and no one in Mel Goodwin's situation could afford to be an unknown quantity. The thing to hope for was that he would get over it. That was undoubtedly what they were all saying at the Pentagon.

Melville Goodwin was still beside me invisibly when I was talking things over with Mr. George Burtheimer at breakfast in Chicago, and he was still beside me when I flew back to New York. Yet it never occurred to me that I would be called into a conference to discuss the love life of Melville Goodwin, until I suddenly heard from General Gooch.

He precipitated himself in the middle of my own affairs, right in the broadcasting company, at a most awkward moment. The army was always egocentric. It never could and it never would understand that civilians might have troubles of their own.

After I had been to Chicago, I naturally expected that Gilbert Frary would return from the Coast precipitously. He reached New York at two o'clock in the afternoon the day after I had arrived from Chicago, and he sent me word through Miss Maynard that he wanted to see me in his office at three. I was sure that he had stopped over in Chicago to see Mr. Burtheimer himself, but I was not worried about this any longer, because I had been over all the ground with Mr. Burtheimer and I had done rather well with him.

There is no need to go into the details here. They were sordid but they were practical. I did not like anything I had done. In fact I was rather surprised at myself now that I had accomplished what I had, for I had never realized that I might be good at business negotiations. At any rate, the whole affair was over and settled by the time Gilbert Frary had arrived in New York, and I was willing and happy to see him in his office at three.

It was a beautiful office, less gay and modern than mine, but much more solid. Gilbert's desk was a Florentine refectory table, and there was a fine tapestry on the wall behind it, and the chairs were Francis I. He had always said they were original Francis Firsts and that you could tell they were from the wormholes. This was not his outer office but the inner office, which he used when he wanted to get away from everything, and his couch in the corner with a pull-over blanket was there to prove it. There was not even an electric clock on the wall. In his sanctum, Gilbert always said, he wanted to be absolutely divorced from time.

I understood, of course, that there was going to be a scene, because Gilbert always liked scenes, so I was entirely prepared, and I closed the door carefully behind me.

"Hello, Gilbert," I said. "How was it on the Coast? Did you come back with a lot of good ideas?"

I did not mean to be unkind about Gilbert's ideas. I only made the remark by way of a conversational opening.

"Sidney," Gilbert said, and his voice sounded choked, and he pulled out a handkerchief and mopped his forehead. "Sidney, may I ask you a single question?"

"Why, yes," I said, "go right ahead, Gilbert."

Gilbert Frary looked at me sadly. He appeared deeply hurt and deeply shocked, and perhaps he was.

"My question can be phrased in a single word, Sidney," he said. "I don't want to be reproachful, Sidney. I don't want to speak about distrustfulness or about what I might call ingratitude. I will not analyze my disillusionment about your integrity. Perhaps there has been some mistake, and I still want to love your integrity and still idealize, if I can, a lovely human relationship. The question I want to ask you, Sidney, is, Why, simply Why?"

"Why what, Gilbert?" I asked.

Gilbert sighed and dabbed his eyes with his cambric handkerchief, and there were genuine tears in them, but then, Gilbert always was emotional.

"Please, Sidney," he said, "don't turn the knife in the wound. For the last forty-eight hours I feel as though I have been impaled on steel."

"I'm sorry if you've suffered, Gilbert," I said, "but then perhaps we have both suffered."

"Sidney," Gilbert said, "before we leave this room I want everything to be as it was formerly between us. Why did you ever mistrust me—of all people, Sidney?"

Since I had worked my way into the driver's seat, there was no reason for any further turning of knives in wounds.

"Perhaps I was wrong, Gilbert," I said. "I'm sorry if I shouldn't have mistrusted you."

"That's a very lovely thing for you to say," Gilbert Frary said. "I'm the one who should be sorry, Sidney. I should have understood your integrity. I should never have suggested even whimsically that you should speak commercials."

"That's all right now, Gilbert," I said. "As long as I know that the sponsor is satisfied with the program, that clears everything. I'm sorry I had to go over your head, but then, you were out on the Coast."

"I cannot see why you are so suspicious," Gilbert said. "That is all that hurts me, Sidney. Suspicion does not coincide with friendship."

"That's quite all right, Gilbert," I told him. "Let's put it this way. Let's say that I lost faith in myself, but it's all right now. It helps me to know that George thinks I'm a valuable piece of property in the face of competitiv bidding. As long as he agrees with my ideas, everything's all right. There's no reason for him or you to worry about the White Wall Rubber Company."

Gilbert Frary sighed.

"But it hurts me to think of your thinking of it, Sidney," he said, "after the long way we have gone together. It isn't like you, Sidney."

"It was probably a great mistake, Gilbert," I said, "but it's perfectly all right now."

"All I want," Gilbert said, "all I've ever wanted, is to have you basically and absolutely happy, Sidney, from every point of view. I cannot blame you wholly. There is no reason why you should ever have known the thought I have expended on you. The program has been a part of my life. Forgive me for having interfered."

"That's all right, Gilbert," I said, "and you won't have to bother about it so much now." I was being gentle with him, though perhaps there was no reason for gentleness under the circumstances, but then, everything was all right now.

"George said a great many lovely things about you," Gilbert said, "but then, why shouldn't he? And I said some lovely things about you, too, to George. All George and I want, all we have ever wanted, is to keep you happy. Sidney, basically what was it that you said to George?"

I could thank Melville Goodwin for my answer, and I felt very grateful to Melville Goodwin.

"I told him let's cut out the horsefeathers," I said, "and if he didn't like me, I had another job, and in the future I'd like to deal with him more closely personally. No reflection on you, Gilbert."

"I always knew," Gilbert Frary said, "that George would think you were a lovely person if he really sat around a table with you."

We both knew exactly where we were with each other, although I knew that neither of us would put it into words. Gilbert still looked at me sadly, but there was a quality of respect in his sadness which he had never displayed before. He must have been ashamed that he had not foreseen the possibility that I would go straight over his head to the sponsor, but it was too late for him to do anything about it now.

"It's a pity you never wanted me to talk to George," I said.

"But, Sidney," Gilbert answered, "I've always thought of you as an artist, to be protected. I always thought that you basically disliked business and did not understand it as an artist. I know differently now."

Yes, he certainly knew differently now, but I felt no thrill of victory, because I did basically dislike business, and now we had reached the business side of the conference. Gilbert's glance sharpened, a contrast to his previous careworn look.

"Now, Sidney," he said, "after this misunderstanding, what is it that will make you happy? Let us sit down and talk this over frankly as we always have, Sidney."

We each sat down in a Francis I chair and watched each other very carefully, but before we could get down to facts, the door of the sanctuary opened. It was Miss Hamilton, Gilbert Frary's secretary, who looked very much like my own Miss Maynard, except that Miss Hamilton was a brunette. Miss Hamilton had made a mistake in opening the door without knocking or, in fact, in opening the door at all, and Gilbert needed to be cross with someone, as he could not be cross with me.

529

"Netta, darling," he said to Miss Hamilton, "on top of everything else, must you interrupt me? I said I must not be disturbed."

There was venom in his voice, and I was sorry for Miss Hamilton.

"It's for Mr. Skelton," Miss Hamilton said. "Miss Maynard has brought an army officer in to see Mr. Skelton, and he's outside now. He would have come in himself if I hadn't. I'm frightfully sorry, Mr. Frary."

"Who?" Gilbert Frary asked. "What officer?"

"His name is General Gooch," Miss Hamilton said. "He says he comes from the General Staff in Washington."

"You'll have to tell him I'm in an important conference," I began, but I knew that no civilian conference was important to General Gooch. I knew it before I had finished speaking, because General Gooch himself had entered Gilbert Frary's sanctum.

"I hope I'm not interrupting anything," he said. General Gooch was in his uniform, wearing the sunburst of the General Staff. He looked at the tapestry behind Gilbert's refectory table, then he looked at Gilbert and finally at me. "I've got a plane waiting and the boss wants to see you in Washington before six o'clock."

"What boss?" I asked.

"God damn it," General Gooch said, "the Chief's office, and we've got to step on it, Sid."

"Why didn't you telephone me?" I asked.

"I've been trying all morning," General Gooch said. "They wouldn't put me through."

I could not blame Gilbert Frary for the way he looked. It was a new experience to him, as it was to me, and General Gooch had obviously forgotten that the war was over.

"Do you know Mr. Frary, General Gooch?" I said, to remind him that the war was over.

"How do you do? I'm sorry to interrupt you gentlemen in this way," General Gooch said, "but there's been a God-damned lot of horsefeathering around here, and I know Mr. Skelton will understand."

It was that beautiful complacency of the army, and it touched me

530

that General Gooch considered me as a part of it and knew that I would understand.

"What's the matter, Goochy?" I asked. It was perfectly all right at this point to call him Goochy.

"It's all fouled the hell up," General Gooch said. "It's about you-know-who, our mutual friend, and I suggested to the boss he'd better see you. It's highly delicate and highly personal. I hope this gentleman will excuse us."

He looked at Gilbert Frary as if he were waiting for him to withdraw.

"Listen, Goochy," I said, "I can't do that. I have to broadcast at seven o'clock."

"Oh, Jesus — " General Gooch began, but I stopped him.

"Now wait a minute," I said. "I'll go down with you afterwards. You'll have to go back to that room of mine and telephone. I'll leave here with you at seven-fifteen, and that's the best I can do."

General Gooch and I stood there for a second, each trying to stare the other down, and I wanted to ask him another question, but it was not the time or place.

"All right," General Gooch said, "I'll do what I can with it. Come on, sister." He nodded to Miss Hamilton, and they both left the inner sanctum.

It was almost as though the ceiling had fallen to put an end to our discussion, and it was too much to expect that either Gilbert Frary or I should be able to adjust ourselves to it casually.

"Sidney," Gilbert Frary asked me, "who is that man?"

"He's an acquaintance of mine," I said. "Don't bother about him now. He's gone, Gilbert."

"I don't see how he ever succeeded in arriving here," Gilbert said.

"I guess he just barged in," I said. "Never mind it now."

"But he says he has a plane waiting," Gilbert Frary said.

"Yes," I answered. "I don't understand it either, but never mind it, Gilbert."

"When I first met you I never dreamed that you had important military connections," Gilbert Frary said.

531

"That's all right," I said, "I never knew it either."

"Can you tell me why they want you?" Gilbert Frary asked.

"No," I said, "but it isn't anything personal, Gilbert. It's something that has happened to somebody else."

"I wish we could use it," Gilbert Frary said. . . . "Some pictures of you boarding the plane. Don't you think it would help the program build-up?"

"No," I said. "This is very private, Gilbert."

Gilbert Frary sighed.

"You have so many lovely connections, Sidney," he said, "that sometimes I have to pinch myself to be sure that I'm awake."

"That's right," I said, "I have a few connections."

Perhaps it was just as well in the future for Gilbert to think of me as an enigmatic character, and he had certainly pinched himself since I had seen Burtheimer in Chicago.

"I wish you would sound more friendly," Gilbert said. "It hurts me, Sidney, if we are not on a warm, confidential basis."

"I'm being friendly," I said.

Gilbert sighed again, but we both knew where we were.

"Where were we in our conversation," he asked, "before this interruption?"

"You wanted to make me happy," I said.

"That's what hurts me," Gilbert Frary said. "Since the very beginning of our association, Sidney, I have always been working for your happiness. If I have been overzealous or unintelligent, it was enthusiasm, Sidney, not lack of integrity."

"You mean," I asked him, "you've been thinking of me selflessly day and night?"

"Yes," Gilbert answered, "absolutely, without a trace of ambiguity, Sidney."

There were polite ways of handling such a problem, as long as we both knew where we were and understood that there was iron beneath the velvet glove.

"I always love to admit it when I'm wrong," I said. "I never should have thought you were trying to run out on me. Can you forgive my suspicious nature, Gilbert?"

532

"Sidney," Gilbert said, "I love you for saying that. It's so absolutely like you."

"I love you, too," I said. "Now let's see how I can be happy."

"But that is all I want," Gilbert said. "Sidney, just name anything."

It was time to get tough, but there was still the velvet glove.

"While this contract lasts," I said, "I'll negotiate all program problems personally with the sponsor instead of going through you. Perhaps we'd better put it in writing, Gilbert."

"Sidney," Gilbert began, "this is so unnecessary. Between friends, a gentlemanly agreement."

"A gentlemanly agreement between friends in writing," I said.

Gilbert had an air of noble resignation.

"George and I only want to have you happy. What else, Sidney?" he asked.

The time had come to lay it on the line.

"The next thing," I said. "You throw this Alan Featherbee the hell out of this shop."

Gilbert laughed. It was a tragic, broken laugh.

"Excuse me, Sidney," he said, "but this is so completely ludicrous. To think that this individual should have been the basis of our trouble. Why didn't you speak to me about him earlier? I only ask you, why?"

"Well," I said, "I'm speaking about him now."

Gilbert spoke gently and soothingly.

"If it gives you a moment's mental ease, Sidney," he said. "And what else?"

"I want loyalty from the bottom up"—I was grateful to Mel Goodwin for this, too. "I want you to fire Art Hertz and let me get my own writer."

"I love it when you speak frankly, Sidney," Gilbert said. "You see so much more clearly than I do. Of course that man has been intriguing between us. We won't let him spoil our friendship, will we? Subconsciously I've always distrusted Art Hertz."

"And while we're on the subject, Miss Maynard had better go, too," I said.

Gilbert thought for a moment and then he smiled brightly.

"I'll tell you exactly what we'll do," he said. "I'll take Miss Maynard and you can have Miss Hamilton. You'll love Miss Hamilton."

"No," I said, "I don't want to love Miss Hamilton. I only want to love you, Gilbert."

"All I can ask is that single monosyllabic question," Gilbert said. "Why? Why didn't you take up all of this with me long ago, Sidney?"

I arose from my Francis I chair. The interview was over, and I shook hands with Gilbert, but I felt no personal triumph.

"It was all a great mistake," I said. "I hadn't realized how valuable they thought I was in Chicago — but I love you, Gilbert." Love would always be different in the show business from other forms of love.

That hypocritical scene had given me a position and a security that I did not personally admire or covet, and if it had not been for Helen and Camilla, I knew that I would never have exerted myself. I was right back in the old groove again. My voice was with me still, and brains were unnecessary again, but at least I had shown a flash of latent business instinct, and things would be simpler now. I had gained in what Gilbert Frary would have called stature.

Melville Goodwin was beside me invisibly when I left Gilbert Frary's office and walked down the corridor past the gray and gold ushers. His methods of procedure had been a galvanizing force to me in that unpleasant interview, and I was indebted to him for a new sense of security. I could even understand what had made me casual and unambitious in the past. Instinctively I had disliked security. I knew this now that I had attained it. I was finally tied down and hemmed in, because this was what my wife wanted, and perhaps security was what any woman most wanted. It was different with Melville Goodwin. I had seen him at the moment when he had attained his own security, and there had been no surrender. I might tell myself that he lacked my sensitiveness or the sort of imagination that instilled fear, but still I envied him with every step I took down that soundproofed, air-conditioned corridor. I still wished to escape from everything around me, but it was too late now. I was a piece of prop-

534

erty now, and we had even talked of television in Chicago. Some day soon it would not only be my voice but my face, and those damned double-breasted suits, and my personal charm of manner, that would be a part of the property. George had come across with a lot of good ideas back there in Chicago. I could not escape from any of it because I was not the man that Melville Goodwin was. I had not the requisite self-belief.

Back in my own office I was conscious of Miss Maynard's avid curiosity, but there was no reason to discuss the future with her. Miss Maynard had bet on the wrong horse, and so had Art Hertz, and she would know what the score was in a very little while. It would all be out on the studio grapevine that there had been a shake-up and that Mr. Frary was not feeling very well.

"That general," she said — "I mean General Gooch — is waiting for you inside, and he's had me put through two telephone calls to Washington. I hope it's what you wanted, Mr. Skelton. Miss Hamilton told me it was what you wanted."

"That's right," I said. "Thanks, Miss Maynard."

She watched me anxiously, striving to read the future. There was no reason to feel sorry for Miss Maynard. She would be assigned elsewhere in the studio.

"I'm frightfully sorry about his bursting in on you and Mr. Frary while you were in conference," Miss Maynard said. "I never dreamed he would do such a thing and neither did Miss Hamilton."

"I don't see how you could have stopped him," I told her.

"Mr. Hertz has been asking for you," Miss Maynard said. "He wants to know when you would care to see the script."

"Tell him in half an hour," I told her.

I wanted to put those inevitable details away from me as far as possible, and I was glad that I could escape from them vicariously through the antics of Melville Goodwin. General Gooch was in my office looking sourly at the blown-up photographs around the wall, and it occurred to me that I would not have to tolerate those pictures any longer. I could remove the whole lot of them, and I could have Helen redecorate the whole place, and Gilbert Frary would not have a word to say about it.

535

"Say, Sid," General Gooch said, "is that you riding on that elephant?"

"That was a tiger hunt in India," I told him.

"Jesus," General Gooch said, "I didn't know you rated elephants. Mel never told me about these pictures."

I told him that Melville Goodwin had never been here. I tried to explain to him that the photographs were not my fault or my idea. They were my problem, I told him, but what was his problem?

"That's me on the elephant," I said, "but what are you doing in here looking at it, Goochy?"

"This place looks as though there might be some liquor around," General Gooch said. "I could do with a shot of bourbon if it's all the same to you. Jesus, what a day, boy, what a day!"

When Miss Maynard brought the ice and glasses, his reactions were similar to those of Robert Goodwin.

"That's really a very nicely stacked up gal," General Gooch said. "Boy, I need this drink."

He drank his whisky neat. He did not need the ice and water. He explained that he had picked up the habit when he was stationed at Bliss. It was a great place, Bliss. During prohibition all you had to do was to cross the bridge into Mexico and you could get anything you wanted, because everything was wide open in Juárez. I could not understand why a description of Juárez was necessary at the moment, but it did not seem advisable to interrupt him, although I began to be afraid that he might be reminded of some good stories about Juárez.

"It's all right," he said, "we've got more time now. The meeting will be at Grimshaw's at twenty-one-thirty, and you have a room at the Mayflower."

It required a moment of mental arithmetic to gather that twenty-one-thirty meant half past nine that evening. He seemed to take it for granted that I understood what everything was all about, and he poured himself another shot of bourbon.

"It's been one hell of a day," he said. "I didn't know until around twelve hundred that Goodwin had blown his top."

"All right," I said, "but maybe you'd better tell me about it, Goochy."

"That's right," he said. "By God, we've got to do something about Goodwin. Say, how much has Goodwin told you?"

For some reason he thought that I had understood the whole situation, and he seemed surprised when I told him that I did not understand anything.

"Oh," General Gooch said, "I thought you were in on this whole picture. Goodwin told me you introduced him to the gal and that you were conversant with the circumstances."

General Gooch scowled at his empty glass. I could see he did not want to tell me any more than was necessary.

"What gal?" I asked. I only asked the question to annoy him.

"God damn it," he said. "This Mrs. Peale. He hasn't got two of them, has he?"

"All right," I said, "what's happened about her now?"

"God damn it," General Gooch said, "don't you know he's planning to marry this Mrs. Peale?"

"No," I said, "I didn't know that."

Of course the idea had been in the back of my mind for a long time, but until the words were snapped at me, without trimmings, I had never honestly believed that things would go so far. I must have always thought that Melville Goodwin would eventually avoid the issue.

"I didn't know," I said again. "I've heard him talk, but what makes you think he's serious?"

I still did not want to believe that it was possible. I still wanted to feel it was preposterous.

"Listen," General Gooch said, and he looked around to see that the door was closed, "when that bastard starts going, he keeps going. You've heard him speak of Lieutenant General Grimshaw, haven't you?"

I thought of Major Foghorn Grimshaw at Bailey, pulling up his badly acting horse and speaking to a young lieutenant who stood in front of his quarters at officers' row, and of Muriel Goodwin's asking him to stay for supper and borrowing some chicken.

"Yes," I said, "I've heard him speak of General Grimshaw, but he's retired now, isn't he?"

"That's right," General Gooch answered, "but Mel's very close to Grimshaw. Well, this morning he told Grimshaw he's leaving the service and marrying this Mrs. Peale."

Goochy had been speaking very gently and slowly, as though someone might overhear us at any moment. There was nothing more assiduously to be avoided, I was thinking, than plain, unadulterated fact.

"What I say is," General Gooch said — "and I ought to know — he's an emotional wound-up son of a bitch. God damn! Why did they put him into Plans?"

"Has he told Mrs. Goodwin?"

My own voice, when I asked, was as low as though we were in a funeral parlor. Then I knew that he could not have told her yet, or General Gooch would not be here.

"No," General Gooch said, "not yet. The Old Man made Mel promise to keep still until they've talked further. Then Grimshaw called up the office. God damn it, it's not too late to handle this some way. Mel has some good friends and they want to get the picture. You see the layout now."

I could see parts of it, but I could not see it all.

"There are right ways and wrong ways of handling these things," General Gooch was saying. "That's why we want the picture. There's a sort of a committee that wants to find out how they can handle this Mrs. Peale."

"Where's Goodwin now?" I asked.

General Gooch contracted the corners of his mouth.

"You know better than to ask that," he said. "Where the hell do you think he would be? Right here in New York City shacked up with this skirt." General Gooch laughed bitterly. "Hell, I don't know why I love the son of a bitch."

I had evidently been cleared for Operation Peale. It was not for me to reason why. It was not for me to argue that I could serve no good purpose by going to Washington.

"All right," I said, "I'll go."

538

"You're damned well right you'll go," he said.

His tone implied that I was personally responsible for the whole problem, but at the same time he looked more cheerful. The thing was in the works now, as they used to say in the army. Mel Goodwin was in the works and there would be some sort of final resolution. As Goochy had said, there was a right way and a wrong way of handling this sort of thing. He must have been sure that this would be handled in the right way, since the proper echelons had taken over. They understood about women and war from every angle in those echelons. General Gooch leaned back in his chair. His glance fell on the bourbon bottle, and he looked away from it reluctantly. It was not a time for too much bourbon, considering the mission, and he was thinking of women and war.

"Now I've never been any God hopper," General Gooch was saying. "I'm an army brat, and ever since I was in diapers I've assumed no sanctimonious attitudes. Hell, these things happen, as I've had occasion to tell Mrs. Gooch. I tell Paula to have a little human charity. Nobody knows all about any individual. Now Mel and Muriel, I should say, always had a happy married life and they've got two fine, clean-cut kids, but I don't know all about it. Paula says I've got one thing to be thankful for — she isn't Muriel Goodwin. Maybe Paula drives me nuts sometimes, but she isn't Muriel Goodwin, and you know how women are. They never take a broad-gauged view like a man. Personally, when it comes to a thing like this, and I've seen plenty, I like to take a broad-gauged regulation view."

General Gooch half closed his eyes, as though he could take the view better by squinting, and he waved his right hand in a broad-gauged gesture and then let it slap down helplessly on his knee.

"Now take Mel," he said. "He's a tactical genius, and I wouldn't be surprised to see him make a corpse get up and walk. He's a damn near perfect officer. I'm his junior and I'm talking out of school, but I'll tell you one trouble with Mel. He doesn't understand women like you and me."

This was the assumption that two men always made when engaged in such a conversation. We both were sophisticates who understood about women.

"Mel got married too young," General Gooch was saying. "That's what happens to a lot of kids. There's something about the Point that makes for early marriage. Hell, whenever you see a pretty girl at the Point, you always think of matrimony, and you want to make an honest woman of every girl you kiss. Now my second year at the Point I had a blind drag . . . oh, hell, never mind it now."

I was sorry to let it go at that, because I should have liked to hear how Cadet Gooch had faced up to natural selection.

"Now you know and I know," General Gooch went on, "that every man gets a label put on him by the crowd when it comes to sex. Mel was one of those boys, as they say around the club, who never looked at another woman. Any gal was always safe with Mel because he never looked at any woman except Muriel. Now maybe you ought to watch that type. They're going to get it someday. I should have foreseen this when Mel cut up in Paris, but then you and I know Paris."

Goochy nodded at me. We were both old roués who knew our Paris.

"Frankly, let's lay it on the line," General Gooch said. "Mel ought to have played around more at the proper age, but, hell, he still would have wanted to make an honest woman out of every gal — and now along comes this Peale. He's an emotional conscientious bastard, if you get what I mean, and with a man, woman trouble starts from conscience. If he had busted loose when he was a captain or even a major, why, hell, that sort of thing is readily handled, but when a man acts like a kid when he's fifty . . . I don't know how we're going to handle this one — not that it hasn't happened to others. Hell, everything happens."

"Maybe no one ought to make an honest woman of anyone after he's fifty," I said. "Perhaps it ought to be a rule."

General Gooch nodded.

"Mel knows that," he said, "but 'Four things greater than all things are, Women and Horses and Power and War,' . . . and you can't stop him when he starts, and when he starts he never thinks about himself. . . . I don't know why it is I love the son of a bitch!"

There was a discreet knock on the door. It was Art Hertz with the script, and the mood and the moment had vanished. General Gooch would never talk to me of women and war again.

"Leave it here with me, Art," I said. "I'll call you if I want any changes."

As General Gooch had said, no one could know everything about any individual, but I was beginning to know more than was decent about Melville Goodwin. The forces that were converging on him now had begun their march in Hallowell years ago, when Muriel had seen to it that he did not look at another girl. Something in him had been unfulfilled, but if he could not stop, at least he was doing what he wanted. I picked up the script and read the old familiar salutation.

"Good evening, friends," I read.

It was vapid and insincere. I was measured and I was safe. I would never throw my heart over a jump. I would never have the bravery or the splendid regardlessness of Melville Goodwin.

I was only asked to Washington to tell some high-ranking friends of Melville Goodwin's, confidentially, what I knew of the character of Dottie Peale. Through it all I felt like a young officer appearing before a board, and I would have preferred to have stood up during the whole interview, although they asked me to sit down. I was simply giving information, and I could read nothing from their expressions as they received it. They listened to me with flattering attention, but I could not gather what they were going to do, if anything. I had not been asked there to discuss their future plans.

General Grimshaw had only been a name to me until then, but he fitted perfectly the portrait I had made of him — a tall, deliberate man whose eyes were ice gray like his hair. His years of complete authority echoed in every inflection of his voice. He would have stood out in any crowd, and not have been mistaken for a retired banker or lawyer. He could have been nothing but a commanding figure in the United States Army. Although he was gracious, I felt nervous whenever he addressed me.

"I'm sure I speak for everyone here," he said, "when I say we are most grateful to you for taking so much time and trouble. You have shed some very real light on this situation, Mr. Skelton. Like you, we are all friends and admirers of Melville Goodwin. I think we can move on from here more confidently."

He did not say where they would move, but there was no doubt that they were not going to sit still, and when they were through with me I was whisked away.

"General Gooch," Foghorn Grimshaw said, "will you please find transportation to return Mr. Skelton to his hotel, and then join us here again?"

"Thank you, sir," I said. "Good night."

Out on the sidewalk General Gooch shook hands with me formally as we stood beside an army car.

"Rattisbone will call for you at eight hundred to take you to the airport," he said. "Good night, Sid."

An iron curtain had fallen and that was all. I was very glad to be leaving that conference. I still felt constrained and unnatural when I tried to get to sleep that night. Even in the morning I still felt that I had been a witness at an inquest. I had told them what they had asked me and if they were taking General Goodwin to pieces and putting him together again, I had nothing further to do with the process. As General Gooch had said, Melville Goodwin was in the works, and I was very glad that I was not in the works with him.

XXXIII

She Had to Say "Poor Sidney"

WHAT with a legal conference and then a correspondents' dinner in the evening, after returning from Chicago, I had not been able to get out to Savin Hill since that Washington broadcast, so there was a great deal I had to tell Helen about Gilbert Frary and the new arrangements when I finally did get home on Friday. Although Helen in her Fortuny gown and the living room with its log fire looked very natural, I felt as though I had returned from overseas and that there should be a lot of unpacked foot lockers and B-4 bags in the hall. I was feeling tired and it did not rest me to answer Helen's questions, but it was reassuring to remember that there would be no broadcast on Saturday or Sunday. I needed time to think.

Helen wanted to know, of course, just what I had done in Chicago and what I had said to Gilbert.

"But I still don't see," she said, "why you had to fly down again to Washington."

It was very hard to explain everything in order to Helen, who had been there quietly in the country.

"I went down to Washington again because Melville Goodwin's going to leave the service and marry Dottie Peale," I said.

After I had explained all about Gilbert Frary and the palace revolution, it did not seem fair to expect me to elaborate on Melville Goodwin. I was tired, but Helen was completely rested.

"Oh dear," she said, "oh dear."

"Let's not discuss it now," I said. "Let's wait until tomorrow morning, Helen. I can do it a whole lot better after I've had some sleep."

543

"Oh dear," Helen said again. "What about Muriel Goodwin?"

I told her that she did not know it yet, or at least I did not think she did.

"That's so dull of you," Helen said. "Of course she must know something."

Perhaps she might know something, but I did not want to discuss it then.

"Listen, Helen," I said. "Why don't we let this thing go for a little while? Tell me about Camilla. How is she doing at school?" but of course Helen did not want to let it go.

"Sid," she said, "look . . . Dottie Peale called up this afternoon."

"She did?" I answered. "What did she want?"

"She invited herself out here for lunch tomorrow," Helen said. "There must be some connection."

"I hope you told her she couldn't come," I said.

"Sid," she answered, "I couldn't do that—but the funny thing was, she never said a word about any of this. She didn't even sound excited—but then, that's like her, isn't it?"

"Yes," I said, "it's like her."

Of course Dottie had to talk to someone, and I could think of us listening to the details blow by blow. Of course I would have had to see her eventually, but I had hoped to have a day or two or three completely free of Melville Goodwin.

"Poor Muriel," Helen said. "After everything she's done for him, and she's just the right wife for him, too. She understands all the queer things that people like him have to do, and it *is* a queer existence, spending all your life learning how to kill people wholesale, when you think of it. After all the years she's spent, making both ends meet and working her fingers to the bone"—it always turned out that the wronged wife had been working her fingers to the bone—"it isn't fair. Somebody ought to tell her."

"All right," I said, "when he gets around to it, maybe Mel Goodwin will tell her."

Helen clasped her hands tightly and stared fixedly at the fire, and her Fortuny dress made me think of the figure of Justice in some late Victorian mural.

"Do you know what I'd do if I were Muriel Goodwin?"

"Listen, Helen," I said, "let's not get theoretical."

"I think I'd kill Dottie."

"Now, Helen," I said, "don't be so conventional."

"When I think of her sitting right here, so contented, crocheting those poor little washcloths for the new place where she was going to live," Helen said, and I found her looking at me indignantly instead of at the fire, "well, if it were I, I'd step out with somebody else and find a new life for myself so fast you wouldn't know it."

"I don't know why you bring us into it," I said, "and besides, don't you think that Mrs. Goodwin is too far along in years to start a new life?"

"Well, I'm not too far along," Helen said. "You'd be surprised if I told you of all the chances I had when you were overseas. Yes, you'd be surprised."

Our discussion had broken into fragments. We were no longer pinned down to anything definite, but then there was always a species of logic in Helen's indefiniteness.

"Listen," I said, "are we talking about you and me or about the Goodwins?"

"Darling," Helen said, "I just want to talk. Here you've been, having an interesting time, and here I've been, shut up here with nobody to talk to except Camilla and Miss Otts."

"But I thought you wanted to live here," I told her, "and what about all the interesting people? What about our new friends, Mr. and Mrs. Tom and Maida Brickley?"

I congratulated myself on remembering the Brickleys' names on top of everything else, and now they were stirred indiscriminately with the other personalities we were discussing.

"Darling," Helen said, "I never said I didn't like it here, and that reminds me that the Brickleys have asked us to dinner tomorrow night." I did not answer. There seemed to be no peace or continuity. It would be quite a day tomorrow, what with Dottie Peale for lunch, and dinner with the Brickleys.

"Darling," Helen said, "I suppose I'm provincial and old-fashioned, and that's why I usually can't seem to get into the spirit of

545

Anglo-Saxon monosyllables, but she's a bitch. I've always tried to be nice about her, but she really is a bitch."

"Who?" I asked. "Mrs. Brickley or Miss Otts?"

"Don't try to be amusing," she said. "There's only one good thing about this, if you want to call it a good thing. It might have been *you,* if she hadn't got all mixed up with the army."

"Me?" I repeated after her, and I felt righteously indignant. "You know everything about Dottie and me."

"Darling," Helen said, "don't you think I had a right to be worried when I heard that you and Dottie were on that trip to Paris? You know, she never wants to let go of anything. You were a piece of personal property, and she was simply furious when we got married."

"Why, no," I said, "she wasn't. She was awfully nice about it. She said how glad she was for me. Don't you remember?"

"Oh, Sid," Helen said, "don't you know anything about bitches? It would have been you if it hadn't been poor old Mel Goodwin, and she would have said it was all your fault basically. She's always been furious at me, and we hate each other's guts. I really don't see how I can be nice to her tomorrow."

Perhaps nothing was ever over, even when you thought it was. I remembered that long flight over the ocean in the darkened plane. I remembered that rococo sitting room in the Ritz in Paris and Dottie whistling in the bedroom. She always whistled when she fixed her face and hair. If Major General Goodwin had not been there, Dottie and I would have been a long way from home. Then I remembered those adjoining bedrooms in that bleak hotel in northern France when Dottie had asked me to kiss her in a friendly way. It was a long way from anywhere.

I pulled myself back into the present. Farouche had dropped his rubber ring on my foot and his doing so relieved the tension. He wagged his beautifully brushed tail expectantly, and Helen looked benign. When I played with Farouche, it meant that I was getting used to everything.

"Darling," Helen said, "we really ought to think about having another baby."

I knew exactly why the idea had occurred to her at that moment.

She was not thinking of the nursery and the bassinet and the good life as much as she was thinking of Dottie Peale.

There always came a time when you wearied of listening to the fallacies of self-justification because you learned finally the basic truth that no one in a jam was in a position to give you anything back. Such people were too busy with their own vagaries even for true gratitude. In the end they always did what they desired, and they might as well have done it from the first instead of making it a problem. This was the way I felt about Dottie Peale. I had studied a great many of her problems, including that of Henry Peale, whom she had not married for money or position — although she knew that everyone had thought she had — and possibly not for love either, in any accepted sense. She had married Henry Peale because she simply had to do something for someone — and there was Henry. This was what she said and what she may even have believed. Then there had been the problem of Dottie's childhood background, which I had studied with her also — why she had not been able to adjust herself to it, and why she had left home and could not possibly go back and marry a boy who, for reasons entirely his own, thought that they were engaged and wrote her letter after letter and even followed her to New York. If Dottie had returned home, as I had once pointed out to her, she could have done a great deal for other people in a selfless way, including her parents, who, though I had never seen them, struck me as having many generous and agreeable traits, in spite of what Dottie said about their narrow-mindedness and medi-ocrity. Dottie could not help it if she always reached for something more than what had been given her and if she was always in revolt. At least this is what she said, and she could illustrate these points by telling many stories about herself in a very interesting way.

Dottie was always shuffling the cards of her past and dealing them out in a sort of intricate solitaire, only for me, as she always said, be-cause I always understood her, and not for anybody else. She was very tired of having herself on her mind, but if you thought of the past, you could understand the present. There was the little private school in that small town — where her dresses had been too plain

547

and the girls had never asked her to their parties — and there had been the birthday party that her mother had made her give. Then came the state college, a dreadful place, and the cousins who had lived on a Midwestern farm, and that column in the local paper about New York by O. O. McIntyre, and the poems of Emily Dickinson and H. L. Mencken's *American Mercury*. I knew about her course in typing and shorthand. I knew how she had watched the trains go east and how she had come to New York herself one summer, thin, aloof and eager, with her overnight case and a dress she had cut from a Butterick pattern, and ten dollars in her purse. I probably knew her as well as anyone, but a time had come when Dottie Peale and I had lived through too many stories.

In the morning I remembered immediately that Dottie had invited herself to lunch. Ever since we had bought the place in Connecticut, she had been saying that she must drop in to see us. Helen had always begged her to wait until everything was decorated, and Dottie had always understood perfectly. She would not drop in suddenly, she said, although she could not wait to see Helen in her new setting. I wished that I did not know so well what Dottie would say and think. I knew she would make me think things that were disloyal to Helen, but this would not be the real reason for her coming. The reason would be to review the pros and cons of her new-found happiness.

Ever since I had worked on the night shift of the newspaper, I had been able to sleep through a morning, and it was after eleven when I awoke. It took me an instant to recollect where I was, something that still happened to me quite frequently at Savin Hill, and then I saw that it was raining and that the bare trees were dripping coldly and moistly against a grim gray sky. I saw that Helen's bed was empty, and then I saw that Camilla was standing beside me. It must have been Camilla's concentrated attention that had finally disturbed my sleep. She had not moved or spoken as I had been pulling my wits together, but suddenly she giggled in the thoughtless, rudimentary manner of childhood.

"Daddy," she said, "you look so funny waking up."

For that matter, Camilla looked pretty funny herself. She was wearing her jodhpurs and her tiny tweed coat and little stock and a gold horseshoe pin. Her hair was in a single braid, clubbed and tied with a black ribbon. She reminded me of an eighteenth-century picture of a child dressed like an adult.

"Hello," I said, "are you going riding?"

Camilla giggled again and nodded.

"You can't," I said, "it's raining."

"Oh, Daddy," Camilla said, "don't be silly. Don't you know that Mr. Delaney has his Saturday class in the indoor ring?"

It was still curious, at least to me, that Camilla should be obliged to learn to ride a horse. The idea was an anachronism. Horses were no longer a necessary means of locomotion. They were only social symbols. Camilla must ride because someday she might meet a nice boy upon another horse and marry him and live happily ever after. Fortunately she had another asset — her mother's eyes and nose and hair, because there might not be any horses or jodhpurs or Mr. Delaneys, the way the world was going. Everyone clung blindly to the hope of eventual security, and the little girl dressed in jodhpurs was a pathetic symbol of that hope. What would happen to Camilla eventually and what could I do about it? I was sure I did not know. Would she be like her mother or would she be like Dottie Peale? The future lay somewhere within her, but I could not read it. There was no solid Victorian future any longer. There were no William Ernest Henleys any longer, making us the masters of our fates and the captains of our souls.

"Mummy told me to tell you to wake up," Camilla said. "Oscar's bringing up your breakfast."

"Where's your mother now?" I asked.

"She's arranging things downstairs," Camilla said. "She acts as if there's going to be a luncheon party."

"It isn't a real party," I told her, "just one lady."

"Well," Camilla said, "good-by, Daddy. Miss Otts is waiting for me, but I'll be back for lunch."

It seemed to me when she had gone that she had left me for good already and that I had never known her. Days were too full and time moved too rapidly. I would not know much about Camilla today because Dottie Peale was coming to lunch and we were going to the Brickleys' to dinner. I remembered what old Mr. Goodwin had said to Melville in the drugstore in Hallowell. There had never been time for him to learn much about Melville Goodwin either. It seemed less and less possible to compress the details of life within the frame of time.

The wailing hum of a vacuum cleaner sounded in the living room as I came down the stairs. Mr. Brown had been brought in from outside to do the rugs, and next he would do the green carpet on the stairs. Mrs. Griscoe, the cleaning woman, was dusting the library. Oscar and Hilda were setting the dining room table, and Williams was waxing the hall floor. Helen was arranging flowers and supervising. The electric waxer and the vacuum cleaner made the house sound like an industrial plant. However, it was to have all the earmarks of a simple informal lunch — just the Skeltons at home.

Helen was wearing a whipcord suit that made her look as efficient as Dottie Peale.

"Everything looks all right, Helen," I said. "Why don't you leave it alone?" It was a useless remark, but the activity made me nervous.

"I don't see how you can sleep in the morning," Helen said. "I've been up since seven. You know how particular she is. She always sees everything."

Helen did not realize that this abnormal neatness was as revealing as untidiness. Women were more vicious and more intolerant than men.

"All right," I said, "but you'll get it looking like a feature piece in *House and Garden*."

Dottie had never let anyone forget that Helen had once worked on a similar magazine.

"You know what she used to say about Tenth Street," Helen said. "I'm not going to have her saying . . ." She stopped and called to Mrs. Griscoe and told her not to forget the powder room.

"What aren't you going to have her say?" I asked.

"I'm not going to have her say, 'Poor Sidney.' I heard her say it once."

In some ways women were surprisingly obtuse. Helen should have known that nothing she could ever do would prevent Dottie from saying, "Poor Sidney."

"Poor Sidney," I could hear her saying as soon as she got back to town, "you should see what Helen's done to him — even the dog with the rubber ring and the little girl like a picture in a Sunday supplement."

"Well," I said, "never mind it, Helen. You can say, 'Poor Mel.'"

Poor Sidney and poor Mel. Both the girls would say it.

"Sidney," Helen said, "I wish you would go upstairs and put on some older clothes so you won't look self-conscious."

"But aren't we both?" I said. "Isn't this whole effort self-conscious?"

"Oh, Sidney," Helen said, "please go upstairs and read the papers. I'm busy and I've got a headache. I want you to mix the Martinis yourself instead of having Oscar bring them in. She won't look natural until she has one in her hand. Dottie and her damn Martinis!"

As General Gooch had said, no one ever knew everything about anybody. I had never realized that Helen, who usually took a charitable view toward everyone, felt so strongly about Dottie Peale.

Upstairs I changed into a suit I had owned for years, before I had met Helen, in fact, which had been in moth balls during the war. It was a suit which I could never bring myself to throw away, because it reminded me of old times. Its knees and elbows were worn thin by old times, and I was reasonably sure that Dottie would remember it. If she did, I could imagine what she would say.

"Poor Sidney," she would say, "in a state of absolute revolt, clinging to that old brown herringbone, the suit that I made him buy before he ever met her. It was pathetic. It made me want to cry." Yet if I wore a new suit, nothing would be improved, because Dottie would say again, "Poor Sidney, completely regimented by that wife of his and overdressed as usual." Nothing would be right for Dottie Peale and nothing would be right for Helen.

I tried to concentrate on the morning news while I listened to the dripping of the rain, but instead I remembered how glad Dottie had seemed to be when Helen and I were married and all the kind things she always said about Helen, and I also recalled the kind things Helen had said about Dottie. At least my mind was off Melville Goodwin, now that I was the vertex of a triangle. It was not Dottie's fault, I was thinking, that she was a girl who could never let anything go entirely. She was a perfect example of the type that could never get on with women, and also she was the type that never got on for long with men.

"Sid," I heard Helen calling, "Sid, please come downstairs. She's here."

Helen had seen before I had that Dottie's town car, driven by Bernard, that chauffeur of hers, was turning into the white-fenced drive. Dottie Peale and I had gone a long, long way since we were working on the paper, and were very young and were very merry. Though middle age had hardly touched me, I felt a twinge of senility as I saw Dottie in the car. We had traveled a long, long way, and only a very little of it together, but here we were.

"Oh, Sid," Helen said, "not that suit," and she could remember my clothes, too, but it was too late to change again, and the car was at the door. I held an umbrella for Dottie while Bernard helped her out, not that she ever needed to be helped. Helen had done right to wear something tailored. Dottie, too, was in a suit, cool and austere, with a topaz brooch at her throat, no noisy bangles — an honest, simple girl.

"Darling," she said, "I'm so glad to see you. How's the country squire?"

Everything was as gay and rural as an Abercrombie & Fitch catalogue, in spite of the rain. "All the way up the road," she went on, "I've been wondering which ancestral mansion could be yours. Bernard called up Williams for the directions, you know. I just couldn't believe it was this one."

"Well, well," I said, "and how's the little city mouse?"

Dottie glanced at me sideways.

"Darling," she said, "I can't wait until I see absolutely everything. It all looks so exactly like you."

"That's just what I've always felt about Seventy-second Street," I said, "but I never could bring myself to tell you."

Dottie gave my arm a savage pinch.

"Oh, Jesus," she said, "shut up. Let's get in out of the rain. . . . Helen, darling, how beautiful this is!"

"Dottie, dear," Helen said, "it's so sweet of you to come out on such an awful day."

Helen and Dottie Peale were being very civilized indeed. There was no rough stuff, scarcely an awkward moment. There were no roundhouse swings or smacks of gloves. There were no cuts from glancing blows. They were so glad to see each other, so fond of each other, so mutually admiring, that it was hard to believe what Helen had said about Dottie. A mutual bond had drawn them together, because they were both so fond of me — Dottie merely in her tender, maternal way. Occasionally they discussed me as though I were not present, but also they had *so* much to say to one another. Dottie could always see everything without appearing to notice, and I knew she was not missing anything.

"Darling," I heard her say, as she and Helen walked arm and arm into the living room, and they seemed to have completely forgotten me in their joy in seeing each other, "no wonder they were sorry to lose you from that magazine. I had lunch with Diana Paul only last week, and Diana was saying that there was no one like you, with restraint and taste combined with so many new ideas. What fun you must have had fixing everything, and you've done it terribly quickly and it's all so perfect. It's — it's like a stage set for that old play *Berkeley Square,* isn't it? And yet it isn't Berkeley Square, dear. It's absolutely you, and you were so right in not consulting Sidney's taste, because Sidney has no taste, has he? It's you in your own setting. I don't really see how you can do any more about anything."

"If you say so," Helen said, "everything must be all right, Dottie, dear. I've been on pins and needles to know what you would think of the house."

Dottie laughed delightfully and affectionately.

"Darling," she said, "you must really learn not to mind what other people think. Hew to the line and let the chips fall where they may, but then there isn't a chip around here anywhere."

"All in order because of you, dear," Helen said. "Sidney doesn't let me forget your love of order for a minute." Then she, too, laughed affectionately. "But now we're on quotations, there is a divinity that shapes our ends, isn't there? Roughhew them how we may."

"Did Sidney teach you that, dear?" Dottie asked. "Sidney's a liberal education for poor girls like you and me, isn't he? You can't help learning from him, just by osmosis. Whose end, darling?"

"Yours," Helen answered, "or mine. Anybody's end."

Dottie laughed and Helen laughed. They both seemed to be having a wonderful time.

"Now, Sidney," Dottie said, and she smiled at me encouragingly, "Helen got that line from you, didn't she? Darlings, I can't tell you how I love being here. Where shall I sit so I won't be roughhewn? I don't want to perch on the wrong museum piece."

"Darling," Helen said, "I've never known a museum piece that didn't suit you."

"Now girls," I said, "suppose you both relax and we'll have a drink."

It was about time under the circumstances, because everything was growing brittle.

"Helen, dear," Dottie said, "Sidney's beginning to look positively corn-fed, isn't he? It's wonderful what you've done to him, darling."

Nothing that had been said would be forgotten, and furthermore it would probably grow to be all my fault when Helen took it up with me later.

"Now, girls," I said, "let's all take it easy, girls."

The round was over when Oscar came in with the cocktail tray.

"Let's have Martinis," I said. "Why don't you make them, Dottie?"

"Oh, no," Dottie said, "let Helen. You make them, darling."

"Sidney," Helen said, "you make them, Sidney."

Both girls were sitting up straight with hands folded in their laps and ankles crossed, like girls in dancing school waiting for a partner. They both looked austerely charming and very pretty, but I thought that Dottie's face looked drawn. The gray light from the north windows was not flattering, and she did not look as happy as she should have, considering everything. I was tempted to cut roughly through

554

her talk and ask her what the news was, as I would have if we had been alone, but then there was Helen, and the amenities. Just as I started with the cocktails, Farouche came in. He was brushed and he had a new bowknot on the top of his cranium, but like Dottie he seemed worried and distrait.

"Oh," Dottie said, "where did you ever come from, you lovely handsome man? Oh, woozums, woozums, woozums!" And she sank down on her knees and threw her arms around Farouche.

Though Farouche submitted to Dottie's embrace like a gentleman, he knew instinctively that her behavior was not genuine, and so did I. Dottie would not have gone overboard in such a manner if she had not been under some sort of tension. I was growing very tired of the feminine character, and I was thinking how many valid reasons there were for men's bars and men's clubs. Helen and I looked at each other, and she raised her eyebrows slightly. Some impulse made me take her hand, and we stood for a moment watching this erratic exhibition between Dottie and Farouche.

"Sid," she said, "hurry with those cocktails. I think we'd all better have a drink."

Such anxiety was not like Helen, who never did approve of cocktails in the middle of the day.

"All right," I said, "all right," and somehow everything was all right. It was as if I had been telling her that I liked everything she had done and that she was not like Dottie Peale. Helen was a neater, sweeter maiden from a cleaner, greener land.

The embrace was over. Dottie was back in her chair again and "Woozums" was wandering about the room distractedly, like an old man looking for his glasses.

"What is he doing?" Dottie asked. "Does he want to go out, Sidney?"

"I think he's looking for his rubber ring," I said.

"Oh, God," Dottie said, "I wish everyone weren't always looking for something. Is he happy when he gets it?"

"Yes," I said, "he seems to be."

"Oh, God," Dottie said, "I wish I could settle for a rubber ring."

For the first time since Dottie's appearance her voice was kind and natural, but her remark was surprising, because it seemed to me that she had finally settled for a rubber ring herself.

"Sid," Helen said, "don't keep stirring. They're cold enough."

I had been exposed to all of Dottie's moods. I could even classify them cold-bloodedly, and she knew I could, and perhaps she both disliked and liked me for it. As I watched her now, she was looking coyly into her Martini. She could hold a glass as carelessly and gracefully as one of those improbable girls in a Sargent portrait handled a handkerchief or fan. I do not mean by this that she drank too much. She despised people who could not manage liquor, especially women. She was just posing as The Girl with the Martini.

"Sid," she said, "did you tell Helen about Gilbert Frary?"

"Yes," I said, "and I won't forget what you did for me, Dot."

"Darling," Dottie said, "anything I did was for Helen, too. It wasn't much—just calling up some people. There's so little anyone can do for anyone else basically. . . . And Helen . . . in case you don't know it, Sid's a very good guy."

"I always had the same idea," Helen answered, "but it's nice to have it confirmed."

The shift in conversation made me wince.

"I'm wonderful," I said, "but don't be so patronizing about it."

Dottie took a delicate sip of her Martini.

"I knew you'd have the subtlety but I didn't know you'd have the guts to do what you did with Frary," she said.

"I couldn't let the home team down," I told her. "If you want to know, I've learned a lot about guts from General Goodwin."

This seemed like a graceful way of bringing Melville Goodwin into the conversation. Even if I did not approve of what had happened, I wanted Dottie to know that my loyalty lay with her and Mel if the chips were down.

"I kept thinking of Mel," I went on, "when I was slugging it out with Gilbert and the boys. You know the way Mel puts it." I was an old friend of Melville Goodwin's now that I had swallowed a Martini. I had almost been with him in the Silver Leaf Armored—almost. "You estimate the situation and then you act." I filled Dottie's glass and filled my own again. "Well, here's to Mel."

It seemed a very handsome thing to say, but Dottie looked at me as though I had been crudely clumsy, and then she blushed. I had not seen Dottie blush for years.

"No, no," she said, "never mind about Mel now. Helen, darling, here's to Sid. I'm awfully glad you've done so much for Sid."

I always disliked sentiment, and the whole thing seemed to be getting out of hand. I saw Helen's eyes open wide in her astonishment.

"God damn it," Dottie said chokingly, "I don't know what's the matter with me."

"Oh, Dottie," I heard Helen say.

First there had been that scene with Farouche, and now Dottie was dabbing her eyes with her handkerchief.

"I don't know what's the matter with me," she said again. "God damn it, don't say anything."

Fortunately I knew exactly what to say.

"Come on," I said, "and pull your socks up, Dot."

"God damn it," Dottie said, "I'm all right now. Give me another drink, Sid."

Her teeth glittered in her most impeccable smile. "Don't look so worried," she said. "It's not alcohol — just nerves, combined with all this sanitary Chippendale. Excuse me, Helen darling."

It was like pulling a rabbit from a hat. It was hard to believe that anything had upset Dottie.

"Why, here's Camilla," I heard Helen saying. "Come in, dear, and shake hands with Mrs. Peale and don't forget to curtsy."

I was singularly moved by the sight of Camilla, out of her riding clothes and all prepared by Helen, like the house, for the visitation of Dottie Peale. She looked so very shy and so small in her patent-leather slippers and her smocked dress of Liberty silk, that for once I seriously felt that I was responsible for her. What might happen to me did not have much value as long as I had done something for Camilla. It was like arriving somewhere safely.

"Why, darling," Dottie Peale said, "how sweet you look. Won't you give me a big kiss, darling?"

Dottie had often told me that she did not like small children and she knew even less than I about how to get along with them. I felt acutely embarrassed, both for her and Camilla, because I was afraid we were going to have a repetition of that exhibition with Farouche. Of course Camilla did not want to give her a big kiss, but I was proud of Camilla and of all the teachings of Helen and Miss Otts. She complied politely and restrainedly and then with the unerring instinct of a child she firmly disengaged herself from Dottie Peale.

"Oh, Helen," Dottie was saying, "she is so sweet, just a pocket edition of you, dear."

Then Camilla moved to where I was sitting and stood leaning lightly against me. I had never thought that she would want to be near me at such a time. I put my arm around her and held her tight.

"Yes," I said, "Camilla does look quite a lot like Helen."

I have often wondered what we all were thinking. I am sure we were all thinking of ourselves in our different ways, because of Camilla.

"I've always wanted to have a little girl," Dottie said.

She always wanted something, but it was not like her to drop all barriers in this way. I had never seen her so insecure, and I could think of nothing to say to fill the embarrassed gap of silence. No one spoke until Dottie spoke again.

"And I don't suppose I ever will," she said, "but then, maybe I wouldn't be very good at it."

By now there was no doubt that Dottie was deeply worried about something, and obviously it was something which she did not wish to discuss in front of Helen. She ate very little all through luncheon, although she said several times how delicious everything tasted. In the living room afterwards she did not touch her coffee, though she had been careful to ask if she could have some saccharine instead of sugar. And I remember her saying how strange it was — once she was always hungry and once she could eat and eat without gaining a single pound, but it was different now. She seemed to be putting off an inevitable moment, while Helen and I both waited. It was like the old story of the man who had dropped one shoe noisily and the man in the room below sending up word to him for heaven's sake to drop the other.

"Helen, dear," she said at last, "would you mind if I took Sid away

558

somewhere for a little while? I don't mind his repeating everything I say, but I don't seem to be able to say it to you both at once."

From the bright way Helen answered, I knew that she was as glad as I that the suspense was over. Why didn't we go into the library, she suggested. She seemed to be turning me over to Dottie very willingly.

"And keep him as long as you like," she said, "and we can all have tea later."

I listened very carefully, but I could find no sharpness in Helen's words, and I had a sense that this disappointed Dottie.

As soon as we reached the library, I knew exactly what Dottie thought of the whole layout, and it placed an undue strain on my loyalty to see her gazing superciliously at the English gentleman's books. All at once she put her arm through mine as though we both were lonely.

"Oh, my God," she said, "poor Sid."

I could not think of an appropriate answer. I wanted to be loyal to Helen, who had tried so hard with that library, but I felt my own self-pity.

"Poor Sid," she said again. "This isn't what you ever wanted, is it, darling?"

"Not exactly," I answered, "but it doesn't really matter. It's a minor detail, Dot."

I might not have had everything, but I had more than she would ever have, and at least I knew that you had to give up some part of yourself to get anything you wanted.

"I know it is," she said. "Sid, I'm awfully glad for you, I really am. . . . And the patter of little feet. This won't be such a bad place for the children's hour."

I wished she did not see everything and know everything. There was never any intellectual privacy when I was with her.

"All right," I said, "that's one way to put it, Dot."

"Damn you," she said, "don't try to be slick about it. All right, I'm jealous of you. God, all this burns me up. I hate you and still I'm glad for you. How the hell did it ever work this way? Oh, God, I'm so unhappy, darling."

Then she threw her arms around me and pressed her head against my shoulder — but not the way she had with Farouche. It was an excellent thing that Helen was not there.

"Oh, Sid," she sobbed, "oh, God!"

"Don't," I said, "don't, Dot."

It was useless to say "don't." There was that destructive driving force inside her. No man, nothing, would ever answer her desire, and unfortunately we both knew it.

"Sid," she said, "please hold me for just a minute. You've got to help me, Sid."

"Help you about what, Dot?" I asked.

She pushed herself away from me, but she continued to hold my hand.

"All right," she said, "all right. Of course you know what. . . . That God-damned brass-hat general of yours, Major General Melville A. Goodwin, and to hell with him! Do you know what he wants? He wants me to marry him and now the whole damned Joint Chiefs of Staff in Washington are beginning to expect me to. Oh, Sidney, I can't. You've got to help me, Sid."

I had never seen her look so empty or defeated. Her words had all her old speciousness, but they had taken a lot out of her. She turned away from me and took a few unsteady steps toward the armchair by the library fireplace, and curiously enough it was the chair that Melville Goodwin had always used. She slumped into it heavily, with none of her beguiling schoolgirl manner. There was no swift moving of the skirt, no crossing of the ankles. Her jacket, so carefully cut to show the arrogant boyish slimness of her figure, was a mass of untidy wrinkles. Her skirt had ridden up above one knee, showing the edge of her slip with its meticulously embroidered border, and nothing could have confirmed her wretchedness more eloquently. For once in her life for a few moments Dottie did not care how she looked. I might have been alone there, surrounded by an aura of Chanel Five and my own disordered thoughts. It was strange how trivial some of them were. Really, I was thinking, Dottie should pull down her dress. She had beautiful legs, but now they were sprawling and inartistic. Really, I was thinking, she ought to sit up, and I sounded aloof and unsympathetic when I answered her, although I did not intend to be.

"Didn't it ever occur to you," I said, "that he might have honorable intentions?"

I should have been beside her with my arm around her, consoling poor Dottie, whom I had known so long, but I did not seem able to throw myself into it.

"Oh, Sid," she said, "please don't. Please say you're fond of me."

"All right," I said, "I'm fond of you, but stop showing your slip."

She arranged things in a single indescribable motion. Suddenly the wrinkles of the jacket were gone and the slip was gone and the skirt and the nylon stockings were all synchronized again.

"For God's sake, sit down yourself," she said.

I thought I had built up a perfect tolerance to Dottie Peale. I should not have cared personally that she could not bring herself to marry a major general in the United States Army with whom I was acquainted. The step had nothing whatsoever to do with my life theoretically, and yet I cared. She had no right to ask for my sympathy, but still she had it.

"Darling," she said, "it's such an awful mess. You are always so right about everything."

"So right about what?" I asked her.

"Oh, about the whole business," she said. "You never did approve of it, did you? Not even back in Paris."

"No," I said, "of course I didn't."

"I don't see why you couldn't have told me more about him," she said. "I never knew he would take everything so seriously. I honestly don't see how I could have known it would go as far as this."

Somehow it was getting to be my fault. Poor Mel Goodwin, I was thinking, who had laid everything he had at her feet. He was worth a thousand of her, but worth did not tip the scale. In the end, when he had given everything, she did not want what he had to offer. It was absolutely like her to draw back in the end. Instinct for survival was working, and Melville Goodwin could go overboard. In any shipwreck it was always women first.

"Didn't you want him to be serious?" I asked.

"Sid, don't you see how I feel?" she asked. "And won't you please sit down and listen? I want to be fair, darling, absolutely fair. Of course I didn't know it would come to this, and he was so unhappy and so completely maladjusted. Sid, I only wanted to make him happy."

I sat down in the other armchair opposite her.

"And so you made him still more maladjusted," I said.

"Darling," she answered, "I wish you'd try to pull yourself together and understand. Of course I know he loves me, but I didn't know he would love me in this way. He's so undeviating, darling. Do you remember that poem he keeps reciting? 'Push off and sitting well in order smite . . .' I'll scream if I hear it again. When the brass wears off there's still more brass." She stopped and looked at me sharply. "And did you ever see those damn clothes of his — that tweed coat and his double-breasted suit?"

I did not answer, but they mattered. Disillusion always came from details.

"I don't mean to be unkind," she said, "and I know part of this is my fault, and I know men always blame women in the end. Of course I was carried away. I've been so lonely, Sid, and well, damn it, he's a man."

"I've heard you say that before," I said.

"Sid," she said, "I know that what I'm saying sounds awful. I still love him — in theory, but it's all too much for me to·manage. Sidney, please be kind."

"All right," I said, "I'm being kind."

I could not unsnarl the raveled ends of her meaning. Her love was always limited, and perhaps she recognized this as she sat there wretchedly, twisting her hands nervously, pulling at the loose edges of her life.

"Darling," she said, "it *did* seem possible at first. I want you please to believe that. I don't suppose I ever thought things out clearly. I didn't want to think, because I was happy. Everything would have been possible if he'd only been a little more like other people, more like you and me, but he's so damned — so damned honest, darling."

562

There was truth in all her sophistry, and her saving grace was that she could see it occasionally. Melville Goodwin *was* more honest than either of us could ever be.

"Darling," she said, "I don't know why I didn't see this coming. Of course we did make plans, but I didn't think he believed them any more than I did. Do you know what he actually wants now? He wants to retire from the service and for us to go away somewhere alone together. He wants us to take a little bungalow or something and live—in Carmel, California, darling." Her voice ended on a higher note.

It was not the incongruity of Carmel, California, that had torn it—this was exactly the place that Melville Goodwin would want to live—and it was not the bungalow. It was the facing of a definite fact and all its implications, including the character of Mel Goodwin himself, in the cold north light.

"And that isn't all,'" she went on. "Darling, do you know what happened yesterday?" She did not expect me to answer, and it was doing her good to tell someone everything. "Darling, yesterday an-other general came, an old one. God, he was polite—something like a priest. Damn it, give me a cigarette."

She was feeling better, or she would not have asked for one, but her hands were shaking.

"What was his name?" I asked.

"Oh, he was someone Mel always talks about," she said. "Grimshaw, Foghorn Grimshaw. Why does everyone have some damned nickname in the army?"

I had often wondered myself, but her words were moving faster.

"And do you know what he wanted? He wanted to tell me all about Mel and he wanted to congratulate me, darling . . . but they don't want Mel to leave the service. They want us to wait until everything can be arranged properly. Time, he kept saying, time. . . . But Mel wants to go to Carmel, or else he wants to be somewhere with troops. Oh, God, I'm ashamed."

"Well," I said, "you ought to be. You haven't any right to ruin Goodwin's life."

"Darling," she said, "I don't want to ruin his life. I'd much rather have ruined yours. We could have gone to hell together, and we would have had a lot of the same ideas." Her face brightened. "Would you like to go to hell with me?"

"No," I said, "not right at the moment, Dot."

"I thought of it when we were on that plane. If Mel hadn't been in Paris . . ." She was retreating from fact again. "All right," she said, "but don't say you never have thought of it. . . . Sid, aren't you going to help me?"

I was thinking of Mel Goodwin and I felt a sudden surge of revolt.

"No," I said. "Damn it, Dottie, if you feel that way, hurry up and tell him so."

"But I don't want to tell him," she said. "There must be some other way. I don't want to hurt him. . . . He believes in me. . . . No one's ever believed in me the way he does."

"He'd better stop," I said.

It was exactly like her, I was thinking, not to be able to say yes and not to be able to say no, and to try to put the burden on someone else.

"Sid," she said, "will you tell him?"

"Certainly not," I said. "Dot, you ought to be ashamed."

"Damn you," Dottie said, "I told you I was ashamed. Can't you be kind to me, Sidney?"

"No," I said.

She was struggling like a struck fish.

"Sid," she said, "suppose I went to see her and just told her everything. Suppose I told her how terrible it is, and it's all a big mistake. I'd rather do that than tell him."

"Who?" I asked.

"Oh, hell!" Dottie said. "Mrs. Goodwin, that dreadful wife of his — Muriel."

"If you do that, he'll lose Muriel, too," I said.

I had never suspected that she would arrive at the old chestnut of the confrontation of the wife and mistress, but as I considered it, I realized that Dottie enjoyed dramatic scenes. Her mind was still vacillating like a needle, between degrees of reason. She was too egocentric to realize that by trying to let herself out the easy way, she might create a situation with Muriel that was irreparable. I could not see Muriel accepting this sort of annunciation.

"Sid," she said, "suppose you tell her."

"Dottie," I said, "I'm not in this, and Mrs. Goodwin isn't either, unless she refuses to take him back. You'll have to take it up with Mel Goodwin, Dot. He's the one you're letting down."

There was not much need for retribution in the life hereafter. You usually paid for the party while you were still on earth.

"Why not face it?" I told her. "You've been through this with other men."

"Darling," Dottie said, "that isn't fair. It wasn't the same with you and me. We had other things on our minds."

We must have both thought about this through a second or two of painful silence. You always had to pay for every party.

"I wasn't referring to you and me," I said. "Let's forget it, Dot."

"Oh, hell," Dottie said. "You didn't believe in Santa Claus. . . . Darling, no one else I've ever known ever threw in everything the way he has. Darling, he must fight like he can love."

I thought of the young Melville Goodwin, just married, just out of the Point, just before he went overseas, walking down Sixth Avenue with Muriel and hearing that old song.

Dottie was sitting up straight. She had picked up all her frankness and confusion and had packed it away. She might have been talking to her lawyer about business matters.

"Sid," she said, "are you going to let me down?"

"No one's letting you down, Dot," I said. "I can't pick up the check."

"By God," Dottie said, "I'll never trust you or anyone again."

She had twisted everything around, as she always could.

"You never have, Dot," I said.

She stood up and I stood up.

"God," she said, "I hate your guts. I guess I'd better be leaving now, but I do want to say good-by to poor Helen. Will you have someone call Bernard, please?"

I opened the library door, and she walked past me. She hated my guts, but then, she had hated them a good many times before and again I was thinking "If you can fight like you can love, good night, Germany."

"Helen darling," I heard her saying, "I'm terribly sorry I kept Sidney so long. I had no idea it was so late, and I have to be back in time for dinner. Sidney's calling Bernard."

I was glad to be able to tell Helen about it all, instead of keeping it to myself. At least there was a chance now of bringing some order into Melville Goodwin's problem. The worst of it was that I had once been almost like Melville Goodwin. Thank God Dottie was gone, I kept thinking.

"You ought not to be so hard on her," Helen said. "She can't help it, Sid."

It all went to show that no one should risk interfering with other people's lives. Dottie and the Goodwins could work it out themselves from now on.

"Don't say you don't care," Helen said. "Of course you care what's going to happen to him and poor Muriel. She certainly must know everything by now."

Helen and I were like good little children who had behaved themselves. We were safe at Savin Hill.

"Why are you so sure she knows?" I asked her.

"Any woman can tell," Helen answered. "It's just a matter of how she's going to take it."

Things never seemed to settle down, there in the country. I never suspected that Muriel Goodwin would be with us all by herself spending Monday night, but then perhaps this was inevitable, since I was growing to be the greatest living authority on Dottie Peale.

XXXIV

And She Never Dropped a Stitch

It was cold and windy on Monday night. The house looked even larger than it had when I had first seen it, now that the trees were bare. Its size engulfed me suddenly, almost like a return to consciousness, as I heard Williams asking me what the orders would be for tomorrow. The wind was whistling past the house. This business of trying to spread myself between New York and Connecticut would be too much, I was afraid, in winter.

"I'll tell you what to do," I said. "Ask Mrs. Skelton tomorrow morning what the plans are."

I wanted to get inside out of the cold, and when I was in the hall, Oscar took my hat and coat.

"I've had my dinner," I told him. "Where's Mrs. Skelton?"

"She's in the living room, sir," Oscar said.

I could not understand why Helen had not come into the hall to meet me as she usually did after my trip from the city. I felt a little neglected, seeing that the house had been Helen's idea. If I had really had my choice, we all would have still been in New York, and I would be entering an apartment just a few blocks away from the office. By the time I reached the living room I was thinking longingly of the place in the Fifties where we had lived.

"Hello, dear," Helen said. "I didn't know you'd be so late. Here's Muriel Goodwin."

Helen spoke as though I were Camilla being prepared for company, and I had certainly not expected any. Not until Helen had mentioned her, did I see that Mrs. Melville Goodwin was seated on the sofa, working on another washcloth, finishing some border stitches quickly so she could leave it and greet me. It was the wash-cloth as much as the apparition of Muriel Goodwin that confused me. My first thought was that it was utterly inappropriate, under the circumstances, for her to be crocheting another of those things, and then I remembered that the threads of Melville Goodwin were being removed from Dottie Peale's tapestry.

"Don't get up. You might drop a stitch," I said.

"Oh, no," she said, "I never drop them," and she held out her hand graciously, as though Helen and I were young people on the post on whom she was making an informal call which she should have made some time before.

"I just called up rather on the spur of the moment," she said. "Helen was most hospitable and sweet and asked me to come out for the night. I had run up to New York to see Pamela Hardee — that's an old army family, really old army, who were stationed with us at Colon — and then I thought of you and Helen, and I thought it might be better for Melville if he were by himself a day longer."

It was an effort for me not to look questioningly at Helen, but the situation was obviously under control, and Muriel Goodwin was the chairman of the board conducting the meeting.

"We've been having such a nice time," she was saying, "talking about everything under the sun all through supper, especially about children and husbands. I told Helen not to call you up. I didn't want you to be worried about my being here."

I wanted very much to know whether Helen had told her any-thing about Dottie Peale, but there was no way of finding out.

"I'm awfully glad to see you," I said.

"I'm glad, too," Mrs. Goodwin answered. "I only had such a short glimpse of you in Washington, Sidney. I was just telling Helen I wished you were both in the service, too — but it's funny, I still keep on feeling as though you were."

At last I felt it might be polite to look at Helen, but she only smiled at me unhelpfully.

"We've only been talking in a very general way," Mrs. Goodwin said again, "about children and husbands, but not about anything in particular."

She seemed anxious for me to know that I had missed nothing, but I knew, as she looked up at me from her work, that she was no longer going to talk about nothing in particular. She was going to talk about everything. It was not a pleasant prospect for the end of any evening.

"Sidney," Helen said, "I think I'd better go upstairs and leave you both together."

"Don't run away, dear," Muriel Goodwin said. "Of course I'm here to talk about the General — but there's nothing you shouldn't hear."

"Sidney," Helen said, "I wish you'd please sit down," and she sounded almost like Dottie Peale. "I don't know why I can't ever stop Sidney from prowling around the room."

"It's all right," Mrs. Goodwin said, and her smile was sympathetically gracious. "Let him if he wants to. Mel often does, when I'm talking things over with him."

"I'm sorry," I said, and I found a chair and pulled it near the sofa where Mrs. Goodwin sat. She waited for me, giving me time to settle myself, and I found myself doing this hastily and guiltily, like a young officer called suddenly into conference. She was patient. She even waited a moment longer than was necessary, and then she spoke again.

"I know you're both fond of Melville," she said. "He has a gift for making friends. I've been very touched by how many people are concerned about him at present. Now General Grimshaw . . . Did Melville ever mention him — Foghorn Grimshaw?"

She smiled again, this time at Helen, and the army had taken over. She was no longer the General's wife dropping in to call. She was closer now to being the spokesman at an army conference, giving a thumbnail sketch of background material.

"You know, dear," she said to Helen, "Sidney made a very favorable impression on General Grimshaw. He went out of his way to speak of Sidney, and Goochy likes Sidney — he was Melville's old chief of staff in France — and Robert liked him so much, too. That's why I can't help feeling that you're all in the family." And she smiled at me again.

Muriel was taking over, and she was running things very well. She was not even being a brave little woman. It was not fair, perhaps, but in a way I could sympathize with Melville Goodwin. He had been away a long time and had become used to running things for himself.

"I admit that General Grimshaw and General Gooch, too, know the General very well," Muriel Goodwin was saying. The only sign of repression that I could detect was her impersonal reference to General Goodwin as "the General." She had raised the barrier of rank and had deliberately made him a symbol, just as Victorian wives had once referred to their husbands as "Mister," even in the bedroom. "But I know the General rather well myself, and I've known him longer than anyone else. I've seen him grow. Now they are talking to me of waiting, and of time curing everything. Of course I know all about waiting. You see, you have to, if you're married in the service . . . but I would really like to know something definite, and no one will tell me."

She had woven a large part of the General's life, and now at last she was getting somewhere. I was forgetting where we were. I was following again in the parade after Melville Goodwin.

"Of course a part of me thinks of Mel as a person and as my husband," she said, "but I realize too that ever since I was a girl in Hallowell, another part of me has always thought of what he means to other people, and what he stands for. I suppose this happens more in the service than anywhere else. If an officer dies, his wife can always remember what he has meant, not only to her, but to the service. Now I've had a good deal to do with making the General what he is."

I was afraid she would speak of self-sacrifice, and it would have disappointed me if she had, but she went straight ahead marshaling her facts.

"Melville has his record, and no one can take that impersonal part of him away from me. He's something more than *my* Melville Goodwin. Do you see what I mean when I say I don't think of him entirely as a person?"

She paused and turned her head toward me abruptly, and her

gray-blue eyes repeated the question. I had often thought how pretty she must have been when she was a girl, and I had no impression of faded beauty now. Although her bluish-gray hair and her plump figure made her look older than Melville Goodwin, she also looked wiser. The motion of her hands stopped. She laid the washcloth gently on her knees, and waited patiently to be sure I understood.

"You mean," I said, "that you think of him as government property?"

She nodded to me quickly and pulled a long loop of thread through with her hook. I noticed that Helen was looking at me in a proud, complacent way that made me hope that I was not becoming a symbol myself.

"I hoped you'd say that," she said. "I'm so glad you understand, and I do hope Helen will. I suppose I'm talking from the point of view of other service wives, and it's hard for people on the outside sometimes to see it. There's been so little ever written about service wives, hasn't there?"

I turned my thoughts dutifully to literature, but I could only recall a few brief sketches of army women in the short stories of Kipling and a few lines in *Departmental Ditties* and *Barrack Room Ballads*. There were also pages from Lever, but then there was Thackeray.

"Well, there are the Newcomes," I said.

Her whole face brightened. Somehow I had never thought of her as reading Thackeray.

"Oh," she said, "the Old Campaigner. I hope you don't think I'm like her. I've always been afraid you might."

"No," I said, "I thought you were at first, but I don't think so now."

She laughed, and when she did, she was almost like a girl who had been paid a compliment.

"Thackeray was so unfair," she said. "He did nicely with the colonel, but when he came to her, he only made a caricature. It's unfair, because army wives really have as much to do with the service as the men. Now take my General. I don't think Melville would ever have made general if I hadn't prodded him sometimes. . . . I wish Melville didn't know this, too. . . . We might have been happier if

I hadn't been so ambitious — but at least I've done something for the service, and the service is more important than Mel or me."

Muriel Goodwin stopped again, and memories of the Goodwins in Tientsin, Schofield, Panama, Benning and Bailey crowded uninvited into the living room. These and certain others had become as vivid to me as the footage of a documentary film. There was little Mel Goodwin fighting that Stickney boy at school, Mel Goodwin studying algebra with Muriel Reece, the first kiss at the Sunday school picnic, Goodwin at the Point, and Goodwin, captain of Company A. I was with him near Château-Thierry when the machine guns opened up. I encountered him walking back wounded in North Africa, and I could hear the enlisted man saying that he was a Goddamned fighting bastard, those words that he wanted on his tombstone. Melville Goodwin had been an officer who earned every cent of money that the taxpayers had paid out on him.

"You know" — and the voice of Muriel Goodwin took over again, like that of a lecturer in a darkened room — "Melville is difficult sometimes. I've sometimes thought he never wanted rank. I don't mean that he's afraid of it, but he's like an absent-minded professor sometimes. Of course we both knew that Melville would be a general one day, when his orders came for the War College, but all Melville really cares about is the practical side of war. I've often thought he'd rather be a colonel, because he would be nearer to the front. Well . . . now he's a general, and I'm very proud. . . . He can't help being a general now . . . and perhaps I've done all I can for him, but I can't bear to think of his not keeping on and being a lieutenant general. . . . Dear me, I've talked a lot, but I've had a reason for it." She laid down her crocheting again and gave me all her attention. "There's not much reason to discuss the personal side of Mel and me," she said. "The boys are all grown up, and besides, I'm old enough to know that certain things do happen some times, but, Sidney . . . I've got to know what to do next . . . and I have to come to you, because he met . . . *her* through you, Sidney."

There was no way of glossing it over, although Helen was always saying that men always stuck together. I could only try to make her think kindly of Melville Goodwin, when there was little reason why she should.

"How much has he told you," I asked, "about all this?"

"Why, he's never told me anything," she said. "Poor Mel, he's only getting ready to tell me, and if you want to know, I'm pretty tired of waiting."

I was relieved to see that Helen was standing up.

"I think I ought to leave you alone here," Helen said. "Don't you really think so?"

"Don't be silly, dear," Mrs. Goodwin said. "I'm the only one who doesn't know all about Mel. Please don't go."

I watched Helen sit down again, and once again, as they put it in Muriel Goodwin's service, I was carrying the ball.

"Of course," I began, "in a place like the ETO . . ." but Muriel Goodwin stopped me.

"Oh, Sidney," she said, "of course I know what men do in a war theater. Of course I know he met her in Paris, and of course I know that her name is Mrs. Peale, and that she's living on Seventy-second Street in New York, and of course I know she's pretty. Mel left her picture in his suitcase — Mel, who always talks about security!"

She laughed in a kindly way that included me in the little joke, but I did not feel like laughing.

"Don't you think it would be easier," I asked her, "if you told me everything else you know, and then we could start from there?"

She nodded, and I could think of her again as young Mrs. Melville Goodwin.

"I knew you'd be loyal to him," she said, "but please don't be like the rest of them and tell me it's a passing phase. I haven't lived all my life with plaster saints" — when I heard that expression, it made me think of Goochy — "in case you haven't noticed, Sidney, there is quite a little sex in the army. There are unattached officers who are feeling lonely, and there are all the marriages that don't seem to work. . . . When I was in Manila and Mel was out on maneuvers, there was someone who wanted me to leave Mel. . . . I can understand what Mel's been going through. I'm only mentioning it to show that I know a few things, Sidney. Men are simple when they fall in love and lose their sense of proportion, and Mel isn't built for it. There's the telephone bill with the New York calls and those trips to New York, and everyone covering up — even Enid. . . . He's like a little boy in some ways. . . . He's even talked to me about her."

"I thought you said he hadn't," I told her.

"Oh, not in that way," she answered, "only subtly — a Mrs. Peale in New York, whom he had met in Paris, and I must meet her, because he would like to know what I thought of her. We ought to meet more outside people — it sounds like Mel, doesn't it? It sounds like any man." There was hardly any bitterness, and she was smiling. "Any woman can tell when her man's infatuated, but what I want to know is . . . does Mel really love her, Sidney? . . . Because if he does . . . he'd better have her. If he wants her, I don't want him." She tossed the washcloth down, and perhaps General Goodwin was crocheted out.

I felt as though I had been thrown hard against the wall of her composure, and I was very glad I was not Melville Goodwin. I was also glad that I did not make my living at the bar, but it was my turn now to do what I could for Mel. I tried to sound measured and confident, and as wise as Foghorn Grimshaw, but it was a very sour attempt.

"Before you make up your mind," I began, "you'd better let me tell you what I can about Mel and Dottie Peale." I cleared my throat as if I were about to deliver a formal address. "I met him in Normandy when I was a PRO. I had never thought much of the brass, but I wish you could have seen him there. If you had, you might not be thinking of him along the lines you are thinking now." I could hear my sincerest radio voice, but I was not satisfied with it. "Well, I was a PRO . . ."

Next I was on the plane again with all those VIPs and Dottie Peale. Then we were in Paris listening to that confidential lecture on the Battle of the Bulge, with the unnecessary guards outside the door.

"Oh dear, they always say that, don't they?" Mrs. Goodwin was saying. "'Git thar fustest with the mostest men.'"

We were in the Ritz again in that alien sitting room, with the pressed duck and the champagne; and Melville Goodwin, warmed by his environment, was the great captain who understood the fog of battle. I was trying to explain Dottie Peale again, as I had often endeavored to explain her to Helen. Dottie always knew how to make men comfortable in the same degree that she made women uncomfortable. There was wistful appeal to her restiveness and her discontent, especially in the neighborhood of a war, where no one could be content. It was inevitable that Melville Goodwin should have been attracted by her. Plenty of other people had sought for a love object in a war zone.

I was doing my best for Melville Goodwin, but neither Helen nor Muriel showed sympathy or enthusiasm. I was only saying that Paris was a long way from home, and behavior was not to be measured according to peacetime standards.

"And besides," I said, "without any reflection on him — as you said yourself — he's a pretty simple guy along those lines."

It was merely, I was saying, what one might call an off moment of infatuation. Dottie would never have given him further thought if it had not been for that incident with the Russian soldier in Berlin. Muriel Goodwin frowned, but she picked up her work again, which gave me a note of hope.

"I thought everything would be the way it always was, when I saw him at the airport," she said.

"It would have been," I told her, "if she hadn't called him up. You can't blame it all on him. She's a very persistent girl."

She was rolling up the washcloth, and I braced myself. She put it in her bag and jerked the mouth of the bag together.

"I know," she said quietly. ". . . Well, that's all there is, isn't it? . . . Helen, I wonder if you have a sleeping pill? I hate small women who think they're perfect, but it's a little hard to take, after all this time. I don't want to be alone with this all night."

I wished I were back in the ETO again, in a world without women, and I wished that Melville Goodwin had died, as he very well might have and should have, in North Africa or Salerno or somewhere along the Rhine.

"You may have a right to be hard on him," I said, "but I don't think he meant this to go so far. He only went overboard after he was assigned to Plans. He wanted to get away from the whole thing."

"Of course I knew he wouldn't like Plans," she went on. "He never knows what's good for him."

"He thinks you had something to do with it," I said.

That technical reference to the army appeared to disturb her more than anything else I had said. She seemed to be more emotionally involved with Plans than she was with Melville Goodwin.

"Of course I had something to do with it," she said. "I've always had to do that sort of thinking for him. He has to be in Plans."

Again I began to feel sympathetic for Melville Goodwin, and suddenly I shared some of his exasperation. If I had not, I would never have spoken so bluntly.

"Well," I said, "men like to lead lives of their own sometimes, or they like to be allowed to think they do. Now take me. I don't always like what's arranged for me either — but I haven't Goodwin's guts." I wished that Helen were not there, and I spoke more rapidly. "You can't always blame men when something gets to be too much."

She did not answer, and I went on right down the line. "Besides, Muriel, there's something you ought to know. . . . Whenever Dottie gets something, she wants something else. She and Mel haven't much in common, you know, and I've an idea she's losing interest in him already."

I felt in my pockets for a pack of cigarettes, but I could not find one, so I got up and walked across the room looking for one.

"In fact, she's told me so," I added.

Dottie Peale was a very clever girl. She could usually get her way in anything. I had given her message to Muriel.

"There are cigarettes on the table beside you, Sidney," Helen said, "not over there, and Mrs. Goodwin — I mean Muriel — might like a cigarette."

"Thank you," Muriel Goodwin said, and she took a white jade

holder from her workbag. "It's pretty, isn't it? Melville gave it to me when we were in Manila. . . . So she's losing interest. . . . Why should she?"

All at once I thought of the time she had handed Melville Goodwin the bayonet at the fairgrounds, and I could almost hear the militia colonel shouting Hooray for Company C.

"That's almost too much, isn't it? That really makes me angry."

She reached in her workbag and pulled out the washcloth. "I know sometimes Mel is — well, heavy, and sometimes he's terribly intense, and if you hear his stories again and again — but she can't have heard them so often. Poor Mel, he's always a problem whenever he's on a staff."

Muriel Goodwin dropped her crocheting abruptly and stood up. "What time is it?" she asked.

It was after eleven o'clock. We had been working for quite a while on Melville Goodwin.

"If I could use the telephone," she said, "I'd better call up Washington. Ellen Grimshaw might still be up, and I can fly down in the morning."

I went with her to the library to turn on the lights.

"I want to speak to Washington, D. C.," she was saying when I left her. "The number is Decatur . . ." and then she was spelling it, "D-e-c-a-t-u-r . . ."

It occurred to me that it was a pity that the late Admiral Decatur was navy and not army.

Helen was standing by the dying embers of the fireplace. Her dark hair, her profile and her velvet housecoat gave her the sentimental look of a Burne-Jones or a Rossetti, and I was sure that her whole pose was planned.

"Helen," I said, "please don't start striking attitudes."

"Sidney," Helen said, "why did you say that in front of her?"

"Say what in front of her?" I asked.

"About your wanting to lead your own life sometimes — right in front of her."

"I said men like to be allowed to think they do," I told her, "and

577

you allow me to think I do — usually. You even make me want to do what you want — usually."

"You didn't say that last part," Helen said. "Sidney, if you want, we can move. You know I'm always willing to do anything you want."

"You know damned well I don't want to move," I said.

At least the air was clearer, and she did not look so aggressively like a Rossetti.

"Let's get this straight," I said. "You're not Mrs. Goodwin, and I'm not Melville Goodwin. Let's just be Mr. and Mrs. Winlock. I'm happier being Winlocks."

"I wish you'd forget about the Winlocks," she said.

"All right," I said, "I'll forget about them."

We stood there waiting. Whether we wanted or not, we were in that constrained position of a host and hostess waiting for their guest to finish her call.

"Sidney?" Helen said.

"Yes?" I said.

"Did you notice? She dropped her washcloth on the floor. Please pick it up and put it on the sofa beside her bag."

"Why?" I asked.

"Because she wouldn't like us to know she forgot it." I picked up the washcloth guiltily and quickly. "She's been trying so hard to be a brave little woman."

"She's the wife of a soldier," I said.

"Don't make fun of her," Helen said. "You know it's been terrible, because nothing ever broke."

"Maybe nothing in her ever has broken," I said. "Maybe nothing in her ever will."

"Sidney," she asked, "do you think she cares about him?"

"Yes," I said, "she cares for what he is."

"You know that isn't what I mean," she said. "If you really love someone, it doesn't matter what he is."

"Of course she loves him," I said, "but love isn't a constant quality. It has its ups and downs like anything else, and it varies all the time."

Helen shook her head.

"It doesn't with a woman," she answered. "It never does."

"Well, it does with a man," I said.

"Well, I love you," Helen said, "and I don't care what you are."

I cared very much, but no one else should have heard us discuss it, especially Muriel Goodwin, and there she was, in the doorway, and I could not tell how long she had been standing there or how much she might have heard — but I knew as soon as she spoke.

"Yes," she said. "Yes, of course I love him, and it is something that doesn't change, even if you think it does."

She had assumed her best reviewing-stand attitude. I remember her blue-gray hair and her black broadcloth suit and even her plump stocky figure, but again I was not conscious of age. There was absolutely nothing to say.

"I wish it weren't so late," she said. Her voice was perfectly steady, but her shoulders began to shake. "I ought to be back in Washington. Please don't say that I don't love him," and then she sobbed, ". . . She must be a damn fool."

It was no place for a man. Muriel Goodwin must have hated to have me see her with all defenses down, and she pulled herself together. "Sidney," she said, "will you give me my bag please? It's where I left it on the sofa."

I was glad that Helen had told me to pick up the washcloth. Muriel Goodwin was looking for a handkerchief, of course, but instead she found the washcloth.

"I never thought I'd cry into this," she said. "I'm sorry, I always hate crying women. Good night, Sidney."

"Let me go up with you," Helen said. "Don't worry about anything now. We can fix everything in the morning."

"Good night, Muriel," I said. "If you need anything, ask Helen, won't you?"

But she did not need anything any longer. She was the General's wife again and I was the young officer on the post, with all the proper loyalties.

"Of course Mel will have to be sent somewhere," she said. "I'm glad I reached Ellen Grimshaw. Mel mustn't ever know. You understand that, don't you?"

579

"Yes," I said.

"And, Sidney . . ."

"Yes?" I said.

"Will you call about a plane reservation, please . . . and it would be nice if I had an alarm clock."

When I was alone, I went into the pantry and poured myself a drink and brought it back into the living room. The women had gone upstairs — my wife and Melville Goodwin's — and in spite of the silence that surrounded me, I did not seem to be entirely by myself. Melville Goodwin seemed to be there with me, and it was not an unpleasant illusion either. I could almost think of myself saying respectfully:

"Sir, won't you have one, too?"

Wherever he was, I was sure that he needed one. His shadow was there with me, but his course had been set. We had been through a lot together, but now it was over. I never liked to drink alone, but I certainly needed a drink.

"Well," I said aloud in that quiet room, "here's looking at you, Mel."

We had been through a lot together, although it was hard to define exactly where our lives had touched. It all was a sort of coincidence to which one grew accustomed in the war. In those unnatural days, the duty, as the navy put it, was forever throwing you into contact with some stranger with whom you were obliged to face some uncertainty and whose character you came to know from every angle. Then there would be new orders. You would pack up and say good-by and move, and in spite of all the closeness and enforced congeniality, you knew that you would never see George, or whoever it was, again. You would never see the sergeant again who took you up to the lines or the pilot who flew you over the ocean and with whom you spent an evening drinking bourbon at Prestwick. You would never see that fresh-faced young lieutenant who had come from the University of Iowa. You would never again, so help you, see that Regular Army bastard, Colonel So-and-so, who made things hot for you in Paris, and you would never see the British major on liaison who was on the trip with you to Cairo. It was always good-by to all that, for none of those people belonged in a peacetime setup, and it was the same with Melville Goodwin. He, too, was a throwback from the war, and he had already become a shadow. He was someone who would never be real again unless there was another war.

This was what I thought, but I had forgotten about the photographs, those signed documents that sealed friendships in the service, and I had forgotten, too, that service friendships were less casual than friendships in an ordinary life. For in the service, friendship took the place of material possession, and I had forgotten service loyalty. I should have known that Melville Goodwin was someone who would never say good-by.

When Muriel Goodwin left at six-thirty the next morning, after kissing Helen, she kissed me also, hastily but efficiently. It was a gesture of affection, but she was also obeying a warmhearted convention of service life. She was indicating that I was in the circle of the close friends of the General. It was the formal embrace used by women in America, as it was used by Latin males in other regions, and she would have kissed Goochy in an identical manner, if he were leaving for parts unknown. There was also a sense of finality to her kiss — like an honorable discharge from the service, accompanied by one of those gallant letters of commendation that were so freely passed around in Washington after V-J Day.

I had asked her, I remember, whether she did not want me to go with her and see her aboard her plane, but she would not hear of this. It would have made her, she said, feel too much like a dear old lady, and Helen and I had done too much for her already, more than we would ever know, and besides, she only had a light overnight bag, if she could not find a porter.

"And, Helen dear," she said, "I have a long piece of Chinese embroidery with a blue border and purple dragons with gold tongues that I couldn't resist buying once from a little man in Baguio. I want to send it to you, because I think it might cheer up the front hall. It would be perfect for that empty space under the stairs. I wish you'd hang it there to remember us by."

I had a quick mental picture, not helped by the unseemly hour, of ornate purple silk stitching against the tropical green wallpaper. She had no taste, in the accepted sense, any more than Mel Goodwin, but, by God, if she did send it, we would hang it there, just to remember them by. It was like the Luger automatic and Adolf Hitler's tea cloth and the kiss — another letter of commendation.

"No," she was saying to Helen, "it isn't too much at all, and besides, I don't think we'll have any place to hang it for quite a while, and we may be where we can pick out something else like it — at least if things work out."

We were standing by the open door watching Williams drive away, and Helen was waving. It was bitter cold and raw at half past six in the morning, and I remember saying to Helen that I was out of the army now, and I remember her answer — that it was just about time.

XXXV

"*Generals Are Human. I Know of None Immune To Error.*" — *Omar N. Bradley*

THOUGH I had thought seriously that my friendship with Melville Goodwin was buried deep in a Never-Never Land, I heard from him exactly six days later. This was surely a short enough lapse, but somehow it seemed like a space of years. In the meantime, the feature story on the General had appeared, a little late for the full news impact, but still it was a good story. His face on the cover of the weekly periodical was a decorative portrait that must have pleased Colonel Flax and everyone else in Public Relations, and I imagined its being passed avidly around the Pentagon. Melville Goodwin's head and shoulders appeared against the background of an American flag, and in one corner was the crossed-rifle emblem of the Infantry. The lines about his eyes and mouth were exaggerated and they made him appear stern, heroic and watchful, but underneath the picture appeared one of those smartly cryptic titles which I was afraid would be painful to the army — *The color of Martinis grows lighter every year.* Phil Bentley had intended this somewhat disconcerting caption to refer to the acceleration of world events, as I saw when I read his Goodwin piece on the inside pages, but I instinctively dreaded its effect on serious-minded parents of draft-age boys at a time when universal military training was a subject for wide discussion. I even thought of calling up Phil Bentley to tell him his idea was unfortunate, but then, Phil had probably been told this already, and it was too late anyway, and besides, it was the Pentagon's problem and not mine.

Actually I had plenty of problems right in the office, what with hirings and firings and reconstruction. On the docket, among other things, was an annual challenge which was just around the corner. Although it was only late November, Miss Jocelyn, my new secretary, had already taken up the subject of Christmas. She had reminded me that I had been asked to make the main speech at the office Christmas party, and she asked if I did not want to prepare a draft of it to get it out of the way, because the editors of the office house organ wanted it in type as soon as possible for the Christmas number. Then after touching on the speech, Miss Jocelyn brought up the subject of Christmas cards. When I reminded her that it was still November, she said, quite correctly, that the office would send them to the right people at the right time, but that we were close to the deadline for having Christmas cards personalized; it would also be wise very soon to make up a list of gifts. Christmas had been a difficult time of year ever since I had married Helen, who took Christmas seriously and emotionally, and it was beginning to appear that Miss Jocelyn had the same ideas.

I would have to make an unusual effort this year about presents. The Yuletide was always an occasion for the healing of old wounds, and it was also a time that bred new hurt feelings, if you were not very careful. It seemed to me that I ought to give some sort of a present to Dottie Peale, although I did not know on what basis we were at the moment. I would also have to give something adequate to George Burtheimer, possibly a case of Scotch. Miss Maynard was no longer working for me, which was all the more reason why I should give her something handsome, and the same was true with Art Hertz. Also, there would have to be something for all the boys in buttons and something particular for Gilbert Frary that would be a permanent monument to affection, something original and intimate, like a first edition of Dickens's *Christmas Carol*. By and large, it had not been an easy day at the office, and besides thinking of the party speech, there was the regular broadcast. I had been writing most of it myself, because the new writer, Billy MacBeth, was not as good as Art Hertz — and I must remember to give him something handsome, too, because after the New Year I would have to make a change.

It was just ten minutes before I was to go on the air, and I was still struggling with all these questions when Miss Jocelyn told me that a General Melville A. Goodwin was on the telephone. She had typed the name on the proper memorandum blank. She knew it must be important, because he had the private number. I could not recall ever having given him that number, but then I remembered that I had given it to General Gooch.

"Tell him to call at seven-twenty," I said.

Miss Jocelyn said she had suggested this already, but she had been told that it was a matter of extreme urgency. That was what he had said — extreme urgency.

I felt resentful, I remember, not only toward him but toward the whole system he represented. I thought of the time that Goochy had barged in unannounced with that summons to Washington, and then there had been the original telephone call from the Pentagon — and it seemed years ago — about helping Colonel Flax with my old friend General Melville Goodwin — the call that had started everything.

War always gave those people too much power. Its fumes still remained in their heads like old Burgundy from the night before. Even the best of them developed a Messiah complex, once they had the rank. If they gave the word, they still expected you to snap into it with pleasure, always secure in the belief that their own affairs were of paramount significance. Goodwin now had so little to do with anything around me that I even found it difficult to believe that I had seen him only a few days before at the airport in Washington. It was nine and a half minutes before I would go on the air, and even his voice seemed far away.

"Look here," he was saying, and he was angry, "I don't want any more of this run-around. I want to speak to Mr. Sidney Skelton."

"You're speaking to him," I answered, "but I've only got a minute, Mel."

"Well, well, Sid," he said. "Say, Sid, where do you think I am?"

"I don't know," I answered.

"Well, I'm right here at the Waldorf and I have a suite. The management gave it to me — no extra charge. Boy, that's what comes of getting a piece about you in the magazines."

Somehow his voice indicated that being at the Waldorf in a suite at no extra charge seemed both to have settled and to have explained everything.

"That sounds wonderful," I said, "but I've only got a minute, Mel."

"Well, drop everything and come up here, will you, Sid? Put this down — rooms fifteen eighty-three and four. It's important."

"I can't," I told him, "I'm going on the air in just eight minutes."

"Oh, hell," he said. "Can't you get someone else to say your piece?"

"No," I said, "of course I can't, Mel."

There was a brief incredulous pause.

"Well, how soon can you get up here?"

"Around half past seven," I said.

"Well, see you make it and don't keep me waiting," he said.

"Yes, sir," I said, and I accented the "sir" in a heavy way that was impertinent.

There was another pause that told me he had caught my meaning.

"Now, now," he said, "what's the matter, son? Are you mad at me about anything?"

"No, sir," I said, and I elaborated the last word again in my sincerest tone, and then he laughed.

"Horsefeathers, boy," he said. "Well, make it nineteen-thirty. Are you happy, boy?"

"No," I said.

"Well, that's too bad," he said, "because I'm feeling God-damn happy."

Almost everyone I knew in New York had first arrived there in a fairly adult state instead of having been born there. We had all reached that city because of legends as old as Horatio Alger. We had all come there to make good and to set the world on fire, and we had all been in a highly impressionable state. In spite of the abrasions and frustrations we might have suffered since, those first impressions of New York were inviolate. No matter how the city grew and changed, its traffic and its skylines and its subway always looked as

586

you first remembered them, gilded by an old magnificence, and among those early visions the most vivid and lasting of them all was always your first hotel.

Mine had been the old Murray Hill. I had dined there with Dottie Peale, after buying marked-down theater tickets at Gray's Drugstore for a show that was fast folding. I cannot remember anything about the play, but it might have been only yesterday that we entered the marble-floored lobby of the Murray Hill and gazed upon the potted palms set among the rococo decorations of a simpler age. It did not matter that the main dining room was already stodgy — it belonged to the Murray Hill, and it had always remained in my mind as a unit of measure, a perpetual standard for gaiety and perfection. I might know better, but my youth and my first wonder and my first brash attempts at sophistication and my first shock at prices on a menu all belonged to the ghost of the Murray Hill. Years afterward whenever there was something special in my life to be celebrated, my instincts turned me back there. The first time I ever invited Helen to dinner and the theater I took her to the Murray Hill, and when I returned from Paris the first time, I stayed at the Murray Hill.

You could not escape those early loyalties easily, so I could see exactly what the Waldorf meant to Melville Goodwin. He had first entered the Waldorf with his bride and he had returned there after World War I. The old building was gone and the immense new structure was nothing like it, but still there was the name.

The outer door was open a crack and he had shouted to me to come in. He was standing in the center of a small impersonal sitting room that looked as functional as he did, and there was no sign of anything about him there except himself, no hat or coat or open suitcase, only Melville Goodwin. He might have just stepped in from somewhere else. Something about his appearance puzzled me for a second — he was wearing one of his older uniforms and not the new one I had seen him in so often since he had returned from overseas. It might have been the same uniform that he had worn in Paris. It had the same used look and the same efficient neatness and even the ribbons had a faded quality. It was a uniform that had been in and out of post tailor shops many times. It looked very well, but the sight of it disturbed me vaguely. It was not what he would ordinarily have worn in New York.

Something had changed in his manner, too. He looked careless and easy, almost as I remembered him at Saint-Lô.

"Well, hello, son," he said. "I'm damned glad to see you," and he did look glad. He gripped my hand hard and slapped me on the shoulder. "I called you up the first time I had a free minute. God damn, you've really got yourself dug in up there. I had a hell of a time getting through to you. How're Helen and Camilla?"

"They're fine," I said, and then I found myself hesitating, because I did not know where to go from there. I did not know whether the ice was thin or thick, and his face showed me nothing, except that he did look happy, but this might have been the service veneer, the officers' club party manner.

"How's Muriel?" I asked. Somehow I was impelled to ask it, and not a line of his smile changed.

"Muriel's fine," he said. "She's busy as a bird dog. By the way, she had a swell time up at your house. She really needed to get away for a while, and that reminds me, she gave me a package to give you to give to Helen — a piece of Chinese embroidery."

"That's awfully kind of her to remember it," I said.

"You know Muriel," he answered. "She's like me — she never forgets anything. I'll get it for you in a minute, but first I want to give you a little call-down, Sid."

"A call-down about what?" I asked.

His smile had gone but his expression was gently paternal, and his words were measured.

"When I try to get you on the telephone, son," he said, "I want to get through to you without telling my life history. Get this arranged in the future when I call you, will you?"

"Yes, sir, I will, sir," I answered. "I'm sorry."

"That's all right," he said. "Have you eaten yet?"

"I'm sorry," I began. "I had some food brought in at half past six."

"That's all right," he said, "I've eaten, too, and now we'd better have a drink. Call up room service, will you, for some ice and glasses? I've got some Scotch. Bink Collamore gave me three bottles. Do you know Bink Collamore?"

"No," I said, "I don't think so."

"You wouldn't have to think, if you had ever met him," he said. "I've been with him all morning. I hadn't seen Bink since Manila. Call up room service, will you, Sid?"

"I really don't need a drink," I said.

"Call up room service," he said. "This is a sort of celebration, son — partly. You telephone and I'll get the bottle."

I was alone in the sitting room while I was calling room service, and he seemed to have vanished so completely that I almost felt he had not been there at all, until he came back and put a fifth of Scotch on the table.

"There," he said, "now the room looks lived in, doesn't it? Say, Sid, it's funny, isn't it, how we've got to be friends — close friends, I mean?"

He had moved me up in the category, which seemed strange to me when I had been thinking of him as part of the past.

"It's funny," he said again, "because you don't often make friends — I mean close friends — after you've got the rank. It's funny but just as soon as I checked in here, I began saying to myself, I've got to see Sid before I push off. I'd have called you earlier today, but I've had a lot of things to clear up."

He sat down opposite me on the edge of an easy chair with his feet drawn under him in that habitual pose that made him always seem ready for anything.

"I didn't know you were pushing off, Mel," I said. "Where are you pushing to?"

His forehead wrinkled and he rubbed his hand over the back of his closely cropped head.

"Why, son," he said, "haven't you heard the news?"

It was like Mel Goodwin and all the rest of them to think that everyone knew when orders had been cut, especially close friends. I had not heard the news, but I remembered Muriel Goodwin's pronouncement — Melville would have to be sent somewhere.

"Of course you haven't heard," he said, "I just keep thinking everybody ought to know. Listen, boy, they've asked for me at SCAP, right from the horse's mouth in Tokyo, and I hardly know anyone on the inside in SCAP. It's a damned tight little crowd. I'm flying out in two days and it's going to be with troops and Goochy's coming over, too. Frizell is coming back. They've been riding the hell out of him over there, but that part's confidential. You know who Frizell is, don't you?"

"No," I said, "I don't think so."

"Listen, Sid," the General said, "it's time you got in touch with the setup. . . . Well, we'll skip it because it's confidential. I'm taking over from Red Frizell. I had it yesterday. It's going to be the beginning of a build-up and it's going to be with troops. Maybe it's going to be a corps command. It's about time they figured on a strategic reserve. God, I'm as happy as a kid. Congratulate the old man, will you, Sid? The only thing that gripes me is that you're not coming, too."

We both stood up and we shook hands formally, the way one should. "Well," I said in my sincerest voice, "congratulations!" I did not know what any of it meant, because I did not know about future plans in the Orient, but I was thinking of Muriel Goodwin.

"Boy," he said, "I'm still slap-happy. I still can't believe I'd get anything like this. Boy, the only thing we need now is a war out there, and things don't look so good in China, do they? I've got a hunch it might happen in Korea."

He was never as dumb as you thought he was going to be. He knew his terrain and he had the prescience. It was the first time I had ever heard a serious mention of Korea.

A discreet knock cut off his flow of words sharply and there was an instant's guilty pause, which was easy to understand. He had thought we were alone and he had been skirting the edges of indiscretion. In fact he had almost stuck his neck out.

"Yes," he called, "who is it?" His voice had a new ring of authority. It was the room waiter with ice and glasses and soda, a timid-looking, middle-aged man, and I did not blame him for looking frightened.

590

"It's only me, sir," he said, "the room waiter, and the suite door was off the latch."

Melville Goodwin glanced at him critically and reached clumsily for change in his right-hand trousers pocket. Uniform pockets were not designed for the graceful extraction of change.

"That's all right," he said. "Give me the check and a pencil. Thank you, waiter."

"Do you wish me to open the soda bottles, sir?" the waiter said.

"All right, all right," Melville Goodwin answered, "open them."

We sat in a frosty silence while the waiter opened the bottles, and Melville Goodwin glanced meaningly toward the suite entry.

"God damn," he said, "I've got to get over being careless. Sid, see that the outside door's locked, will you? Close that entry door, too." He was on his feet, removing the cap from the whisky bottle, when I returned from my mission, but I was sure he had taken a quick look in the bedroom. It was a simple little observation of military security. He had almost been indiscreet, but he was still as happy as a kid.

"Boy," he said, "suppose we forget my last few remarks, just on general security principles, but if you knew what I know."

"Well, I don't," I told him. "It's all right, I can't put any of it together."

He was pouring out the Scotch and putting ice in the glasses.

"That's so," he said. "It's all right as long as you don't know who Frizell is," and it did not seem to occur to him that he might have made me anxious to find out about the mysterious stranger named Frizell. It was often that way with security. "But, boy, I'll tell you this — it's just about time they had an activator in that setup, but picking me out ahead of all that South Pacific crowd . . . I'm on record to say that's something. Of course some damn fools might say it was a demotion after Plans, but not for me it isn't. They wouldn't give it to anybody without a top combat record, and boy, I'm here to say I'm proud."

He sat down on the edge of his chair again. He was lost in the glow of that unknown new assignment, and he had the shining morning face of Shakespeare's schoolboy.

591

"Well, here's to you, Mel," I said. "Here's luck."

"Thanks," he said, "maybe I'll need it, but at the same time, I think I've got what it's going to take to handle this one. God, I wish I could give you the whole blueprint — and you ought to have seen Goochy when he got the word, and you ought to have seen Muriel. . . . All this talk about an apartment in Washington . . . you ought to have seen her when she got the word. She was just as surprised as I was. She's acting just the way she did when we started off for Bailey. You wouldn't have thought any of us were grown-up."

"I wish I could have seen her," I said.

Melville Goodwin shook the ice softly in his glass.

"You know," he said, "it reminds me of that poem."

"You mean the one about Ulysses?" I asked.

"That's it," he said, "exactly. 'Push off and sitting well in order smite' — and it's a nice thing from Muriel's point of view. There's quite a little dog connected with it, not that I give a damn, but Muriel has a weakness for putting on the dog. Do you know what?"

"What?" I asked.

"Well, just confidentially, we're moving into Frizell's quarters, and I've got the word on them today. He has one of those houses in Tokyo that belonged to the Mitsuis — you know, part European and part Japanese — with dwarf gardens and all the old servants in kimonos and all paid for by the occupation. It will be something for Muriel to get her teeth into. Muriel's really going to get something, and maybe it's about time."

I was familiar with the sort of real estate in Tokyo to which he was referring, half grotesque and half beautiful. I had a vision of miniature rock gardens, of stunted pines and azaleas and little pools — a setting for the usually ludicrous and unsuccessful effort of a wealthy Japanese to reconcile the East and West. Part of the house would be an overelaborated London villa stuffed with heavy carpets and velvet hangings and furnished with contorted imitations of European period pieces upholstered in suffocating velvet, and then, like an austere rebuke, would come the traditional Japanese dwelling in back, chaste and exquisite, with its scrolls, its matting, its sliding partitions and its rice-paper windows.

"Yes, maybe it's about time that Muriel had something," I said.

It was a strange world, I was thinking, and it was moving so fast that it was impossible to keep up with it any longer — for me, but not for Melville Goodwin, who had the service right behind him and his own simple lexicon of belief. He was safe again, safer than I would ever be in this changing world. There had been a stormy moment of maladjustment, but it was gone. He was off again, behaving exactly as he should, able to shed experience, but still some thought made him stare solemnly at his glass.

"You know," he said, "it's queer how a thing like this clarifies your thinking and changes your point of view. I don't seem to be the same person I was before I got the word. I don't know what's been the matter with me lately." He looked at me with cold deceptive innocence. "You follow what I mean, don't you?"

"Yes," I said carefully, "I guess I do, partly."

He could see things without intermediate shadows. I knew he was facing an awkward moment of confession, but his frankness saved the awkwardness.

"All right," he said, "let's lay it on the line. I had never thought of myself as being humanly inexperienced, but by God, I must have been. Let's lay it on the line. Maybe I don't understand about women, Sid. Let's leave it at that, shall we?"

He had almost said all that was necessary. The clear truth of his innocence explained his aberration. He was not the sort of person who understood women, and this was almost enough to close the incident.

"Say," he said, "did you ever hear the story about the southern gentleman of the old school who felt that he ought to give his son a little briefing on sex?"

"No, I don't think I ever have," I answered.

He was about to push off on another of his stories, and he smiled in anticipation.

"Well, it goes this way. When he was face to face with the boy, there didn't seem to be a damned thing to say. That's the point, not one damned thing, and that's the way I feel about sex right now. All he could say was, 'Listen, son, you're getting to be a big boy now and you're going out and around, and all I can tell you is this: Never put sweetening in your liquor, and try to tell the truth.'"

Melville Goodwin looked at me expectantly, as though he had told one of his best stories, and he was disappointed when I made no comment.

"Well, maybe that's all there is to it," he said. "Maybe I did sort of sweeten up my liquor. . . . All right, I know now what that gentleman of the old school meant. Take Dottie Peale. Maybe I ought to have run around some when I was younger. I don't know what I was thinking of. Isn't that the damnedest thing?"

He looked at me curiously, but I did not answer.

"You always knew I was being a damn fool, didn't you?"

"Well, I wouldn't put it quite that way," I said.

"Horsefeathers," he said. "I had never faced up to it, that's all — not that she isn't a nice girl. She's a very remarkable person."

"That's so," I answered, "she's remarkable."

"It's sort of rugged, isn't it," he said, "to go to someone and just say you've been a damn fool, but I like to think I tell the truth."

"You mean you've seen Dottie?" I asked.

"Hell, yes," he said. "You didn't think I'd write her a 'Dear John' letter, did you? Hell, yes, I saw Dottie at five this afternoon."

He set his drink on the table and smoothed the wrinkles in his blouse. Perhaps he should have left his story at that. Whatever had happened belonged to no one but him and Dottie Peale.

"I don't know much about these things, but she was wonderful," he said. "I don't know how she ever managed it, but she made it seem all right. She never let me feel for a minute that I was ducking out. In fact she made it all seem like something to be proud of. I'll never forget her, Sid."

For some reason or other, nothing in that confession sounded tawdry or shopworn, when every element in it should have. Something in Melville Goodwin prevented it. There was always a quality in him of simple fact that raised him above the obvious. There was a metal in him that life had never tarnished, though it possessed a confusing luster for people like Dottie Peale and me. He was a stranger from a strange world which we could never touch.

"Yes, by God, I *am* proud of it," he said. He shook his glass slowly, watching the ice cubes carefully. "Of course," he went on, "I took this up with Muriel last night. It all just came over me. I had to tell her I'd been a God-damned fool, and she was wonderful. She said it was only decent to clear it as quickly as possible with Dottie. She even helped me plan what to say."

He was watching me, and sometimes he had a way of seeing everything, and he must have read something in my expression.

"You would have done that, wouldn't you," he asked, "if you had been in my shoes?"

"No," I said, "I don't think so. I don't believe I'd have had the guts. No, I wouldn't have done it in just that way."

He shook his head slowly.

"That isn't guts," he said. "It's only truth. There are some things you have to lay on the line — some things. For instance . . ." He picked up his drink again. "There's the flag, for instance."

"What?" I said.

I could not see why Old Glory should enter into it, but then he had always been an Old Glory Boy.

"There's the flag," he said again, "and there's taking care of the men and never telling them to do anything that you won't do yourself. That has nothing to do with guts." His eyes narrowed slightly. He could always see more than you thought he was going to. "You think I'm a pretty simple guy, don't you?"

"No, sir," I said, "I wouldn't call you simple."

"Well, it doesn't make a damned bit of difference," he said. "I don't know how it is but I feel like a good boy who has done the right thing. Say, Sid, do you know what I'd like to do tonight?"

"No," I answered.

"Well, it's just a whim," he said, and he looked at me doubtfully. "I don't know when we'll get the chance again. How about our staying here tonight and polishing off some of this liquor in a serious way?"

It was a curious sort of ending and yet somehow it seemed appropriate. It meant that he was human after all, and it was a way of bridging a gap that divided us.

". . . Just because we've seen a hell of a lot together," he said, "just because — oh, hell, there isn't any reason."

"Well, I don't mind," I said.

"Boy," he said, "I knew you'd be right with me." When he smiled, he looked like young Mel Goodwin from the Point.

"There used to be a bugler at Bailey," Melville Goodwin was saying. "His last name was Lowther — funny that this should come back to me now. He was always getting into trouble, but he could really blow the calls. Even when he was in the pen, the Old Man used to order him out under guard to play taps. By God, when you heard that man do taps, it would hit you in the heels. It always eased you down and made everything clear — all the answers in the book. I remember what the Old Man said one night when taps was over — that was old Jupiter Jones. I'll tell you some good ones about him later. He was sitting on his veranda with a bottle of Old Home Elixir for his cough, when Lowther marched by on his way back to the pen — the guard behind him, bayonet and everything. The Old Man had a real sense of humor. . . .

" 'Lieutenant,' he said to me, 'go down, will you, and see that that son-of-a-bitching bugler is locked in tight. I want him where you can get at him so he can blow taps over me when I die.'

"It's funny I should remember a thing like that, but you really should have heard him. . . . It really was the answer. . . . I sort of wish we had that son-of-a-bitching bugler here now. . . ."